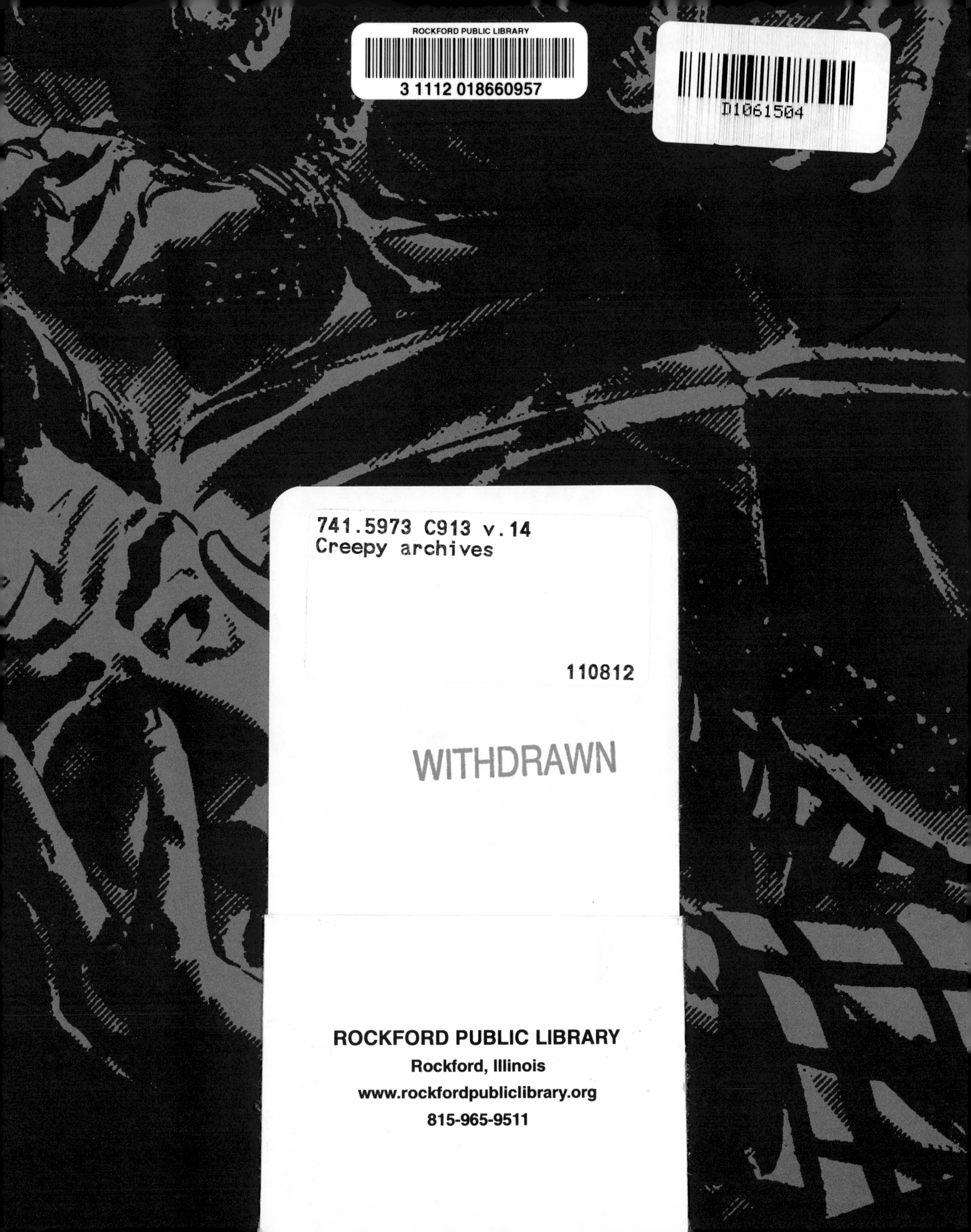

CREEPY™

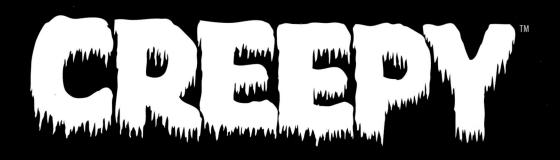

ARTISTS

Adolfo Abellan	José Ortiz
Vicente Alcazar	Martin Salvador
Vaughn Bodé	Leopold Sánchez
Howard Chaykin	Sanjulian
Richard Corben	John Severin
Ken Kelly	Leo Summers
Esteban Maroto	Tom Sutton
Isidro Mones	Larry Todd
Paul Neary	Bernie Wrightson

WRITERS

Ambrose Bierce	Isidro Mones
Gerry Boudreau	Edgar Allan Poe
Jack Butterworth	Greg Potter
Archie Goodwin	Jeff Rovin
Budd Lewis	Steve Skeates
Rich Margopoulos	Jim Stenstrum
Doug Moench	Tom Sutton
Carl Wessler	

EDITORS

Bill DuBay	Jeff Rovin
Archie Goodwin	James Warren

CREEPY
VOLUME FOURTEEN
COLLECTING CREEPY 64-68
DARK HORSE ARCHIVES

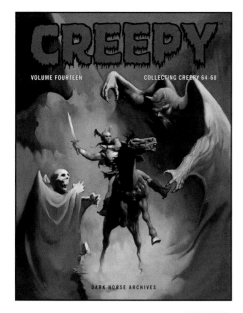

OUR COVER:
Warning: The Brain Surgeon General has determined that the ensuing pages may contain more shocking revelations and flabbergasting twists than the human mind can handle!

PUBLISHER
Mike Richardson

EDITOR
Philip R. Simon

CONSULTING EDITOR
Dan Braun

ASSISTANT EDITOR
Everett Patterson

DESIGNER
Heather Doornink

DIGITAL PRODUCTION
Ryan Jorgensen

Color restoration on "An Angel Shy of Hell," "The Raven," "Anti-Christmas," and "Bowser" by José Villarrubia.

CREEPY™

ARCHIVES - VOLUME FOURTEEN

NEW COMIC COMPANY:
Josh Braun, Dan Braun, Rick Brookwell, Craig Haffner

PUBLISHED BY DARK HORSE BOOKS, A DIVISION OF DARK HORSE COMICS, INC., 10956 SE MAIN STREET, MILWAUKIE, OREGON 97222. TO FIND A COMICS SHOP IN YOUR AREA, CALL THE COMIC SHOP LOCATOR SERVICE: (888) 266-4226.

DARKHORSE.COM
FIRST EDITION: OCTOBER 2012 – ISBN 978-1-59582-772-2
1 3 5 7 9 10 8 6 4 2
PRINTED AT 1010 PRINTING INTERNATIONAL, LTD.,
GUANGDONG PROVINCE, CHINA

FOREWORD

by Joshua Hale Fialkov

By the time I was born, many of the things I would one day grow to love were already gone. Hammer films, film noir, EC Comics—all distant memories while I was coming through the birth canal. Luckily for me, *Creepy* and *Eerie* made it until my fourth birthday, which was still a few years shy of my comics reading, but close enough that I can still feel like one of my passions in life coexisted with me, however briefly.

I discovered *Creepy* when I was nine or ten years old. My older brother would take me with him to the stores Phantom of the Attic (still going strong all these years later) and Eide's (not so much) in Pittsburgh, Pennsylvania, and as he'd pick up his issues of *Vigilante* and *Batman*, I'd dig through the long boxes looking for *Teenage Mutant Ninja Turtles* comics, which, as you might not remember, were originally in magazine format. Which put me smack dab in the *Creepy*, *Eerie*, and *Vampirella* section.

I'd already fallen in love with the EC anthology series by then, and so immediately clamored to try these oversized, gorgeous magazines. What was inside was something I'd never imagined. Like a nightmare come to life in the most splendid way possible, issue to issue, month in and month out, *Creepy* was the best there was in horror, and the ghastly things contained within the dusty newsprint pages would shape me for life. My mother would say "scar," but I'll go with "shape" instead.

So, now, a couple of decades later, I find myself constantly going back to my stack of *Creepy* and *Eerie* for inspiration, for education, and, more often, for the fun. These stories are from a different era, when telling a great story was the central goal, rather than marketing and crossovers and brand identity. In fact, the mentality seems to have been "Let our brand identity be totally amazing stories told brilliantly." Which has been something I've always aspired to.

This collection you hold in your hands is a gift. A gift of the magic that comics hold, and specifically, the power that the old Warren magazines could wield. A perfect marriage of words and pictures into a chillingly lyrical package that deserves to be not on your bookshelf, but on your coffee table and being read by every person, comics reader or otherwise, that steps foot into your home.

The boundaries these comics pushed (and not just the ones of taste) were epic and effortless. The sense of spirit and adventure goes beyond just honoring the EC comics that came before them, managing to nearly eclipse them in terms of significance and quality—at least to those of us who make comics for a living. They stand as a perfect example of commerce meeting art and both coming up far better for it.

Take, for example, issue #64. Six stories in service of a cover. A cover was commissioned, and the accompanying story was never completed. Instead, Jim and Archie and the gang sent the cover out for their pools of talent to write their own versions of just what that story was about.

What you got was six radically different takes by some of the best guys in comics (including Tom Sutton, cocreator of my current gig, *I,Vampire*, over at DC Comics!) on a cover that's equal parts ghastly and stirring. Two of those takes are by the masterful Doug Moench, which, without a credit to tell you otherwise, you would never mistake for being written by the same guy.

This issue, it should be noted, was Archie Goodwin's final issue of *Creepy*, and no better testament to his ability to get the very best out of the talent around him exists. Even in Archie's absence (the odd reprint issue aside), the book continued in both his and Jim Warren's image for years and years to come (and gorgeous deluxe hardcover collections

to come, too!). There just was no better horror comic on the stands at the time, and I'd argue, no offense to my friends and publishers, nor since. These are the very gold standard that all horror, for me, is judged against.

That being said, this book also makes me extremely sad. As one of a handful of horror writers still grinding away in comics, *Creepy* (and *Eerie*) stands as a testament to a bygone era, where the absolute top industry talents were given free reign to tell the type of stories that they were passionate about. Where horror wasn't seen as some flaky subgenre of superhero comics (themselves a pretty damn flaky subgenre). Where imagination and creativity trumped safe corporate confines. Where major publishers saw the value in genres other than men in tights.

It was a different world then, obviously, where you could still make money from magazines and pamphlets, and you weren't competing with an infinite supply of movies and video games a click of the mouse away. But, I'd argue, what these comics have that you see less and less of these days is sheer and utter joy. So much of what makes comics great comes from the head-scratchingly bold choices made by our forebearers. Every story contains a piece of their creative hearts, and coupling that with their talent and skill, they made every damn page of every issue a classic.

Maybe I'm wearing rose-colored glasses. I don't know. What I do know is that for twenty years, Warren Publishing published the stories that inspired me to do what I do.

So now, sit back, relax, and try not to wet yourself, as you read some of the best horror stories ever written from the best horror magazine that ever was. It feels so good to go back there.

—Joshua Hale Fialkov
March 2011, North Hollywood, CA

Joshua Hale Fialkov is the Eisner, Harvey, and Emmy Award–nominated writer of graphic novels including *Elk's Run*, *Tumor*, *Echoes*, and *The Last of the Greats*. He's also written *I, Vampire* for DC Comics, *Doctor Who* for IDW Publishing, and *Vampirella* for Harris Comics. Find out more about him online at TheFialkov.com.

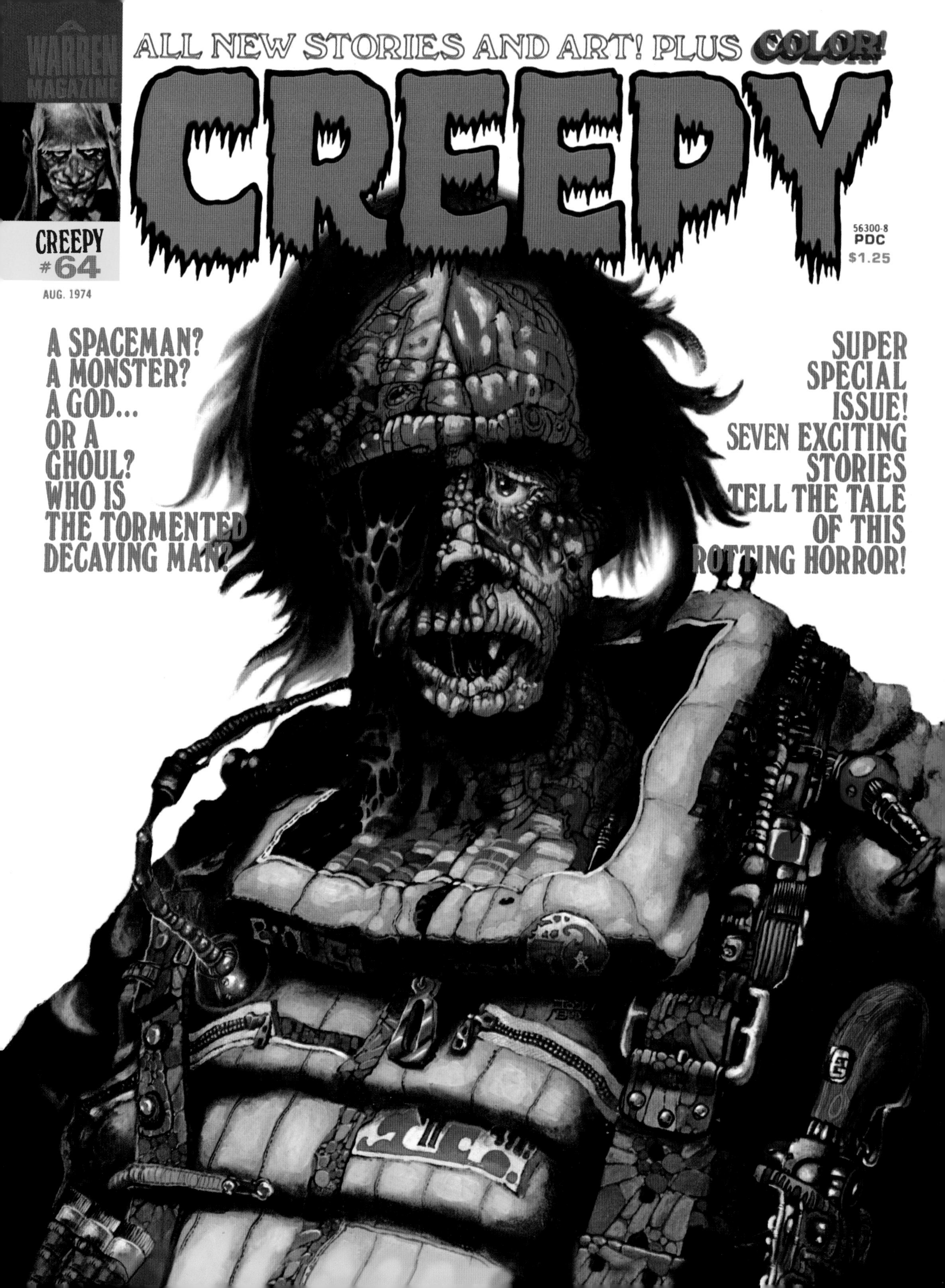
WARREN MAGAZINE
CREEPY #64
AUG. 1974
ALL NEW STORIES AND ART! PLUS COLOR!
CREEPY
56300-8
PDC
$1.25
A SPACEMAN? A MONSTER? A GOD... OR A GHOUL? WHO IS THE TORMENTED DECAYING MAN?
SUPER SPECIAL ISSUE! SEVEN EXCITING STORIES TELL THE TALE OF THIS ROTTING HORROR!

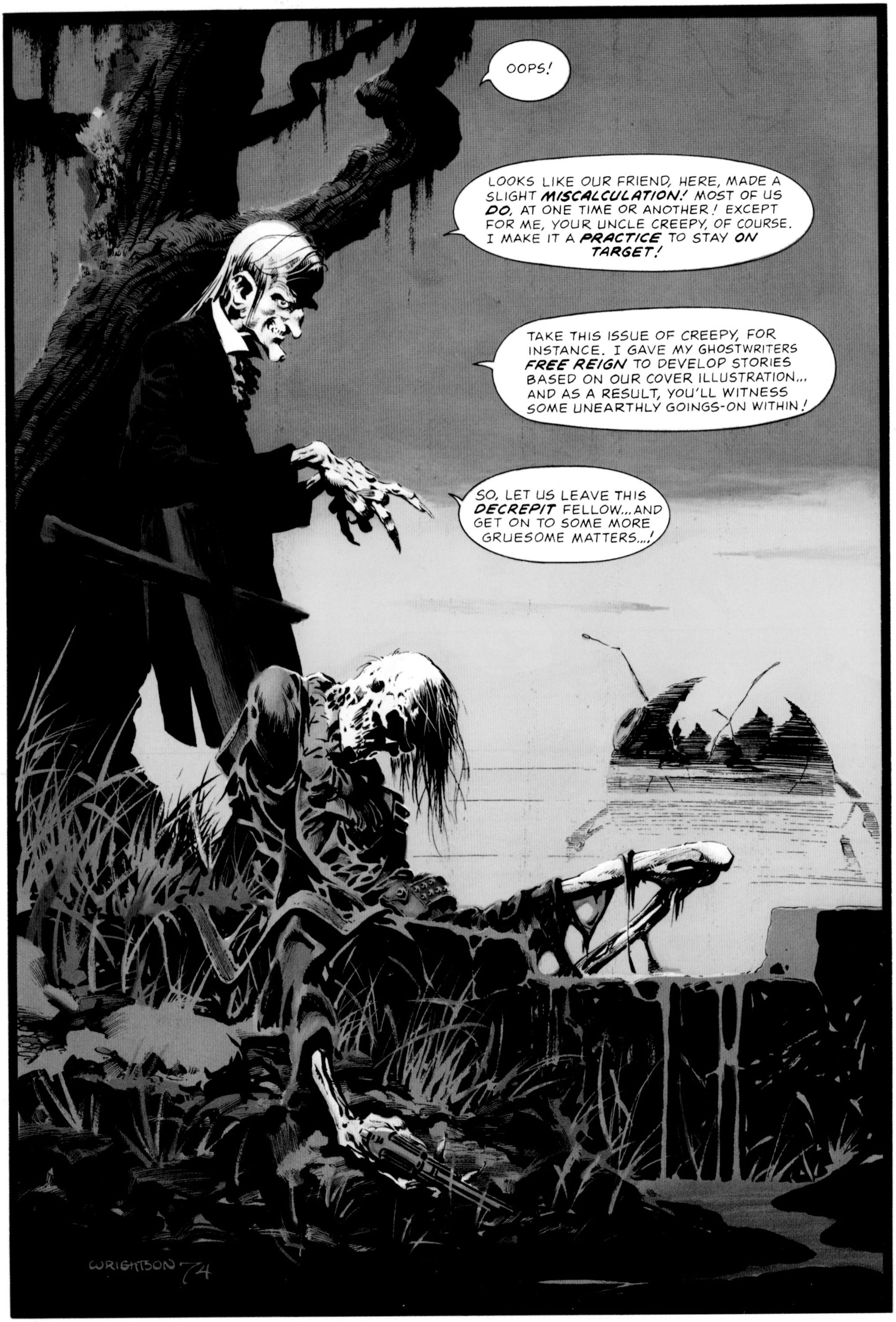
OOPS!
LOOKS LIKE OUR FRIEND, HERE, MADE A SLIGHT MISCALCULATION! MOST OF US DO, AT ONE TIME OR ANOTHER! EXCEPT FOR ME, YOUR UNCLE CREEPY, OF COURSE. I MAKE IT A PRACTICE TO STAY ON TARGET!
TAKE THIS ISSUE OF CREEPY, FOR INSTANCE. I GAVE MY GHOSTWRITERS FREE REIGN TO DEVELOP STORIES BASED ON OUR COVER ILLUSTRATION... AND AS A RESULT, YOU'LL WITNESS SOME UNEARTHLY GOINGS-ON WITHIN!
SO, LET US LEAVE THIS DECREPIT FELLOW... AND GET ON TO SOME MORE GRUESOME MATTERS...!
WRIGHTSON '74

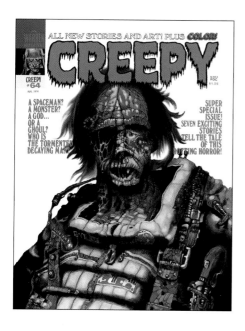

ALL NEW STORIES AND ART! PLUS COLOR!

CREEPY

CREEPY #64

A SPACEMAN?
A MONSTER?
A GOD...
OR A GHOUL?
WHO IS THE TORMENTED DECAYING MA...

SUPER SPECIAL ISSUE!
SEVEN EXCITING STORIES TELL THE TALE OF THIS ...TING HORROR!

Editor-In-Chief
& Publisher
JAMES WARREN

Senior Editor
W.B. DuBAY

Editor
ARCHIE GOODWIN

Associate Editor
JEFF ROVIN

Production Mgr.
W.R. MOHALLEY

Cover
LARRY TODD
& VAUGHN BODE

Interior Color
RICH CORBEN
W.B. DuBAY
Circulation Director
AB SIDEMAN

Artists
This Issue
VINCENTE ALCAZAR
HOWARD CHAYKIN
RICH CORBEN
ESTEBAN MAROTO
PAUL NEARY
LEO SUMMERS
TOM SUTTON
BERNI WRIGHTSON

Writers
This Issue
RICH MARGOPOULOS
DOUG MOENCH
JEFF ROVIN
STEVE SKEATES
JIM STENSTRUM
TOM SUTTON

CREEPY

CONTENTS ISSUE NO. 64 AUGUST 1974

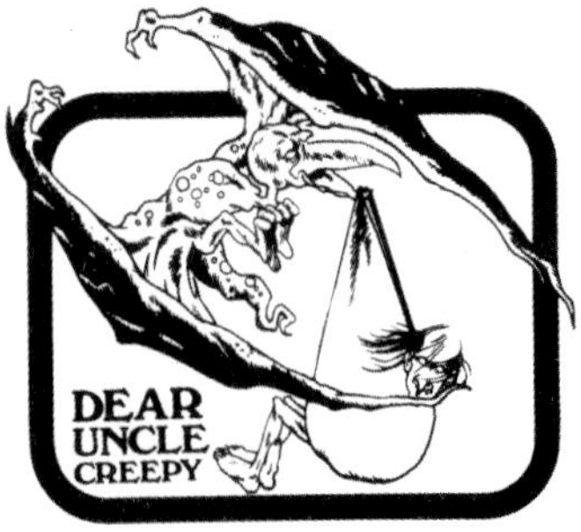
DEAR
UNCLE
CREEPY

"The art quality is more than I could ask!"

All I can say about CREEPY #62 is that it's got to be one of your best issues to date. The quality of its art is more than I could possibly ask for. When **Al Williamson** and **Angelo Torres** left the magazine, much of the macabre terror which had originally been there, vanished. Now, though, you have presented a talent to replace those two. I speak of **Berni Wrightson.** His beautiful drawings set off by his equally as lovely inks, give the story a perfect atmosphere. Whatever you do, don't let him go.

GLEN NETHERCUT
Stockton, Calif.

I have always thought CREEPY was an average magazine, but now that **Berni Wrightson** is illustrating stories, CREEPY is the **best! Berni's** rendition of **Edgar Allan Poe's** "The Black Cat" was fantastic.

As long as you keep **Wrightson** as one of your artists, I'll be one of your most faithful fans.

KEVIN FOWLER
Springville, Utah

I just finished reading CREEPY #62. It was **fabulous!** Only recently have I started buying your whole line of magazines. But I keep asking myself why I never started earlier. I've followed **Berni Wrightson** for many moons, but "The Black Cat" has to be his best story ever! I hope he's in many, many **more** issues to come.

One of my favorite stories in CREEPY #62 was "Survior or Savior." The plot was great, but the art was out of this world. **Gonzalo Mayo!** Man, can he draw!

The main reason I buy CREEPY, EERIE, and VAMPIRELLA is to broaden my knowledge of comic book art, and to enjoy some of the greatest stories in black and white! (And color! Keep up the good work, **Rich Corben!**)

SCOTT WORRALL
Saginaw, Miss.

My monstrous mag has been accused of being many things, Scott . . . Horrifying, nauseating, depraved, disgusting, terror-iffic, beastly, chilling, and even funny. But to my knowledge no one's ever come up with BROADENING before, heh, heh. The closest EERIE can do to that is FATTENING!

I've been a fan of yours ever since I bought my first CREEPY. In the old days (when I first became acquainted with your ironic humor and pathos) there were several reasons for my reading so astutely your amusing publication. Now it seems there is no longer anything to be admired or worth even a casual reading.

I say this with regret for in the past I really enjoyed reading CREEPY! For instance, you **used** to have **Reed Crandall** and others illustrating the interior stories, and **Frank Frazetta** doing all the covers. **Frazetta** was an all-time great and I don't think anyone will come along to equal the **works of art** he created for your covers.

But, we can't bring back the past. And maybe we don't want to. We must look toward brighter prospects for the future. Keeping this in mind, you are doing admirably well, considering the tragic loss of these fine artists.

Nonetheless, the quality of **subject matter** has noticeably fallen down from the previous great "heights."

Your stories now are of the same basic subject matter in some cases, but noticeably **altered.** I guess you try to cater to what you think a portion of the public reading your mag will enjoy. By this, I mean **Science-fiction.**

Now, I enjoy s-f, but only when it is admirably composed, with characters seemingly true-to-life. When you try to introduce s-f (even s-f not composed by a notable person) into a comic format, you're negating the thing which gives a story reality. **Imagination!** This is the living entity of the s-f genre. When you illustrate a s-f story, you destroy this quality. Imagination, without literal reins, can soar to unguessable heights; illustrations impose such a rein.

Science-fiction was not originated to be used by comic artists because of this inalienable fact. Because s-f (and fantasy) "plays" so much with the imagination, is the main reason I object to it in your book.

CREEPY (and EERIE and VAMPIRELLA) has, in my opinion, evolved into just another **comic book.** You editors are, in part, responsible. I'm not balling you out, but I would like to see **all** your books reattain your previous heights of "literary magnificence."

GEORGE BARTLETT
Detroit, Mich.

We're trying, George.

After being a CREEPY fan for approximately eight years, I feel it's time I wrote some suggestions and criticisms.

First, publish a regular **science-fiction** magazine. This would not only end the s-f controversy in CREEPY and EERIE, but also provide s-f fans like me with a unique magazine of their own.

Second, some of your readers enjoy serials or character stories. I don't and I'm sure others feel the same. So, let CREEPY be left as is, a fine mag of short horror tales. Give your readers a choice of a series book (EERIE) or a non-series effort.

Third, CREEPY has long been the best in illustrated horror, but there's a dangerous trend developing which could end that fine tradition. **Humor** stories have found their way into recent issues. **Humor has no place in a horror book!** I hope you consider this to be worth discussion.

BILL GOOD
Ontario, Canada

Humor adds variety, Bill. What do you other readers think?

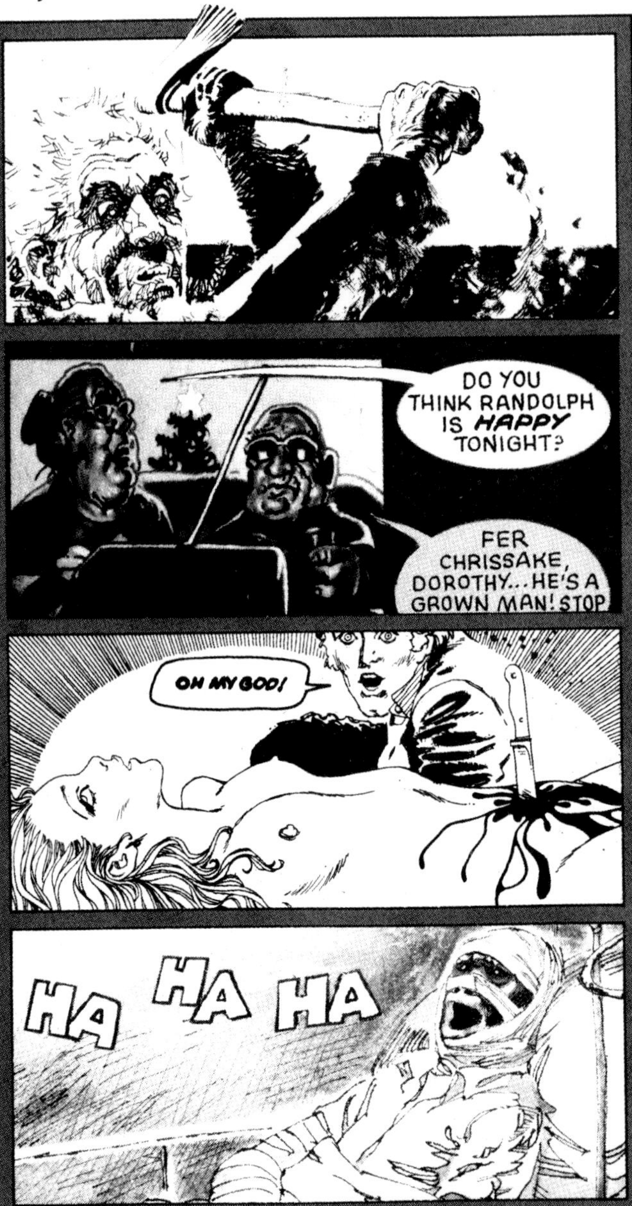
DO YOU THINK RANDOLPH IS HAPPY TONIGHT?
FER CHRISSAKE, DOROTHY... HE'S A GROWN MAN! STOP
OH MY GOD!
HA HA HA

Reader Mike Oliveri cites four examples wherein Warren writers have scripted stories, seemingly exceeding the limits of good taste: Steve Skeates' nude girl from "Bed of Roses" (CREEPY #54), Bill DuBay's use of verbal profanity in "Bless Us, Father" (CREEPY #59), Fernando Fernandez' maniacal protagonist of "Diary of a Killer" (VAMPIRELLA #30), and the all-too-real amputee in Skeates' "Twisted Medicine" (CREEPY #61).

The following thoughtful and concerned letter from Mike Oliveri seemed deserving of a much fuller and more serious treatment than the limitations our letters page usually permit. We think it's of sufficient interest to justify the extra space we're providing to present Mike's letter uncut and unedited.

I've been with you since CREEPY #9, and the **Warren** magazines are my favorite comics. But **Warren** publications are just getting sicker and sicker. It's just too damn much.

First there were the nude women. Fine. No problem. A picture of a lovely young lady in the nude is delightfully sexy, and even sophisticated if artistically drawn. But that progressed in **Warren** magazines to where the pictures were of **dead** nude young ladies. That's no longer sexy; it's sick. And if it **is** sexy to **you**, that's **really** sick. If you publish such things because you think they're sexy to **me**, that's a first-order insult. When you started showing the nude young body with a knife sticking out of it and blood running, that's full-fledged perversity of the vilest degree.

The next step towards grossness was your use of Lord's-name-in-vain cursing. That has **no** place in a magazine whose readers have an average age of 17 or 18, if **that** high. Why couldn't you be satisfied with "damn" and "hell?" If you have to escalate, use "bitch" and "bastard." Even "shit" would be better. At least those only offend people's sense of good taste. They don't offend their religion as well.

The next low point, which occurred about the same time, was abundant use of homicidal maniac stories. Man, they **really** turn me off. The one by **Fernando Fernandez** was especially disgusting (VAMPIRELLA #30). **Fernandez'** excellent writing, plot, and art did **not**, at all, compensate for the utter obscenity in the maniac's thoughts of getting pleasure from knifing and hacking people.

And now "Twisted Medicine" by **Steve Skeates** in CREEPY #61 goes one step further, if that's possible. The use of a snap ending built around a first-person narrator who is deaf, blind, and handless is completely beyond redemption. And to use that as the story's "hook" . . . Words can not express my **revulsion** of the story and the people responsible for it. The utter insensitivity this displays towards my fellow man simply curdled my stomach. It's immoral in the true sense of the word. I find it unbelievable that a writer, an editor, and a publisher could stoop so low to find something to have a story about. It's pornography to me in the way the Supreme Court defines pornography . . . as being whatever offends community standards. I am an offended community of one.

Warren magazines strive for adulthood. They approach the level of real literature and they're **at** the level of real art. They seek and achieve cultural relevancy. Being there, they can't cop out now! They can't now say to me, "Aw, man, don't get so uptight. It's only a comic book story." It's not **just** a comic book story when it's about a blind, deaf, cripple. If it's about the Crypt Keeper and a rotted corpse coming back from the grave, that's okay. That's fantasy. But when it's about something as realistic as what **real** people suffer, and you compound that by using it as a plot device, that's **unspeakable.**

(And don't give me the hogwash about real things don't go away by us ignoring them, and we're only free if we can make light of our woes, and handicapped people don't want pity, etc. That line of reasoning in this situation is b.s. and you know it.)

Has it never occurred to you that youngsters with physical defects themselves read your publications? Did you see for instance the letter in BATMAN #256 about the reader whose burden of muscular dystrophy affliction was lightened by the fun of reading BATMAN? It actually brought tears to my eyes. It's not unlikely he read CREEPY too!

I used to be embarrassed (being 26 years old) to let people know I read comic books. Now I'm ashamed because of the depravity in them. Some **Warrens** I simply cannot show to my friends; they might think I liked that stuff.

This letter will, I'm sure, never see the light of publication. I don't think you'd have the guts to print it. It doesn't say, "Dear Uncle Creepy," or "Bring back **Frazetta**," or "I love Vampirella." It's real. **Skeates'** story was real. **Too** real to be **acceptable!** And that realness, being used as the "E.C." shock ending, was nothing other than just cheap **shit!**

Wertham was **not—never was**—completely wrong, you know.

What'll be next, **Warren?** Homosexuality? Or dead babies with their eyes hanging out?

MICHAEL OLIVERI
Washington, DC

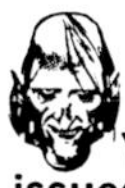

You raise a good many issues which, while I may not agree with most of them, are well worth discussing, Mike. I'm sorry you cheapened an otherwise worthwhile letter with the "I don't think you'd have the guts to print it" gambit which is usually the sign of someone anxious to get their letter in print rather than raise any kind of serious issue.

If we were afraid to receive or publish criticism, we either wouldn't have a letter column or else we'd make up our own letters. And if some letters say, "Dear Uncle Creepy, Bring back Frazetta," etc., it's because they reflect what some of our readers ARE saying. It doesn't make them less valid . . . Or less real.

That said, I'd like to go on to something else in your letter, something I AGREE with: "Warren magazines strive for adulthood. They approach the level of real literature, and they're AT the level of real art. They seek and achieve cultural relevancy." Mike, you don't do any of that by restricting yourself to doing over and over again the same TYPE of story you did ten years, or five years, or two years ago, or by doing them in the same WAY. You constantly search and explore new areas and new approaches to your genre, hoping you hit upon a valid way to expand it. This isn't just true of Warren Publications, it's true of television and movies, of books and records, of any form of mass communication.

In the course of such searching and exploring, bad taste and excesses are inevitable. On occasion, we're guilty of both. It's the price of TRYING. Without that freedom to fail, you're reduced to constantly playing "safe," being repetitive, and, inevitably, dull and moribund. We don't want that, and I don't think you do either. What has kept Warren one of the tops in the field is that most of the time, our "trying" doesn't end in failure, but success.

Before writing this, I reread the two stories you cite, Mike. "Twisted Medicine" I consider to be a success. It's strong and shocking, yes, but obviously structured to make a very valid comparison between the stock, artificial horror we unthinkingly accept as entertainment, and the tragic, horror of real-life as wrought by war. If just another "snap" ending had been our aim, we certainly could have set up the script and art to exploit the conclusion far more vividly. There'd be no foreshadowing of the narrator's fate as appears on page 56. In fact, his whole background, thoughts and feelings would have been played down to better preserve the "surprise." What shocks about the story is its great and terrible TRUTH. If this truth had been presented with the insensitivity you claim, Mike, I think "Twisted Medicine" would be immensely forgettable. I don't think it is!

But I didn't want to get involved with trying to argue you into liking a story you obviously didn't. The point I want to make is that if we were REALLY the pornographers of violence and depravity you imply, our whole approach would be different. We'd never bother paying high rates to artists of Leo Summers or Fernando Fernandez' sensitivity; we'd hire any hack who could shove blood and gore from every panel. We'd never use complex stories, functioning on multiple levels as "Twisted Medicine" did. That might confuse a reader or make him think. No, we'd want gross, blatant yarns to scream our intent.

THAT'S the point. Our INTENTION. We ARE striving for "the level of real literature," you and others seem to want, Mike. But you also seem to want us to impose limits, in language, in subject, that "real literature" never would. We feel we know and respect our audience, and gauge our content accordingly. If we err, we'd rather it be in OVERESTIMATING what they can appreciate. We try NOT to err, Mike, but it's good having readers who CARE enough to write in when they feel we do. Thanks.

ARCHIE GOODWIN, Editor

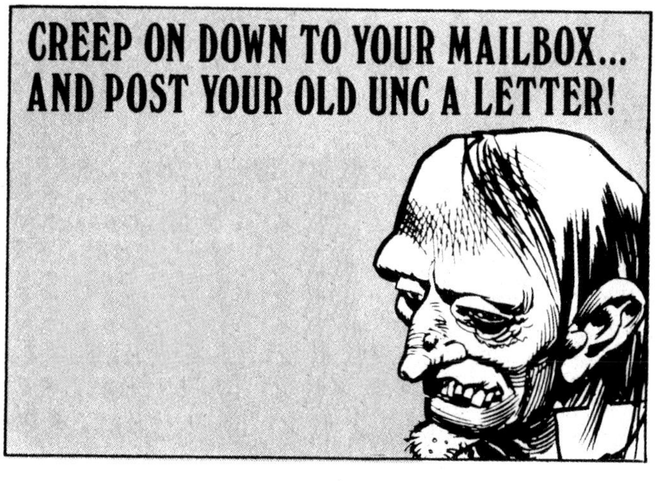
CREEP ON DOWN TO YOUR MAILBOX...
AND POST YOUR OLD UNC A LETTER!

CREEPY'S CATACOMBS

THE STORY AND SOUL OF
FERNANDO FERNANDEZ
THE MAN WHO IS WHAT HE DRAWS

I was asked for the story of my life, that Warren Publishing might run a brief biography," wrote **Fernando Fernandez**, one of our most illustrative artists, "and I wrote it. But," he continued, "after reading it several times, I realized that this just wasn't my life."

We read the information with interest, but were convinced by **Fernando** not to run it.

"Any artist's or illustrator's life," he believes, "is just that: his art! The facts, dates, and numbers tell you nothing about the man!" And so, based on this idea, we allowed one of our finest artists free reign to discuss his career.

"Whether the art is 'fine' or whether it is commercial," he began, "is of little importance to the true creator. What he does care about is his work itself, and how it is a reflection of his inner self."

"A man's art is where he feels . . . where he breathes. He is driven on, always wanting to improve, to go on seeking the self which he does not understand."

"He keeps looking for this identity, which is as vital a part of himself as food and water."

"And this, quite honestly, is not only **my** story, but that of anyone who has ever sought to create art in any form."

His point is a valid one, which suggests that it is not really important when or where an artist was born, or where he went to school. For art, as nature, eggs us on, beyond our control. One can only suspect that this is the way it was meant to be. Without this drive, we would all be content to do second-best.

And, we think, **Fernando's** dedication is reflected in his exceptional work!

Nowhere has Fernando's idea of art as a mirror of life been more evident than in the sensitive renderings of "Rendezvous," Vampirella #35.

THE FACE THAT LAUNCHED AN ISSUE OF CREEPY!

Jim Warren loved it, "It's going to make a **great** cover!" He was talking about the off-beat—and more than a little horrifying—portrait recently completed by **Larry Todd** and **Vaughn Bode**. Larry was to write and draw a story to go with the cover, called, intriguingly, "Philadelphia Pilot." Then, **Larry** got busy with his underground comix activities, and the story never materialized.

Enter Editor **Bill DuBay**. Here's this cover, striking, but a sharp stylistic break with the usual CREEPY, EERIE, or VAMPIRELLA cover; so different, it seemed to cry for something different inside to accompany it. When **several** writers showed interest in doing stories, Bill **had** it. Why not an **entire issue** based on the cover?

That was the idea and **this** is the issue. The stories were done gradually, over **two** years, as the right people became available. The result is something **unique** in comics history . . . And unique, we hope, in entertaining **you**!

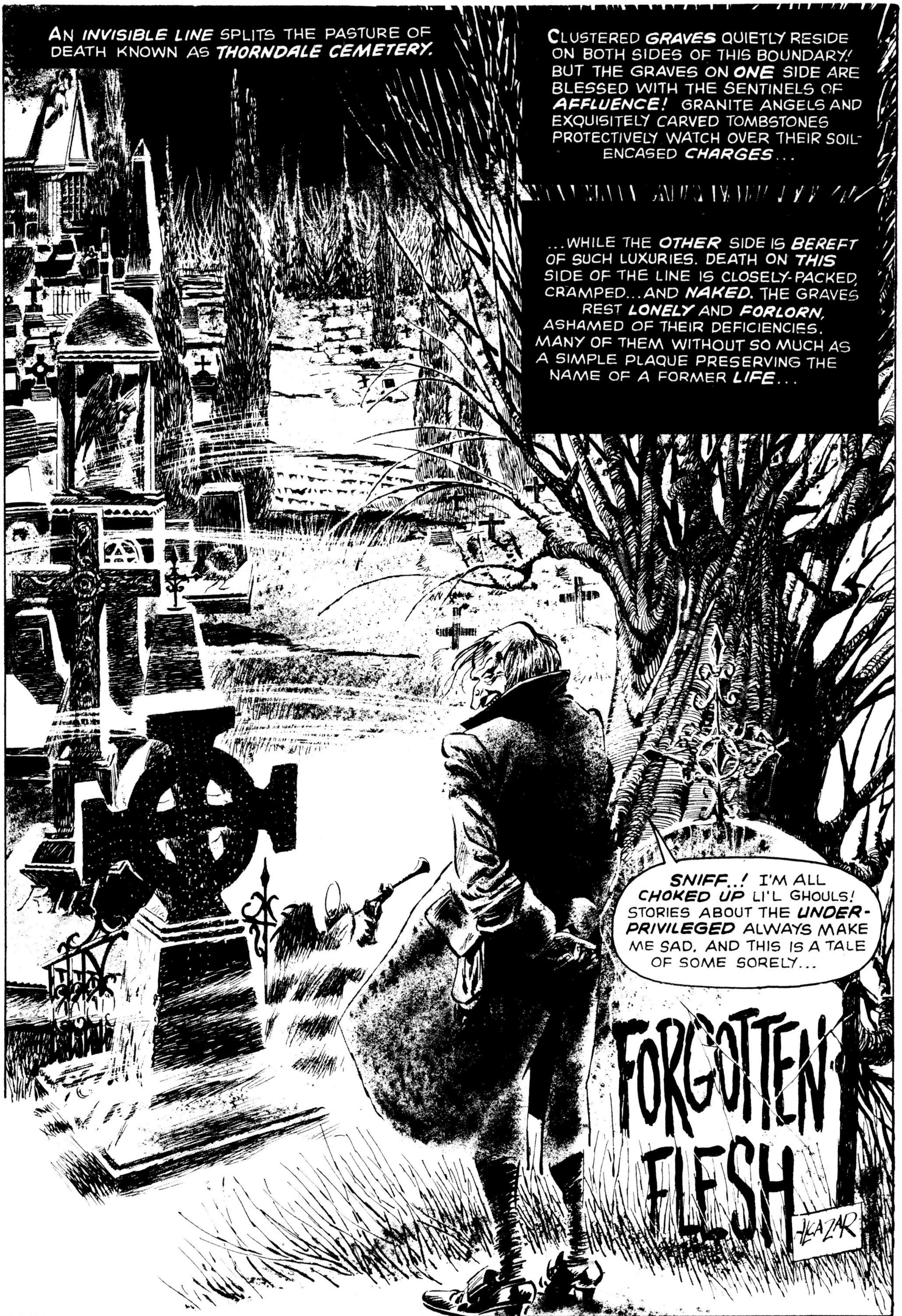
AN INVISIBLE LINE SPLITS THE PASTURE OF DEATH KNOWN AS THORNDALE CEMETERY.
CLUSTERED GRAVES QUIETLY RESIDE ON BOTH SIDES OF THIS BOUNDARY! BUT THE GRAVES ON ONE SIDE ARE BLESSED WITH THE SENTINELS OF AFFLUENCE! GRANITE ANGELS AND EXQUISITELY CARVED TOMBSTONES PROTECTIVELY WATCH OVER THEIR SOIL-ENCASED CHARGES...
...WHILE THE OTHER SIDE IS BEREFT OF SUCH LUXURIES. DEATH ON THIS SIDE OF THE LINE IS CLOSELY-PACKED, CRAMPED... AND NAKED. THE GRAVES REST LONELY AND FORLORN, ASHAMED OF THEIR DEFICIENCIES. MANY OF THEM WITHOUT SO MUCH AS A SIMPLE PLAQUE PRESERVING THE NAME OF A FORMER LIFE...
SNIFF..! I'M ALL CHOKED UP LI'L GHOULS! STORIES ABOUT THE UNDER-PRIVILEGED ALWAYS MAKE ME SAD. AND THIS IS A TALE OF SOME SORELY...
FORGOTTEN FLESH
ALCAZAR

STORY: DOUG MOENCH / ART: VICENTE ALCAZAR

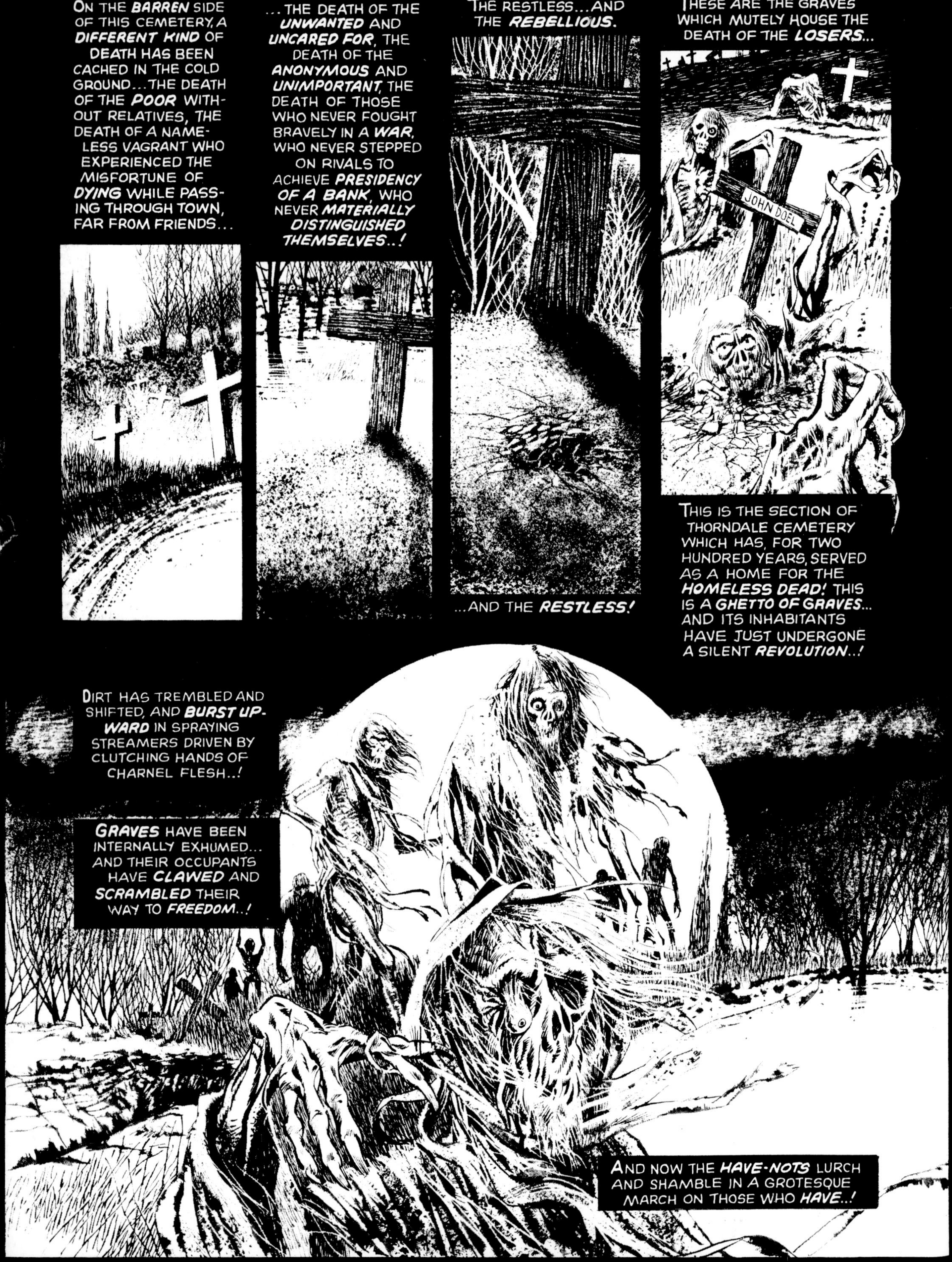

ON THE BARREN SIDE OF THIS CEMETERY, A DIFFERENT KIND OF DEATH HAS BEEN CACHED IN THE COLD GROUND... THE DEATH OF THE POOR WITHOUT RELATIVES, THE DEATH OF A NAMELESS VAGRANT WHO EXPERIENCED THE MISFORTUNE OF DYING WHILE PASSING THROUGH TOWN, FAR FROM FRIENDS...
...THE DEATH OF THE UNWANTED AND UNCARED FOR, THE DEATH OF THE ANONYMOUS AND UNIMPORTANT, THE DEATH OF THOSE WHO NEVER FOUGHT BRAVELY IN A WAR, WHO NEVER STEPPED ON RIVALS TO ACHIEVE PRESIDENCY OF A BANK, WHO NEVER MATERIALLY DISTINGUISHED THEMSELVES..!
THE RESTLESS... AND THE REBELLIOUS.
...AND THE RESTLESS!
THESE ARE THE GRAVES WHICH MUTELY HOUSE THE DEATH OF THE LOSERS...
JOHN DOE
THIS IS THE SECTION OF THORNDALE CEMETERY WHICH HAS, FOR TWO HUNDRED YEARS, SERVED AS A HOME FOR THE HOMELESS DEAD! THIS IS A GHETTO OF GRAVES... AND ITS INHABITANTS HAVE JUST UNDERGONE A SILENT REVOLUTION..!
DIRT HAS TREMBLED AND SHIFTED, AND BURST UPWARD IN SPRAYING STREAMERS DRIVEN BY CLUTCHING HANDS OF CHARNEL FLESH..!
GRAVES HAVE BEEN INTERNALLY EXHUMED... AND THEIR OCCUPANTS HAVE CLAWED AND SCRAMBLED THEIR WAY TO FREEDOM..!
AND NOW THE HAVE-NOTS LURCH AND SHAMBLE IN A GROTESQUE MARCH ON THOSE WHO HAVE..!

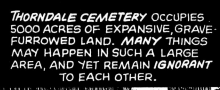

THORNDALE CEMETERY OCCUPIES 5000 ACRES OF EXPANSIVE, GRAVE-FURROWED LAND. MANY THINGS MAY HAPPEN IN SUCH A LARGE AREA, AND YET REMAIN IGNORANT TO EACH OTHER.

FAR FROM REBELLIOUS CORPSES, YET NOT SO FAR FROM TWO SCAVENGERS OF DEATH, SITS THE SIMPLE COTTAGE OF THORNDALE CEMETERY'S CARETAKER...HE WHO MAKES HIS LIVING TENDING THE DEAD..!

GHOULS IS WHAT WE'RE CALLED, LARCH! GHOULS! AND WHAT FOR? FOR THE SIMPLE FACT WE NEED TO EAT, AND WE TAKE THINGS TO BUY FOOD FROM THOSE WHAT AIN'T EVER GONNA EAT AGAIN!

SHUT UP AND DIG, SWINERT!

ALMOST TIME TO MAKE MY ROUNDS, LUCRETIA...

FROM THIS FANCY TOMBSTONE, I'LL BE DAMNABLY SURPRISED IF WE DON'T FIND THE TICKET TO HEAPS OF MEAT AND POTATOES INSIDE THE CASKET...

SHUT UP AND DIG, LARCH!

NOW DON'T YOU WORRY, LUCRETIA...

...I'LL BE BACK SOON.

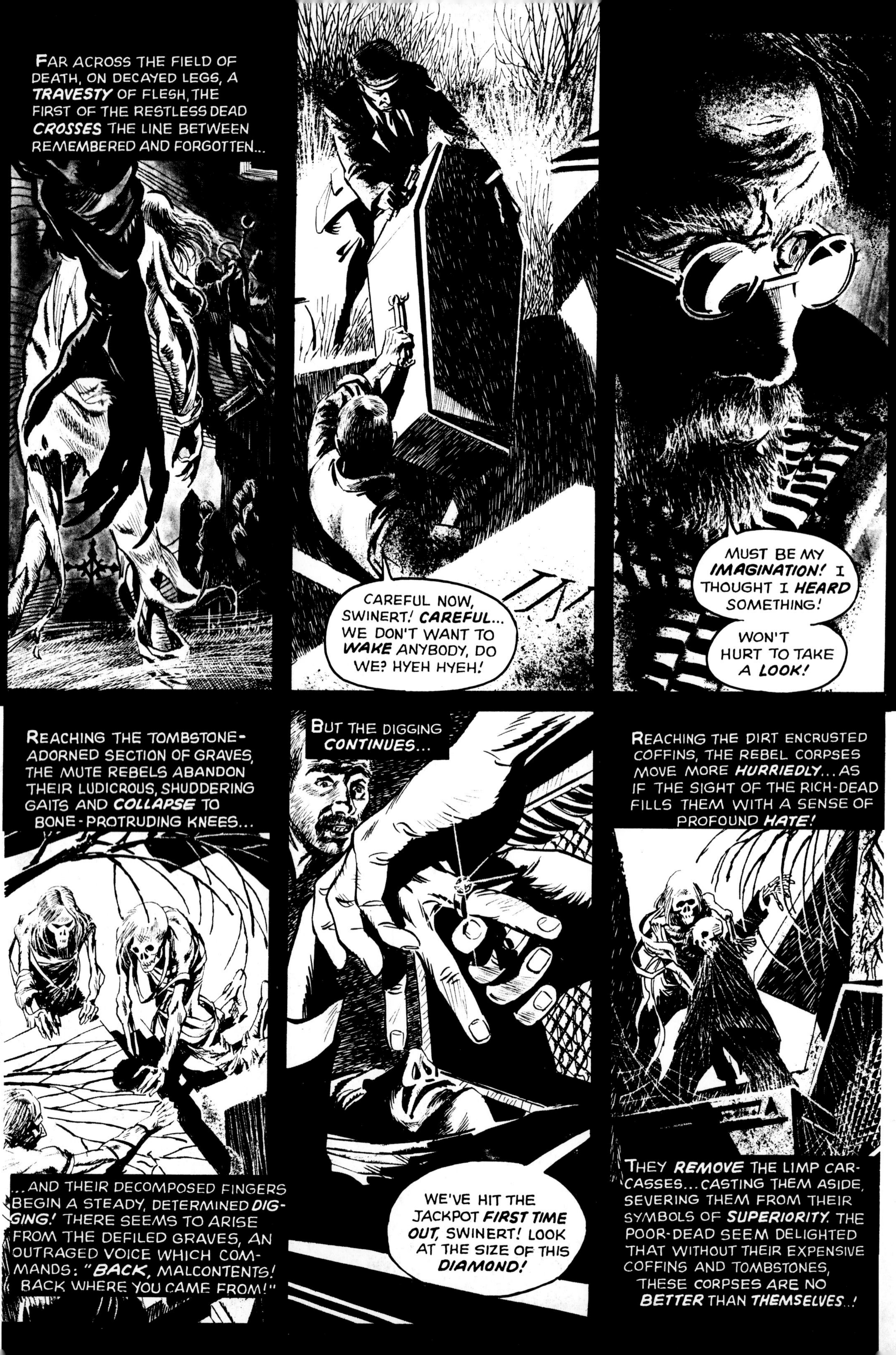
FAR ACROSS THE FIELD OF DEATH, ON DECAYED LEGS, A TRAVESTY OF FLESH, THE FIRST OF THE RESTLESS DEAD CROSSES THE LINE BETWEEN REMEMBERED AND FORGOTTEN...
CAREFUL NOW, SWINERT! CAREFUL... WE DON'T WANT TO WAKE ANYBODY, DO WE? HYEH HYEH!
MUST BE MY IMAGINATION! I THOUGHT I HEARD SOMETHING!
WON'T HURT TO TAKE A LOOK!
REACHING THE TOMBSTONE-ADORNED SECTION OF GRAVES, THE MUTE REBELS ABANDON THEIR LUDICROUS, SHUDDERING GAITS AND COLLAPSE TO BONE-PROTRUDING KNEES...
...AND THEIR DECOMPOSED FINGERS BEGIN A STEADY, DETERMINED DIGGING! THERE SEEMS TO ARISE FROM THE DEFILED GRAVES, AN OUTRAGED VOICE WHICH COMMANDS: "BACK, MALCONTENTS! BACK WHERE YOU CAME FROM!"
BUT THE DIGGING CONTINUES...
WE'VE HIT THE JACKPOT FIRST TIME OUT, SWINERT! LOOK AT THE SIZE OF THIS DIAMOND!
REACHING THE DIRT ENCRUSTED COFFINS, THE REBEL CORPSES MOVE MORE HURRIEDLY... AS IF THE SIGHT OF THE RICH-DEAD FILLS THEM WITH A SENSE OF PROFOUND HATE!
THEY REMOVE THE LIMP CARCASSES... CASTING THEM ASIDE, SEVERING THEM FROM THEIR SYMBOLS OF SUPERIORITY. THE POOR-DEAD SEEM DELIGHTED THAT WITHOUT THEIR EXPENSIVE COFFINS AND TOMBSTONES, THESE CORPSES ARE NO BETTER THAN THEMSELVES..!

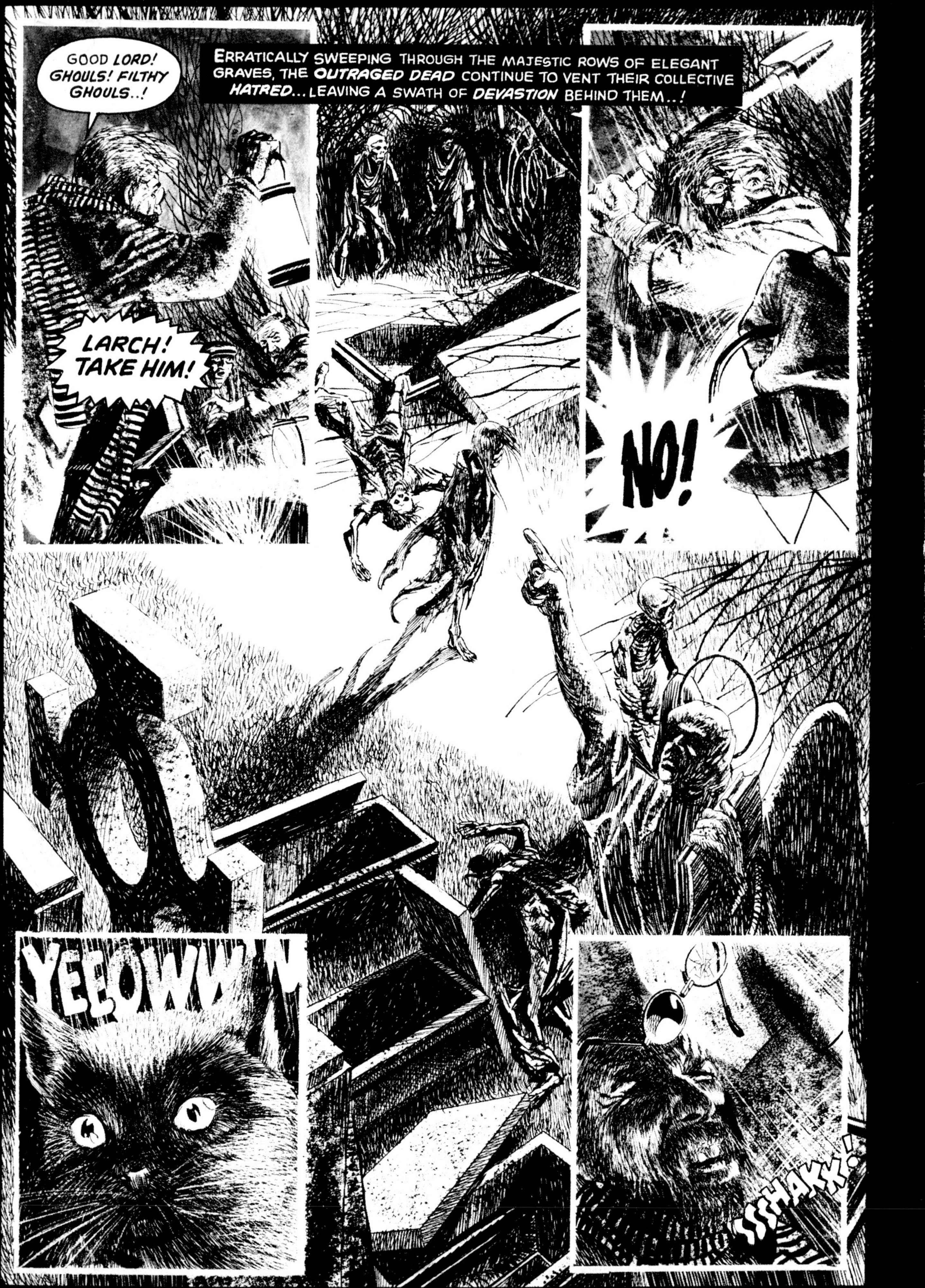
GOOD LORD! GHOULS! FILTHY GHOULS..!
ERRATICALLY SWEEPING THROUGH THE MAJESTIC ROWS OF ELEGANT GRAVES, THE OUTRAGED DEAD CONTINUE TO VENT THEIR COLLECTIVE HATRED... LEAVING A SWATH OF DEVASTION BEHIND THEM..!
LARCH! TAKE HIM!
NO!
YEEOWWW'N
SSSHAKK!

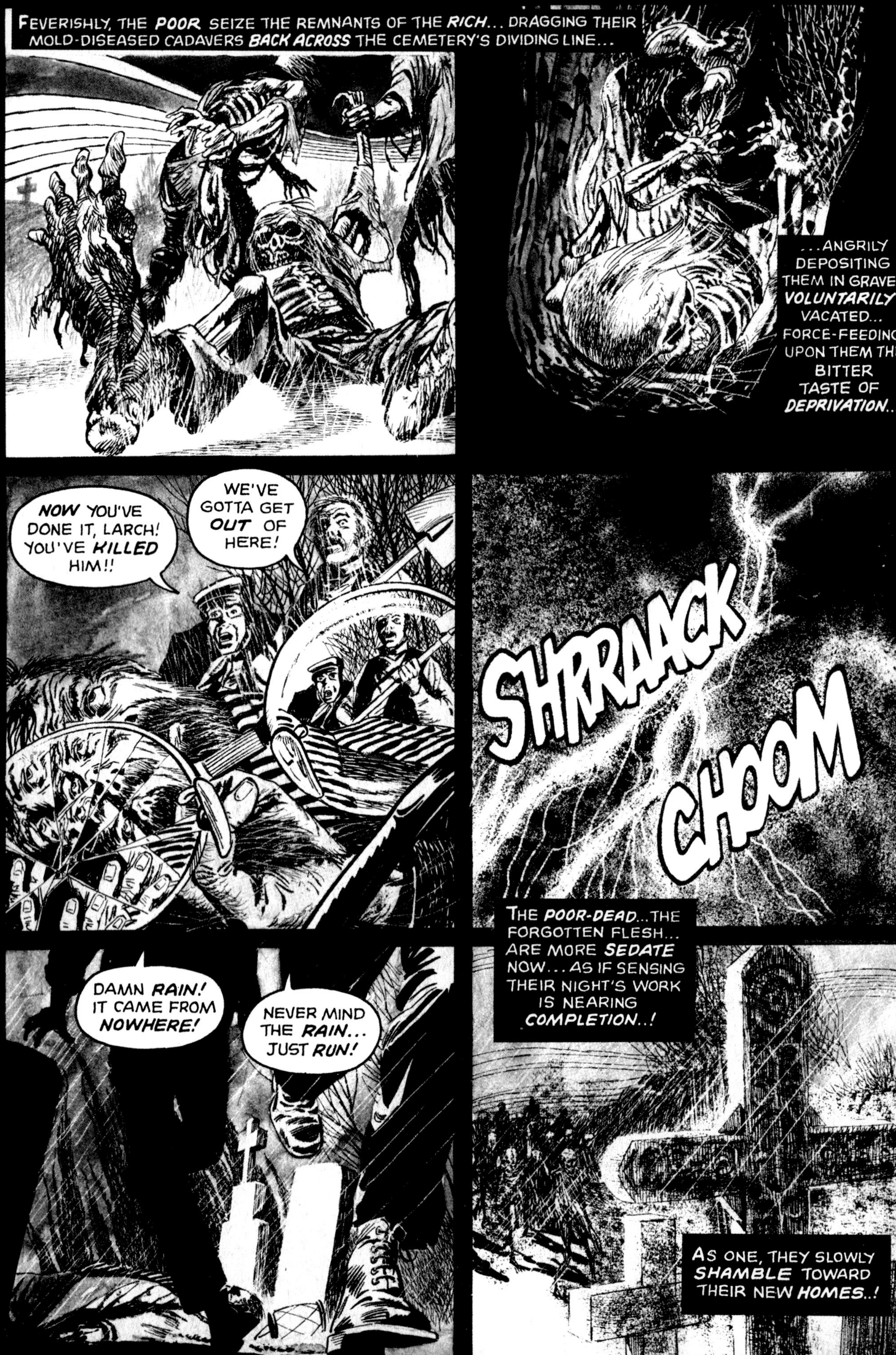
FEVERISHLY, THE POOR SEIZE THE REMNANTS OF THE RICH... DRAGGING THEIR MOLD-DISEASED CADAVERS BACK ACROSS THE CEMETERY'S DIVIDING LINE...
...ANGRILY DEPOSITING THEM IN GRAVES VOLUNTARILY VACATED... FORCE-FEEDING UPON THEM THE BITTER TASTE OF DEPRIVATION..!
NOW YOU'VE DONE IT, LARCH! YOU'VE KILLED HIM!!
WE'VE GOTTA GET OUT OF HERE!
SHRRAACK
CHOOM
DAMN RAIN! IT CAME FROM NOWHERE!
NEVER MIND THE RAIN... JUST RUN!
THE POOR-DEAD... THE FORGOTTEN FLESH... ARE MORE SEDATE NOW... AS IF SENSING THEIR NIGHT'S WORK IS NEARING COMPLETION..!
AS ONE, THEY SLOWLY SHAMBLE TOWARD THEIR NEW HOMES..!

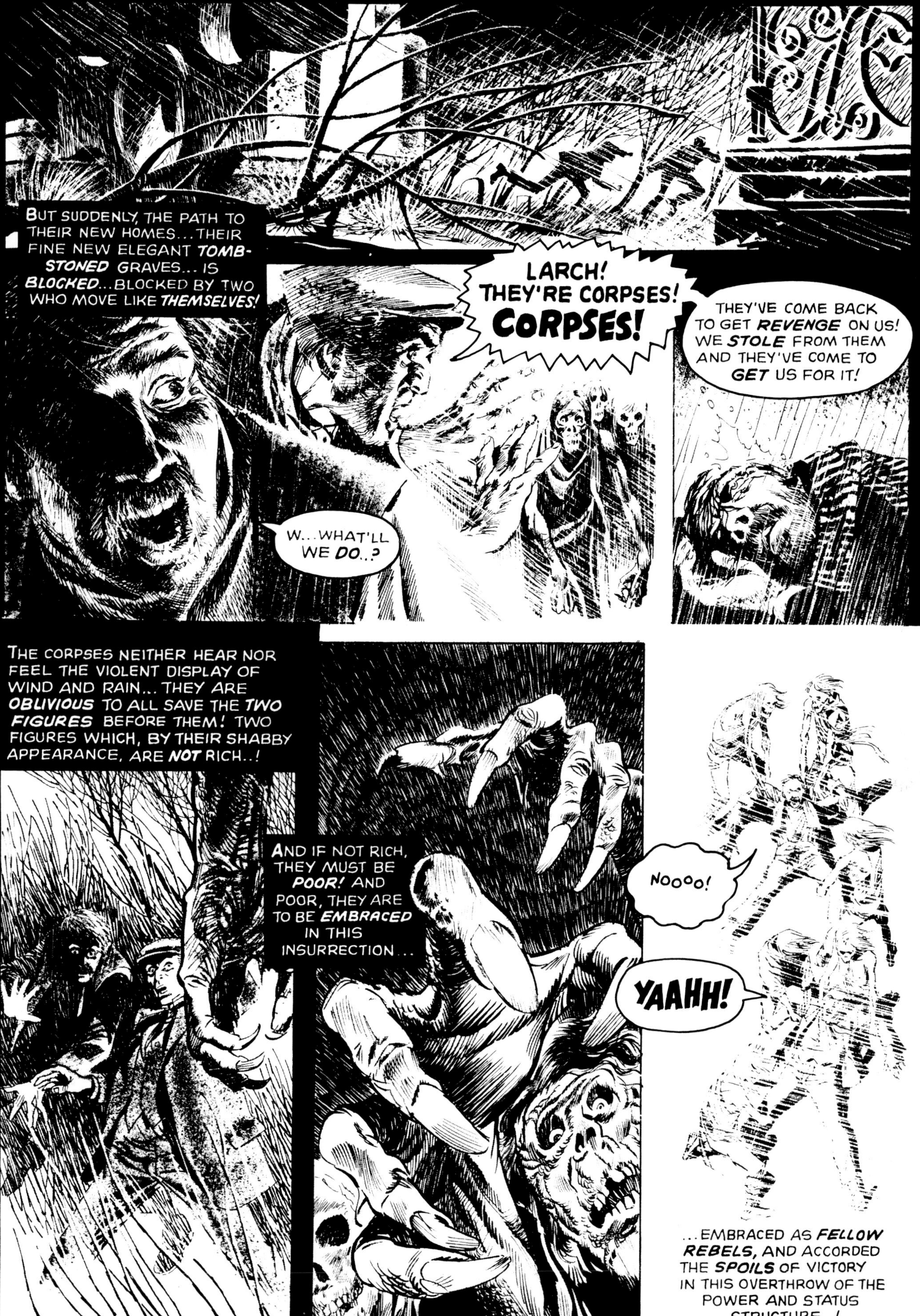

BUT SUDDENLY, THE PATH TO THEIR NEW HOMES... THEIR FINE NEW ELEGANT TOMB-STONED GRAVES... IS BLOCKED... BLOCKED BY TWO WHO MOVE LIKE THEMSELVES!
LARCH! THEY'RE CORPSES! CORPSES!
THEY'VE COME BACK TO GET REVENGE ON US! WE STOLE FROM THEM AND THEY'VE COME TO GET US FOR IT!
W... WHAT'LL WE DO..?
THE CORPSES NEITHER HEAR NOR FEEL THE VIOLENT DISPLAY OF WIND AND RAIN... THEY ARE OBLIVIOUS TO ALL SAVE THE TWO FIGURES BEFORE THEM! TWO FIGURES WHICH, BY THEIR SHABBY APPEARANCE, ARE NOT RICH..!
AND IF NOT RICH, THEY MUST BE POOR! AND POOR, THEY ARE TO BE EMBRACED IN THIS INSURRECTION...
NOOOO!
YAAHH!
...EMBRACED AS FELLOW REBELS, AND ACCORDED THE SPOILS OF VICTORY IN THIS OVERTHROW OF THE POWER AND STATUS STRUCTURE..!

BEING *EQUALS*, THE CORPSES REASON, THESE TWO MUST ALSO BE HEIR TO FINE *NEW HOMES* THEY HAVE NEVER HAD *BEFORE!*

NO! GOD! NOoo...

BUT WHY THEN DO THEY *STRUGGLE* AND *SCREAM* AS THEY ARE THROWN INTO SUCH *ELEGANT GRAVES..?*

NO MATTER. THEY ARE SOON *QUIET,* COMPLACENT BENEATH THEIR NEW BLANKETS OF EARTH!

AND THE EARTH IS BEATEN SNUGLY *OVER* THEM BY THE FURY OF A HEAVEN-BOLTED *DELUGE..!*

THE CORPSES ARE *SATISFIED* WITH WHAT THEY HAVE DONE. THEIR *TRANQUIL FEELING* CONTRASTS SHARPLY WITH THE CHAOTIC MAELSTROM NATURE HAS UNLEASHED AROUND THEM!

COMPLACENTLY, THEY ASSUME *OCCUPANCY* OF THE USURPED GRAVES..!

THE CORPSES LIE *STILL* NOW, RESTING IN SERENE PEACE AS THE RELENTLESS HURRICANE *RIPS* THROUGH THE CEMETERY, UPROOTING *TREES* AND *TOMBSTONES* ALIKE...

...AND DISTRIBUTING THEM *EQUALLY* THROUGHOUT THE WIND-TORN GRAVEYARD... *DESTROYING* THE INVISIBLE LINE BETWEEN THE *HAVES* AND THE *HAVE-NOTS..!*

AND IN THE MORNING, YOU WOULD *SWEAR* THAT EVERYONE IN THORNDALE CEMETERY WAS *HAPPY..!*

ALMOST..!

MEEOWRR?

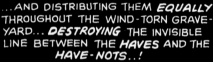

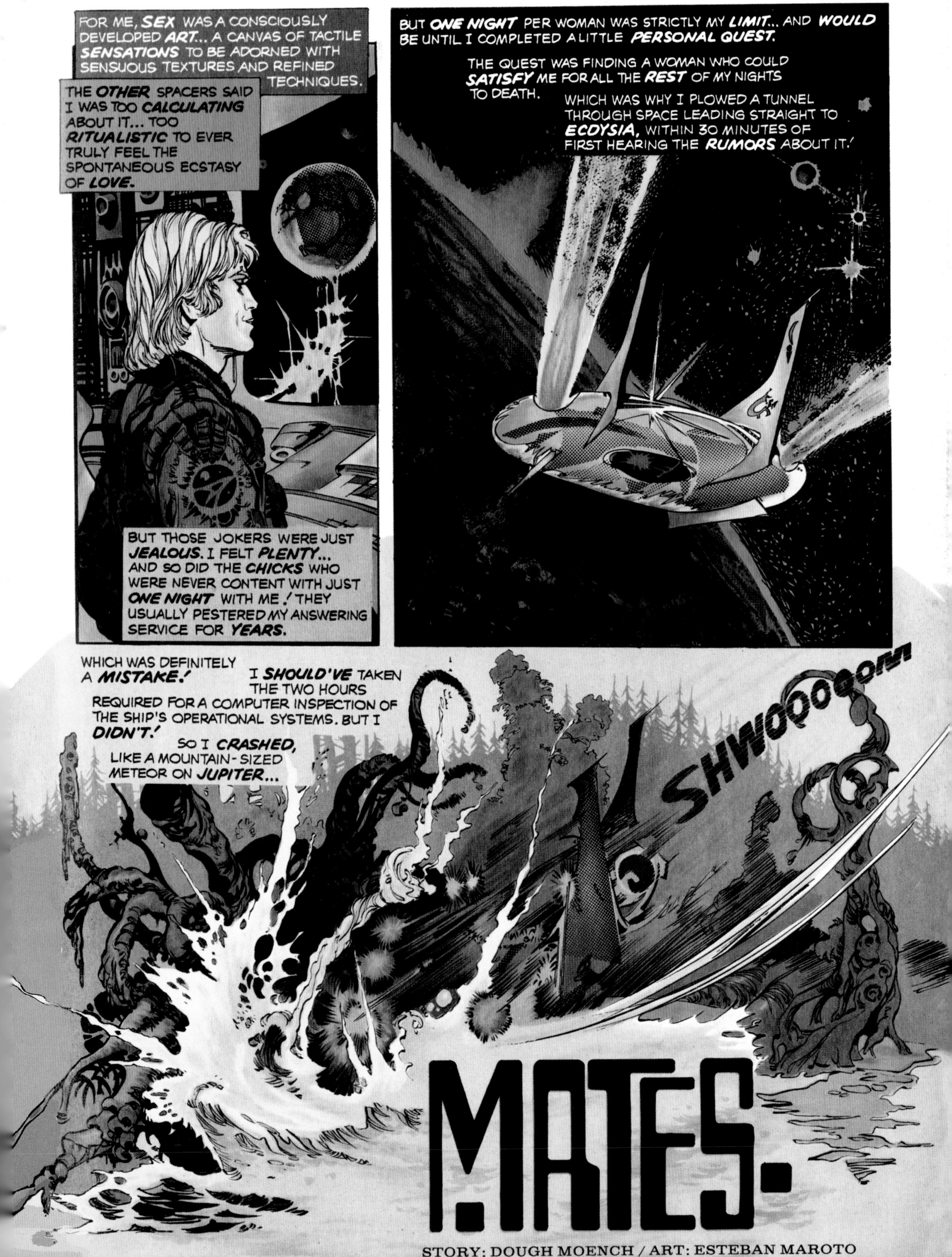

FOR ME, SEX WAS A CONSCIOUSLY DEVELOPED ART... A CANVAS OF TACTILE SENSATIONS TO BE ADORNED WITH SENSUOUS TEXTURES AND REFINED TECHNIQUES.
THE OTHER SPACERS SAID I WAS TOO CALCULATING ABOUT IT... TOO RITUALISTIC TO EVER TRULY FEEL THE SPONTANEOUS ECSTASY OF LOVE.
BUT THOSE JOKERS WERE JUST JEALOUS. I FELT PLENTY... AND SO DID THE CHICKS WHO WERE NEVER CONTENT WITH JUST ONE NIGHT WITH ME.' THEY USUALLY PESTERED MY ANSWERING SERVICE FOR YEARS.
BUT ONE NIGHT PER WOMAN WAS STRICTLY MY LIMIT... AND WOULD BE UNTIL I COMPLETED A LITTLE PERSONAL QUEST.
THE QUEST WAS FINDING A WOMAN WHO COULD SATISFY ME FOR ALL THE REST OF MY NIGHTS TO DEATH.
WHICH WAS WHY I PLOWED A TUNNEL THROUGH SPACE LEADING STRAIGHT TO ECDYSIA, WITHIN 30 MINUTES OF FIRST HEARING THE RUMORS ABOUT IT.'
WHICH WAS DEFINITELY A MISTAKE.'
I SHOULD'VE TAKEN THE TWO HOURS REQUIRED FOR A COMPUTER INSPECTION OF THE SHIP'S OPERATIONAL SYSTEMS. BUT I DIDN'T.'
SO I CRASHED, LIKE A MOUNTAIN-SIZED METEOR ON JUPITER...
SHWOOOOOOM
MATES
STORY: DOUGH MOENCH / ART: ESTEBAN MAROTO

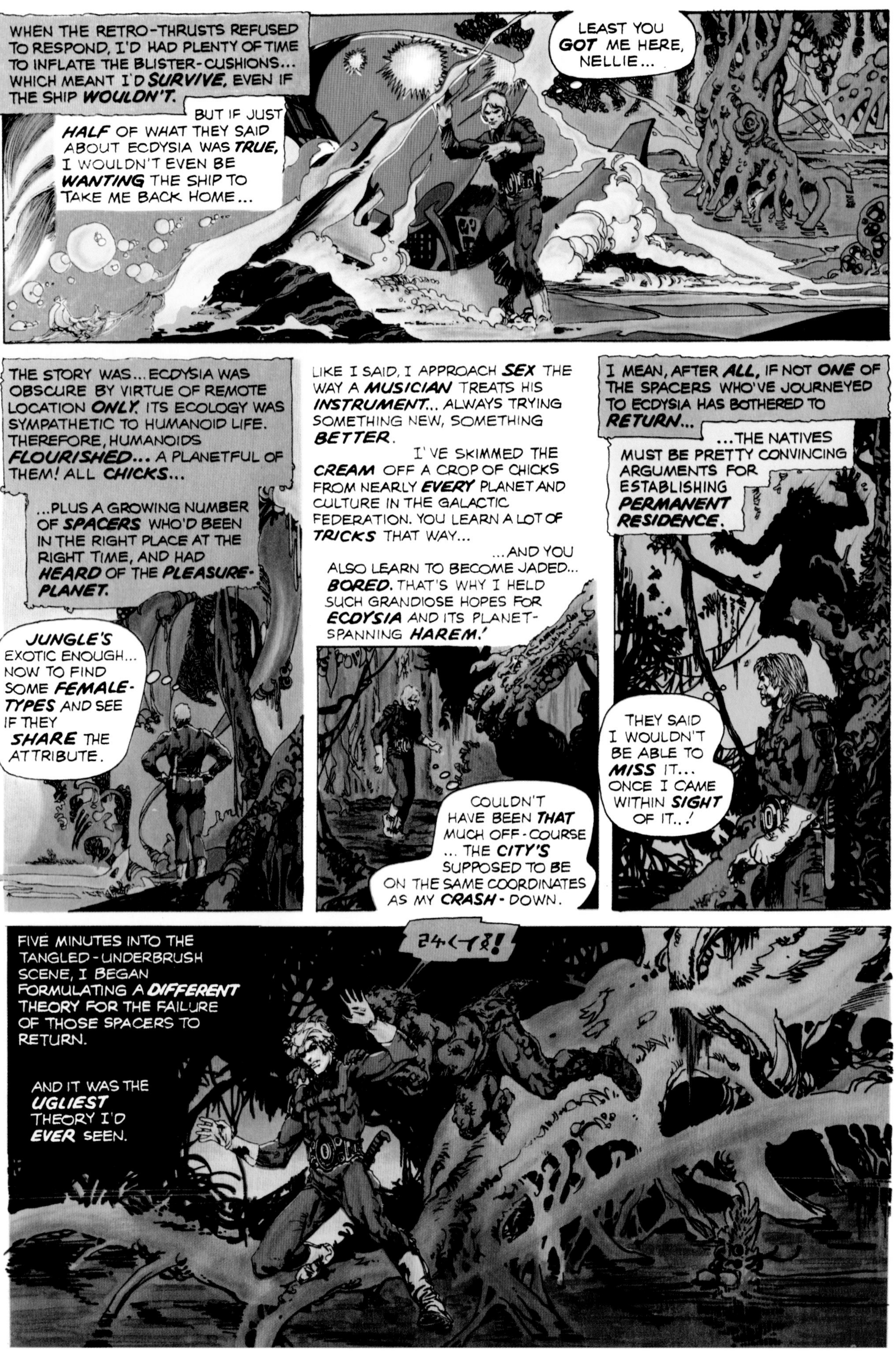
WHEN THE RETRO-THRUSTS REFUSED TO RESPOND, I'D HAD PLENTY OF TIME TO INFLATE THE BLISTER-CUSHIONS... WHICH MEANT I'D SURVIVE, EVEN IF THE SHIP WOULDN'T.
LEAST YOU GOT ME HERE, NELLIE...
BUT IF JUST HALF OF WHAT THEY SAID ABOUT ECDYSIA WAS TRUE, I WOULDN'T EVEN BE WANTING THE SHIP TO TAKE ME BACK HOME...
THE STORY WAS... ECDYSIA WAS OBSCURE BY VIRTUE OF REMOTE LOCATION ONLY. ITS ECOLOGY WAS SYMPATHETIC TO HUMANOID LIFE. THEREFORE, HUMANOIDS FLOURISHED... A PLANETFUL OF THEM! ALL CHICKS...
...PLUS A GROWING NUMBER OF SPACERS WHO'D BEEN IN THE RIGHT PLACE AT THE RIGHT TIME, AND HAD HEARD OF THE PLEASURE-PLANET.
JUNGLE'S EXOTIC ENOUGH... NOW TO FIND SOME FEMALE-TYPES AND SEE IF THEY SHARE THE ATTRIBUTE.
LIKE I SAID, I APPROACH SEX THE WAY A MUSICIAN TREATS HIS INSTRUMENT... ALWAYS TRYING SOMETHING NEW, SOMETHING BETTER.
I'VE SKIMMED THE CREAM OFF A CROP OF CHICKS FROM NEARLY EVERY PLANET AND CULTURE IN THE GALACTIC FEDERATION. YOU LEARN A LOT OF TRICKS THAT WAY...
...AND YOU ALSO LEARN TO BECOME JADED... BORED. THAT'S WHY I HELD SUCH GRANDIOSE HOPES FOR ECDYSIA AND ITS PLANET-SPANNING HAREM!
COULDN'T HAVE BEEN THAT MUCH OFF-COURSE... THE CITY'S SUPPOSED TO BE ON THE SAME COORDINATES AS MY CRASH-DOWN.
I MEAN, AFTER ALL, IF NOT ONE OF THE SPACERS WHO'VE JOURNEYED TO ECDYSIA HAS BOTHERED TO RETURN...
...THE NATIVES MUST BE PRETTY CONVINCING ARGUMENTS FOR ESTABLISHING PERMANENT RESIDENCE.
THEY SAID I WOULDN'T BE ABLE TO MISS IT... ONCE I CAME WITHIN SIGHT OF IT...!
FIVE MINUTES INTO THE TANGLED-UNDERBRUSH SCENE, I BEGAN FORMULATING A DIFFERENT THEORY FOR THE FAILURE OF THOSE SPACERS TO RETURN.
AND IT WAS THE UGLIEST THEORY I'D EVER SEEN.

BUT I REALLY DIDN'T *WANT* TO *BELIEVE* THAT ALL THOSE LUST-CRAZED SPACERS HAD BEEN *PREVENTED* FROM LEAVING ECDYSIA...

...SO I DECIDED TO PROVE FOR MYSELF THAT A SPACER EQUIPPED WITH STANDARD GEAR COULD *AVOID* ANY POTENTIAL PREVENTION.

"STANDARD GEAR" BEING A *LASER-SLASHER...!*

I *SLASHED...*

...LEAVING THE *LASER* TO DO THE *REST.*

SPRAKSHHH

AH-*AH,* HANDSOME... MUSTN'T TOUCH THE *MAGIC WAND.*

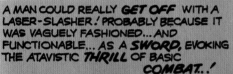

A MAN COULD REALLY *GET OFF* WITH A LASER-SLASHER*!* PROBABLY BECAUSE IT WAS VAGUELY FASHIONED... AND FUNCTIONABLE... AS A *SWORD,* EVOKING THE ATAVISTIC *THRILL* OF BASIC *COMBAT..!*

OF COURSE, THE FACT THAT EACH THRUST OR SLASH MET WITH A BURST OF CRACKLING *SPARKS,* SEARED *FLESH,* AND ERUPTING *GORE* HELPED A LITTLE...

SHHKRAK- PSSSSS

...HELPED IN MORE WAYS THAN *ONE!*

THE SIZZLING CARCASS *REEKED...* MAKING ME ANXIOUS TO FORGE *AHEAD...*

...TOWARD THE FABULOUS RACE OF CHICKS WHO HAD DEVOTED THEMSELVES TO THE ARTFUL GROOMING OF *SEX.* DEFINITELY *MY* KIND OF CHICKS..!

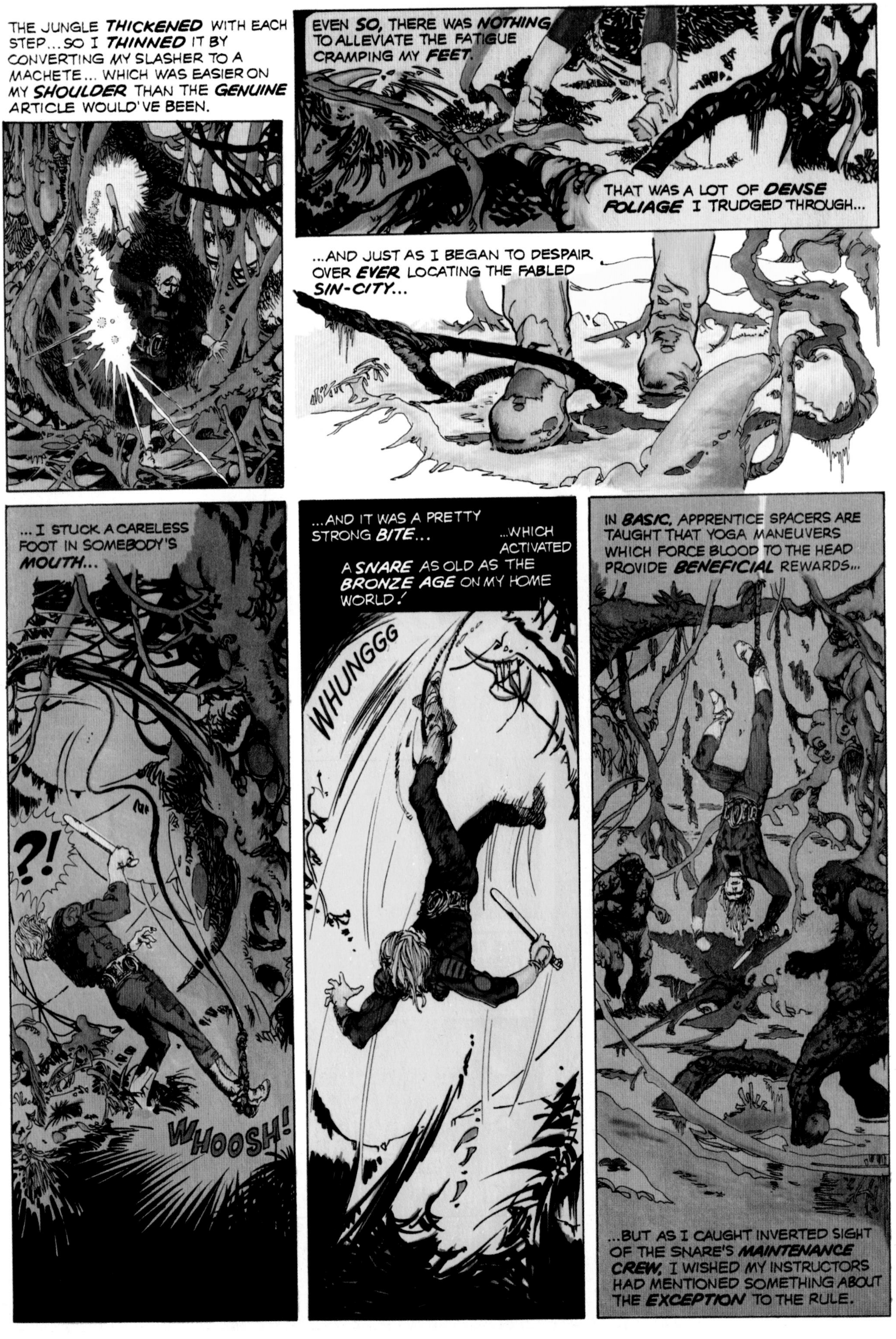
THE JUNGLE THICKENED WITH EACH STEP... SO I THINNED IT BY CONVERTING MY SLASHER TO A MACHETE... WHICH WAS EASIER ON MY SHOULDER THAN THE GENUINE ARTICLE WOULD'VE BEEN.
EVEN SO, THERE WAS NOTHING TO ALLEVIATE THE FATIGUE CRAMPING MY FEET.
THAT WAS A LOT OF DENSE FOLIAGE I TRUDGED THROUGH...
...AND JUST AS I BEGAN TO DESPAIR OVER EVER LOCATING THE FABLED SIN-CITY...
...I STUCK A CARELESS FOOT IN SOMEBODY'S MOUTH...
?!
WHOOSH!
...AND IT WAS A PRETTY STRONG BITE...
...WHICH ACTIVATED
A SNARE AS OLD AS THE BRONZE AGE ON MY HOME WORLD!
WHUNGGG
IN BASIC, APPRENTICE SPACERS ARE TAUGHT THAT YOGA MANEUVERS WHICH FORCE BLOOD TO THE HEAD PROVIDE BENEFICIAL REWARDS...
...BUT AS I CAUGHT INVERTED SIGHT OF THE SNARE'S MAINTENANCE CREW, I WISHED MY INSTRUCTORS HAD MENTIONED SOMETHING ABOUT THE EXCEPTION TO THE RULE.

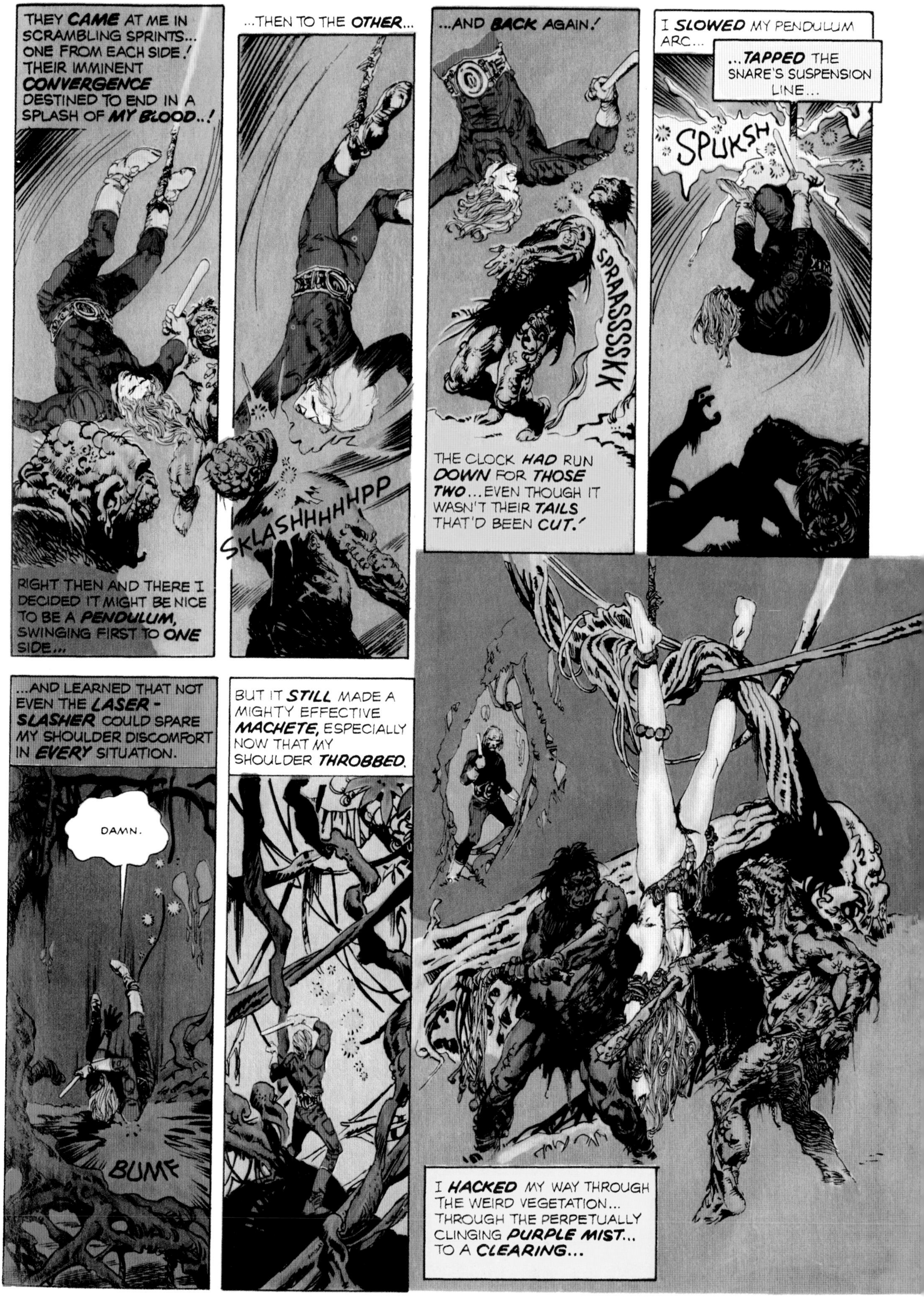
THEY CAME AT ME IN SCRAMBLING SPRINTS... ONE FROM EACH SIDE! THEIR IMMINENT CONVERGENCE DESTINED TO END IN A SPLASH OF MY BLOOD..!
RIGHT THEN AND THERE I DECIDED IT MIGHT BE NICE TO BE A PENDULUM, SWINGING FIRST TO ONE SIDE...
...THEN TO THE OTHER...
SKLASHHHHHPP
...AND BACK AGAIN!
SPRAASSSSKK
THE CLOCK HAD RUN DOWN FOR THOSE TWO... EVEN THOUGH IT WASN'T THEIR TAILS THAT'D BEEN CUT!
I SLOWED MY PENDULUM ARC...
...TAPPED THE SNARE'S SUSPENSION LINE...
SPUKSH
...AND LEARNED THAT NOT EVEN THE LASER-SLASHER COULD SPARE MY SHOULDER DISCOMFORT IN EVERY SITUATION.
DAMN.
BUMF
BUT IT STILL MADE A MIGHTY EFFECTIVE MACHETE, ESPECIALLY NOW THAT MY SHOULDER THROBBED.
I HACKED MY WAY THROUGH THE WEIRD VEGETATION... THROUGH THE PERPETUALLY CLINGING PURPLE MIST... TO A CLEARING...

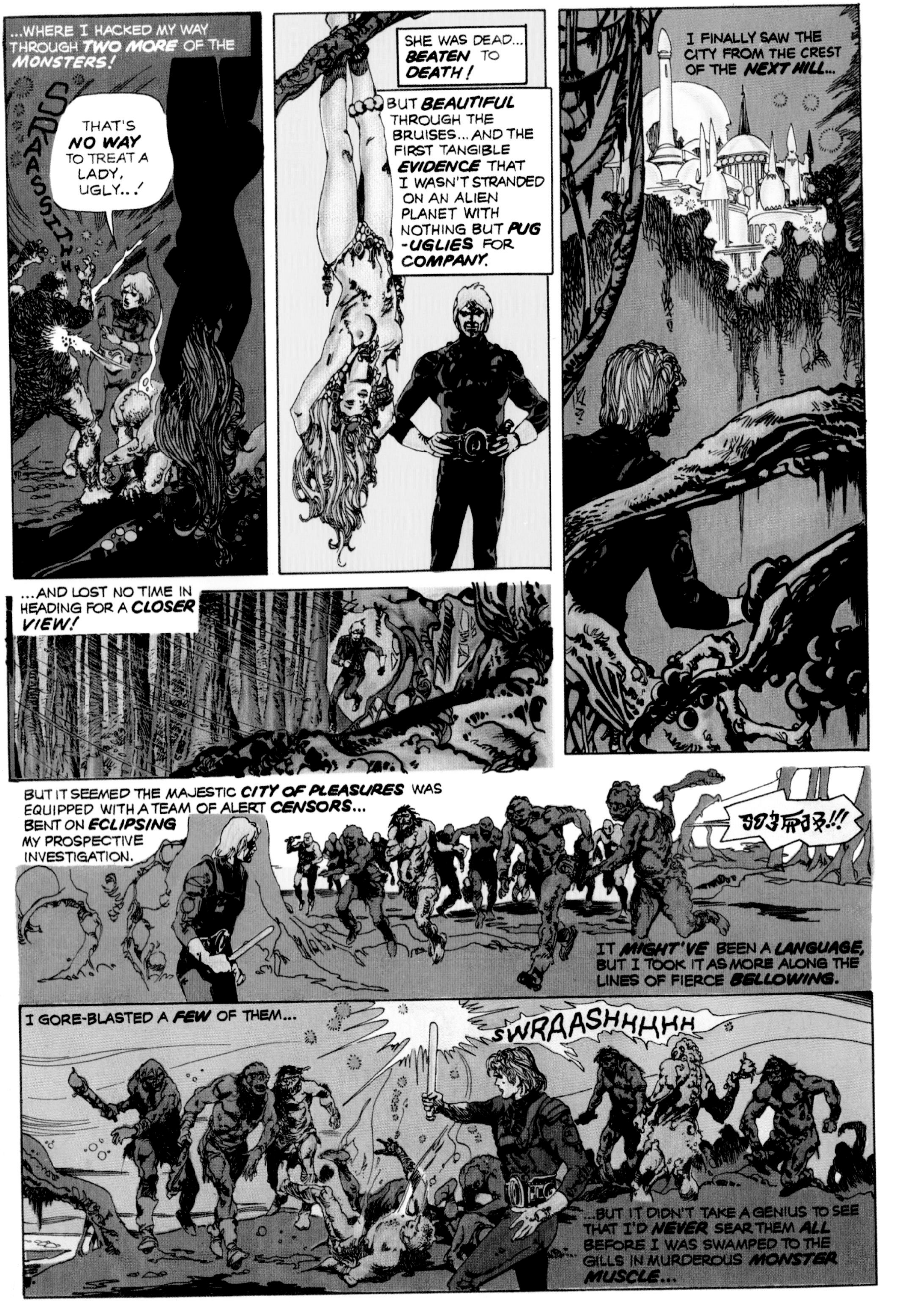

...WHERE I HACKED MY WAY THROUGH TWO MORE OF THE MONSTERS!
SRRAASSSHHH
THAT'S NO WAY TO TREAT A LADY, UGLY..!
SHE WAS DEAD... BEATEN TO DEATH!
BUT BEAUTIFUL THROUGH THE BRUISES...AND THE FIRST TANGIBLE EVIDENCE THAT I WASN'T STRANDED ON AN ALIEN PLANET WITH NOTHING BUT PUG-UGLIES FOR COMPANY.
I FINALLY SAW THE CITY FROM THE CREST OF THE NEXT HILL...
...AND LOST NO TIME IN HEADING FOR A CLOSER VIEW!
BUT IT SEEMED THE MAJESTIC CITY OF PLEASURES WAS EQUIPPED WITH A TEAM OF ALERT CENSORS... BENT ON ECLIPSING MY PROSPECTIVE INVESTIGATION.
IT MIGHT'VE BEEN A LANGUAGE, BUT I TOOK IT AS MORE ALONG THE LINES OF FIERCE BELLOWING.
I GORE-BLASTED A FEW OF THEM...
SWRAASHHHHH
...BUT IT DIDN'T TAKE A GENIUS TO SEE THAT I'D NEVER SEAR THEM ALL BEFORE I WAS SWAMPED TO THE GILLS IN MURDEROUS MONSTER MUSCLE...

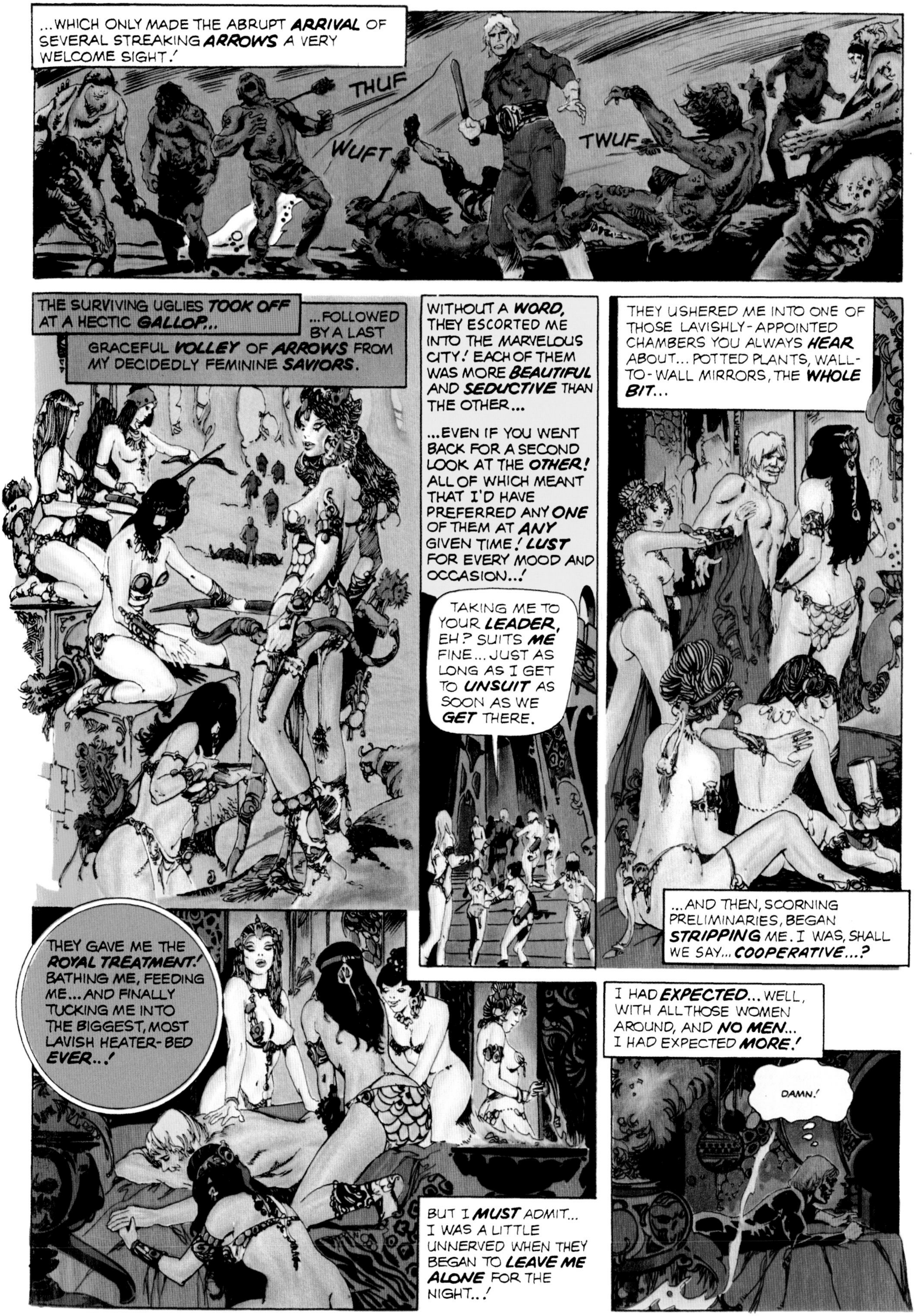
...WHICH ONLY MADE THE ABRUPT ARRIVAL OF SEVERAL STREAKING ARROWS A VERY WELCOME SIGHT.!
THUF
WUFT
TWUF
THE SURVIVING UGLIES TOOK OFF AT A HECTIC GALLOP...
...FOLLOWED BY A LAST
GRACEFUL VOLLEY OF ARROWS FROM MY DECIDEDLY FEMININE SAVIORS.
WITHOUT A WORD, THEY ESCORTED ME INTO THE MARVELOUS CITY! EACH OF THEM WAS MORE BEAUTIFUL AND SEDUCTIVE THAN THE OTHER...
...EVEN IF YOU WENT BACK FOR A SECOND LOOK AT THE OTHER! ALL OF WHICH MEANT THAT I'D HAVE PREFERRED ANY ONE OF THEM AT ANY GIVEN TIME! LUST FOR EVERY MOOD AND OCCASION..!
TAKING ME TO YOUR LEADER, EH? SUITS ME FINE... JUST AS LONG AS I GET TO UNSUIT AS SOON AS WE GET THERE.
THEY USHERED ME INTO ONE OF THOSE LAVISHLY-APPOINTED CHAMBERS YOU ALWAYS HEAR ABOUT... POTTED PLANTS, WALL-TO-WALL MIRRORS, THE WHOLE BIT...
...AND THEN, SCORNING PRELIMINARIES, BEGAN STRIPPING ME. I WAS, SHALL WE SAY... COOPERATIVE...?
THEY GAVE ME THE ROYAL TREATMENT! BATHING ME, FEEDING ME... AND FINALLY TUCKING ME INTO THE BIGGEST, MOST LAVISH HEATER-BED EVER...!
BUT I MUST ADMIT... I WAS A LITTLE UNNERVED WHEN THEY BEGAN TO LEAVE ME ALONE FOR THE NIGHT..!
I HAD EXPECTED... WELL, WITH ALL THOSE WOMEN AROUND, AND NO MEN... I HAD EXPECTED MORE!
DAMN!

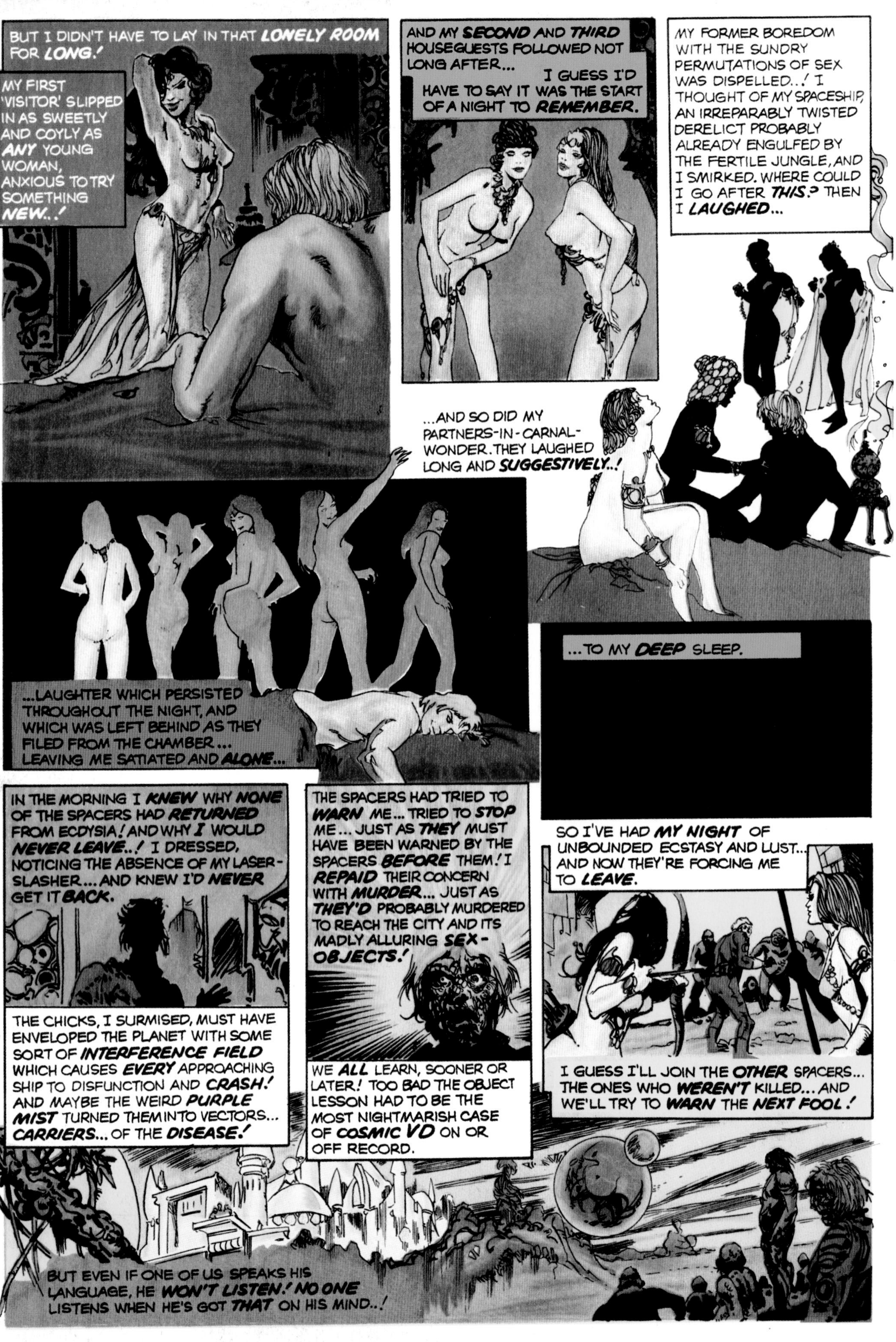

BUT I DIDN'T HAVE TO LAY IN THAT LONELY ROOM FOR LONG.!
MY FIRST 'VISITOR' SLIPPED IN AS SWEETLY AND COYLY AS ANY YOUNG WOMAN, ANXIOUS TO TRY SOMETHING NEW..!
AND MY SECOND AND THIRD HOUSEGUESTS FOLLOWED NOT LONG AFTER...
I GUESS I'D HAVE TO SAY IT WAS THE START OF A NIGHT TO REMEMBER.
MY FORMER BOREDOM WITH THE SUNDRY PERMUTATIONS OF SEX WAS DISPELLED..! I THOUGHT OF MY SPACESHIP, AN IRREPARABLY TWISTED DERELICT PROBABLY ALREADY ENGULFED BY THE FERTILE JUNGLE, AND I SMIRKED. WHERE COULD I GO AFTER THIS? THEN I LAUGHED...
...AND SO DID MY PARTNERS-IN-CARNAL-WONDER. THEY LAUGHED LONG AND SUGGESTIVELY..!
...LAUGHTER WHICH PERSISTED THROUGHOUT THE NIGHT, AND WHICH WAS LEFT BEHIND AS THEY FILED FROM THE CHAMBER... LEAVING ME SATIATED AND ALONE...
...TO MY DEEP SLEEP.
IN THE MORNING I KNEW WHY NONE OF THE SPACERS HAD RETURNED FROM ECDYSIA! AND WHY I WOULD NEVER LEAVE..! I DRESSED, NOTICING THE ABSENCE OF MY LASER-SLASHER... AND KNEW I'D NEVER GET IT BACK.
THE CHICKS, I SURMISED, MUST HAVE ENVELOPED THE PLANET WITH SOME SORT OF INTERFERENCE FIELD WHICH CAUSES EVERY APPROACHING SHIP TO DISFUNCTION AND CRASH! AND MAYBE THE WEIRD PURPLE MIST TURNED THEM INTO VECTORS... CARRIERS... OF THE DISEASE!
THE SPACERS HAD TRIED TO WARN ME... TRIED TO STOP ME... JUST AS THEY MUST HAVE BEEN WARNED BY THE SPACERS BEFORE THEM! I REPAID THEIR CONCERN WITH MURDER... JUST AS THEY'D PROBABLY MURDERED TO REACH THE CITY AND ITS MADLY ALLURING SEX-OBJECTS!
WE ALL LEARN, SOONER OR LATER! TOO BAD THE OBJECT LESSON HAD TO BE THE MOST NIGHTMARISH CASE OF COSMIC VD ON OR OFF RECORD.
SO I'VE HAD MY NIGHT OF UNBOUNDED ECSTASY AND LUST... AND NOW THEY'RE FORCING ME TO LEAVE.
I GUESS I'LL JOIN THE OTHER SPACERS... THE ONES WHO WEREN'T KILLED... AND WE'LL TRY TO WARN THE NEXT FOOL!
BUT EVEN IF ONE OF US SPEAKS HIS LANGUAGE, HE WON'T LISTEN! NO ONE LISTENS WHEN HE'S GOT THAT ON HIS MIND..!

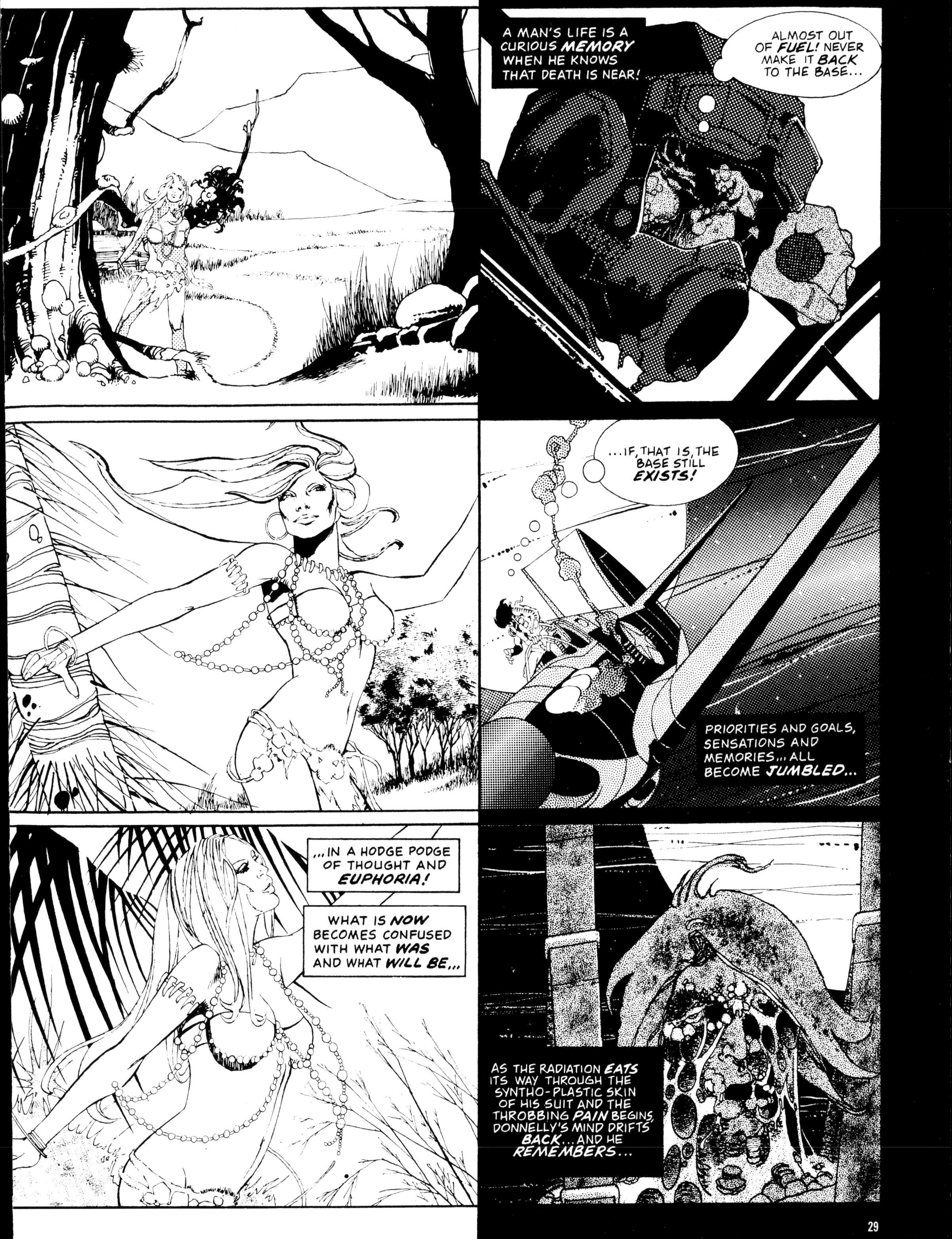
A MAN'S LIFE IS A CURIOUS MEMORY WHEN HE KNOWS THAT DEATH IS NEAR!
ALMOST OUT OF FUEL! NEVER MAKE IT BACK TO THE BASE...
...IF, THAT IS, THE BASE STILL EXISTS!
PRIORITIES AND GOALS, SENSATIONS AND MEMORIES... ALL BECOME JUMBLED...
...IN A HODGE PODGE OF THOUGHT AND EUPHORIA!
WHAT IS NOW BECOMES CONFUSED WITH WHAT WAS AND WHAT WILL BE...
AS THE RADIATION EATS ITS WAY THROUGH THE SYNTHO-PLASTIC SKIN OF HIS SUIT AND THE THROBBING PAIN BEGINS, DONNELLY'S MIND DRIFTS BACK... AND HE REMEMBERS...

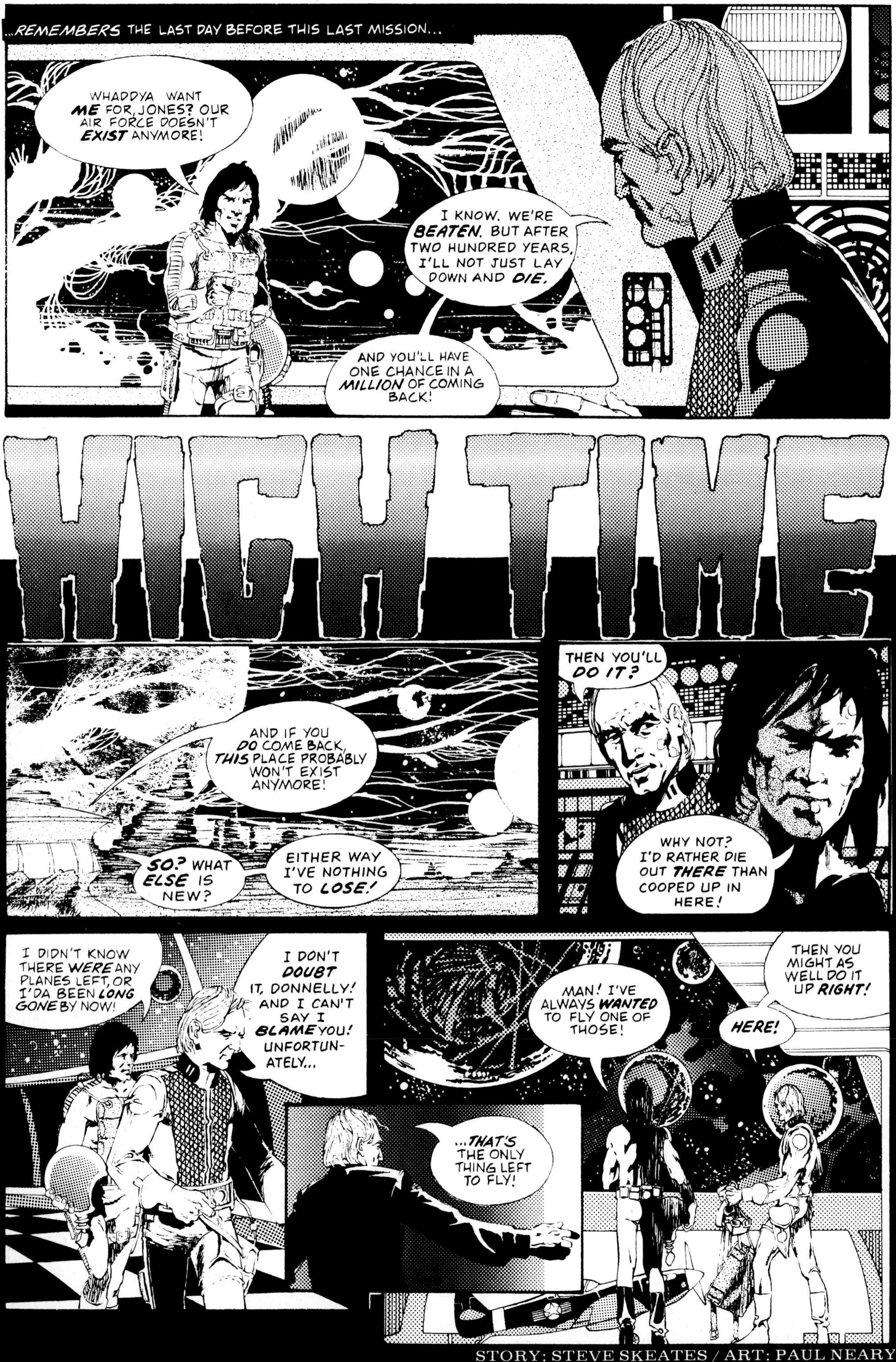
...REMEMBERS THE LAST DAY BEFORE THIS LAST MISSION...
WHADDYA WANT ME FOR, JONES? OUR AIR FORCE DOESN'T EXIST ANYMORE!
I KNOW. WE'RE BEATEN. BUT AFTER TWO HUNDRED YEARS, I'LL NOT JUST LAY DOWN AND DIE.
AND YOU'LL HAVE ONE CHANCE IN A MILLION OF COMING BACK!
HIGH TIME
AND IF YOU DO COME BACK, THIS PLACE PROBABLY WON'T EXIST ANYMORE!
SO? WHAT ELSE IS NEW?
EITHER WAY I'VE NOTHING TO LOSE!
THEN YOU'LL DO IT?
WHY NOT? I'D RATHER DIE OUT THERE THAN COOPED UP IN HERE!
I DIDN'T KNOW THERE WERE ANY PLANES LEFT, OR I'DA BEEN LONG GONE BY NOW!
I DON'T DOUBT IT, DONNELLY! AND I CAN'T SAY I BLAME YOU! UNFORTUN-ATELY...
...THAT'S THE ONLY THING LEFT TO FLY!
MAN! I'VE ALWAYS WANTED TO FLY ONE OF THOSE!
THEN YOU MIGHT AS WELL DO IT UP RIGHT!
HERE!

STORY: STEVE SKEATES / ART: PAUL NEARY

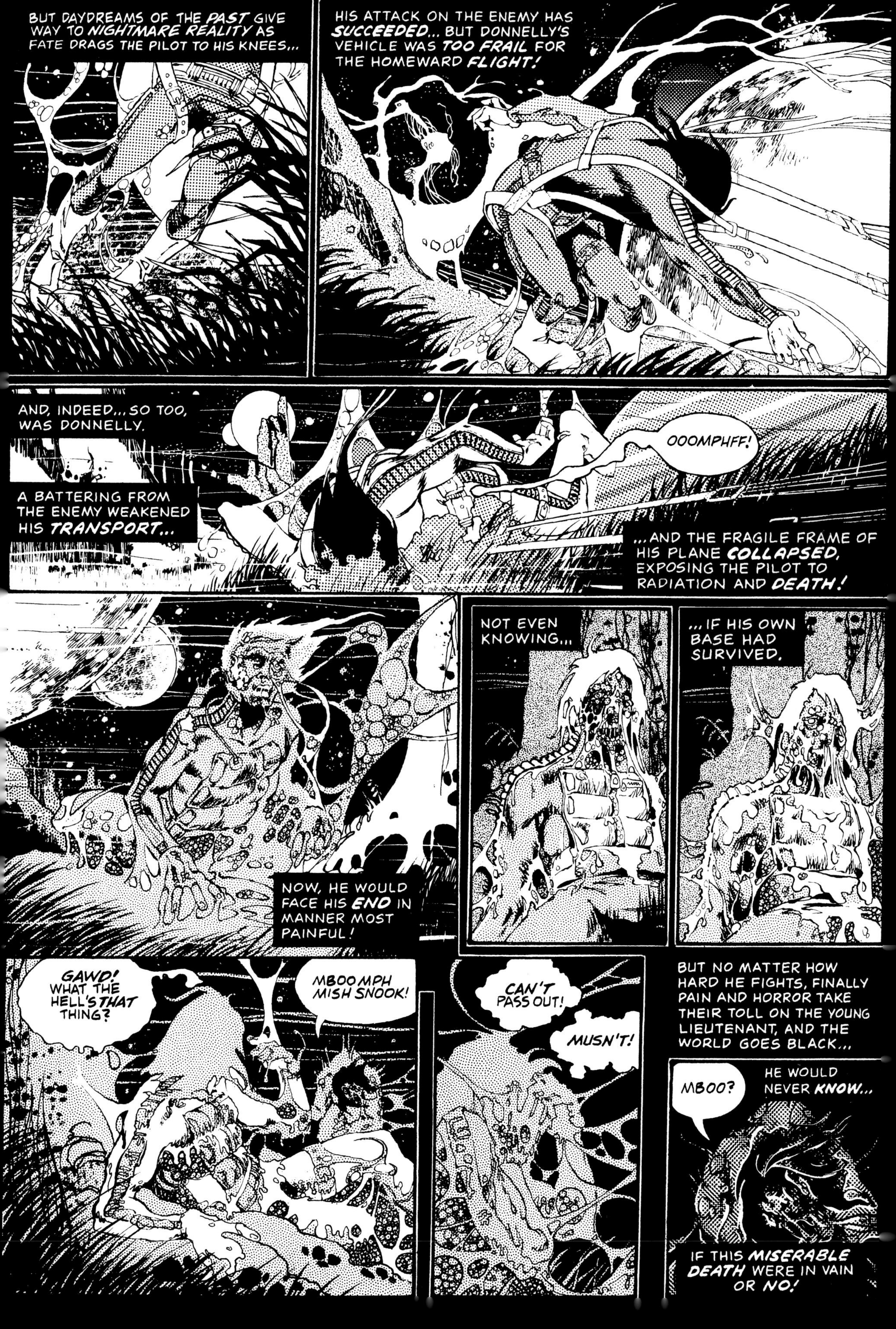
BUT DAYDREAMS OF THE PAST GIVE WAY TO NIGHTMARE REALITY AS FATE DRAGS THE PILOT TO HIS KNEES...
HIS ATTACK ON THE ENEMY HAS SUCCEEDED... BUT DONNELLY'S VEHICLE WAS TOO FRAIL FOR THE HOMEWARD FLIGHT!
AND, INDEED... SO TOO, WAS DONNELLY.
A BATTERING FROM THE ENEMY WEAKENED HIS TRANSPORT...
OOOMPHFF!
...AND THE FRAGILE FRAME OF HIS PLANE COLLAPSED, EXPOSING THE PILOT TO RADIATION AND DEATH!
NOW, HE WOULD FACE HIS END IN MANNER MOST PAINFUL!
NOT EVEN KNOWING...
...IF HIS OWN BASE HAD SURVIVED.
GAWD! WHAT THE HELL'S THAT THING?
MBOOMPH MISH SNOOK!
CAN'T PASS OUT!
MUSN'T!
BUT NO MATTER HOW HARD HE FIGHTS, FINALLY PAIN AND HORROR TAKE THEIR TOLL ON THE YOUNG LIEUTENANT, AND THE WORLD GOES BLACK...
MBOO?
HE WOULD NEVER KNOW...
IF THIS MISERABLE DEATH WERE IN VAIN OR NO!

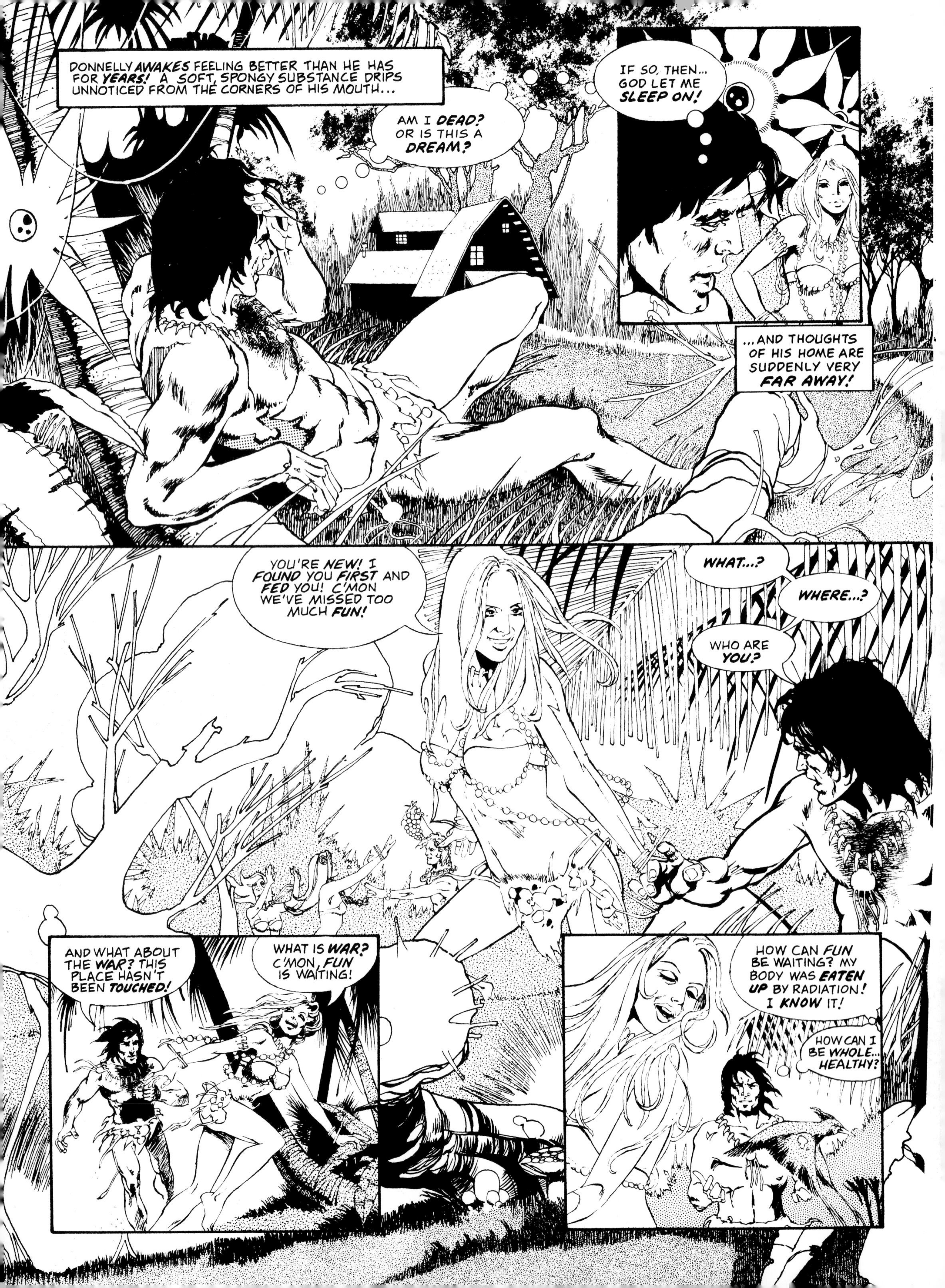

DONNELLY AWAKES FEELING BETTER THAN HE HAS FOR YEARS! A SOFT, SPONGY SUBSTANCE DRIPS UNNOTICED FROM THE CORNERS OF HIS MOUTH...
AM I DEAD? OR IS THIS A DREAM?
IF SO, THEN... GOD LET ME SLEEP ON!
...AND THOUGHTS OF HIS HOME ARE SUDDENLY VERY FAR AWAY!
YOU'RE NEW! I FOUND YOU FIRST AND FED YOU! C'MON WE'VE MISSED TOO MUCH FUN!
WHAT...?
WHERE...?
WHO ARE YOU?
AND WHAT ABOUT THE WAR? THIS PLACE HASN'T BEEN TOUCHED!
WHAT IS WAR? C'MON, FUN IS WAITING!
HOW CAN FUN BE WAITING? MY BODY WAS EATEN UP BY RADIATION! I KNOW IT!
HOW CAN I BE WHOLE... HEALTHY?

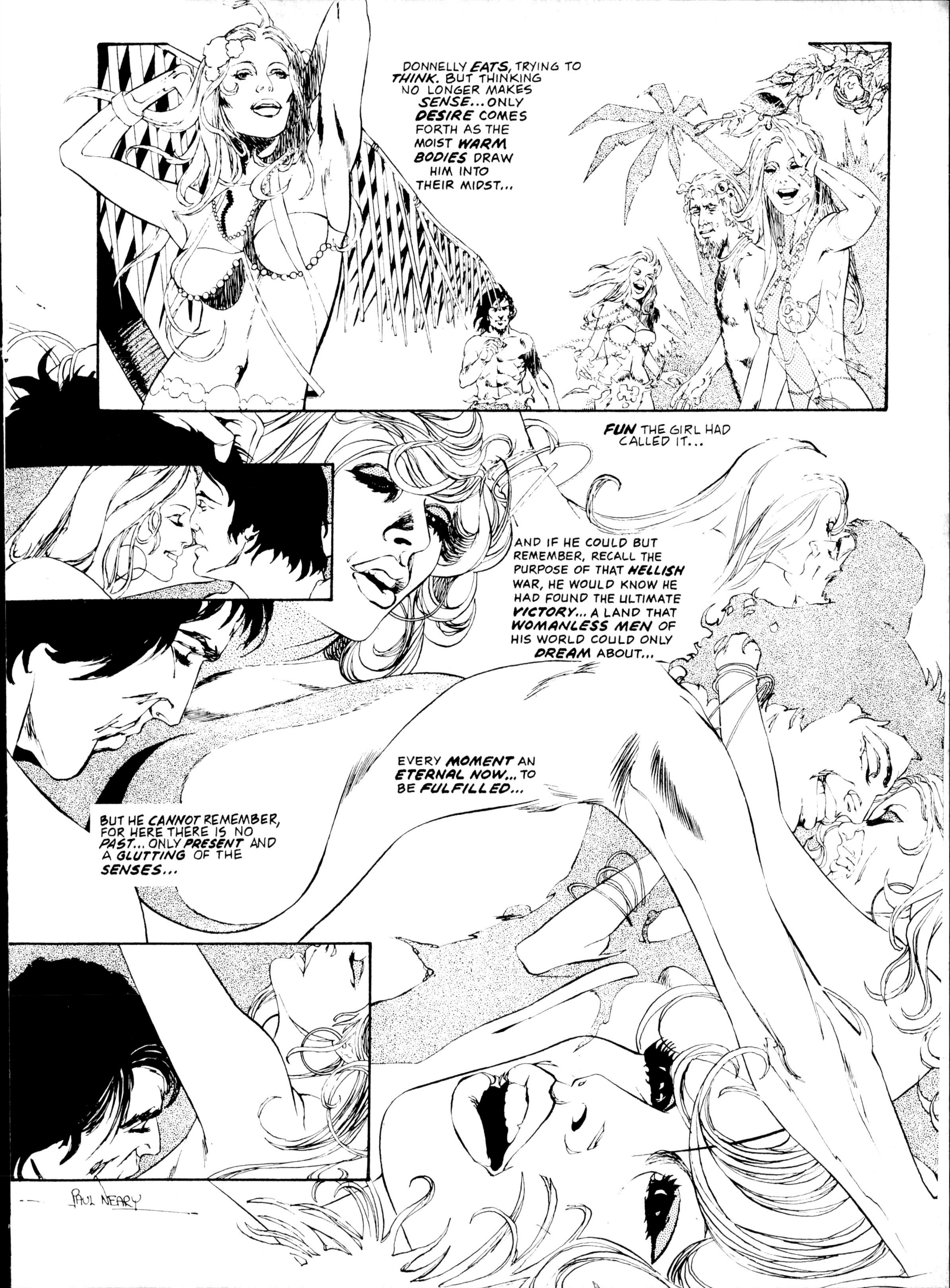
DONNELLY EATS, TRYING TO THINK. BUT THINKING NO LONGER MAKES SENSE... ONLY DESIRE COMES FORTH AS THE MOIST WARM BODIES DRAW HIM INTO THEIR MIDST...
FUN THE GIRL HAD CALLED IT...
AND IF HE COULD BUT REMEMBER, RECALL THE PURPOSE OF THAT HELLISH WAR, HE WOULD KNOW HE HAD FOUND THE ULTIMATE VICTORY... A LAND THAT WOMANLESS MEN OF HIS WORLD COULD ONLY DREAM ABOUT...
EVERY MOMENT AN ETERNAL NOW... TO BE FULFILLED...
BUT HE CANNOT REMEMBER, FOR HERE THERE IS NO PAST... ONLY PRESENT AND A GLUTTING OF THE SENSES...
PAUL NEARY

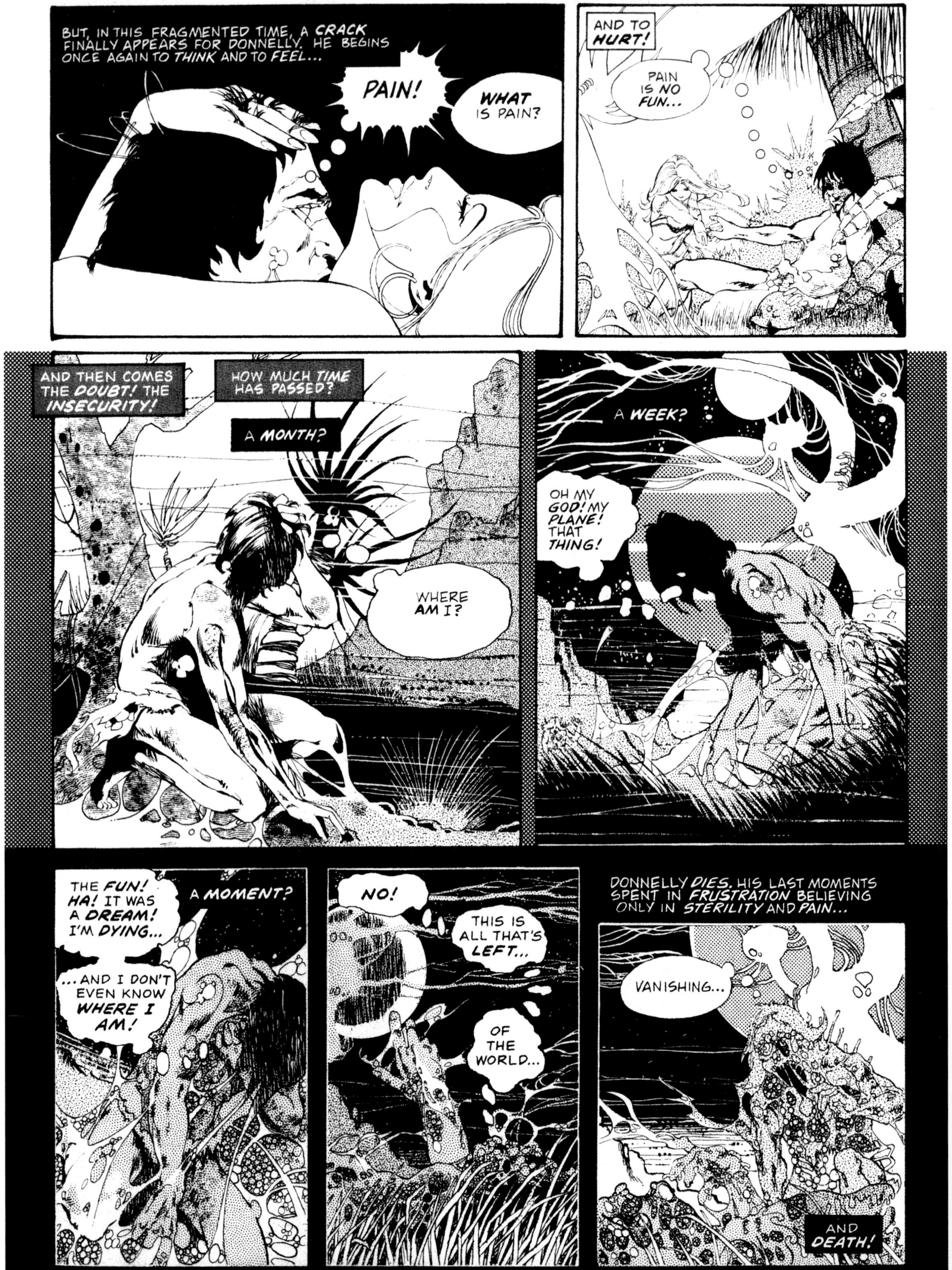
BUT, IN THIS FRAGMENTED TIME, A CRACK FINALLY APPEARS FOR DONNELLY. HE BEGINS ONCE AGAIN TO THINK AND TO FEEL...
PAIN!
WHAT IS PAIN?
AND TO HURT!
PAIN IS NO FUN...
AND THEN COMES THE DOUBT! THE INSECURITY!
HOW MUCH TIME HAS PASSED?
A MONTH?
WHERE AM I?
A WEEK?
OH MY GOD! MY PLANE! THAT THING!
THE FUN! HA! IT WAS A DREAM! I'M DYING...
A MOMENT?
...AND I DON'T EVEN KNOW WHERE I AM!
NO!
THIS IS ALL THAT'S LEFT...
OF THE WORLD...
DONNELLY DIES. HIS LAST MOMENTS SPENT IN FRUSTRATION BELIEVING ONLY IN STERILITY AND PAIN...
VANISHING...
AND DEATH!

GONE!

EVERYBODY GETS *GONE!*

SHE LOOKS *ABOUT*...LOOKS TO THE *OTHERS* AND NOTICES THAT FAMILIAR *SLIGHT CHANGE*...TOO MUCH *TIME* HAS PASSED...

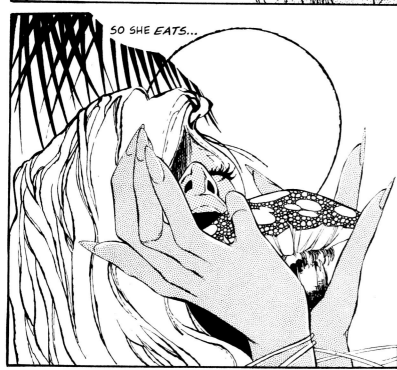

SO SHE *EATS*...

...AND THINGS ARE *BETTER* AGAIN!

SOMEDAY *I* WILL BE GONE!

BUT NOT *NOW!*

NOW IT IS *HIGH TIME!*

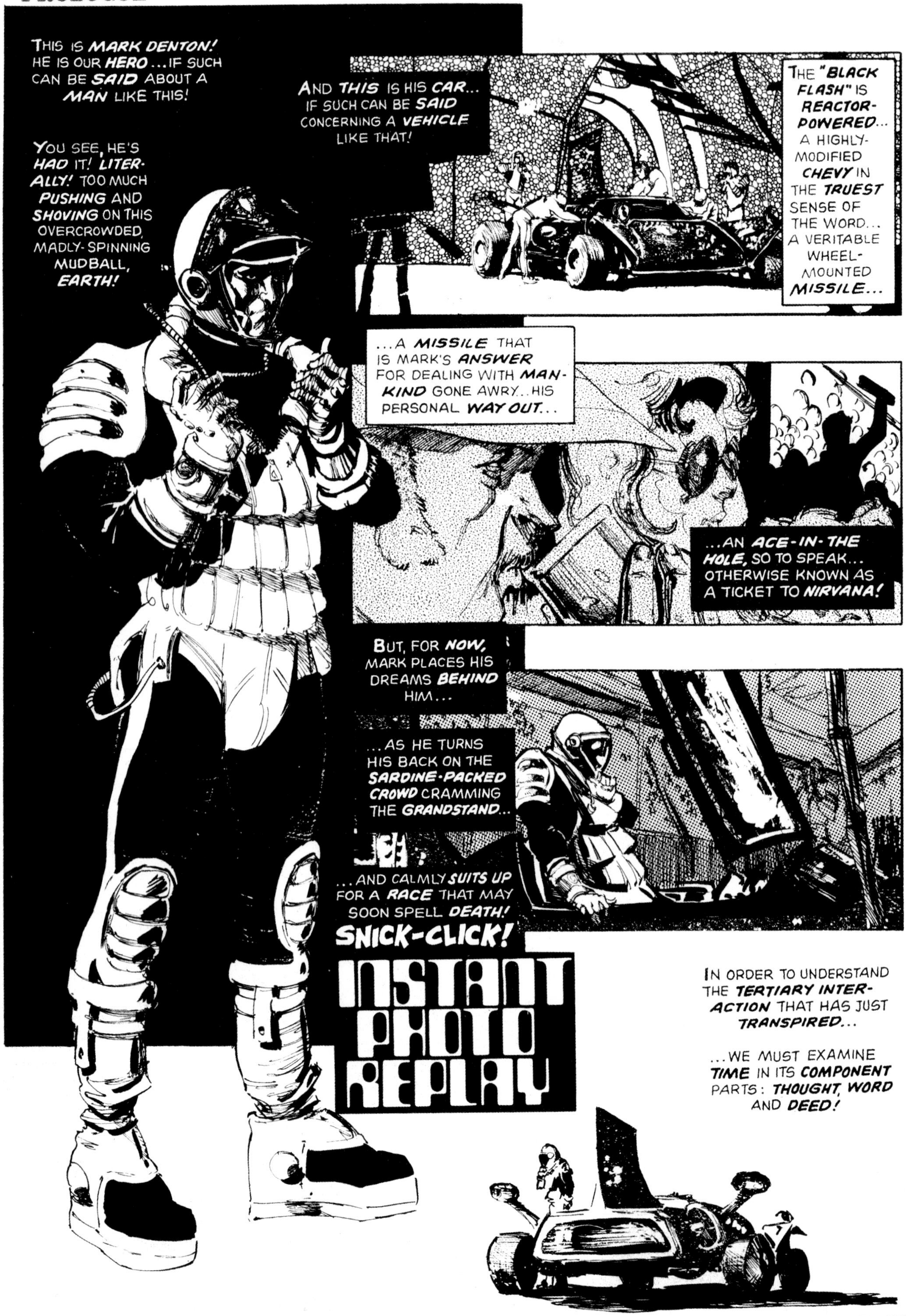
THIS IS MARK DENTON! HE IS OUR HERO... IF SUCH CAN BE SAID ABOUT A MAN LIKE THIS!
YOU SEE, HE'S HAD IT! LITER-ALLY! TOO MUCH PUSHING AND SHOVING ON THIS OVERCROWDED, MADLY-SPINNING MUDBALL, EARTH!
AND THIS IS HIS CAR... IF SUCH CAN BE SAID CONCERNING A VEHICLE LIKE THAT!
THE "BLACK FLASH" IS REACTOR-POWERED... A HIGHLY-MODIFIED CHEVY IN THE TRUEST SENSE OF THE WORD... A VERITABLE WHEEL-MOUNTED MISSILE...
...A MISSILE THAT IS MARK'S ANSWER FOR DEALING WITH MAN-KIND GONE AWRY... HIS PERSONAL WAY OUT...
...AN ACE-IN-THE HOLE, SO TO SPEAK... OTHERWISE KNOWN AS A TICKET TO NIRVANA!
BUT, FOR NOW, MARK PLACES HIS DREAMS BEHIND HIM...
...AS HE TURNS HIS BACK ON THE SARDINE-PACKED CROWD CRAMMING THE GRANDSTAND...
...AND CALMLY SUITS UP FOR A RACE THAT MAY SOON SPELL DEATH!
SNICK-CLICK!
INSTANT PHOTO REPLAY
IN ORDER TO UNDERSTAND THE TERTIARY INTER-ACTION THAT HAS JUST TRANSPIRED...
...WE MUST EXAMINE TIME IN ITS COMPONENT PARTS: THOUGHT, WORD AND DEED!

STORY: RICH MARGOPPOULOS / ART: HOWARD CHAYKIN

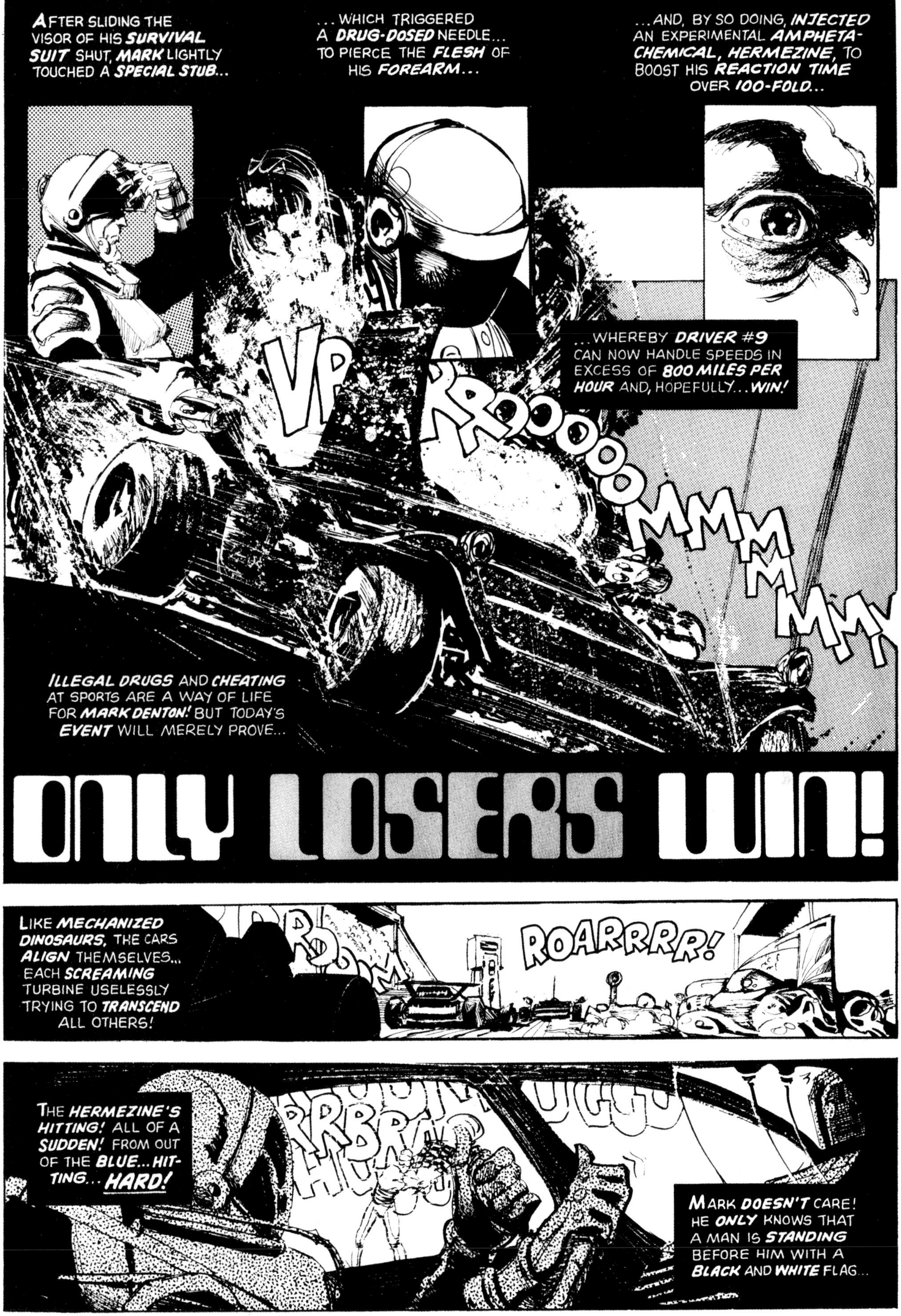

AFTER SLIDING THE VISOR OF HIS SURVIVAL SUIT SHUT, MARK LIGHTLY TOUCHED A SPECIAL STUB...
...WHICH TRIGGERED A DRUG-DOSED NEEDLE... TO PIERCE THE FLESH OF HIS FOREARM...
...AND, BY SO DOING, INJECTED AN EXPERIMENTAL AMPHETA-CHEMICAL, HERMEZINE, TO BOOST HIS REACTION TIME OVER 100-FOLD...
...WHEREBY DRIVER #9 CAN NOW HANDLE SPEEDS IN EXCESS OF 800 MILES PER HOUR AND, HOPEFULLY... WIN!
VRRROOOOMMMMMMMM
ILLEGAL DRUGS AND CHEATING AT SPORTS ARE A WAY OF LIFE FOR MARK DENTON! BUT TODAY'S EVENT WILL MERELY PROVE...
ONLY LOSERS WIN!
LIKE MECHANIZED DINOSAURS, THE CARS ALIGN THEMSELVES... EACH SCREAMING TURBINE USELESSLY TRYING TO TRANSCEND ALL OTHERS!
ROARRRRR!
THE HERMEZINE'S HITTING! ALL OF A SUDDEN! FROM OUT OF THE BLUE... HIT-TING... HARD!
MARK DOESN'T CARE! HE ONLY KNOWS THAT A MAN IS STANDING BEFORE HIM WITH A BLACK AND WHITE FLAG...

...AND, THAT THE **CHECKERED MATERIAL** IS NOW ARCING DOWN... **FALLING**...

...**FLOATING** WITH ALMOST **INFINITE** SLOWNESS...

...AS THE **BOOSTER-DRUG** TWISTS REALITY INTO **TURTLE-MOTION**...

...AND...

HIGGGAMMIONNN!!!!!!

VARRROOOOOOOOOOMM

...THE **RACE** IS **ON**, LADIES AND GENTLEMEN!

THCLIK

THIS IS **HOWARD BOSWELL** ON THE OUTSKIRTS OF **LOS ANGELES, CALIFORNIA**... WHILE IN THE **DISTANCE** ANOTHER **ANNUAL SPEEDWAY EVENT** GETS UNDER WAY!

SOMEHOW, THE RAW **EXCITEMENT**... THE SHEER **THRILL** OF IT ALL... HAS A **WAY** OF GETTING INTO ONE'S **BLOOD**!

BUT ENOUGH **OPINION**! TIME TO **SWITCH** YOU TO **GABE SILVERMAN** IN THE JUDGES' **CUBICAL**! ...**GABE**?

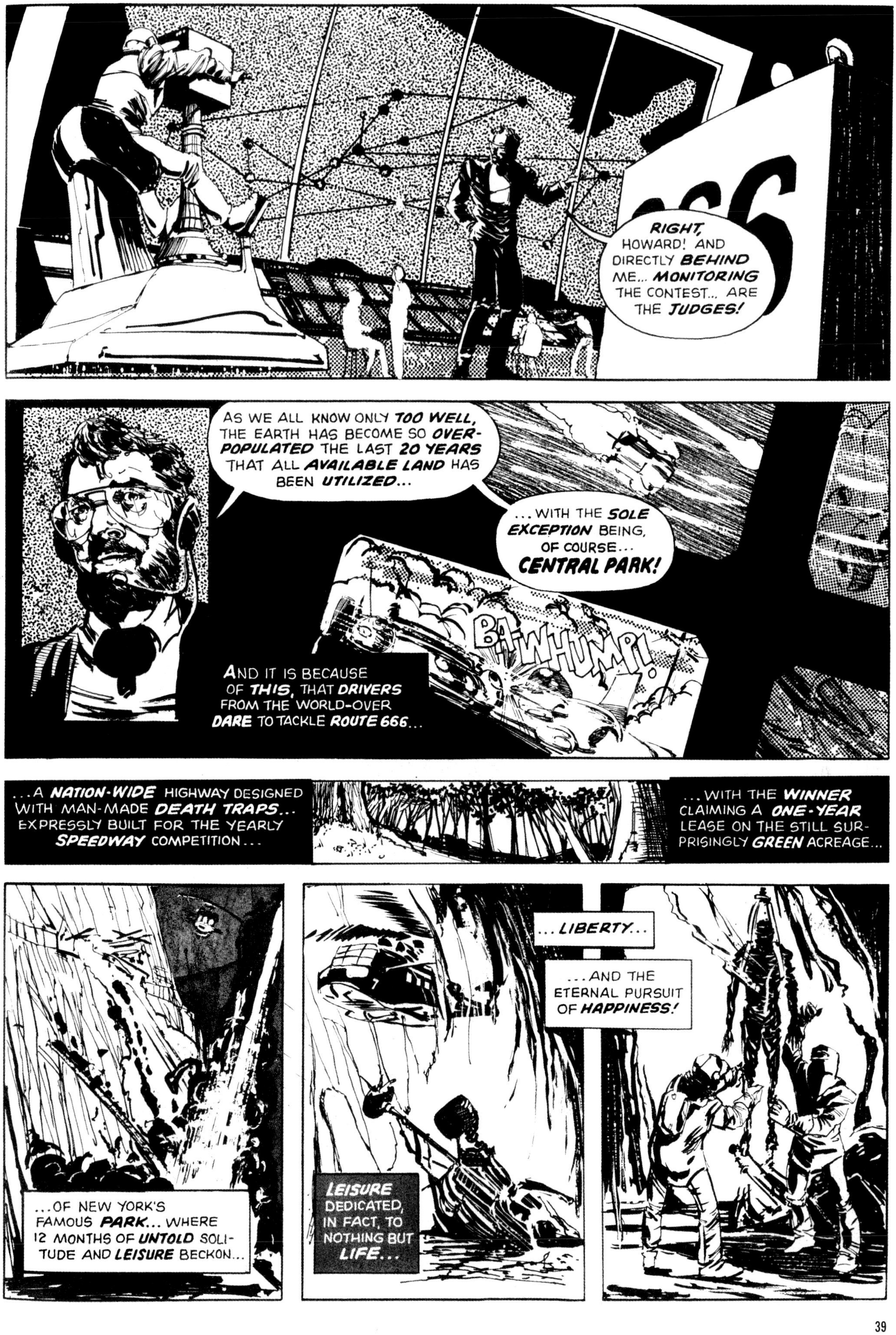
RIGHT, HOWARD! AND DIRECTLY BEHIND ME... MONITORING THE CONTEST... ARE THE JUDGES!
AS WE ALL KNOW ONLY TOO WELL, THE EARTH HAS BECOME SO OVER-POPULATED THE LAST 20 YEARS THAT ALL AVAILABLE LAND HAS BEEN UTILIZED...
...WITH THE SOLE EXCEPTION BEING, OF COURSE... CENTRAL PARK!
BAWHUMP!
AND IT IS BECAUSE OF THIS, THAT DRIVERS FROM THE WORLD-OVER DARE TO TACKLE ROUTE 666...
...A NATION-WIDE HIGHWAY DESIGNED WITH MAN-MADE DEATH TRAPS... EXPRESSLY BUILT FOR THE YEARLY SPEEDWAY COMPETITION...
...WITH THE WINNER CLAIMING A ONE-YEAR LEASE ON THE STILL SURPRISINGLY GREEN ACREAGE...
...OF NEW YORK'S FAMOUS PARK... WHERE 12 MONTHS OF UNTOLD SOLITUDE AND LEISURE BECKON...
LEISURE DEDICATED, IN FACT, TO NOTHING BUT LIFE...
...LIBERTY...
...AND THE ETERNAL PURSUIT OF HAPPINESS!

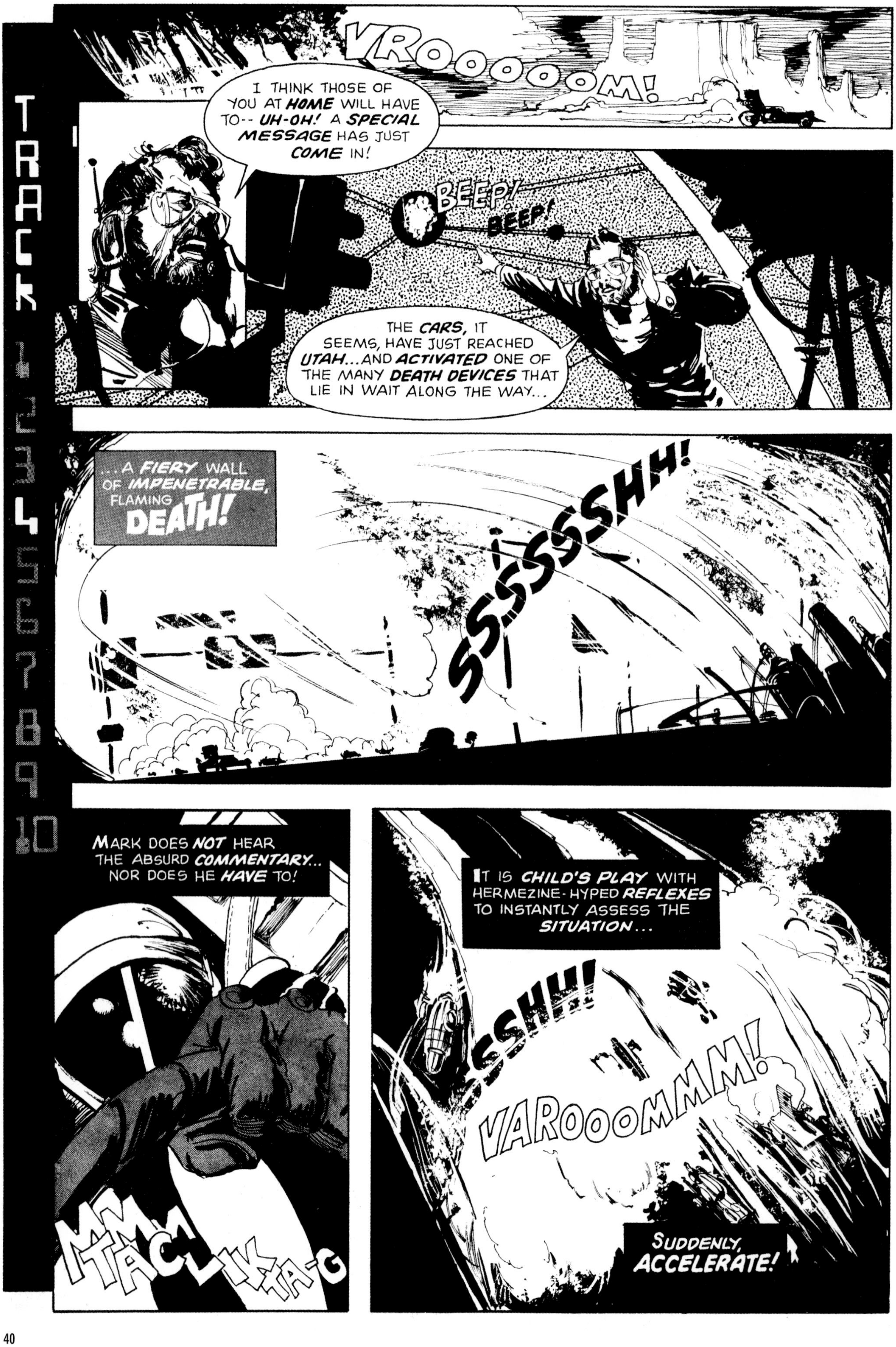

VROOOOOM!
I THINK THOSE OF YOU AT HOME WILL HAVE TO-- UH-OH! A SPECIAL MESSAGE HAS JUST COME IN!
BEEP! BEEP!
THE CARS, IT SEEMS, HAVE JUST REACHED UTAH...AND ACTIVATED ONE OF THE MANY DEATH DEVICES THAT LIE IN WAIT ALONG THE WAY...
...A FIERY WALL OF IMPENETRABLE, FLAMING DEATH!
SSSSSSHH!
MARK DOES NOT HEAR THE ABSURD COMMENTARY... NOR DOES HE HAVE TO!
MMM TAC CLIK TA-G
IT IS CHILD'S PLAY WITH HERMEZINE-HYPED REFLEXES TO INSTANTLY ASSESS THE SITUATION...
SSHH!
VAROOOMMM!
SUDDENLY, ACCELERATE!

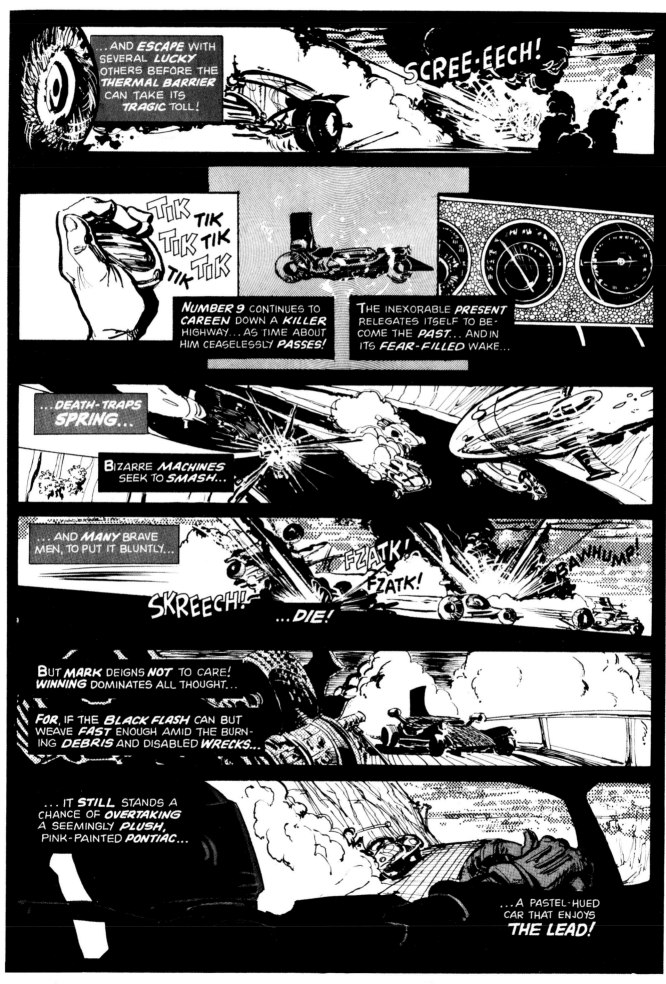

...AND *ESCAPE* WITH SEVERAL *LUCKY* OTHERS BEFORE THE *THERMAL BARRIER* CAN TAKE ITS *TRAGIC* TOLL!

SCREE-EECH!

TIK TIK TIK TIK TIK TIK

NUMBER 9 CONTINUES TO *CAREEN* DOWN A *KILLER* HIGHWAY... AS TIME ABOUT HIM CEASELESSLY *PASSES!*

THE INEXORABLE *PRESENT* RELEGATES ITSELF TO BECOME THE *PAST*... AND IN ITS *FEAR-FILLED* WAKE...

...*DEATH-TRAPS* SPRING...

BIZARRE *MACHINES* SEEK TO *SMASH*...

...AND *MANY* BRAVE MEN, TO PUT IT BLUNTLY...

SKREECH!!

FZATK! FZATK!

...*DIE!*

BAWHUMP!

BUT *MARK* DEIGNS *NOT* TO CARE! *WINNING* DOMINATES ALL THOUGHT...

FOR, IF THE *BLACK FLASH* CAN BUT WEAVE *FAST* ENOUGH AMID THE BURNING *DEBRIS* AND DISABLED *WRECKS*...

...IT *STILL* STANDS A CHANCE OF *OVERTAKING* A SEEMINGLY *PLUSH*, PINK-PAINTED *PONTIAC*...

...A PASTEL-HUED CAR THAT ENJOYS *THE LEAD!*

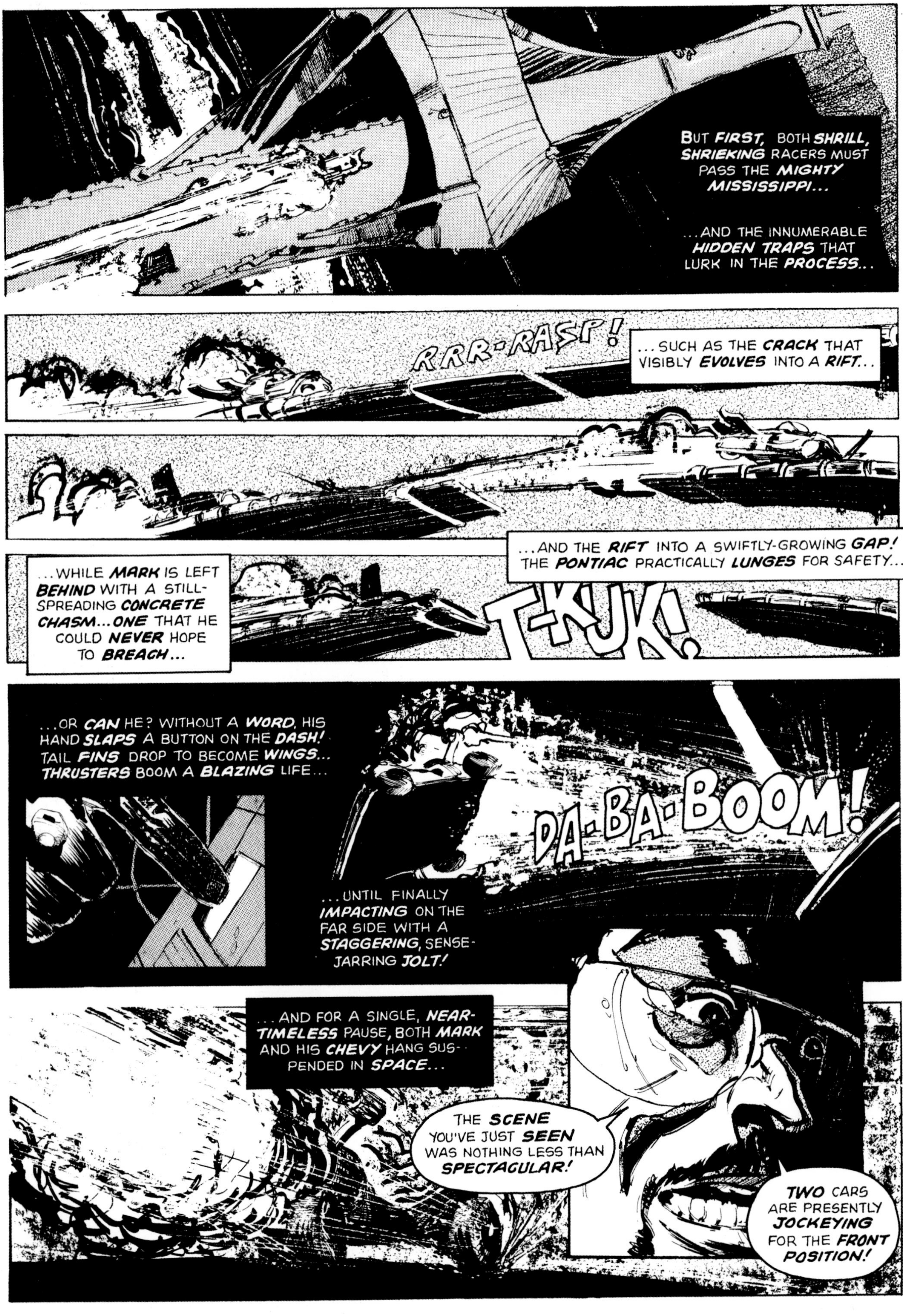

But first, both shrill, shrieking racers must pass the mighty Mississippi...
...and the innumerable hidden traps that lurk in the process...
RRR-RASP!
...such as the crack that visibly evolves into a rift...
...and the rift into a swiftly-growing gap! The Pontiac practically lunges for safety...
...while Mark is left behind with a still-spreading concrete chasm...one that he could never hope to breach...
T-KUK!
...or can he? Without a word, his hand slaps a button on the dash! Tail fins drop to become wings... thrusters boom a blazing life...
DA-BA-BOOM!
...until finally impacting on the far side with a staggering, sense-jarring jolt!
...and for a single, near-timeless pause, both Mark and his Chevy hang suspended in space...
The scene you've just seen was nothing less than spectacular!
Two cars are presently jockeying for the front position!

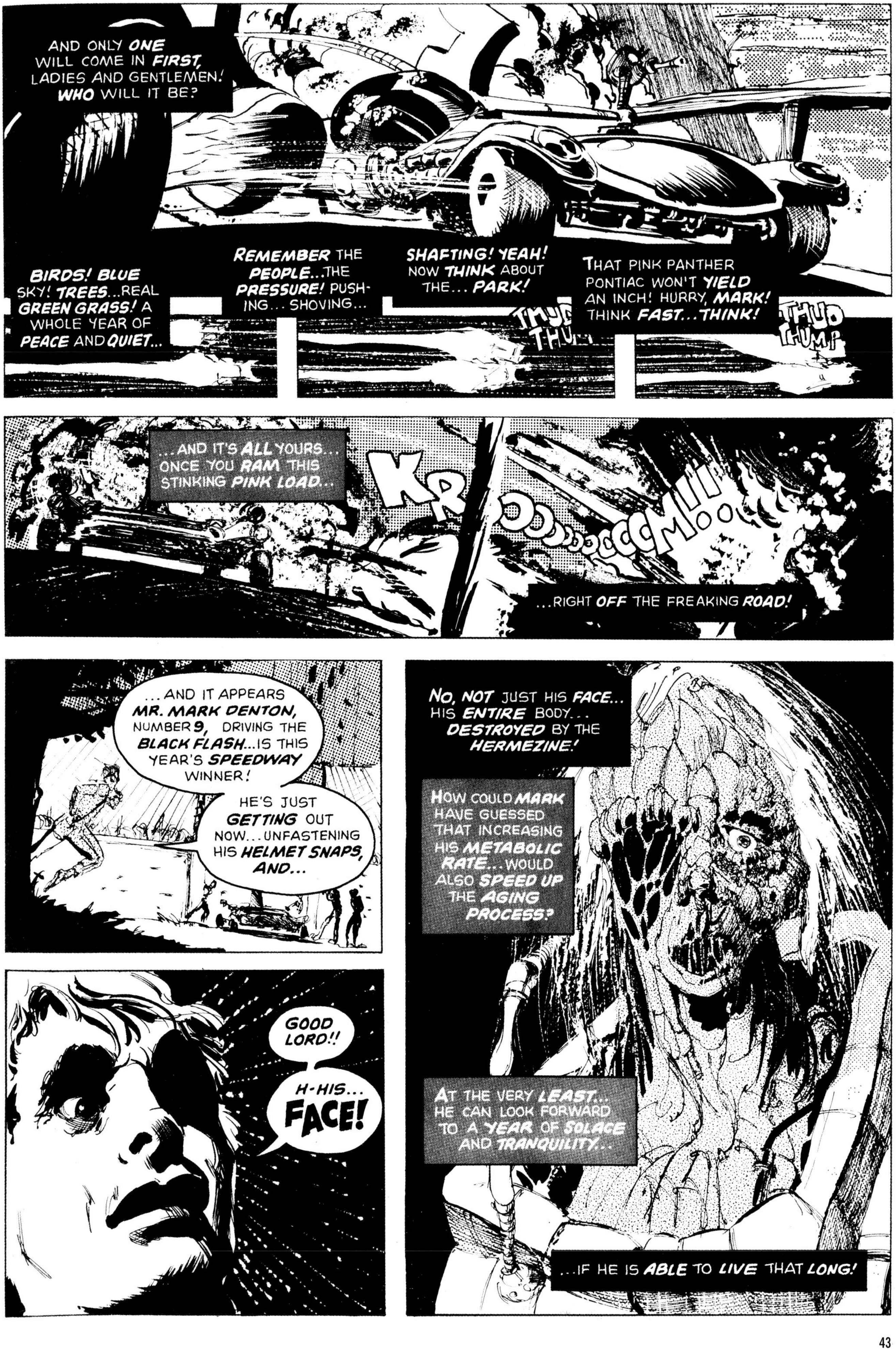
AND ONLY ONE WILL COME IN FIRST, LADIES AND GENTLEMEN! WHO WILL IT BE?
BIRDS! BLUE SKY! TREES...REAL GREEN GRASS! A WHOLE YEAR OF PEACE AND QUIET...
REMEMBER THE PEOPLE...THE PRESSURE! PUSHING... SHOVING...
SHAFTING! YEAH! NOW THINK ABOUT THE... PARK!
THAT PINK PANTHER PONTIAC WON'T YIELD AN INCH! HURRY, MARK! THINK FAST...THINK!
THUD THUMP
THUD THUMP
...AND IT'S ALL YOURS... ONCE YOU RAM THIS STINKING PINK LOAD...
KAROOOOOOOOOOM!!
...RIGHT OFF THE FREAKING ROAD!
...AND IT APPEARS MR. MARK DENTON, NUMBER 9, DRIVING THE BLACK FLASH...IS THIS YEAR'S SPEEDWAY WINNER!
HE'S JUST GETTING OUT NOW...UNFASTENING HIS HELMET SNAPS, AND...
GOOD LORD!!
H-HIS... FACE!
NO, NOT JUST HIS FACE... HIS ENTIRE BODY... DESTROYED BY THE HERMEZINE!
HOW COULD MARK HAVE GUESSED THAT INCREASING HIS METABOLIC RATE...WOULD ALSO SPEED UP THE AGING PROCESS?
AT THE VERY LEAST... HE CAN LOOK FORWARD TO A YEAR OF SOLACE AND TRANQUILITY...
...IF HE IS ABLE TO LIVE THAT LONG!

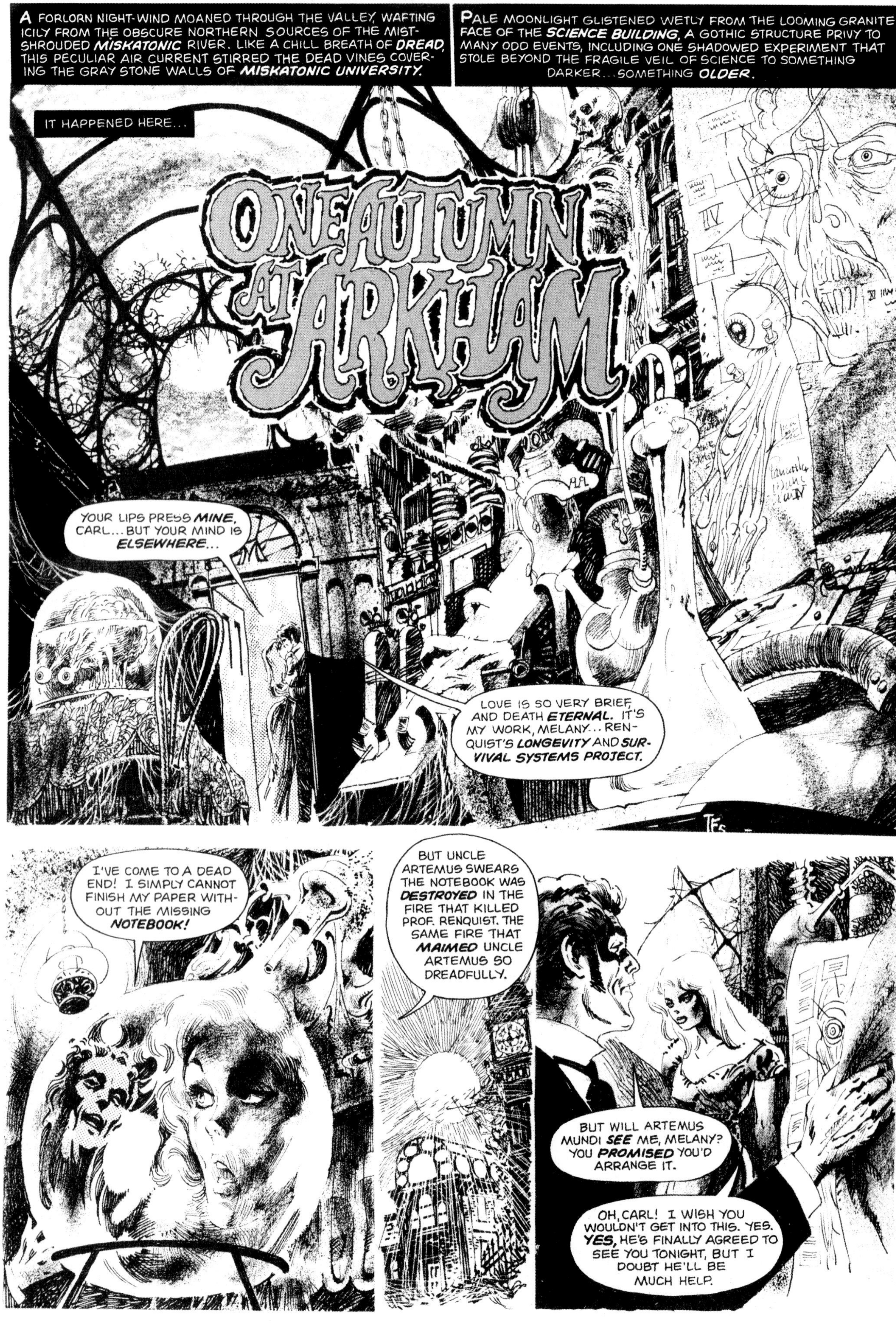
A FORLORN NIGHT-WIND MOANED THROUGH THE VALLEY, WAFTING ICILY FROM THE OBSCURE NORTHERN SOURCES OF THE MIST-SHROUDED MISKATONIC RIVER. LIKE A CHILL BREATH OF DREAD, THIS PECULIAR AIR CURRENT STIRRED THE DEAD VINES COVERING THE GRAY STONE WALLS OF MISKATONIC UNIVERSITY.
PALE MOONLIGHT GLISTENED WETLY FROM THE LOOMING GRANITE FACE OF THE SCIENCE BUILDING, A GOTHIC STRUCTURE PRIVY TO MANY ODD EVENTS, INCLUDING ONE SHADOWED EXPERIMENT THAT STOLE BEYOND THE FRAGILE VEIL OF SCIENCE TO SOMETHING DARKER... SOMETHING OLDER.
IT HAPPENED HERE...
ONE AUTUMN AT ARKHAM
YOUR LIPS PRESS MINE, CARL... BUT YOUR MIND IS ELSEWHERE...
LOVE IS SO VERY BRIEF, AND DEATH ETERNAL. IT'S MY WORK, MELANY... RENQUIST'S LONGEVITY AND SURVIVAL SYSTEMS PROJECT.
I'VE COME TO A DEAD END! I SIMPLY CANNOT FINISH MY PAPER WITHOUT THE MISSING NOTEBOOK!
BUT UNCLE ARTEMUS SWEARS THE NOTEBOOK WAS DESTROYED IN THE FIRE THAT KILLED PROF. RENQUIST. THE SAME FIRE THAT MAIMED UNCLE ARTEMUS SO DREADFULLY.
BUT WILL ARTEMUS MUNDI SEE ME, MELANY? YOU PROMISED YOU'D ARRANGE IT.
OH, CARL! I WISH YOU WOULDN'T GET INTO THIS. YES. YES, HE'S FINALLY AGREED TO SEE YOU TONIGHT, BUT I DOUBT HE'LL BE MUCH HELP.

STORY AND ART: TOM SUTTON

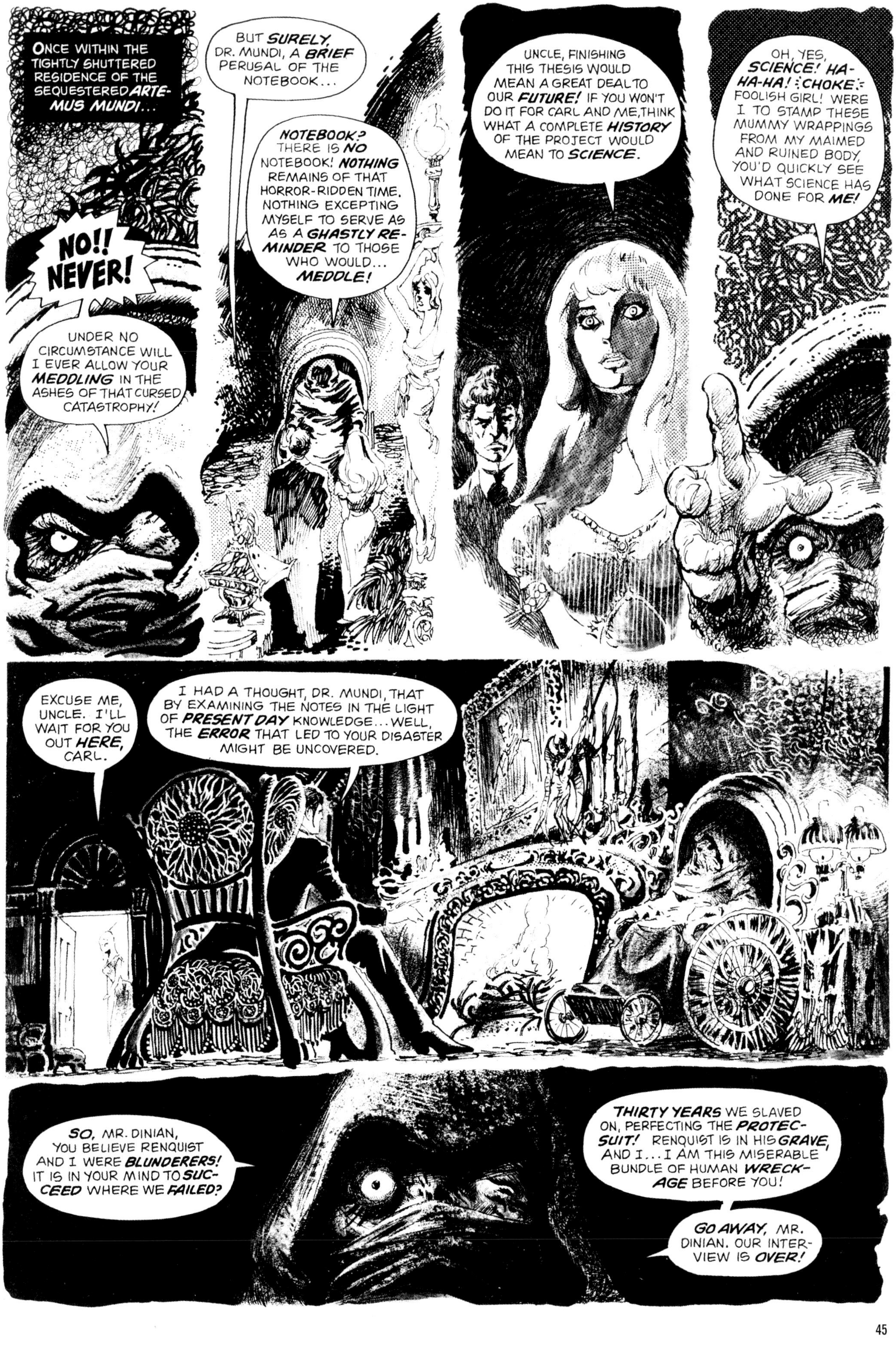

Once within the tightly shuttered residence of the sequestered Artemus Mundi...
NO!! NEVER!
UNDER NO CIRCUMSTANCE WILL I EVER ALLOW YOUR MEDDLING IN THE ASHES OF THAT CURSED CATASTROPHY!
BUT SURELY, DR. MUNDI, A BRIEF PERUSAL OF THE NOTEBOOK...
NOTEBOOK? THERE IS NO NOTEBOOK! NOTHING REMAINS OF THAT HORROR-RIDDEN TIME. NOTHING EXCEPTING MYSELF TO SERVE AS AS A GHASTLY REMINDER TO THOSE WHO WOULD... MEDDLE!
UNCLE, FINISHING THIS THESIS WOULD MEAN A GREAT DEAL TO OUR FUTURE! IF YOU WON'T DO IT FOR CARL AND ME, THINK WHAT A COMPLETE HISTORY OF THE PROJECT WOULD MEAN TO SCIENCE.
OH, YES, SCIENCE! HA-HA-HA! :CHOKE: FOOLISH GIRL! WERE I TO STAMP THESE MUMMY WRAPPINGS FROM MY MAIMED AND RUINED BODY, YOU'D QUICKLY SEE WHAT SCIENCE HAS DONE FOR ME!
EXCUSE ME, UNCLE. I'LL WAIT FOR YOU OUT HERE, CARL.
I HAD A THOUGHT, DR. MUNDI, THAT BY EXAMINING THE NOTES IN THE LIGHT OF PRESENT DAY KNOWLEDGE... WELL, THE ERROR THAT LED TO YOUR DISASTER MIGHT BE UNCOVERED.
SO, MR. DINIAN, YOU BELIEVE RENQUIST AND I WERE BLUNDERERS! IT IS IN YOUR MIND TO SUCCEED WHERE WE FAILED?
THIRTY YEARS WE SLAVED ON, PERFECTING THE PROTEC-SUIT! RENQUIST IS IN HIS GRAVE, AND I... I AM THIS MISERABLE BUNDLE OF HUMAN WRECKAGE BEFORE YOU!
GO AWAY, MR. DINIAN. OUR INTERVIEW IS OVER!

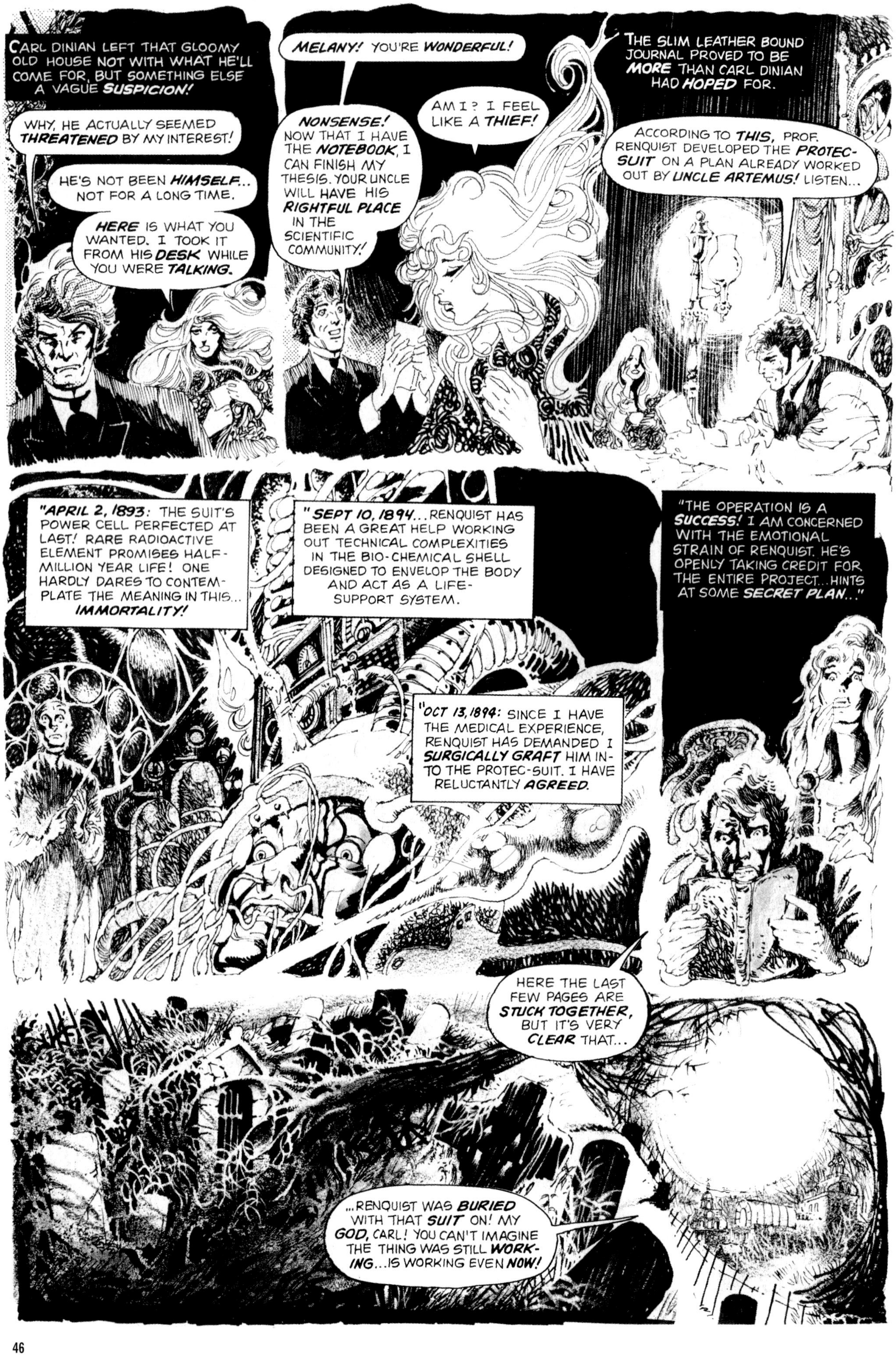
CARL DINIAN LEFT THAT GLOOMY OLD HOUSE NOT WITH WHAT HE'LL COME FOR, BUT SOMETHING ELSE A VAGUE SUSPICION!
WHY, HE ACTUALLY SEEMED THREATENED BY MY INTEREST!
HE'S NOT BEEN HIMSELF... NOT FOR A LONG TIME.
HERE IS WHAT YOU WANTED. I TOOK IT FROM HIS DESK WHILE YOU WERE TALKING.
MELANY! YOU'RE WONDERFUL!
AM I? I FEEL LIKE A THIEF!
NONSENSE! NOW THAT I HAVE THE NOTEBOOK, I CAN FINISH MY THESIS. YOUR UNCLE WILL HAVE HIS RIGHTFUL PLACE IN THE SCIENTIFIC COMMUNITY!
THE SLIM LEATHER BOUND JOURNAL PROVED TO BE MORE THAN CARL DINIAN HAD HOPED FOR.
ACCORDING TO THIS, PROF. RENQUIST DEVELOPED THE PROTEC-SUIT ON A PLAN ALREADY WORKED OUT BY UNCLE ARTEMUS! LISTEN...
"APRIL 2, 1893: THE SUIT'S POWER CELL PERFECTED AT LAST! RARE RADIOACTIVE ELEMENT PROMISES HALF-MILLION YEAR LIFE! ONE HARDLY DARES TO CONTEMPLATE THE MEANING IN THIS... IMMORTALITY!
"SEPT 10, 1894... RENQUIST HAS BEEN A GREAT HELP WORKING OUT TECHNICAL COMPLEXITIES IN THE BIO-CHEMICAL SHELL DESIGNED TO ENVELOP THE BODY AND ACT AS A LIFE-SUPPORT SYSTEM.
"OCT 13, 1894: SINCE I HAVE THE MEDICAL EXPERIENCE, RENQUIST HAS DEMANDED I SURGICALLY GRAFT HIM INTO THE PROTEC-SUIT. I HAVE RELUCTANTLY AGREED.
"THE OPERATION IS A SUCCESS! I AM CONCERNED WITH THE EMOTIONAL STRAIN OF RENQUIST. HE'S OPENLY TAKING CREDIT FOR THE ENTIRE PROJECT... HINTS AT SOME SECRET PLAN..."
HERE THE LAST FEW PAGES ARE STUCK TOGETHER, BUT IT'S VERY CLEAR THAT...
...RENQUIST WAS BURIED WITH THAT SUIT ON! MY GOD, CARL! YOU CAN'T IMAGINE THE THING WAS STILL WORKING... IS WORKING EVEN NOW!

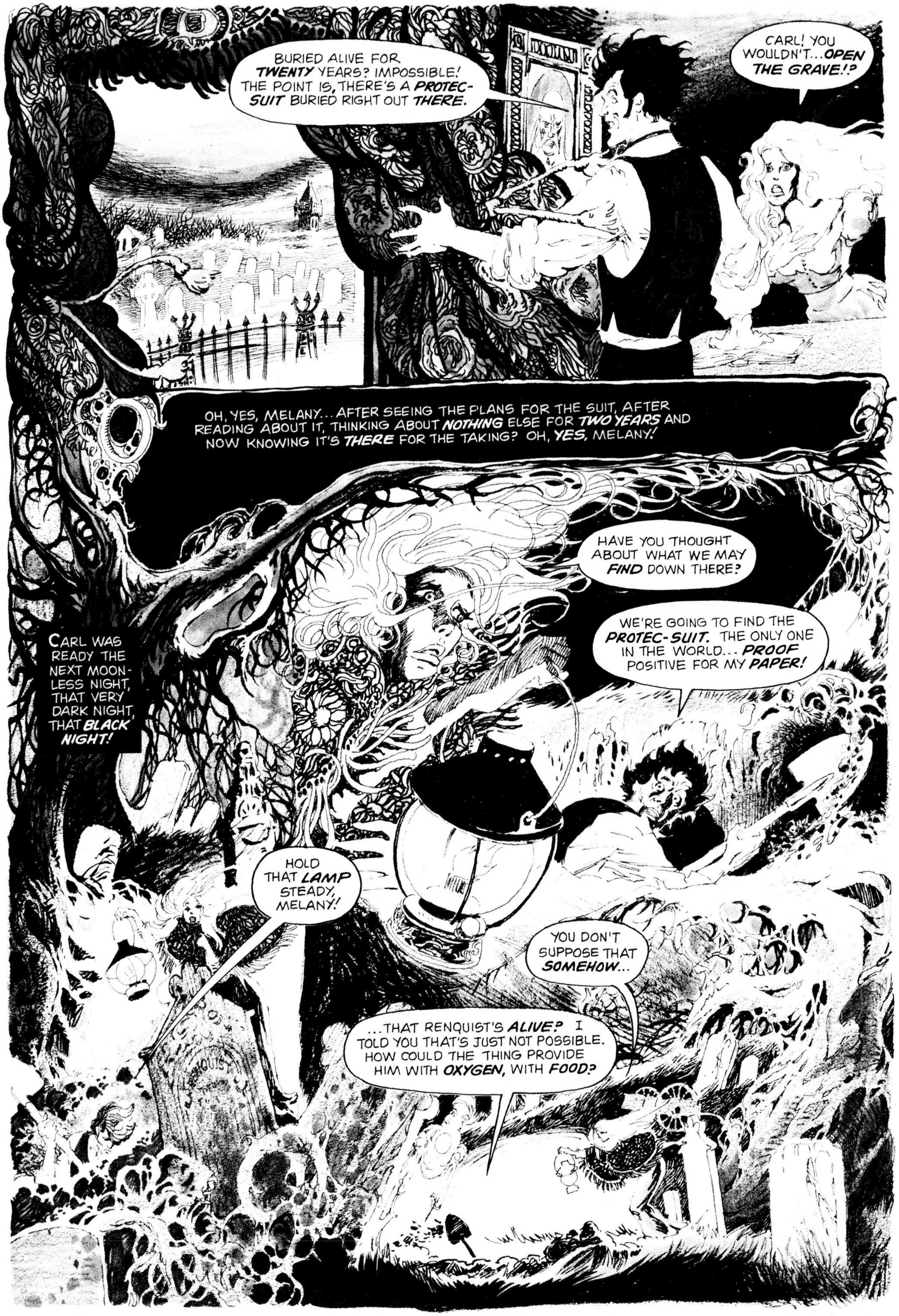
BURIED ALIVE FOR TWENTY YEARS? IMPOSSIBLE! THE POINT IS, THERE'S A PROTEC-SUIT BURIED RIGHT OUT THERE.
CARL! YOU WOULDN'T...OPEN THE GRAVE!?
OH, YES, MELANY... AFTER SEEING THE PLANS FOR THE SUIT, AFTER READING ABOUT IT, THINKING ABOUT NOTHING ELSE FOR TWO YEARS AND NOW KNOWING IT'S THERE FOR THE TAKING? OH, YES, MELANY!
CARL WAS READY THE NEXT MOONLESS NIGHT, THAT VERY DARK NIGHT, THAT BLACK NIGHT!
HAVE YOU THOUGHT ABOUT WHAT WE MAY FIND DOWN THERE?
WE'RE GOING TO FIND THE PROTEC-SUIT. THE ONLY ONE IN THE WORLD... PROOF POSITIVE FOR MY PAPER!
HOLD THAT LAMP STEADY, MELANY!
YOU DON'T SUPPOSE THAT SOMEHOW...
...THAT RENQUIST'S ALIVE? I TOLD YOU THAT'S JUST NOT POSSIBLE. HOW COULD THE THING PROVIDE HIM WITH OXYGEN, WITH FOOD?

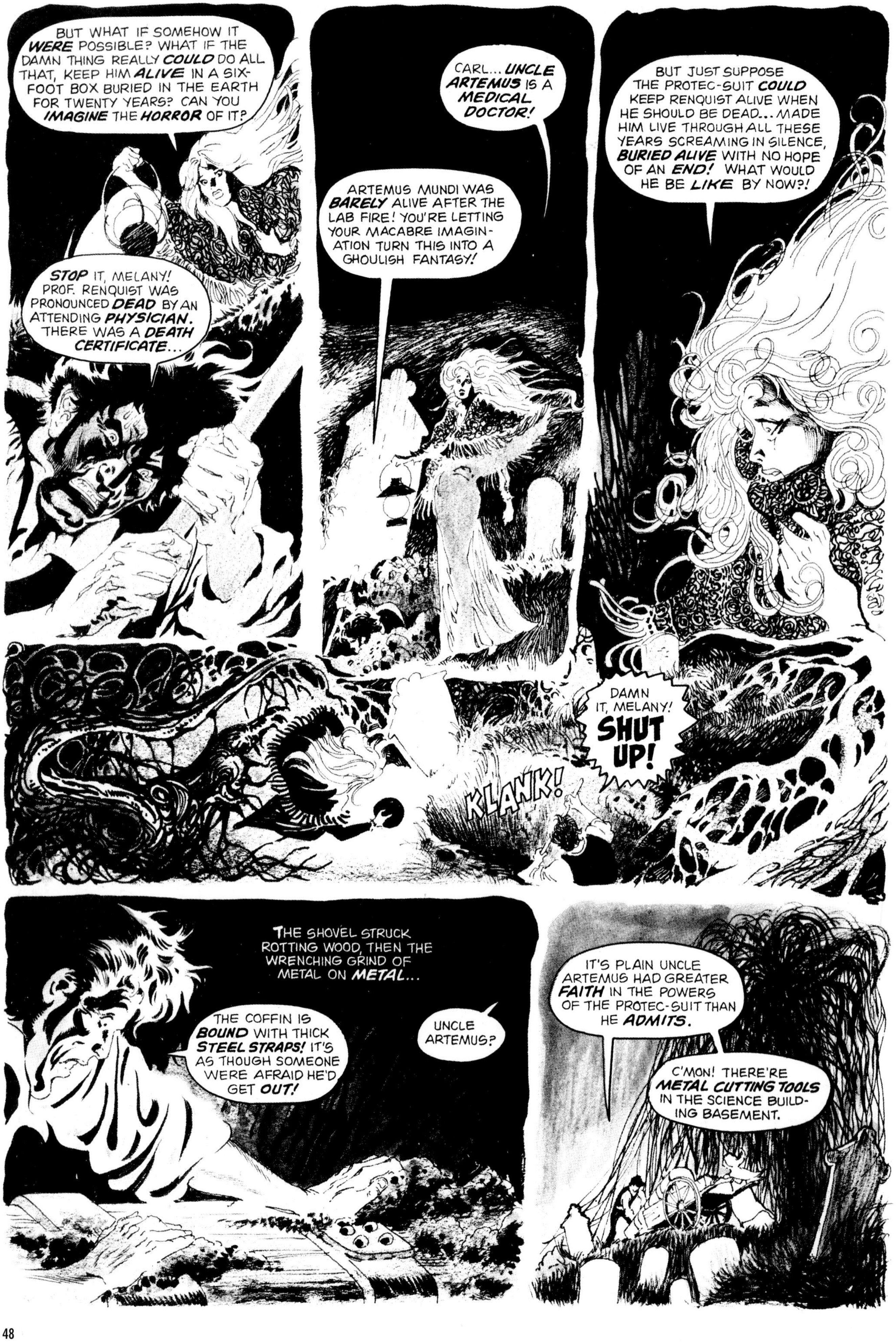
BUT WHAT IF SOMEHOW IT WERE POSSIBLE? WHAT IF THE DAMN THING REALLY COULD DO ALL THAT, KEEP HIM ALIVE IN A SIX-FOOT BOX BURIED IN THE EARTH FOR TWENTY YEARS? CAN YOU IMAGINE THE HORROR OF IT?
STOP IT, MELANY! PROF. RENQUIST WAS PRONOUNCED DEAD BY AN ATTENDING PHYSICIAN. THERE WAS A DEATH CERTIFICATE...
CARL... UNCLE ARTEMUS IS A MEDICAL DOCTOR!
ARTEMUS MUNDI WAS BARELY ALIVE AFTER THE LAB FIRE! YOU'RE LETTING YOUR MACABRE IMAGINATION TURN THIS INTO A GHOULISH FANTASY!
BUT JUST SUPPOSE THE PROTEC-SUIT COULD KEEP RENQUIST ALIVE WHEN HE SHOULD BE DEAD... MADE HIM LIVE THROUGH ALL THESE YEARS SCREAMING IN SILENCE, BURIED ALIVE WITH NO HOPE OF AN END! WHAT WOULD HE BE LIKE BY NOW?!
DAMN IT, MELANY! SHUT UP!
KLANK!
THE SHOVEL STRUCK ROTTING WOOD, THEN THE WRENCHING GRIND OF METAL ON METAL...
THE COFFIN IS BOUND WITH THICK STEEL STRAPS! IT'S AS THOUGH SOMEONE WERE AFRAID HE'D GET OUT!
UNCLE ARTEMUS?
IT'S PLAIN UNCLE ARTEMUS HAD GREATER FAITH IN THE POWERS OF THE PROTEC-SUIT THAN HE ADMITS.
C'MON! THERE'RE METAL CUTTING TOOLS IN THE SCIENCE BUILDING BASEMENT.

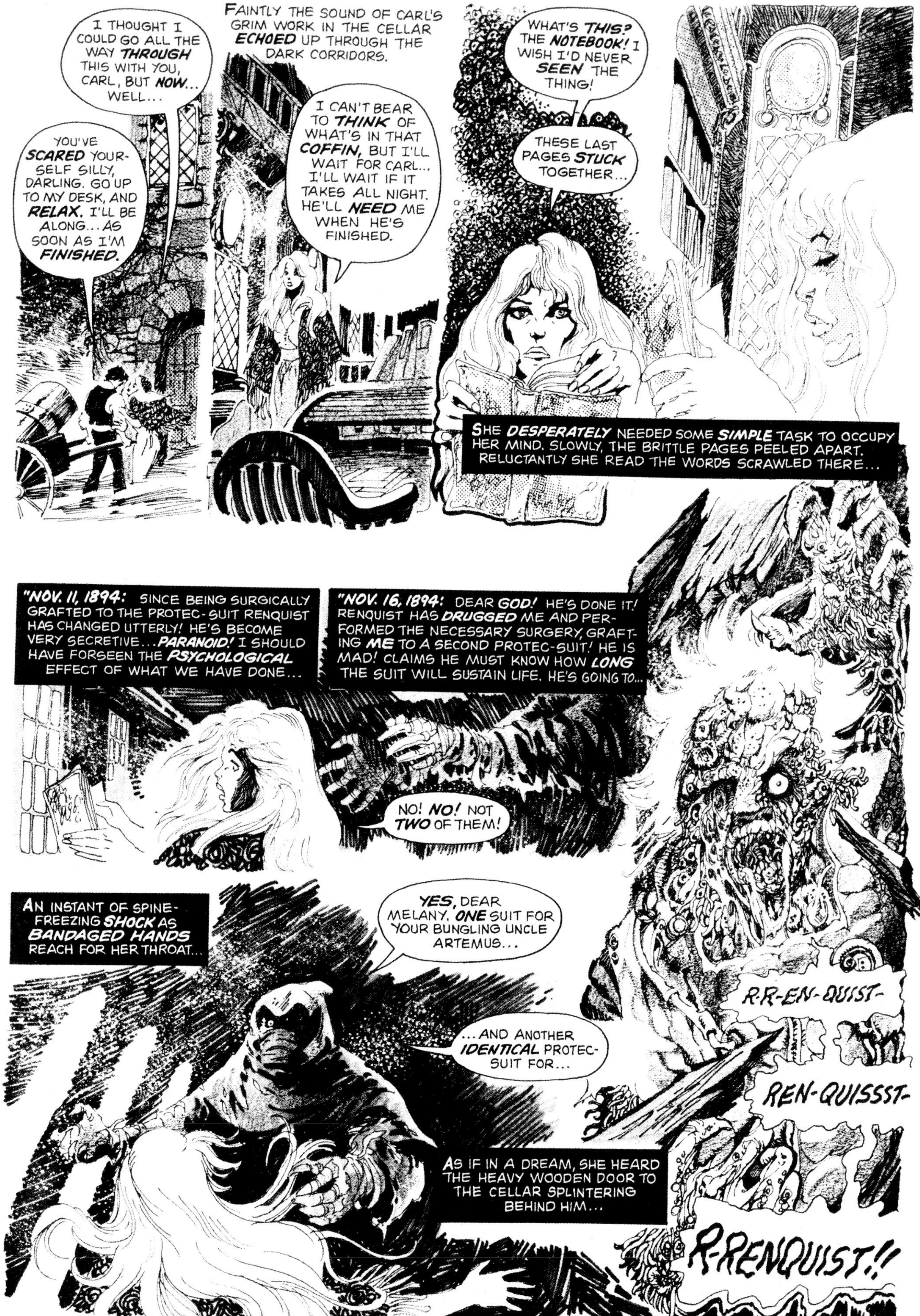

I THOUGHT I COULD GO ALL THE WAY THROUGH THIS WITH YOU, CARL, BUT NOW... WELL...
YOU'VE SCARED YOURSELF SILLY, DARLING. GO UP TO MY DESK, AND RELAX. I'LL BE ALONG... AS SOON AS I'M FINISHED.
FAINTLY THE SOUND OF CARL'S GRIM WORK IN THE CELLAR ECHOED UP THROUGH THE DARK CORRIDORS.
I CAN'T BEAR TO THINK OF WHAT'S IN THAT COFFIN, BUT I'LL WAIT FOR CARL... I'LL WAIT IF IT TAKES ALL NIGHT. HE'LL NEED ME WHEN HE'S FINISHED.
WHAT'S THIS? THE NOTEBOOK! I WISH I'D NEVER SEEN THE THING!
THESE LAST PAGES STUCK TOGETHER...
SHE DESPERATELY NEEDED SOME SIMPLE TASK TO OCCUPY HER MIND. SLOWLY, THE BRITTLE PAGES PEELED APART. RELUCTANTLY SHE READ THE WORDS SCRAWLED THERE...
"NOV. 11, 1894: SINCE BEING SURGICALLY GRAFTED TO THE PROTEC-SUIT RENQUIST HAS CHANGED UTTERLY! HE'S BECOME VERY SECRETIVE... PARANOID! I SHOULD HAVE FORSEEN THE PSYCHOLOGICAL EFFECT OF WHAT WE HAVE DONE...
"NOV. 16, 1894: DEAR GOD! HE'S DONE IT! RENQUIST HAS DRUGGED ME AND PERFORMED THE NECESSARY SURGERY, GRAFTING ME TO A SECOND PROTEC-SUIT! HE IS MAD! CLAIMS HE MUST KNOW HOW LONG THE SUIT WILL SUSTAIN LIFE. HE'S GOING TO...
NO! NO! NOT TWO OF THEM!
AN INSTANT OF SPINE-FREEZING SHOCK AS BANDAGED HANDS REACH FOR HER THROAT...
YES, DEAR MELANY, ONE SUIT FOR YOUR BUNGLING UNCLE ARTEMUS...
...AND ANOTHER IDENTICAL PROTEC-SUIT FOR...
R-R-EN-QUIST-
REN-QUISSST-
AS IF IN A DREAM, SHE HEARD THE HEAVY WOODEN DOOR TO THE CELLAR SPLINTERING BEHIND HIM...
R-RENQUIST!!

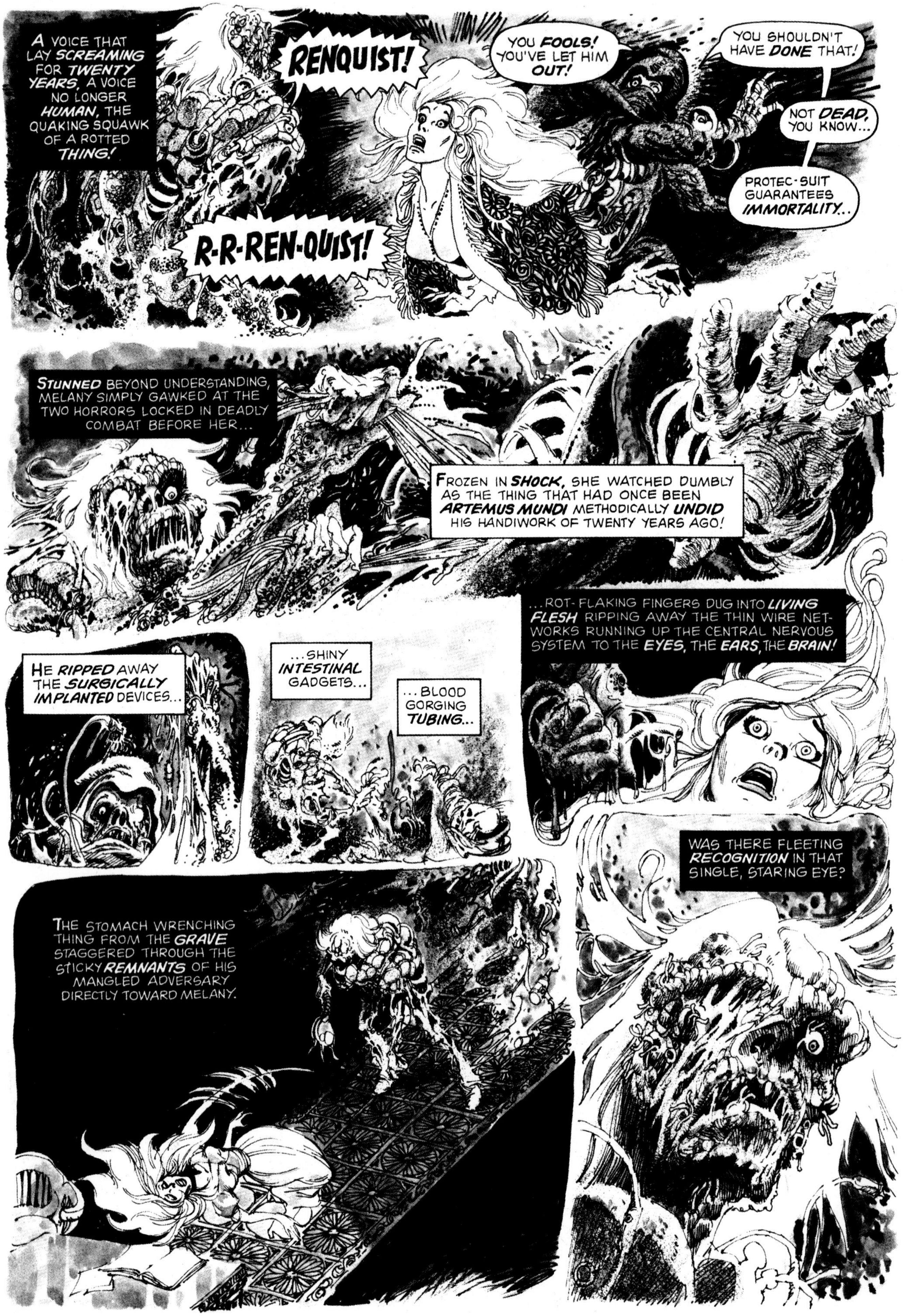
A VOICE THAT LAY SCREAMING FOR TWENTY YEARS, A VOICE NO LONGER HUMAN, THE QUAKING SQUAWK OF A ROTTED THING!
RENQUIST!
YOU FOOLS! YOU'VE LET HIM OUT!
YOU SHOULDN'T HAVE DONE THAT!
NOT DEAD, YOU KNOW...
PROTEC-SUIT GUARANTEES IMMORTALITY...
R-R-REN-QUIST!
STUNNED BEYOND UNDERSTANDING, MELANY SIMPLY GAWKED AT THE TWO HORRORS LOCKED IN DEADLY COMBAT BEFORE HER...
FROZEN IN SHOCK, SHE WATCHED DUMBLY AS THE THING THAT HAD ONCE BEEN ARTEMUS MUNDI METHODICALLY UNDID HIS HANDIWORK OF TWENTY YEARS AGO!
HE RIPPED AWAY THE SURGICALLY IMPLANTED DEVICES...
...SHINY INTESTINAL GADGETS...
...BLOOD GORGING TUBING...
...ROT-FLAKING FINGERS DUG INTO LIVING FLESH RIPPING AWAY THE THIN WIRE NET-WORKS RUNNING UP THE CENTRAL NERVOUS SYSTEM TO THE EYES, THE EARS, THE BRAIN!
THE STOMACH WRENCHING THING FROM THE GRAVE STAGGERED THROUGH THE STICKY REMNANTS OF HIS MANGLED ADVERSARY DIRECTLY TOWARD MELANY.
WAS THERE FLEETING RECOGNITION IN THAT SINGLE, STARING EYE?

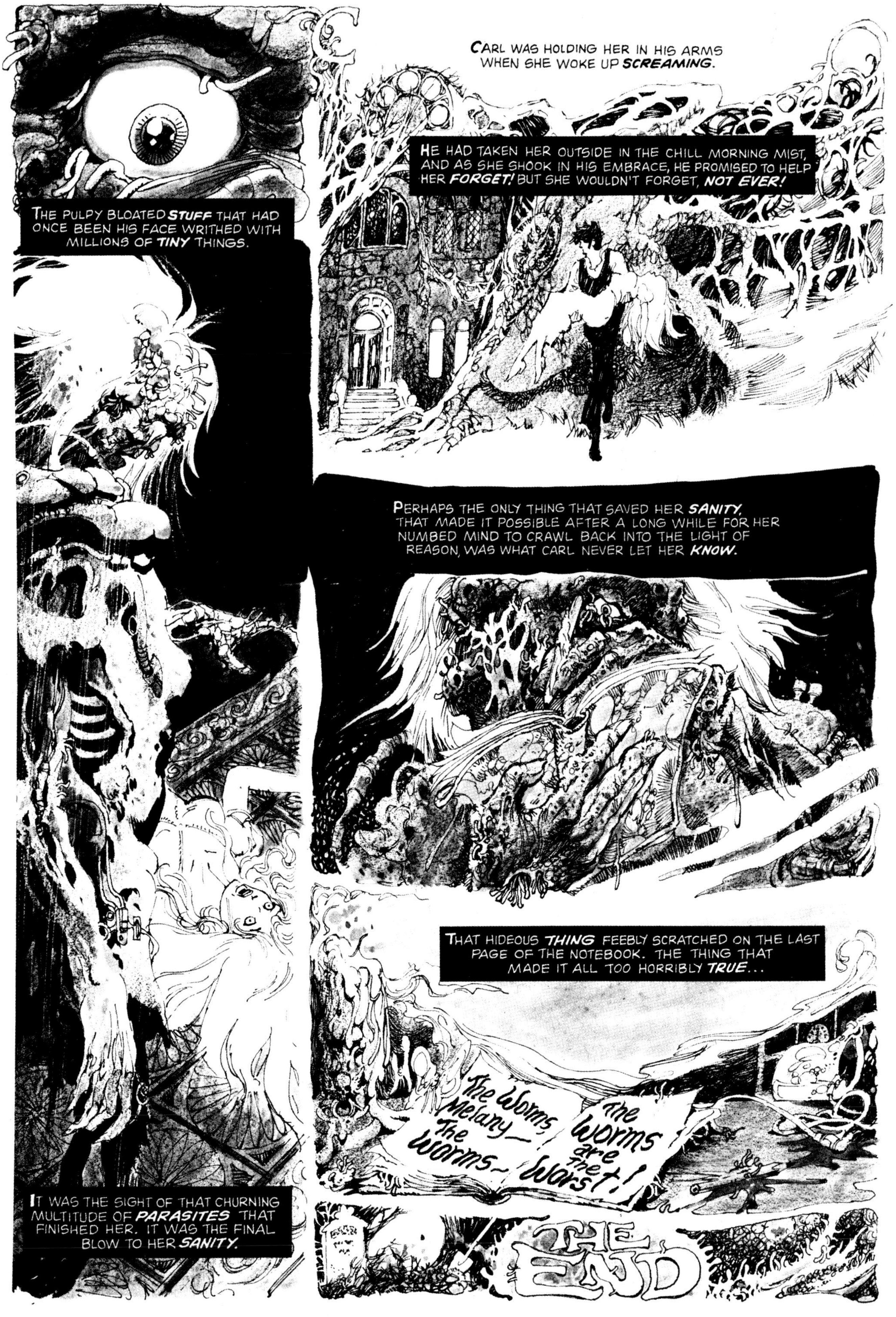

THE PULPY BLOATED STUFF THAT HAD ONCE BEEN HIS FACE WRITHED WITH MILLIONS OF TINY THINGS.
IT WAS THE SIGHT OF THAT CHURNING MULTITUDE OF PARASITES THAT FINISHED HER. IT WAS THE FINAL BLOW TO HER SANITY.
CARL WAS HOLDING HER IN HIS ARMS WHEN SHE WOKE UP SCREAMING.
HE HAD TAKEN HER OUTSIDE IN THE CHILL MORNING MIST, AND AS SHE SHOOK IN HIS EMBRACE, HE PROMISED TO HELP HER FORGET! BUT SHE WOULDN'T FORGET, NOT EVER!
PERHAPS THE ONLY THING THAT SAVED HER SANITY, THAT MADE IT POSSIBLE AFTER A LONG WHILE FOR HER NUMBED MIND TO CRAWL BACK INTO THE LIGHT OF REASON, WAS WHAT CARL NEVER LET HER KNOW.
THAT HIDEOUS THING FEEBLY SCRATCHED ON THE LAST PAGE OF THE NOTEBOOK. THE THING THAT MADE IT ALL TOO HORRIBLY TRUE...
The Worms Melany— The Worms—
The Worms are the Worst!
THE END

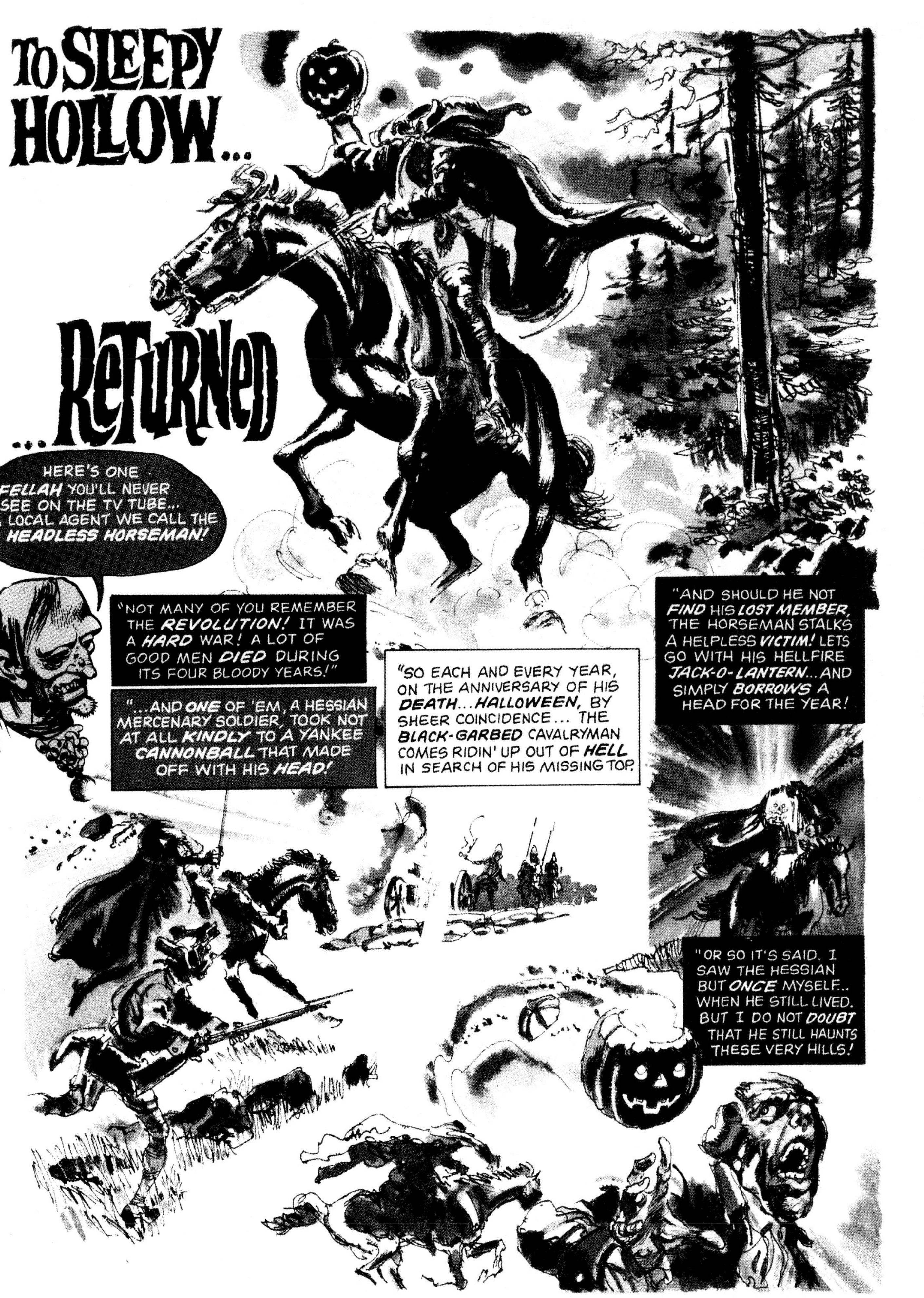
TO SLEEPY HOLLOW...
...RETURNED
HERE'S ONE FELLAH YOU'LL NEVER SEE ON THE TV TUBE... A LOCAL AGENT WE CALL THE HEADLESS HORSEMAN!
"NOT MANY OF YOU REMEMBER THE REVOLUTION! IT WAS A HARD WAR! A LOT OF GOOD MEN DIED DURING ITS FOUR BLOODY YEARS!"
"...AND ONE OF 'EM, A HESSIAN MERCENARY SOLDIER, TOOK NOT AT ALL KINDLY TO A YANKEE CANNONBALL THAT MADE OFF WITH HIS HEAD!
"SO EACH AND EVERY YEAR, ON THE ANNIVERSARY OF HIS DEATH...HALLOWEEN, BY SHEER COINCIDENCE... THE BLACK-GARBED CAVALRYMAN COMES RIDIN' UP OUT OF HELL IN SEARCH OF HIS MISSING TOP.
"AND SHOULD HE NOT FIND HIS LOST MEMBER, THE HORSEMAN STALKS A HELPLESS VICTIM! LETS GO WITH HIS HELLFIRE JACK-O-LANTERN...AND SIMPLY BORROWS A HEAD FOR THE YEAR!
"OR SO IT'S SAID. I SAW THE HESSIAN BUT ONCE MYSELF.. WHEN HE STILL LIVED. BUT I DO NOT DOUBT THAT HE STILL HAUNTS THESE VERY HILLS!

STORY: JEFF ROVIN / ART: LEO SUMMERS

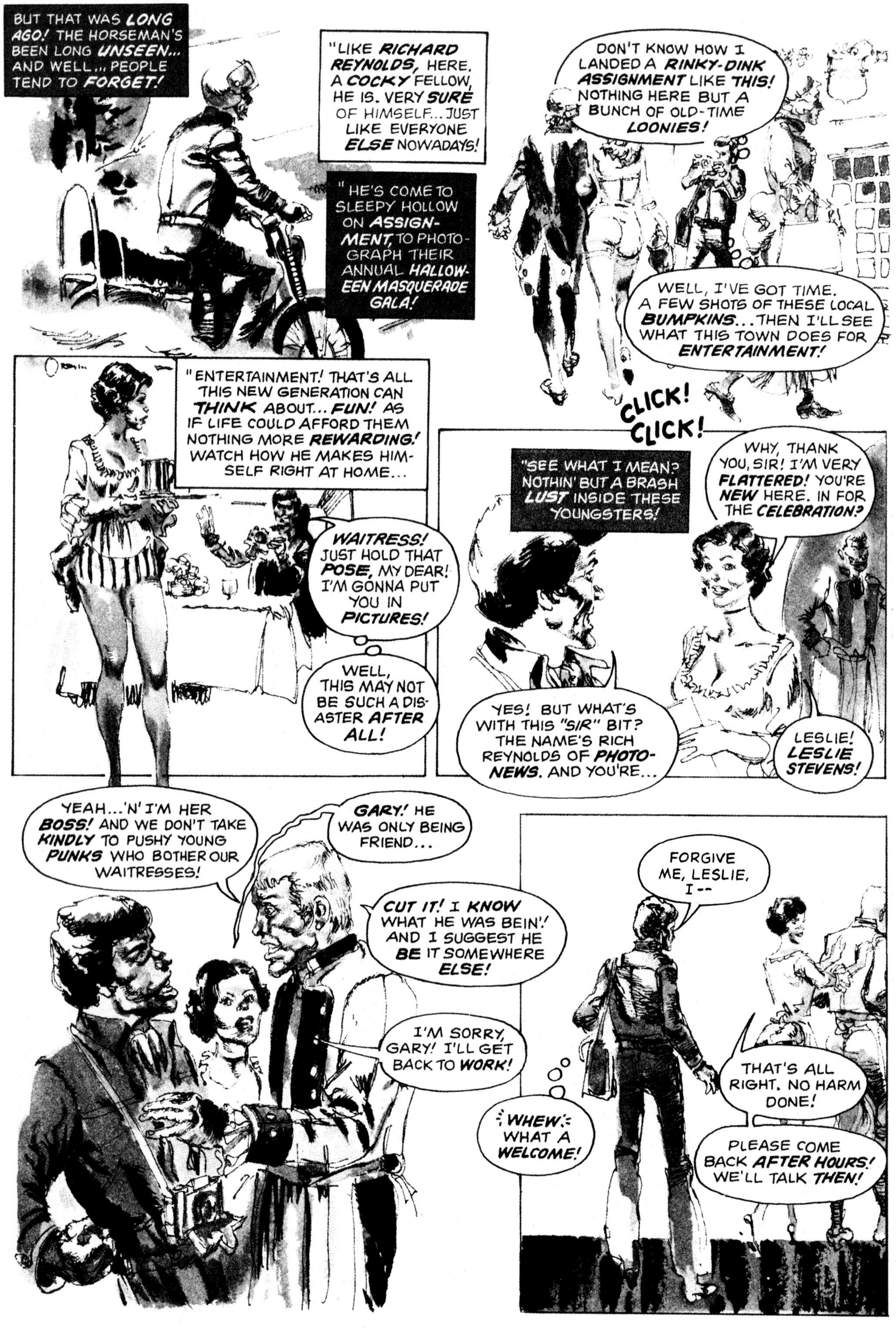

BUT THAT WAS LONG AGO! THE HORSEMAN'S BEEN LONG UNSEEN... AND WELL... PEOPLE TEND TO FORGET!
"LIKE RICHARD REYNOLDS, HERE. A COCKY FELLOW, HE IS. VERY SURE OF HIMSELF... JUST LIKE EVERYONE ELSE NOWADAYS!
"HE'S COME TO SLEEPY HOLLOW ON ASSIGNMENT, TO PHOTOGRAPH THEIR ANNUAL HALLOWEEN MASQUERADE GALA!
DON'T KNOW HOW I LANDED A RINKY-DINK ASSIGNMENT LIKE THIS! NOTHING HERE BUT A BUNCH OF OLD-TIME LOONIES!
WELL, I'VE GOT TIME. A FEW SHOTS OF THESE LOCAL BUMPKINS... THEN I'LL SEE WHAT THIS TOWN DOES FOR ENTERTAINMENT!
"ENTERTAINMENT! THAT'S ALL THIS NEW GENERATION CAN THINK ABOUT... FUN! AS IF LIFE COULD AFFORD THEM NOTHING MORE REWARDING! WATCH HOW HE MAKES HIMSELF RIGHT AT HOME...
WAITRESS! JUST HOLD THAT POSE, MY DEAR! I'M GONNA PUT YOU IN PICTURES!
WELL, THIS MAY NOT BE SUCH A DISASTER AFTER ALL!
CLICK! CLICK!
"SEE WHAT I MEAN? NOTHIN' BUT A BRASH LUST INSIDE THESE YOUNGSTERS!
WHY, THANK YOU, SIR! I'M VERY FLATTERED! YOU'RE NEW HERE. IN FOR THE CELEBRATION?
YES! BUT WHAT'S WITH THIS "SIR" BIT? THE NAME'S RICH REYNOLDS OF PHOTO-NEWS. AND YOU'RE...
LESLIE! LESLIE STEVENS!
YEAH...'N' I'M HER BOSS! AND WE DON'T TAKE KINDLY TO PUSHY YOUNG PUNKS WHO BOTHER OUR WAITRESSES!
GARY! HE WAS ONLY BEING FRIEND...
CUT IT! I KNOW WHAT HE WAS BEIN'! AND I SUGGEST HE BE IT SOMEWHERE ELSE!
I'M SORRY, GARY! I'LL GET BACK TO WORK!
FORGIVE ME, LESLIE, I --
WHEW! WHAT A WELCOME!
THAT'S ALL RIGHT. NO HARM DONE!
PLEASE COME BACK AFTER HOURS! WE'LL TALK THEN!

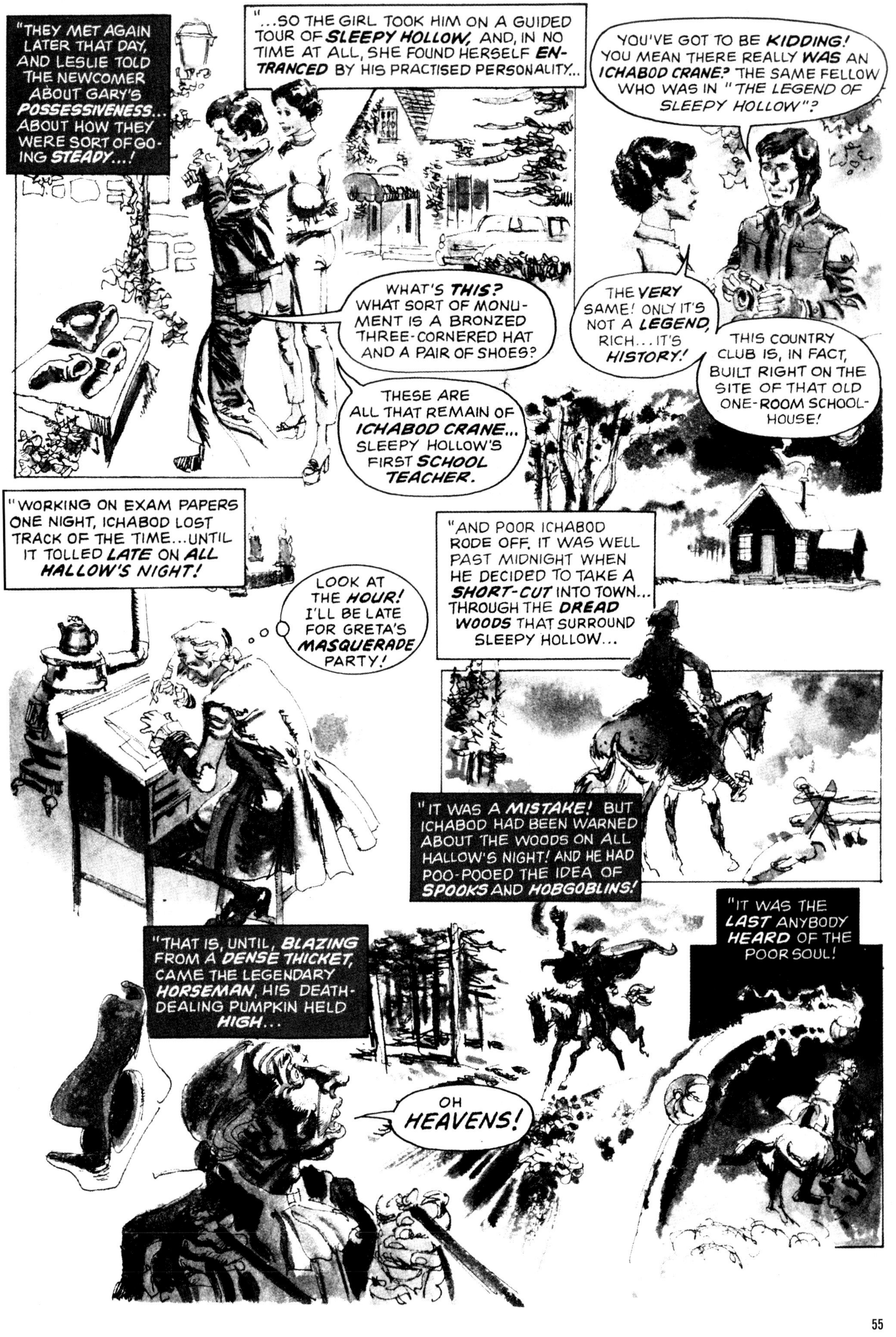

"THEY MET AGAIN LATER THAT DAY, AND LESLIE TOLD THE NEWCOMER ABOUT GARY'S POSSESSIVENESS... ABOUT HOW THEY WERE SORT OF GO-ING STEADY...!
"...SO THE GIRL TOOK HIM ON A GUIDED TOUR OF SLEEPY HOLLOW, AND, IN NO TIME AT ALL, SHE FOUND HERSELF EN-TRANCED BY HIS PRACTISED PERSONALITY...
WHAT'S THIS? WHAT SORT OF MONU-MENT IS A BRONZED THREE-CORNERED HAT AND A PAIR OF SHOES?
THESE ARE ALL THAT REMAIN OF ICHABOD CRANE... SLEEPY HOLLOW'S FIRST SCHOOL TEACHER.
YOU'VE GOT TO BE KIDDING! YOU MEAN THERE REALLY WAS AN ICHABOD CRANE? THE SAME FELLOW WHO WAS IN "THE LEGEND OF SLEEPY HOLLOW"?
THE VERY SAME! ONLY IT'S NOT A LEGEND, RICH... IT'S HISTORY!
THIS COUNTRY CLUB IS, IN FACT, BUILT RIGHT ON THE SITE OF THAT OLD ONE-ROOM SCHOOL-HOUSE!
"WORKING ON EXAM PAPERS ONE NIGHT, ICHABOD LOST TRACK OF THE TIME... UNTIL IT TOLLED LATE ON ALL HALLOW'S NIGHT!
LOOK AT THE HOUR! I'LL BE LATE FOR GRETA'S MASQUERADE PARTY!
"AND POOR ICHABOD RODE OFF. IT WAS WELL PAST MIDNIGHT WHEN HE DECIDED TO TAKE A SHORT-CUT INTO TOWN... THROUGH THE DREAD WOODS THAT SURROUND SLEEPY HOLLOW...
"IT WAS A MISTAKE! BUT ICHABOD HAD BEEN WARNED ABOUT THE WOODS ON ALL HALLOW'S NIGHT! AND HE HAD POO-POOED THE IDEA OF SPOOKS AND HOBGOBLINS!
"THAT IS, UNTIL, BLAZING FROM A DENSE THICKET, CAME THE LEGENDARY HORSEMAN, HIS DEATH-DEALING PUMPKIN HELD HIGH...
OH HEAVENS!
"IT WAS THE LAST ANYBODY HEARD OF THE POOR SOUL!

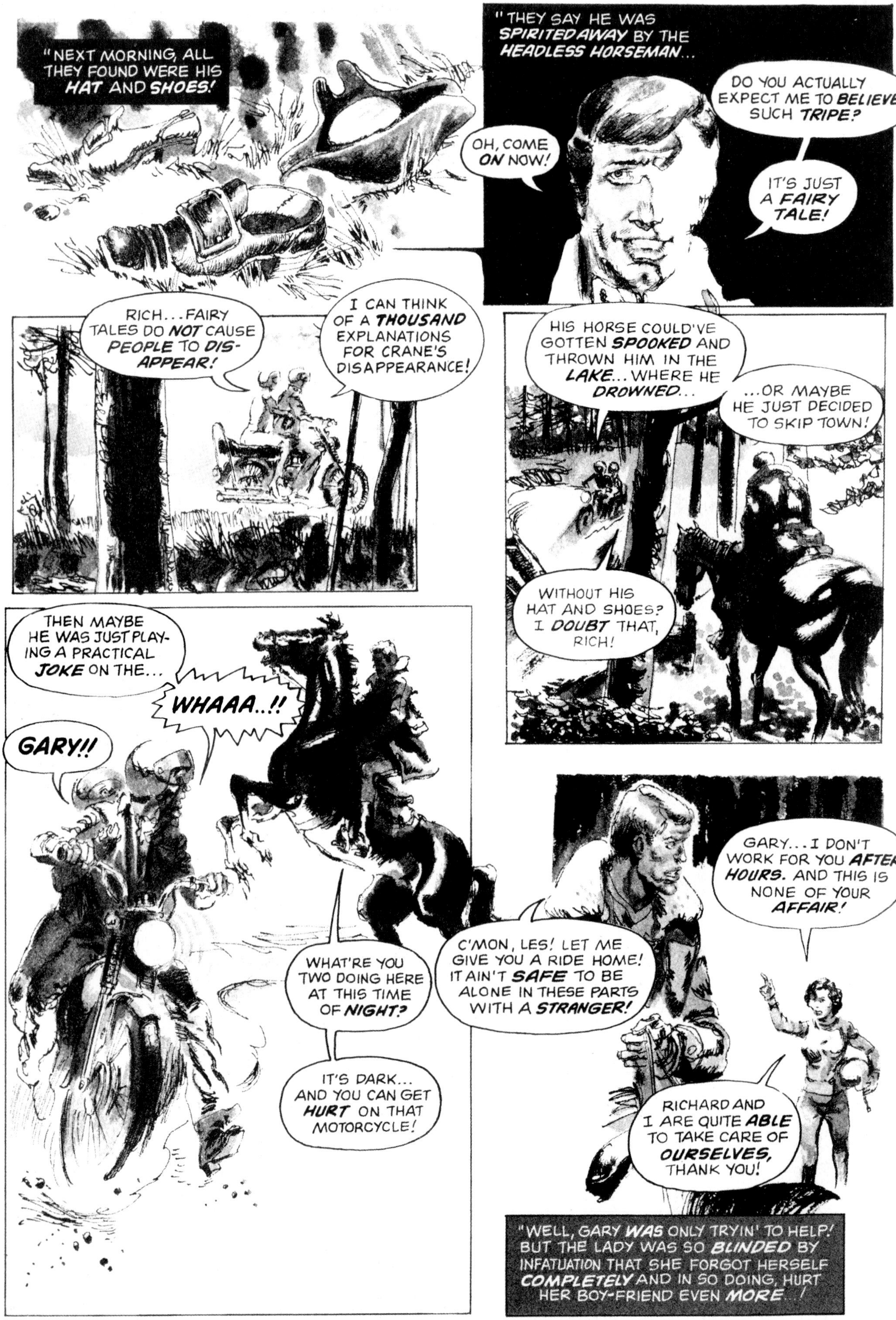
"NEXT MORNING, ALL THEY FOUND WERE HIS HAT AND SHOES!
"THEY SAY HE WAS SPIRITED AWAY BY THE HEADLESS HORSEMAN...
DO YOU ACTUALLY EXPECT ME TO BELIEVE SUCH TRIPE?
OH, COME ON NOW!
IT'S JUST A FAIRY TALE!
RICH...FAIRY TALES DO NOT CAUSE PEOPLE TO DIS-APPEAR!
I CAN THINK OF A THOUSAND EXPLANATIONS FOR CRANE'S DISAPPEARANCE!
HIS HORSE COULD'VE GOTTEN SPOOKED AND THROWN HIM IN THE LAKE... WHERE HE DROWNED...
...OR MAYBE HE JUST DECIDED TO SKIP TOWN!
WITHOUT HIS HAT AND SHOES? I DOUBT THAT, RICH!
THEN MAYBE HE WAS JUST PLAY-ING A PRACTICAL JOKE ON THE...
WHAAA..!!
GARY!!
WHAT'RE YOU TWO DOING HERE AT THIS TIME OF NIGHT?
IT'S DARK... AND YOU CAN GET HURT ON THAT MOTORCYCLE!
C'MON, LES! LET ME GIVE YOU A RIDE HOME! IT AIN'T SAFE TO BE ALONE IN THESE PARTS WITH A STRANGER!
GARY... I DON'T WORK FOR YOU AFTER HOURS. AND THIS IS NONE OF YOUR AFFAIR!
RICHARD AND I ARE QUITE ABLE TO TAKE CARE OF OURSELVES, THANK YOU!
"WELL, GARY WAS ONLY TRYIN' TO HELP! BUT THE LADY WAS SO BLINDED BY INFATUATION THAT SHE FORGOT HERSELF COMPLETELY AND IN SO DOING, HURT HER BOY-FRIEND EVEN MORE...!

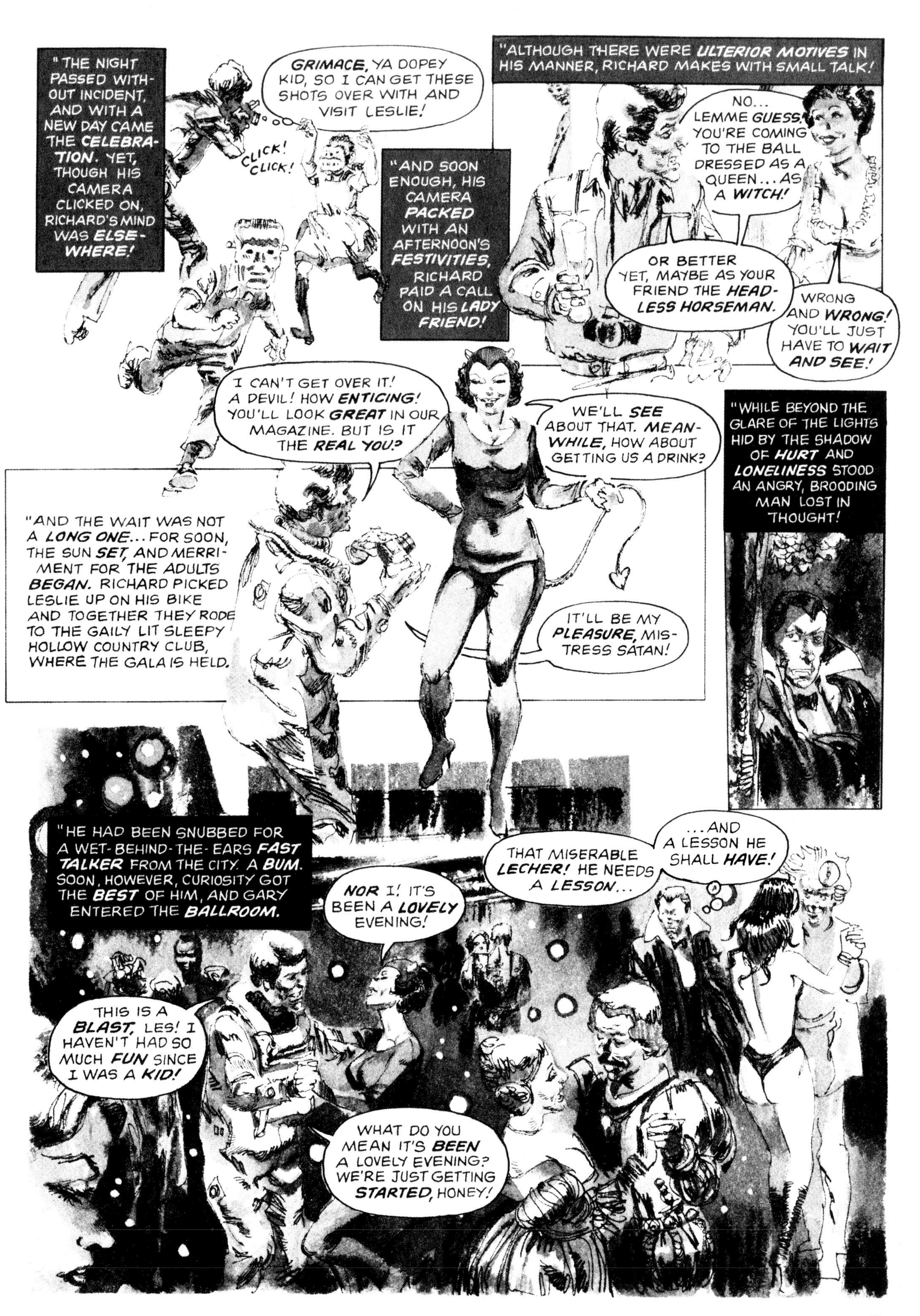
"THE NIGHT PASSED WITHOUT INCIDENT, AND WITH A NEW DAY CAME THE CELEBRATION. YET, THOUGH HIS CAMERA CLICKED ON, RICHARD'S MIND WAS ELSEWHERE!
GRIMACE, YA DOPEY KID, SO I CAN GET THESE SHOTS OVER WITH AND VISIT LESLIE!
CLICK! CLICK!
"AND SOON ENOUGH, HIS CAMERA PACKED WITH AN AFTERNOON'S FESTIVITIES, RICHARD PAID A CALL ON HIS LADY FRIEND!
"ALTHOUGH THERE WERE ULTERIOR MOTIVES IN HIS MANNER, RICHARD MAKES WITH SMALL TALK!
NO... LEMME GUESS. YOU'RE COMING TO THE BALL DRESSED AS A QUEEN... AS A WITCH!
OR BETTER YET, MAYBE AS YOUR FRIEND THE HEADLESS HORSEMAN.
WRONG AND WRONG! YOU'LL JUST HAVE TO WAIT AND SEE!
"AND THE WAIT WAS NOT A LONG ONE... FOR SOON, THE SUN SET, AND MERRIMENT FOR THE ADULTS BEGAN. RICHARD PICKED LESLIE UP ON HIS BIKE AND TOGETHER THEY RODE TO THE GAILY LIT SLEEPY HOLLOW COUNTRY CLUB, WHERE THE GALA IS HELD.
I CAN'T GET OVER IT! A DEVIL! HOW ENTICING! YOU'LL LOOK GREAT IN OUR MAGAZINE. BUT IS IT THE REAL YOU?
WE'LL SEE ABOUT THAT. MEANWHILE, HOW ABOUT GETTING US A DRINK?
IT'LL BE MY PLEASURE, MISTRESS SATAN!
"WHILE BEYOND THE GLARE OF THE LIGHTS HID BY THE SHADOW OF HURT AND LONELINESS STOOD AN ANGRY, BROODING MAN LOST IN THOUGHT!
"HE HAD BEEN SNUBBED FOR A WET-BEHIND-THE-EARS FAST TALKER FROM THE CITY. A BUM. SOON, HOWEVER, CURIOSITY GOT THE BEST OF HIM, AND GARY ENTERED THE BALLROOM.
THIS IS A BLAST, LES! I HAVEN'T HAD SO MUCH FUN SINCE I WAS A KID!
NOR I! IT'S BEEN A LOVELY EVENING!
WHAT DO YOU MEAN IT'S BEEN A LOVELY EVENING? WE'RE JUST GETTING STARTED, HONEY!
THAT MISERABLE LECHER! HE NEEDS A LESSON...
...AND A LESSON HE SHALL HAVE!

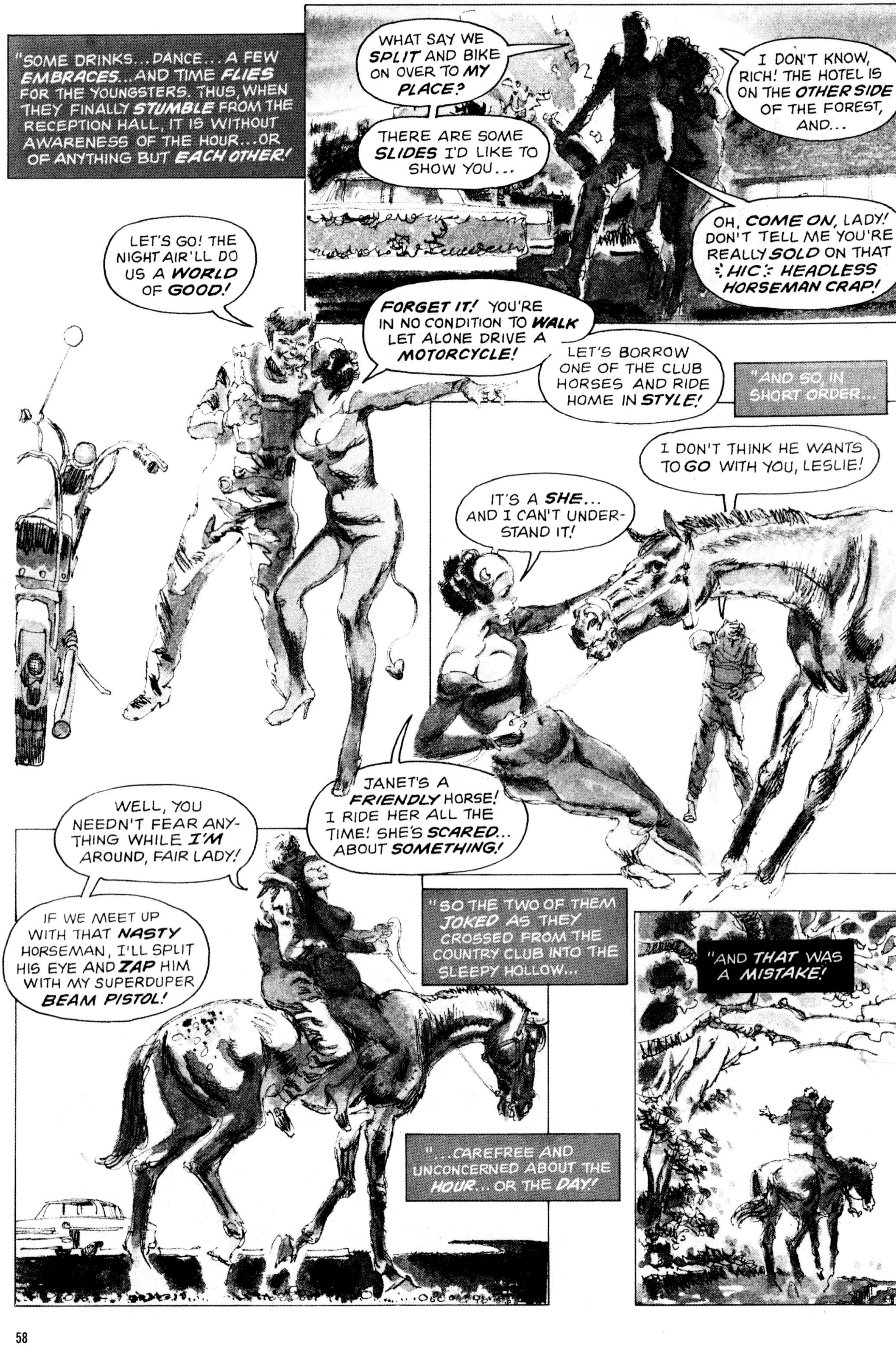
"SOME DRINKS... DANCE... A FEW EMBRACES... AND TIME FLIES FOR THE YOUNGSTERS. THUS, WHEN THEY FINALLY STUMBLE FROM THE RECEPTION HALL, IT IS WITHOUT AWARENESS OF THE HOUR... OR OF ANYTHING BUT EACH OTHER!
WHAT SAY WE SPLIT AND BIKE ON OVER TO MY PLACE?
THERE ARE SOME SLIDES I'D LIKE TO SHOW YOU...
I DON'T KNOW, RICH! THE HOTEL IS ON THE OTHER SIDE OF THE FOREST, AND...
OH, COME ON, LADY! DON'T TELL ME YOU'RE REALLY SOLD ON THAT HIC HEADLESS HORSEMAN CRAP!
LET'S GO! THE NIGHT AIR'LL DO US A WORLD OF GOOD!
FORGET IT! YOU'RE IN NO CONDITION TO WALK LET ALONE DRIVE A MOTORCYCLE!
LET'S BORROW ONE OF THE CLUB HORSES AND RIDE HOME IN STYLE!
"AND SO, IN SHORT ORDER...
I DON'T THINK HE WANTS TO GO WITH YOU, LESLIE!
IT'S A SHE... AND I CAN'T UNDERSTAND IT!
JANET'S A FRIENDLY HORSE! I RIDE HER ALL THE TIME! SHE'S SCARED... ABOUT SOMETHING!
WELL, YOU NEEDN'T FEAR ANYTHING WHILE I'M AROUND, FAIR LADY!
IF WE MEET UP WITH THAT NASTY HORSEMAN, I'LL SPLIT HIS EYE AND ZAP HIM WITH MY SUPERDUPER BEAM PISTOL!
"SO THE TWO OF THEM JOKED AS THEY CROSSED FROM THE COUNTRY CLUB INTO THE SLEEPY HOLLOW...
"...CAREFREE AND UNCONCERNED ABOUT THE HOUR... OR THE DAY!
"AND THAT WAS A MISTAKE!

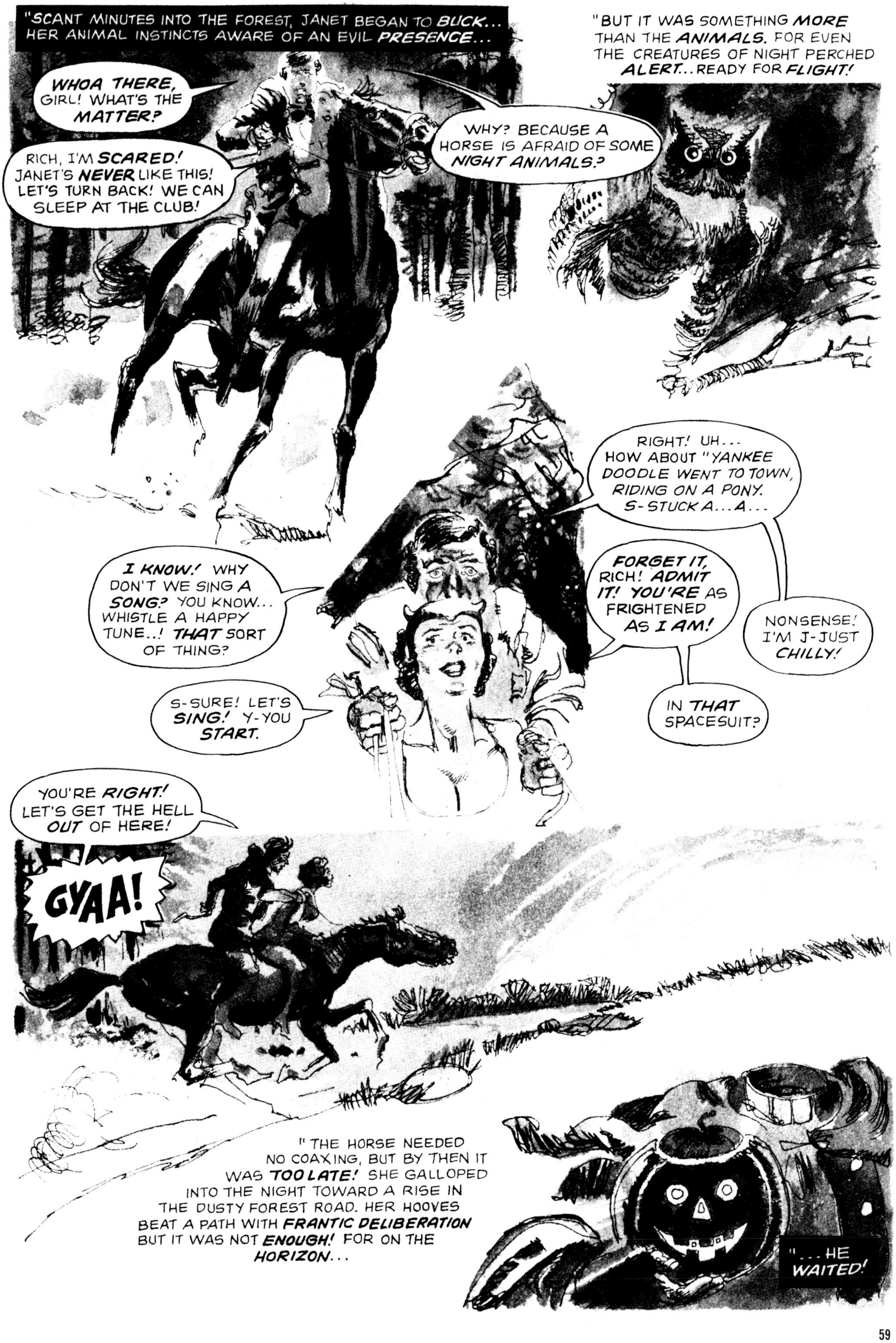
"SCANT MINUTES INTO THE FOREST, JANET BEGAN TO BUCK... HER ANIMAL INSTINCTS AWARE OF AN EVIL PRESENCE...
WHOA THERE, GIRL! WHAT'S THE MATTER?
RICH, I'M SCARED! JANET'S NEVER LIKE THIS! LET'S TURN BACK! WE CAN SLEEP AT THE CLUB!
WHY? BECAUSE A HORSE IS AFRAID OF SOME NIGHT ANIMALS?
"BUT IT WAS SOMETHING MORE THAN THE ANIMALS. FOR EVEN THE CREATURES OF NIGHT PERCHED ALERT...READY FOR FLIGHT!
I KNOW! WHY DON'T WE SING A SONG? YOU KNOW... WHISTLE A HAPPY TUNE..! THAT SORT OF THING?
S-SURE! LET'S SING! Y-YOU START.
RIGHT! UH... HOW ABOUT "YANKEE DOODLE WENT TO TOWN, RIDING ON A PONY. S-STUCK A...A...
FORGET IT, RICH! ADMIT IT! YOU'RE AS FRIGHTENED AS I AM!
NONSENSE! I'M J-JUST CHILLY!
IN THAT SPACESUIT?
YOU'RE RIGHT! LET'S GET THE HELL OUT OF HERE!
GYAA!
" THE HORSE NEEDED NO COAXING, BUT BY THEN IT WAS TOO LATE! SHE GALLOPED INTO THE NIGHT TOWARD A RISE IN THE DUSTY FOREST ROAD. HER HOOVES BEAT A PATH WITH FRANTIC DELIBERATION BUT IT WAS NOT ENOUGH! FOR ON THE HORIZON...
"...HE WAITED!

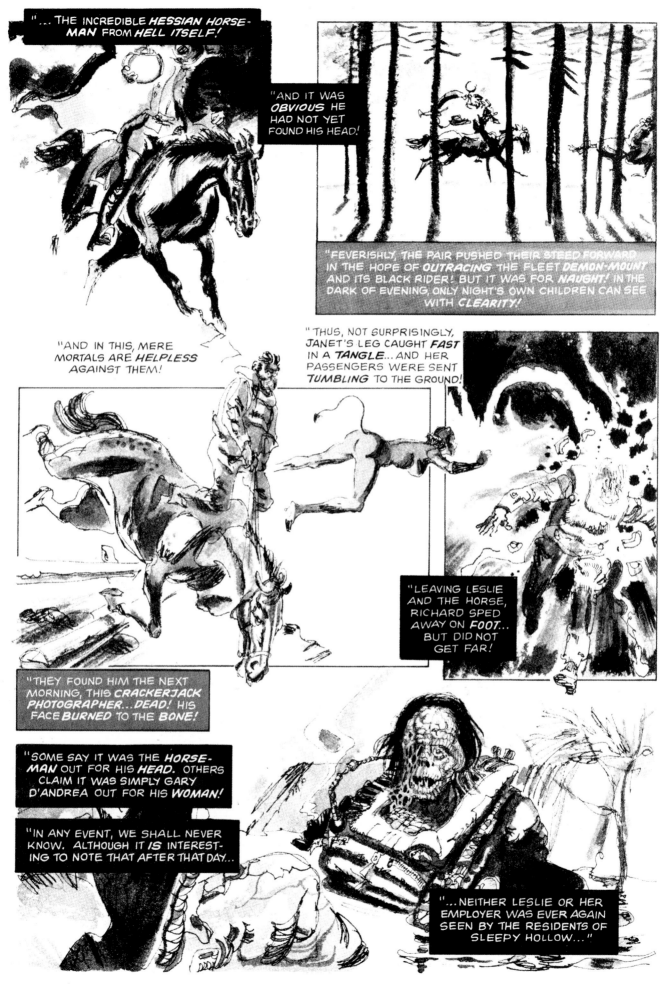

"...THE INCREDIBLE *HESSIAN HORSE-MAN* FROM *HELL ITSELF!*

"AND IT WAS *OBVIOUS* HE HAD NOT YET FOUND HIS HEAD!

"FEVERISHLY, THE PAIR PUSHED THEIR STEED FORWARD IN THE HOPE OF *OUTRACING* THE FLEET *DEMON-MOUNT* AND ITS BLACK RIDER! BUT IT WAS FOR *NAUGHT!* IN THE DARK OF EVENING, ONLY NIGHT'S OWN CHILDREN CAN SEE WITH *CLEARITY!*

"AND IN THIS, MERE MORTALS ARE *HELPLESS* AGAINST THEM!

"THUS, NOT SURPRISINGLY, JANET'S LEG CAUGHT *FAST* IN A *TANGLE*...AND HER PASSENGERS WERE SENT *TUMBLING* TO THE GROUND!

"LEAVING LESLIE AND THE HORSE, RICHARD SPED AWAY ON *FOOT*...BUT DID NOT GET FAR!

"THEY FOUND HIM THE NEXT MORNING, THIS *CRACKERJACK PHOTOGRAPHER*...DEAD! HIS FACE *BURNED* TO THE *BONE!*

"SOME SAY IT WAS THE *HORSE-MAN* OUT FOR HIS *HEAD.* OTHERS CLAIM IT WAS SIMPLY GARY D'ANDREA OUT FOR HIS *WOMAN!*

"IN ANY EVENT, WE SHALL NEVER KNOW. ALTHOUGH IT *IS* INTERESTING TO NOTE THAT AFTER THAT DAY...

"...NEITHER LESLIE OR HER EMPLOYER WAS EVER AGAIN SEEN BY THE RESIDENTS OF SLEEPY HOLLOW..."

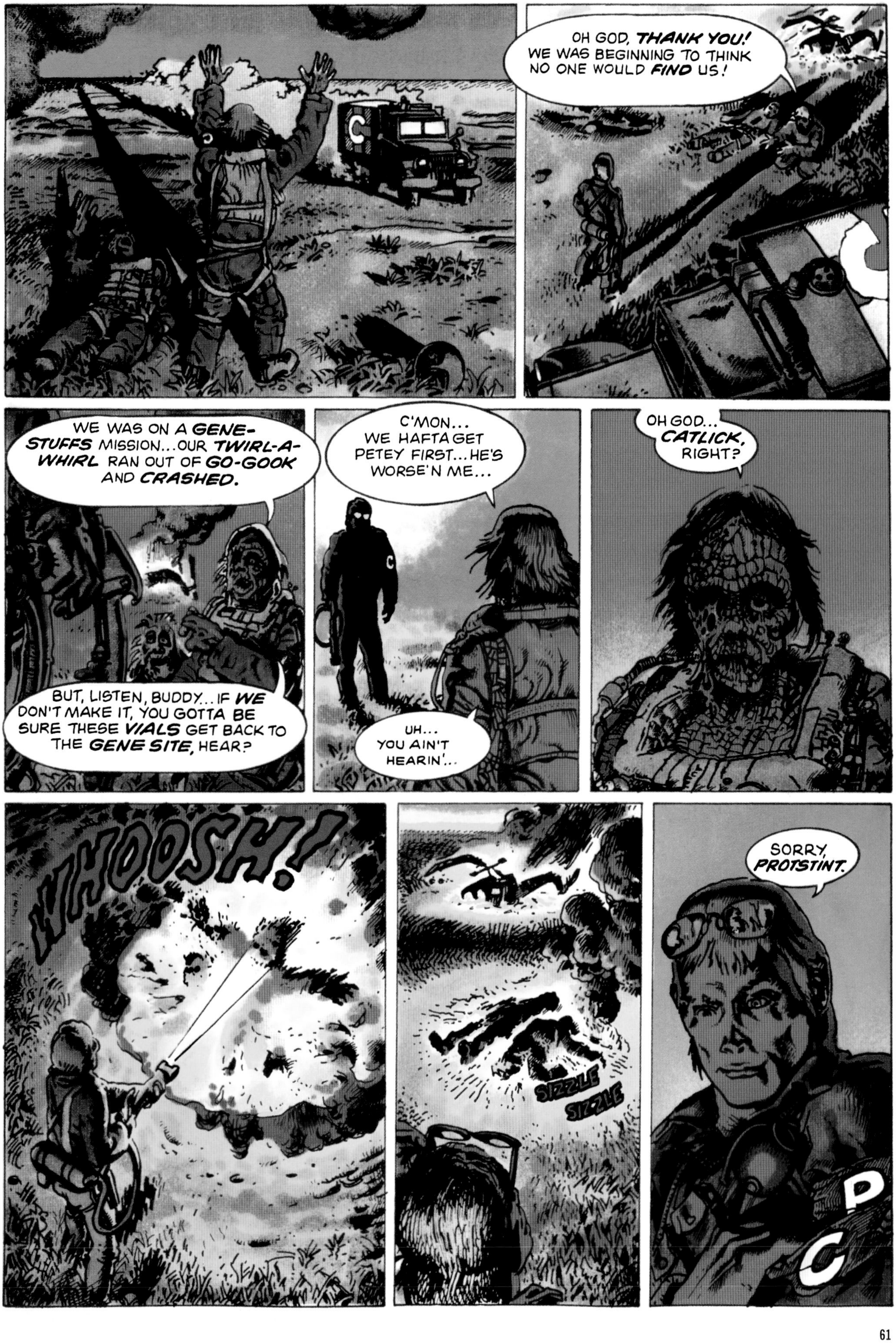
OH GOD, THANK YOU! WE WAS BEGINNING TO THINK NO ONE WOULD FIND US!
WE WAS ON A GENE-STUFFS MISSION...OUR TWIRL-A-WHIRL RAN OUT OF GO-GOOK AND CRASHED.
BUT, LISTEN, BUDDY...IF WE DON'T MAKE IT, YOU GOTTA BE SURE THESE VIALS GET BACK TO THE GENE SITE, HEAR?
C'MON... WE HAFTA GET PETEY FIRST...HE'S WORSE'N ME...
UH... YOU AIN'T HEARIN'...
OH GOD... CATLICK, RIGHT?
WHOOSH!
SIZZLE
SIZZLE
SORRY, PROTSTINT.
P
C

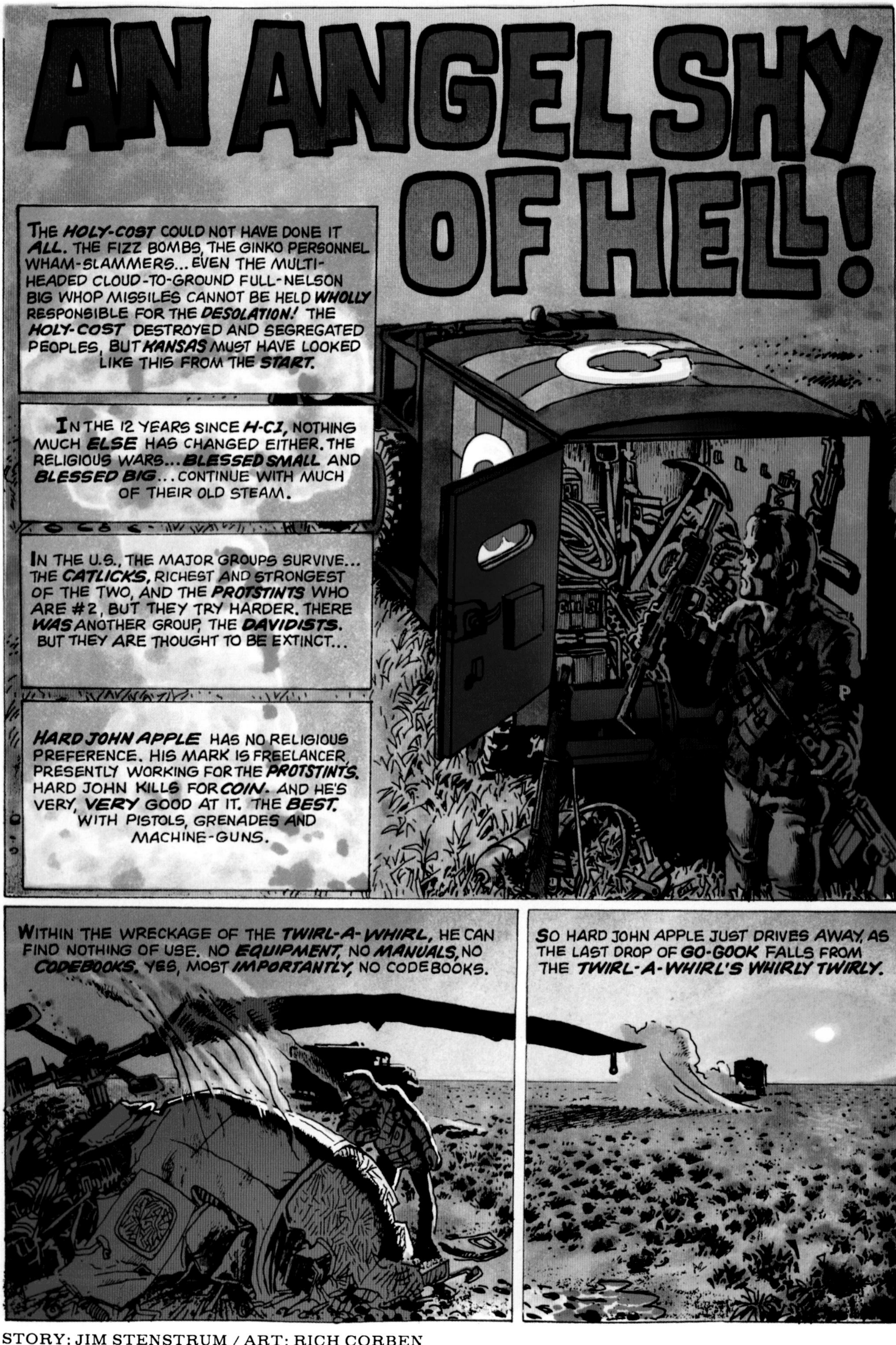

AN ANGEL SHY OF HELL!
THE HOLY-COST COULD NOT HAVE DONE IT ALL. THE FIZZ BOMBS, THE GINKO PERSONNEL WHAM-SLAMMERS... EVEN THE MULTI-HEADED CLOUD-TO-GROUND FULL-NELSON BIG WHOP MISSILES CANNOT BE HELD WHOLLY RESPONSIBLE FOR THE DESOLATION! THE HOLY-COST DESTROYED AND SEGREGATED PEOPLES, BUT KANSAS MUST HAVE LOOKED LIKE THIS FROM THE START.
IN THE 12 YEARS SINCE H-C1, NOTHING MUCH ELSE HAS CHANGED EITHER. THE RELIGIOUS WARS... BLESSED SMALL AND BLESSED BIG... CONTINUE WITH MUCH OF THEIR OLD STEAM.
IN THE U.S., THE MAJOR GROUPS SURVIVE... THE CATLICKS, RICHEST AND STRONGEST OF THE TWO, AND THE PROTSTINTS WHO ARE #2, BUT THEY TRY HARDER. THERE WAS ANOTHER GROUP, THE DAVIDISTS. BUT THEY ARE THOUGHT TO BE EXTINCT...
HARD JOHN APPLE HAS NO RELIGIOUS PREFERENCE. HIS MARK IS FREELANCER, PRESENTLY WORKING FOR THE PROTSTINTS. HARD JOHN KILLS FOR COIN. AND HE'S VERY, VERY GOOD AT IT. THE BEST. WITH PISTOLS, GRENADES AND MACHINE-GUNS.
WITHIN THE WRECKAGE OF THE TWIRL-A-WHIRL, HE CAN FIND NOTHING OF USE. NO EQUIPMENT, NO MANUALS, NO CODEBOOKS. YES, MOST IMPORTANTLY, NO CODEBOOKS.
SO HARD JOHN APPLE JUST DRIVES AWAY, AS THE LAST DROP OF GO-GOOK FALLS FROM THE TWIRL-A-WHIRL'S WHIRLY TWIRLY.

STORY: JIM STENSTRUM / ART: RICH CORBEN

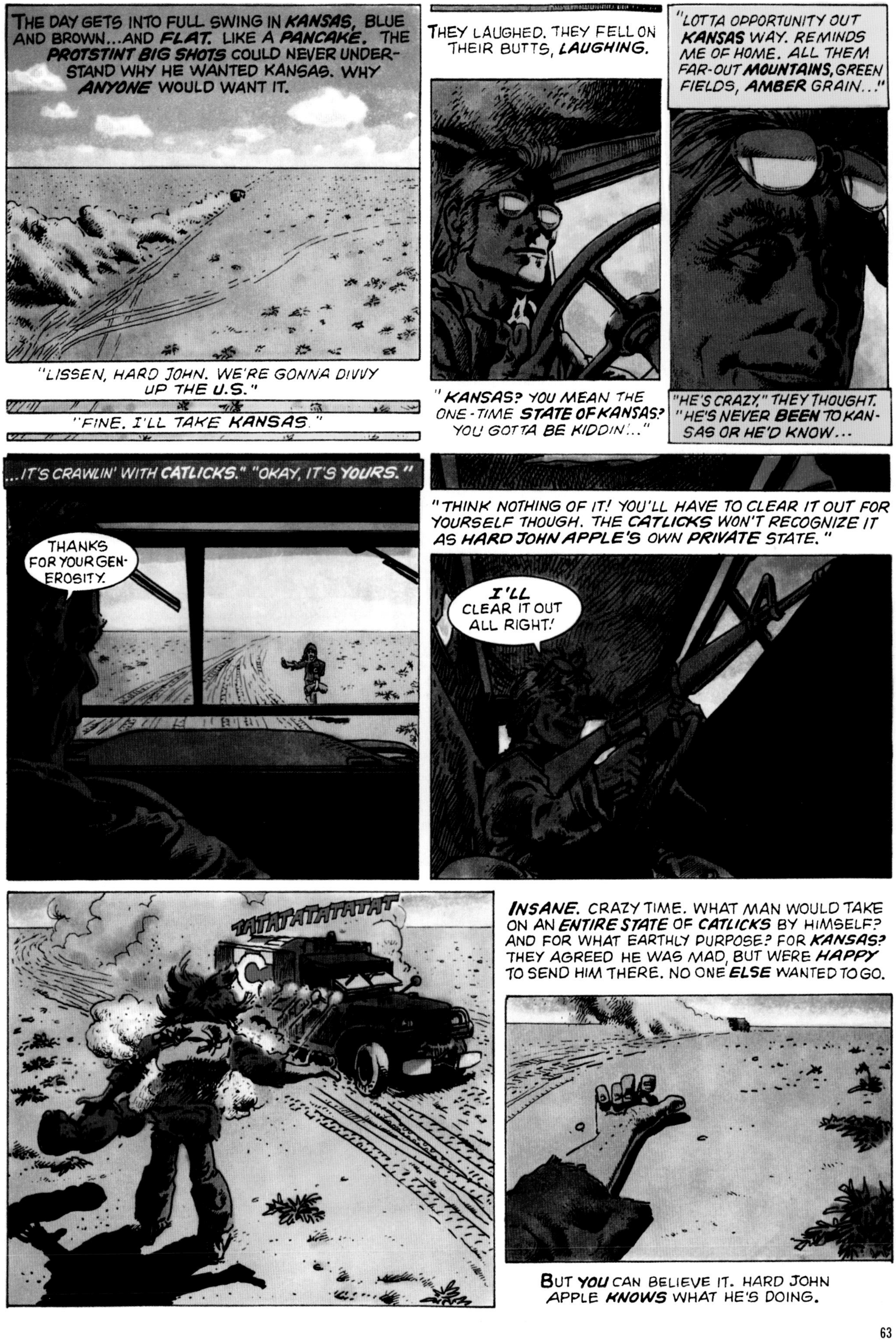
THE DAY GETS INTO FULL SWING IN KANSAS, BLUE AND BROWN...AND FLAT. LIKE A PANCAKE. THE PROTSTINT BIG SHOTS COULD NEVER UNDERSTAND WHY HE WANTED KANSAS. WHY ANYONE WOULD WANT IT.
"LISSEN, HARD JOHN. WE'RE GONNA DIVVY UP THE U.S."
"FINE. I'LL TAKE KANSAS."
THEY LAUGHED. THEY FELL ON THEIR BUTTS, LAUGHING.
"KANSAS? YOU MEAN THE ONE-TIME STATE OF KANSAS? YOU GOTTA BE KIDDIN'..."
"LOTTA OPPORTUNITY OUT KANSAS WAY. REMINDS ME OF HOME. ALL THEM FAR-OUT MOUNTAINS, GREEN FIELDS, AMBER GRAIN..."
"HE'S CRAZY," THEY THOUGHT. "HE'S NEVER BEEN TO KANSAS OR HE'D KNOW...
...IT'S CRAWLIN' WITH CATLICKS." "OKAY, IT'S YOURS."
THANKS FOR YOUR GENEROSITY.
"THINK NOTHING OF IT! YOU'LL HAVE TO CLEAR IT OUT FOR YOURSELF THOUGH. THE CATLICKS WON'T RECOGNIZE IT AS HARD JOHN APPLE'S OWN PRIVATE STATE."
I'LL CLEAR IT OUT ALL RIGHT!
TATATATATATATAT
INSANE. CRAZY TIME. WHAT MAN WOULD TAKE ON AN ENTIRE STATE OF CATLICKS BY HIMSELF? AND FOR WHAT EARTHLY PURPOSE? FOR KANSAS? THEY AGREED HE WAS MAD, BUT WERE HAPPY TO SEND HIM THERE. NO ONE ELSE WANTED TO GO.
BUT YOU CAN BELIEVE IT. HARD JOHN APPLE KNOWS WHAT HE'S DOING.

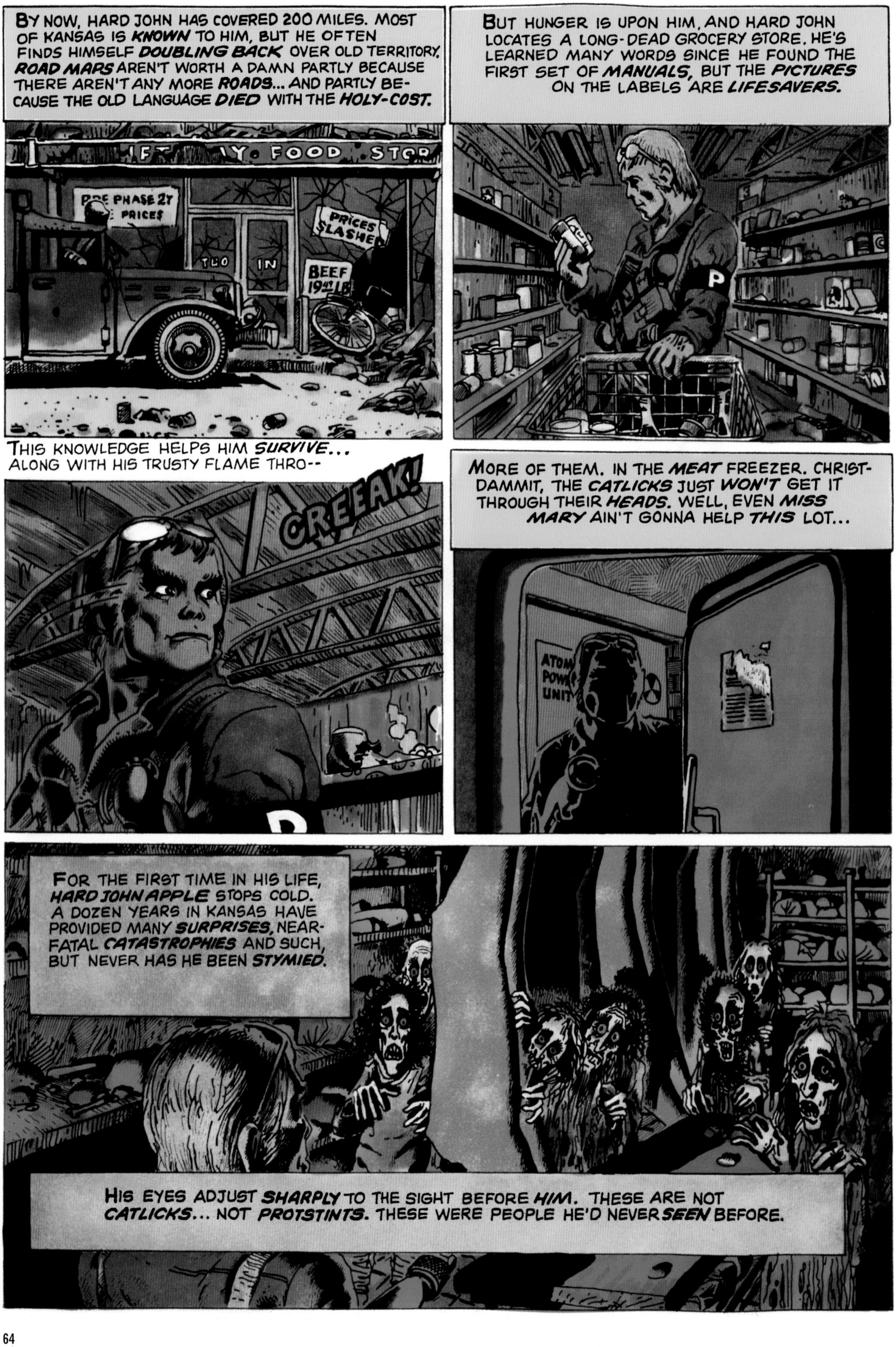
BY NOW, HARD JOHN HAS COVERED 200 MILES. MOST OF KANSAS IS *KNOWN* TO HIM, BUT HE OFTEN FINDS HIMSELF *DOUBLING BACK* OVER OLD TERRITORY. *ROAD MAPS* AREN'T WORTH A DAMN PARTLY BECAUSE THERE AREN'T ANY MORE *ROADS*... AND PARTLY BECAUSE THE OLD LANGUAGE *DIED* WITH THE *HOLY-COST.*
FOOD
PHASE 27
PRICES
PRICES
BEEF
IN
BUT HUNGER IS UPON HIM, AND HARD JOHN LOCATES A LONG-DEAD GROCERY STORE. HE'S LEARNED MANY WORDS SINCE HE FOUND THE FIRST SET OF *MANUALS*, BUT THE *PICTURES* ON THE LABELS ARE *LIFESAVERS.*
P
THIS KNOWLEDGE HELPS HIM *SURVIVE*... ALONG WITH HIS TRUSTY FLAME THRO--
CREEAK!
MORE OF THEM. IN THE *MEAT* FREEZER. CHRIST-DAMMIT, THE *CATLICKS* JUST *WON'T* GET IT THROUGH THEIR *HEADS*. WELL, EVEN *MISS MARY* AIN'T GONNA HELP *THIS* LOT...
FOR THE FIRST TIME IN HIS LIFE, *HARD JOHN APPLE* STOPS COLD. A DOZEN YEARS IN KANSAS HAVE PROVIDED MANY *SURPRISES*, NEAR-FATAL *CATASTROPHIES* AND SUCH, BUT NEVER HAS HE BEEN *STYMIED.*
HIS EYES ADJUST *SHARPLY* TO THE SIGHT BEFORE *HIM*. THESE ARE NOT *CATLICKS*... NOT *PROTSTINTS*. THESE WERE PEOPLE HE'D NEVER *SEEN* BEFORE.

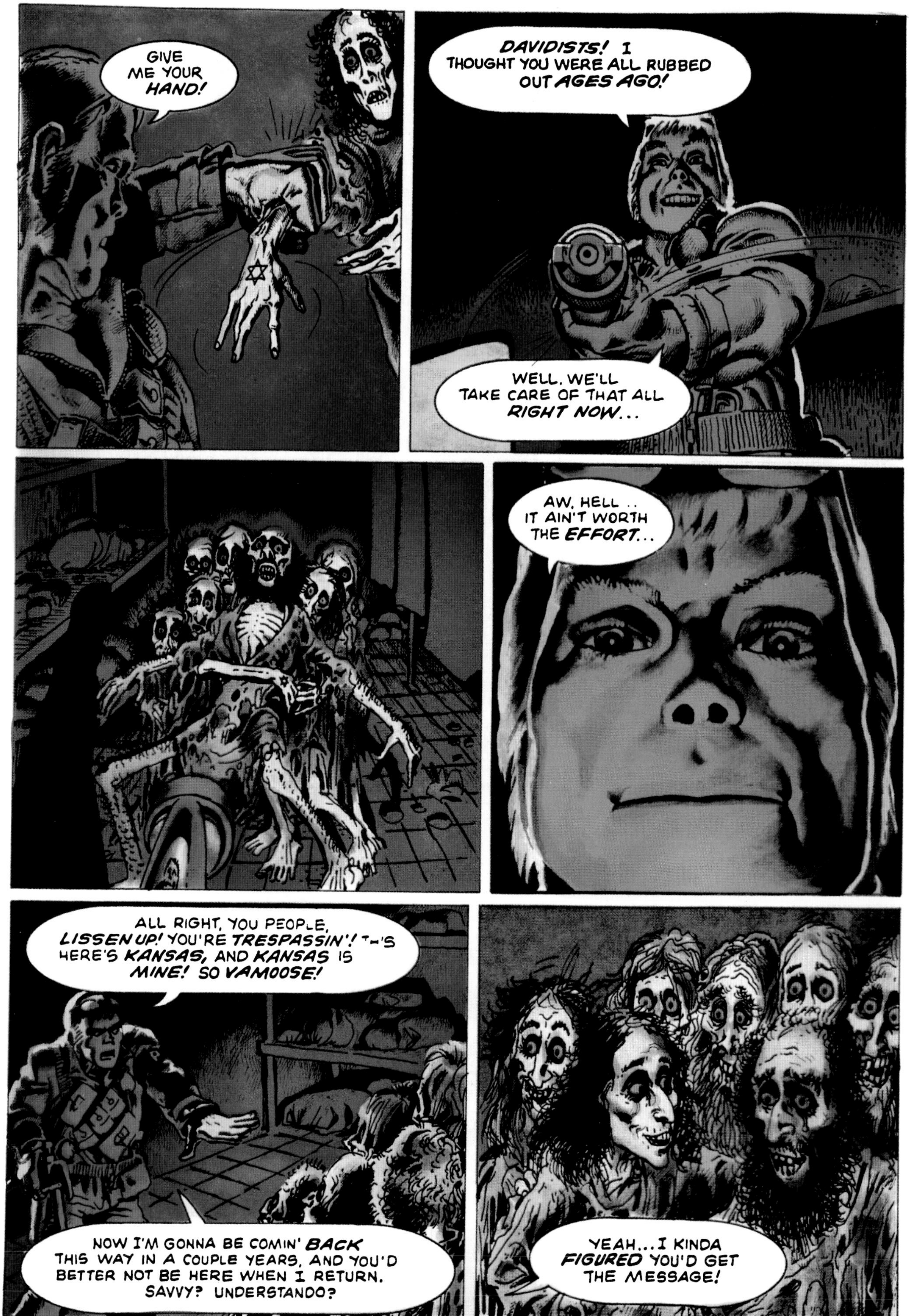

GIVE ME YOUR *HAND!*
DAVIDISTS! I THOUGHT YOU WERE ALL RUBBED OUT *AGES AGO!*
WELL, WE'LL TAKE CARE OF THAT ALL *RIGHT NOW...*
AW, HELL .. IT AIN'T WORTH THE *EFFORT...*
ALL RIGHT, YOU PEOPLE, *LISSEN UP!* YOU'RE *TRESPASSIN'!* TH'S HERE'S *KANSAS,* AND *KANSAS* IS *MINE!* SO *VAMOOSE!*
NOW I'M GONNA BE COMIN' *BACK* THIS WAY IN A COUPLE YEARS, AND YOU'D BETTER NOT BE HERE WHEN I RETURN. SAVVY? UNDERSTANDO?
YEAH... I KINDA *FIGURED* YOU'D GET THE MESSAGE!

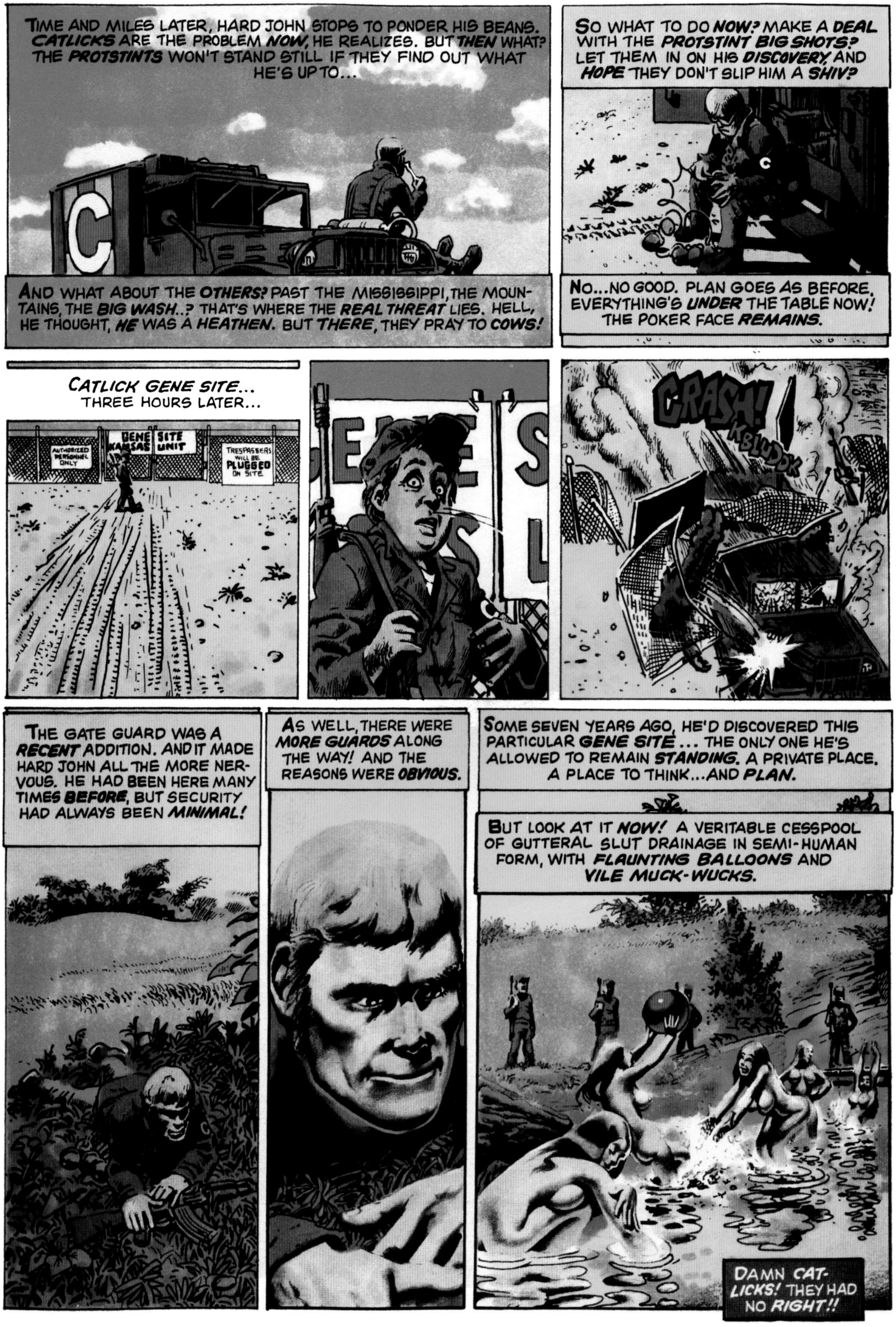
TIME AND MILES LATER, HARD JOHN STOPS TO PONDER HIS BEANS. CATLICKS ARE THE PROBLEM NOW, HE REALIZES. BUT THEN WHAT? THE PROTSTINTS WON'T STAND STILL IF THEY FIND OUT WHAT HE'S UP TO...
AND WHAT ABOUT THE OTHERS? PAST THE MISSISSIPPI, THE MOUNTAINS, THE BIG WASH..? THAT'S WHERE THE REAL THREAT LIES. HELL, HE THOUGHT, HE WAS A HEATHEN. BUT THERE, THEY PRAY TO COWS!
SO WHAT TO DO NOW? MAKE A DEAL WITH THE PROTSTINT BIG SHOTS? LET THEM IN ON HIS DISCOVERY, AND HOPE THEY DON'T SLIP HIM A SHIV?
NO...NO GOOD. PLAN GOES AS BEFORE. EVERYTHING'S UNDER THE TABLE NOW! THE POKER FACE REMAINS.
CATLICK GENE SITE... THREE HOURS LATER...
GENE SITE KANSAS UNIT
AUTHORIZED PERSONNEL ONLY
TRESPASSERS WILL BE PLUGGED ON SITE
CRASH!
KBLUDDK
THE GATE GUARD WAS A RECENT ADDITION. AND IT MADE HARD JOHN ALL THE MORE NERVOUS. HE HAD BEEN HERE MANY TIMES BEFORE, BUT SECURITY HAD ALWAYS BEEN MINIMAL!
AS WELL, THERE WERE MORE GUARDS ALONG THE WAY! AND THE REASONS WERE OBVIOUS.
SOME SEVEN YEARS AGO, HE'D DISCOVERED THIS PARTICULAR GENE SITE... THE ONLY ONE HE'S ALLOWED TO REMAIN STANDING. A PRIVATE PLACE. A PLACE TO THINK...AND PLAN.
BUT LOOK AT IT NOW! A VERITABLE CESSPOOL OF GUTTERAL SLUT DRAINAGE IN SEMI-HUMAN FORM, WITH FLAUNTING BALLOONS AND VILE MUCK-WUCKS.
DAMN CATLICKS! THEY HAD NO RIGHT!!

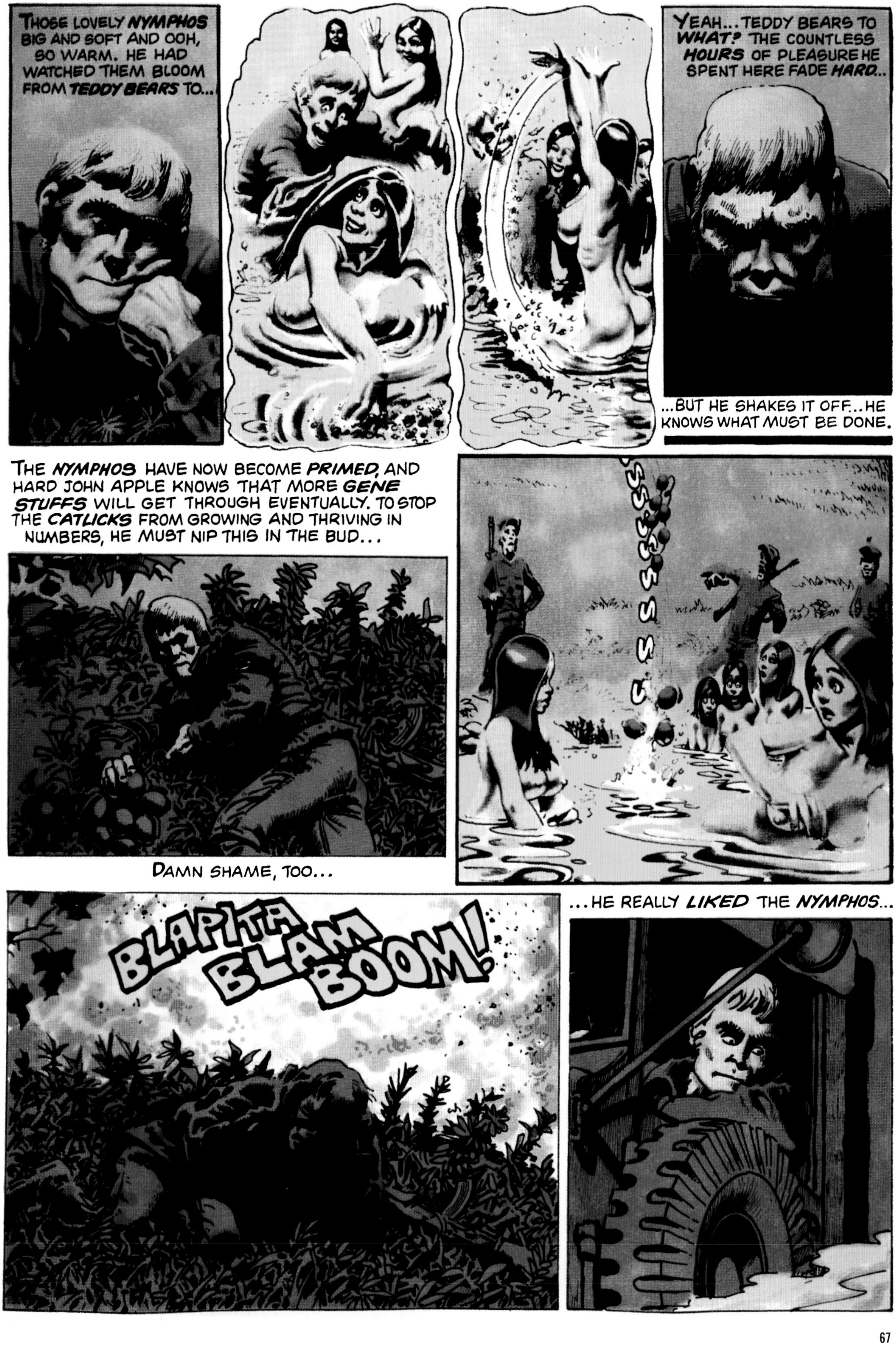
THOSE LOVELY NYMPHOS BIG AND SOFT AND OOH, SO WARM. HE HAD WATCHED THEM BLOOM FROM TEDDY BEARS TO...
YEAH... TEDDY BEARS TO WHAT? THE COUNTLESS HOURS OF PLEASURE HE SPENT HERE FADE HARD...
...BUT HE SHAKES IT OFF... HE KNOWS WHAT MUST BE DONE.
THE NYMPHOS HAVE NOW BECOME PRIMED, AND HARD JOHN APPLE KNOWS THAT MORE GENE STUFFS WILL GET THROUGH EVENTUALLY. TO STOP THE CATLICKS FROM GROWING AND THRIVING IN NUMBERS, HE MUST NIP THIS IN THE BUD...
DAMN SHAME, TOO...
SSSSSS
...HE REALLY LIKED THE NYMPHOS...
BLAPITA BLAM BOOM!

DUSK. SCATTERINGS OF CLOUD DISSIPATE IN A BLOOD RED SKY, AS THE SUN TURNS ITS FACE.
HARD JOHN APPLE IS HOME AFTER A LONG HARD DAY OF KILLING.
MOVING PAST HIS HIDDEN FORTIFICATIONS, HARD JOHN COMES TO A HALT ON CONCRETE SURFACE.
FOR HIM, RELIGIOUS SERVICES ARE ABOUT TO BEGIN. HE PULLS A TOP SECRET OPERATIONS MANUAL FROM THE SEAT.
U.S. AIR FORCE
TOP SECRET OPERATIONS MANUAL
AND, SETTLING HIMSELF ON THE HOOD OF HIS TRUCK, HE MOMENTARILY PAUSES BEFORE BEGINNING THE MANUAL. HE LOOKS OUTWARD, AND ALL HIS DAILY MISGIVINGS, THE THREAT OF THE CATLICKS, THE PROTSTINTS, AND ALL THE OTHERS DISSOLVES FROM HIS MIND. HE FEELS SECURE.
SOON, WHENEVER HE CAN GAIN A STRONG UNDERSTANDING OF THIS STRANGE LANGUAGE ENG-LISH AND THE EVEN STRANGER LINGO OF THE AIR FORCE CODEBOOKS AND MANUALS, THEN HE WOULD KNOW ALL HE WOULD EVER NEED KNOW.
AS HARD JOHN APPLE READS, HE LOOKS OUT OVER HIS MANY HIDDEN ICBM SILOS, ONLY PART OF THE DOZENS KANSAS OFFERS AND STILL MUCH OF A MYSTERY TO HIM, AND GOES BACK TO HIS MANUAL WITH EVEN MORE DETERMINATION...
SOON, HE COULD GET DOWN TO SOME SERIOUS KILLING.

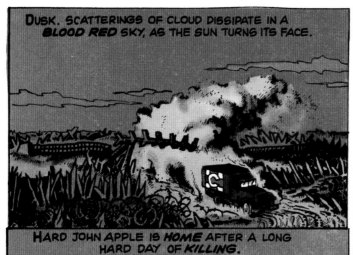

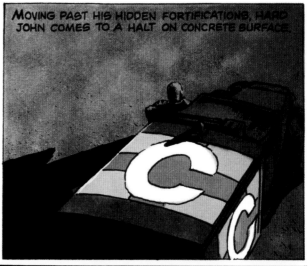

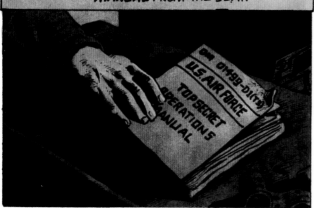

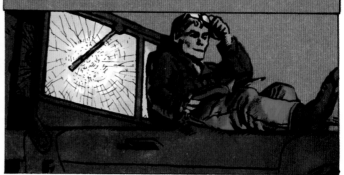

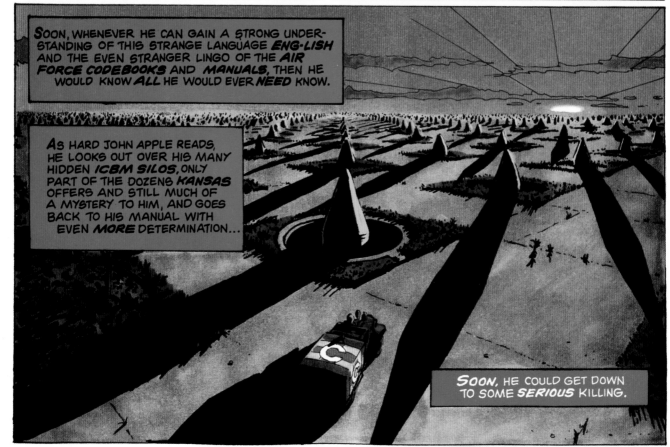

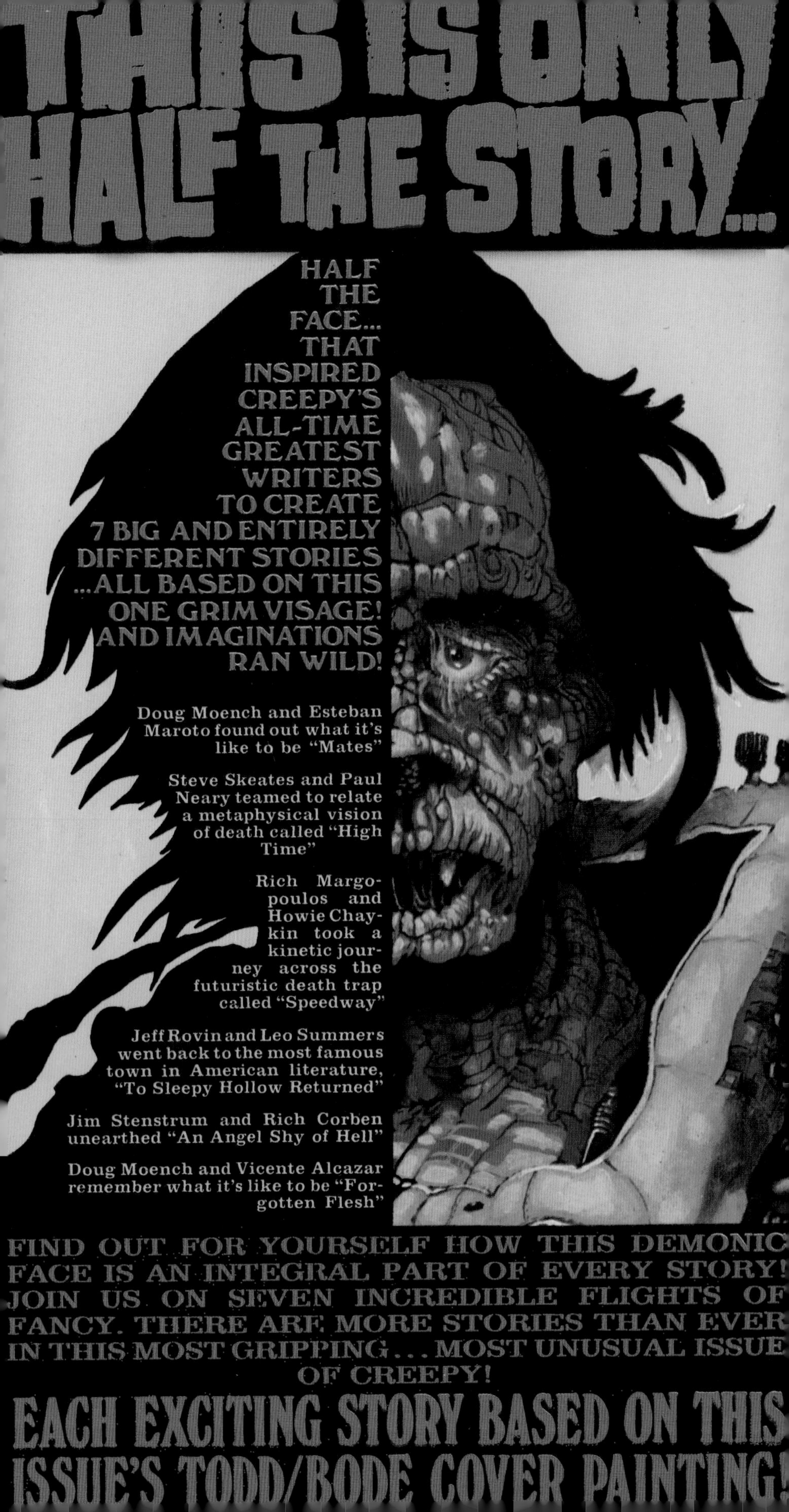
THIS IS ONLY HALF THE STORY...
HALF THE FACE... THAT INSPIRED CREEPY'S ALL-TIME GREATEST WRITERS TO CREATE 7 BIG AND ENTIRELY DIFFERENT STORIES ...ALL BASED ON THIS ONE GRIM VISAGE! AND IMAGINATIONS RAN WILD!
Doug Moench and Esteban Maroto found out what it's like to be "Mates"
Steve Skeates and Paul Neary teamed to relate a metaphysical vision of death called "High Time"
Rich Margopoulos and Howie Chaykin took a kinetic journey across the futuristic death trap called "Speedway"
Jeff Rovin and Leo Summers went back to the most famous town in American literature, "To Sleepy Hollow Returned"
Jim Stenstrum and Rich Corben unearthed "An Angel Shy of Hell"
Doug Moench and Vicente Alcazar remember what it's like to be "Forgotten Flesh"
FIND OUT FOR YOURSELF HOW THIS DEMONIC FACE IS AN INTEGRAL PART OF EVERY STORY! JOIN US ON SEVEN INCREDIBLE FLIGHTS OF FANCY. THERE ARE MORE STORIES THAN EVER IN THIS MOST GRIPPING . . . MOST UNUSUAL ISSUE OF CREEPY!
EACH EXCITING STORY BASED ON THIS ISSUE'S TODD/BODE COVER PAINTING!

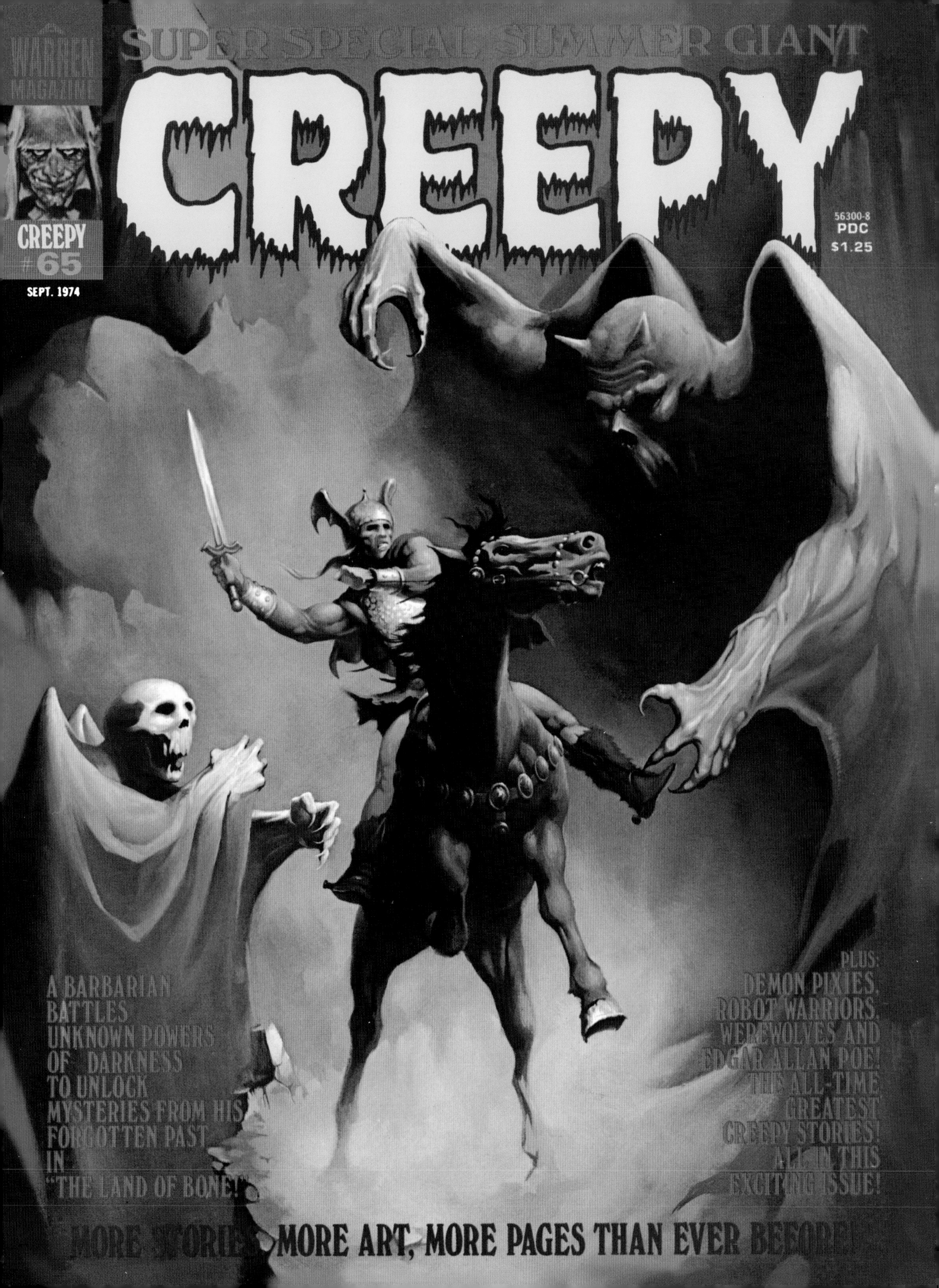
A WARREN MAGAZINE
SUPER SPECIAL SUMMER GIANT
CREEPY
CREEPY #65
SEPT. 1974
56300-8
PDC
$1.25
A BARBARIAN BATTLES UNKNOWN POWERS OF DARKNESS TO UNLOCK MYSTERIES FROM HIS FORGOTTEN PAST IN "THE LAND OF BONE!"
PLUS: DEMON PIXIES, ROBOT WARRIORS, WEREWOLVES AND EDGAR ALLAN POE! THE ALL-TIME GREATEST CREEPY STORIES! ALL IN THIS EXCITING ISSUE!
MORE STORIES, MORE ART, MORE PAGES THAN EVER BEFORE!

DINOSAUR SCENES HOBBY KITS

ALL-PLASTIC MONSTERS TO BUILD AND DISPLAY

DIMETRODON

NEW! 10" long replica of the finned lizard. With the ferocious beast is a prehistoric dragonfly. One of the earliest dinosaurs. It's fin was an incredible weather vane! #24105/$3.20

TYRANNOSAURUS REX

NEW! The King of the Dinosaurs, the most powerful creature ever to roam the earth. This kit, when fully assembled, stands nearly 3 feet tall! An amazing plastic kit. #24106/$12.99

ANKYLOSAURUS

NEW! An indestructible dinosaur, due to his mace-like tail and spiked armor shell. A vegatarian, but an incredibly strong animal. One of the last of the dinosaurs. #24104/$2.79

PLUS THESE 14 EXCITING FAVORITES!

GIANT BIRD: Called Phororhacos, this is a large meat-eating bird. Could not fly, but was an enormous 6' tall. Kit is a large 6", and features all details, such as 4-toes and the devastating jaw. #2434/$2.50

SPIKED DINOSAUR: The Styracosaurus, cousin to the Triceratops. Multi-spiked shield on head and horn on nose kept the meat-eaters at a great distance. Kit is over a foot long; pit him against 'Rex!' #2435/$5.00

SABER-TOOTH TIGER: Kit is over 8" long, and features the most ferocious mammal ever to walk the earth. Our ancestors were this monster's breakfast! Pit him against the Mammoth, his blood-enemy! #2420/$2.00

GIANT WOOLLY MAMMOTH: The best-known of the prehistoric monsters. Kit is over 14" long, and features the long-tusked beast in all of his glory. Mammoth was plant-eater, although strong. #2438/$6.00

TAR PIT SCENE: Here is a perfect setting for your Mammoth, Tiger, and other Mammals. Kit comes complete with setting, tree, sunken Rhino, and prehistoric vulture. Scene of death and devastation. #2417/$3.00

CRO-MAGNON WOMAN: A perfect and necessary companion for the Cro-Magnon man. She, too, is over 4" tall, and is posed so as to be frightened of monsters. Put her in cave, tending home, while hubby hunts. #2422/$2.00

PREHISTORIC CAVE: Built to scale so that prehistoric humans can be placed inside. Hide your people from the dangerous dinosaurs that lurk without! Detailed interior of cave to keep cavemen busy. #2418/$3.00

BUILD AN ENTIRE PREHISTORIC WORLD

Here is an incredible world of monsters against men. Create an entire diorama of prehistoric life with these exciting prehistoric kits. Featured are all of the best-known dinosaurs and early mammals. A challenging set of hobby kits; a must for all fans of early life on our world.

Build 'em & display!

JUNGLE SWAMP: Over 60 parts in this recreation of an ages-old prehistoric marshland. Includes flying reptiles, cave-horse, prehistoric bird, pool, trees, and dinosaurian plants. Over a large 13" long. #2435/$3.00

CRO-MAGNON MAN: Here he is, in all of his spear-throwing glory. Man is 4" tall, and can be put in battle against the Tiger, or any of the other prehistoric dangers. Perfectly proportioned for cave. #2423/$2.00

GIANT ALLOSAURUS: This kit is over 10" high, and stars the deadly cousin of the Tyrannosaur. Creature was 30' tall, and lived in what is now the United States. Have him fight the Triceratops. #2419/$3.00

FLYING REPTILE: The Pteranodon, the first of the winged reptiles. Kit features bird with 18-1/2" wingspan. Creature would pluck fish from the sea to eat; had poor eyesight, but flew by sonar like bat. #2424/$2.00

NEANDERTHAL MAN: This is one of the first cavemen. Lived in what is now Europe, and could live in temperatures of extreme cold. Kit is 4-1/2" high, with detailed human features. Put him in cave! #2421/$2.00

CAVE BEAR: A big 6" tall kit, and a most powerful beast of the Pleistocene period. He was exclusively vegetarian. This animal was an amazing 1/3 taller than any bear of today. Worshipped by cults. #2433/$2.50

THREE-HORNED DINOSAUR: This model kit is over 13" long, and features the Triceratops, a monster that grew to over 20' long. Two deadly horns on head were used to combat predatory dinosaurs. #2436/$5.00

To order any of these items, please see last page of this magazine for convenient RUSH ORDER FORM.

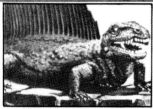

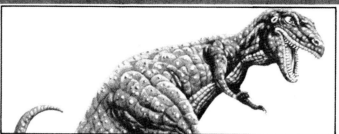

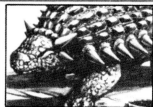

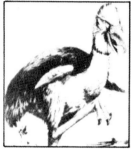

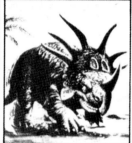

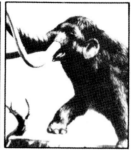

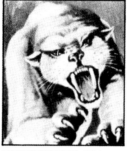

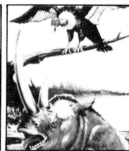

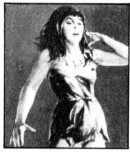

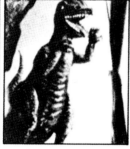

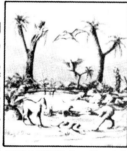

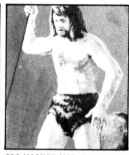

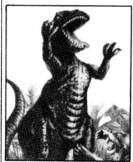

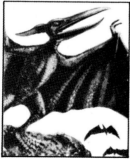

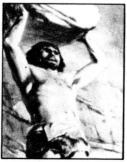

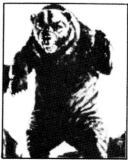

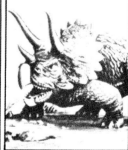

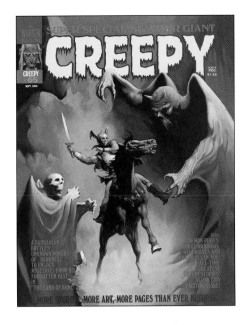

Editor-in-Chief
& Publisher
JAMES WARREN

Senior Editor
W.B. DuBAY

Production Manager
W.R. MOHALLEY

Circulation Director
AB SIDEMAN

Cover
KEN KELLY

Back Cover
ALBERT MICHINI

Artists
This Issue
AURALEON
JOSE BEA
JAIME BROCAL
REED CRANDALL
JORGE B. GALVEZ
LUIS GARCIA
ESTEBAN MAROTO
FELIX MAS
RAMON TORRENTS

Writers
This Issue
JOSE BEA
GARDNER FOX
ARCHIE GOODWIN
RICH MARGOPOULOS
DONALD F. McGREGOR
DOUG MOENCH
BUDDY SAUNDERS
STEVE SKEATES
JAMES STENSTRUM

CREEPY

CONTENTS ISSUE NO. 65 SEPTEMBER 1974

These stories are reprinted in previous volumes of *Creepy Archives*.

FILM BOOKS

FRANKENSTEIN AND MALTESE FALCON

Here are two exciting high-quality paperback books featuring photographs from every scene in the classic films FRANKENSTEIN and THE MALTESE FALCON. And, beneath every photograph, is the dialogue from that particular scene. Next best thing to owning the films.

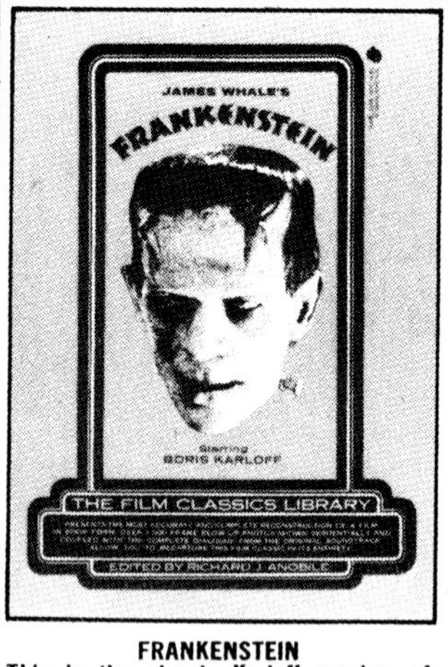
JAMES WHALE'S
FRANKENSTEIN
Starring BORIS KARLOFF
THE FILM CLASSICS LIBRARY
EDITED BY RICHARD J. ANOBILE

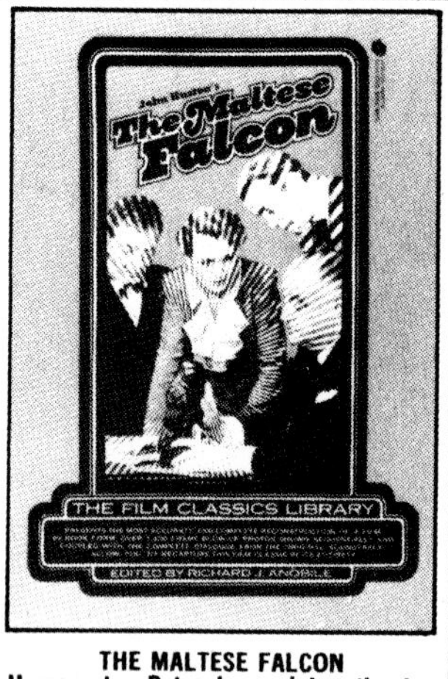
The Maltese Falcon
THE FILM CLASSICS LIBRARY
EDITED BY RICHARD J. ANOBILE

FRANKENSTEIN
This is the classic Karloff version of Frankenstein. Starring Colin Clive, Dwight Frye, and Karloff, this remains one of the great horror films. And here are all the scenes from that film, including the birth of the monster, his oft-censored killing of a girl, and his death in a burning windmill. Over 1,000 photographs, along with every word of dialogue from the film. And, there is a surprise introduction to the film; rare and seldom seen. Size 9" x 12". #21124 . . . $4.95.

THE MALTESE FALCON
Horror star Peter Lorre joins the immortal Humphrey Bogart and Sydney Greenstreet in this scene-by-scene photo journal of the greatest mystery movie of all-time. The film tells of Detective Sam Spade's search for a stolen art object. His search is dangerous, and holds as many surprises for the agent as for the reader. The book is in the form of 1,400 photographs from the film, and contains all of the film's dialogue. Size 9"x12". #21125/$4.95

WEREWOLF NOSE!

TURN YOURSELF INTO A WOLFMAN!

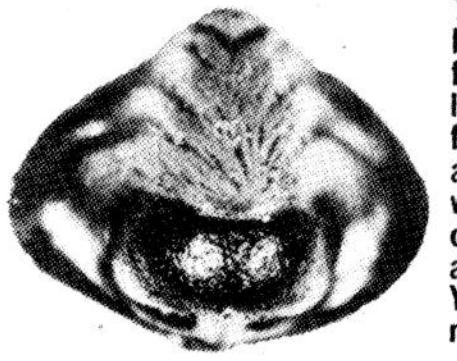

Now you can own the same unique, high quality latex appliance that was used to turn Lon Chaney Jr. into his monstrous characterization, The Wolfman. Apply to your face with spirit gum (available at most drug stores) or with Creepy Skin paste, advertised below. And, when the hand-painted nose is fixed on your face, apply the gruesome Face Fur, available below. You will be a complete werewolf. There are two large air-holes in the appliance, for easy breathing. So life-like, you'll scare your friends to death! Become a make-up artist. And, while you're at it, order our fangs, glowing eyes, and other make-up items. You may be the next Westmore. #2666/$1.39

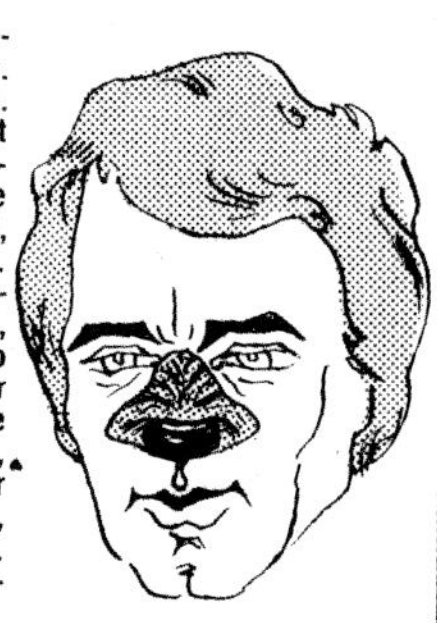

CREEPY SKIN

STICKS ON THE SKIN TO MAKE LUMPS 'N BUMPS

Here's a horrid looking gook to give your skin a new dimension. Sticks by itself without glue; completely realistic. Or, use it to attach other appliances to your face . . . such as the Werewolf nose. A positively grotesque substance, to scare your family #2668/ 49¢

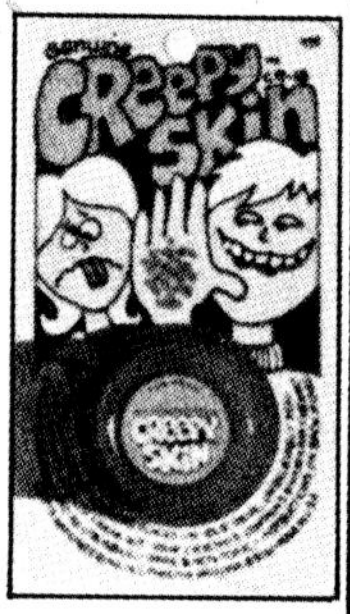
Creepy Skin

FACE FUR

SELF-ADHESIVE WOLFMAN WOOL FOR HANDS OR FACE

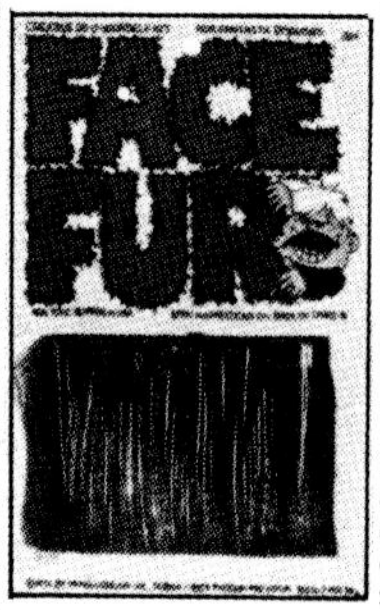
FACE FUR

Transform yourself from man to wolfman with this fuzzy flock of face fur, direct from the werewolf's lair. With Creepy Skin and Werewolf nose, the horrid hair will make you the complete lycanthrope. Frighten the daylights out of your friends or people in the street. #2667/ 59¢

ASTONISHING! BRAND-NEW VINYL WHOLE-HEAD HORROR MASKS!

NEW! FROM HOLLYWOOD! VINYL MOVIE MONSTER MASKS!

They fit the whole head. Sturdy flexible but unbreakable all-weather vinyl masks. Reasonably priced so you can buy 'em ALL! All great!

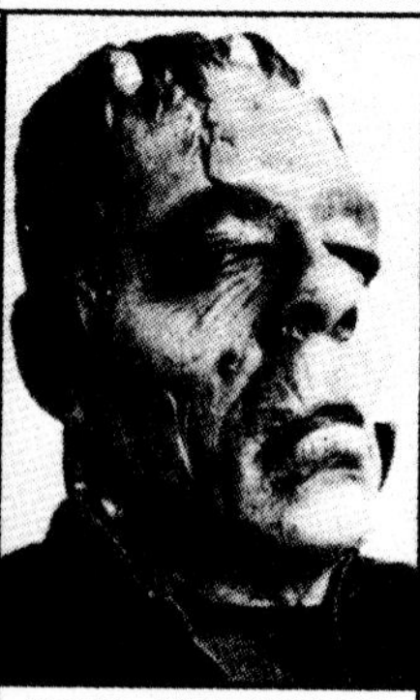

"THIN" FRANKENSTEIN! For the narrow-minded, this long-face Frank's a must! "THIN" FRANKENSTEIN $8.95 #2555

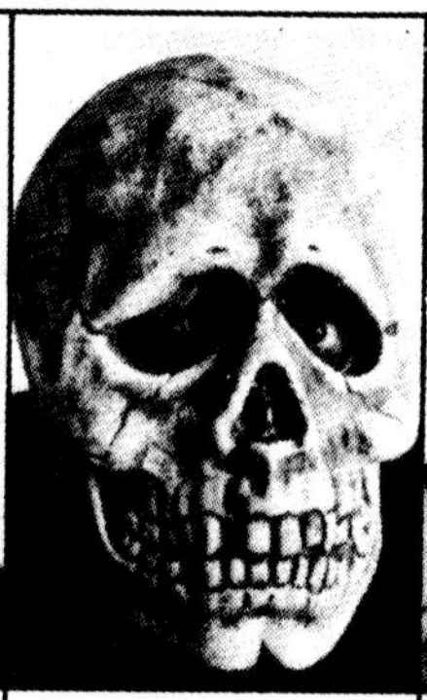

THE SKULL! Immense, oversized skull! Classic for the Calcium Clique! And quite cracked! #2556 THE SKULL $8.95

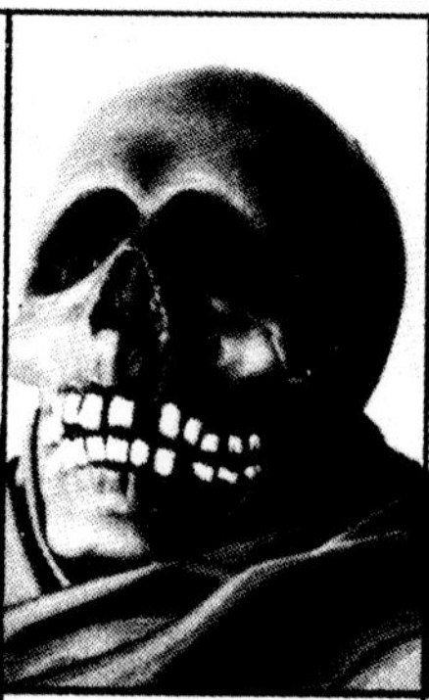

VERMILLION SKULL! A fearful fiery Roasting Red! The hard-headed hit of Hades! #2557 VERMILLION SKULL $8.95

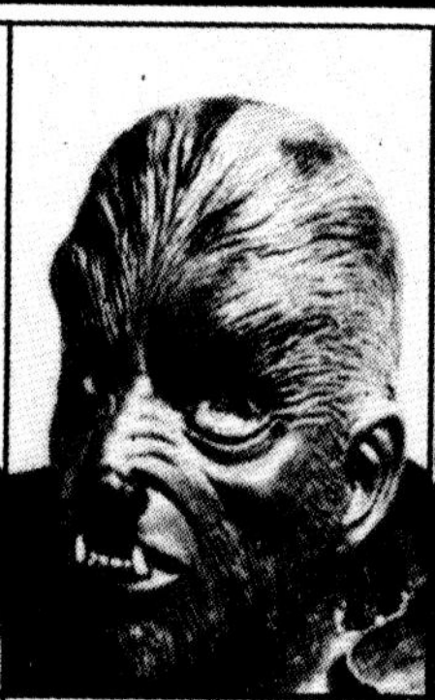

WOLFMAN! Really new-FANGled way to break friends & influential people! #2558 WOLFMAN $8.95

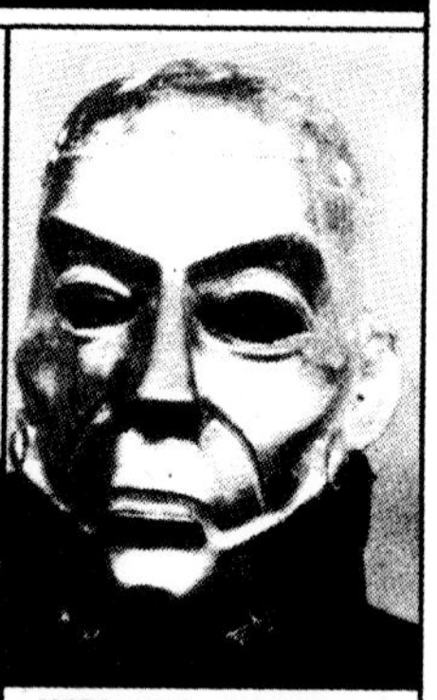

METALUNA ROBOT! A metal man, shining silvery. It could be YOU! #2559 METALUNA ROBOT $8.95

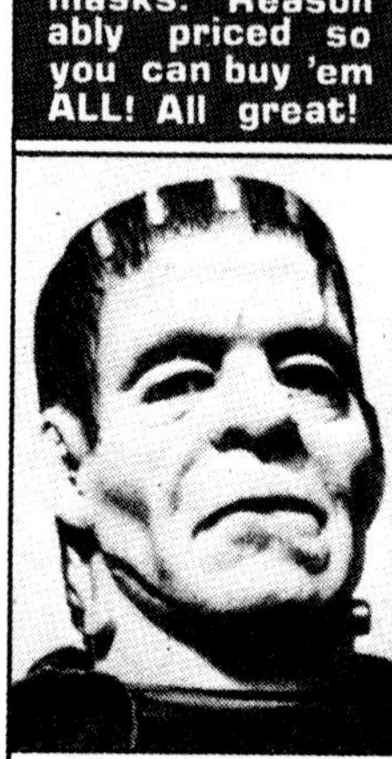

"WIDE" FRANKENSTEIN! The square-headed monster buff will DEMAND this #2560 "WIDE" FRANKENSTEIN $8.95

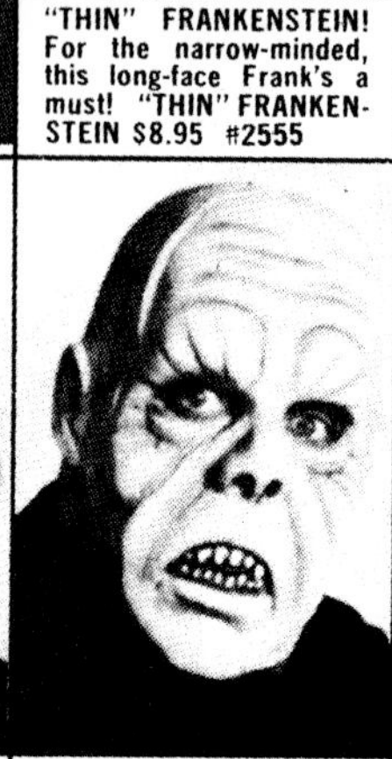

THE PHANTOM! His skull-like face and flaring nostrils could make a statue sweat blood! #2561 THE PHANTOM $8.95

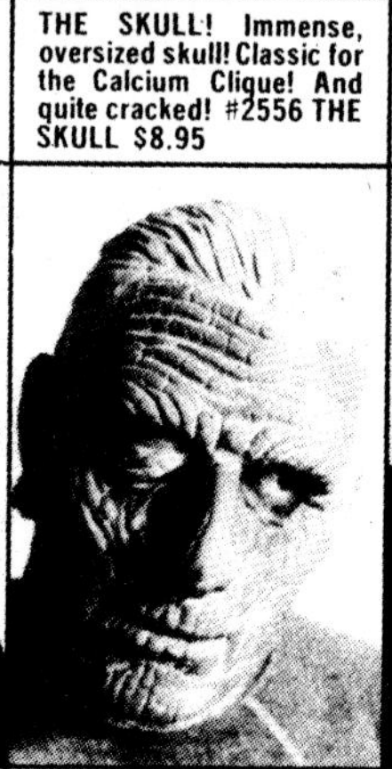

THE MUMMY! He leers at you from the AGES, this ghost-propelled corpse of Tainted Tannis! #2562 THE MUMMY $8.95

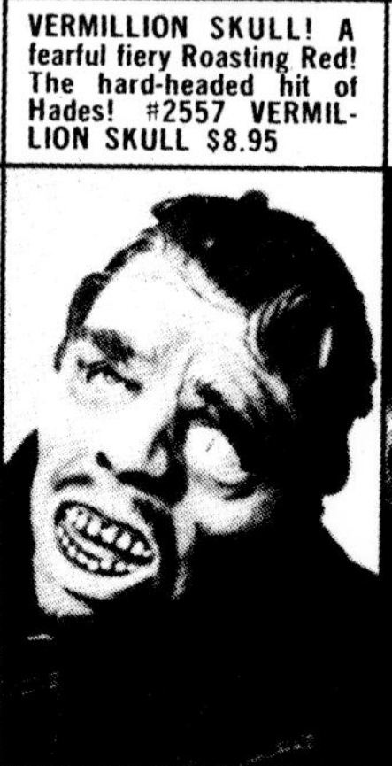

THE HUNCHBACK! Deformed creature cursed to slink through countless catacombs! #2563 THE HUNCHBACK $8.95

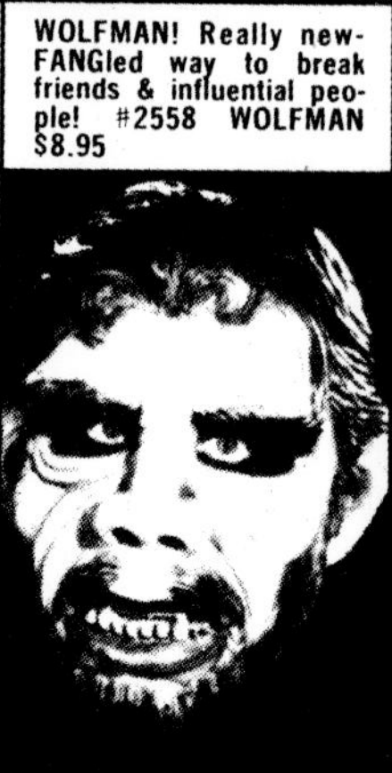

MR. HYDE! The first and last (choking) word in beast-men! The sallow-eyed Fiend of Fiends! #2564 MR. HYDE $8.95

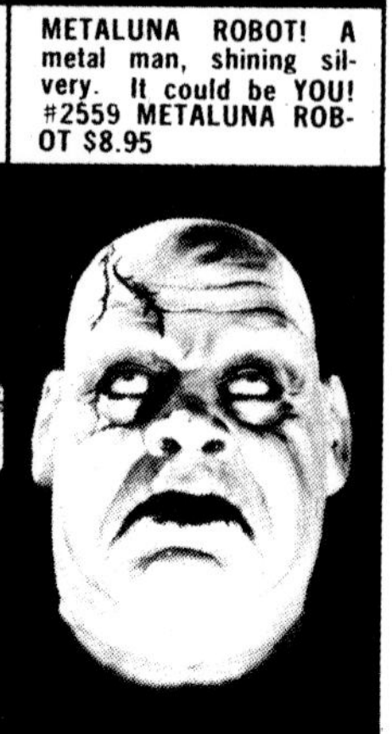

TOR JOHNSON! One of the greatest character actors of all time! Now YOU can be him! Perfect! #2565 TOR JOHNSON $8.95

To order any of these items, please see last page of this magazine for convenient RUSH ORDER FORM.

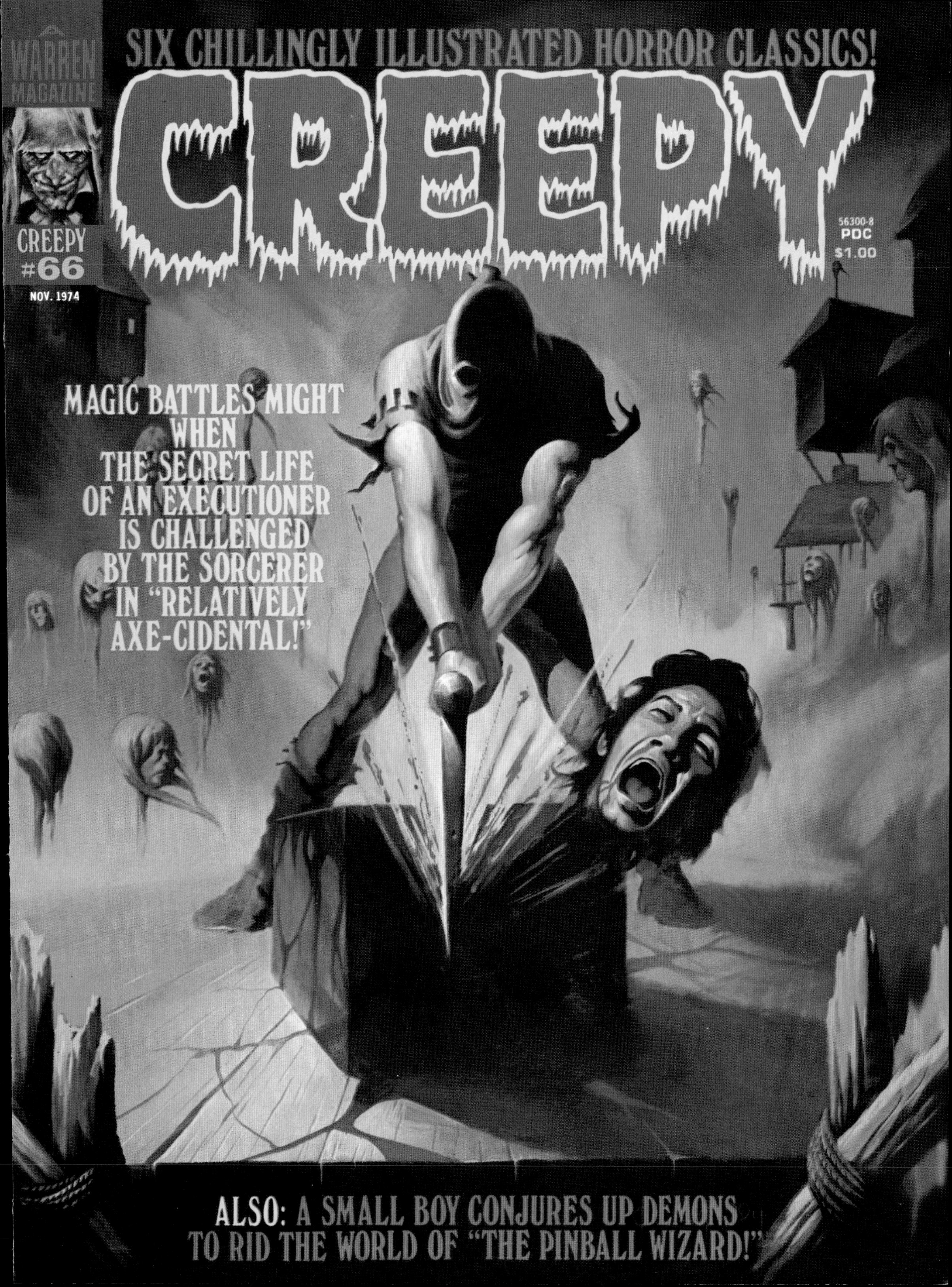
WARREN MAGAZINE
SIX CHILLINGLY ILLUSTRATED HORROR CLASSICS!
CREEPY
CREEPY #66
NOV. 1974
56300-8
PDC
$1.00
MAGIC BATTLES MIGHT WHEN THE SECRET LIFE OF AN EXECUTIONER IS CHALLENGED BY THE SORCERER IN "RELATIVELY AXE-CIDENTAL!"
ALSO: A SMALL BOY CONJURES UP DEMONS TO RID THE WORLD OF "THE PINBALL WIZARD!"

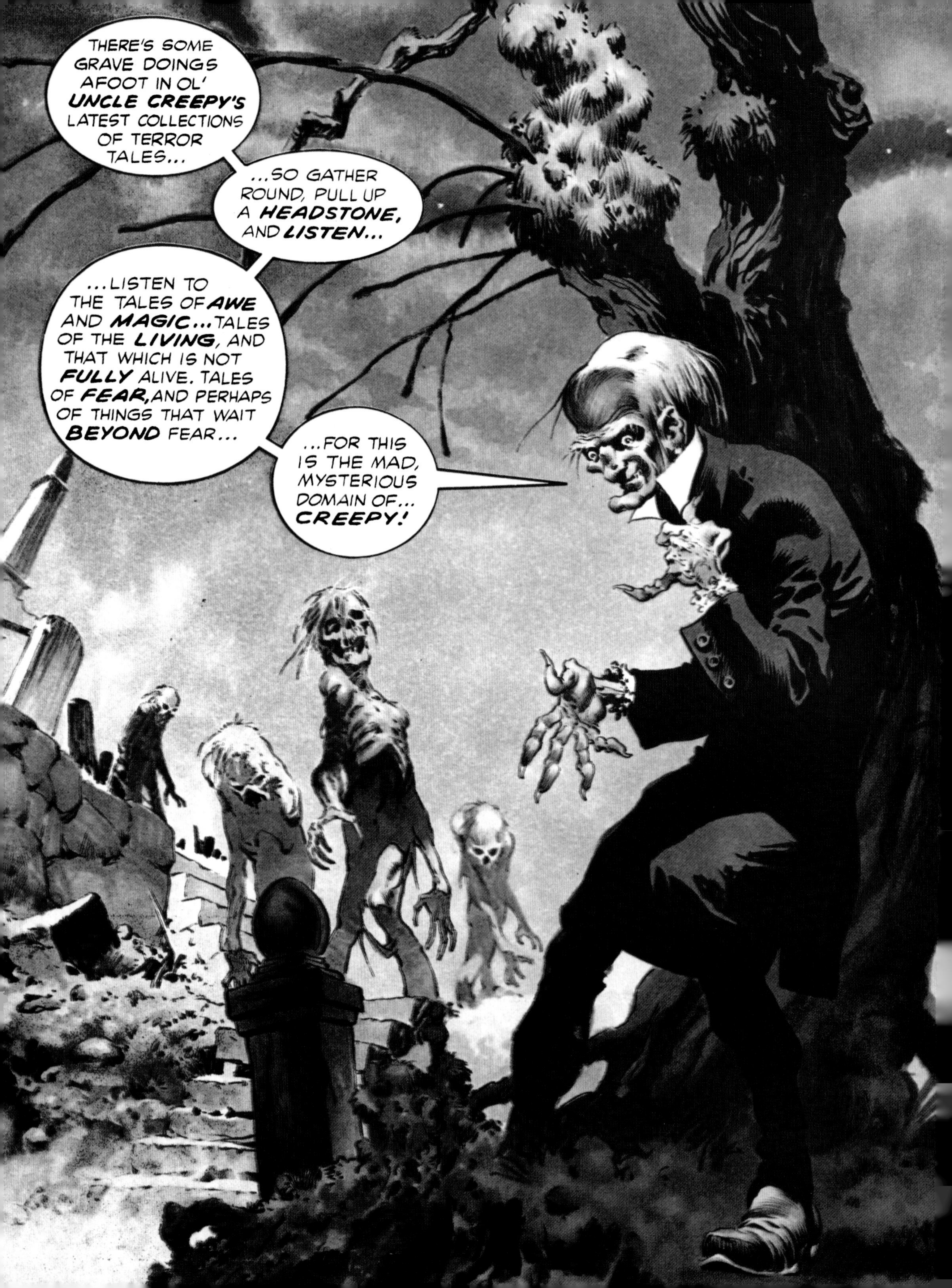
THERE'S SOME GRAVE DOINGS AFOOT IN OL' UNCLE CREEPY'S LATEST COLLECTIONS OF TERROR TALES...
...SO GATHER ROUND, PULL UP A HEADSTONE, AND LISTEN...
...LISTEN TO THE TALES OF AWE AND MAGIC...TALES OF THE LIVING, AND THAT WHICH IS NOT FULLY ALIVE. TALES OF FEAR, AND PERHAPS OF THINGS THAT WAIT BEYOND FEAR...
...FOR THIS IS THE MAD, MYSTERIOUS DOMAIN OF... CREEPY!

SIX CHILLINGLY ILLUSTRATED HORROR CLASSICS!
CREEPY
CREEPY #66
MAGIC BATTLES MIGHT WHEN THE SECRET LIFE OF AN EXECUTIONER IS CHALLENGED BY THE SORCERER IN "RELATIVELY AXE-CIDENTAL!"
ALSO: A SMALL BOY CONJURES UP DEMONS TO RID THE WORLD OF "THE PINBALL WIZARD!"

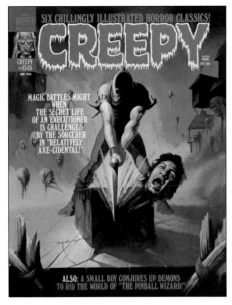

OUR COVER:
Hated and mistrusted by his own family and neighbors, the Executioner worked in the loneliest profession of all. This awe-inspiring figure is captured here by artist Ken Kelly.

Editor-In-Chief
& Publisher
JAMES WARREN

Editor
W.B. DuBAY

Production Manager
W.R. MOHALLEY

Circulation Director
AB SIDEMAN

Artists This Issue
ADOLPHO ABELLAN
VINCENTE ALCAZAR
RICHARD CORBEN
ISIDRO MONES
JOSE ORTIZ
MARTIN SALVADOR
BERNI WRIGHTSON

Writers This Issue
GERRY BOUDREAU
ARCHIE GOODWIN
BUDD LEWIS
DOUG MOENCH
GREG POTTER

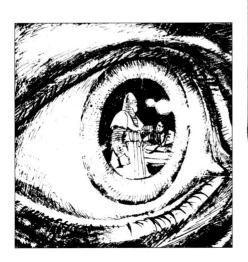

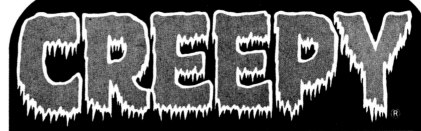

CREEPY®

CONTENTS

ISSUE NO. 66
NOVEMBER 1974

DEAR UNCLE CREEPY

"Each and every panel is fit to be framed!"

Even a casual browser couldn't help but notice the cover of CREEPY #64. The highly imaginative and macabre painting by **Larry Todd** and **Vaughn Bode** was one of your best!

Warren magazines always have small, subtle things which make their product just a little bit better. Coloring the letter pages yellow is one of them. It is so much more interesting to look at than drab white pages.

My favorite story in the issue was "Mates." **Doug Moench**'s highly original plot, combined with his realistic dialogue, seems the perfect counterpart for **Estaban Maroto**'s graceful art. **Maroto**'s figures seem to pulsate with life and beauty.

The two color sections were also a welcome treat!

REX MUNSEE
Wattsburg, Penn.

First "The Black Cat" in #62. Then "Jenifer" in #63. Now **Tom Sutton**'s "One Autumn in Arkham" in #64! Who can deny that **Warren** is still the best in the black-and-white field?

KEN PETERS
Manhasset, N.Y.

"An Angel Shy of Hell" was one of the favorites of the seven tales written around our special cover by Larry Todd and Vaughn Bode. Corben did it again!

After reading **Michael Oliveri**'s letter to you in CREEPY #64, I'd have to say that I agree with him somewhat. I've been reading CREEPY since issue #5 and I like good horror stories. But your recent trend seems to be leaning toward **shock** stories, rather than horror.

Horror stories can be an art form. Good craftsmanship beats sensationalism any day. Good writers do not need the sex-and-violence syndrome to appeal to their readers. It seems that many of your writers are trying to see just how close to the boundaries of bad taste they can come, in their desire to produce some new atrocity that hasn't been seen before.

The world doesn't need any more insanity than it already has. You would do better to try to bring it a little **class**!

LARRY GUERNSEZ
Phoenix, Ariz.

CREEPY #64 certainly was impressive. "Mates" was truly exceptional, largely due to **Esteban Maroto**'s exceptional art! **Rich Corben**'s story, as always, was excellent. I'd like to see more of Hard John Apple.

Let's also see more of **Paul Neary**. His work is deft and masterful, and he has quite a feel for the fantastic!

ED O'REILLEY
Oxford, Ohio

I have just read the latest CREEPY and I feel that it is unfair what people say about the quality of your stories. I have been reading your magazine for about two years, and feel that each individual story has its own way of entertaining the reader. You deserve a great deal of credit for your prolific and diversified work.

I hope you will go on as you have been. I thank you for letting me express my feelings.

GARY ROBUDIE
Melrose, Ala.

I am writing in regard to the page-long letter and response which appeared in CREEPY #64. I'm sure you've had an ample share of similar responses from other readers, screaming over their moral and aesthetic wounds, and of course, always threatening the loss of their patronage.

I have only one reaction to this social bellowing. And that is to say . . . you're a **success**!

To be more specific, you have successfully managed to shatter the level of aesthetic entropy which, in any field of art or literature, is a difficult but necessary accomplishment. Progress is only made when individuals push the already established limits, and open the doors to new and unexplored regions.

The concept of artistic anarchy is perhaps too much for the general public to accept. But please continue your efforts to bring a more mature type of comic entertainment to the masses.

THOMAS HUMPHERIES
Minneapolis, Minn.

You bring up an interesting point, Thomas. The question of artistic anarchy has two sides to it. Should society impose restrictions and censures on the boundaries of an artist's imagination? We think not. But on the other hand, should the artist use this license to impose tasteless personal fantasies upon the community? More often, that is an abuse of license rather than use of it.

We at Warren have stressed often that we are an entertainment magazine. As such, we must appeal to our readers sensibilities through strong storytelling and equally strong art. We do indeed wish to shatter the level of aesthetic entropy, but we don't feel that this is a justification for abandoning good taste. We strive to remain within its realm at all times. This is an equally important factor in determining our success or failure and it is the reason we took Michael Oliveri's letter so seriously.

I have just finished reading CREEPY #63 and it chilled me to the bone. My wife thinks I am crazy to read your magazines because I can't get to sleep for hours afterwards. The story "Demon in the Cockpit" was a real frenzy, but then, the color sections are usually my favorite part of the magazine.

BRUCE GOLDRING
Sasketchawan, Canada

I like the idea of your color center sections. But you should try to improve the quality. Most of them look like black and white strips with color added as an afterthought.

Rich Corben's color work is great. But often they are printed so dark, the colors become muddy.

Why don't you do your color sections like you do your covers . . . with painted figures!

If **Penthouse** and **Playboy** can do it, why can't you?

DON KEIFER
Maywood, N.J.

Keep **Ken Kelly** on your covers! He is magnificent! His paintings on issues #62 and #63 were the best you have had in a long time.

When is **Archie Goodwin** going to write some new stories for your pages? He's always been a tremendous talent. I look **forward** to his work.

BILL MARKS
St. Marys, Penn.

Archie's in this very issue, Bill. Look for "Solitude" on page 25.

As I sit here reading CREEPY #63, my mind blows with the flip of every page! This issue was truly an artistic masterpiece!

Berni Wrightson! Those two words make any comic reader run circles in ecstacy. The inside cover was an apt example of his beautiful work. But the high point of the issue was "Jenifer." Each and every panel was fit to be framed! I've seldom seen **Wrightson** work in tone, and this story shows him in his artistic prime.

Now for the **Rich Corben** color feature! It is an artistic phantasmagoria! This man is changing the drab color impression of comics into a rainbow of colors. The story was good too, but the ending was a bit predictable.

I almost forgot to praise **Ken Kelly**'s finest cover to date. I'm glad he's returned to **Warren**. Let him do big things for you.

KEN MEYER
Hill AFB, Utah

"Jenifer stole the issue!"

I think I can justifiably be called one of your oldest fans, having picked up issue number one of CREEPY a long, long time ago. It gives me great pleasure to see your magazine beginning to attain once again the heights of great art that made you one of the finest magazines in the world.

Thank you for many hours of reading pleasure.

LAURENT GUREWITCH
Geneva, N.Y.

In the letter column of CREEPY #64, **Michael Oliveri** raises an issue broader than that of mere good taste. He raises questions of what is or is not acceptable in the graphic-story medium. But there can never **be** any generalized guidelines, because the medium itself cannot be generalized.

Different comics are aimed at different audiences and what is acceptable in one may not be acceptable in another. To cite an obvious example: VAMPIRELLA's costume is more revealing than that of **Bat Girl**, while **Little Annie Fanny** usually ends each adventure in the nude. Yet each one is considered acceptable in the media in which it appears.

It has been my understanding that **Warren** magazines were aimed at a more mature audience. Possibly because the higher price tends to keep them out of the hands of the very young. It is only fair then that those who pay the price should expect more for their money. Indeed, **Warren** magazines should be more adventuresome than they already are! When they err, it is more often on the side of conservatism.

As long as publishers adopt the thesis that comics are produced for children who need to be protected from the real world, you may as well forget about turning out an art form and be content with publishing trash.

That will be the day I stop reading CREEPY.

BRIAN CADEN
Cincinnati, Ohio

Our sentiments exactly, Brian. Our primary goal is to ENTERTAIN. But to do that, we must give the reader something that is both substantial and stimulating. Readers will not be entertained by something that insults their intelligence. Even Mr. Oliveri will have to admit that while he may not LIKE everything we do, our stories make him stop and THINK ... enough to write his letter.

CREEPY #63 featured the best cover **Ken Kelly** has done in a long time. The nymatoid in the doctor's uniform reminded me of the "Mannikins of Horror" segment of the movie, **Asylum**. But that did not take away from the story's fine plot and setting.

It was "Jenifer" by **Bruce Jones** and **Berni Wrightson** that stole the issue, however!

MIKE KAROL
Taunton, Mass.

Words alone couldn't describe the demonic gleam that set in my eyes after reading CREEPY #63.

"Jenifer" was perhaps the most disturbing pathos-horror story that **Warren** has ever presented. It is a masterpiece, in the true sense of the word.

Berni Wrightson's illustrative genius brought it to the pinnacle of graphic terror. He is a truly gifted artist (and writer, as we have seen from his other tales).

JIM GALLAGHER
Cherry Hill, N.J.

Here are a few comments on CREEPY #63:

"Jenifer." Haunting and exceptional. **Berni Wrightson's** art is a cross between **Graham Ingles** and **Wally Wood**.

"Ghost of A Chance" was a pure formula story. Vampires should be avoided for the remainder of the century.

My feelings toward "Fishbait" were ambivalent. It had a good ending, but **Leo Summers'** art lacked the visual impact needed to make it work.

"The Clone" can only be described as a total failure.

GARY DAVIS
Portland, Ore.

I was very disappointed by **Michael Oliveri's** letter in CREEPY #64. He cut down your magazines so badly, you probably could have walked under a snake. But I take exception with much of what he says.

Why is it so terrible to feature a story about the handicapped? The movie **Frankenstein** had the hunchbacked character Igor. No one got upset about **him**.

If you were attempting to portray a handicapped person in a derogatory light, you could have done it easily. Instead, the story in question portrayed a sympathetic and human individual.

Mr. Oliveri is forgetting one important thing ... the handicapped are **people**, too!

ALAN BORDEN
Virginia Beach, Va.

The controversial theme behind Doug Moench and Esteban Maroto's "Mates" caused a stir among CREEPY readers.

I glanced at the cover of CREEPY #63 and knew it was going to be a great issue. I was right. My favorite story was "A Touch of Terror."

MARC PECORELLA
Brooklyn, N.Y.

CREEPY #63 was a pretty good issue! The inside cover was great and "Jenifer" was an excellent story, if not a classic! **Berni Wrightson** put mood and feeling into his art, which very few of your artists can do. I hope you will let him do a color story soon.

GREG AUGUSTINE
No. Highlands, Cal.

I am writing to congratulate you on the addition of **Berni Wrightson** to your ranks. His work in your recent issues shows that he is second only to **Frank Frazetta**. What took you so long to catch him?

A quick closing question: Are you ever going to bring back your yearbooks?

TIM MORRELL
Brookfield, Wi.

The yearbooks are still with us in the form of our Super Special Issues, such as you saw last month.

I applaud the return of **Jim Stenstrum** to your ranks after too long an absence from the written word. His past efforts had already proved him to be one of your most innovative writers. But "An Angel Shy of Hell" in CREEPY #64 is worthy of special comment.

The concept of Hard John Apple represented a none too subtle attack on religion, something that has been brewing in the **Warren** wings for many a year. In a way, the story seemed not to want to drift that way, and it could have been a bit less harsh had some of the pretentious narration been rewritten.

Visually it is an impressive story, although a bit crowded. And it had an ending that **Warren Publishing** can be proud of.

SERGIUS KOBISH
Minneapolis, Minn.

Ken Kelly's cover for CREEPY #63 was not up to par, nor was the color section by **Rich Corben**. It looked rushed. Perhaps **Corben** needs a rest!

But I still look forward to #64!

MICHAEL POCHMARA
Allen Park, Mich.

Let me make this perfectly clear!

Why not take a chance on a 300 year-old creep? Write! Send letters to:

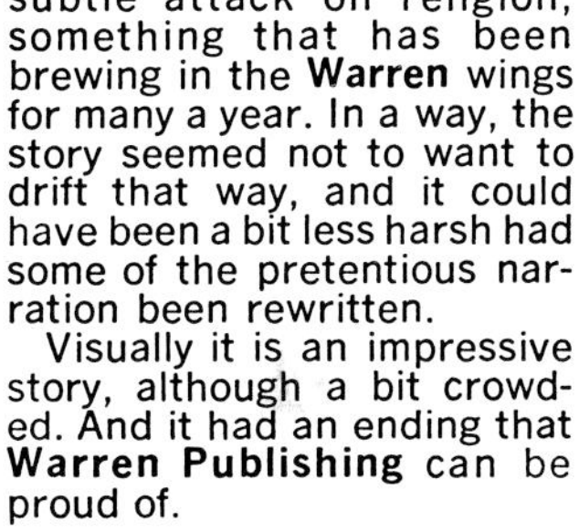

CREEPY'S CATACOMBS

WARREN'S NEWEST ARTIST
GONZALO MAYO
THE MAN BEHIND A SERIES!

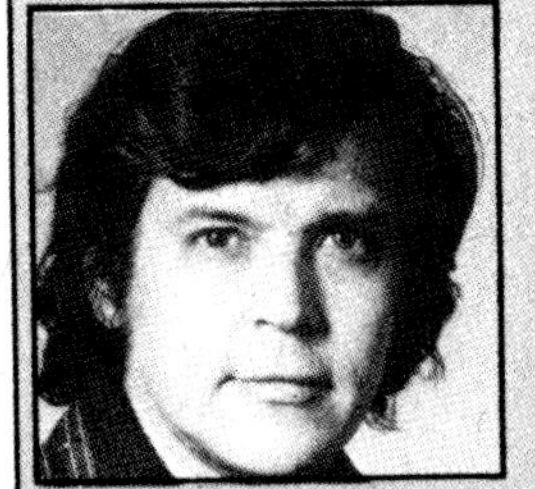

When **Gonzalo Mayo** made his debut in the **Warren** magazines, in CREEPY #60, readers hailed him as the artistic find of the century. Since that time, however, **Gonzalo** seemed to have disappeared from comics completely. Not so. For the past several months, the versatile illustrator has been working on a special book-length project, soon to appear in the pages of EERIE magazine. Like our **Dax The Warrior** annual, in EERIE #59, **Gonzalo's** feature will focus on the exploits of a legendary hero . . . The Spanish Lord, **El Cid.**

Gonzalo, who was born thirty-two years ago in Peru, only recently moved to New York City to begin work as a **Warren** staff artist. "I've been illustrating comics for ten years," **Gonzalo** cites. "I've done every type of story, every type of comic imaginable, including the European publications of **Tarzan.** But I've achieved one of my major ambitions by becoming part of the **Warren** family of artists."

However, comics are not the only thing **Gonzalo** has illustrated. "At sixteen, I began to work professionally," he claims. "I worked as a staff artist for Panamerican Television. I've done both serious illustrations and simple cartoons for book, magazine and newspaper publishers, both in the Americas and overseas."

Gonzalo cites two reasons for selecting comics as his artistic homeground. "I like to tell stories," he boasts. "That, coupled with fond memories of reading **Batman, Captain Marvel** and **Flash Gordon** when I was a child, seemed to point me in only one direction . . . straight at the comics!"

Besides being an artist whose work is suddenly in great demand, **Gonzalo** is also a family man. His wife, Jessica, is one of those rare women of delicate beauty. She is even more radiant now that she is expecting her third baby. **Gonzalo** and his wife have two other children, Edgar and Sandra.

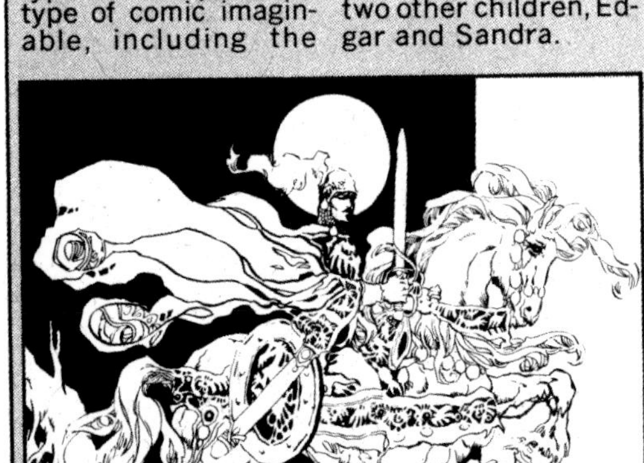

El Cid is coming! In legendary exploits against long-forgotten horrors of the past, the great Spanish hero will make his forthcoming debut in a special issue of EERIE, by Gonzalo Mayo.

IN DEFENSE OF A NAME!

Recently we received a letter from **James Lind** of Cleveland, Ohio:

"I don't understand it. **Rich Corben** doesn't have a **Spanish** surname. Why do you use him in your magazines?"

In the same week, we heard from **Sam Martinelli** of Dallas, Texas:

"Some time ago, I sent you a complete comic story that I had both written and drawn. While I have never had anything published professionally, I feel my artwork is even better than **Frank Frazetta's.** Yet, you've returned it with a rejection slip. **Why?** Because I'm not **Mexican?**"

A third letter was sent from **Gordon Whitman** of Pittsburgh, California.

"Gonzalez, Maroto, Sanchez, Ortiz! It seems that I'm seeing nothing but **Spaniards** in your magazines these days."

Although the tone of each of the above letters varies, misters **Lind, Martinelli** and **Whitman** are essentially asking the same question: Why do the **Warren** magazines use so many **Spanish** artists?

We have only **one** answer for that. Here, at **Warren Publishing,** we use the finest artists in the **world** to produce quality comics. We have found that some of the best artists in comics today, come from **Spain!** But, whether we have to go to **Spain** for a **Gonzalez, Maroto, Sanchez** or **Ortiz** . . . or to **England** for a **Neary,** or into **America's** heartland for a **Corben** or a **Wrightson,** we feel strongly that the artists who appear in our magazines are the **finest** men illustrating comics today.

Our first responsibility is to present the best work possible to our readers. We feel that we are doing just that. We are proud of our artists, proud of their work. We are proud to have the best of **Spain, England** and **America** working together, to give you what we hope to be some of the finest comics in the **world!**

THE CREATIVE MAN

KEN KELLY: DOODLING COVER ARTIST!

We at Warren Publishing take pride in presenting the work of some of the finest artists in comics. Unfortunately, our readers see only a limited view of these men's talents; that which fits into the format of our magazines. Like most people, artists have many sides to them. As does their work. This column explores the men behind our magazines of illustrated horror. It probes their projects and dreams, their ideas and ideals. Within this column we'll see art outside the field of horror comics . . . other sides to the multi-talented Warren illustrators.

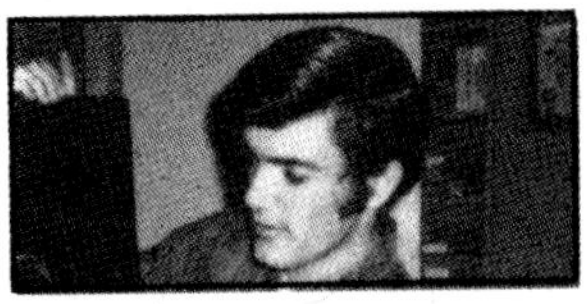

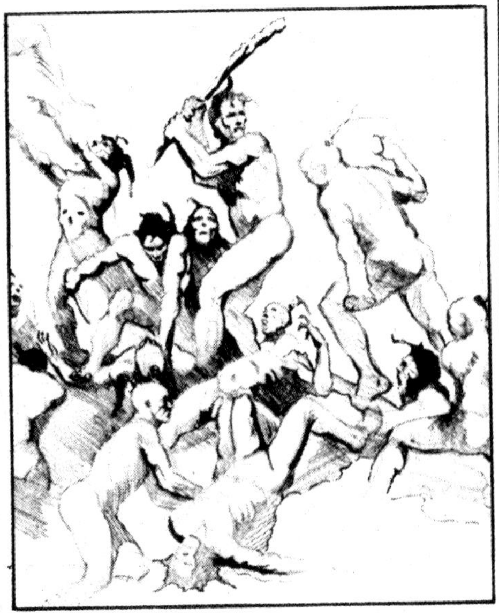

There are many sides to **Ken Kelly.** To his wife and children, he is the stranger who sleeps days and spends his nights slopping up the house with his paints. To his fellow artists, **Ken** is "that kid over at **Warren** who's been showing a lot of **promise** . . . for the past **six years!**" To the **Warren** editorial staff, he's **Moses** trucking from the Mount with a cover painting under each arm, just in time to make a deadline.

But to thousands of comic book fans, **Ken** is the luckiest guy in the world. His art teacher and mentor is the reknown **Frank Frazetta.**

"**Frank's** an incredible guy," claims **Ken.** "Besides being the most talented artist this side of **Michelangelo,** he's been a great friend, a challenging coach, and unbelievably patient with me. I owe him a lot!"

There's another side to **Ken Kelly** that few people see. In fact, he doesn't like to show anyone . . . not even his mentor and teacher. He doodles. "I like the human figure," **Ken** points out. "I could spend **days** sketching it. In fact, if my family didn't have this bad habit of **eating** . . . this would be the only type of art I'd do."

Here then is a sample of the type of artwork **Ken Kelly** enjoys most. He would never allow us to show this to anyone . . . so we had to **steal** it from him! **Surprise,** Ken!

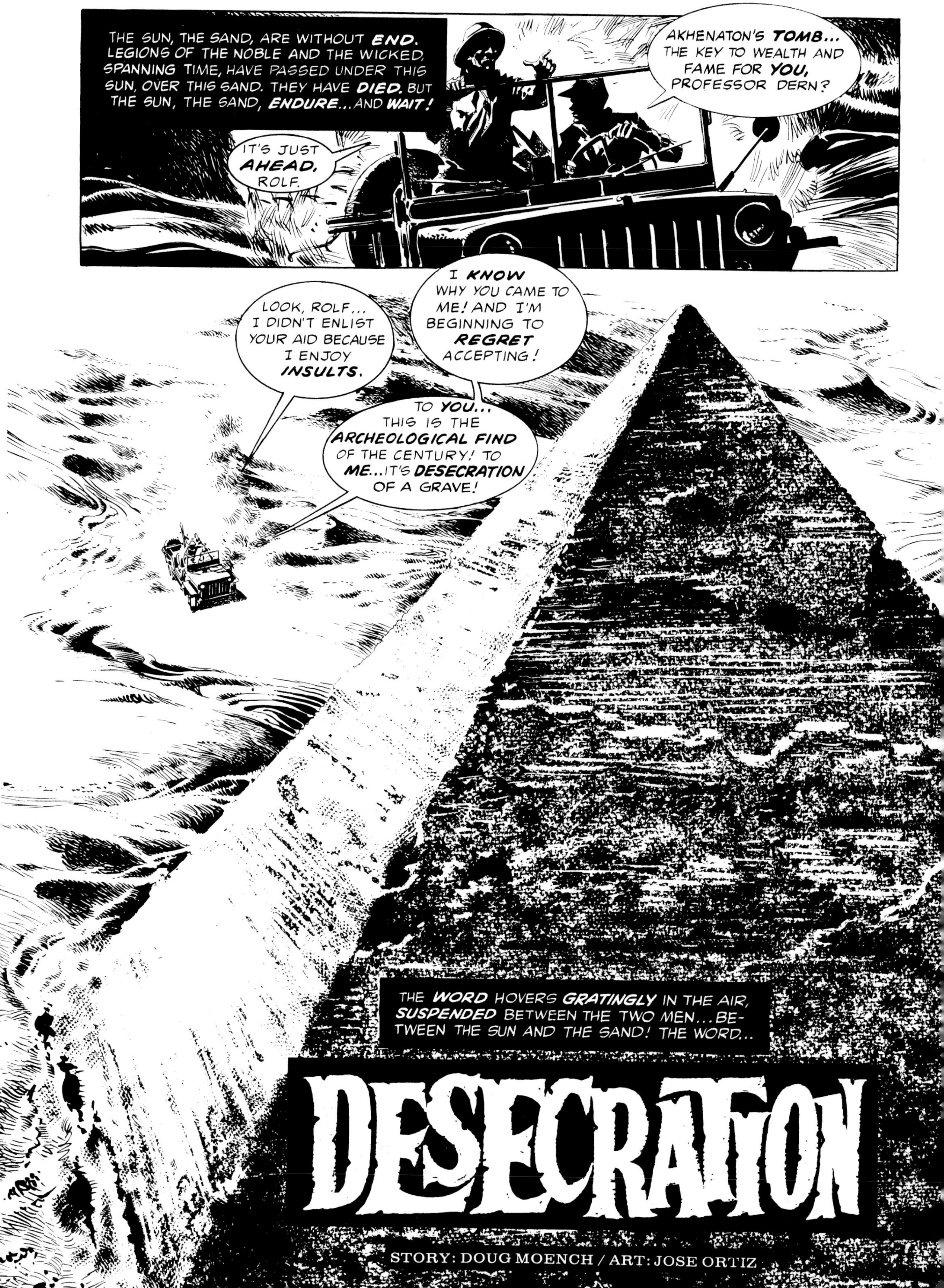
THE SUN, THE SAND, ARE WITHOUT END. LEGIONS OF THE NOBLE AND THE WICKED, SPANNING TIME, HAVE PASSED UNDER THIS SUN, OVER THIS SAND. THEY HAVE DIED. BUT THE SUN, THE SAND, ENDURE...AND WAIT!
AKHENATON'S TOMB... THE KEY TO WEALTH AND FAME FOR YOU, PROFESSOR DERN?
IT'S JUST AHEAD, ROLF.
LOOK, ROLF... I DIDN'T ENLIST YOUR AID BECAUSE I ENJOY INSULTS.
I KNOW WHY YOU CAME TO ME! AND I'M BEGINNING TO REGRET ACCEPTING!
TO YOU... THIS IS THE ARCHEOLOGICAL FIND OF THE CENTURY! TO ME...IT'S DESECRATION OF A GRAVE!
THE WORD HOVERS GRATINGLY IN THE AIR, SUSPENDED BETWEEN THE TWO MEN...BETWEEN THE SUN AND THE SAND! THE WORD...
DESECRATION
STORY: DOUG MOENCH / ART: JOSE ORTIZ

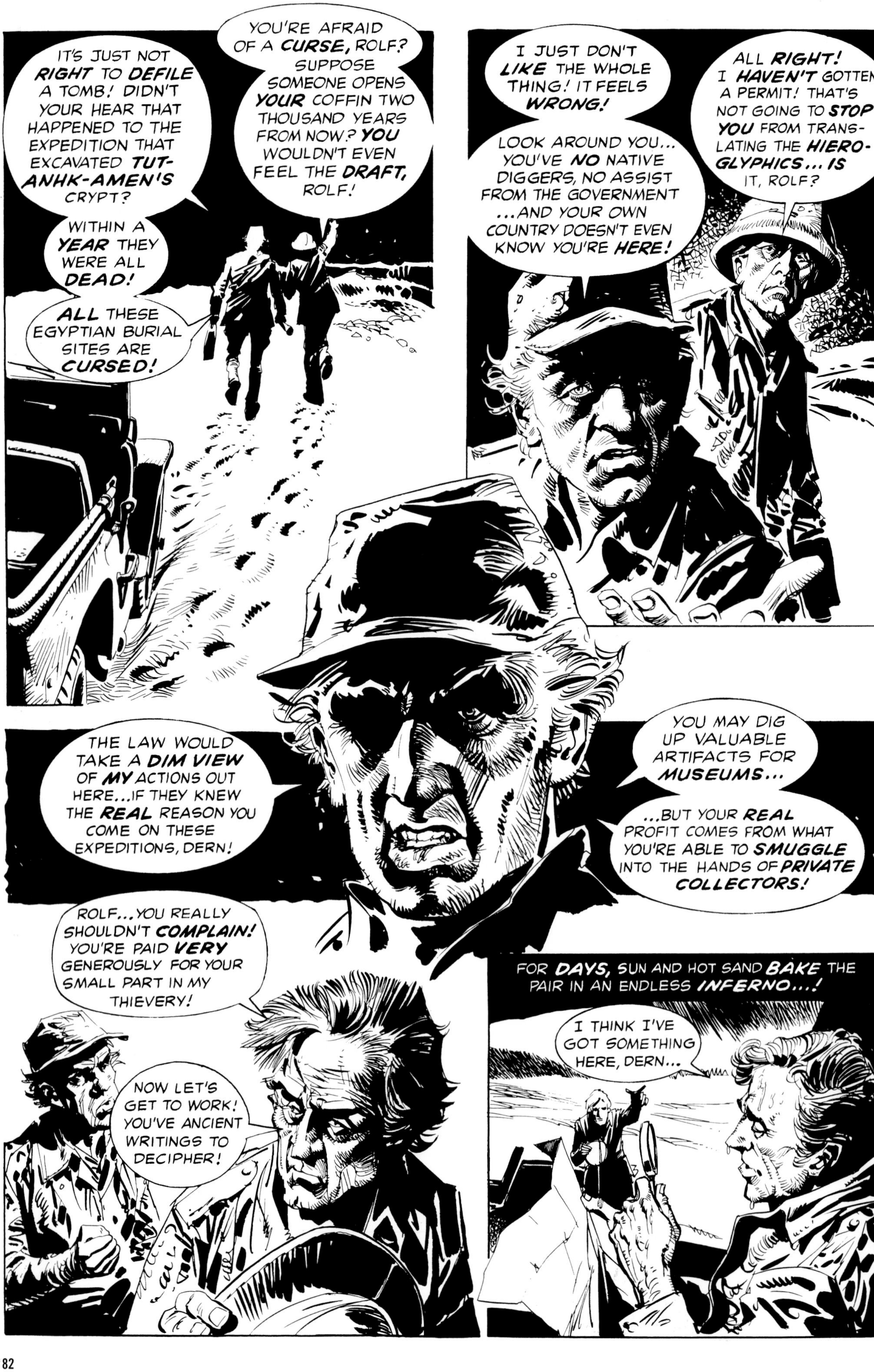
IT'S JUST NOT RIGHT TO DEFILE A TOMB! DIDN'T YOUR HEAR THAT HAPPENED TO THE EXPEDITION THAT EXCAVATED TUT-ANHK-AMEN'S CRYPT?
WITHIN A YEAR THEY WERE ALL DEAD!
ALL THESE EGYPTIAN BURIAL SITES ARE CURSED!
YOU'RE AFRAID OF A CURSE, ROLF? SUPPOSE SOMEONE OPENS YOUR COFFIN TWO THOUSAND YEARS FROM NOW? YOU WOULDN'T EVEN FEEL THE DRAFT, ROLF!
I JUST DON'T LIKE THE WHOLE THING! IT FEELS WRONG!
LOOK AROUND YOU... YOU'VE NO NATIVE DIGGERS, NO ASSIST FROM THE GOVERNMENT ...AND YOUR OWN COUNTRY DOESN'T EVEN KNOW YOU'RE HERE!
ALL RIGHT! I HAVEN'T GOTTEN A PERMIT! THAT'S NOT GOING TO STOP YOU FROM TRANSLATING THE HIEROGLYPHICS... IS IT, ROLF?
THE LAW WOULD TAKE A DIM VIEW OF MY ACTIONS OUT HERE...IF THEY KNEW THE REAL REASON YOU COME ON THESE EXPEDITIONS, DERN!
YOU MAY DIG UP VALUABLE ARTIFACTS FOR MUSEUMS...
...BUT YOUR REAL PROFIT COMES FROM WHAT YOU'RE ABLE TO SMUGGLE INTO THE HANDS OF PRIVATE COLLECTORS!
ROLF...YOU REALLY SHOULDN'T COMPLAIN! YOU'RE PAID VERY GENEROUSLY FOR YOUR SMALL PART IN MY THIEVERY!
NOW LET'S GET TO WORK! YOU'VE ANCIENT WRITINGS TO DECIPHER!
FOR DAYS, SUN AND HOT SAND BAKE THE PAIR IN AN ENDLESS INFERNO...!
I THINK I'VE GOT SOMETHING HERE, DERN...

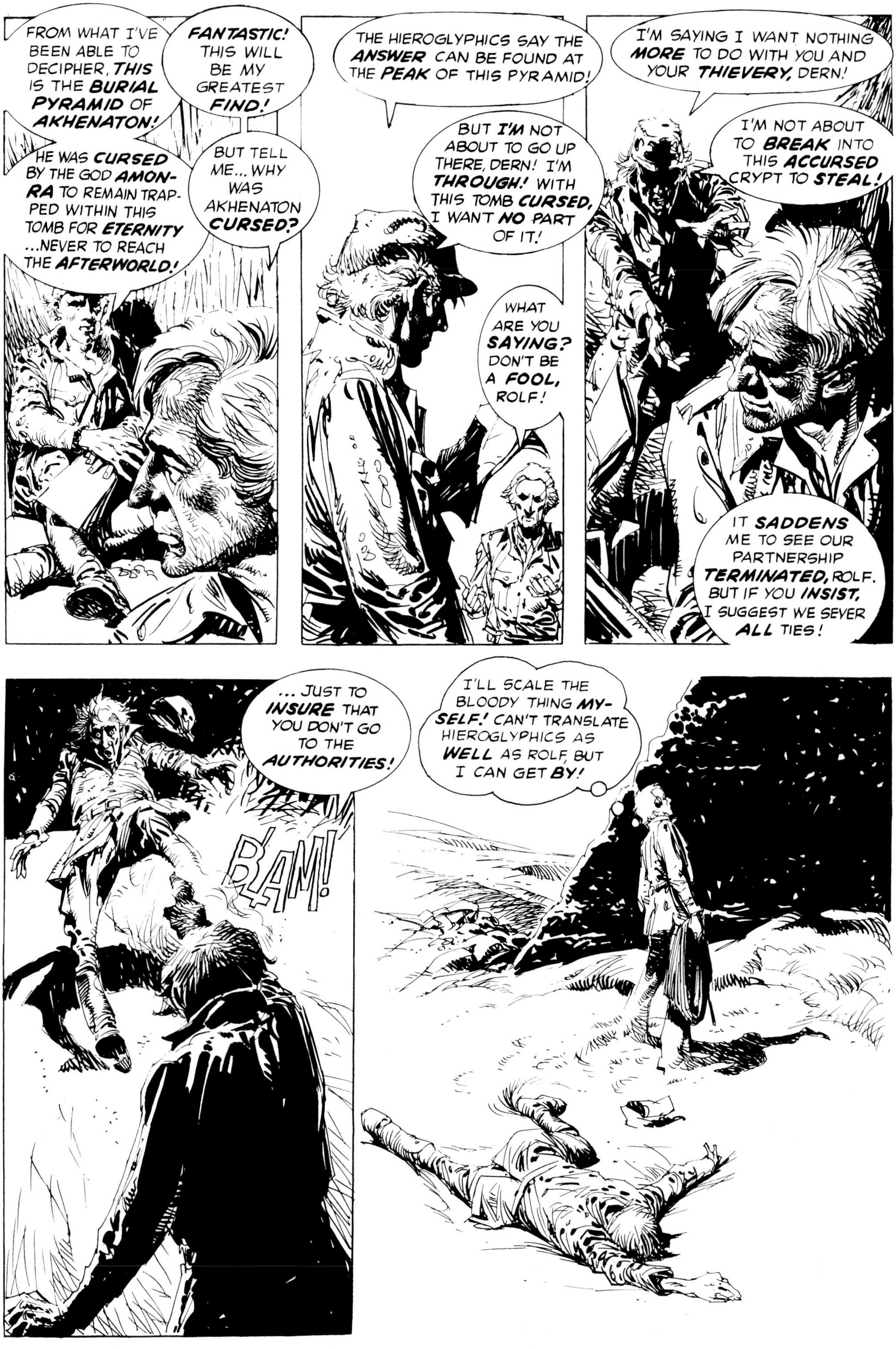
FROM WHAT I'VE BEEN ABLE TO DECIPHER, THIS IS THE BURIAL PYRAMID OF AKHENATON!
FANTASTIC! THIS WILL BE MY GREATEST FIND!
HE WAS CURSED BY THE GOD AMON-RA TO REMAIN TRAP-PED WITHIN THIS TOMB FOR ETERNITY ...NEVER TO REACH THE AFTERWORLD!
BUT TELL ME... WHY WAS AKHENATON CURSED?
THE HIEROGLYPHICS SAY THE ANSWER CAN BE FOUND AT THE PEAK OF THIS PYRAMID!
BUT I'M NOT ABOUT TO GO UP THERE, DERN! I'M THROUGH! WITH THIS TOMB CURSED, I WANT NO PART OF IT!
WHAT ARE YOU SAYING? DON'T BE A FOOL, ROLF!
I'M SAYING I WANT NOTHING MORE TO DO WITH YOU AND YOUR THIEVERY, DERN!
I'M NOT ABOUT TO BREAK INTO THIS ACCURSED CRYPT TO STEAL!
IT SADDENS ME TO SEE OUR PARTNERSHIP TERMINATED, ROLF. BUT IF YOU INSIST, I SUGGEST WE SEVER ALL TIES!
... JUST TO INSURE THAT YOU DON'T GO TO THE AUTHORITIES!
BLAM!
I'LL SCALE THE BLOODY THING MY-SELF! CAN'T TRANSLATE HIEROGLYPHICS AS WELL AS ROLF, BUT I CAN GET BY!

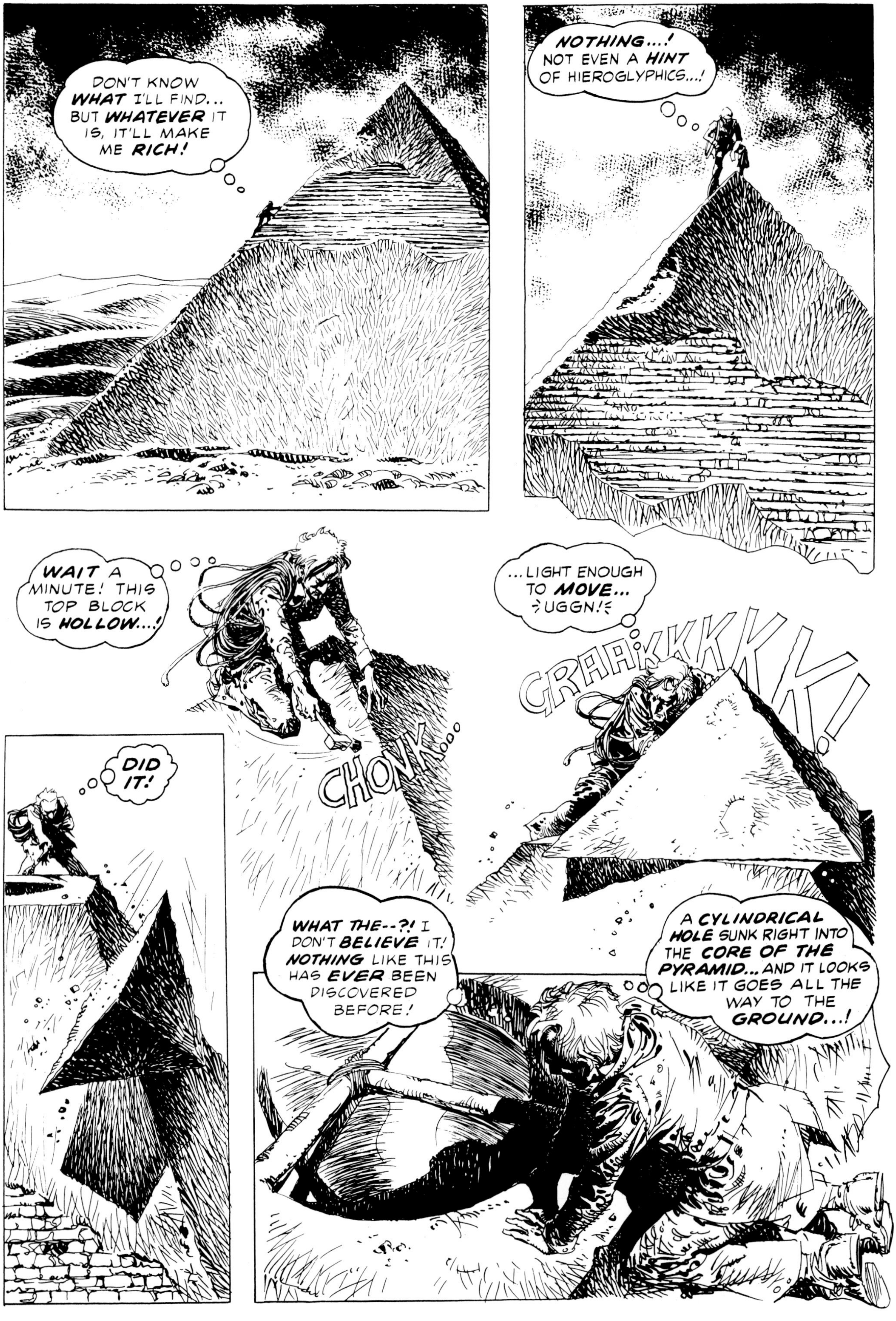
DON'T KNOW WHAT I'LL FIND... BUT WHATEVER IT IS, IT'LL MAKE ME RICH!
NOTHING...! NOT EVEN A HINT OF HIEROGLYPHICS...!
WAIT A MINUTE! THIS TOP BLOCK IS HOLLOW...!
...LIGHT ENOUGH TO MOVE... UGGN!
CHONK...
GRAAKKKKK!
DID IT!
WHAT THE--?! I DON'T BELIEVE IT! NOTHING LIKE THIS HAS EVER BEEN DISCOVERED BEFORE!
A CYLINDRICAL HOLE SUNK RIGHT INTO THE CORE OF THE PYRAMID... AND IT LOOKS LIKE IT GOES ALL THE WAY TO THE GROUND...!

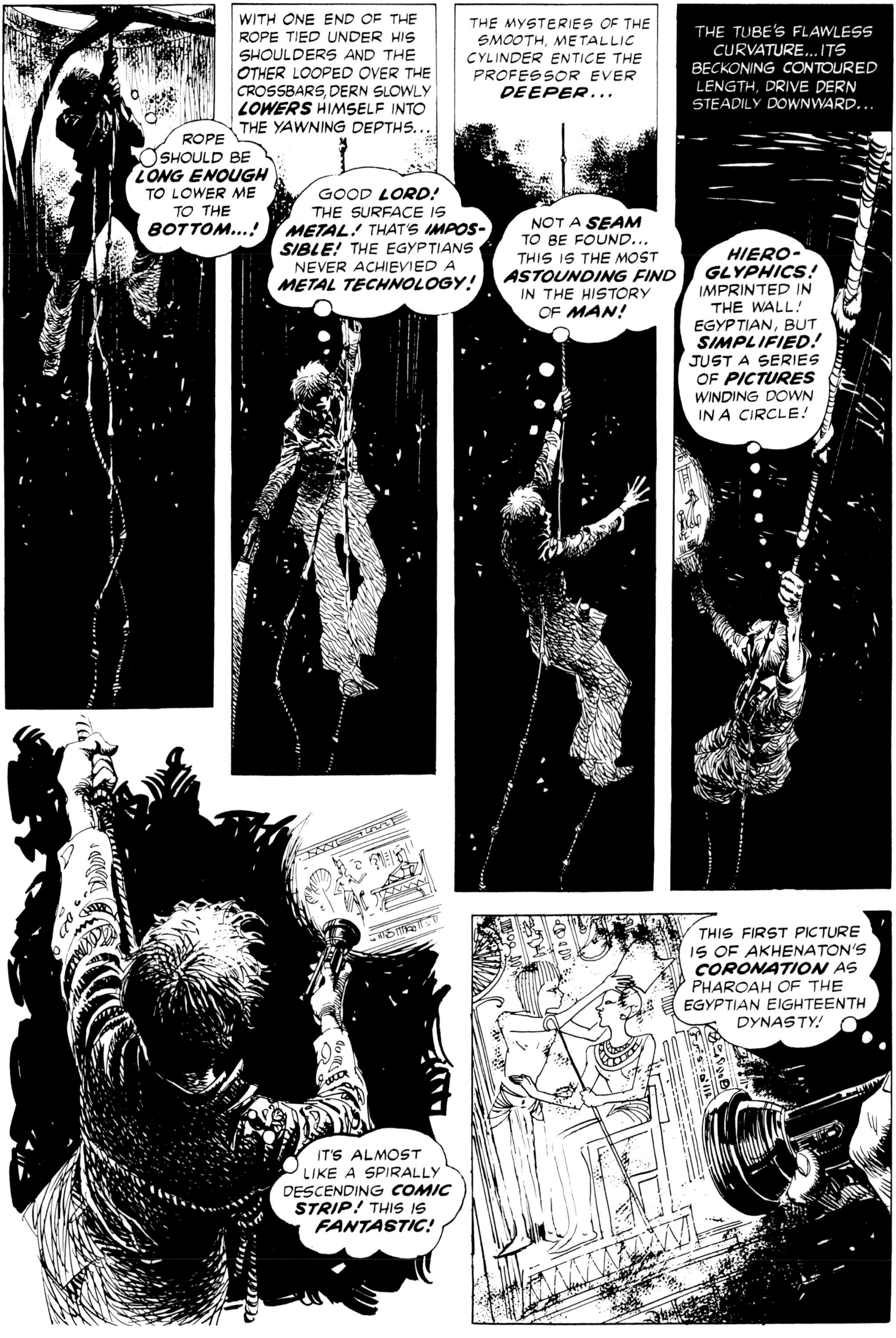
ROPE SHOULD BE LONG ENOUGH TO LOWER ME TO THE BOTTOM...!
WITH ONE END OF THE ROPE TIED UNDER HIS SHOULDERS AND THE OTHER LOOPED OVER THE CROSSBARS, DERN SLOWLY LOWERS HIMSELF INTO THE YAWNING DEPTHS...
GOOD LORD! THE SURFACE IS METAL! THAT'S IMPOSSIBLE! THE EGYPTIANS NEVER ACHIEVIED A METAL TECHNOLOGY!
THE MYSTERIES OF THE SMOOTH, METALLIC CYLINDER ENTICE THE PROFESSOR EVER DEEPER...
NOT A SEAM TO BE FOUND... THIS IS THE MOST ASTOUNDING FIND IN THE HISTORY OF MAN!
THE TUBE'S FLAWLESS CURVATURE...ITS BECKONING CONTOURED LENGTH, DRIVE DERN STEADILY DOWNWARD...
HIEROGLYPHICS! IMPRINTED IN THE WALL! EGYPTIAN, BUT SIMPLIFIED! JUST A SERIES OF PICTURES WINDING DOWN IN A CIRCLE!
IT'S ALMOST LIKE A SPIRALLY DESCENDING COMIC STRIP! THIS IS FANTASTIC!
THIS FIRST PICTURE IS OF AKHENATON'S CORONATION AS PHAROAH OF THE EGYPTIAN EIGHTEENTH DYNASTY!

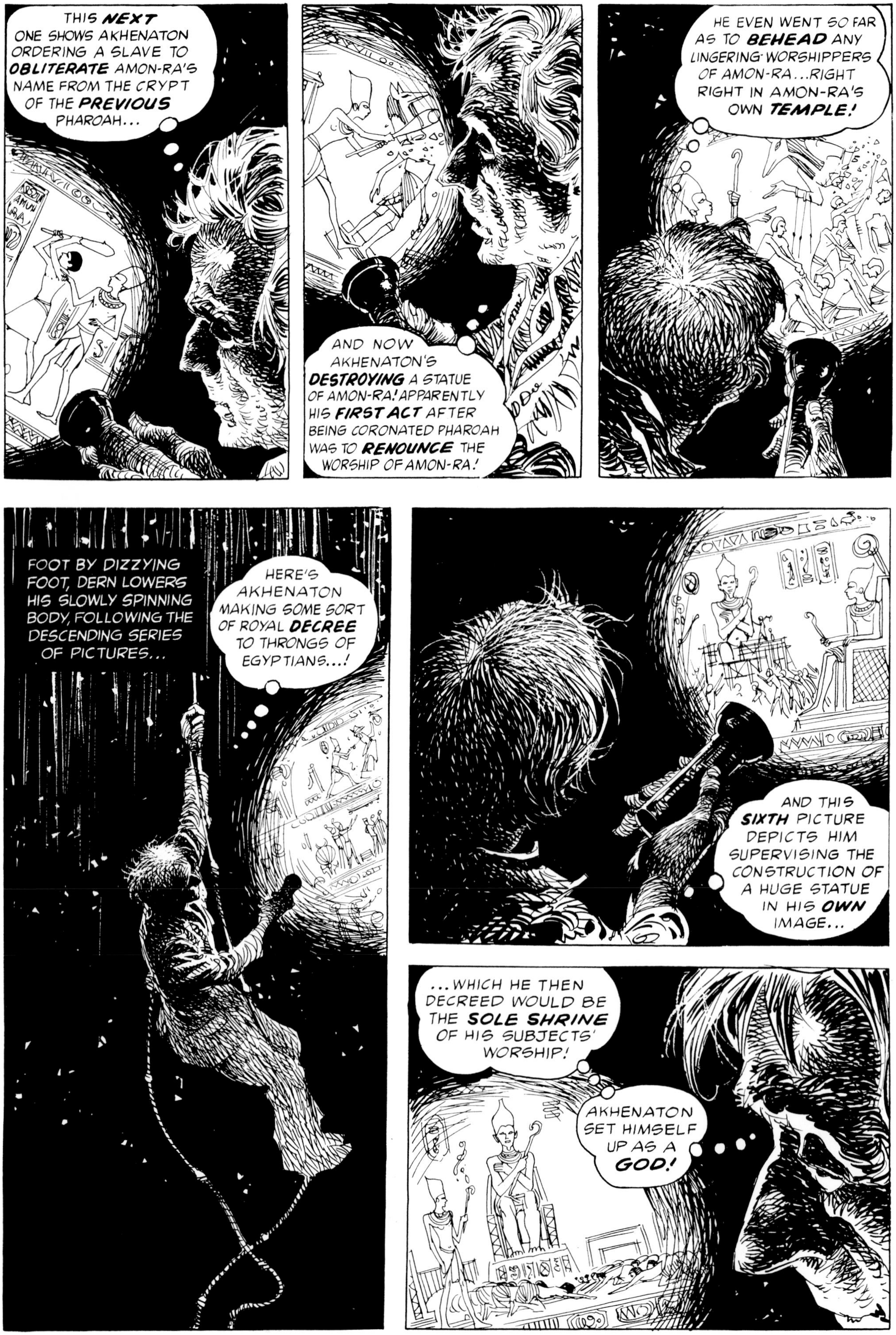
THIS NEXT ONE SHOWS AKHENATON ORDERING A SLAVE TO OBLITERATE AMON-RA'S NAME FROM THE CRYPT OF THE PREVIOUS PHAROAH...
AMUN RA
AND NOW AKHENATON'S DESTROYING A STATUE OF AMON-RA! APPARENTLY HIS FIRST ACT AFTER BEING CORONATED PHAROAH WAS TO RENOUNCE THE WORSHIP OF AMON-RA!
HE EVEN WENT SO FAR AS TO BEHEAD ANY LINGERING WORSHIPPERS OF AMON-RA...RIGHT RIGHT IN AMON-RA'S OWN TEMPLE!
FOOT BY DIZZYING FOOT, DERN LOWERS HIS SLOWLY SPINNING BODY, FOLLOWING THE DESCENDING SERIES OF PICTURES...
HERE'S AKHENATON MAKING SOME SORT OF ROYAL DECREE TO THRONGS OF EGYPTIANS...!
AND THIS SIXTH PICTURE DEPICTS HIM SUPERVISING THE CONSTRUCTION OF A HUGE STATUE IN HIS OWN IMAGE...
...WHICH HE THEN DECREED WOULD BE THE SOLE SHRINE OF HIS SUBJECTS' WORSHIP!
AKHENATON SET HIMSELF UP AS A GOD!

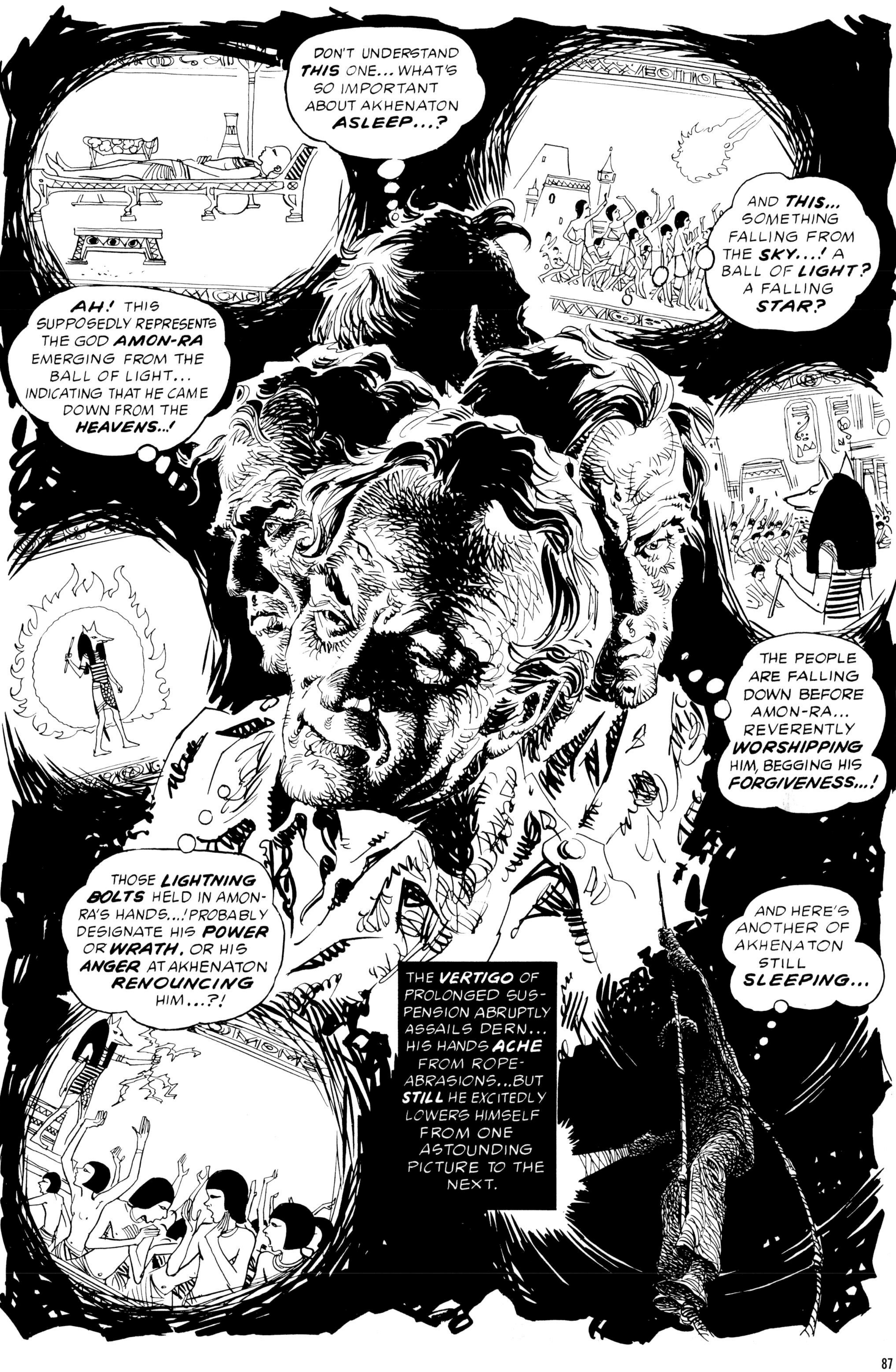
DON'T UNDERSTAND THIS ONE... WHAT'S SO IMPORTANT ABOUT AKHENATON ASLEEP...?
AND THIS... SOMETHING FALLING FROM THE SKY...! A BALL OF LIGHT? A FALLING STAR?
AH! THIS SUPPOSEDLY REPRESENTS THE GOD AMON-RA EMERGING FROM THE BALL OF LIGHT... INDICATING THAT HE CAME DOWN FROM THE HEAVENS...!
THE PEOPLE ARE FALLING DOWN BEFORE AMON-RA... REVERENTLY WORSHIPPING HIM, BEGGING HIS FORGIVENESS...!
THOSE LIGHTNING BOLTS HELD IN AMON-RA'S HANDS...! PROBABLY DESIGNATE HIS POWER OR WRATH. OR HIS ANGER AT AKHENATON RENOUNCING HIM...?!
AND HERE'S ANOTHER OF AKHENATON STILL SLEEPING...
THE VERTIGO OF PROLONGED SUSPENSION ABRUPTLY ASSAILS DERN... HIS HANDS ACHE FROM ROPE-ABRASIONS... BUT STILL HE EXCITEDLY LOWERS HIMSELF FROM ONE ASTOUNDING PICTURE TO THE NEXT.

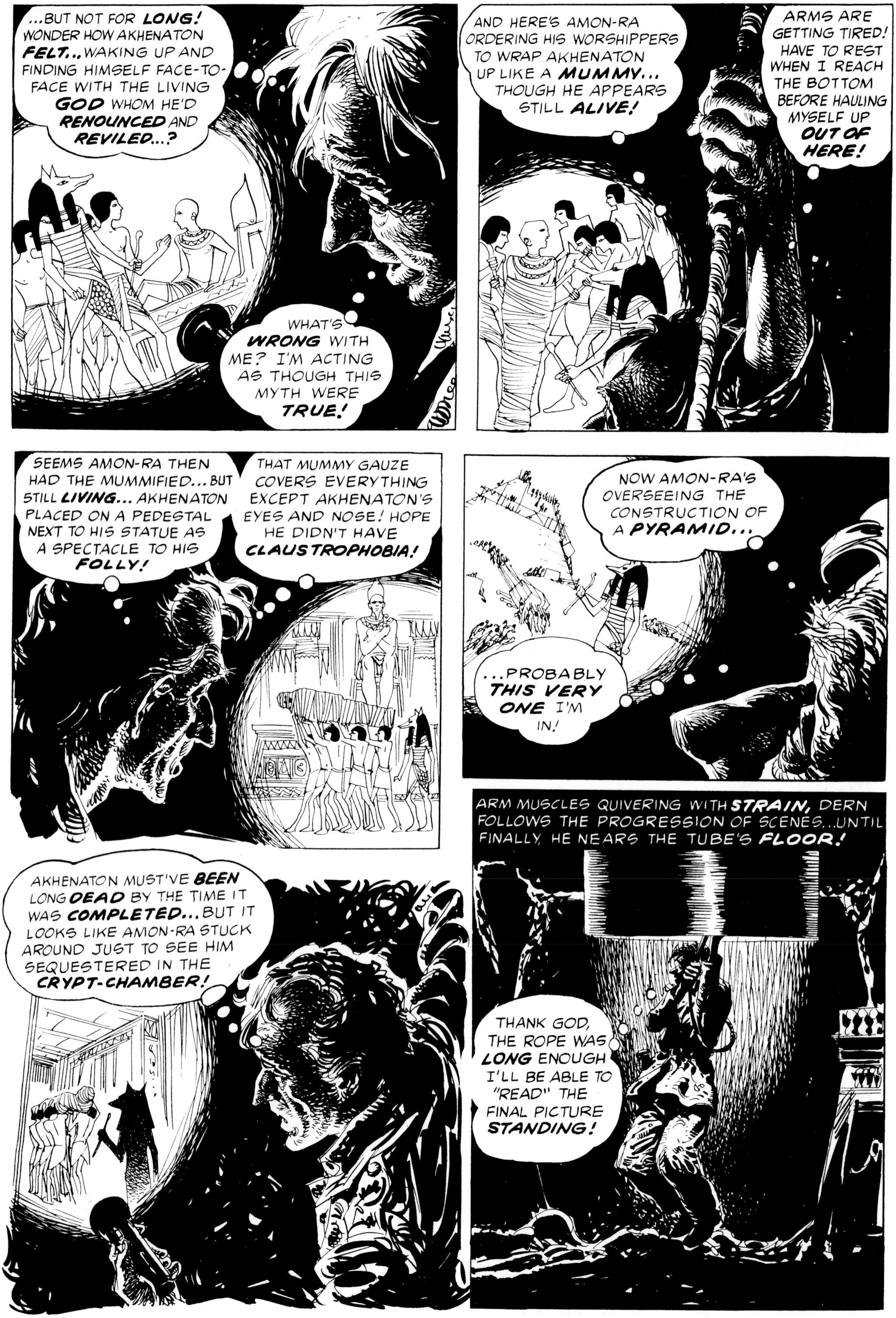
...BUT NOT FOR LONG! WONDER HOW AKHENATON FELT... WAKING UP AND FINDING HIMSELF FACE-TO-FACE WITH THE LIVING GOD WHOM HE'D RENOUNCED AND REVILED...?
WHAT'S WRONG WITH ME? I'M ACTING AS THOUGH THIS MYTH WERE TRUE!
AND HERE'S AMON-RA ORDERING HIS WORSHIPPERS TO WRAP AKHENATON UP LIKE A MUMMY... THOUGH HE APPEARS STILL ALIVE!
ARMS ARE GETTING TIRED! HAVE TO REST WHEN I REACH THE BOTTOM BEFORE HAULING MYSELF UP OUT OF HERE!
SEEMS AMON-RA THEN HAD THE MUMMIFIED... BUT STILL LIVING... AKHENATON PLACED ON A PEDESTAL NEXT TO HIS STATUE AS A SPECTACLE TO HIS FOLLY!
THAT MUMMY GAUZE COVERS EVERYTHING EXCEPT AKHENATON'S EYES AND NOSE! HOPE HE DIDN'T HAVE CLAUSTROPHOBIA!
NOW AMON-RA'S OVERSEEING THE CONSTRUCTION OF A PYRAMID...
...PROBABLY THIS VERY ONE I'M IN!
AKHENATON MUST'VE BEEN LONG DEAD BY THE TIME IT WAS COMPLETED... BUT IT LOOKS LIKE AMON-RA STUCK AROUND JUST TO SEE HIM SEQUESTERED IN THE CRYPT-CHAMBER!
ARM MUSCLES QUIVERING WITH STRAIN, DERN FOLLOWS THE PROGRESSION OF SCENES... UNTIL FINALLY, HE NEARS THE TUBE'S FLOOR!
THANK GOD, THE ROPE WAS LONG ENOUGH I'LL BE ABLE TO "READ" THE FINAL PICTURE STANDING!

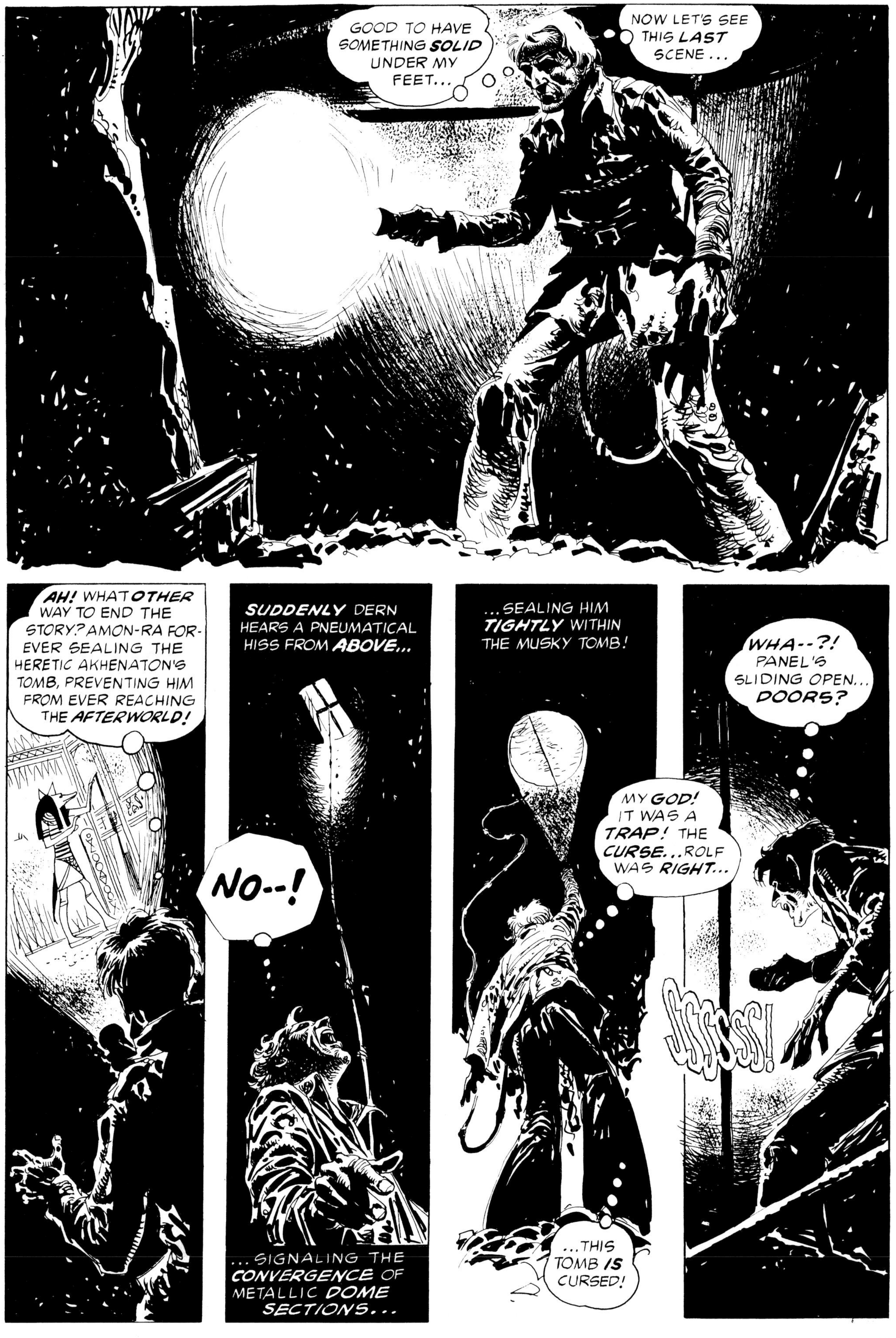
GOOD TO HAVE SOMETHING SOLID UNDER MY FEET...
NOW LET'S SEE THIS LAST SCENE...
AH! WHAT OTHER WAY TO END THE STORY? AMON-RA FOREVER SEALING THE HERETIC AKHENATON'S TOMB, PREVENTING HIM FROM EVER REACHING THE AFTERWORLD!
SUDDENLY DERN HEARS A PNEUMATICAL HISS FROM ABOVE...
NO--!
...SIGNALING THE CONVERGENCE OF METALLIC DOME SECTIONS...
...SEALING HIM TIGHTLY WITHIN THE MUSKY TOMB!
MY GOD! IT WAS A TRAP! THE CURSE...ROLF WAS RIGHT...
...THIS TOMB IS CURSED!
WHA--?! PANEL'S SLIDING OPEN... DOORS?
SSSSSS!

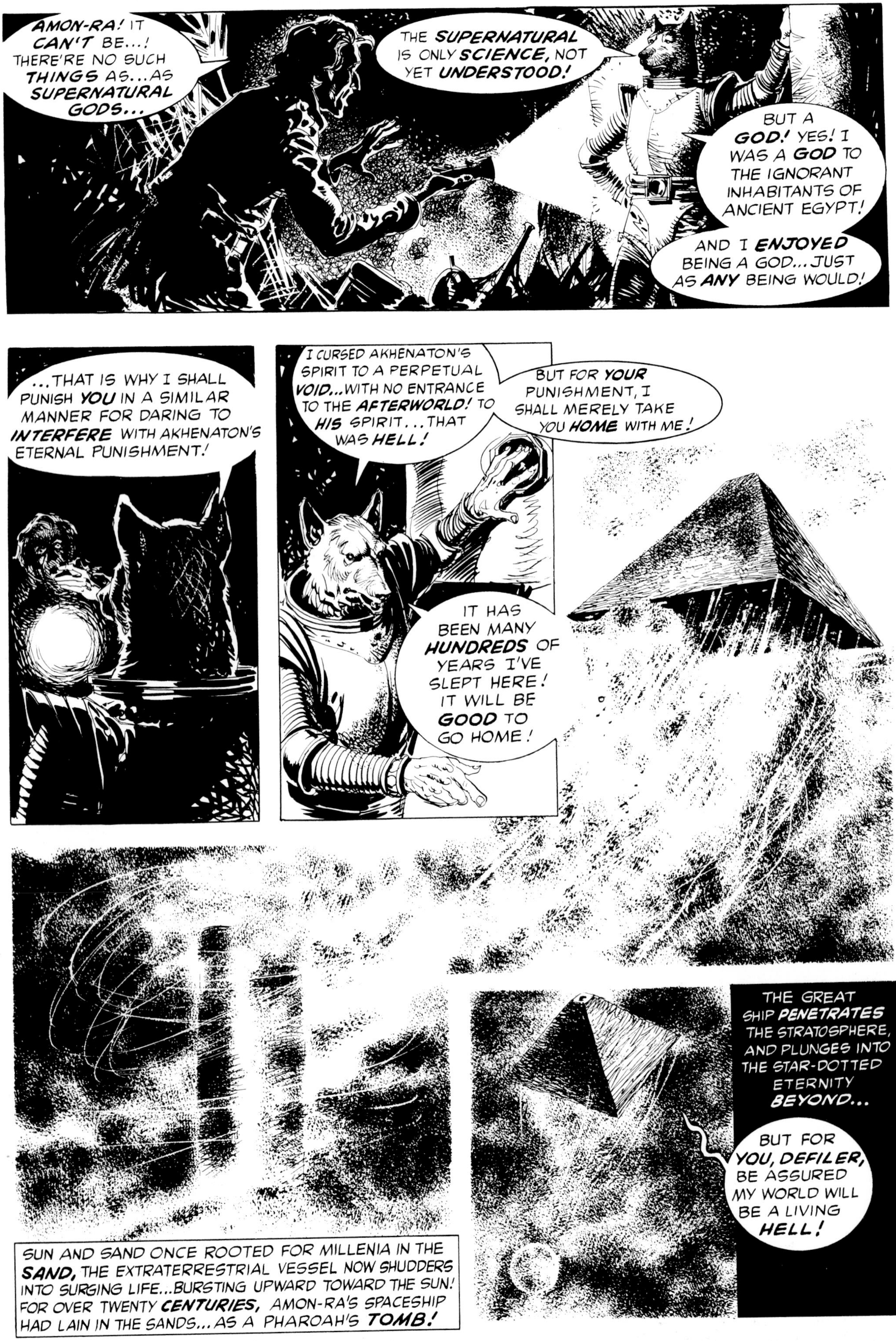

AMON-RA! IT CAN'T BE...! THERE'RE NO SUCH THINGS AS...AS SUPERNATURAL GODS...
THE SUPERNATURAL IS ONLY SCIENCE, NOT YET UNDERSTOOD!
BUT A GOD! YES! I WAS A GOD TO THE IGNORANT INHABITANTS OF ANCIENT EGYPT!
AND I ENJOYED BEING A GOD... JUST AS ANY BEING WOULD!
...THAT IS WHY I SHALL PUNISH YOU IN A SIMILAR MANNER FOR DARING TO INTERFERE WITH AKHENATON'S ETERNAL PUNISHMENT!
I CURSED AKHENATON'S SPIRIT TO A PERPETUAL VOID...WITH NO ENTRANCE TO THE AFTERWORLD! TO HIS SPIRIT...THAT WAS HELL!
BUT FOR YOUR PUNISHMENT, I SHALL MERELY TAKE YOU HOME WITH ME!
IT HAS BEEN MANY HUNDREDS OF YEARS I'VE SLEPT HERE! IT WILL BE GOOD TO GO HOME!
SUN AND SAND ONCE ROOTED FOR MILLENIA IN THE SAND, THE EXTRATERRESTRIAL VESSEL NOW SHUDDERS INTO SURGING LIFE...BURSTING UPWARD TOWARD THE SUN! FOR OVER TWENTY CENTURIES, AMON-RA'S SPACESHIP HAD LAIN IN THE SANDS... AS A PHAROAH'S TOMB!
THE GREAT SHIP PENETRATES THE STRATOSPHERE, AND PLUNGES INTO THE STAR-DOTTED ETERNITY BEYOND...
BUT FOR YOU, DEFILER, BE ASSURED MY WORLD WILL BE A LIVING HELL!

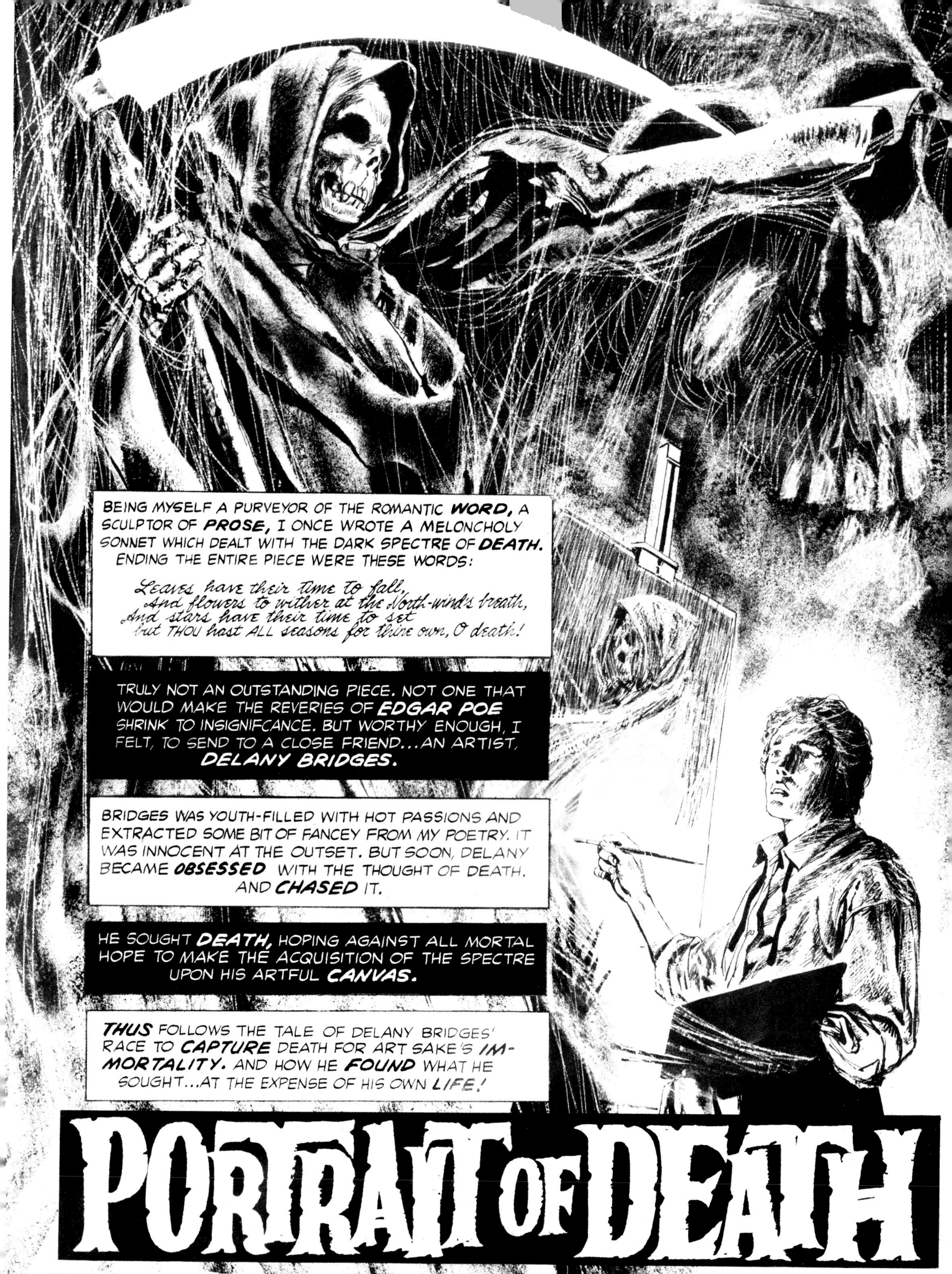
BEING MYSELF A PURVEYOR OF THE ROMANTIC WORD, A SCULPTOR OF PROSE, I ONCE WROTE A MELONCHOLY SONNET WHICH DEALT WITH THE DARK SPECTRE OF DEATH. ENDING THE ENTIRE PIECE WERE THESE WORDS:
Leaves have their time to fall,
And flowers to wither at the North-wind's breath,
And stars have their time to set
but THOU hast ALL seasons for thine own, O death!
TRULY NOT AN OUTSTANDING PIECE. NOT ONE THAT WOULD MAKE THE REVERIES OF EDGAR POE SHRINK TO INSIGNIFCANCE. BUT WORTHY ENOUGH, I FELT, TO SEND TO A CLOSE FRIEND... AN ARTIST, DELANY BRIDGES.
BRIDGES WAS YOUTH-FILLED WITH HOT PASSIONS AND EXTRACTED SOME BIT OF FANCEY FROM MY POETRY. IT WAS INNOCENT AT THE OUTSET. BUT SOON, DELANY BECAME OBSESSED WITH THE THOUGHT OF DEATH. AND CHASED IT.
HE SOUGHT DEATH, HOPING AGAINST ALL MORTAL HOPE TO MAKE THE ACQUISITION OF THE SPECTRE UPON HIS ARTFUL CANVAS.
THUS FOLLOWS THE TALE OF DELANY BRIDGES' RACE TO CAPTURE DEATH FOR ART SAKE'S IMMORTALITY. AND HOW HE FOUND WHAT HE SOUGHT... AT THE EXPENSE OF HIS OWN LIFE!
PORTRAIT OF DEATH

STORY: BUDD LEWIS / ART: VICENTE ALCAZAR

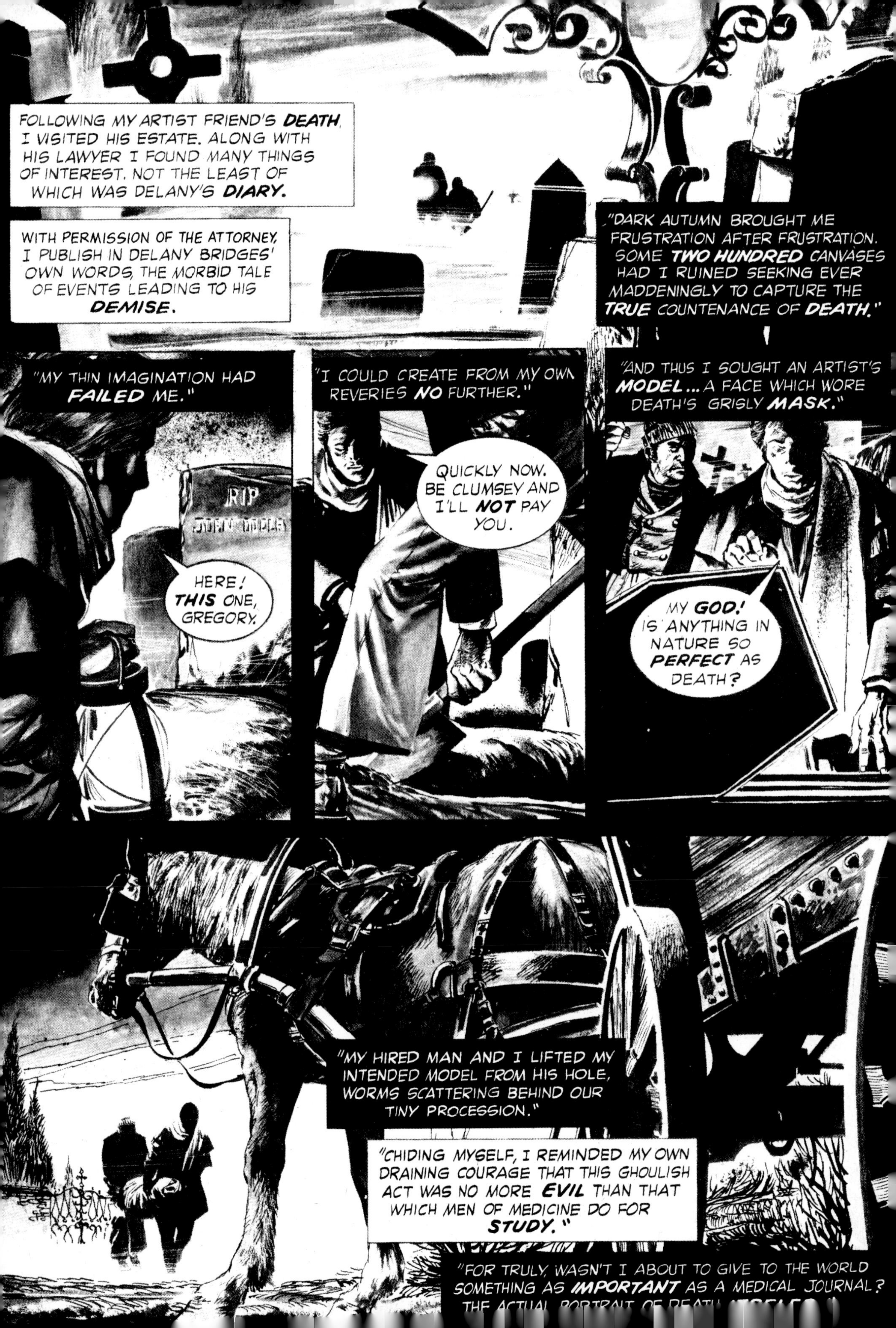
FOLLOWING MY ARTIST FRIEND'S DEATH, I VISITED HIS ESTATE. ALONG WITH HIS LAWYER I FOUND MANY THINGS OF INTEREST. NOT THE LEAST OF WHICH WAS DELANY'S DIARY.
WITH PERMISSION OF THE ATTORNEY, I PUBLISH IN DELANY BRIDGES' OWN WORDS, THE MORBID TALE OF EVENTS LEADING TO HIS DEMISE.
"DARK AUTUMN BROUGHT ME FRUSTRATION AFTER FRUSTRATION. SOME TWO HUNDRED CANVASES HAD I RUINED SEEKING EVER MADDENINGLY TO CAPTURE THE TRUE COUNTENANCE OF DEATH."
"MY THIN IMAGINATION HAD FAILED ME."
RIP
HERE! THIS ONE, GREGORY.
"I COULD CREATE FROM MY OWN REVERIES NO FURTHER."
QUICKLY NOW. BE CLUMSEY AND I'LL NOT PAY YOU.
"AND THUS I SOUGHT AN ARTIST'S MODEL... A FACE WHICH WORE DEATH'S GRISLY MASK."
MY GOD! IS ANYTHING IN NATURE SO PERFECT AS DEATH?
"MY HIRED MAN AND I LIFTED MY INTENDED MODEL FROM HIS HOLE, WORMS SCATTERING BEHIND OUR TINY PROCESSION."
"CHIDING MYSELF, I REMINDED MY OWN DRAINING COURAGE THAT THIS GHOULISH ACT WAS NO MORE EVIL THAN THAT WHICH MEN OF MEDICINE DO FOR STUDY."
"FOR TRULY, WASN'T I ABOUT TO GIVE TO THE WORLD SOMETHING AS IMPORTANT AS A MEDICAL JOURNAL? THE ACTUAL PORTRAIT OF DEATH

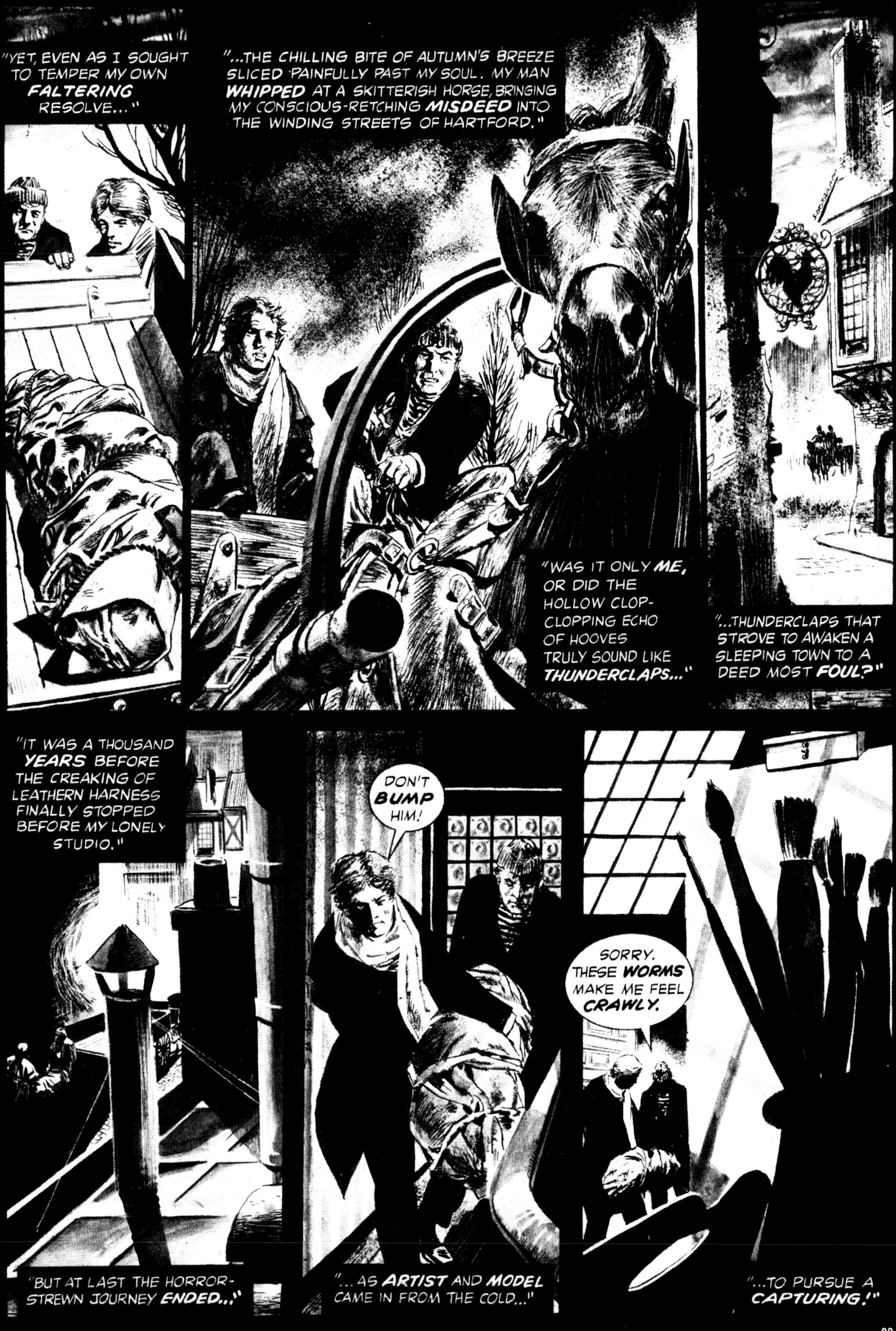
"YET, EVEN AS I SOUGHT TO TEMPER MY OWN FALTERING RESOLVE..."
"...THE CHILLING BITE OF AUTUMN'S BREEZE SLICED PAINFULLY PAST MY SOUL. MY MAN WHIPPED AT A SKITTERISH HORSE, BRINGING MY CONSCIOUS-RETCHING MISDEED INTO THE WINDING STREETS OF HARTFORD."
"WAS IT ONLY ME, OR DID THE HOLLOW CLOP-CLOPPING ECHO OF HOOVES TRULY SOUND LIKE THUNDERCLAPS..."
"...THUNDERCLAPS THAT STROVE TO AWAKEN A SLEEPING TOWN TO A DEED MOST FOUL?"
"IT WAS A THOUSAND YEARS BEFORE THE CREAKING OF LEATHERN HARNESS FINALLY STOPPED BEFORE MY LONELY STUDIO."
"BUT AT LAST THE HORROR-STREWN JOURNEY ENDED..."
DON'T BUMP HIM!
"...AS ARTIST AND MODEL CAME IN FROM THE COLD..."
SORRY. THESE WORMS MAKE ME FEEL CRAWLY.
"...TO PURSUE A CAPTURING!"

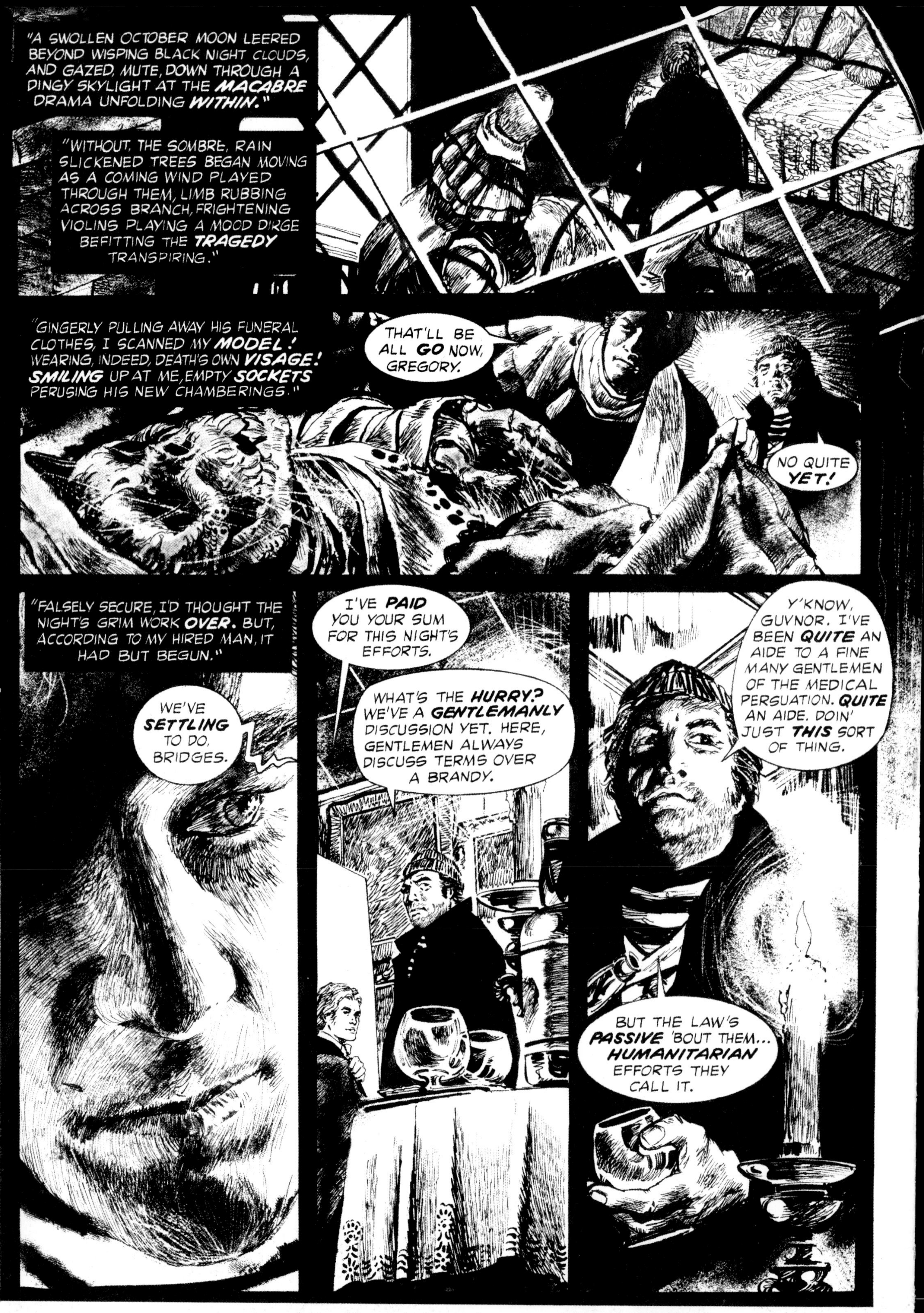
"A SWOLLEN OCTOBER MOON LEERED BEYOND WISPING BLACK NIGHT CLOUDS, AND GAZED, MUTE, DOWN THROUGH A DINGY SKYLIGHT AT THE MACABRE DRAMA UNFOLDING WITHIN."
"WITHOUT, THE SOMBRE, RAIN SLICKENED TREES BEGAN MOVING AS A COMING WIND PLAYED THROUGH THEM, LIMB RUBBING ACROSS BRANCH, FRIGHTENING VIOLINS PLAYING A MOOD DIRGE BEFITTING THE TRAGEDY TRANSPIRING."
"GINGERLY PULLING AWAY HIS FUNERAL CLOTHES, I SCANNED MY MODEL! WEARING, INDEED, DEATH'S OWN VISAGE! SMILING UP AT ME, EMPTY SOCKETS PERUSING HIS NEW CHAMBERINGS."
THAT'LL BE ALL GO NOW, GREGORY.
NO QUITE YET!
"FALSELY SECURE, I'D THOUGHT THE NIGHT'S GRIM WORK OVER. BUT, ACCORDING TO MY HIRED MAN, IT HAD BUT BEGUN."
WE'VE SETTLING TO DO, BRIDGES.
I'VE PAID YOU YOUR SUM FOR THIS NIGHT'S EFFORTS.
WHAT'S THE HURRY? WE'VE A GENTLEMANLY DISCUSSION YET. HERE, GENTLEMEN ALWAYS DISCUSS TERMS OVER A BRANDY.
Y'KNOW, GUVNOR. I'VE BEEN QUITE AN AIDE TO A FINE MANY GENTLEMEN OF THE MEDICAL PERSUATION. QUITE AN AIDE. DOIN' JUST THIS SORT OF THING.
BUT THE LAW'S PASSIVE 'BOUT THEM... HUMANITARIAN EFFORTS THEY CALL IT.

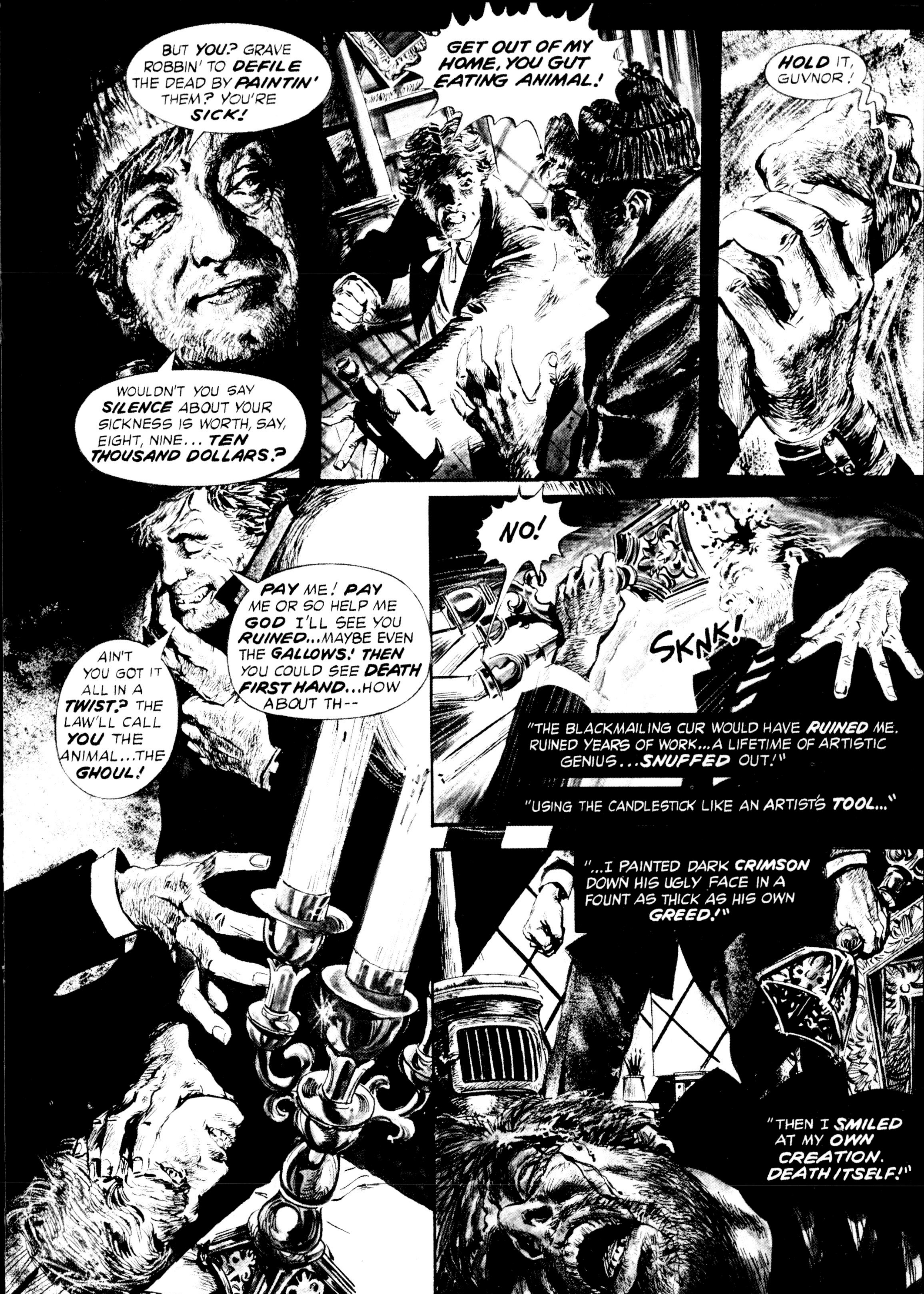

BUT YOU? GRAVE ROBBIN' TO DEFILE THE DEAD BY PAINTIN' THEM? YOU'RE SICK!
WOULDN'T YOU SAY SILENCE ABOUT YOUR SICKNESS IS WORTH, SAY, EIGHT, NINE... TEN THOUSAND DOLLARS?
GET OUT OF MY HOME, YOU GUT EATING ANIMAL!
HOLD IT, GUVNOR!
AIN'T YOU GOT IT ALL IN A TWIST? THE LAW'LL CALL YOU THE ANIMAL...THE GHOUL!
PAY ME! PAY ME OR SO HELP ME GOD I'LL SEE YOU RUINED...MAYBE EVEN THE GALLOWS! THEN YOU COULD SEE DEATH FIRST HAND...HOW ABOUT TH--
NO!
SKNK!
"THE BLACKMAILING CUR WOULD HAVE RUINED ME. RUINED YEARS OF WORK...A LIFETIME OF ARTISTIC GENIUS...SNUFFED OUT!"
"USING THE CANDLESTICK LIKE AN ARTIST'S TOOL..."
"...I PAINTED DARK CRIMSON DOWN HIS UGLY FACE IN A FOUNT AS THICK AS HIS OWN GREED!"
"THEN I SMILED AT MY OWN CREATION. DEATH ITSELF!"

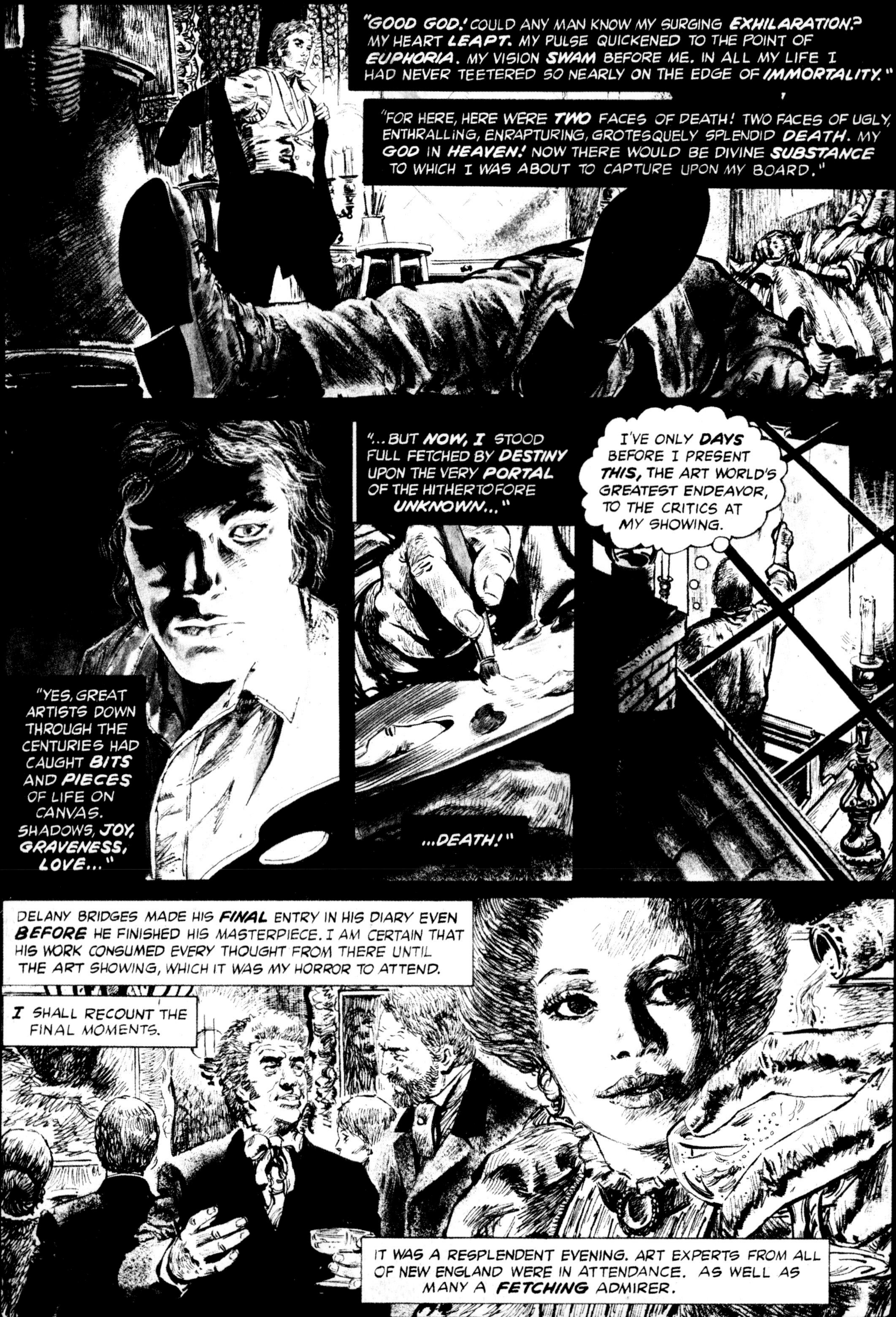
"GOOD GOD! COULD ANY MAN KNOW MY SURGING EXHILARATION? MY HEART LEAPT. MY PULSE QUICKENED TO THE POINT OF EUPHORIA. MY VISION SWAM BEFORE ME. IN ALL MY LIFE I HAD NEVER TEETERED SO NEARLY ON THE EDGE OF IMMORTALITY."
"FOR HERE, HERE WERE TWO FACES OF DEATH! TWO FACES OF UGLY, ENTHRALLING, ENRAPTURING, GROTESQUELY SPLENDID DEATH. MY GOD IN HEAVEN! NOW THERE WOULD BE DIVINE SUBSTANCE TO WHICH I WAS ABOUT TO CAPTURE UPON MY BOARD."
"YES, GREAT ARTISTS DOWN THROUGH THE CENTURIES HAD CAUGHT BITS AND PIECES OF LIFE ON CANVAS. SHADOWS, JOY, GRAVENESS, LOVE..."
"...BUT NOW, I STOOD FULL FETCHED BY DESTINY UPON THE VERY PORTAL OF THE HITHERTOFORE UNKNOWN..."
...DEATH!"
I'VE ONLY DAYS BEFORE I PRESENT THIS, THE ART WORLD'S GREATEST ENDEAVOR, TO THE CRITICS AT MY SHOWING.
DELANY BRIDGES MADE HIS FINAL ENTRY IN HIS DIARY EVEN BEFORE HE FINISHED HIS MASTERPIECE. I AM CERTAIN THAT HIS WORK CONSUMED EVERY THOUGHT FROM THERE UNTIL THE ART SHOWING, WHICH IT WAS MY HORROR TO ATTEND.
I SHALL RECOUNT THE FINAL MOMENTS.
IT WAS A RESPLENDENT EVENING. ART EXPERTS FROM ALL OF NEW ENGLAND WERE IN ATTENDANCE. AS WELL AS MANY A FETCHING ADMIRER.

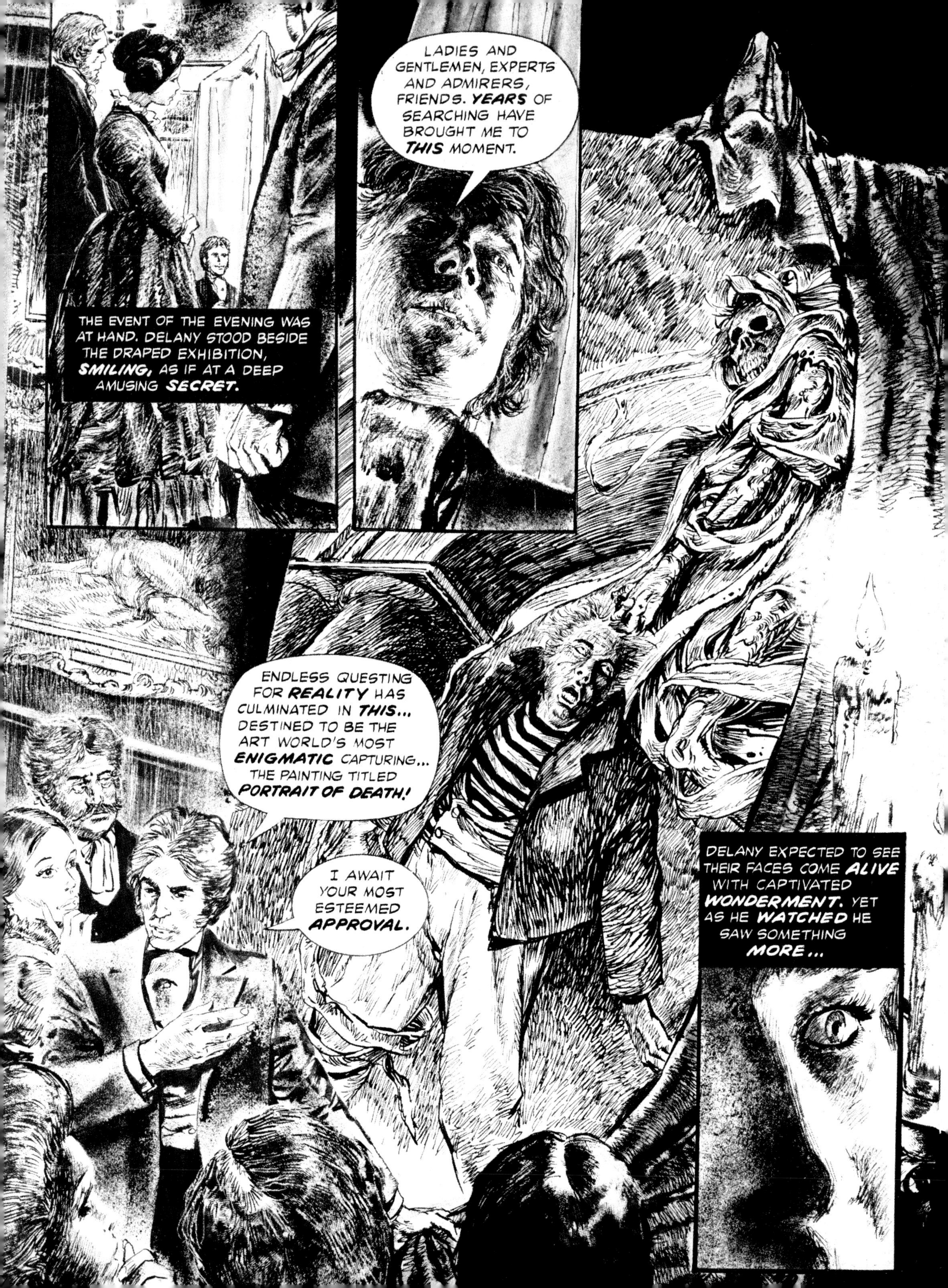
THE EVENT OF THE EVENING WAS AT HAND. DELANY STOOD BESIDE THE DRAPED EXHIBITION, SMILING, AS IF AT A DEEP AMUSING SECRET.
LADIES AND GENTLEMEN, EXPERTS AND ADMIRERS, FRIENDS. YEARS OF SEARCHING HAVE BROUGHT ME TO THIS MOMENT.
ENDLESS QUESTING FOR REALITY HAS CULMINATED IN THIS... DESTINED TO BE THE ART WORLD'S MOST ENIGMATIC CAPTURING... THE PAINTING TITLED PORTRAIT OF DEATH!
I AWAIT YOUR MOST ESTEEMED APPROVAL.
DELANY EXPECTED TO SEE THEIR FACES COME ALIVE WITH CAPTIVATED WONDERMENT. YET AS HE WATCHED HE SAW SOMETHING MORE...

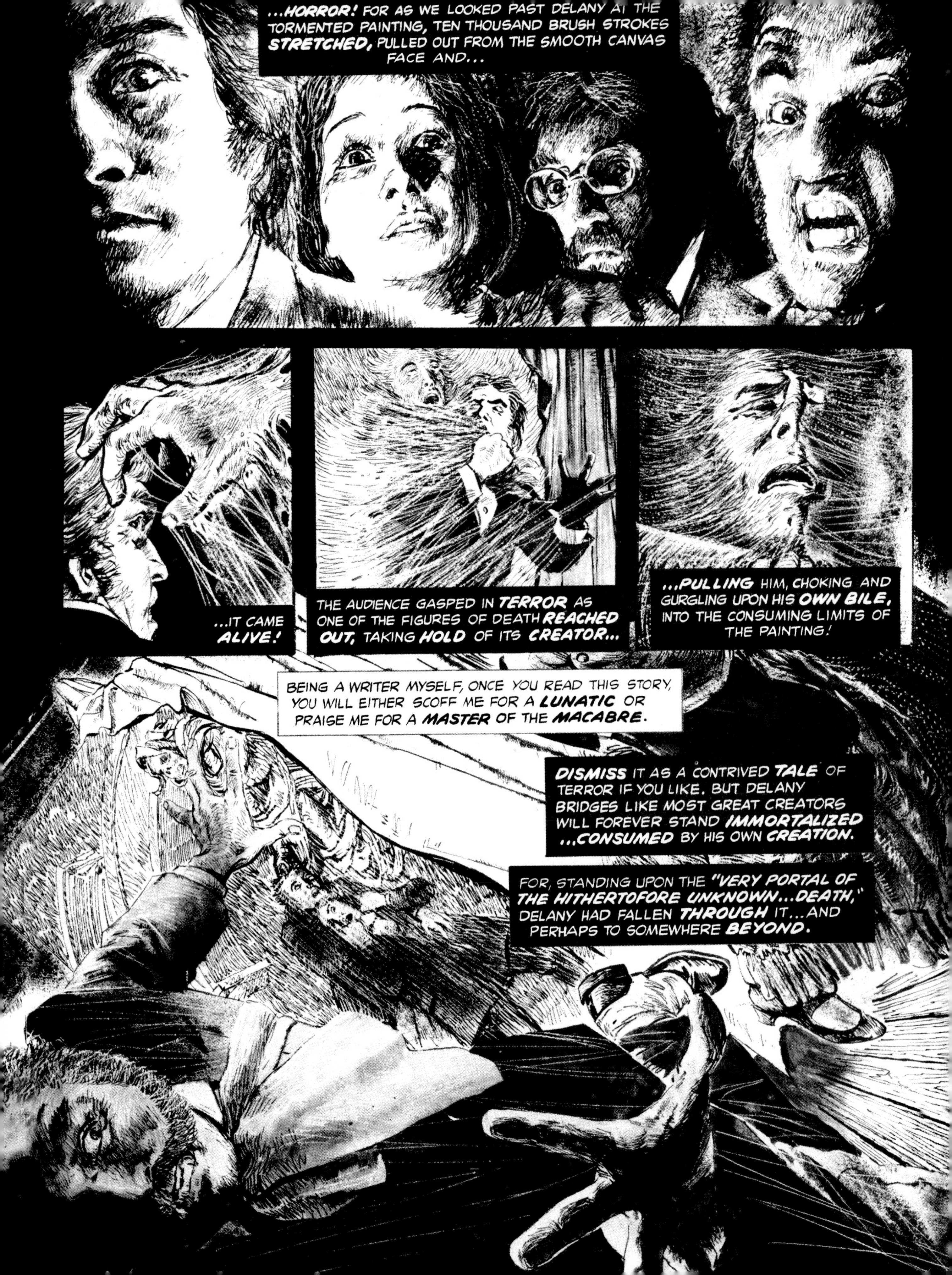
...HORROR! FOR AS WE LOOKED PAST DELANY AT THE TORMENTED PAINTING, TEN THOUSAND BRUSH STROKES STRETCHED, PULLED OUT FROM THE SMOOTH CANVAS FACE AND...
...IT CAME ALIVE!
THE AUDIENCE GASPED IN TERROR AS ONE OF THE FIGURES OF DEATH REACHED OUT, TAKING HOLD OF ITS CREATOR...
...PULLING HIM, CHOKING AND GURGLING UPON HIS OWN BILE, INTO THE CONSUMING LIMITS OF THE PAINTING!
BEING A WRITER MYSELF, ONCE YOU READ THIS STORY, YOU WILL EITHER SCOFF ME FOR A LUNATIC OR PRAISE ME FOR A MASTER OF THE MACABRE.
DISMISS IT AS A CONTRIVED TALE OF TERROR IF YOU LIKE. BUT DELANY BRIDGES LIKE MOST GREAT CREATORS WILL FOREVER STAND IMMORTALIZED ...CONSUMED BY HIS OWN CREATION.
FOR, STANDING UPON THE "VERY PORTAL OF THE HITHERTOFORE UNKNOWN...DEATH," DELANY HAD FALLEN THROUGH IT...AND PERHAPS TO SOMEWHERE BEYOND.

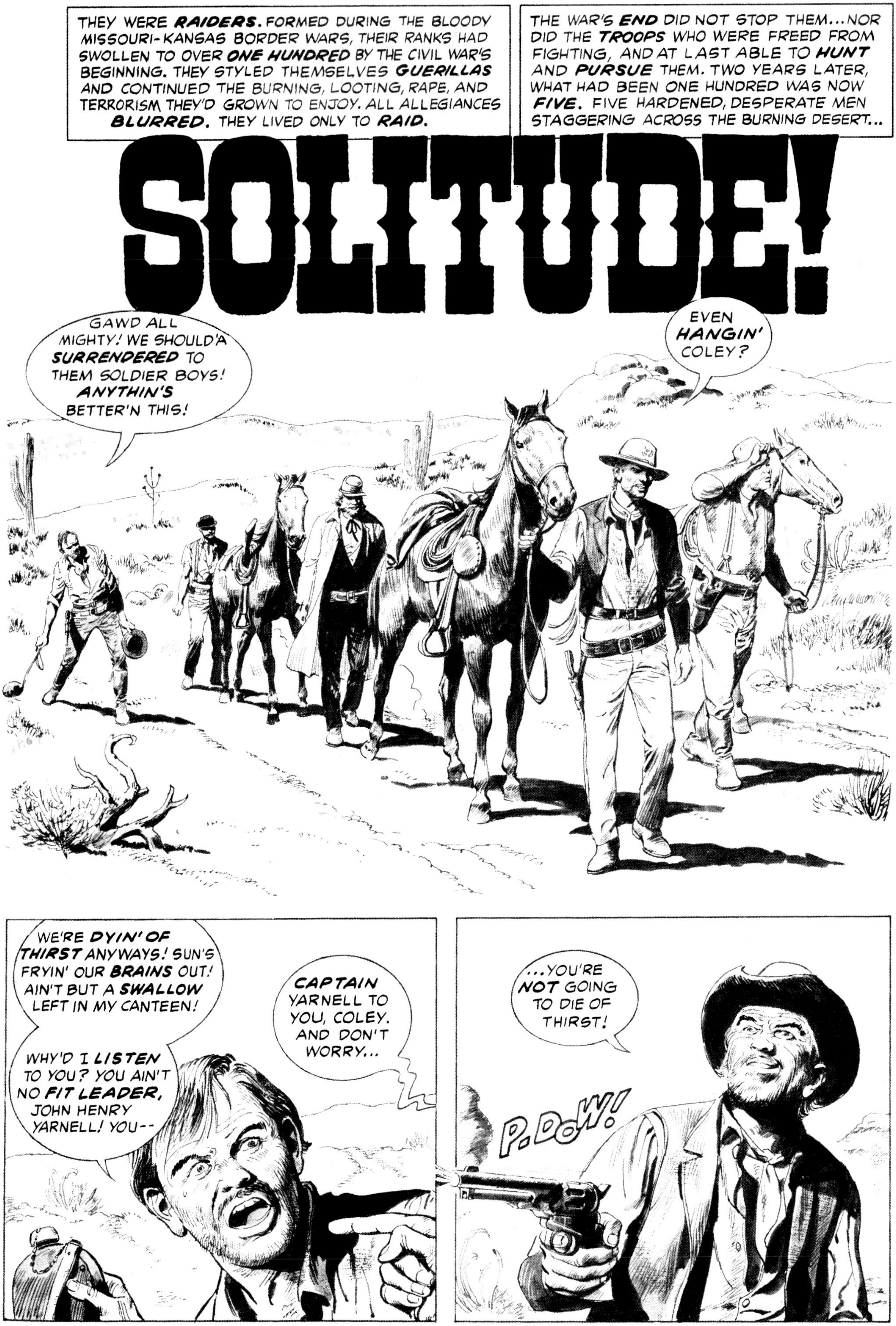
THEY WERE RAIDERS. FORMED DURING THE BLOODY MISSOURI-KANSAS BORDER WARS, THEIR RANKS HAD SWOLLEN TO OVER ONE HUNDRED BY THE CIVIL WAR'S BEGINNING. THEY STYLED THEMSELVES GUERILLAS AND CONTINUED THE BURNING, LOOTING, RAPE, AND TERRORISM THEY'D GROWN TO ENJOY. ALL ALLEGIANCES BLURRED. THEY LIVED ONLY TO RAID.
THE WAR'S END DID NOT STOP THEM... NOR DID THE TROOPS WHO WERE FREED FROM FIGHTING, AND AT LAST ABLE TO HUNT AND PURSUE THEM. TWO YEARS LATER, WHAT HAD BEEN ONE HUNDRED WAS NOW FIVE. FIVE HARDENED, DESPERATE MEN STAGGERING ACROSS THE BURNING DESERT...
SOLITUDE!
GAWD ALL MIGHTY! WE SHOULD'A SURRENDERED TO THEM SOLDIER BOYS! ANYTHIN'S BETTER'N THIS!
EVEN HANGIN' COLEY?
WE'RE DYIN' OF THIRST ANYWAYS! SUN'S FRYIN' OUR BRAINS OUT! AIN'T BUT A SWALLOW LEFT IN MY CANTEEN!
WHY'D I LISTEN TO YOU? YOU AIN'T NO FIT LEADER, JOHN HENRY YARNELL! YOU--
CAPTAIN YARNELL TO YOU, COLEY. AND DON'T WORRY...
...YOU'RE NOT GOING TO DIE OF THIRST!
P-DOW!

STORY: ARCHIE GOODWIN / ART: MARTIN SALVADOR

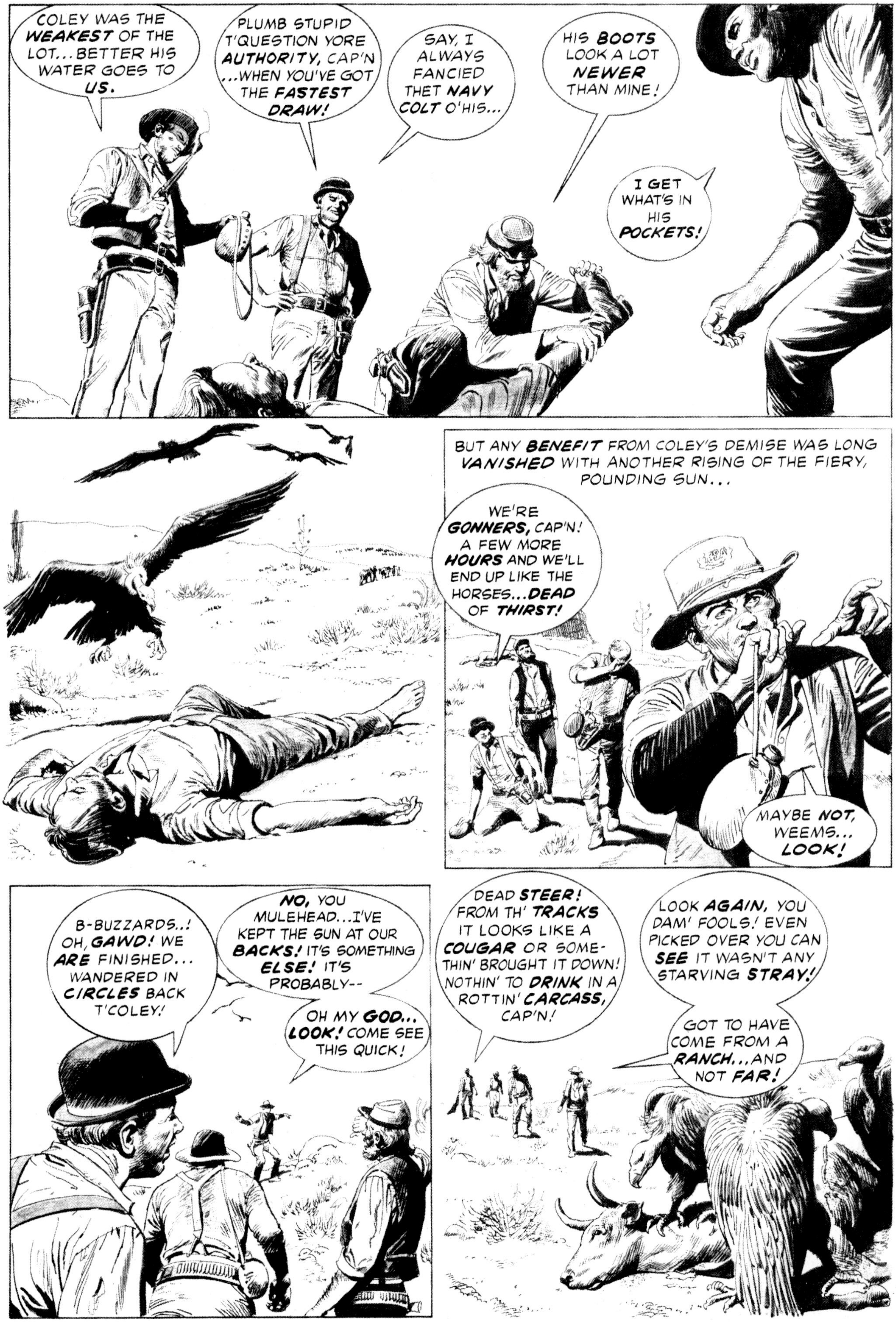
COLEY WAS THE WEAKEST OF THE LOT... BETTER HIS WATER GOES TO US.
PLUMB STUPID T'QUESTION YORE AUTHORITY, CAP'N ...WHEN YOU'VE GOT THE FASTEST DRAW!
SAY, I ALWAYS FANCIED THET NAVY COLT O'HIS...
HIS BOOTS LOOK A LOT NEWER THAN MINE!
I GET WHAT'S IN HIS POCKETS!
BUT ANY BENEFIT FROM COLEY'S DEMISE WAS LONG VANISHED WITH ANOTHER RISING OF THE FIERY, POUNDING SUN...
WE'RE GONNERS, CAP'N! A FEW MORE HOURS AND WE'LL END UP LIKE THE HORSES...DEAD OF THIRST!
MAYBE NOT, WEEMS... LOOK!
B-BUZZARDS..! OH, GAWD! WE ARE FINISHED... WANDERED IN CIRCLES BACK T'COLEY!
NO, YOU MULEHEAD...I'VE KEPT THE SUN AT OUR BACKS! IT'S SOMETHING ELSE! IT'S PROBABLY--
OH MY GOD... LOOK! COME SEE THIS QUICK!
DEAD STEER! FROM TH' TRACKS IT LOOKS LIKE A COUGAR OR SOME-THIN' BROUGHT IT DOWN! NOTHIN' TO DRINK IN A ROTTIN' CARCASS, CAP'N!
LOOK AGAIN, YOU DAM' FOOLS! EVEN PICKED OVER YOU CAN SEE IT WASN'T ANY STARVING STRAY!
GOT TO HAVE COME FROM A RANCH...AND NOT FAR!

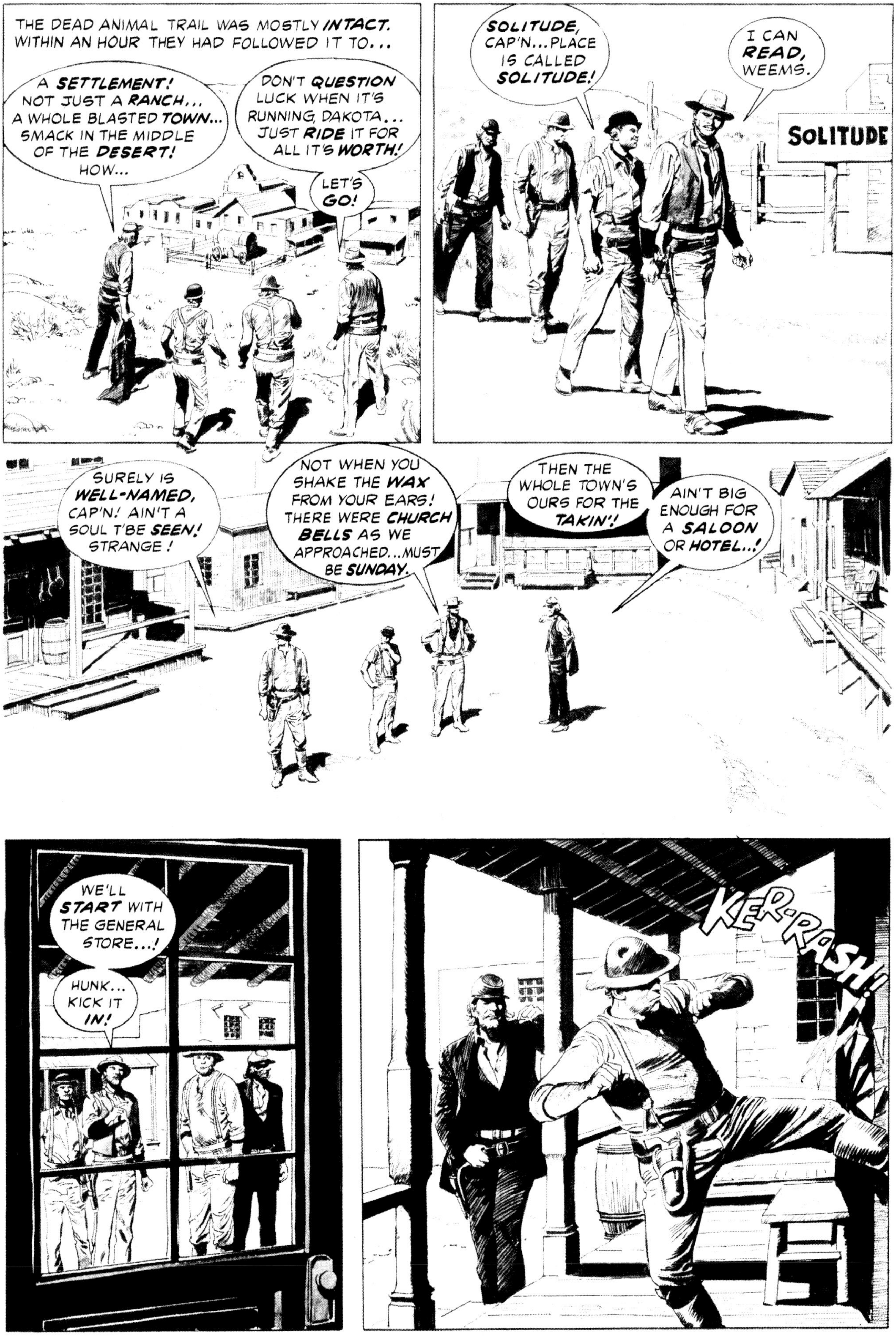
THE DEAD ANIMAL TRAIL WAS MOSTLY INTACT. WITHIN AN HOUR THEY HAD FOLLOWED IT TO...
A SETTLEMENT! NOT JUST A RANCH... A WHOLE BLASTED TOWN... SMACK IN THE MIDDLE OF THE DESERT! HOW...
DON'T QUESTION LUCK WHEN IT'S RUNNING, DAKOTA... JUST RIDE IT FOR ALL IT'S WORTH!
LET'S GO!
SOLITUDE, CAP'N... PLACE IS CALLED SOLITUDE!
I CAN READ, WEEMS.
SOLITUDE
SURELY IS WELL-NAMED, CAP'N! AIN'T A SOUL T'BE SEEN! STRANGE!
NOT WHEN YOU SHAKE THE WAX FROM YOUR EARS! THERE WERE CHURCH BELLS AS WE APPROACHED...MUST BE SUNDAY.
THEN THE WHOLE TOWN'S OURS FOR THE TAKIN'!
AIN'T BIG ENOUGH FOR A SALOON OR HOTEL...!
WE'LL START WITH THE GENERAL STORE...!
HUNK... KICK IT IN!
KER-RASH!

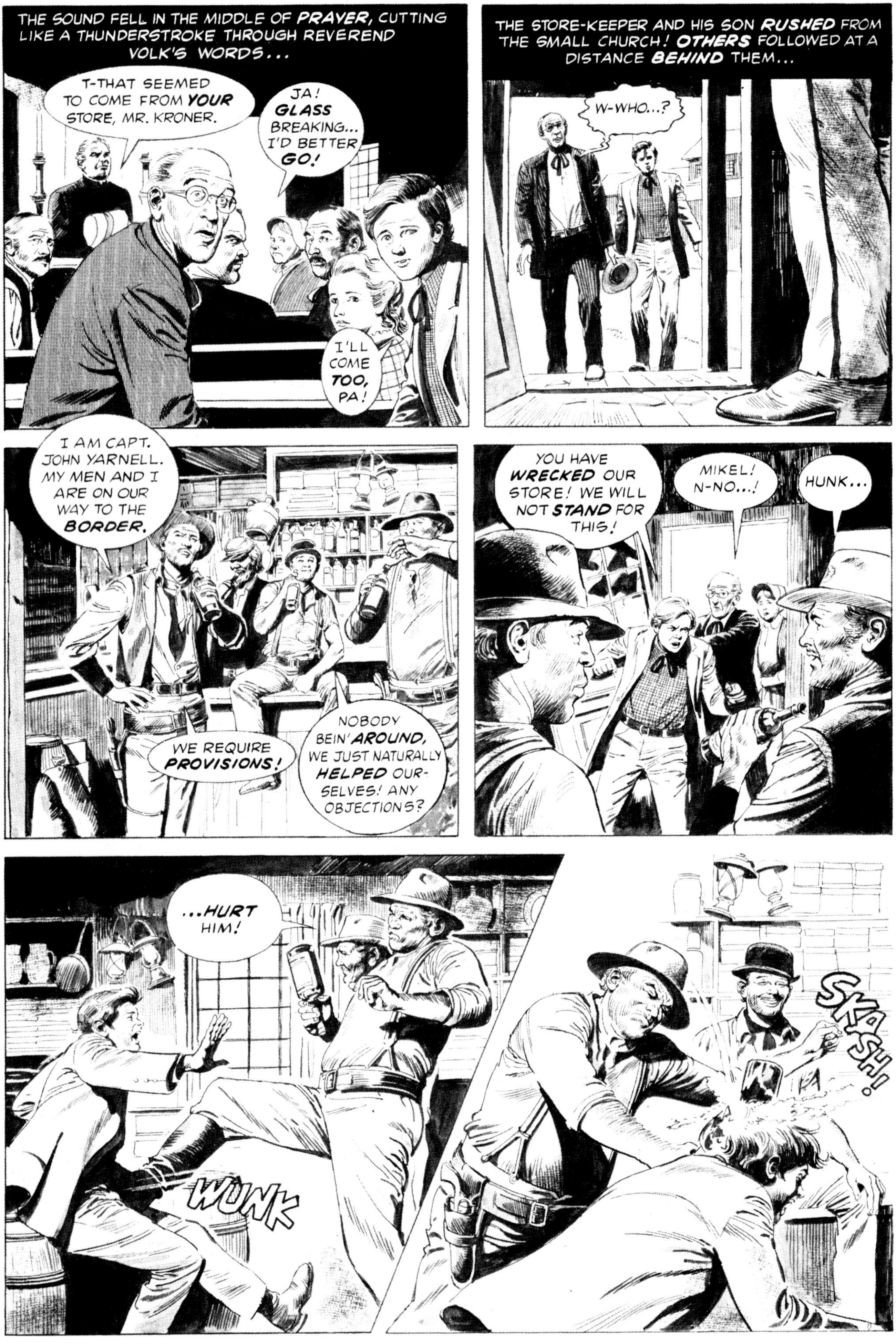

THE SOUND FELL IN THE MIDDLE OF PRAYER, CUTTING LIKE A THUNDERSTROKE THROUGH REVEREND VOLK'S WORDS...
T-THAT SEEMED TO COME FROM YOUR STORE, MR. KRONER.
JA! GLASS BREAKING... I'D BETTER GO!
I'LL COME TOO, PA!
THE STORE-KEEPER AND HIS SON RUSHED FROM THE SMALL CHURCH! OTHERS FOLLOWED AT A DISTANCE BEHIND THEM...
W-WHO...?
I AM CAPT. JOHN YARNELL. MY MEN AND I ARE ON OUR WAY TO THE BORDER.
WE REQUIRE PROVISIONS!
NOBODY BEIN' AROUND, WE JUST NATURALLY HELPED OUR-SELVES! ANY OBJECTIONS?
YOU HAVE WRECKED OUR STORE! WE WILL NOT STAND FOR THIS!
MIKEL! N-NO...!
HUNK...
...HURT HIM!
WUNK
SKASH!

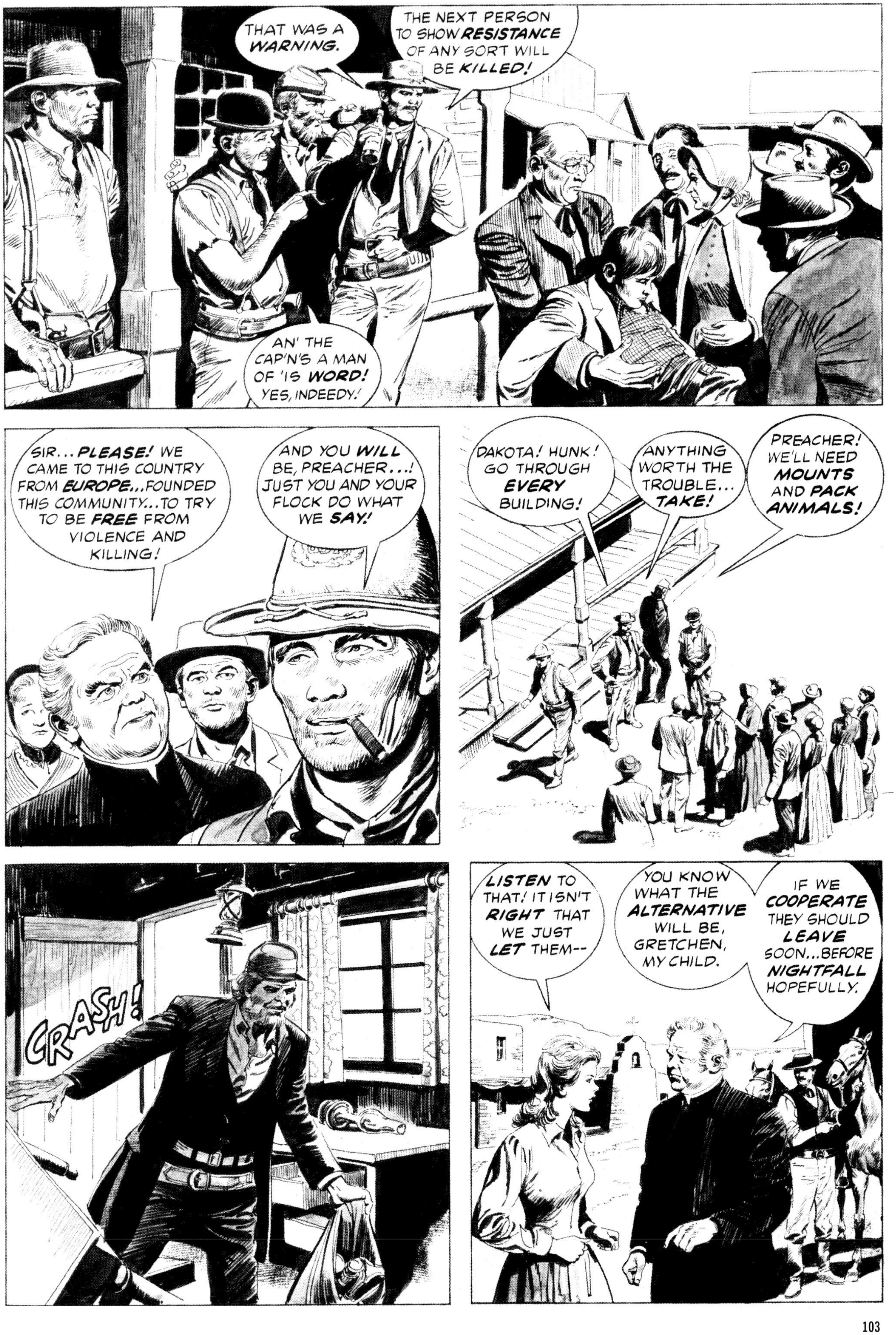

THAT WAS A WARNING.
THE NEXT PERSON TO SHOW RESISTANCE OF ANY SORT WILL BE KILLED!
AN' THE CAP'N'S A MAN OF 'IS WORD! YES, INDEEDY!
SIR... PLEASE! WE CAME TO THIS COUNTRY FROM EUROPE...FOUNDED THIS COMMUNITY...TO TRY TO BE FREE FROM VIOLENCE AND KILLING!
AND YOU WILL BE, PREACHER...! JUST YOU AND YOUR FLOCK DO WHAT WE SAY!
DAKOTA! HUNK! GO THROUGH EVERY BUILDING!
ANYTHING WORTH THE TROUBLE... TAKE!
PREACHER! WE'LL NEED MOUNTS AND PACK ANIMALS!
CRASH!
LISTEN TO THAT! IT ISN'T RIGHT THAT WE JUST LET THEM--
YOU KNOW WHAT THE ALTERNATIVE WILL BE, GRETCHEN, MY CHILD.
IF WE COOPERATE THEY SHOULD LEAVE SOON...BEFORE NIGHTFALL HOPEFULLY.

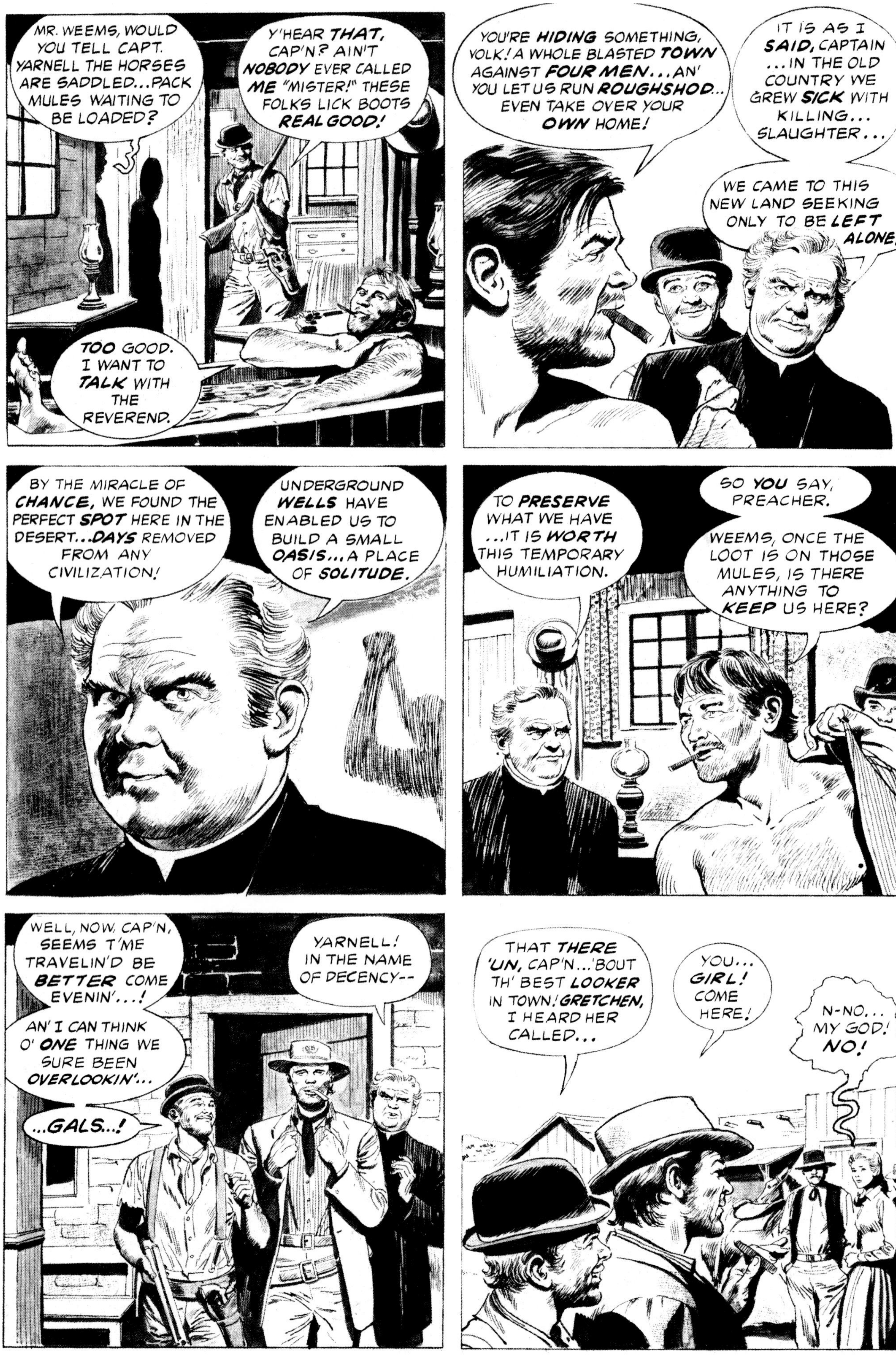
MR. WEEMS, WOULD YOU TELL CAPT. YARNELL THE HORSES ARE SADDLED...PACK MULES WAITING TO BE LOADED?
Y'HEAR THAT, CAP'N? AIN'T NOBODY EVER CALLED ME "MISTER!" THESE FOLKS LICK BOOTS REAL GOOD!
TOO GOOD. I WANT TO TALK WITH THE REVEREND.
YOU'RE HIDING SOMETHING, VOLK! A WHOLE BLASTED TOWN AGAINST FOUR MEN...AN' YOU LET US RUN ROUGHSHOD... EVEN TAKE OVER YOUR OWN HOME!
IT IS AS I SAID, CAPTAIN ...IN THE OLD COUNTRY WE GREW SICK WITH KILLING... SLAUGHTER...
WE CAME TO THIS NEW LAND SEEKING ONLY TO BE LEFT ALONE!
BY THE MIRACLE OF CHANCE, WE FOUND THE PERFECT SPOT HERE IN THE DESERT...DAYS REMOVED FROM ANY CIVILIZATION!
UNDERGROUND WELLS HAVE ENABLED US TO BUILD A SMALL OASIS...A PLACE OF SOLITUDE.
TO PRESERVE WHAT WE HAVE ...IT IS WORTH THIS TEMPORARY HUMILIATION.
SO YOU SAY, PREACHER.
WEEMS, ONCE THE LOOT IS ON THOSE MULES, IS THERE ANYTHING TO KEEP US HERE?
WELL, NOW, CAP'N, SEEMS T'ME TRAVELIN'D BE BETTER COME EVENIN'...!
AN' I CAN THINK O' ONE THING WE SURE BEEN OVERLOOKIN'...
...GALS...!
YARNELL! IN THE NAME OF DECENCY--
THAT THERE 'UN, CAP'N...'BOUT TH' BEST LOOKER IN TOWN! GRETCHEN, I HEARD HER CALLED...
YOU... GIRL! COME HERE!
N-NO... MY GOD! NO!

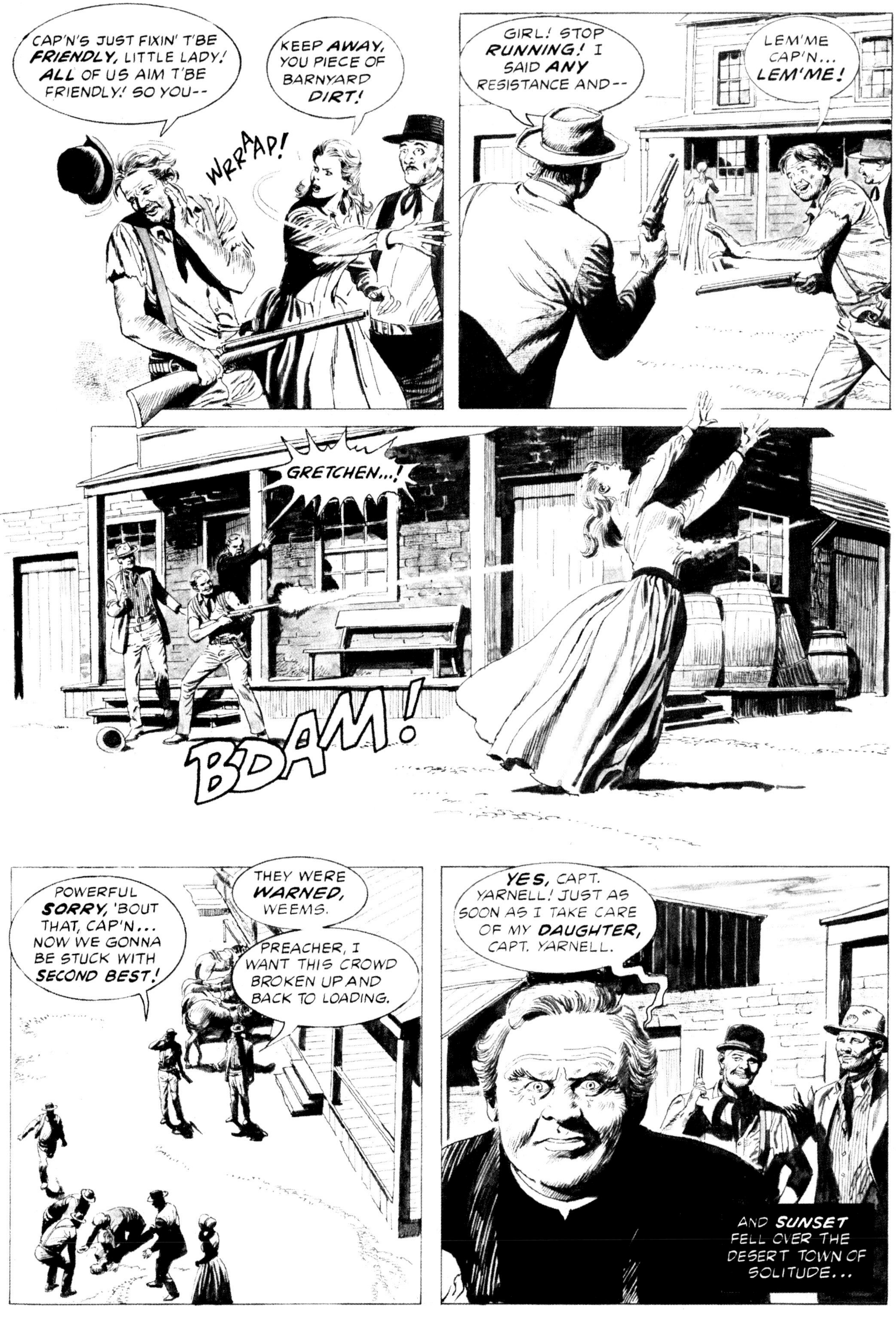
CAP'N'S JUST FIXIN' T'BE FRIENDLY, LITTLE LADY! ALL OF US AIM T'BE FRIENDLY! SO YOU--
KEEP AWAY, YOU PIECE OF BARNYARD DIRT!
WRRAAP!
GIRL! STOP RUNNING! I SAID ANY RESISTANCE AND--
LEM'ME CAP'N... LEM'ME!
GRETCHEN...!
BDAM!
POWERFUL SORRY, 'BOUT THAT, CAP'N... NOW WE GONNA BE STUCK WITH SECOND BEST!
THEY WERE WARNED, WEEMS.
PREACHER, I WANT THIS CROWD BROKEN UP AND BACK TO LOADING.
YES, CAPT. YARNELL! JUST AS SOON AS I TAKE CARE OF MY DAUGHTER, CAPT. YARNELL.
AND SUNSET FELL OVER THE DESERT TOWN OF SOLITUDE...

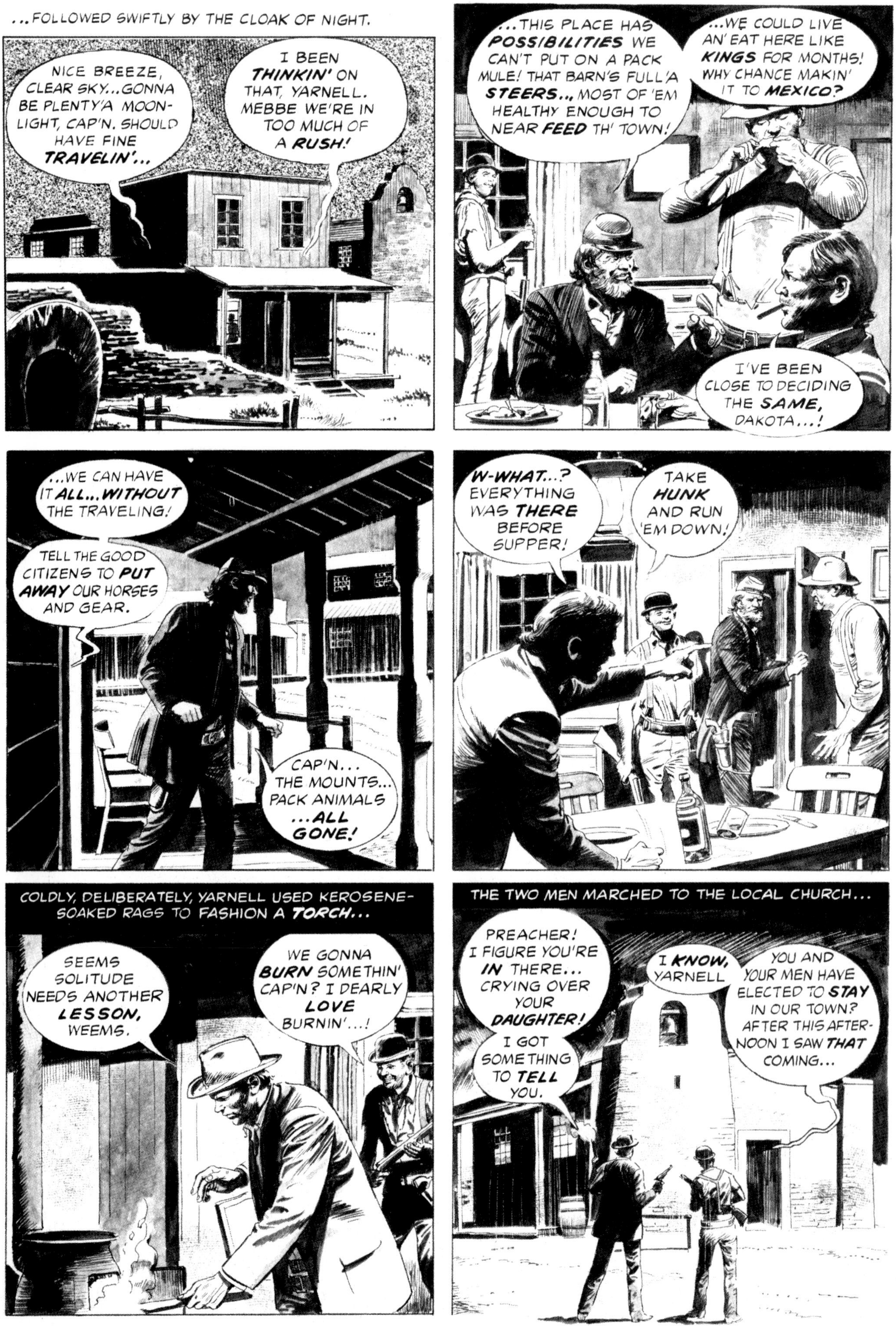
...FOLLOWED SWIFTLY BY THE CLOAK OF NIGHT.
NICE BREEZE, CLEAR SKY...GONNA BE PLENTY'A MOON-LIGHT, CAP'N. SHOULD HAVE FINE TRAVELIN'...
I BEEN THINKIN' ON THAT, YARNELL. MEBBE WE'RE IN TOO MUCH OF A RUSH!
...THIS PLACE HAS POSSIBILITIES WE CAN'T PUT ON A PACK MULE! THAT BARN'S FULL'A STEERS... MOST OF 'EM HEALTHY ENOUGH TO NEAR FEED TH' TOWN!
...WE COULD LIVE AN' EAT HERE LIKE KINGS FOR MONTHS! WHY CHANCE MAKIN' IT TO MEXICO?
I'VE BEEN CLOSE TO DECIDING THE SAME, DAKOTA...!
...WE CAN HAVE IT ALL...WITHOUT THE TRAVELING!
TELL THE GOOD CITIZENS TO PUT AWAY OUR HORSES AND GEAR.
CAP'N... THE MOUNTS... PACK ANIMALS ...ALL GONE!
W-WHAT...? EVERYTHING WAS THERE BEFORE SUPPER!
TAKE HUNK AND RUN 'EM DOWN!
COLDLY, DELIBERATELY, YARNELL USED KEROSENE-SOAKED RAGS TO FASHION A TORCH...
SEEMS SOLITUDE NEEDS ANOTHER LESSON, WEEMS.
WE GONNA BURN SOMETHIN' CAP'N? I DEARLY LOVE BURNIN'...!
THE TWO MEN MARCHED TO THE LOCAL CHURCH...
PREACHER! I FIGURE YOU'RE IN THERE... CRYING OVER YOUR DAUGHTER!
I GOT SOMETHING TO TELL YOU.
I KNOW, YARNELL
YOU AND YOUR MEN HAVE ELECTED TO STAY IN OUR TOWN? AFTER THIS AFTERNOON I SAW THAT COMING...

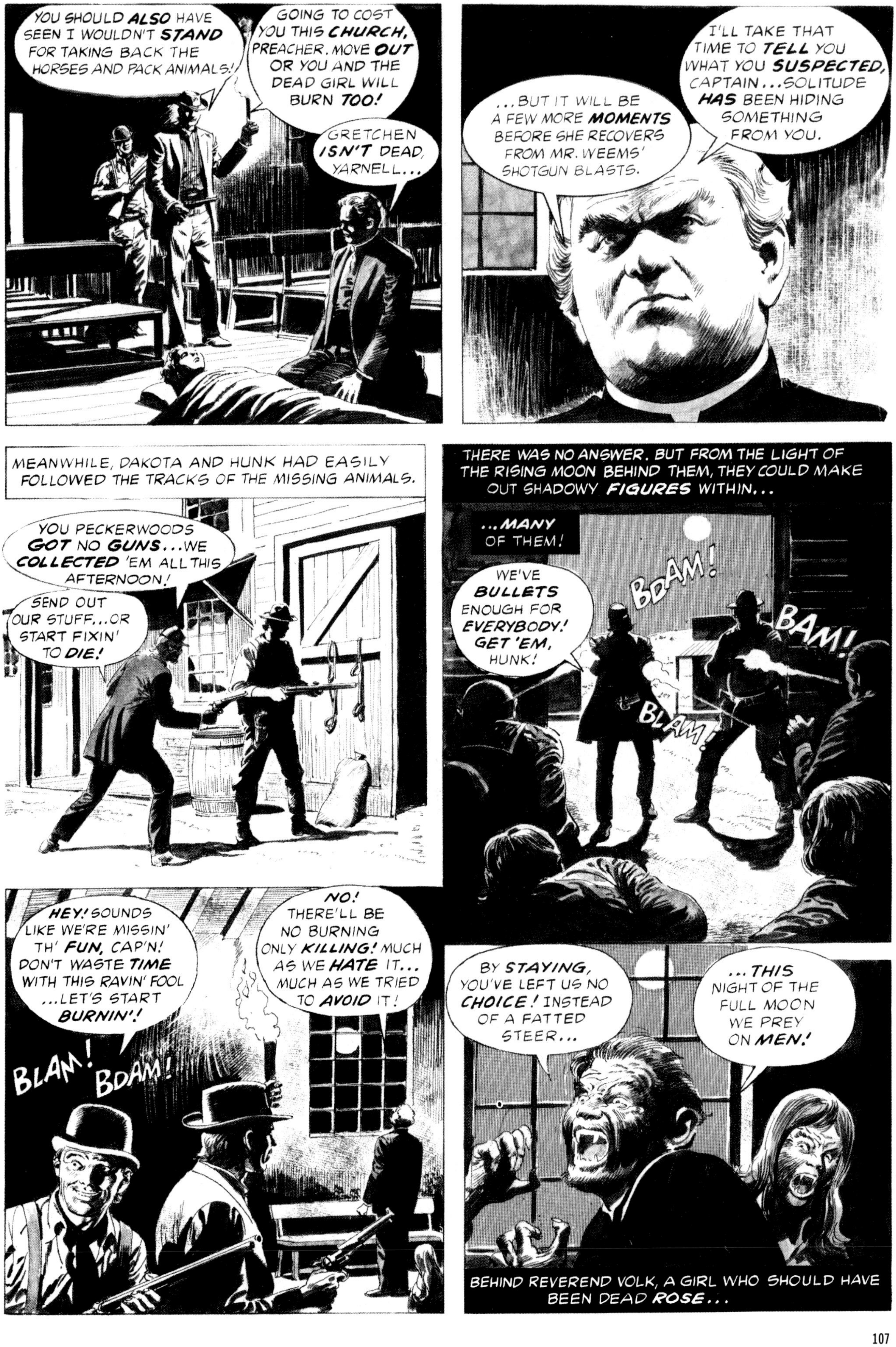
YOU SHOULD ALSO HAVE SEEN I WOULDN'T STAND FOR TAKING BACK THE HORSES AND PACK ANIMALS!
GOING TO COST YOU THIS CHURCH, PREACHER. MOVE OUT OR YOU AND THE DEAD GIRL WILL BURN TOO!
GRETCHEN ISN'T DEAD, YARNELL...
...BUT IT WILL BE A FEW MORE MOMENTS BEFORE SHE RECOVERS FROM MR. WEEMS' SHOTGUN BLASTS.
I'LL TAKE THAT TIME TO TELL YOU WHAT YOU SUSPECTED, CAPTAIN...SOLITUDE HAS BEEN HIDING SOMETHING FROM YOU.
MEANWHILE, DAKOTA AND HUNK HAD EASILY FOLLOWED THE TRACKS OF THE MISSING ANIMALS.
YOU PECKERWOODS GOT NO GUNS...WE COLLECTED 'EM ALL THIS AFTERNOON!
SEND OUT OUR STUFF...OR START FIXIN' TO DIE!
THERE WAS NO ANSWER. BUT FROM THE LIGHT OF THE RISING MOON BEHIND THEM, THEY COULD MAKE OUT SHADOWY FIGURES WITHIN...
...MANY OF THEM!
WE'VE BULLETS ENOUGH FOR EVERYBODY! GET 'EM, HUNK!
BDAM!
BAM!
BLAM!
HEY! SOUNDS LIKE WE'RE MISSIN' TH' FUN, CAP'N! DON'T WASTE TIME WITH THIS RAVIN' FOOL ...LET'S START BURNIN'!
NO! THERE'LL BE NO BURNING ONLY KILLING! MUCH AS WE HATE IT... MUCH AS WE TRIED TO AVOID IT!
BLAM! BDAM!
BY STAYING, YOU'VE LEFT US NO CHOICE! INSTEAD OF A FATTED STEER...
...THIS NIGHT OF THE FULL MOON WE PREY ON MEN!
BEHIND REVEREND VOLK, A GIRL WHO SHOULD HAVE BEEN DEAD ROSE...

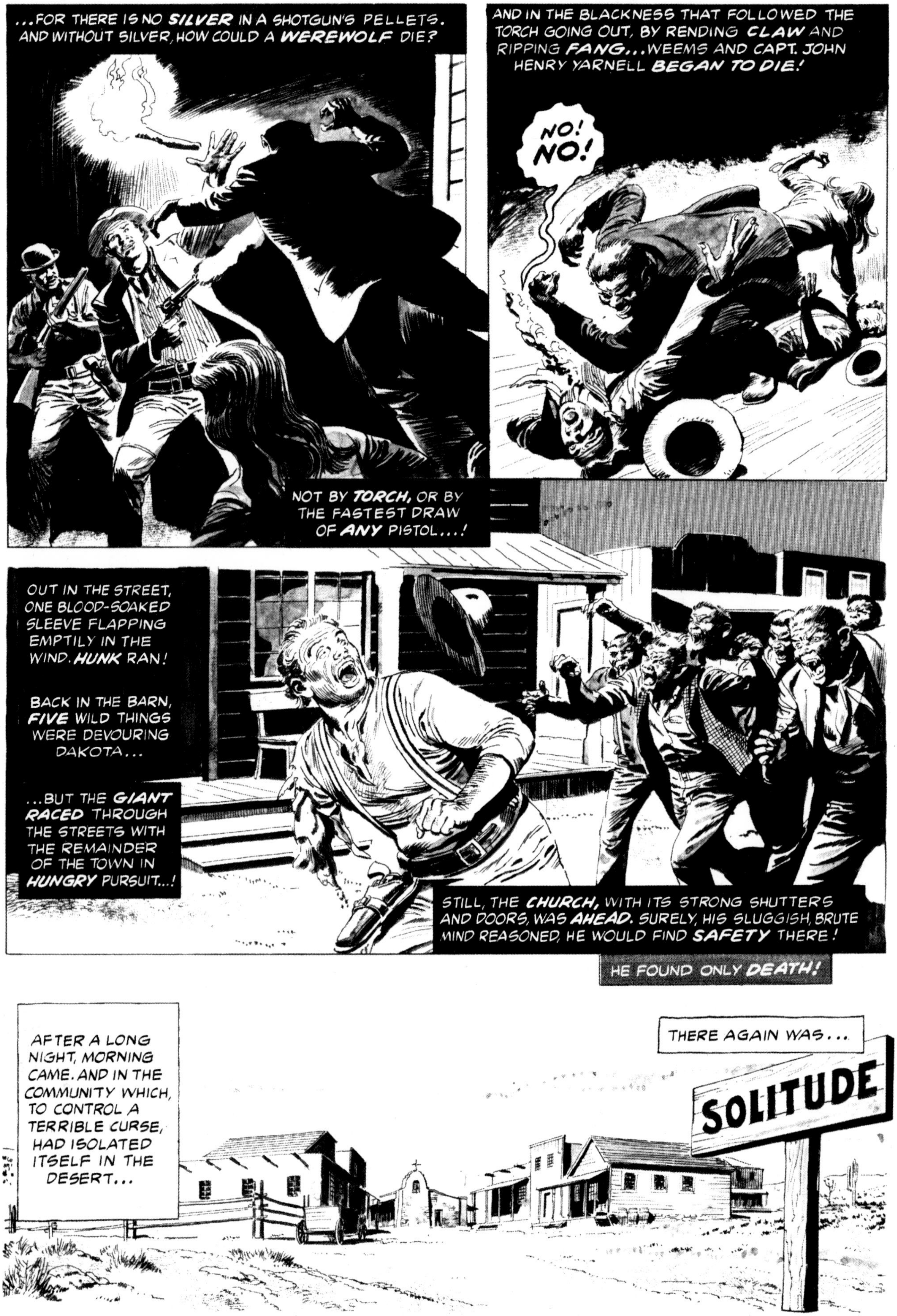

...FOR THERE IS NO SILVER IN A SHOTGUN'S PELLETS. AND WITHOUT SILVER, HOW COULD A WEREWOLF DIE?
NOT BY TORCH, OR BY THE FASTEST DRAW OF ANY PISTOL...!
AND IN THE BLACKNESS THAT FOLLOWED THE TORCH GOING OUT, BY RENDING CLAW AND RIPPING FANG...WEEMS AND CAPT. JOHN HENRY YARNELL BEGAN TO DIE!
NO! NO!
OUT IN THE STREET, ONE BLOOD-SOAKED SLEEVE FLAPPING EMPTILY IN THE WIND. HUNK RAN!
BACK IN THE BARN, FIVE WILD THINGS WERE DEVOURING DAKOTA...
...BUT THE GIANT RACED THROUGH THE STREETS WITH THE REMAINDER OF THE TOWN IN HUNGRY PURSUIT...!
STILL, THE CHURCH, WITH ITS STRONG SHUTTERS AND DOORS, WAS AHEAD. SURELY, HIS SLUGGISH, BRUTE MIND REASONED, HE WOULD FIND SAFETY THERE!
HE FOUND ONLY DEATH!
AFTER A LONG NIGHT, MORNING CAME. AND IN THE COMMUNITY WHICH, TO CONTROL A TERRIBLE CURSE, HAD ISOLATED ITSELF IN THE DESERT...
THERE AGAIN WAS...
SOLITUDE

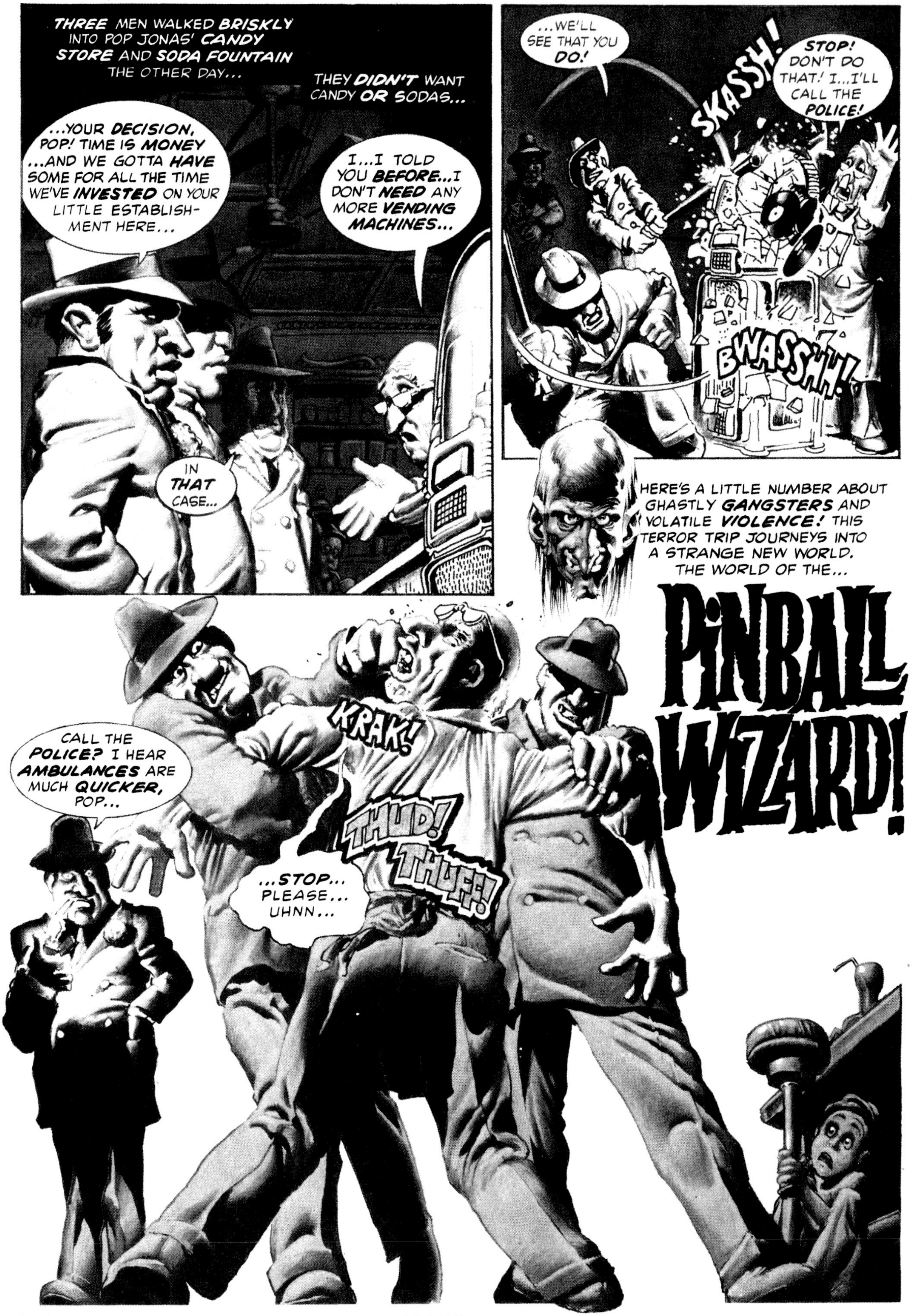
THREE MEN WALKED BRISKLY INTO POP JONAS' CANDY STORE AND SODA FOUNTAIN THE OTHER DAY...
THEY DIDN'T WANT CANDY OR SODAS...
...YOUR DECISION, POP! TIME IS MONEY ...AND WE GOTTA HAVE SOME FOR ALL THE TIME WE'VE INVESTED ON YOUR LITTLE ESTABLISHMENT HERE...
I...I TOLD YOU BEFORE...I DON'T NEED ANY MORE VENDING MACHINES...
IN THAT CASE...
...WE'LL SEE THAT YOU DO!
SKASSH!
STOP! DON'T DO THAT! I...I'LL CALL THE POLICE!
BWASSHH!
HERE'S A LITTLE NUMBER ABOUT GHASTLY GANGSTERS AND VOLATILE VIOLENCE! THIS TERROR TRIP JOURNEYS INTO A STRANGE NEW WORLD. THE WORLD OF THE...
PINBALL WIZARD!
KRAK!
CALL THE POLICE? I HEAR AMBULANCES ARE MUCH QUICKER, POP...
THUD!
THUFF!
...STOP... PLEASE... UHNN...

STORY: DOUG MOENCH / ART: RICHARD CORBEN

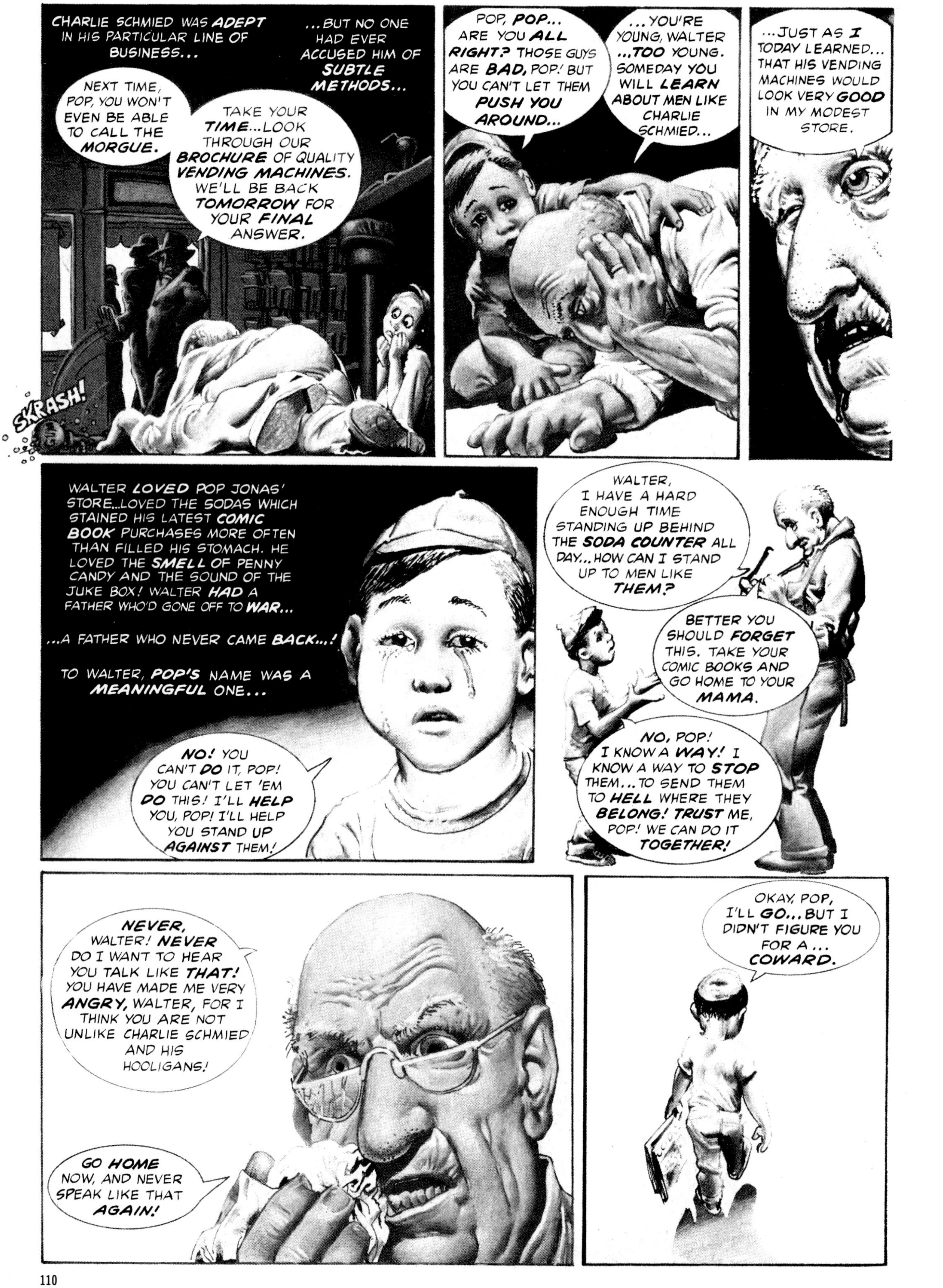
CHARLIE SCHMIED WAS ADEPT IN HIS PARTICULAR LINE OF BUSINESS...
...BUT NO ONE HAD EVER ACCUSED HIM OF SUBTLE METHODS...
NEXT TIME, POP, YOU WON'T EVEN BE ABLE TO CALL THE MORGUE.
TAKE YOUR TIME...LOOK THROUGH OUR BROCHURE OF QUALITY VENDING MACHINES. WE'LL BE BACK TOMORROW FOR YOUR FINAL ANSWER.
SKRASH!
POP, POP... ARE YOU ALL RIGHT? THOSE GUYS ARE BAD, POP! BUT YOU CAN'T LET THEM PUSH YOU AROUND...
...YOU'RE YOUNG, WALTER ...TOO YOUNG. SOMEDAY YOU WILL LEARN ABOUT MEN LIKE CHARLIE SCHMIED...
...JUST AS I TODAY LEARNED... THAT HIS VENDING MACHINES WOULD LOOK VERY GOOD IN MY MODEST STORE.
WALTER LOVED POP JONAS' STORE...LOVED THE SODAS WHICH STAINED HIS LATEST COMIC BOOK PURCHASES MORE OFTEN THAN FILLED HIS STOMACH. HE LOVED THE SMELL OF PENNY CANDY AND THE SOUND OF THE JUKE BOX! WALTER HAD A FATHER WHO'D GONE OFF TO WAR...
...A FATHER WHO NEVER CAME BACK...!
TO WALTER, POP'S NAME WAS A MEANINGFUL ONE...
NO! YOU CAN'T DO IT, POP! YOU CAN'T LET 'EM DO THIS! I'LL HELP YOU, POP! I'LL HELP YOU STAND UP AGAINST THEM!
WALTER, I HAVE A HARD ENOUGH TIME STANDING UP BEHIND THE SODA COUNTER ALL DAY...HOW CAN I STAND UP TO MEN LIKE THEM?
BETTER YOU SHOULD FORGET THIS. TAKE YOUR COMIC BOOKS AND GO HOME TO YOUR MAMA.
NO, POP! I KNOW A WAY! I KNOW A WAY TO STOP THEM...TO SEND THEM TO HELL WHERE THEY BELONG! TRUST ME, POP! WE CAN DO IT TOGETHER!
NEVER, WALTER! NEVER DO I WANT TO HEAR YOU TALK LIKE THAT! YOU HAVE MADE ME VERY ANGRY, WALTER, FOR I THINK YOU ARE NOT UNLIKE CHARLIE SCHMIED AND HIS HOOLIGANS!
GO HOME NOW, AND NEVER SPEAK LIKE THAT AGAIN!
OKAY, POP, I'LL GO...BUT I DIDN'T FIGURE YOU FOR A ... COWARD.

CHARLIE SCHMIED IS AN *ENERGETIC* MAN, AND BEGINS EACH NEW DAY AS IF IT WERE HIS *FIRST* ON A NEW JOB...! HE DEALS IN *MERCHANDISE*, NOT IN *SCRUPLES*...

LOTTA *PIN-BALL MACHINES* HERE TO PEDDLE...AND I KNOW *JUST* THE MAN *RIPE* FOR A SALE...

ALWAYS *SAID* A PINBALL MACHINE'D LOOK REAL *NICE* IN *POP JONAS'* STORE... *REAL NICE.*

SUCH A *MESS* THOSE CRIMINALS MADE LAST NIGHT! I AM AN *HONEST* MAN. I DO NOT *DESERVE* SUCH TREATMENT...AND I DO *NOT* DESERVE TO BE THOUGHT OF AS A *COWARD* BY WALTER!

WALTER IS SO *YOUNG*... HE LOOKS *UP* TO ME, CONSIDERS ME HIS *IDEAL.* I *MUST* BE A GOOD EXAMPLE TO HIM... I *MUST!*

I WILL *REFUSE* THEIR VENDING MACHINES...

MORNING, POP. LOOK OVER OUR *BROCHURE?* WE GOT A NICE *NEW* MODEL FOR YA...A *PINBALL MACHINE.*

I DON'T *NEED* ANY PROTECTION! THE *POLICE* WILL PROTECT ME! AND FOR THE *LAST TIME,* I DON'T NEED ANY OF YOUR *PINBALL MACHINES!*

NOW *GET OUT* OF HERE!

REFUSING US WON'T *LOOK GOOD,* POP. OUR *OTHER* CUSTOMERS MIGHT GET THE IDEA THAT *THEY* CAN REFUSE US TOO. SINCE YOU HAVEN'T *LEARNED,* POP...WE'RE GONNA HAVE TO MAKE AN *EXAMPLE* OF YOU FOR THE *OTHERS*...

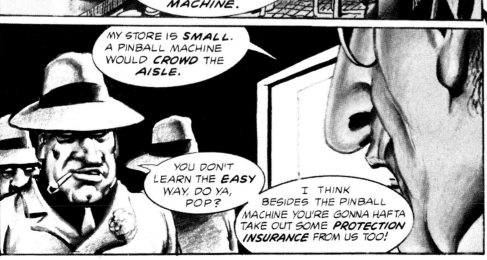

MY STORE IS *SMALL.* A PINBALL MACHINE WOULD *CROWD* THE AISLE.

YOU DON'T LEARN THE *EASY* WAY, DO YA, POP?

I THINK BESIDES THE PINBALL MACHINE YOU'RE GONNA HAFTA TAKE OUT SOME *PROTECTION INSURANCE* FROM US TOO!

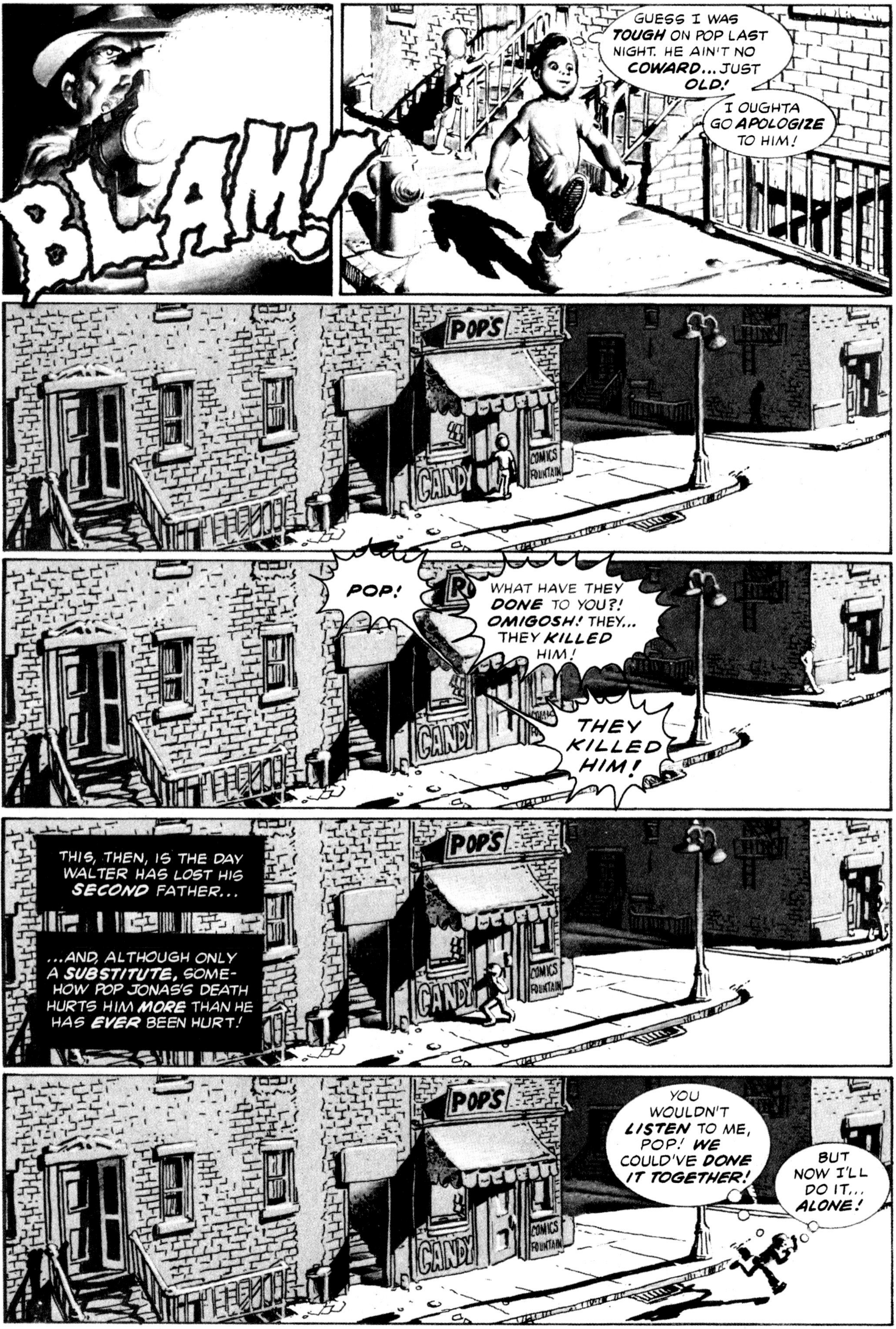
BLAM!
GUESS I WAS TOUGH ON POP LAST NIGHT. HE AIN'T NO COWARD... JUST OLD!
I OUGHTA GO APOLOGIZE TO HIM!
POP'S
CANDY
COMICS FOUNTAIN
POP!
WHAT HAVE THEY DONE TO YOU?! OMIGOSH! THEY... THEY KILLED HIM!
THEY KILLED HIM!
THIS, THEN, IS THE DAY WALTER HAS LOST HIS SECOND FATHER...
...AND, ALTHOUGH ONLY A SUBSTITUTE, SOMEHOW POP JONAS'S DEATH HURTS HIM MORE THAN HE HAS EVER BEEN HURT!
POP'S
YOU WOULDN'T LISTEN TO ME, POP! WE COULD'VE DONE IT TOGETHER!
BUT NOW I'LL DO IT... ALONE!

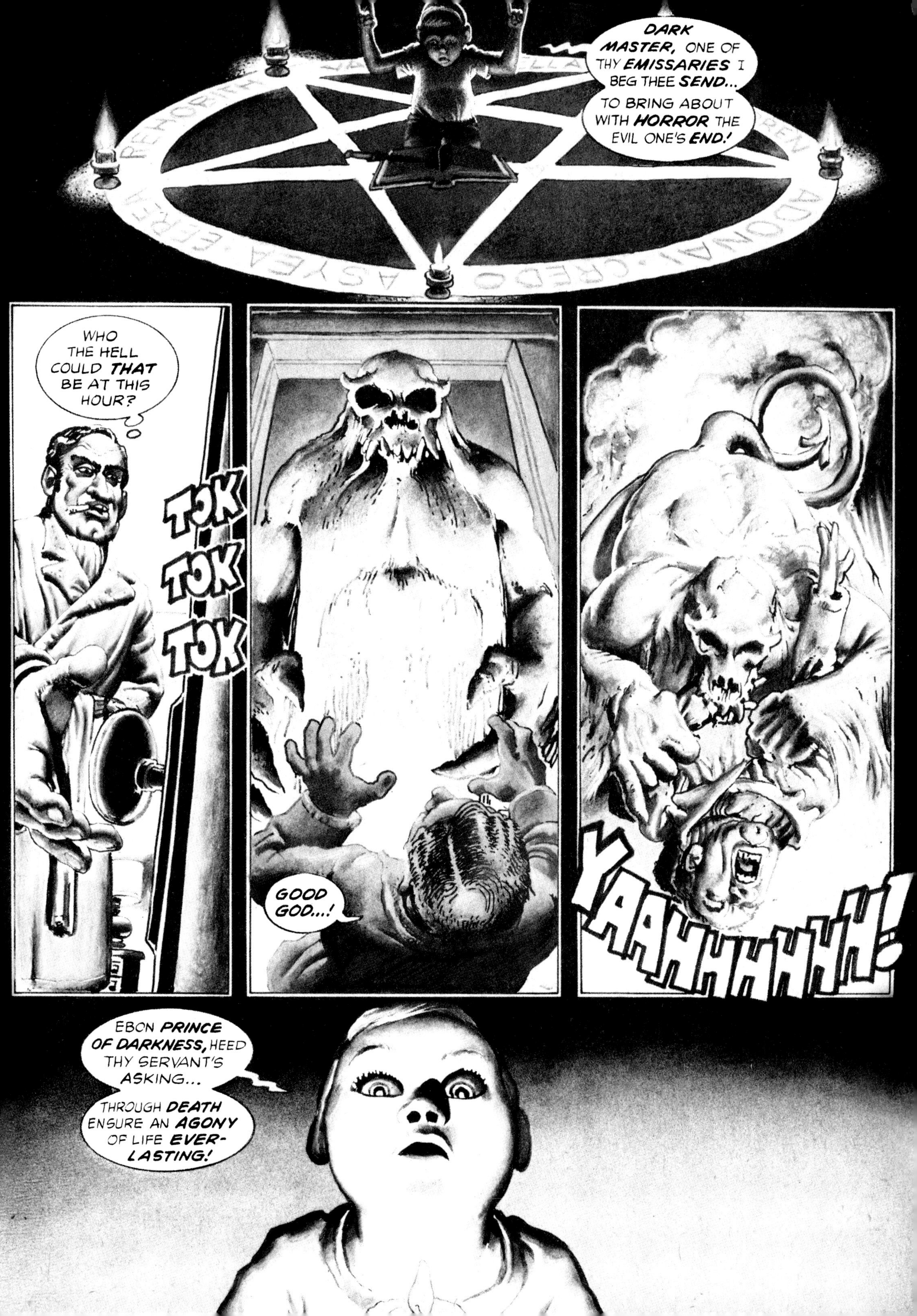
DARK MASTER, ONE OF THY EMISSARIES I BEG THEE SEND...
TO BRING ABOUT WITH HORROR THE EVIL ONE'S END!
WHO THE HELL COULD THAT BE AT THIS HOUR?
TOK
TOK
TOK
GOOD GOD...!
YAAHHHHHH!
EBON PRINCE OF DARKNESS, HEED THY SERVANT'S ASKING...
THROUGH DEATH ENSURE AN AGONY OF LIFE EVER-LASTING!

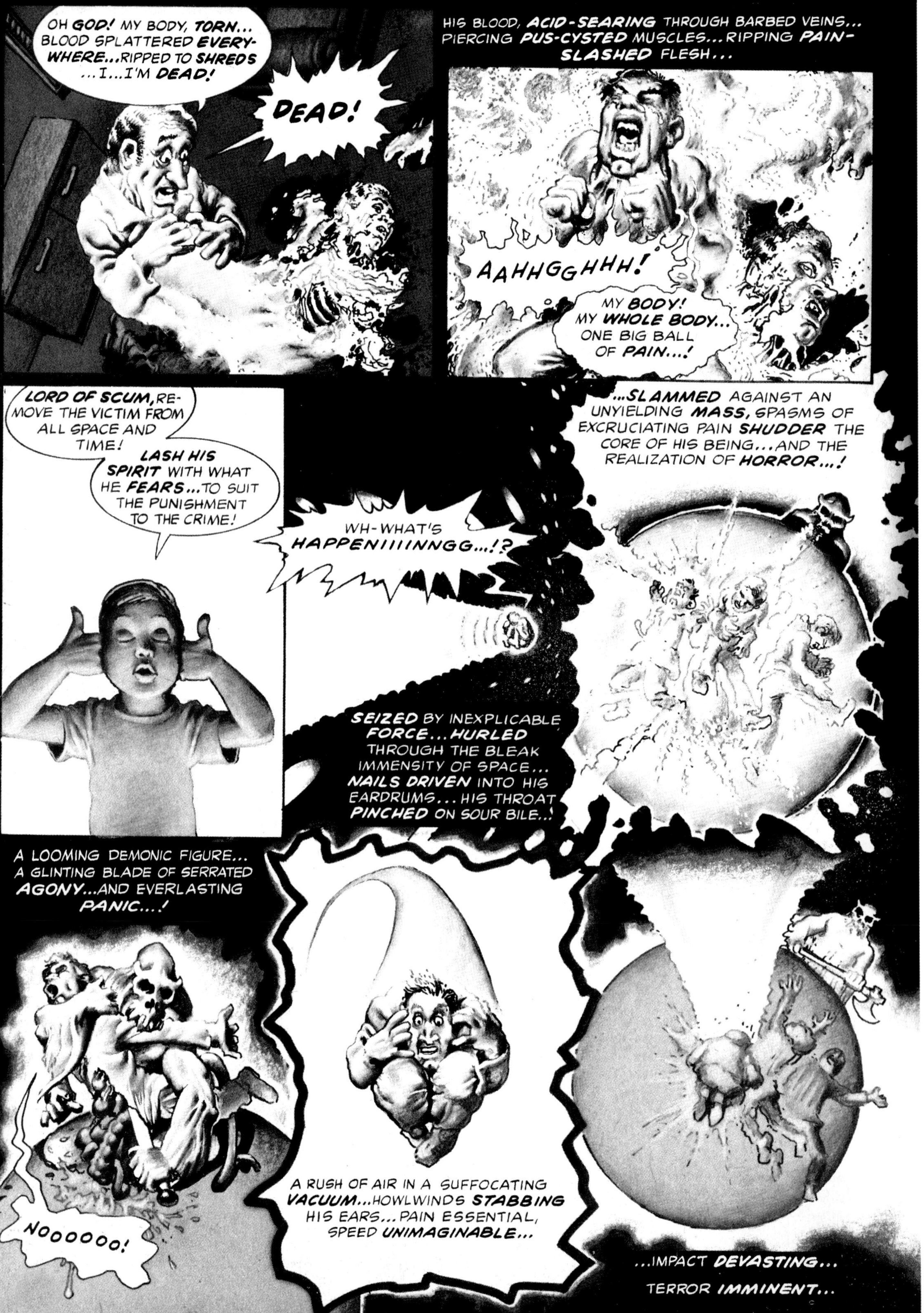
OH GOD! MY BODY, TORN... BLOOD SPLATTERED EVERY-WHERE...RIPPED TO SHREDS ...I...I'M DEAD!
DEAD!
HIS BLOOD, ACID-SEARING THROUGH BARBED VEINS... PIERCING PUS-CYSTED MUSCLES...RIPPING PAIN-SLASHED FLESH...
AAHHGGHHH!
MY BODY! MY WHOLE BODY... ONE BIG BALL OF PAIN...!
LORD OF SCUM, RE-MOVE THE VICTIM FROM ALL SPACE AND TIME!
LASH HIS SPIRIT WITH WHAT HE FEARS...TO SUIT THE PUNISHMENT TO THE CRIME!
WH-WHAT'S HAPPENIIIINNGG...!?
SEIZED BY INEXPLICABLE FORCE...HURLED THROUGH THE BLEAK IMMENSITY OF SPACE... NAILS DRIVEN INTO HIS EARDRUMS... HIS THROAT PINCHED ON SOUR BILE...!
...SLAMMED AGAINST AN UNYIELDING MASS, SPASMS OF EXCRUCIATING PAIN SHUDDER THE CORE OF HIS BEING...AND THE REALIZATION OF HORROR...!
A LOOMING DEMONIC FIGURE... A GLINTING BLADE OF SERRATED AGONY...AND EVERLASTING PANIC...!
NOOOOOOO!
A RUSH OF AIR IN A SUFFOCATING VACUUM...HOWLWINDS STABBING HIS EARS...PAIN ESSENTIAL, SPEED UNIMAGINABLE...
...IMPACT DEVASTING...
TERROR IMMINENT...

...INEXORABLE...

...ALL-CONSUMING!

HURTLING *AGAIN*, WITH EVER-INCESSANT *PAIN*... HURTLING THROUGH EMPTINESS ON A COLLISION COURSE WITH UNMITIGATED *HORROR*...

...IN THE FORM OF MANY FLASHING FANGED SCRABBLING DEMON-*GHOULS* WITH SHARP *SHARP* TALONS...RAKING *FIRE* AND *SIZZLING* FLESH...

AND SO IT GOES... ...THROUGH AN *INFINITY* OF *TORTURE*... SUFFERING *DEATH* COMPOUNDED AND TRANSCENDED BY EACH *SUCCESSIVE* DEATH...!

A *TOTAL* PERPETUAL *PUNISHMENT* GEARED TO *SUIT THE CRIME*...

...INITIATED BY A GRIEF-STRICKEN, *VENGEANCE-BENT LITTLE BOY*... DABBLING IN THE *DARKLING ARTS*...

A LITTLE BOY, WHO IN HIS OWN STRANGE WAY, HAS DEALT OUT AN ODD FORM OF *JUSTICE!*

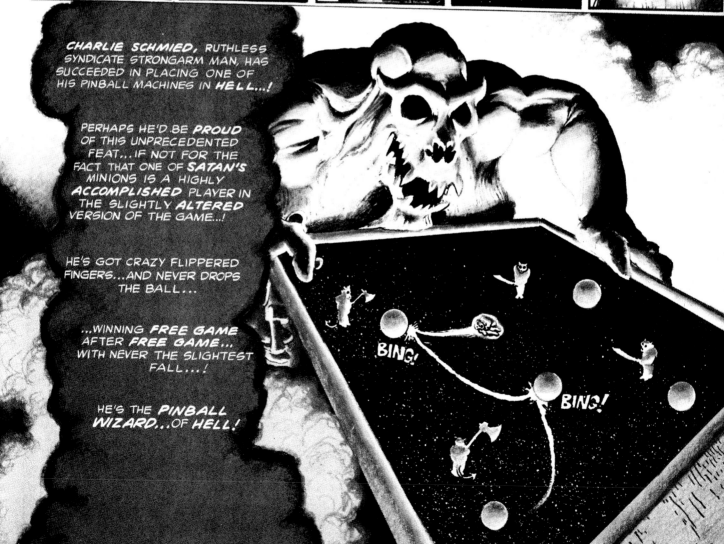

CHARLIE SCHMIED, RUTHLESS SYNDICATE STRONGARM MAN, HAS SUCCEEDED IN PLACING ONE OF HIS PINBALL MACHINES IN *HELL*...!

PERHAPS HE'D BE *PROUD* OF THIS UNPRECEDENTED FEAT...IF NOT FOR THE FACT THAT ONE OF *SATAN'S* MINIONS IS A HIGHLY *ACCOMPLISHED* PLAYER IN THE SLIGHTLY *ALTERED* VERSION OF THE GAME...!

HE'S GOT CRAZY FLIPPERED FINGERS...AND NEVER DROPS THE BALL...

...WINNING *FREE GAME* AFTER *FREE GAME*... WITH NEVER THE SLIGHTEST FALL...!

HE'S THE *PINBALL WIZARD*...OF HELL!

BING!

BING!

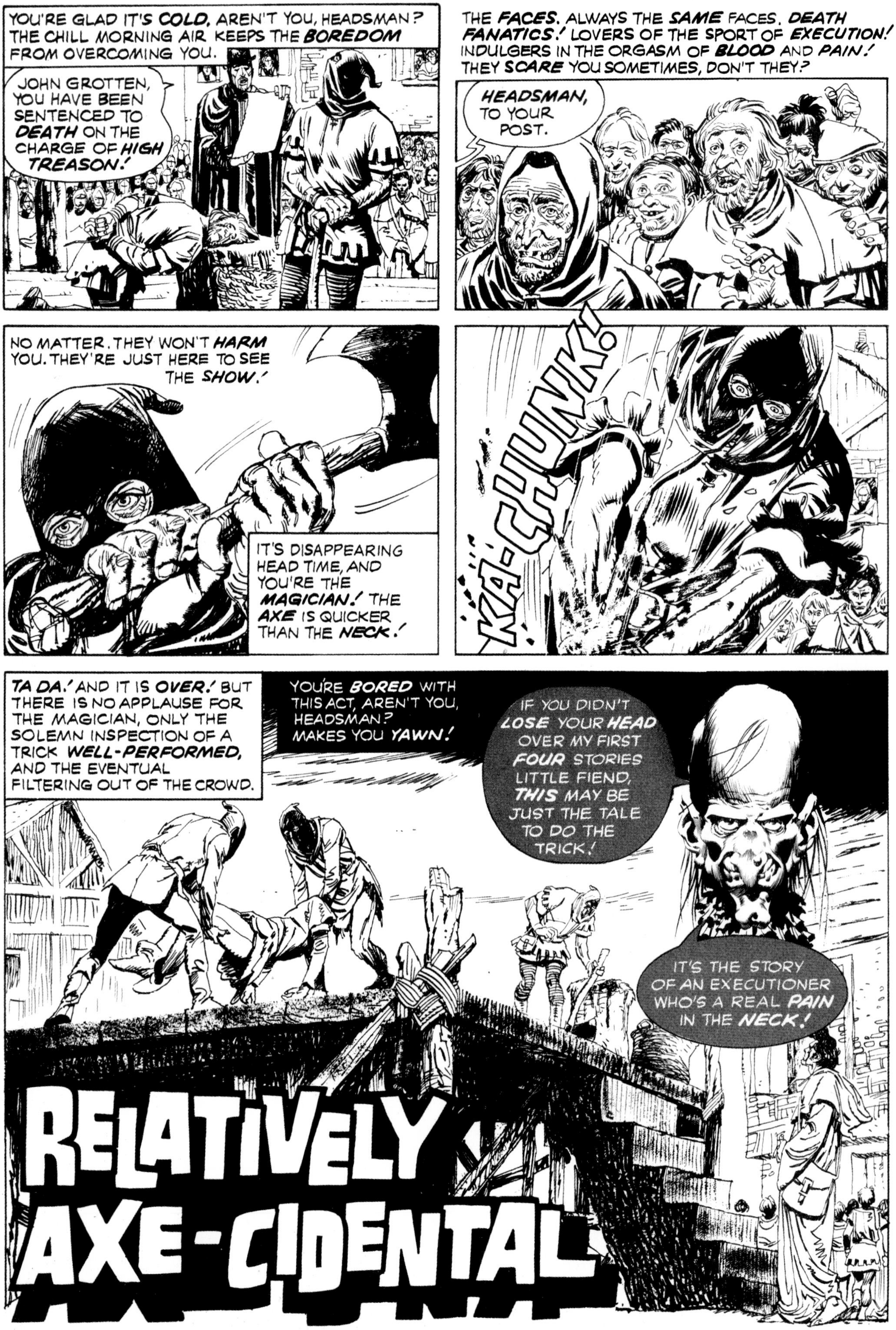
YOU'RE GLAD IT'S COLD, AREN'T YOU, HEADSMAN? THE CHILL MORNING AIR KEEPS THE BOREDOM FROM OVERCOMING YOU.
JOHN GROTTEN, YOU HAVE BEEN SENTENCED TO DEATH ON THE CHARGE OF HIGH TREASON!
THE FACES. ALWAYS THE SAME FACES. DEATH FANATICS! LOVERS OF THE SPORT OF EXECUTION! INDULGERS IN THE ORGASM OF BLOOD AND PAIN! THEY SCARE YOU SOMETIMES, DON'T THEY?
HEADSMAN, TO YOUR POST.
NO MATTER. THEY WON'T HARM YOU. THEY'RE JUST HERE TO SEE THE SHOW!
IT'S DISAPPEARING HEAD TIME, AND YOU'RE THE MAGICIAN! THE AXE IS QUICKER THAN THE NECK!
KA-CHUNK!
TA DA! AND IT IS OVER! BUT THERE IS NO APPLAUSE FOR THE MAGICIAN, ONLY THE SOLEMN INSPECTION OF A TRICK WELL-PERFORMED, AND THE EVENTUAL FILTERING OUT OF THE CROWD.
YOU'RE BORED WITH THIS ACT, AREN'T YOU, HEADSMAN? MAKES YOU YAWN!
IF YOU DIDN'T LOSE YOUR HEAD OVER MY FIRST FOUR STORIES LITTLE FIEND, THIS MAY BE JUST THE TALE TO DO THE TRICK!
IT'S THE STORY OF AN EXECUTIONER WHO'S A REAL PAIN IN THE NECK!
RELATIVELY AXE-CIDENTAL

STORY: GREG POTTER / ART: ADOLFO ABELLAN

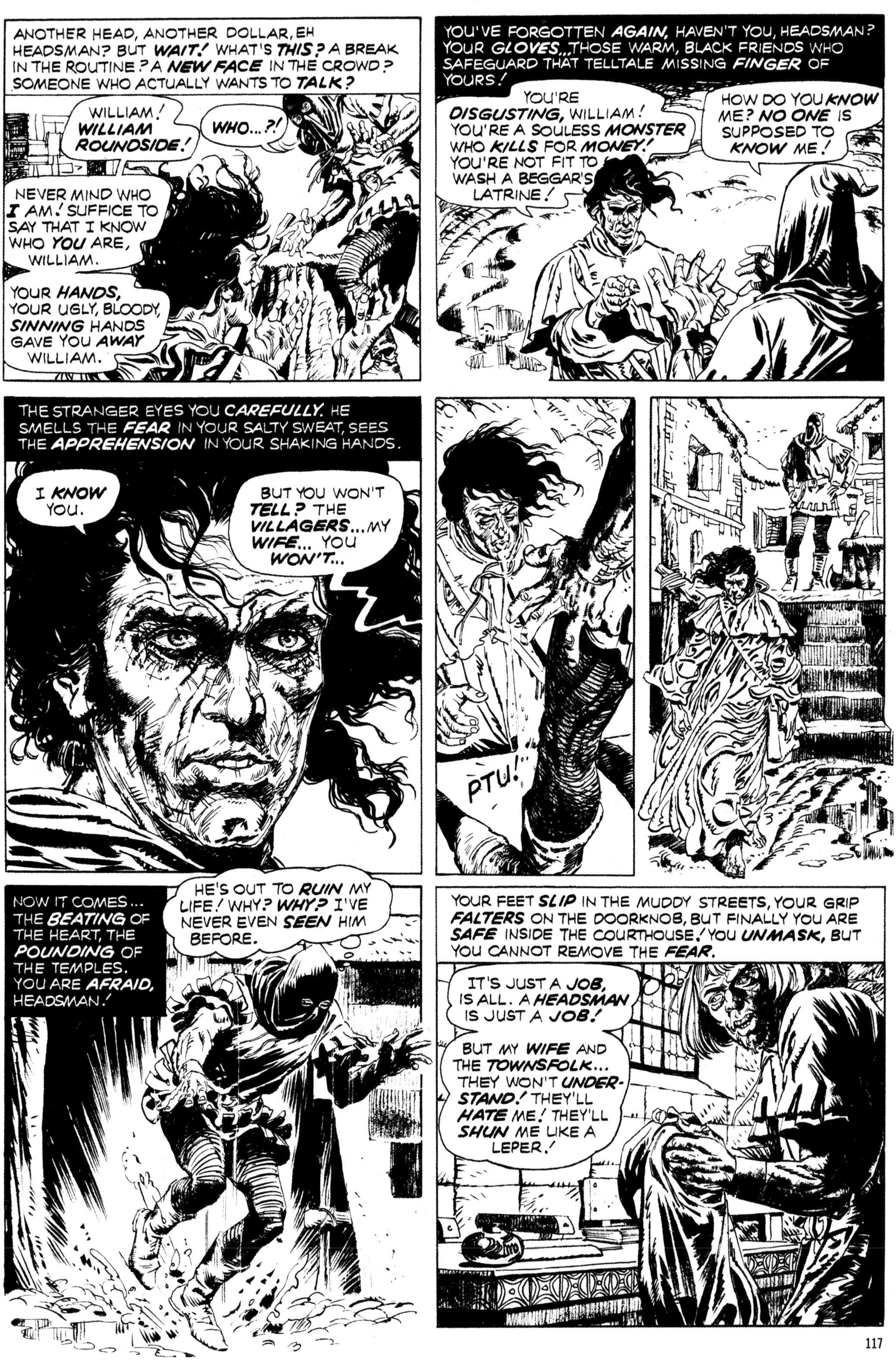
ANOTHER HEAD, ANOTHER DOLLAR, EH HEADSMAN? BUT WAIT! WHAT'S THIS? A BREAK IN THE ROUTINE? A NEW FACE IN THE CROWD? SOMEONE WHO ACTUALLY WANTS TO TALK?
WILLIAM! WILLIAM ROUNDSIDE!
WHO...?!
NEVER MIND WHO I AM! SUFFICE TO SAY THAT I KNOW WHO YOU ARE, WILLIAM.
YOUR HANDS, YOUR UGLY, BLOODY, SINNING HANDS GAVE YOU AWAY WILLIAM.
YOU'VE FORGOTTEN AGAIN, HAVEN'T YOU, HEADSMAN? YOUR GLOVES... THOSE WARM, BLACK FRIENDS WHO SAFEGUARD THAT TELLTALE MISSING FINGER OF YOURS!
YOU'RE DISGUSTING, WILLIAM! YOU'RE A SOULESS MONSTER WHO KILLS FOR MONEY! YOU'RE NOT FIT TO WASH A BEGGAR'S LATRINE!
HOW DO YOU KNOW ME? NO ONE IS SUPPOSED TO KNOW ME!
THE STRANGER EYES YOU CAREFULLY. HE SMELLS THE FEAR IN YOUR SALTY SWEAT, SEES THE APPREHENSION IN YOUR SHAKING HANDS.
I KNOW YOU.
BUT YOU WON'T TELL? THE VILLAGERS... MY WIFE... YOU WON'T...
PTU!
NOW IT COMES... THE BEATING OF THE HEART, THE POUNDING OF THE TEMPLES. YOU ARE AFRAID, HEADSMAN!
HE'S OUT TO RUIN MY LIFE! WHY? WHY? I'VE NEVER EVEN SEEN HIM BEFORE.
YOUR FEET SLIP IN THE MUDDY STREETS, YOUR GRIP FALTERS ON THE DOORKNOB, BUT FINALLY YOU ARE SAFE INSIDE THE COURTHOUSE! YOU UNMASK, BUT YOU CANNOT REMOVE THE FEAR.
IT'S JUST A JOB, IS ALL. A HEADSMAN IS JUST A JOB!
BUT MY WIFE AND THE TOWNSFOLK... THEY WON'T UNDER-STAND! THEY'LL HATE ME! THEY'LL SHUN ME LIKE A LEPER!

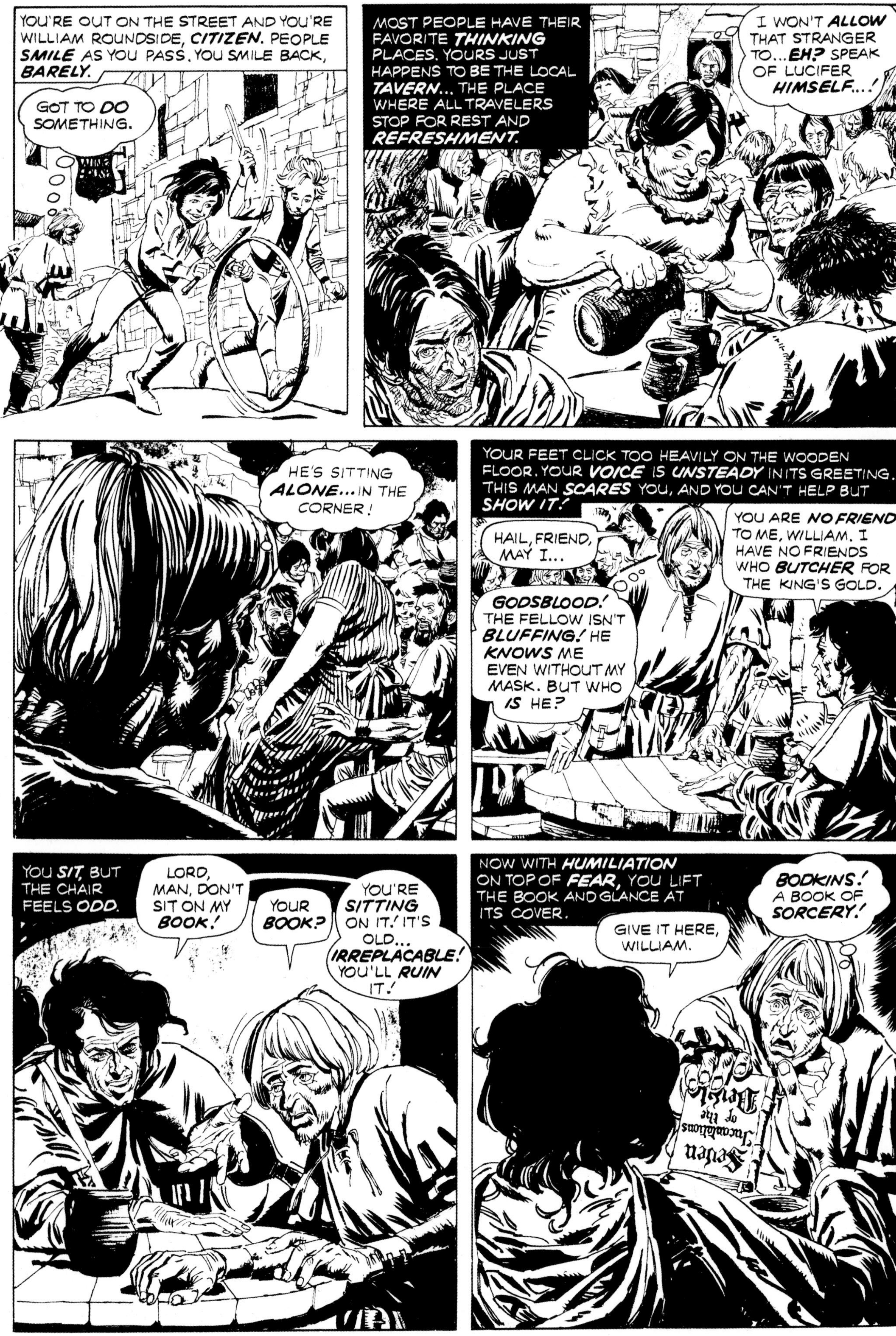
YOU'RE OUT ON THE STREET AND YOU'RE WILLIAM ROUNDSIDE, CITIZEN. PEOPLE SMILE AS YOU PASS. YOU SMILE BACK, BARELY.
GOT TO DO SOMETHING.
MOST PEOPLE HAVE THEIR FAVORITE THINKING PLACES. YOURS JUST HAPPENS TO BE THE LOCAL TAVERN... THE PLACE WHERE ALL TRAVELERS STOP FOR REST AND REFRESHMENT.
I WON'T ALLOW THAT STRANGER TO... EH? SPEAK OF LUCIFER HIMSELF...!
HE'S SITTING ALONE... IN THE CORNER!
YOUR FEET CLICK TOO HEAVILY ON THE WOODEN FLOOR. YOUR VOICE IS UNSTEADY IN ITS GREETING. THIS MAN SCARES YOU, AND YOU CAN'T HELP BUT SHOW IT!
HAIL, FRIEND, MAY I...
YOU ARE NO FRIEND TO ME, WILLIAM. I HAVE NO FRIENDS WHO BUTCHER FOR THE KING'S GOLD.
GODSBLOOD! THE FELLOW ISN'T BLUFFING! HE KNOWS ME EVEN WITHOUT MY MASK. BUT WHO IS HE?
YOU SIT, BUT THE CHAIR FEELS ODD.
LORD, MAN, DON'T SIT ON MY BOOK!
YOUR BOOK?
YOU'RE SITTING ON IT! IT'S OLD... IRREPLACABLE! YOU'LL RUIN IT!
NOW WITH HUMILIATION ON TOP OF FEAR, YOU LIFT THE BOOK AND GLANCE AT ITS COVER.
GIVE IT HERE, WILLIAM.
BODKINS! A BOOK OF SORCERY!

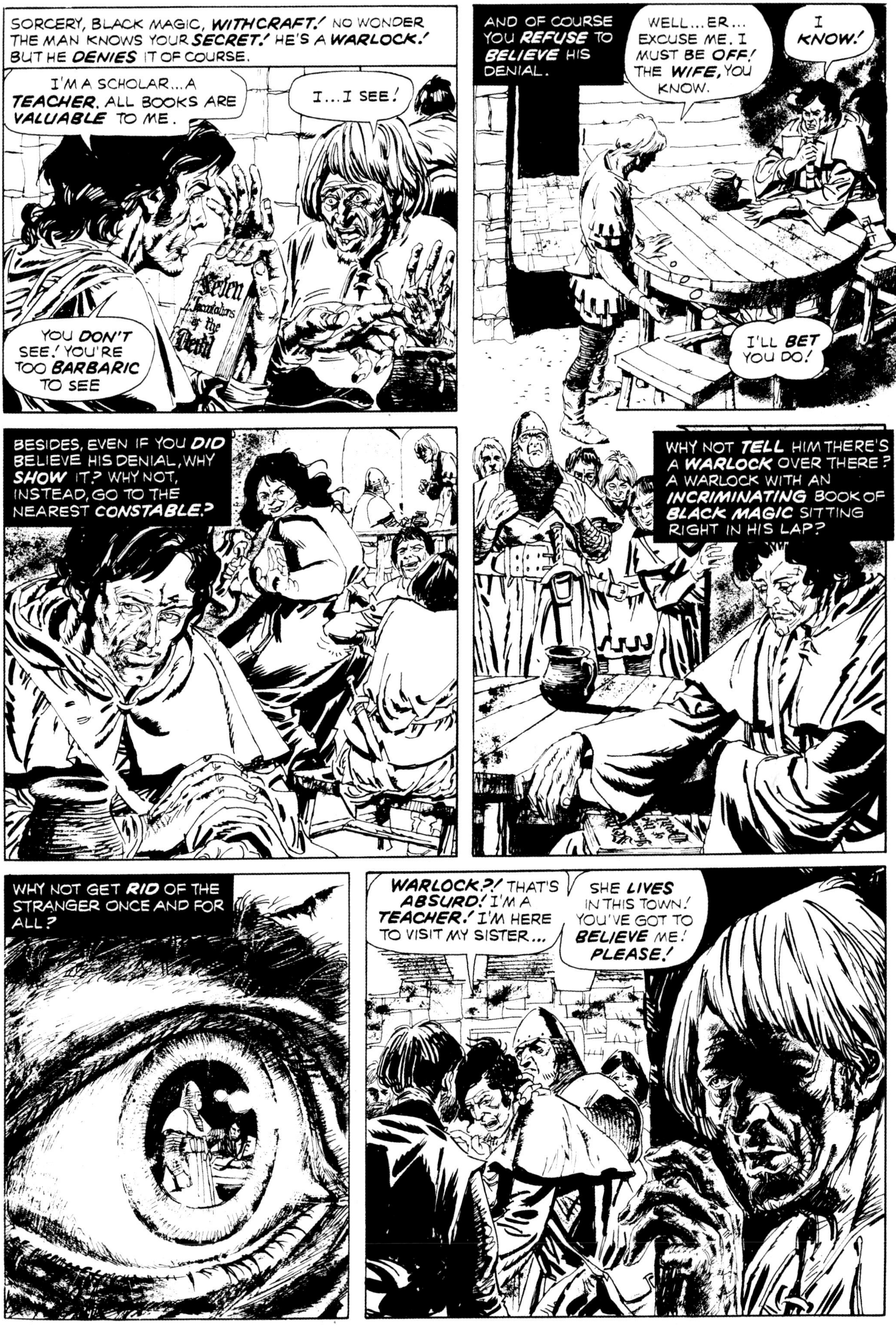
SORCERY, BLACK MAGIC, WITCHCRAFT! NO WONDER THE MAN KNOWS YOUR SECRET! HE'S A WARLOCK! BUT HE DENIES IT OF COURSE.
I'M A SCHOLAR...A TEACHER. ALL BOOKS ARE VALUABLE TO ME.
I...I SEE!
YOU DON'T SEE! YOU'RE TOO BARBARIC TO SEE
Seven Incantations of the Devil
AND OF COURSE YOU REFUSE TO BELIEVE HIS DENIAL.
WELL...ER... EXCUSE ME. I MUST BE OFF! THE WIFE, YOU KNOW.
I KNOW!
I'LL BET YOU DO!
BESIDES, EVEN IF YOU DID BELIEVE HIS DENIAL, WHY SHOW IT? WHY NOT, INSTEAD, GO TO THE NEAREST CONSTABLE?
WHY NOT TELL HIM THERE'S A WARLOCK OVER THERE? A WARLOCK WITH AN INCRIMINATING BOOK OF BLACK MAGIC SITTING RIGHT IN HIS LAP?
WHY NOT GET RID OF THE STRANGER ONCE AND FOR ALL?
WARLOCK?! THAT'S ABSURD! I'M A TEACHER! I'M HERE TO VISIT MY SISTER...
SHE LIVES IN THIS TOWN! YOU'VE GOT TO BELIEVE ME! PLEASE!

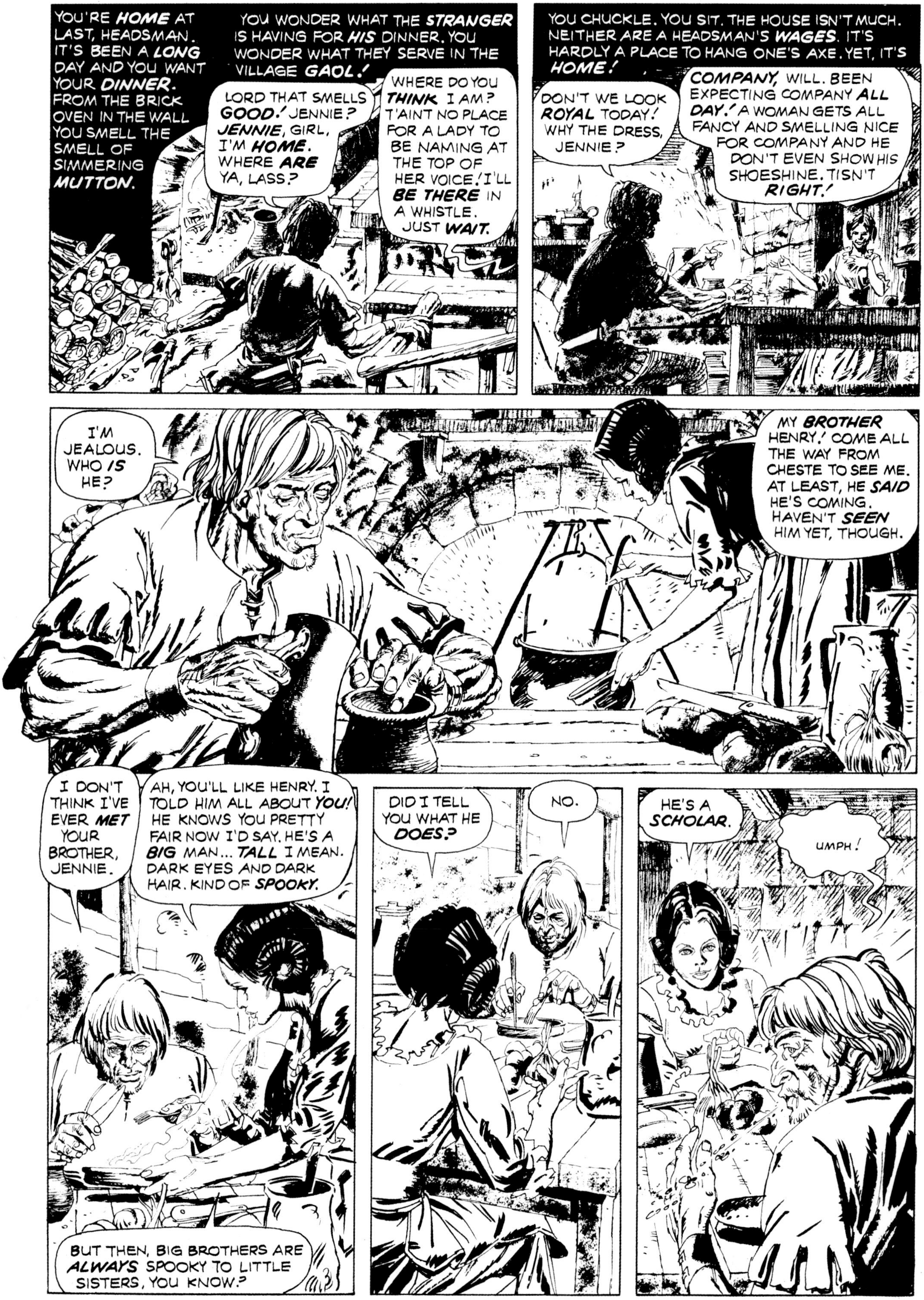

YOU'RE HOME AT LAST, HEADSMAN. IT'S BEEN A LONG DAY AND YOU WANT YOUR DINNER. FROM THE BRICK OVEN IN THE WALL YOU SMELL THE SMELL OF SIMMERING MUTTON.
YOU WONDER WHAT THE STRANGER IS HAVING FOR HIS DINNER. YOU WONDER WHAT THEY SERVE IN THE VILLAGE GAOL!
LORD THAT SMELLS GOOD! JENNIE? JENNIE, GIRL, I'M HOME. WHERE ARE YA, LASS?
WHERE DO YOU THINK I AM? T'AINT NO PLACE FOR A LADY TO BE NAMING AT THE TOP OF HER VOICE! I'LL BE THERE IN A WHISTLE. JUST WAIT.
YOU CHUCKLE. YOU SIT. THE HOUSE ISN'T MUCH. NEITHER ARE A HEADSMAN'S WAGES. IT'S HARDLY A PLACE TO HANG ONE'S AXE. YET, IT'S HOME!
DON'T WE LOOK ROYAL TODAY! WHY THE DRESS, JENNIE?
COMPANY, WILL. BEEN EXPECTING COMPANY ALL DAY! A WOMAN GETS ALL FANCY AND SMELLING NICE FOR COMPANY AND HE DON'T EVEN SHOW HIS SHOESHINE. TISN'T RIGHT!
I'M JEALOUS. WHO IS HE?
MY BROTHER HENRY! COME ALL THE WAY FROM CHESTE TO SEE ME. AT LEAST, HE SAID HE'S COMING. HAVEN'T SEEN HIM YET, THOUGH.
I DON'T THINK I'VE EVER MET YOUR BROTHER, JENNIE.
AH, YOU'LL LIKE HENRY. I TOLD HIM ALL ABOUT YOU! HE KNOWS YOU PRETTY FAIR NOW I'D SAY. HE'S A BIG MAN... TALL I MEAN. DARK EYES AND DARK HAIR. KIND OF SPOOKY.
BUT THEN, BIG BROTHERS ARE ALWAYS SPOOKY TO LITTLE SISTERS, YOU KNOW?
DID I TELL YOU WHAT HE DOES?
NO.
HE'S A SCHOLAR.
UMPH!

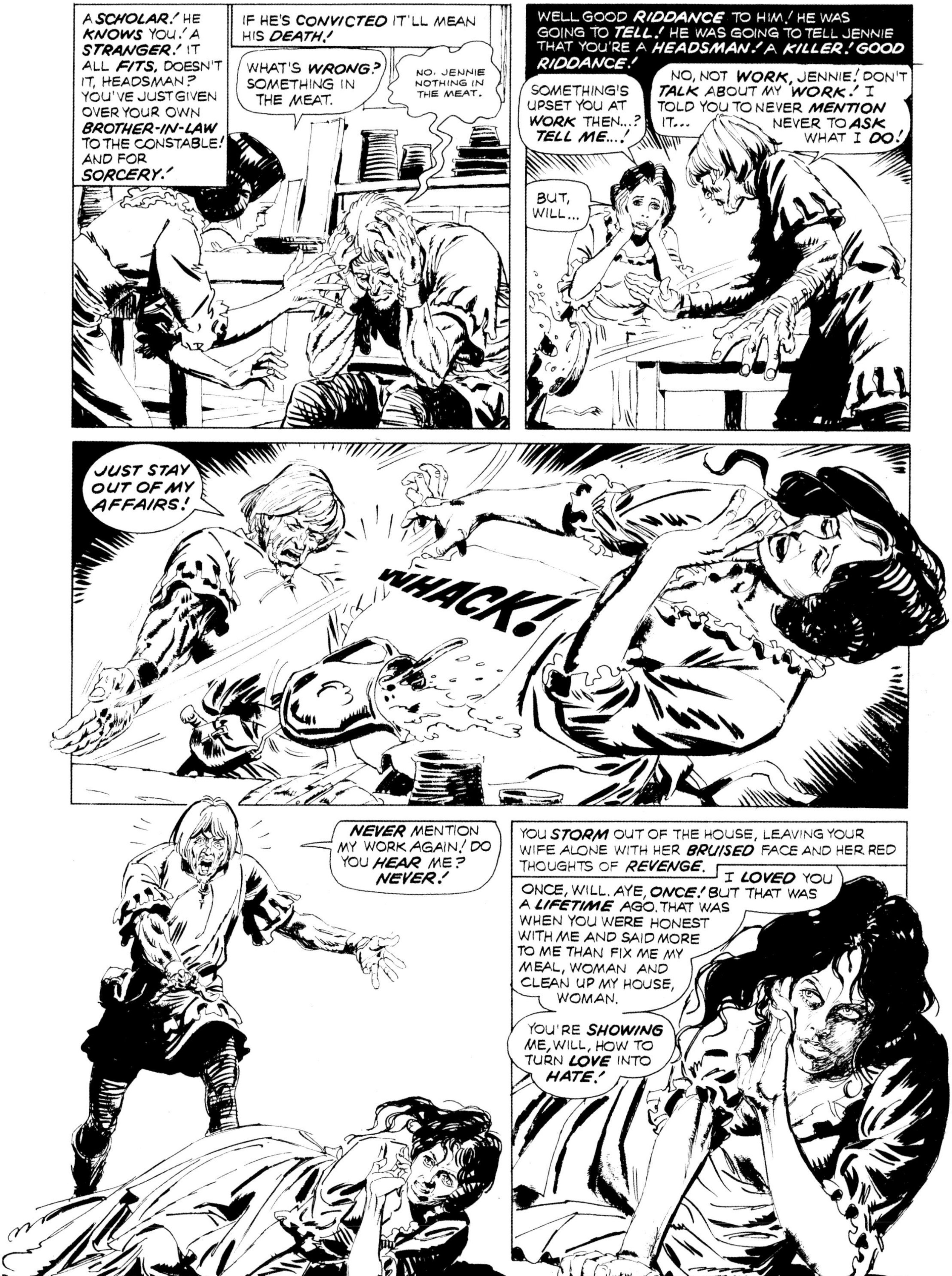
A SCHOLAR! HE KNOWS YOU! A STRANGER! IT ALL FITS, DOESN'T IT, HEADSMAN? YOU'VE JUST GIVEN OVER YOUR OWN BROTHER-IN-LAW TO THE CONSTABLE! AND FOR SORCERY!
IF HE'S CONVICTED IT'LL MEAN HIS DEATH!
WHAT'S WRONG? SOMETHING IN THE MEAT.
NO, JENNIE NOTHING IN THE MEAT.
WELL GOOD RIDDANCE TO HIM! HE WAS GOING TO TELL! HE WAS GOING TO TELL JENNIE THAT YOU'RE A HEADSMAN! A KILLER! GOOD RIDDANCE!
SOMETHING'S UPSET YOU AT WORK THEN...? TELL ME...!
NO, NOT WORK, JENNIE! DON'T TALK ABOUT MY 'WORK'! I TOLD YOU TO NEVER MENTION IT... NEVER TO ASK WHAT I DO!
BUT, WILL...
JUST STAY OUT OF MY AFFAIRS!
WHACK!
NEVER MENTION MY WORK AGAIN! DO YOU HEAR ME? NEVER!
YOU STORM OUT OF THE HOUSE, LEAVING YOUR WIFE ALONE WITH HER BRUISED FACE AND HER RED THOUGHTS OF REVENGE.
I LOVED YOU ONCE, WILL. AYE, ONCE! BUT THAT WAS A LIFETIME AGO. THAT WAS WHEN YOU WERE HONEST WITH ME AND SAID MORE TO ME THAN FIX ME MY MEAL, WOMAN AND CLEAN UP MY HOUSE, WOMAN.
YOU'RE SHOWING ME, WILL, HOW TO TURN LOVE INTO HATE!

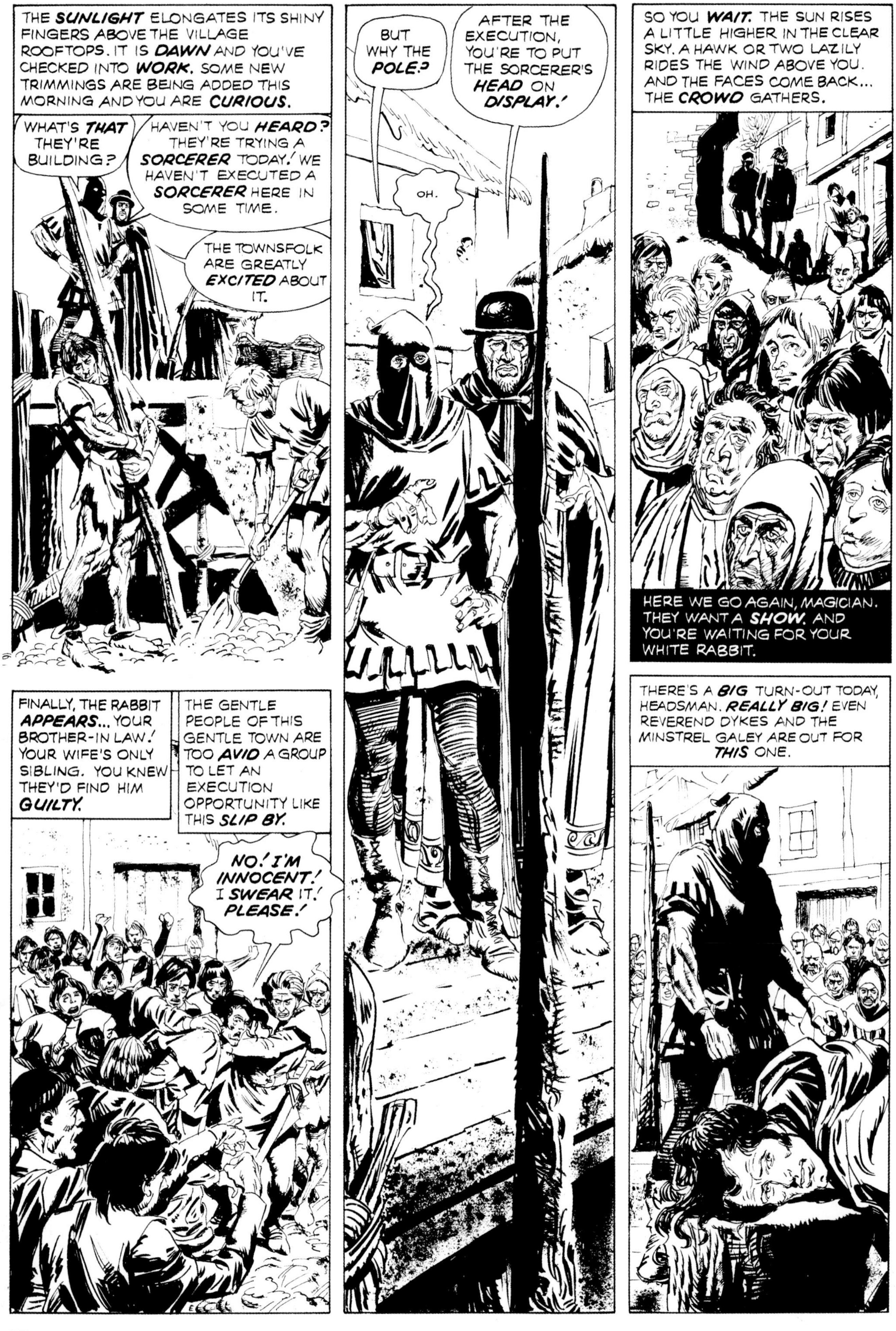

THE SUNLIGHT ELONGATES ITS SHINY FINGERS ABOVE THE VILLAGE ROOFTOPS. IT IS DAWN AND YOU'VE CHECKED INTO WORK. SOME NEW TRIMMINGS ARE BEING ADDED THIS MORNING AND YOU ARE CURIOUS.
WHAT'S THAT THEY'RE BUILDING?
HAVEN'T YOU HEARD? THEY'RE TRYING A SORCERER TODAY! WE HAVEN'T EXECUTED A SORCERER HERE IN SOME TIME.
THE TOWNSFOLK ARE GREATLY EXCITED ABOUT IT.
BUT WHY THE POLE?
AFTER THE EXECUTION, YOU'RE TO PUT THE SORCERER'S HEAD ON DISPLAY!
OH.
SO YOU WAIT. THE SUN RISES A LITTLE HIGHER IN THE CLEAR SKY. A HAWK OR TWO LAZILY RIDES THE WIND ABOVE YOU. AND THE FACES COME BACK... THE CROWD GATHERS.
HERE WE GO AGAIN, MAGICIAN. THEY WANT A SHOW. AND YOU'RE WAITING FOR YOUR WHITE RABBIT.
FINALLY, THE RABBIT APPEARS... YOUR BROTHER-IN LAW! YOUR WIFE'S ONLY SIBLING. YOU KNEW THEY'D FIND HIM GUILTY.
THE GENTLE PEOPLE OF THIS GENTLE TOWN ARE TOO AVID A GROUP TO LET AN EXECUTION OPPORTUNITY LIKE THIS SLIP BY.
NO! I'M INNOCENT! I SWEAR IT! PLEASE!
THERE'S A BIG TURN-OUT TODAY, HEADSMAN. REALLY BIG! EVEN REVEREND DYKES AND THE MINSTREL GALEY ARE OUT FOR THIS ONE.

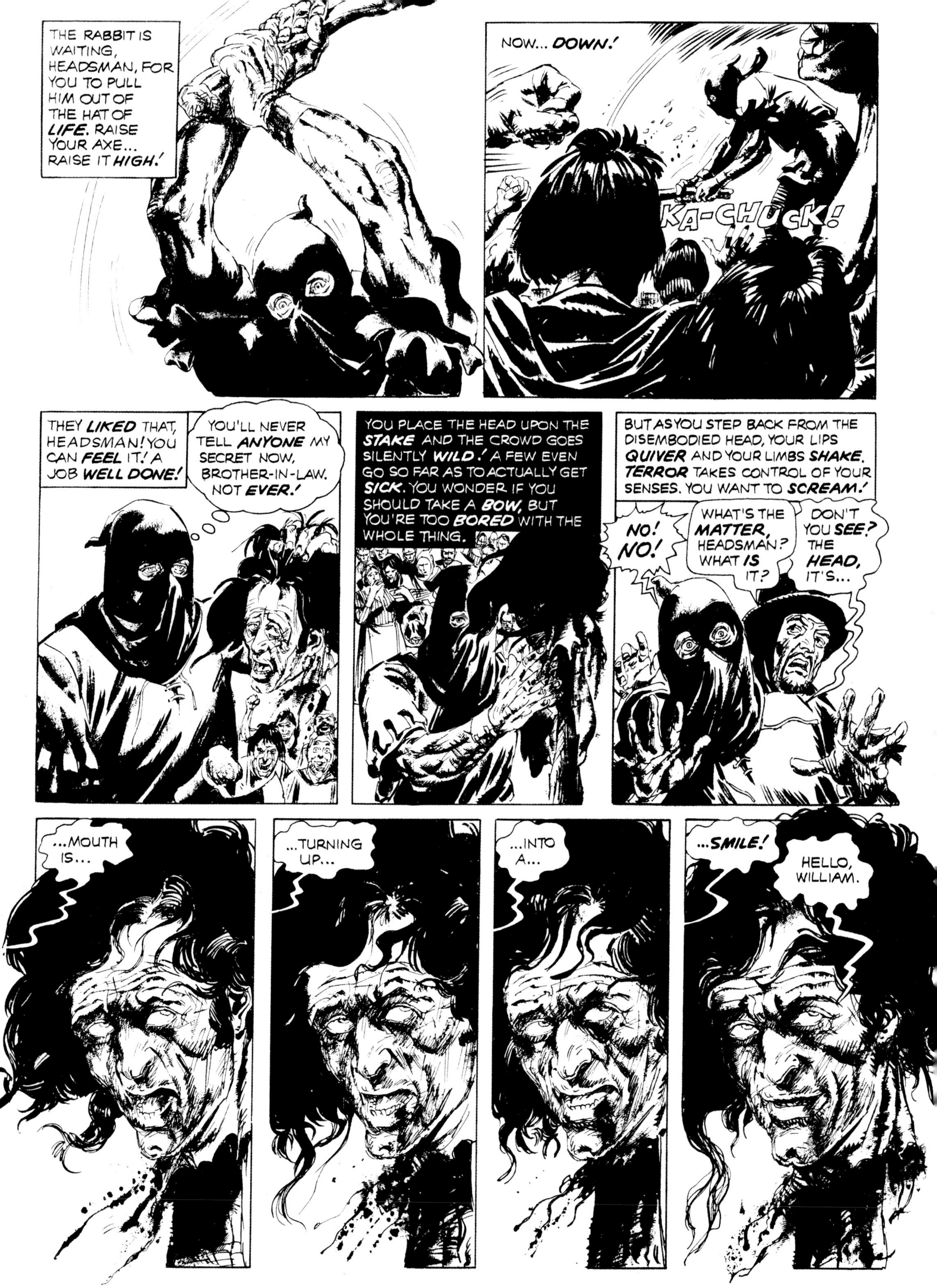
THE RABBIT IS WAITING, HEADSMAN, FOR YOU TO PULL HIM OUT OF THE HAT OF LIFE. RAISE YOUR AXE... RAISE IT HIGH!
NOW... DOWN!
KA-CHUCK!
THEY LIKED THAT, HEADSMAN! YOU CAN FEEL IT! A JOB WELL DONE!
YOU'LL NEVER TELL ANYONE MY SECRET NOW, BROTHER-IN-LAW. NOT EVER!
YOU PLACE THE HEAD UPON THE STAKE AND THE CROWD GOES SILENTLY WILD! A FEW EVEN GO SO FAR AS TO ACTUALLY GET SICK. YOU WONDER IF YOU SHOULD TAKE A BOW, BUT YOU'RE TOO BORED WITH THE WHOLE THING.
BUT AS YOU STEP BACK FROM THE DISEMBODIED HEAD, YOUR LIPS QUIVER AND YOUR LIMBS SHAKE. TERROR TAKES CONTROL OF YOUR SENSES. YOU WANT TO SCREAM!
NO! NO!
WHAT'S THE MATTER, HEADSMAN? WHAT IS IT?
DON'T YOU SEE? THE HEAD, IT'S...
...MOUTH IS...
...TURNING UP...
...INTO A...
...SMILE!
HELLO, WILLIAM.

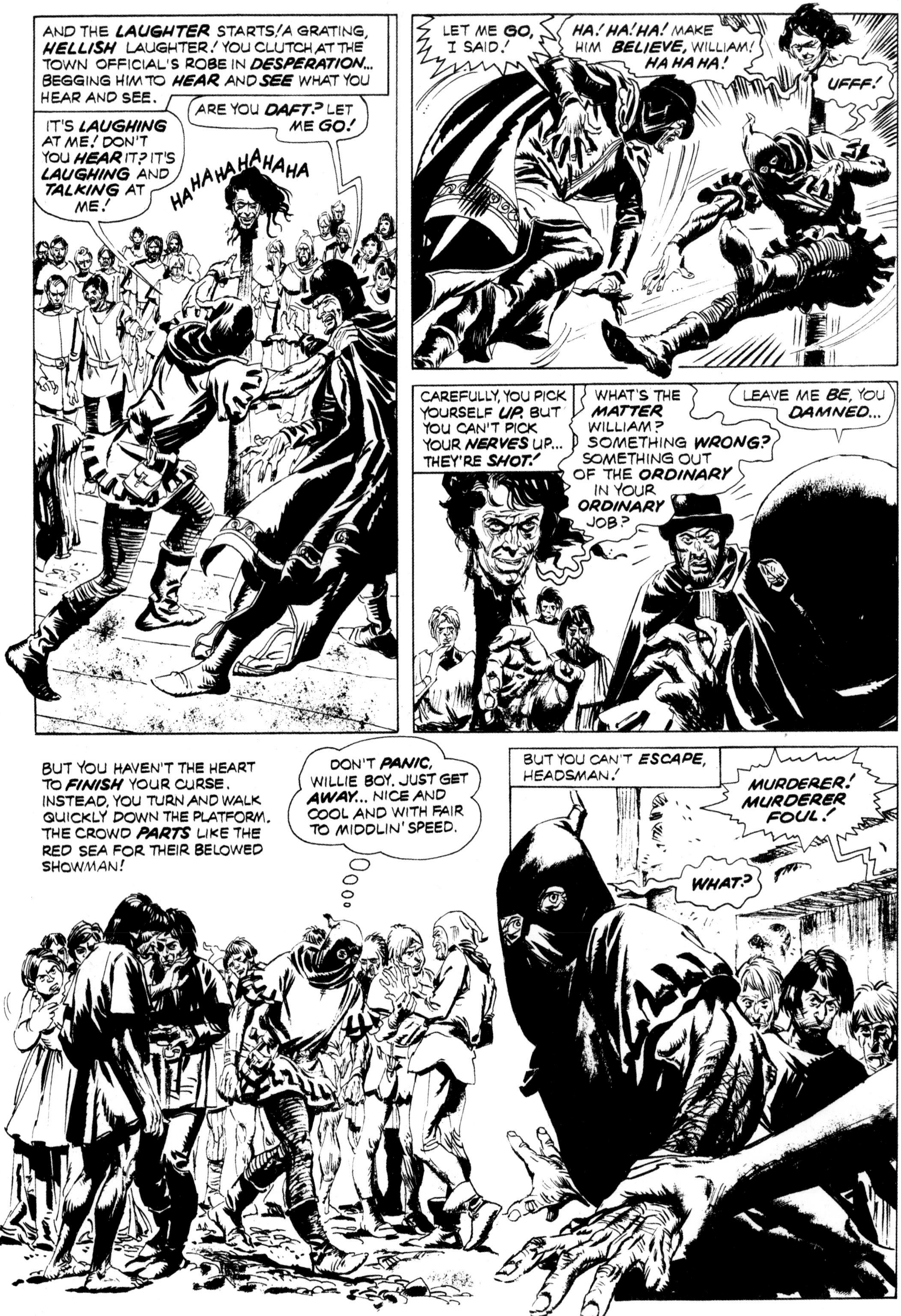

AND THE LAUGHTER STARTS! A GRATING, HELLISH LAUGHTER! YOU CLUTCH AT THE TOWN OFFICIAL'S ROBE IN DESPERATION... BEGGING HIM TO HEAR AND SEE WHAT YOU HEAR AND SEE.
IT'S LAUGHING AT ME! DON'T YOU HEAR IT? IT'S LAUGHING AND TALKING AT ME!
ARE YOU DAFT? LET ME GO!
HAHAHAHAHAHAHA
LET ME GO, I SAID!
HA! HA! HA! MAKE HIM BELIEVE, WILLIAM! HA HA HA!
UFFF!
CAREFULLY, YOU PICK YOURSELF UP. BUT YOU CAN'T PICK YOUR NERVES UP... THEY'RE SHOT!
WHAT'S THE MATTER WILLIAM? SOMETHING WRONG? SOMETHING OUT OF THE ORDINARY IN YOUR ORDINARY JOB?
LEAVE ME BE, YOU DAMNED...
BUT YOU HAVEN'T THE HEART TO FINISH YOUR CURSE. INSTEAD, YOU TURN AND WALK QUICKLY DOWN THE PLATFORM. THE CROWD PARTS LIKE THE RED SEA FOR THEIR BELOWED SHOWMAN!
DON'T PANIC, WILLIE BOY. JUST GET AWAY... NICE AND COOL AND WITH FAIR TO MIDDLIN' SPEED.
BUT YOU CAN'T ESCAPE, HEADSMAN!
MURDERER! MURDERER FOUL!
WHAT?

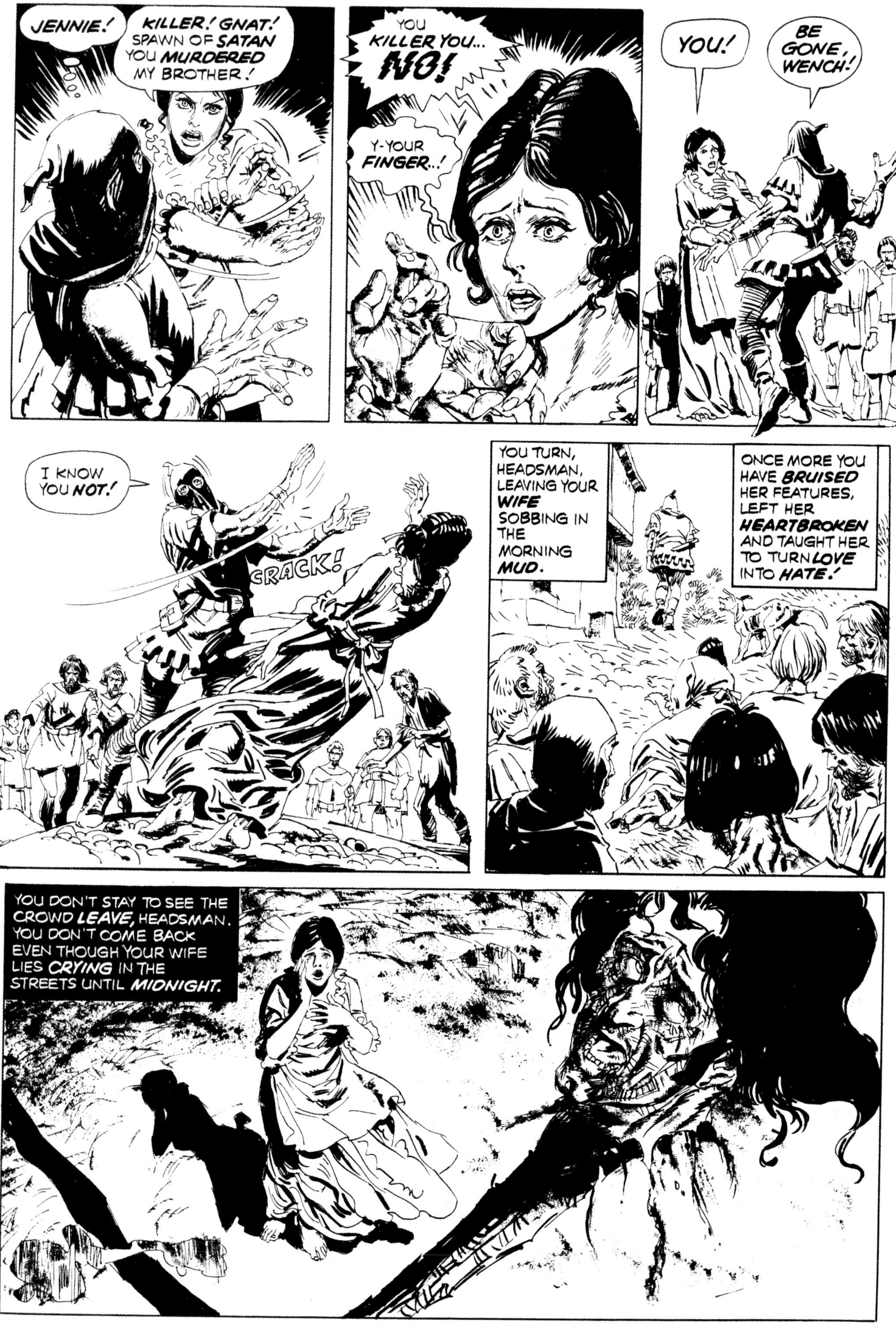

JENNIE!
KILLER! GNAT! SPAWN OF SATAN YOU MURDERED MY BROTHER!
YOU KILLER YOU... NO!
Y-YOUR FINGER..!
YOU!
BE GONE, WENCH!
I KNOW YOU NOT!
CRACK!
YOU TURN, HEADSMAN, LEAVING YOUR WIFE SOBBING IN THE MORNING MUD.
ONCE MORE YOU HAVE BRUISED HER FEATURES, LEFT HER HEARTBROKEN AND TAUGHT HER TO TURN LOVE INTO HATE!
YOU DON'T STAY TO SEE THE CROWD LEAVE, HEADSMAN. YOU DON'T COME BACK EVEN THOUGH YOUR WIFE LIES CRYING IN THE STREETS UNTIL MIDNIGHT.

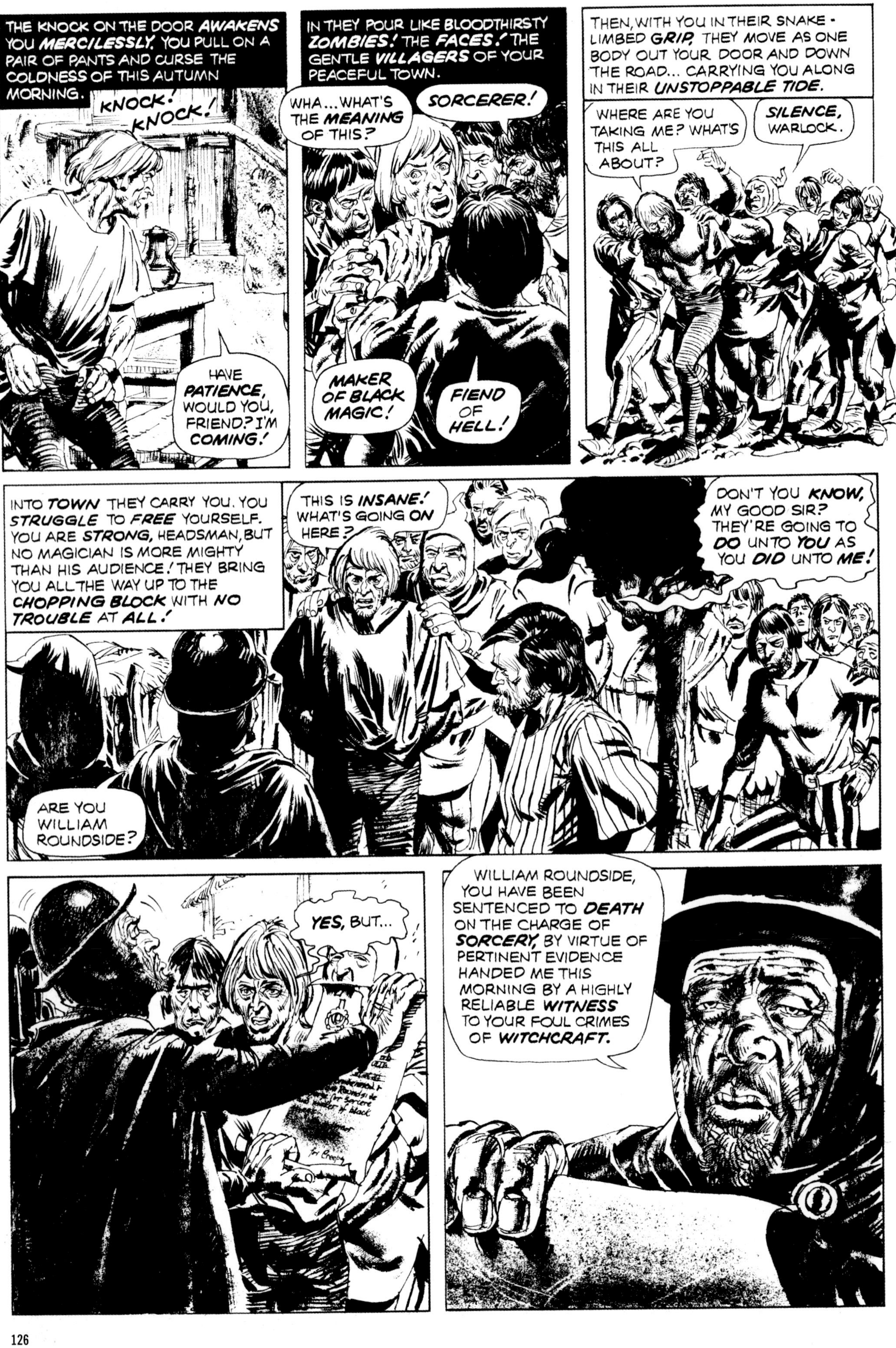

THE KNOCK ON THE DOOR AWAKENS YOU MERCILESSLY. YOU PULL ON A PAIR OF PANTS AND CURSE THE COLDNESS OF THIS AUTUMN MORNING.
KNOCK! KNOCK!
HAVE PATIENCE, WOULD YOU, FRIEND? I'M COMING!
IN THEY POUR LIKE BLOODTHIRSTY ZOMBIES! THE FACES! THE GENTLE VILLAGERS OF YOUR PEACEFUL TOWN.
WHA... WHAT'S THE MEANING OF THIS?
SORCERER!
MAKER OF BLACK MAGIC!
FIEND OF HELL!
THEN, WITH YOU IN THEIR SNAKE-LIMBED GRIP, THEY MOVE AS ONE BODY OUT YOUR DOOR AND DOWN THE ROAD... CARRYING YOU ALONG IN THEIR UNSTOPPABLE TIDE.
WHERE ARE YOU TAKING ME? WHAT'S THIS ALL ABOUT?
SILENCE, WARLOCK.
INTO TOWN THEY CARRY YOU. YOU STRUGGLE TO FREE YOURSELF. YOU ARE STRONG, HEADSMAN, BUT NO MAGICIAN IS MORE MIGHTY THAN HIS AUDIENCE! THEY BRING YOU ALL THE WAY UP TO THE CHOPPING BLOCK WITH NO TROUBLE AT ALL!
THIS IS INSANE! WHAT'S GOING ON HERE?
DON'T YOU KNOW, MY GOOD SIR? THEY'RE GOING TO DO UNTO YOU AS YOU DID UNTO ME!
ARE YOU WILLIAM ROUNDSIDE?
YES, BUT...
WILLIAM ROUNDSIDE, YOU HAVE BEEN SENTENCED TO DEATH ON THE CHARGE OF SORCERY, BY VIRTUE OF PERTINENT EVIDENCE HANDED ME THIS MORNING BY A HIGHLY RELIABLE WITNESS TO YOUR FOUL CRIMES OF WITCHCRAFT.

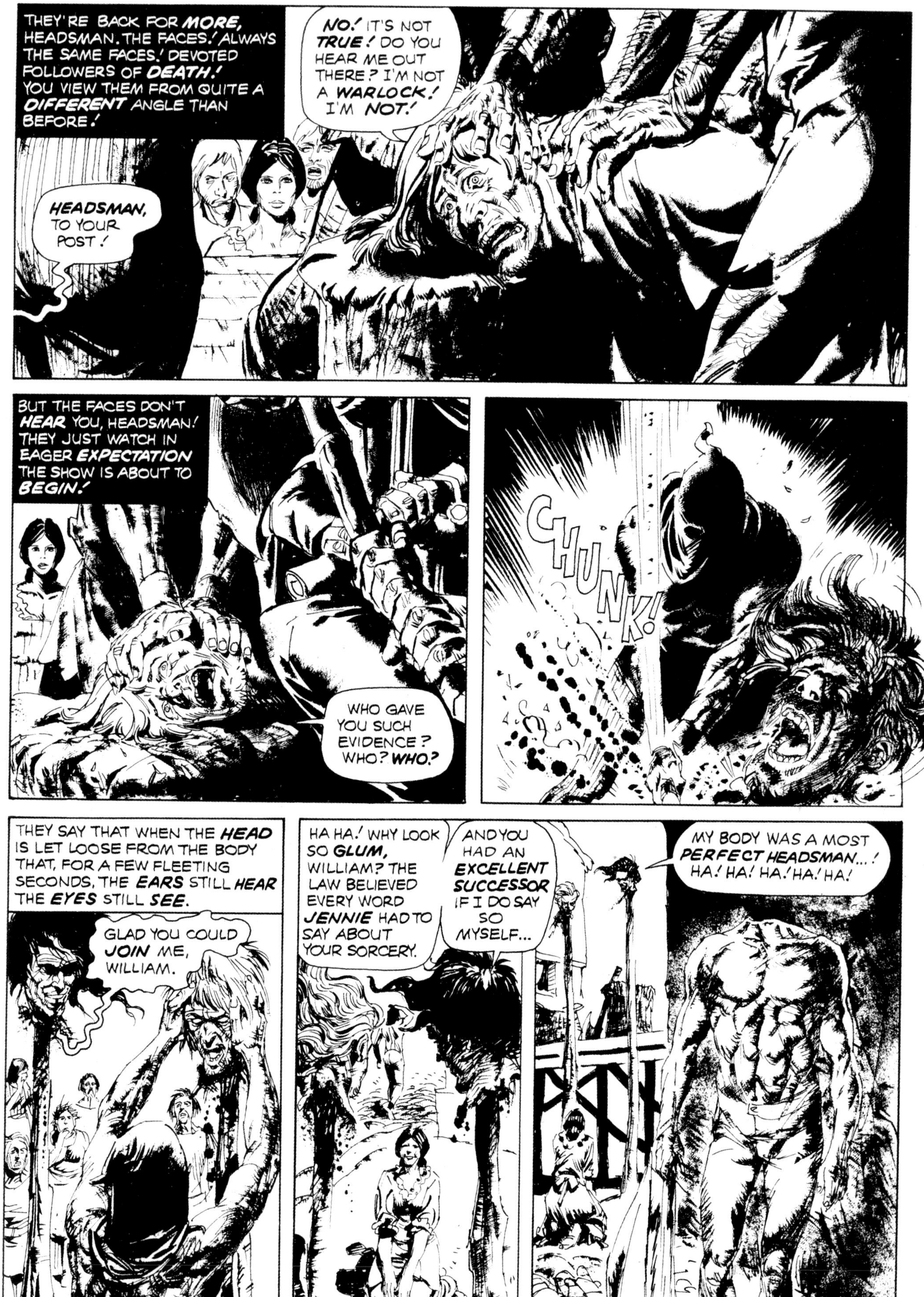
THEY'RE BACK FOR MORE, HEADSMAN. THE FACES! ALWAYS THE SAME FACES! DEVOTED FOLLOWERS OF DEATH! YOU VIEW THEM FROM QUITE A DIFFERENT ANGLE THAN BEFORE!
NO! IT'S NOT TRUE! DO YOU HEAR ME OUT THERE? I'M NOT A WARLOCK! I'M NOT!
HEADSMAN, TO YOUR POST!
BUT THE FACES DON'T HEAR YOU, HEADSMAN! THEY JUST WATCH IN EAGER EXPECTATION THE SHOW IS ABOUT TO BEGIN!
WHO GAVE YOU SUCH EVIDENCE? WHO? WHO?
CHUNK!
THEY SAY THAT WHEN THE HEAD IS LET LOOSE FROM THE BODY THAT, FOR A FEW FLEETING SECONDS, THE EARS STILL HEAR THE EYES STILL SEE.
GLAD YOU COULD JOIN ME, WILLIAM.
HA HA! WHY LOOK SO GLUM, WILLIAM? THE LAW BELIEVED EVERY WORD JENNIE HAD TO SAY ABOUT YOUR SORCERY.
AND YOU HAD AN EXCELLENT SUCCESSOR IF I DO SAY SO MYSELF...
MY BODY WAS A MOST PERFECT HEADSMAN...! HA! HA! HA! HA! HA!

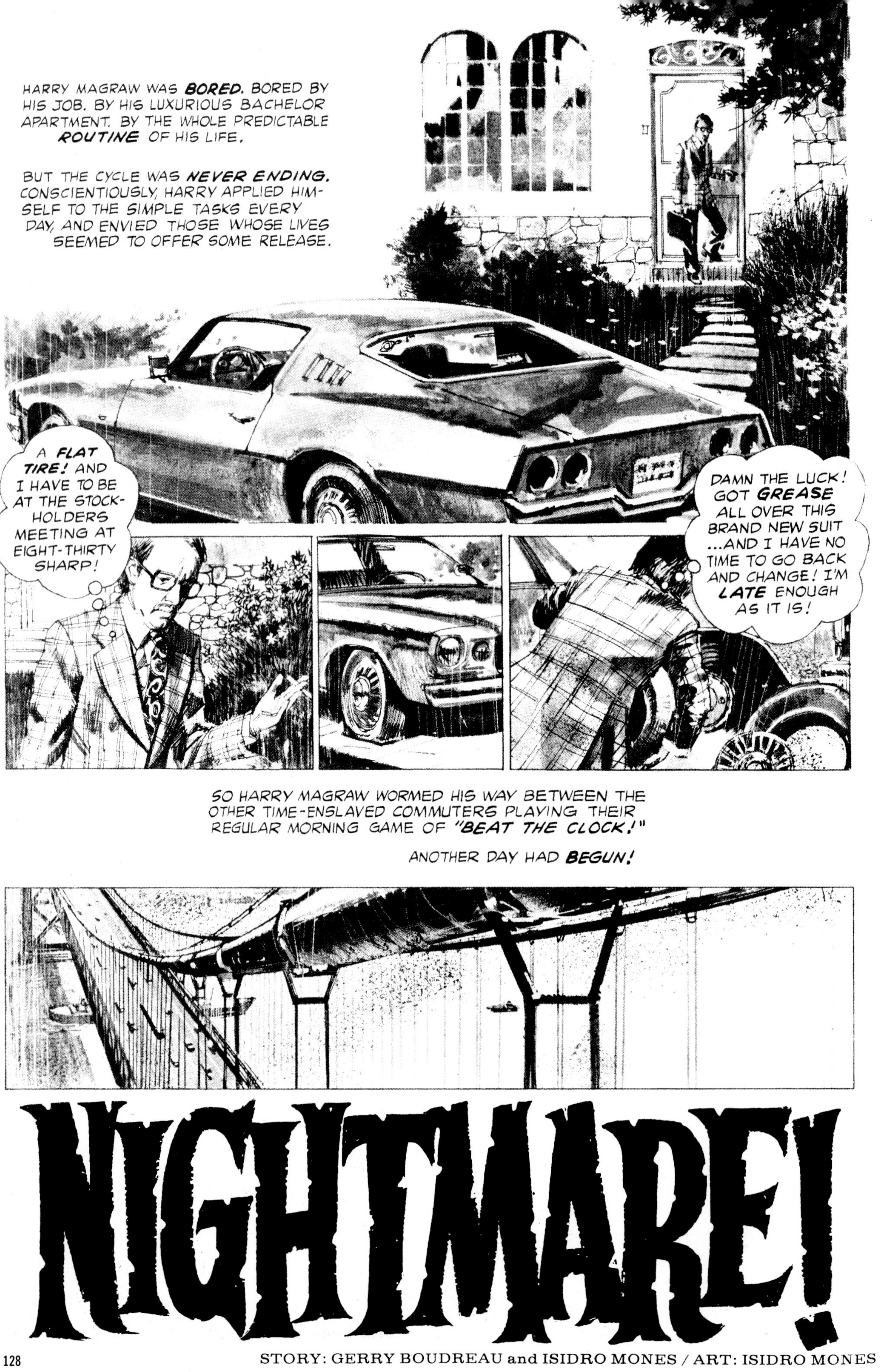
HARRY MAGRAW WAS BORED. BORED BY HIS JOB. BY HIS LUXURIOUS BACHELOR APARTMENT. BY THE WHOLE PREDICTABLE ROUTINE OF HIS LIFE.
BUT THE CYCLE WAS NEVER ENDING. CONSCIENTIOUSLY, HARRY APPLIED HIMSELF TO THE SIMPLE TASKS EVERY DAY, AND ENVIED THOSE WHOSE LIVES SEEMED TO OFFER SOME RELEASE.
A FLAT TIRE! AND I HAVE TO BE AT THE STOCKHOLDERS MEETING AT EIGHT-THIRTY SHARP!
DAMN THE LUCK! GOT GREASE ALL OVER THIS BRAND NEW SUIT ...AND I HAVE NO TIME TO GO BACK AND CHANGE! I'M LATE ENOUGH AS IT IS!
SO HARRY MAGRAW WORMED HIS WAY BETWEEN THE OTHER TIME-ENSLAVED COMMUTERS PLAYING THEIR REGULAR MORNING GAME OF "BEAT THE CLOCK!"
ANOTHER DAY HAD BEGUN!

NIGHTMARE!

STORY: GERRY BOUDREAU and ISIDRO MONES / ART: ISIDRO MONES

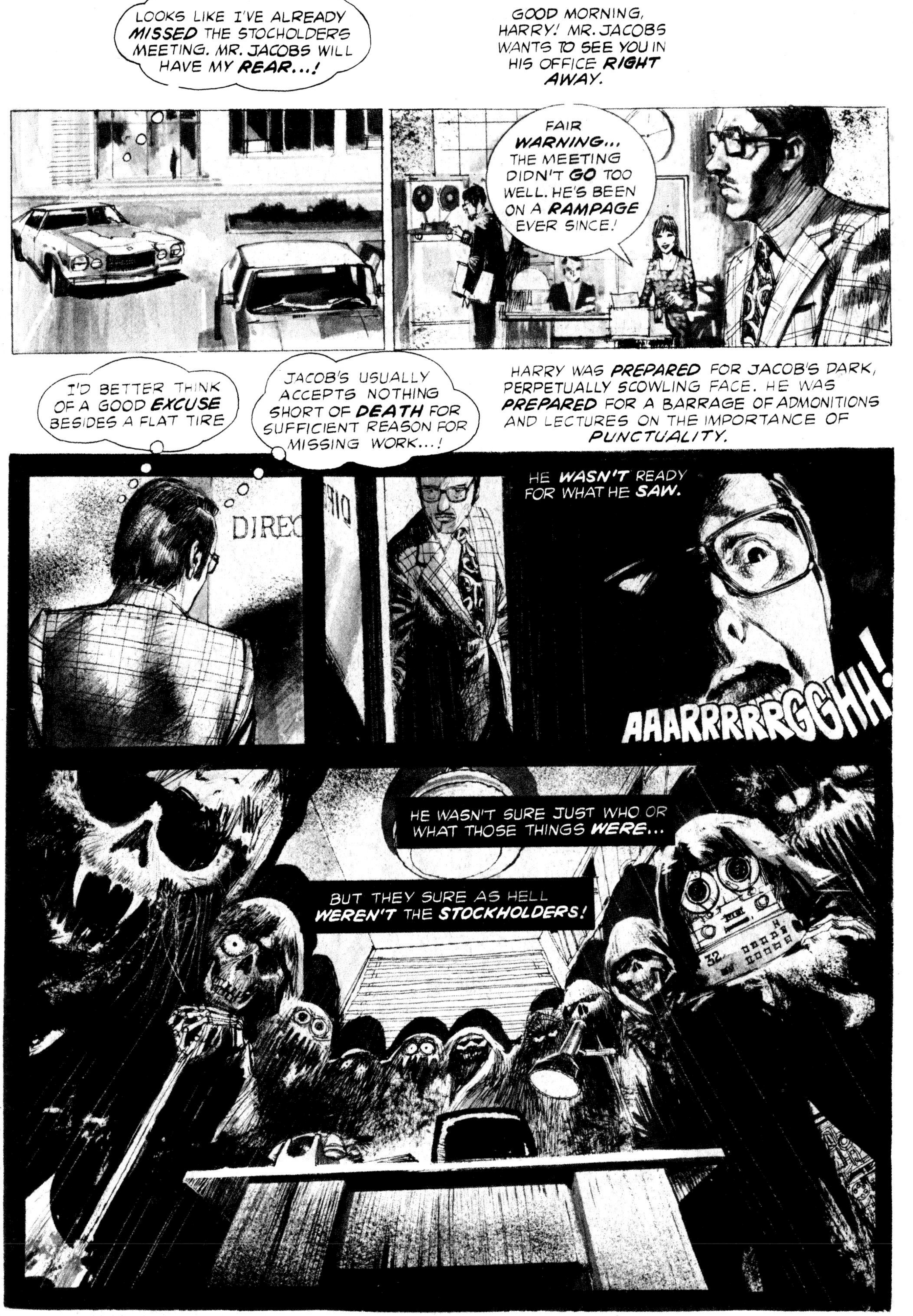

LOOKS LIKE I'VE ALREADY MISSED THE STOCHOLDERS MEETING. MR. JACOBS WILL HAVE MY REAR...!
GOOD MORNING, HARRY! MR. JACOBS WANTS TO SEE YOU IN HIS OFFICE RIGHT AWAY.
FAIR WARNING... THE MEETING DIDN'T GO TOO WELL. HE'S BEEN ON A RAMPAGE EVER SINCE!
I'D BETTER THINK OF A GOOD EXCUSE BESIDES A FLAT TIRE
JACOB'S USUALLY ACCEPTS NOTHING SHORT OF DEATH FOR SUFFICIENT REASON FOR MISSING WORK...!
HARRY WAS PREPARED FOR JACOB'S DARK, PERPETUALLY SCOWLING FACE. HE WAS PREPARED FOR A BARRAGE OF ADMONITIONS AND LECTURES ON THE IMPORTANCE OF PUNCTUALITY.
DIREC
HE WASN'T READY FOR WHAT HE SAW.
AAARRRRRGGHH!
HE WASN'T SURE JUST WHO OR WHAT THOSE THINGS WERE...
BUT THEY SURE AS HELL WEREN'T THE STOCKHOLDERS!

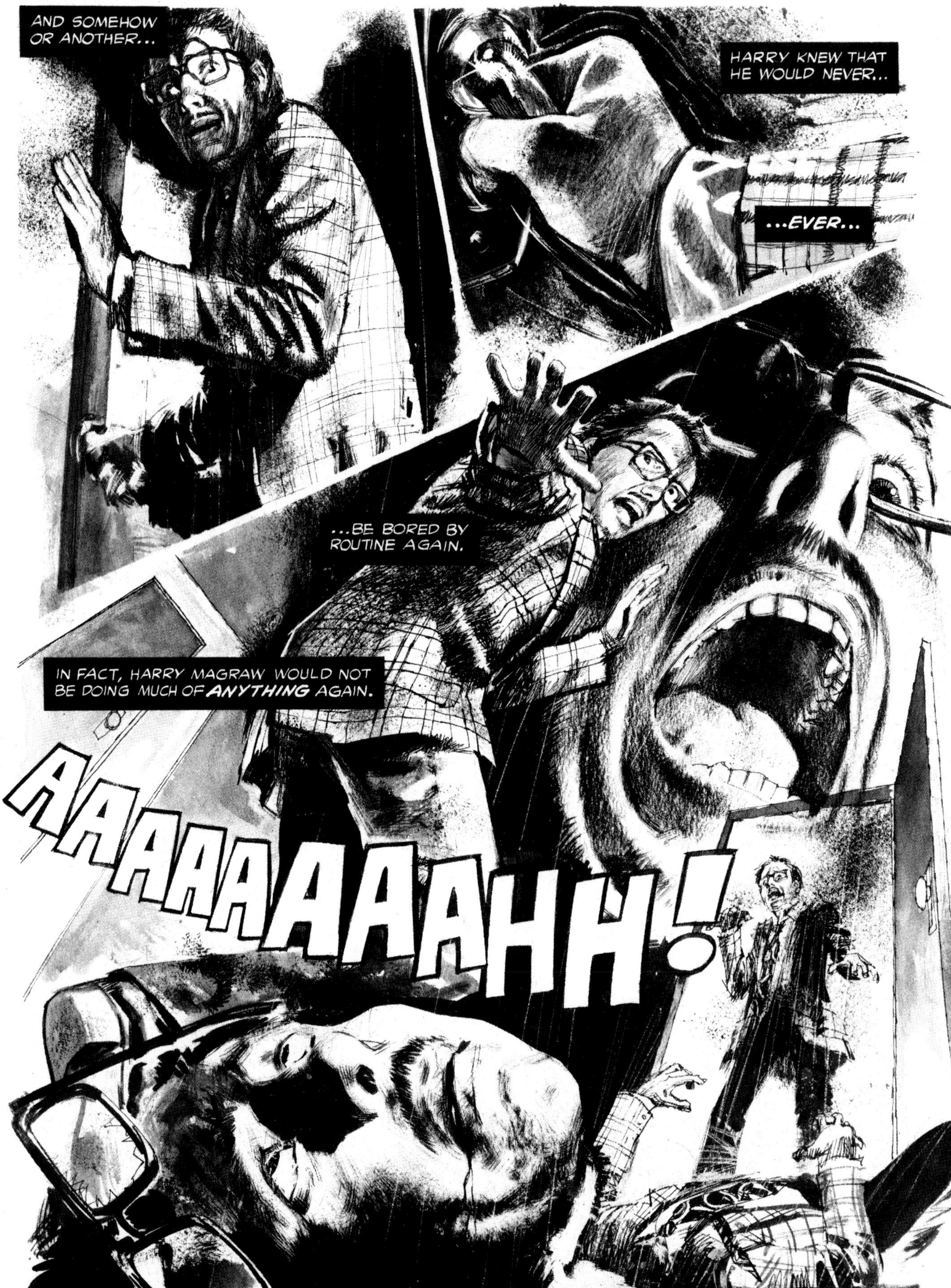
AND SOMEHOW OR ANOTHER...
HARRY KNEW THAT HE WOULD NEVER...
...EVER...
...BE BORED BY ROUTINE AGAIN.
IN FACT, HARRY MAGRAW WOULD NOT BE DOING MUCH OF ANYTHING AGAIN.
AAAAAAAAAAHH!

HARRY WAS AWARE OF EVERY **SOUND** IN THE SURROUNDING DARKNESS... THE THROBBING OF HIS **PULSE**, THE TICKING OF THE ALARM CLOCK, HIS OWN ERRATIC **BREATHING**...

THE SAME **NIGHT-MARE** AGAIN! THAT'S THE THIRD NIGHT THIS WEEK I'VE HAD THE SAME WEIRD **DREAM**...! MUST BE PUTTING IN TOO MUCH TIME AT THE OFFICE...

FOUR IN THE MORNING... AND I'M TOO NERVOUS TO GO BACK TO **SLEEP**! WHY DIDN'T I LISTEN TO MY MOTHER AND GET **MARRIED**! IT'S TIMES LIKE THIS WHEN SLEEPING ALONE CAN BE A REAL **PAIN**!

WHY IS IT PEOPLE REGRET THINGS THEY **DIDN'T** DO FAR MORE THAN THINGS THEY **DID**?

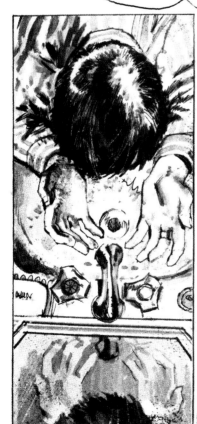

A **DRINK**! I SURE NEED SOMETHING TO STEADY MY **NERVES** RIGHT NOW...!

EMPTY! THAT'S FUNNY...

I DON'T REMEMBER DRINKING THE REST OF THE BOTTLE.

WELL, THERE'S MORE IN THE BASEMENT...!

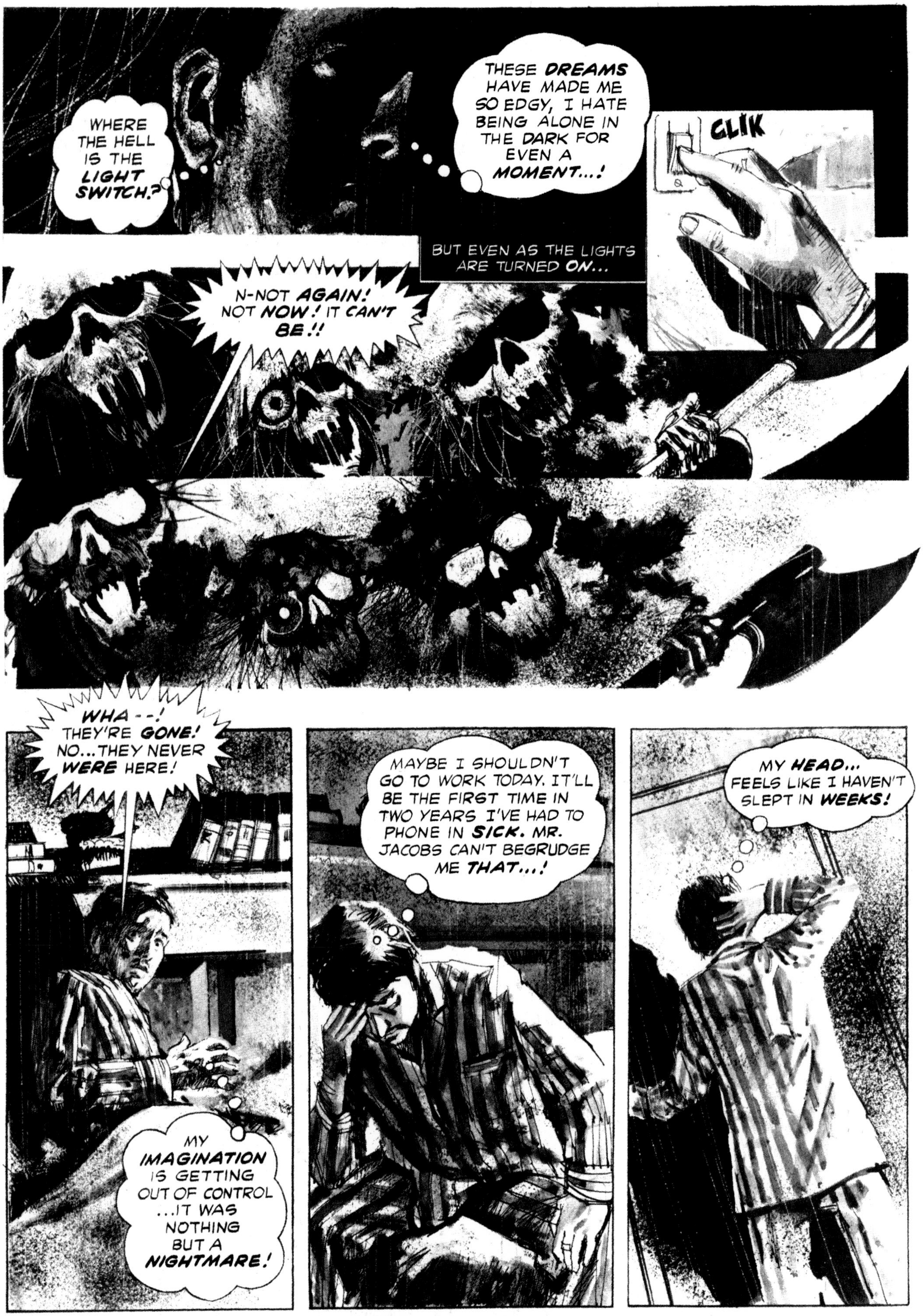
WHERE THE HELL IS THE LIGHT SWITCH?
THESE DREAMS HAVE MADE ME SO EDGY, I HATE BEING ALONE IN THE DARK FOR EVEN A MOMENT...!
GLIK
BUT EVEN AS THE LIGHTS ARE TURNED ON...
N-NOT AGAIN! NOT NOW! IT CAN'T BE!!
WHA--! THEY'RE GONE! NO...THEY NEVER WERE HERE!
MY IMAGINATION IS GETTING OUT OF CONTROL ...IT WAS NOTHING BUT A NIGHTMARE!
MAYBE I SHOULDN'T GO TO WORK TODAY. IT'LL BE THE FIRST TIME IN TWO YEARS I'VE HAD TO PHONE IN SICK. MR. JACOBS CAN'T BEGRUDGE ME THAT...!
MY HEAD... FEELS LIKE I HAVEN'T SLEPT IN WEEKS!

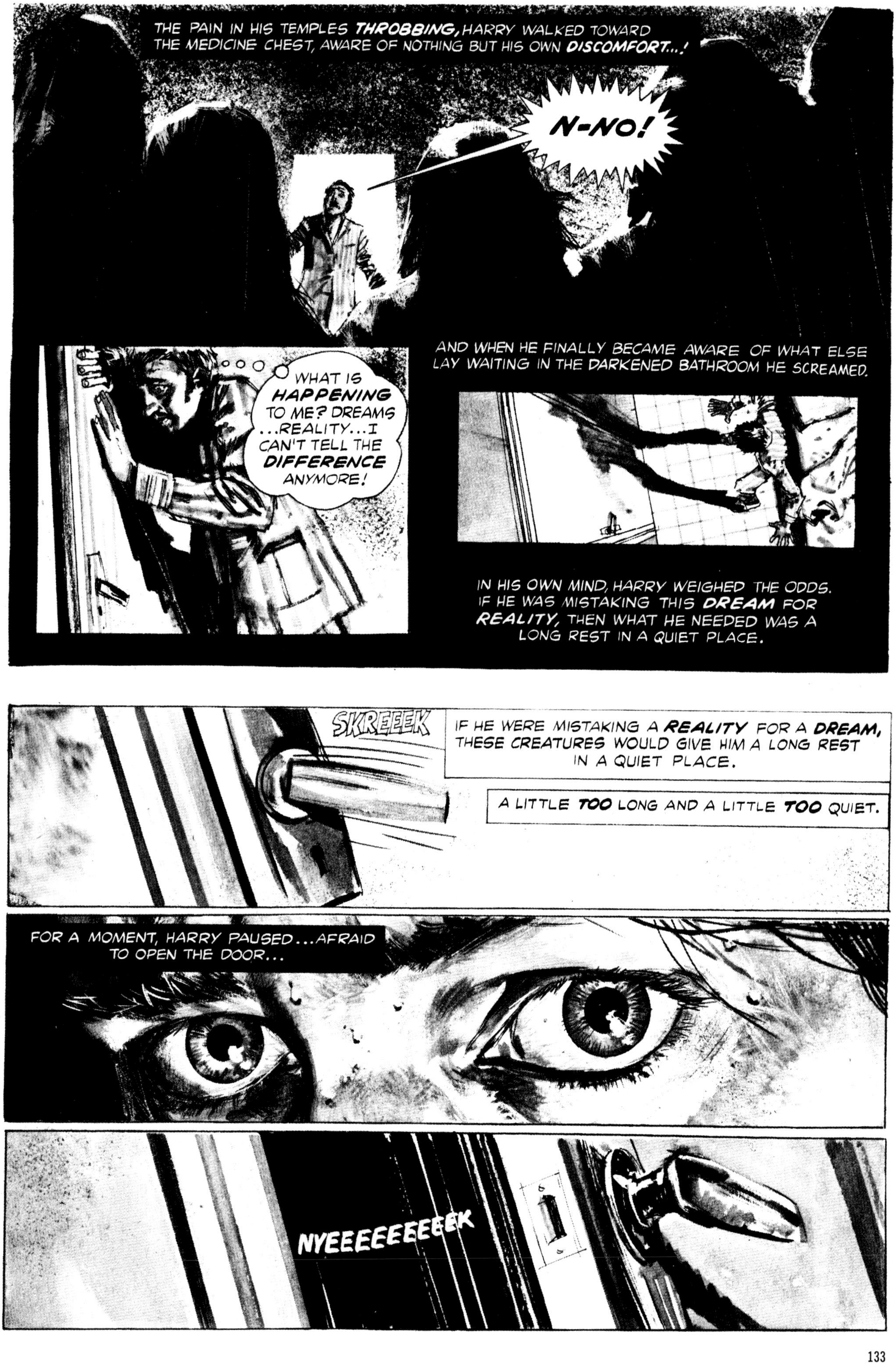

THE PAIN IN HIS TEMPLES THROBBING, HARRY WALKED TOWARD THE MEDICINE CHEST, AWARE OF NOTHING BUT HIS OWN DISCOMFORT...!
N-NO!
AND WHEN HE FINALLY BECAME AWARE OF WHAT ELSE LAY WAITING IN THE DARKENED BATHROOM HE SCREAMED.
WHAT IS HAPPENING TO ME? DREAMS ...REALITY...I CAN'T TELL THE DIFFERENCE ANYMORE!
IN HIS OWN MIND, HARRY WEIGHED THE ODDS. IF HE WAS MISTAKING THIS DREAM FOR REALITY, THEN WHAT HE NEEDED WAS A LONG REST IN A QUIET PLACE.
SKREEEK
IF HE WERE MISTAKING A REALITY FOR A DREAM, THESE CREATURES WOULD GIVE HIM A LONG REST IN A QUIET PLACE.
A LITTLE TOO LONG AND A LITTLE TOO QUIET.
FOR A MOMENT, HARRY PAUSED...AFRAID TO OPEN THE DOOR...
NYEEEEEEEEEK

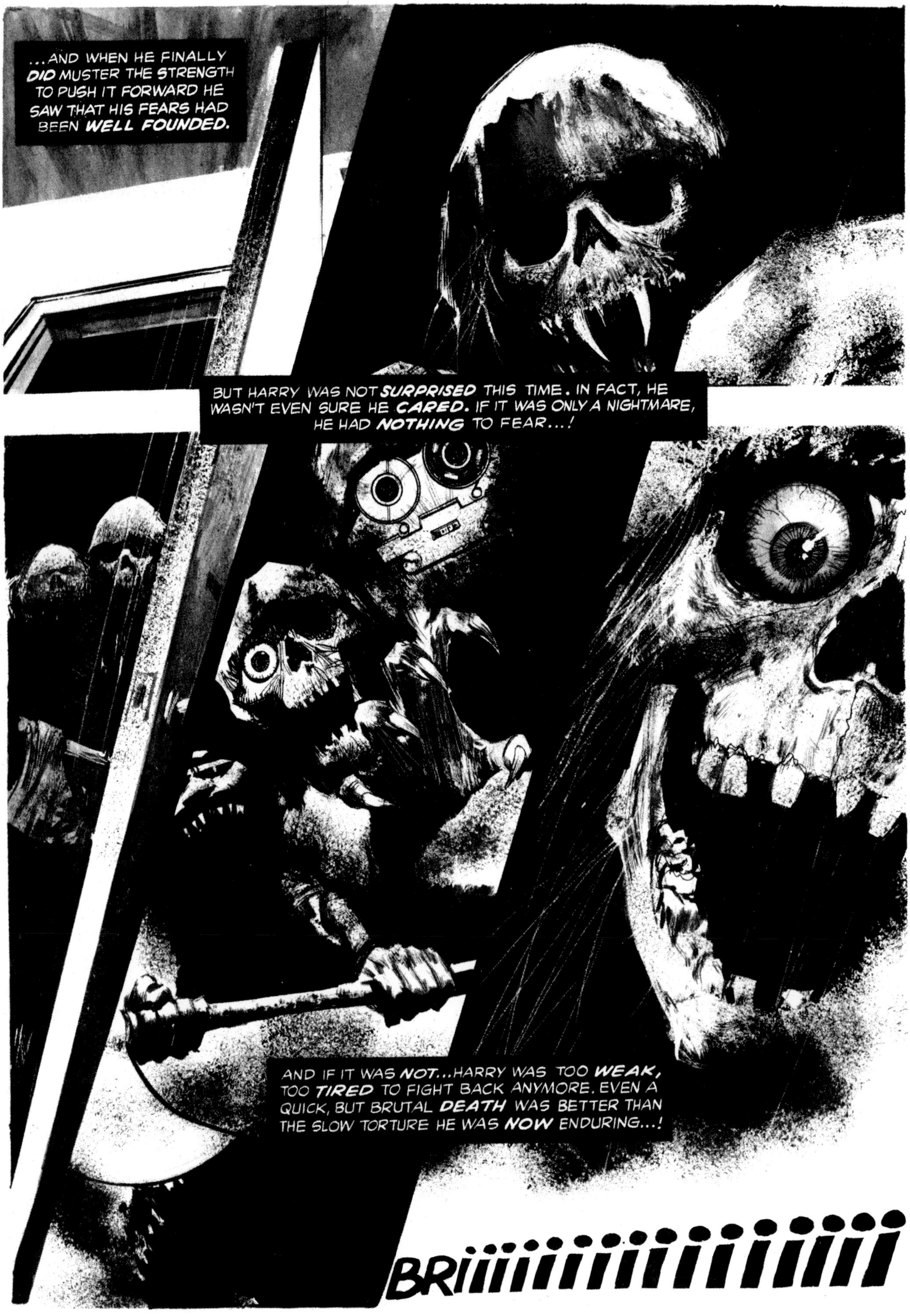
...AND WHEN HE FINALLY DID MUSTER THE STRENGTH TO PUSH IT FORWARD HE SAW THAT HIS FEARS HAD BEEN WELL FOUNDED.
BUT HARRY WAS NOT SURPRISED THIS TIME. IN FACT, HE WASN'T EVEN SURE HE CARED. IF IT WAS ONLY A NIGHTMARE, HE HAD NOTHING TO FEAR...!
AND IF IT WAS NOT...HARRY WAS TOO WEAK, TOO TIRED TO FIGHT BACK ANYMORE. EVEN A QUICK, BUT BRUTAL DEATH WAS BETTER THAN THE SLOW TORTURE HE WAS NOW ENDURING...!
BRiiiiiiiiiiiiiiii

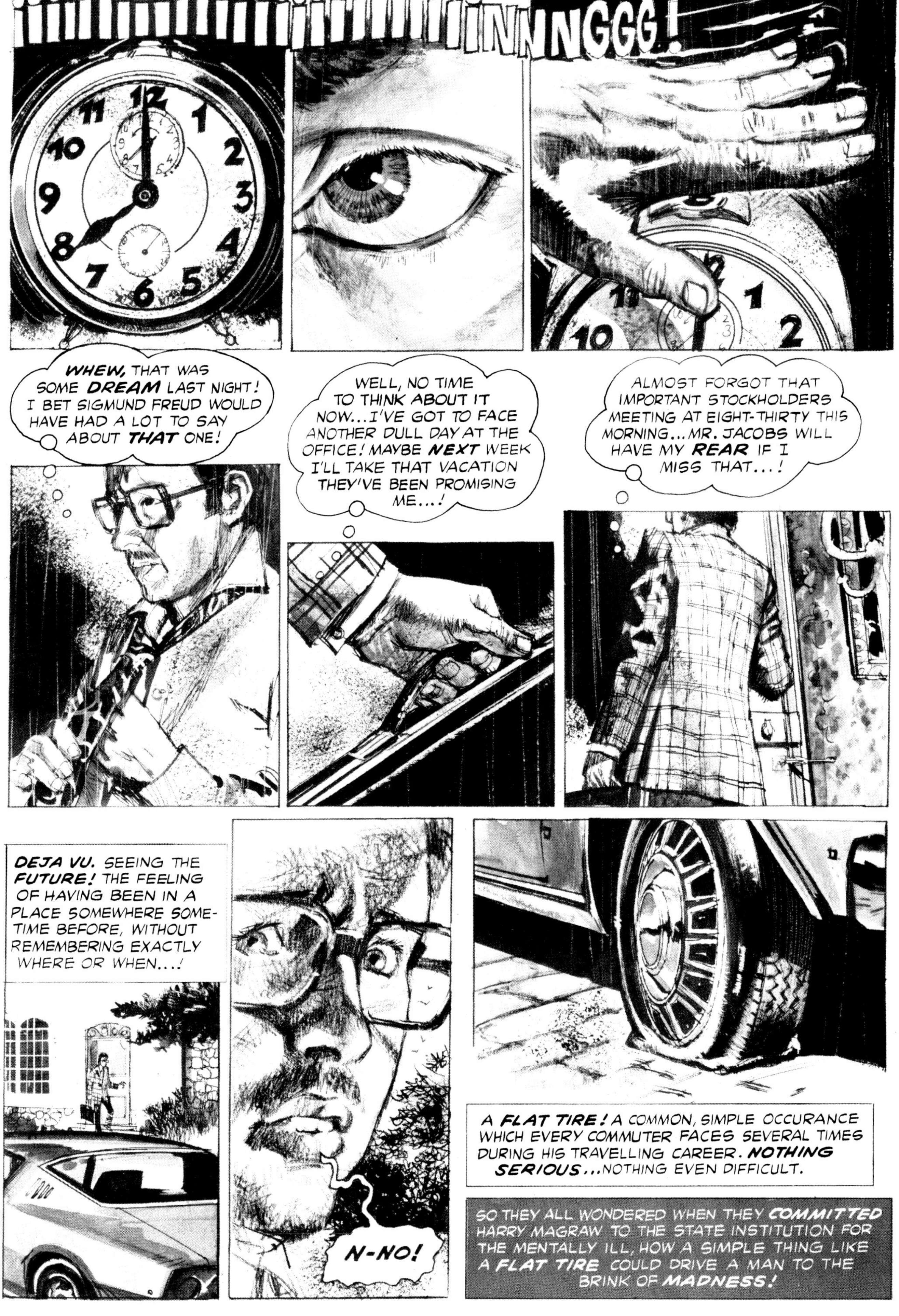
IIIIIIIIIIIIIIIIIIIIIIIIIIIIINNNGGG!
WHEW, THAT WAS SOME DREAM LAST NIGHT! I BET SIGMUND FREUD WOULD HAVE HAD A LOT TO SAY ABOUT THAT ONE!
WELL, NO TIME TO THINK ABOUT IT NOW...I'VE GOT TO FACE ANOTHER DULL DAY AT THE OFFICE! MAYBE NEXT WEEK I'LL TAKE THAT VACATION THEY'VE BEEN PROMISING ME...!
ALMOST FORGOT THAT IMPORTANT STOCKHOLDERS MEETING AT EIGHT-THIRTY THIS MORNING...MR. JACOBS WILL HAVE MY REAR IF I MISS THAT...!
DEJA VU. SEEING THE FUTURE! THE FEELING OF HAVING BEEN IN A PLACE SOMEWHERE SOMETIME BEFORE, WITHOUT REMEMBERING EXACTLY WHERE OR WHEN...!
N-NO!
A FLAT TIRE! A COMMON, SIMPLE OCCURANCE WHICH EVERY COMMUTER FACES SEVERAL TIMES DURING HIS TRAVELLING CAREER. NOTHING SERIOUS...NOTHING EVEN DIFFICULT.
SO THEY ALL WONDERED WHEN THEY COMMITTED HARRY MAGRAW TO THE STATE INSTITUTION FOR THE MENTALLY ILL, HOW A SIMPLE THING LIKE A FLAT TIRE COULD DRIVE A MAN TO THE BRINK OF MADNESS!

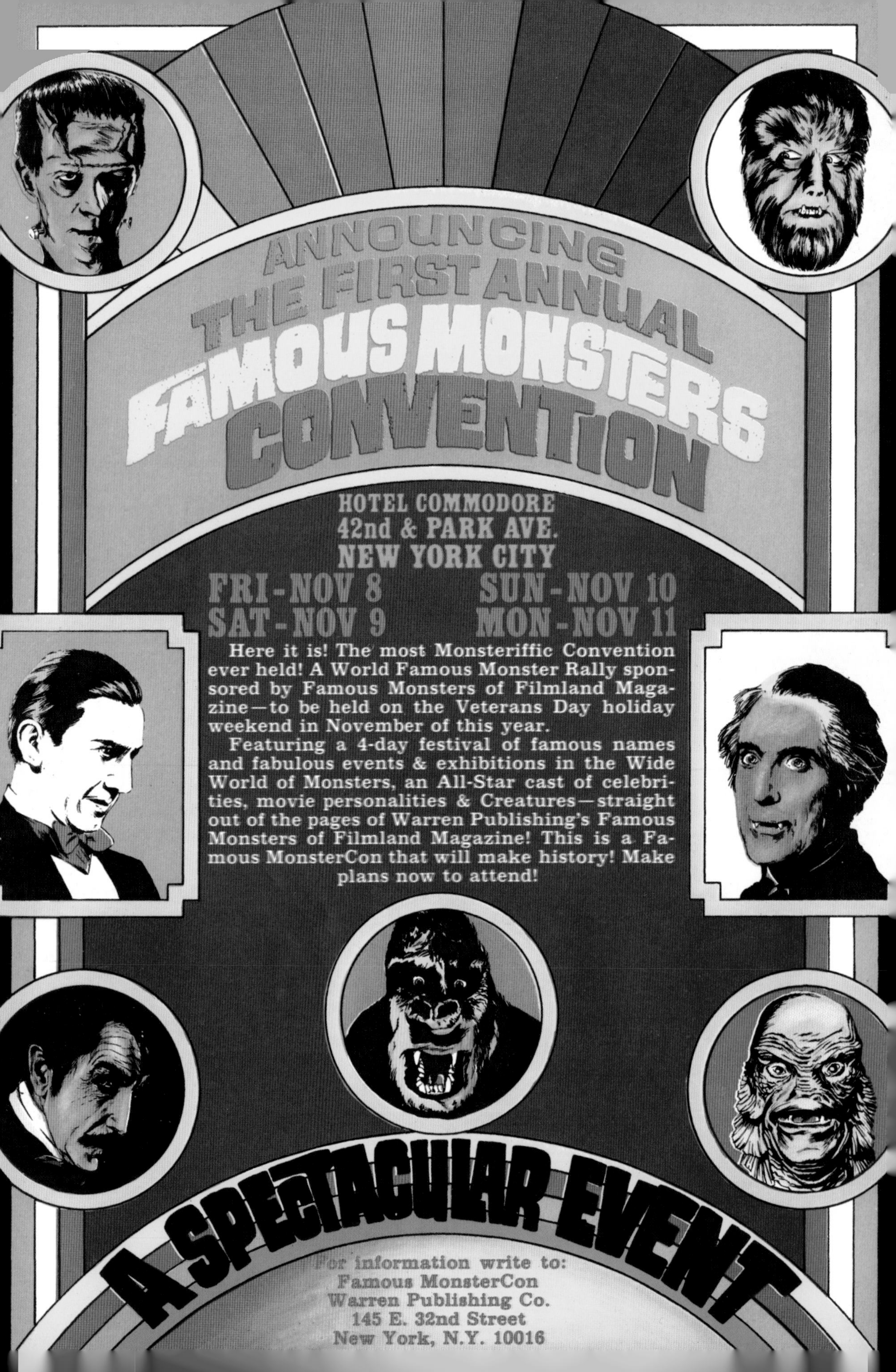
ANNOUNCING
THE FIRST ANNUAL
FAMOUS MONSTERS
CONVENTION
HOTEL COMMODORE
42nd & PARK AVE.
NEW YORK CITY
FRI-NOV 8
SAT-NOV 9
SUN-NOV 10
MON-NOV 11
Here it is! The most Monsteriffic Convention ever held! A World Famous Monster Rally sponsored by Famous Monsters of Filmland Magazine—to be held on the Veterans Day holiday weekend in November of this year.
Featuring a 4-day festival of famous names and fabulous events & exhibitions in the Wide World of Monsters, an All-Star cast of celebrities, movie personalities & Creatures—straight out of the pages of Warren Publishing's Famous Monsters of Filmland Magazine! This is a Famous MonsterCon that will make history! Make plans now to attend!
A SPECTACULAR EVENT
For information write to:
Famous MonsterCon
Warren Publishing Co.
145 E. 32nd Street
New York, N.Y. 10016

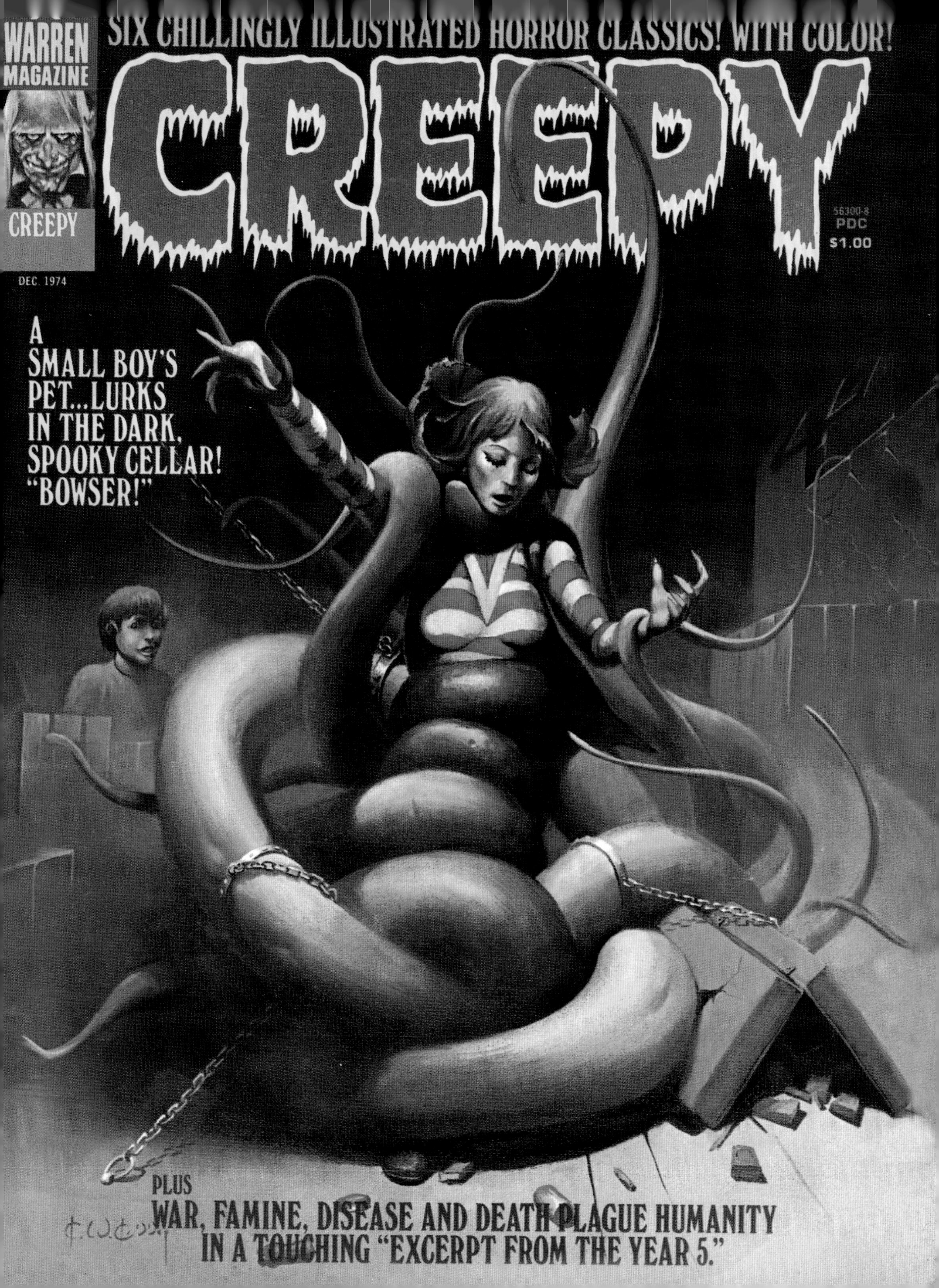
WARREN MAGAZINE
SIX CHILLINGLY ILLUSTRATED HORROR CLASSICS! WITH COLOR!
CREEPY
CREEPY
56300-8
PDC
$1.00
DEC. 1974
A SMALL BOY'S PET...LURKS IN THE DARK, SPOOKY CELLAR! "BOWSER!"
PLUS
WAR, FAMINE, DISEASE AND DEATH PLAGUE HUMANITY
IN A TOUCHING "EXCERPT FROM THE YEAR 5."

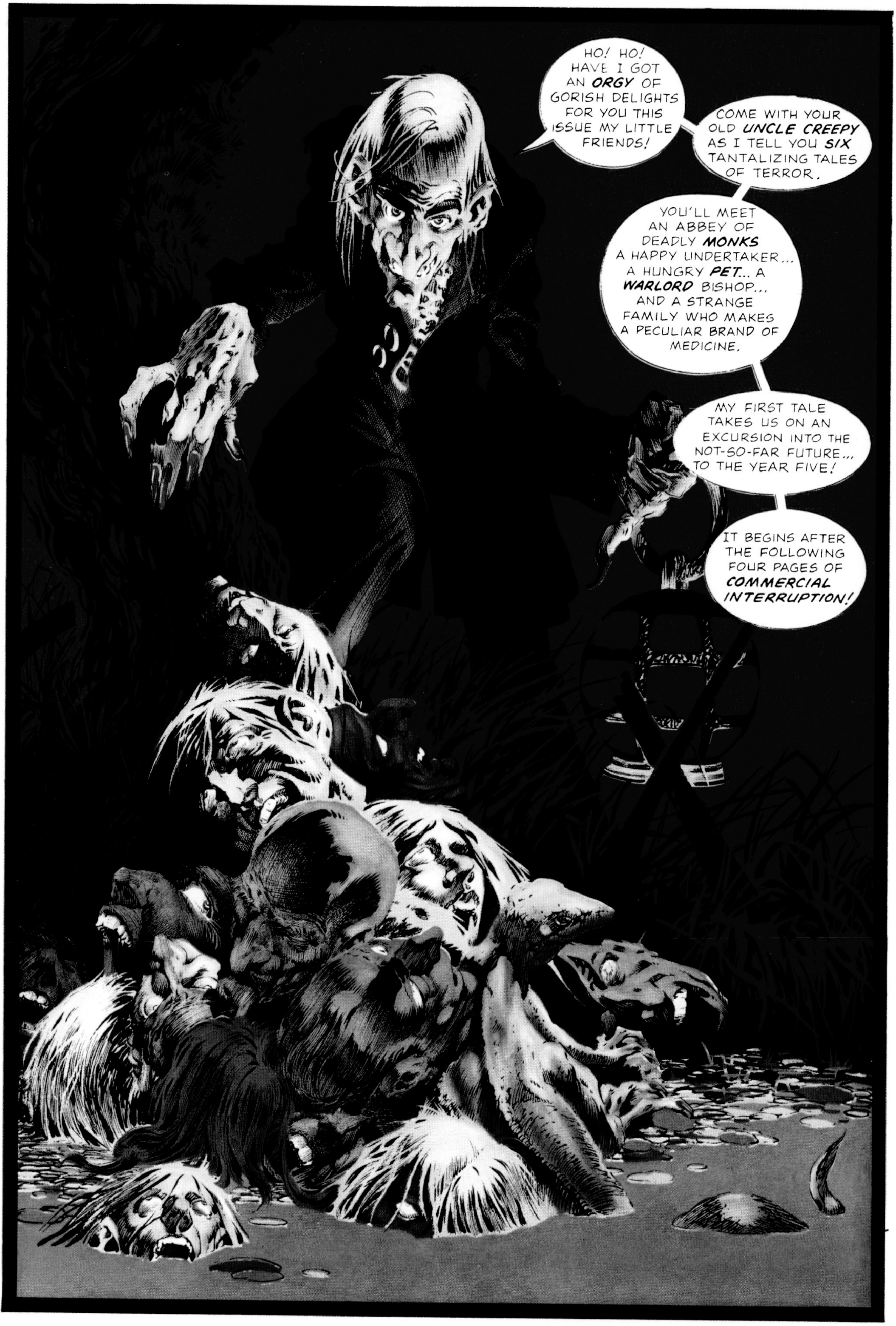
HO! HO! HAVE I GOT AN ORGY OF GORISH DELIGHTS FOR YOU THIS ISSUE MY LITTLE FRIENDS!
COME WITH YOUR OLD UNCLE CREEPY AS I TELL YOU SIX TANTALIZING TALES OF TERROR.
YOU'LL MEET AN ABBEY OF DEADLY MONKS A HAPPY UNDERTAKER... A HUNGRY PET... A WARLORD BISHOP... AND A STRANGE FAMILY WHO MAKES A PECULIAR BRAND OF MEDICINE.
MY FIRST TALE TAKES US ON AN EXCURSION INTO THE NOT-SO-FAR FUTURE... TO THE YEAR FIVE!
IT BEGINS AFTER THE FOLLOWING FOUR PAGES OF COMMERCIAL INTERRUPTION!

WARREN MAGAZINE
SIX CHILLINGLY ILLUSTRATED HORROR CLASSICS! WITH COLOR!
CREEPY
A SMALL BOY'S PET...LURKS IN THE DARK. SPOOKY CELLAR! "BOWSER!"
PLUS WAR, FAMINE, DISEASE AND DEATH PLAGUE HUMANITY IN A TOUCHING "EXCERPT FROM THE YEAR 5."

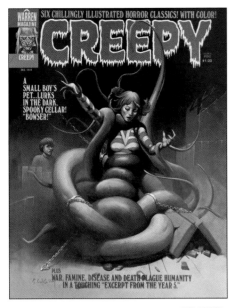

OUR COVER:
A small boy's pet runs rampant, eating stray dogs . . . and Avon ladies. Ken Kelly illustrates this issue's color story by Rich Corben and Jan Strnad. "Bowser!"

Editor-In-Chief & Publisher
JAMES WARREN

Editor
W.B. DuBAY

Production Manager
W.R. MOHALLEY

Circulation Director
AB SIDEMAN

Artists This Issue
ADOLFO ABELLAN
VICENTE ALCAZAR
RICHARD CORBEN
ISIDRO MONES
JOSE ORTIZ
MARTIN SALVADOR
BERNI WRIGHTSON

Writers This Issue
JACK BUTTERWORTH
BUDD LEWIS
JAN STRNAD
CARL WESSLER

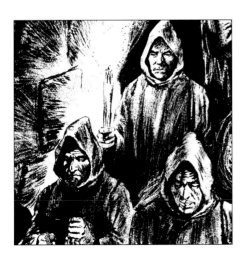

CREEPY

CONTENTS

ISSUE NO. 67
DECEMBER 1974

As explained in the letters column for *Creepy* #69, the story "Bowser" by Jan Strnad and Richard Corben did not actually appear in this issue—it was replaced by Richard Corben's adaptation of Edgar Allan Poe's "The Raven" due to a bindery error and ran much later in Creepy #132. But take heart, monster lovers! "Bowser" appears on page 269 in this volume as a special bonus treat, and "Bowser" can also be found in *Creepy Presents Richard Corben*! —Your Cousin Eerie

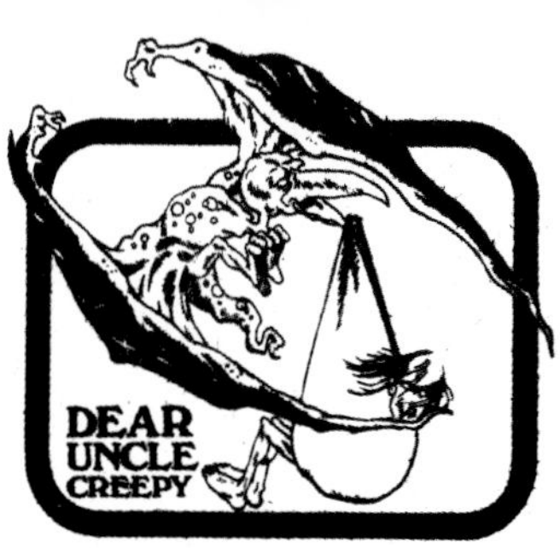
DEAR UNCLE CREEPY

"Horror comics serve a magic-escape function."

Do CREEPY stories exceed the limits of good taste? This controversial question was posed by Michael Oliveri in a lengthy missive published in our August issue. His letter generated so much response, that we are devoting our column this issue to that topic. The following are only a few of the many hundreds of thought-provoking letters received from our readers.

Michael Oliveri's letter in the August issue was indeed worthwhile and deserved more thought than you gave it.

It's true that so-called "real" literature does not usually put limits on the amount of trash it feeds the public. But I've always thought of **Warren** as something **special**. The use of pornography to make your stories real is not necessary. Offending someone's religion by using **the Lord's** name in vain does not make your stories more true-to-life for your readers. And the use of too much gore doesn't, either. **Any** comic company can make you sick, if that is their goal. But **Warren,** and only **Warren,** can emotionally involve you in a horror story.

Keep up the good work, but try to keep down the gore and pornography.

ALAN RICHARD
Humeston, Iowa

Issue #64 was good. Damn good! Sort of an off-shoot for those science fiction anthologies that revolve around a single theme. It is a novel idea that worked well in the comics format.

I didn't read the story of the blinded, deaf and handless character in question, but from the tone of his letter **Mr. Oliveri** was offended.

Being a handicapped adult myself, (Cerebral Palsy) I must admit to being desirous of pity at times. But I feel that's normal. You mean to say, **Mr. Oliveri,** that **you** never feel blue? Is everything always **right** for **you?** I don't believe that!

Also, I don't object to a writer using a handicapped character as a villain or hero. I loved that **Hawaii Five-O** episode about the amputee-killer. I actually got a charge out of seeing a handicapped person playing the heavy.

True, the handicapped have been stereotyped in a certain way and there should be more anti-stereotyped handicaps portrayed as everyday people. But I see no harm in having a villain being disabled in some way.

Although I disagree with Mr. Oliveri on this single point, I respect him for having spoken out. I hate it when people let someone else do their thinking for them. When that happens, censorship follows . . . simply because someone is too lazy to think for himself, or stand up for what he believes in.

RAYMOND J. BOWIE, JR.
Somerville, Mass.

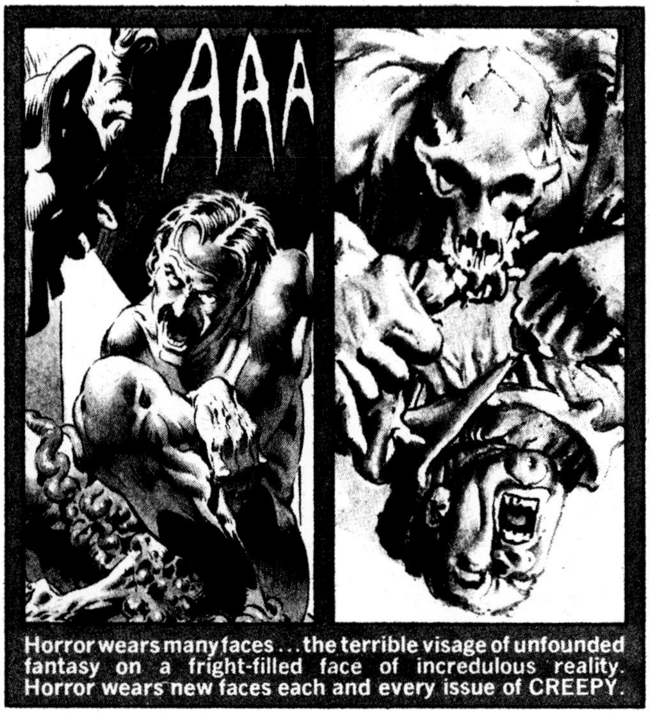
AAA

Horror wears many faces . . . the terrible visage of unfounded fantasy on a fright-filled face of incredulous reality. Horror wears new faces each and every issue of CREEPY.

If **Michael Oliveri** considers it within his religious realms to say "bitch," "bastard," "damn," or "hell," what, may I ask, in the Good-Lord's-Name (no offense intended, **Mike**) do you have against "Fer Chrissake?" I'm actually **puzzled.**

Language ("shit," "fer Chrissake," and "Oh, Jesus" included) is an essential part of **realism. And horror magazines need all they can get!** It's hard to be **realistic** about half-decayed flesh, murderous Zombies or ravenous werewolves grubbing their way in the dark.

Mike, if it's escape from reality you want, there's always **Mother Goose** and **Dr. Seuss!**

HAL MAHAFFEY
Franklin, Penn.

I sadly agree with most of **Michael Oliveri**'s letter. Far too many issues of CREEPY in the past **few** years, have come off as being completely formularized. While some literacy has crept in, **(Archie Goodwin** termed it as a story functioning on "multiple levels") the stories still leave much to be desired.

It's funny that you talk about hiring hacks if you only wanted to portray blood and violence. It's funny because **no** company ever claims to hire hacks.

While many of your artists do, **in fact,** have a great deal of **sensitivity,** as you call it, **most** do not. You've been using too many artists from the **Esteban Maroto** school of pretty-pictures-but-bad-story-flow. Lately, I've been buying the **Warren** books just for the **Rich Corben** or **Berni Wrightson** stories. I'm barely able to even skim over your other tales.

Mr. Oliveri is correct, for the most part, when he refers to your use of needless violence and sex. I'm **all** for beautiful, arty naked women, but only to further the storyline. Unfortunately, too many stories are hacked out with nude women thrown in to **titillate**. Physical violence (in all its graphic detail) is tossed in to **nauseate**.

Violence, for the most part, need **rarely** be depicted. Its suggestion is enough, because the mind is its own best artist.

I think that CREEPY is headed **back on the right track,** though. From a short year ago, when **I looked forward to** nothing, **I now find myself** awaiting at least a color **Corben** story, and possibly something by **Wrightson.** That's two out of six.

HARVEY SOBEL
Commack, N.Y.

I've just read my first CREEPY, at the age of 33, and was astounded by **Michael Oliveri**'s letter. I assume that anyone buying a horror-theme comic in the first place is in an odd position to complain about the magazine being **horrible.**

I would also imagine that the parents of an amputee or deformed or mentally unstable youth would be downright sadistic to buy him **any** horror-theme magazine. It just **isn't** the market you'd want to reach. Or expect to.

I think **Mr. Oliveri** has overlooked the magic-escape function of the magazine. **It's only a magazine!** We want to read CREEPY to escape a world that has more subtle and present horrors. If that were not enough, the quality of the artwork is so outstanding as to elevate the reaction. **Fernando Fernandez'** axe-wielding maniac is a delight in black and white composition, and certainly less horrible than a flesh and blood maniac, simply because of the genius put into the frame by the artist!

More horrible, more realistic terrors were painted by **Francisco Goya!** Should we then turn his canvases to the wall?

I suppose I'm writing because, as a child I used to read horror comics. Then along came the do-gooders implying homosexual relationships between super-heroes, and the effects of scary stories on growing children. And we lost, for a while, a really interesting and important media. So when I hear someone who wishes to okay horror to the extent that **they** aren't shocked, it's not only a paradox (horror **involves** shock) but somehow a **threat!**

Consider the bland quality of most American television programs, which strive to remain non-offensive to **everyone!**

Anyway, I am impressed with the really **superior** quality of your artists, and found the storylines generally tight and effective, especially "Mates" and "High Time."

I might add that humor is an effective counterpoint to horror, each heightening the effect of the other. I teach creative writing. I wouldn't be ashamed to recommend your magazine to students trying to write a good, tight story. I'm glad I found you!

I can't even add "Bring back **Frazetta!"** (Who is **Frazetta? Was Frazetta?**) Or, how did CREEPY become an Uncle? Whose?

MRS. HOWARD GENE
Dallas, Texas

"Horror is subjective reality!"

What difference does it make if the dead girl **did** or did **not** have clothes on? The point is, she's **dead.** In some cases, it is better artistically if the figure is disrobed.

BOB ALLEN
Laredo, Texas

This is in response to **Michael Oliveri**'s letter. He makes some valid points. So does **Archie Goodwin** in his reply.

Unfortunately, like **Mr. Oliveri,** I am worried that "excessive experimentation" may lead beyond the limits of decency.

I immensely enjoy the **Warren** magazines. I also enjoyed **EC** comics as a youngster. However, in the final analysis, **EC** carried their "striving" for new material **too far!** Extremism in any form of communication is an invitation to general public condemnation.

I do not believe in censorship. Yet sometimes society feels compelled to use it as a last resort when material with completely negative values becomes detrimental to social welfare. (i.e.: The correlation between television violence and juvenile crime.) Excesses often breed still further excesses until many people feel a **halt** must be called.

What killed **EC** comics was their treating, in some cases, of the immoral as though it were moral. **EC** used as its justification, the excuse that it was portraying the **real** world; that things do not always end happily, nor does justice always prevail. But it was a shoddy defense.

The **Warren** magazines, however, are to be **commended,** in the main, for not publishing this sort of trash. Ghosts, goblins, vampires, headless horsemen, etc., are fantasy creations. They may, with a thin thread of justice running through the plots, be treated as gothic horror. Homocidal maniacs, on the other hand, are characterizations from life, and should have a moral **raison d'etre.**

We all know that people are beaten, raped, strangled, dismembered, murdered, etc., and that the criminals sometimes escape punishment. But of what value is a **story** in which such a pervert is allowed to escape his just deserts? And what effect does it have on an impressionable ten or twelve year old when he reads that crime seemingly pays?

Keep the **gothic** horror, **Mr. Warren,** but, please use **discretion.**

RON BAKER
Erving, Mass.

Once again, the readers of illustrated story magazines must endure the indignant ranting of a moralistic **zealot.** His letter fairly reeks of religious indoctrination, narrowminded condescension toward the attitudes of others, and puerile sentimentality. As far as he is concerned, the only possibility is that his point of view is right!

"Do not," says the zealot, "view the world as it **is!** Instead, view it as I **want** it to be! Do not remind me of the 'real' reality as I drift in my artificial one; because, if you do, you are sick!"

The zealot creates his own limited world with its own standard of right and wrong, good and bad, suitability and unsuitability, with little reference to the "real world." And, if given the opportunity, he will impose these standards on others whether they like them or not.

The illustrated story is a mode of communication which contains literature, whose subject matter should be all of the manifestations of man. There is no conclusive evidence, derived from scientific investigation, that indicates certain story themes harm the minds of the healthy.

The unfounded attempts of certain individuals to single out the illustrated story and limit the subject matter available to it must be of no consequence. To allow these individuals to impose their personal standards of suitability on this medium of communication amounts to a **rape** of the freedom of thought and of the press.

To be worthy of reading, these illustrated stories must be powerful enough to **offend** someone. If they were so diluted as to insure no offense, even to a person of the most sensitive nature, they would have little to offer beyond their bland inoffensiveness.

As a man of thirty-five years educated with experience at the Ph.D. level, a teacher in college and high school for ten years, I know my mind is capable of deciding what I want to see or read. I neither need nor want the guidance or protection which the zealots are ever willing to provide.

Illustrated story magazines are an interesting alternative in the adventure of life. Please do not limit your artists or writers. Produce the **best** material you can. The **Warren** magazines are the most beautiful of their kind available today. I thank you for producing them. They enrich my life.

CHARLES W. HOWIE, JR.
Manomet, Mass.

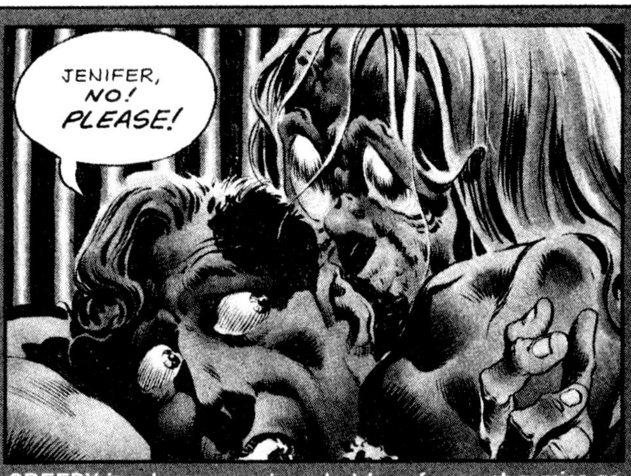
JENIFER, NO! PLEASE!

CREEPY is a horror comic . . . but how far must comics go to portray the ultimate in terror? How far can they go? Our readers tell us in this issue's letters column!

Michael Oliveri seemed disturbed by the use of the Lord's name in vain. I do hate to be the one to break this news to him, but the sad, ugly fact is that many people **do** swear. Didn't I see Mr. Oliveri himself use bitch, bastard and shit in his letter. It was a comic book **first.** I've never seen these words in a **story.**

However, I'm **for** the use of swearing in **Warren** stories.

Swearing is a fact of life. If a horror story mirrors life, it becomes that much more realistic and horrifying. Horror doesn't work well in fantasy, simply because you don't believe it. It is at its best when **real** people, in **real** situations, encounter **real** horrors. For me to believe in a story, I require all the little obscurely accurate traits of human nature the writer can furnish. When I find myself trapped within the strict confines of a gory story, I squirm. And the story is a success. Swearing, deformity and perversions may shock, yet they are artistically valid because they are universally real. And please, it has taken the comics industry twenty years to recover from **Dr. Wertham**'s onslaughts.

CREEPY may be a horror magazine, but it hasn't yet revived "Seduction Of The Innocent" from its deserved death.

LARRY PURSELLEY
Ft. Worth, Tex.

Michael Oliveri makes many interesting comments. But I agree with only **one** . . . the part about the dead, disrobed woman.

Why did she **have** to be naked? Now, I have no qualms about nudity, but I don't like **useless** nudity.

As for his comments on verbal obscentities. Mr. Oliveri has to be living in the dark ages. I'm barely 14, just out of the ninth grade, and the cursing in your magazine is nothing compared to the cursing I hear around school. And in the elementary school, I sometimes wonder if it isn't **worse!**

The prime purpose in my reading your magazine is to be scared or thrilled by your stories. Now no one over 12 years old is really scared by vampires, werewolves, etc. The stories that scare me are the ones that are **real!** When I read a story about a homocidal maniac, I keep looking over my shoulder to see if there is a man with an axe behind me, ready to bury it in my head. I thoroughly agree with **Archie Goodwin**'s comments on "Twisted Medicine." It indeed was true-to-life, very tragic horror. But then, there's **nothing** wrong with realism!

Mr. Oliveri wrote an interesting letter. I didn't agree with it, but I'm glad you printed it!

STEVE FLAA
Wayzata, Minn.

Let me make this perfectly clear!

Why not take a chance on a 300 year-old creep? Write! Send letters to:

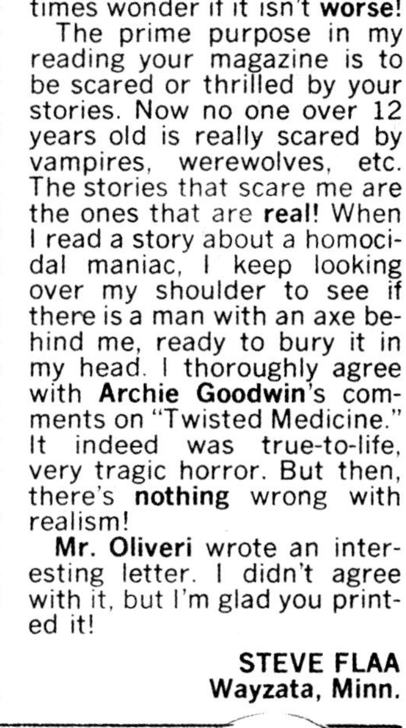

CREEPY'S CATACOMBS

ONCE UPON A TIME AT WARREN...

All is quiet in the editorial office of **Warren Publishing**, except for the staccato hammering of editor **Bill DuBay**'s typewriter. In a large sunny room, **Sherry Berne** is busy designing advertising pages, while colorist, **Michele Brand** is just beginning a new story. Editorial assistant **Louise Jones** is busy putting the finishing touches on Captain Company ad copy.

Suddenly, through the door, with a noise like ten thousand raging pygmies, bursts **"Super Barbarian,"** with cries of **"Kill! Pillage!"**

He attacks the chairs with a flailing mailing tube, overthrowing them in fierce, one-sided combat, then proceeds to vanquish the desks and drawing boards in mere seconds.

Having overcome all obstacles, he retires to his studio to assume again the mild-mannered identity of **"The Kid,"** otherwise known as **Bill Mohalley**, production manager. (Someone remarks that **"The Kid"** must have made that deadline on **Famous Monsters** after all.)

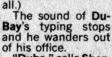

SHERRY BERNE

LOUISE JONES

MICHELE BRAND

BILL MOHALLEY

The sound of **DuBay**'s typing stops and he wanders out of his office.

"Dube," calls **Sherry,** "I have to have twelve more ad pages in **Creepy.**"

"No way, Bernowitz!" growls **DuBay.** "What are you doing to that ad page anyway? Where's the copy? Where's the art? Where's my **name?**"

"And **Brand**, what can I do to hassle **you** today? You call yourself a **colorist?** Look at that page? You've got to **mold** things, **Brand.** Make them **three-dimensional!** Make believe you're **Rich Corben!**"

"And **Jones!** Are you still on those ads? You've been on those ads for an **hour.** Why haven't you finished those letters pages and that editorial I gave you ten minutes ago?"

"GO AWAY! SHOO! SCATT! GET OUT OF HERE AND LET US DO SOME WORK!" scream **Sherry, Michele** and **Louise** in unison. Then a sympathetic voice intones, "What's the matter, **Dube?** Are you **stuck** again? Is that why you're hassling us?"

"Yeah," admits **DuBay.** "If you had two seconds in a hardware store to grab something you could conceal in the palm of your hand before being abducted in a flying saucer, what would you take?"

"Well..."

"I would..."

"Why don't you..."

"That's great!" bellows **DuBay.** "You know, you guys are a lot of help!" He makes a flying leap for his sanctum and his typewriter.

From the carpeted recesses of **DuBay**'s office, there is a muffled shout. "You guys really do do good work," and the typing resumes.

"He's been reading those 'encourage your staff' articles in the office management magazine again," murmurs **Sherry.**

CONTROVERSY IN THE COMICS

Sex. Cannibalism. Religion. Abortion. Divorce. Mercy-killing. Racism. Prostitution. What do these eight subjects have in common? They're controversial topics that have long been **avoided** by the comics industry. They're considered by many to be **"heavy"** subjects, too relevant, thought-provoking or "touchy" to be treated properly in a medium as light as the comic book.

But we at **Warren Publishing** think **differently.** We feel that many readers of today's **horror** comics have matured **beyond** a need for **mythical horror.** Some **Warren** readers seem to want more than **vampires, werewolves** and **zombies.** We receive letters every day suggesting topics of modern, every-day horrors from which readers would like to see stories written. And in response to those letters, we try to include a proportionate amount of true-to-life horror in each issue of CREEPY, EERIE and VAMPIRELLA.

This month you'll find both relevance and controversy in a world depleted of resources and food in **"Excerpts From The Year Five,"** our lead story in the January issue of **CREEPY.** The subject of cannibalism is touched upon briefly, in a way to show its true horror... but its occasional necessity.

In the same magazine, the church comes under fire. **"Holy War"** digs into the all-too-real terrors of the religious-political struggles of the middle ages and the depressing realities of why thousands of lives were lost in the Crusades.

Another view of religion... with a touch of vigilanteism and a dash of prostitution turns up in a new series in this month's **EERIE** Magazine. **"The Butcher"** probes the religious beliefs of mobsters in the early 1930's. While in the same issue, **"The Spook"** offers a look at white and black men's relations in a racist, pro-slavery South. It's all very **real.** Some will argue it is **too** real for escapist **comic book** literature.

In the months ahead, we'll be featuring stories touching on other taboo but ever present subjects of controversy in today's headlines: euthanasia, or mercy killing, suicide, abortion, political freedom and the drug question. Each story will deal with the realities and the horrors of its particular subject on a human, personal level. **You won't see sensationalism** masked by **relevance,** nor will you see unadulterated **gore** in the guise of **childish comic book action.** Each subject will be treated in an adult manner, stressing **entertainment** and **feeling** first, posing a question as to the moral correctness of the topic, second.

In all cases, **Warren Publishing** recognizes its responsibility to provide wholesome, informative entertainment. No matter if our subject be werewolves and zombies, or suicides and divorces, never will the **Warren** magazines step beyond the limits of **good taste.**

And for those readers who want the classic horror that has been found in the **Warren** comic magazinee since their inception more than ten years ago, there'll be a sprinkling of that old-fashioned horror mixed among the relevant topics discussed above.

We'll also offer occasional adaptations of **Edgar Allan Poe, H.P. Lovecraft** and **Ambrose Bierce** masterpieces... with a moderate blend of our own EERIE/VAMPIRELLA continuing series.

With an average of six new stories in each issue of every **Warren** magazine, we think we have something for **everyone.**

We hope you'll agree.

THE CREATIVE MAN
GERRY BOUDREAU: PORTRAIT ARTIST?

What is **Gerry Boudreau**'s name doing in a column devoted to Warren **artists?** He's a **writer,** true enough, but when he's not poking away at his typewriter, he can often be found sketching furiously with pen, pencil or any convenient implement.

"Although I've had no formal art training, I can't remember a time when I didn't like to draw," says **Gerry.** "Even as a kid, I would sketch faces from newspapers, magazines, comic books... anybody or anything that would sit still long enough for me to commit it to paper."

Even now, his primary interest is in drawing faces. "I love sketching actors," **Gerry** claims. "Most of them have such expressive and distinctive faces, it is a challenge to find and capture those details that make them so popular with fans."

Among the film stars who can be found in **Gerry**'s sketchbook are **Clint Eastwood, Diana Rigg, Peter Cushing,** and many others.

EXCERPTS FROM THE YEAR FIVE!

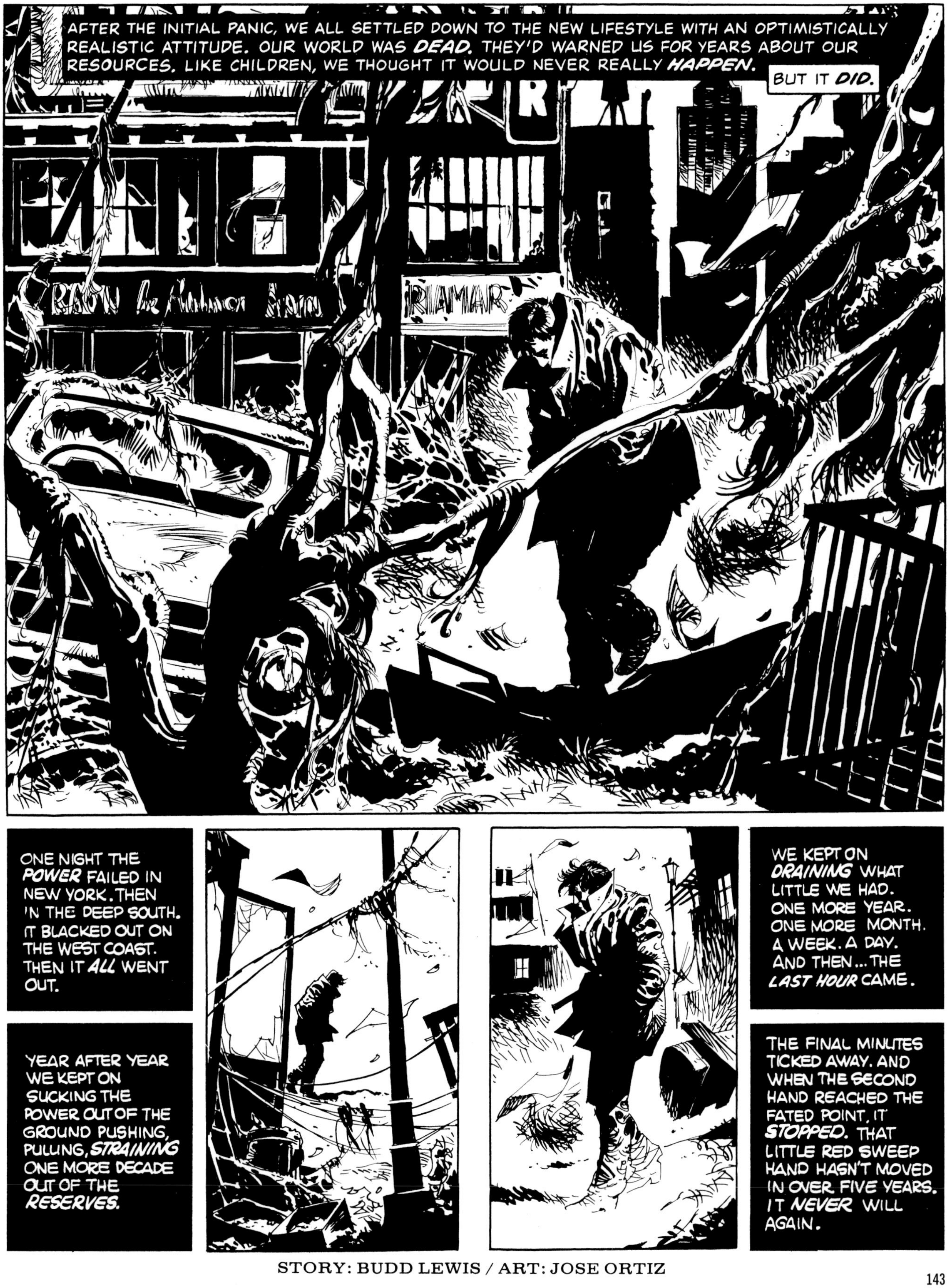
AFTER THE INITIAL PANIC, WE ALL SETTLED DOWN TO THE NEW LIFESTYLE WITH AN OPTIMISTICALLY REALISTIC ATTITUDE. OUR WORLD WAS DEAD. THEY'D WARNED US FOR YEARS ABOUT OUR RESOURCES. LIKE CHILDREN, WE THOUGHT IT WOULD NEVER REALLY HAPPEN.
BUT IT DID.
RIAMAR
ONE NIGHT THE POWER FAILED IN NEW YORK. THEN IN THE DEEP SOUTH. IT BLACKED OUT ON THE WEST COAST. THEN IT ALL WENT OUT.
YEAR AFTER YEAR WE KEPT ON SUCKING THE POWER OUT OF THE GROUND PUSHING, PULLING, STRAINING ONE MORE DECADE OUT OF THE RESERVES.
WE KEPT ON DRAINING WHAT LITTLE WE HAD. ONE MORE YEAR. ONE MORE MONTH. A WEEK. A DAY. AND THEN... THE LAST HOUR CAME.
THE FINAL MINUTES TICKED AWAY. AND WHEN THE SECOND HAND REACHED THE FATED POINT, IT STOPPED. THAT LITTLE RED SWEEP HAND HASN'T MOVED IN OVER FIVE YEARS. IT NEVER WILL AGAIN.

STORY: BUDD LEWIS / ART: JOSE ORTIZ

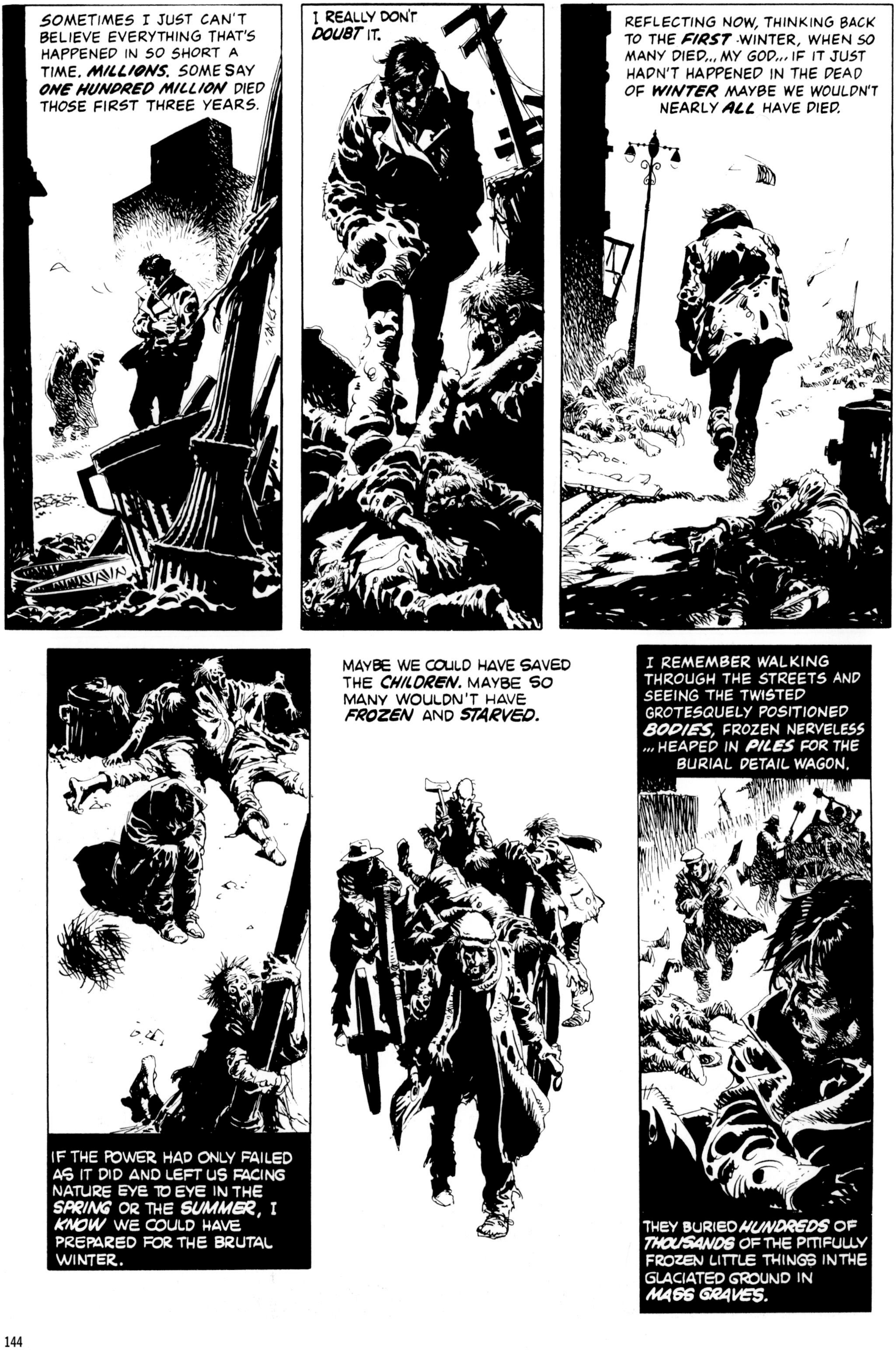
SOMETIMES I JUST CAN'T BELIEVE EVERYTHING THAT'S HAPPENED IN SO SHORT A TIME. MILLIONS. SOME SAY ONE HUNDRED MILLION DIED THOSE FIRST THREE YEARS.
I REALLY DON'T DOUBT IT.
REFLECTING NOW, THINKING BACK TO THE FIRST WINTER, WHEN SO MANY DIED... MY GOD... IF IT JUST HADN'T HAPPENED IN THE DEAD OF WINTER MAYBE WE WOULDN'T NEARLY ALL HAVE DIED.
IF THE POWER HAD ONLY FAILED AS IT DID AND LEFT US FACING NATURE EYE TO EYE IN THE SPRING OR THE SUMMER, I KNOW WE COULD HAVE PREPARED FOR THE BRUTAL WINTER.
MAYBE WE COULD HAVE SAVED THE CHILDREN. MAYBE SO MANY WOULDN'T HAVE FROZEN AND STARVED.
I REMEMBER WALKING THROUGH THE STREETS AND SEEING THE TWISTED GROTESQUELY POSITIONED BODIES, FROZEN NERVELESS ... HEAPED IN PILES FOR THE BURIAL DETAIL WAGON.
THEY BURIED HUNDREDS OF THOUSANDS OF THE PITIFULLY FROZEN LITTLE THINGS IN THE GLACIATED GROUND IN MASS GRAVES.

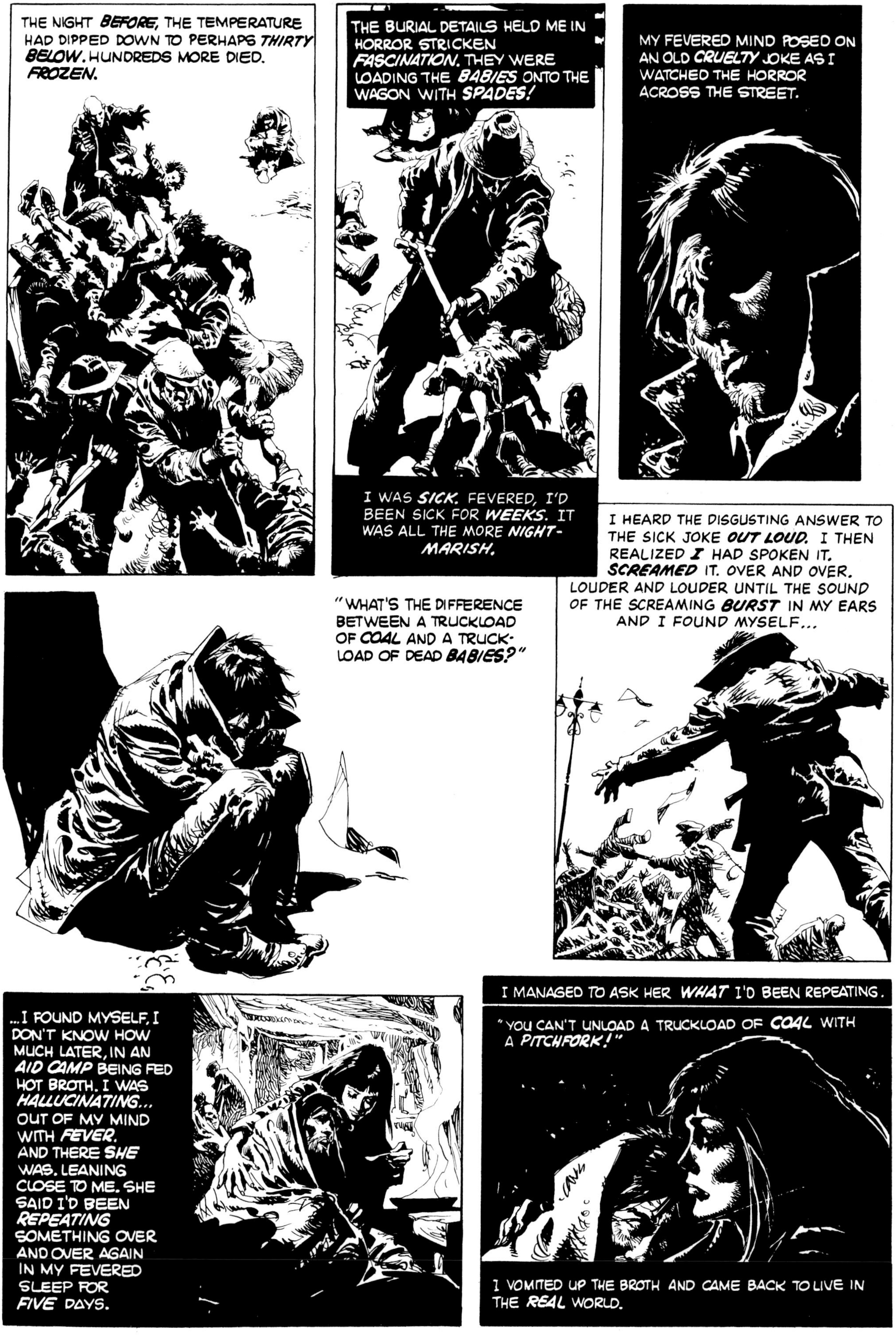

THE NIGHT BEFORE, THE TEMPERATURE HAD DIPPED DOWN TO PERHAPS THIRTY BELOW. HUNDREDS MORE DIED. FROZEN.
THE BURIAL DETAILS HELD ME IN HORROR STRICKEN FASCINATION. THEY WERE LOADING THE BABIES ONTO THE WAGON WITH SPADES!
I WAS SICK. FEVERED, I'D BEEN SICK FOR WEEKS. IT WAS ALL THE MORE NIGHT-MARISH.
MY FEVERED MIND POSED ON AN OLD CRUELTY JOKE AS I WATCHED THE HORROR ACROSS THE STREET.
"WHAT'S THE DIFFERENCE BETWEEN A TRUCKLOAD OF COAL AND A TRUCK-LOAD OF DEAD BABIES?"
I HEARD THE DISGUSTING ANSWER TO THE SICK JOKE OUT LOUD. I THEN REALIZED I HAD SPOKEN IT. SCREAMED IT. OVER AND OVER. LOUDER AND LOUDER UNTIL THE SOUND OF THE SCREAMING BURST IN MY EARS AND I FOUND MYSELF...
...I FOUND MYSELF, I DON'T KNOW HOW MUCH LATER, IN AN AID CAMP BEING FED HOT BROTH. I WAS HALLUCINATING... OUT OF MY MIND WITH FEVER. AND THERE SHE WAS. LEANING CLOSE TO ME. SHE SAID I'D BEEN REPEATING SOMETHING OVER AND OVER AGAIN IN MY FEVERED SLEEP FOR FIVE DAYS.
I MANAGED TO ASK HER WHAT I'D BEEN REPEATING.
"YOU CAN'T UNLOAD A TRUCKLOAD OF COAL WITH A PITCHFORK!"
I VOMITED UP THE BROTH AND CAME BACK TO LIVE IN THE REAL WORLD.

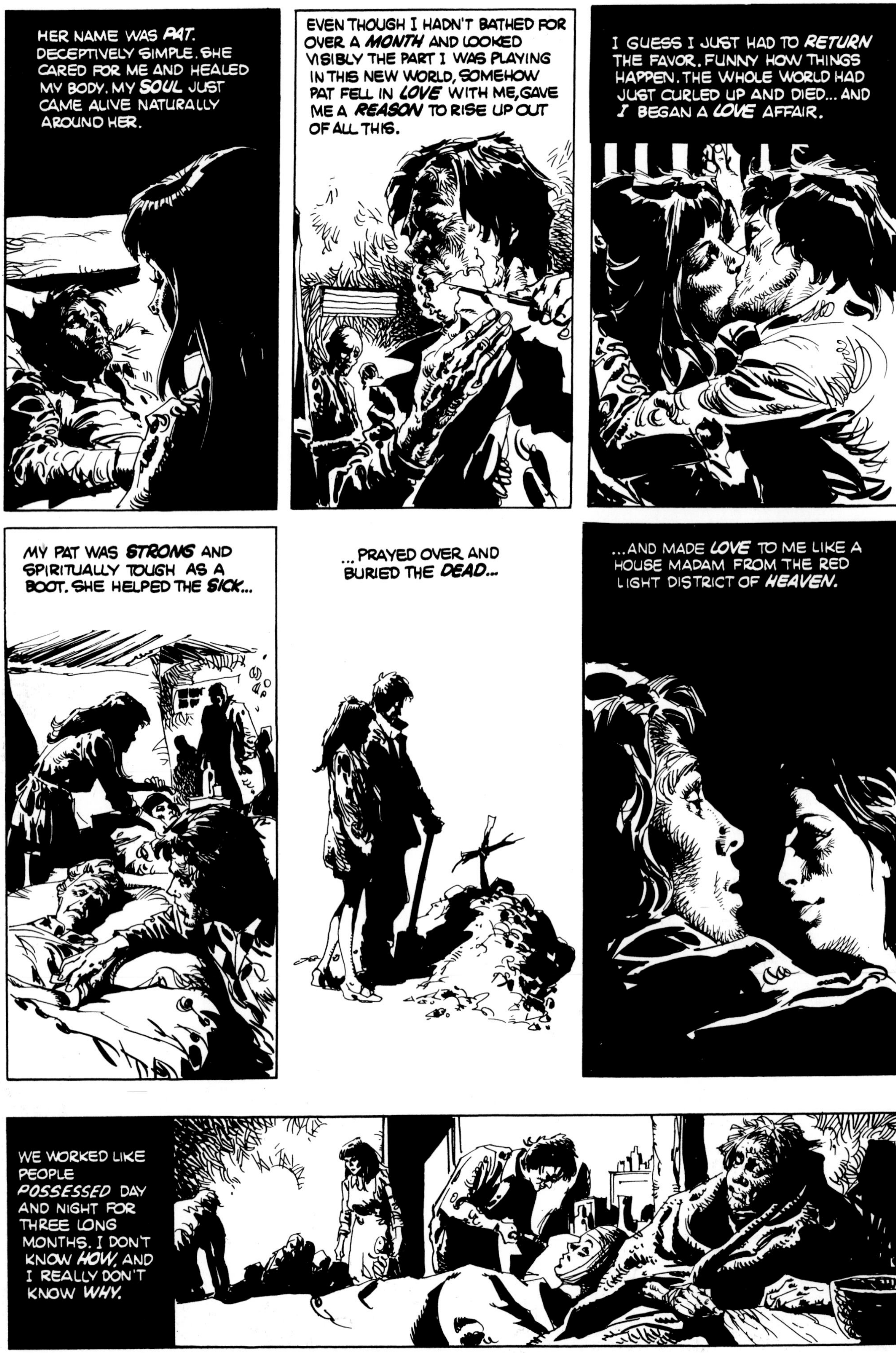
HER NAME WAS PAT. DECEPTIVELY SIMPLE. SHE CARED FOR ME AND HEALED MY BODY. MY SOUL JUST CAME ALIVE NATURALLY AROUND HER.
EVEN THOUGH I HADN'T BATHED FOR OVER A MONTH AND LOOKED VISIBLY THE PART I WAS PLAYING IN THIS NEW WORLD, SOMEHOW PAT FELL IN LOVE WITH ME, GAVE ME A REASON TO RISE UP OUT OF ALL THIS.
I GUESS I JUST HAD TO RETURN THE FAVOR. FUNNY HOW THINGS HAPPEN. THE WHOLE WORLD HAD JUST CURLED UP AND DIED... AND I BEGAN A LOVE AFFAIR.
MY PAT WAS STRONG AND SPIRITUALLY TOUGH AS A BOOT. SHE HELPED THE SICK...
...PRAYED OVER AND BURIED THE DEAD...
...AND MADE LOVE TO ME LIKE A HOUSE MADAM FROM THE RED LIGHT DISTRICT OF HEAVEN.
WE WORKED LIKE PEOPLE POSSESSED DAY AND NIGHT FOR THREE LONG MONTHS. I DON'T KNOW HOW, AND I REALLY DON'T KNOW WHY.

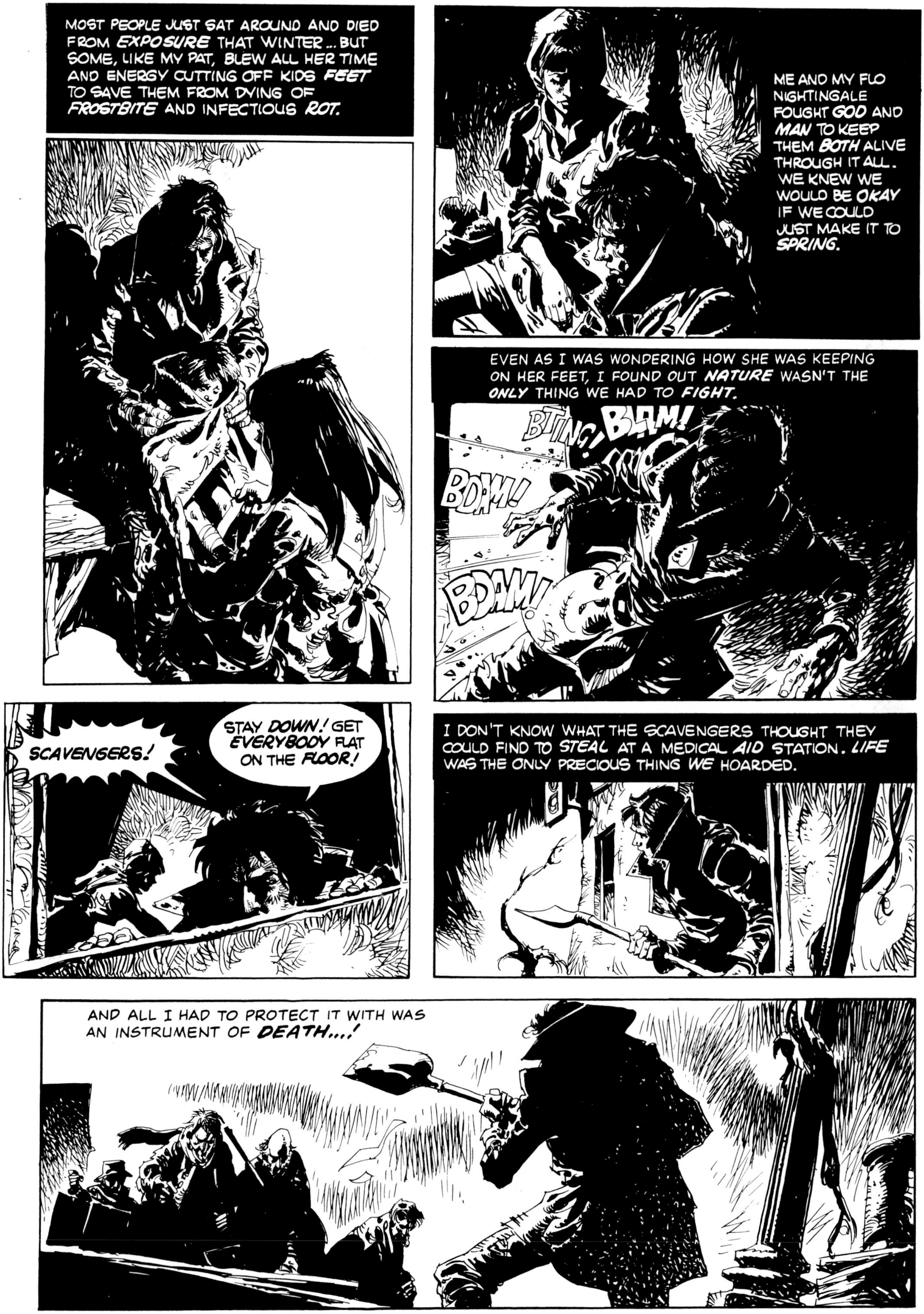
MOST PEOPLE JUST SAT AROUND AND DIED FROM EXPOSURE THAT WINTER... BUT SOME, LIKE MY PAT, BLEW ALL HER TIME AND ENERGY CUTTING OFF KIDS FEET TO SAVE THEM FROM DYING OF FROSTBITE AND INFECTIOUS ROT.
ME AND MY FLO NIGHTINGALE FOUGHT GOD AND MAN TO KEEP THEM BOTH ALIVE THROUGH IT ALL. WE KNEW WE WOULD BE OKAY IF WE COULD JUST MAKE IT TO SPRING.
EVEN AS I WAS WONDERING HOW SHE WAS KEEPING ON HER FEET, I FOUND OUT NATURE WASN'T THE ONLY THING WE HAD TO FIGHT.
BTING!
BLAM!
BDAM!
BDAM!
SCAVENGERS!
STAY DOWN! GET EVERYBODY FLAT ON THE FLOOR!
I DON'T KNOW WHAT THE SCAVENGERS THOUGHT THEY COULD FIND TO STEAL AT A MEDICAL AID STATION. LIFE WAS THE ONLY PRECIOUS THING WE HOARDED.
AND ALL I HAD TO PROTECT IT WITH WAS AN INSTRUMENT OF DEATH...!

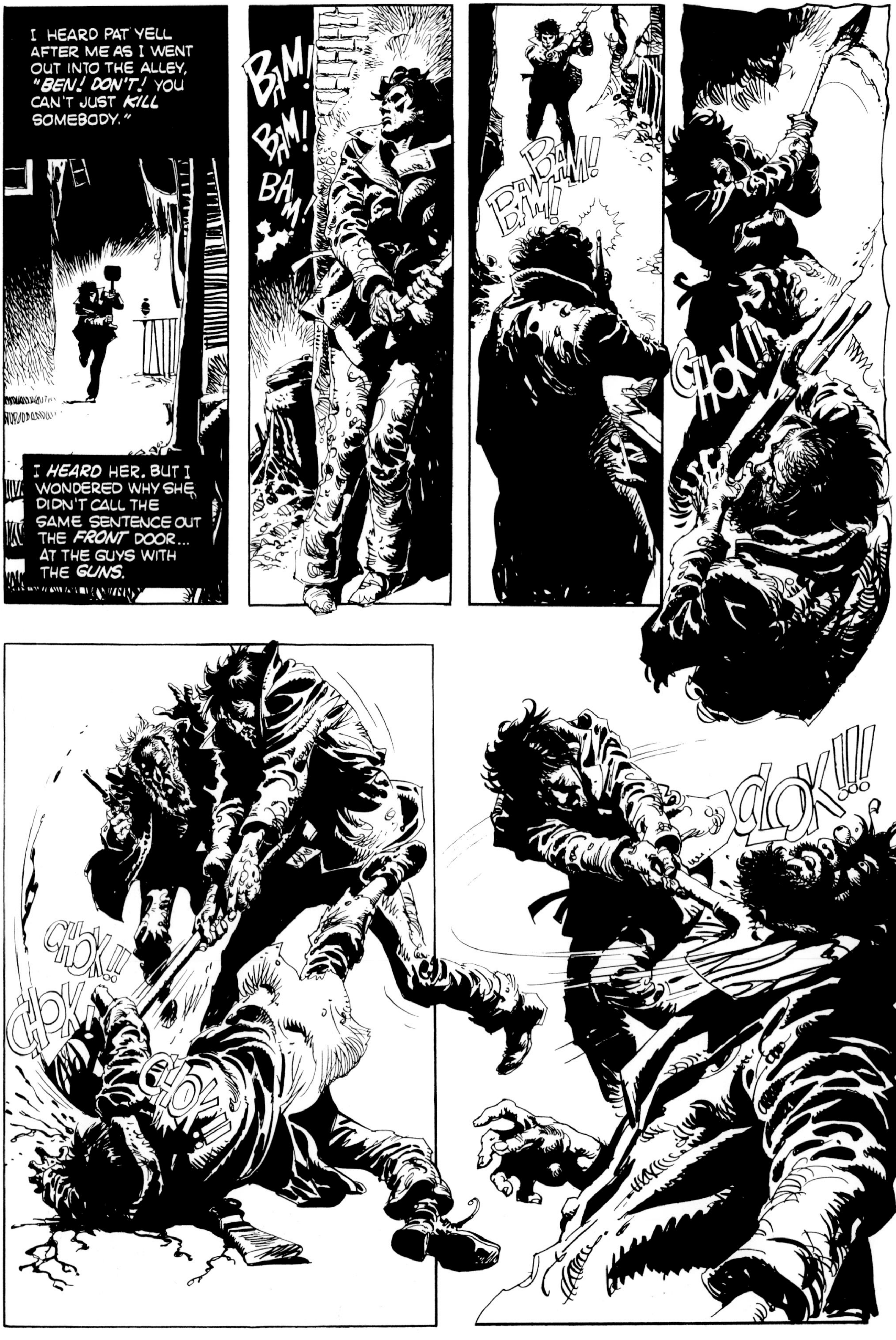
I HEARD PAT YELL AFTER ME AS I WENT OUT INTO THE ALLEY, "BEN! DON'T! YOU CAN'T JUST KILL SOMEBODY."
I HEARD HER. BUT I WONDERED WHY SHE DIDN'T CALL THE SAME SENTENCE OUT THE FRONT DOOR... AT THE GUYS WITH THE GUNS.
BAM!
BAM!
BAM!
BAM!
BAM!
CHOK!!
CHOK!!
CHOK!
CHOK!!
CLOK!!!

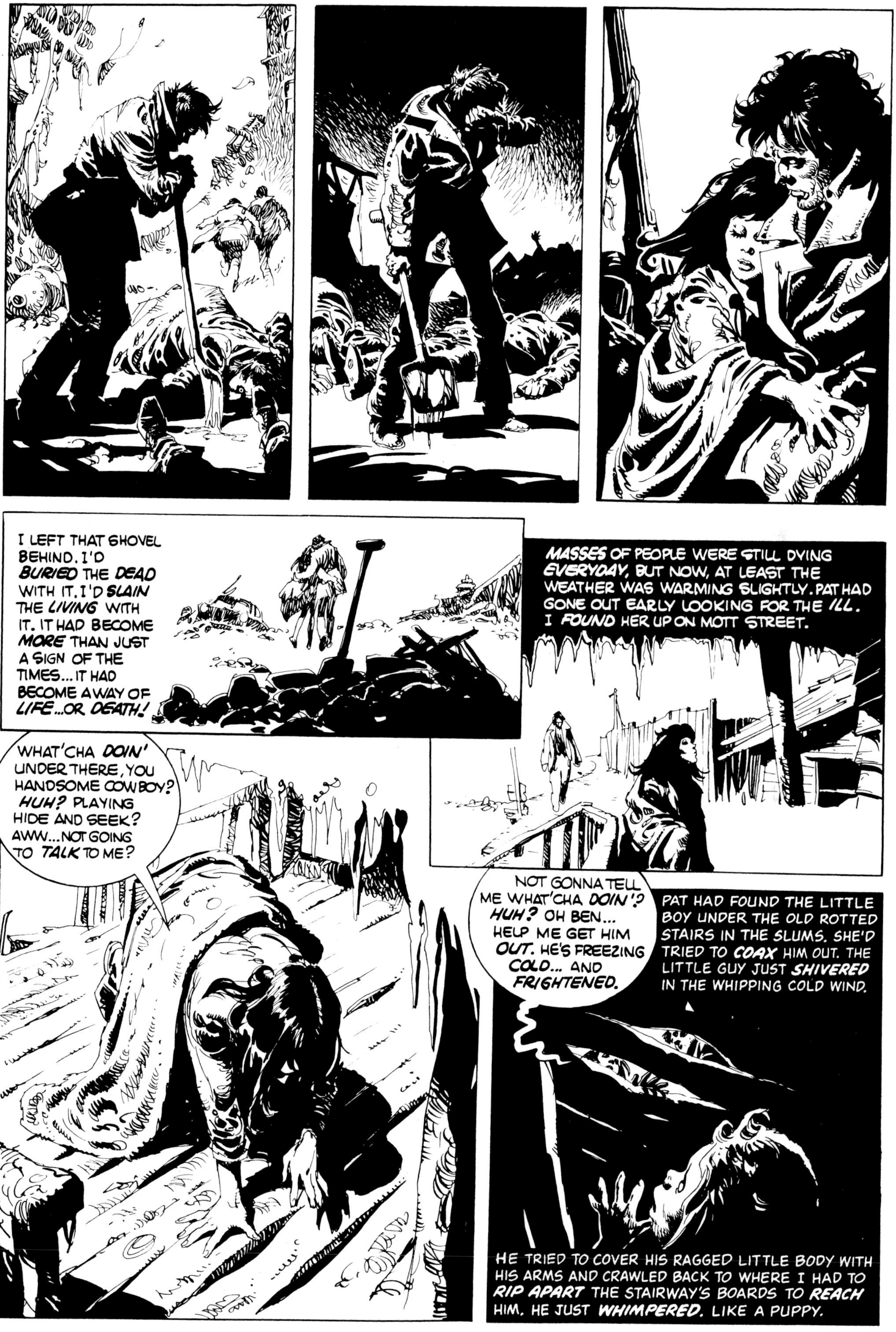
I LEFT THAT SHOVEL BEHIND. I'D BURIED THE DEAD WITH IT. I'D SLAIN THE LIVING WITH IT. IT HAD BECOME MORE THAN JUST A SIGN OF THE TIMES... IT HAD BECOME A WAY OF LIFE...OR DEATH!
MASSES OF PEOPLE WERE STILL DYING EVERYDAY, BUT NOW, AT LEAST THE WEATHER WAS WARMING SLIGHTLY. PAT HAD GONE OUT EARLY LOOKING FOR THE ILL. I FOUND HER UP ON MOTT STREET.
WHAT'CHA DOIN' UNDER THERE, YOU HANDSOME COWBOY? HUH? PLAYING HIDE AND SEEK? AWW...NOT GOING TO TALK TO ME?
NOT GONNA TELL ME WHAT'CHA DOIN'? HUH? OH BEN... HELP ME GET HIM OUT. HE'S FREEZING COLD... AND FRIGHTENED.
PAT HAD FOUND THE LITTLE BOY UNDER THE OLD ROTTED STAIRS IN THE SLUMS. SHE'D TRIED TO COAX HIM OUT. THE LITTLE GUY JUST SHIVERED IN THE WHIPPING COLD WIND.
HE TRIED TO COVER HIS RAGGED LITTLE BODY WITH HIS ARMS AND CRAWLED BACK TO WHERE I HAD TO RIP APART THE STAIRWAY'S BOARDS TO REACH HIM. HE JUST WHIMPERED. LIKE A PUPPY.

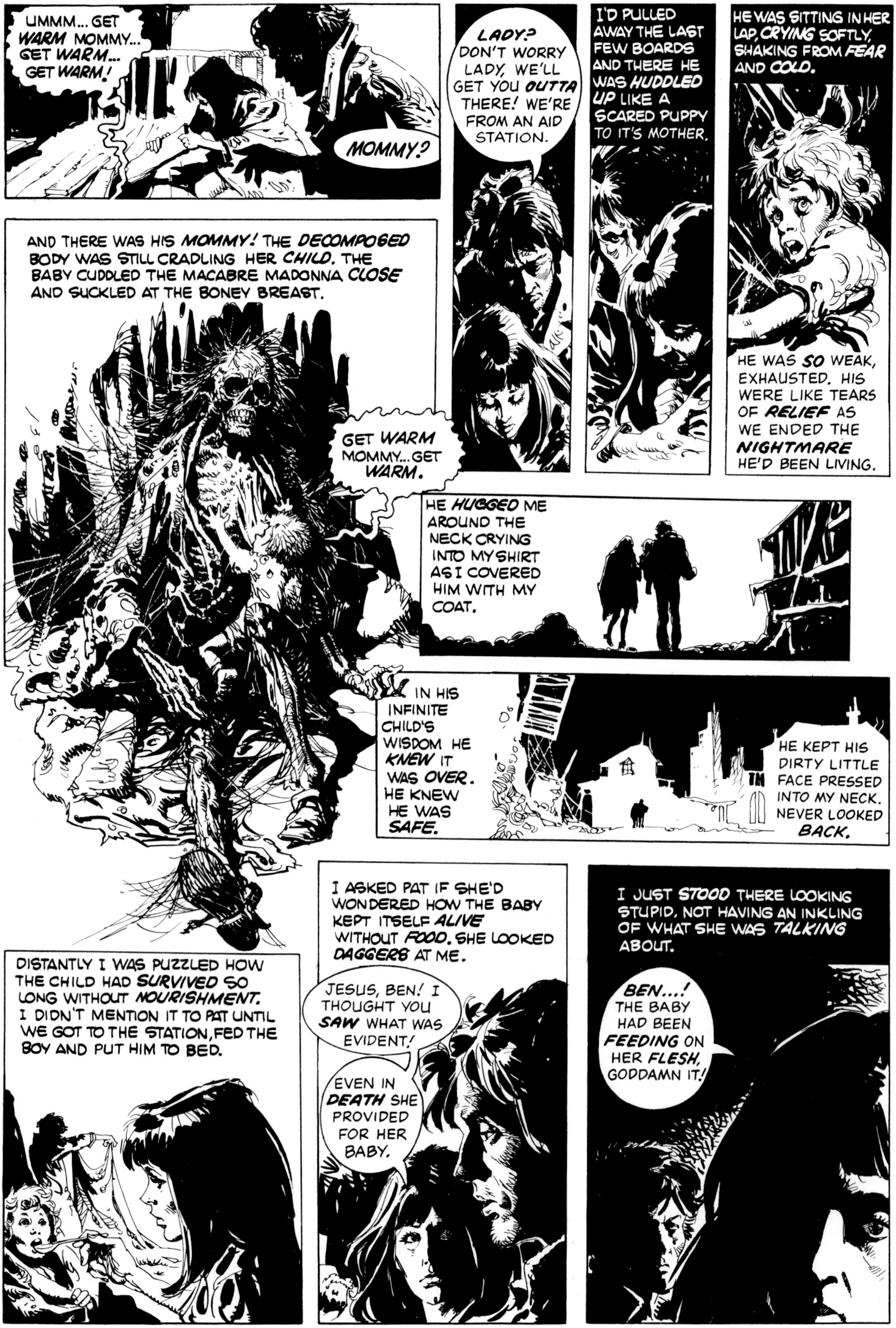

UMMM... GET WARM MOMMY... GET WARM... GET WARM!
MOMMY?
LADY? DON'T WORRY LADY, WE'LL GET YOU OUTTA THERE! WE'RE FROM AN AID STATION.
I'D PULLED AWAY THE LAST FEW BOARDS AND THERE HE WAS HUDDLED UP LIKE A SCARED PUPPY TO IT'S MOTHER.
HE WAS SITTING IN HER LAP, CRYING SOFTLY, SHAKING FROM FEAR AND COLD.
HE WAS SO WEAK, EXHAUSTED. HIS WERE LIKE TEARS OF RELIEF AS WE ENDED THE NIGHTMARE HE'D BEEN LIVING.
AND THERE WAS HIS MOMMY! THE DECOMPOSED BODY WAS STILL CRADLING HER CHILD. THE BABY CUDDLED THE MACABRE MADONNA CLOSE AND SUCKLED AT THE BONEY BREAST.
GET WARM MOMMY... GET WARM.
HE HUGGED ME AROUND THE NECK CRYING INTO MY SHIRT AS I COVERED HIM WITH MY COAT.
IN HIS INFINITE CHILD'S WISDOM HE KNEW IT WAS OVER. HE KNEW HE WAS SAFE.
HE KEPT HIS DIRTY LITTLE FACE PRESSED INTO MY NECK. NEVER LOOKED BACK.
DISTANTLY I WAS PUZZLED HOW THE CHILD HAD SURVIVED SO LONG WITHOUT NOURISHMENT. I DIDN'T MENTION IT TO PAT UNTIL WE GOT TO THE STATION, FED THE BOY AND PUT HIM TO BED.
I ASKED PAT IF SHE'D WONDERED HOW THE BABY KEPT ITSELF ALIVE WITHOUT FOOD. SHE LOOKED DAGGERS AT ME.
JESUS, BEN! I THOUGHT YOU SAW WHAT WAS EVIDENT!
EVEN IN DEATH SHE PROVIDED FOR HER BABY.
I JUST STOOD THERE LOOKING STUPID, NOT HAVING AN INKLING OF WHAT SHE WAS TALKING ABOUT.
BEN...! THE BABY HAD BEEN FEEDING ON HER FLESH, GODDAMN IT!

SHE *CRIED*. AND I HELD HER. AND I GUESS *I* WAS CRYING TOO. NOT FOR HER OR ME OR THE BABY OR THE MOTHER... NOT FOR THE SITUATION OR THE DEAD OR THE DYING... NOT FOR THE LIVING OR THE UNBORN... BUT JUST BECAUSE IT WAS THE *ONLY* THING *LEFT* TO DO.

THE WEATHER WAS GETTING MUCH BETTER. THE SNOW HAD NEARLY ALL MELTED. SPRING WASN'T FAR AWAY AND IT WAS MY GENTLE PAT THAT WAS RESPONSIBLE FOR *THOUSANDS* OF US BEING THERE TO APPRECIATE IT!

GOD, SHE WAS *TIRED!* BUT SHE KEPT GOING.

THERE WERE ABOUT FIFTY PEOPLE HERE THAT GROUPED TOGETHER. THEY ALL WORKED WITH PAT AND I IN THE AID STATION, GIVING *LIFE* TO THOSE IN *NEED*.

WE TOOK THE LITTLE FELLOW FROM MOTT STREET. NAMED HIM BENNIE. THERE WAS ALWAYS ROOM FOR *NEW* ADDITIONS TO THE GROUP.

I WAS CAUTIOUS ABOUT *STRANGERS*. I NEVER GOT OVER HAVING TO *KILL* THOSE SCAVENGERS. BUT PAT *WELCOMED* ANY AND ALL. HER LOVE FOR LIFE *MADE* PARADISE. AND IT WAS THAT *SAME* LOVE THAT *DESTROYED* IT AGAIN.

IT WAS THOSE *PEOPLE* WHO CAME INTO CAMP. *STRANGE* PEOPLE. EVEN *SAID* THEY WERE *DEVIL WORSHIPPERS*. I WANTED THEM *OUT*... BUT PAT WELCOMED THEM TO *STAY*.

THEY STAYED *DAYS WAITING*. CHANTING RITUALS. *SCARING* EVERYONE.

THEN ONE NIGHT, I HEARD BENNIE *SCREAMING*... AND I KNEW THEY *KIDNAPPED* HIM!

WITH MY HEART BEATING IN MY TEMPLES, I *JUMPED* OUT OF *BED*...

...AND *RAN* AFTER THEM!

GOD *NO!*

BAM! BAM! BAM!

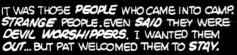

THE UNHOLY MOTHERS HAD *SLIT* BENNY UP THE MIDDLE.

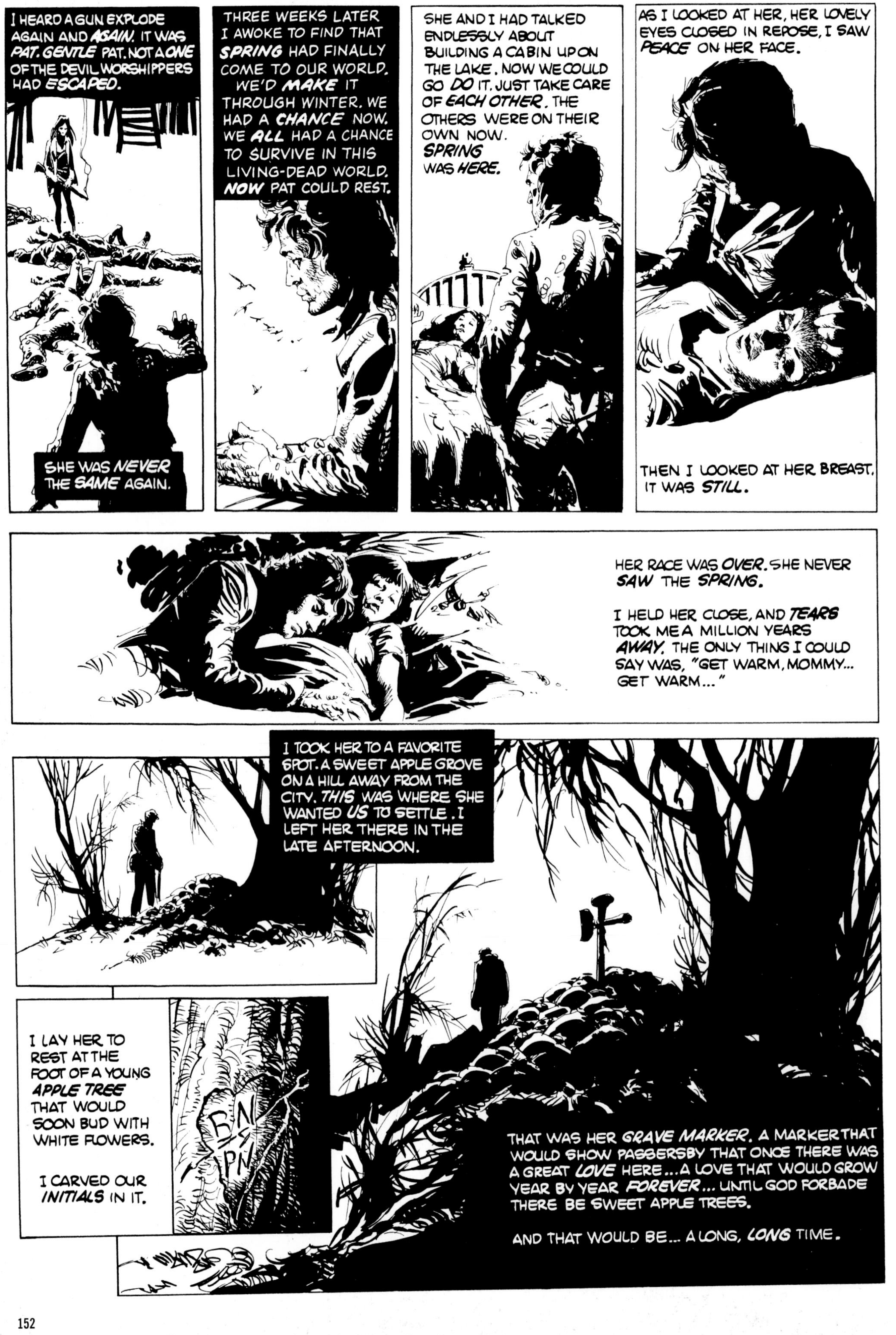
I HEARD A GUN EXPLODE AGAIN AND AGAIN. IT WAS PAT. GENTLE PAT. NOT A ONE OF THE DEVIL WORSHIPPERS HAD ESCAPED.
SHE WAS NEVER THE SAME AGAIN.
THREE WEEKS LATER I AWOKE TO FIND THAT SPRING HAD FINALLY COME TO OUR WORLD.
WE'D MAKE IT THROUGH WINTER. WE HAD A CHANCE NOW. WE ALL HAD A CHANCE TO SURVIVE IN THIS LIVING-DEAD WORLD. NOW PAT COULD REST.
SHE AND I HAD TALKED ENDLESSLY ABOUT BUILDING A CABIN UP ON THE LAKE. NOW WE COULD GO DO IT. JUST TAKE CARE OF EACH OTHER. THE OTHERS WERE ON THEIR OWN NOW. SPRING WAS HERE.
AS I LOOKED AT HER, HER LOVELY EYES CLOSED IN REPOSE, I SAW PEACE ON HER FACE.
THEN I LOOKED AT HER BREAST. IT WAS STILL.
HER RACE WAS OVER. SHE NEVER SAW THE SPRING.
I HELD HER CLOSE, AND TEARS TOOK ME A MILLION YEARS AWAY. THE ONLY THING I COULD SAY WAS, "GET WARM, MOMMY... GET WARM..."
I TOOK HER TO A FAVORITE SPOT. A SWEET APPLE GROVE ON A HILL AWAY FROM THE CITY. THIS WAS WHERE SHE WANTED US TO SETTLE. I LEFT HER THERE IN THE LATE AFTERNOON.
I LAY HER TO REST AT THE FOOT OF A YOUNG APPLE TREE THAT WOULD SOON BUD WITH WHITE FLOWERS.
I CARVED OUR INITIALS IN IT.
BN PN
THAT WAS HER GRAVE MARKER. A MARKER THAT WOULD SHOW PASSERSBY THAT ONCE THERE WAS A GREAT LOVE HERE... A LOVE THAT WOULD GROW YEAR BY YEAR FOREVER... UNTIL GOD FORBADE THERE BE SWEET APPLE TREES.
AND THAT WOULD BE... A LONG, LONG TIME.

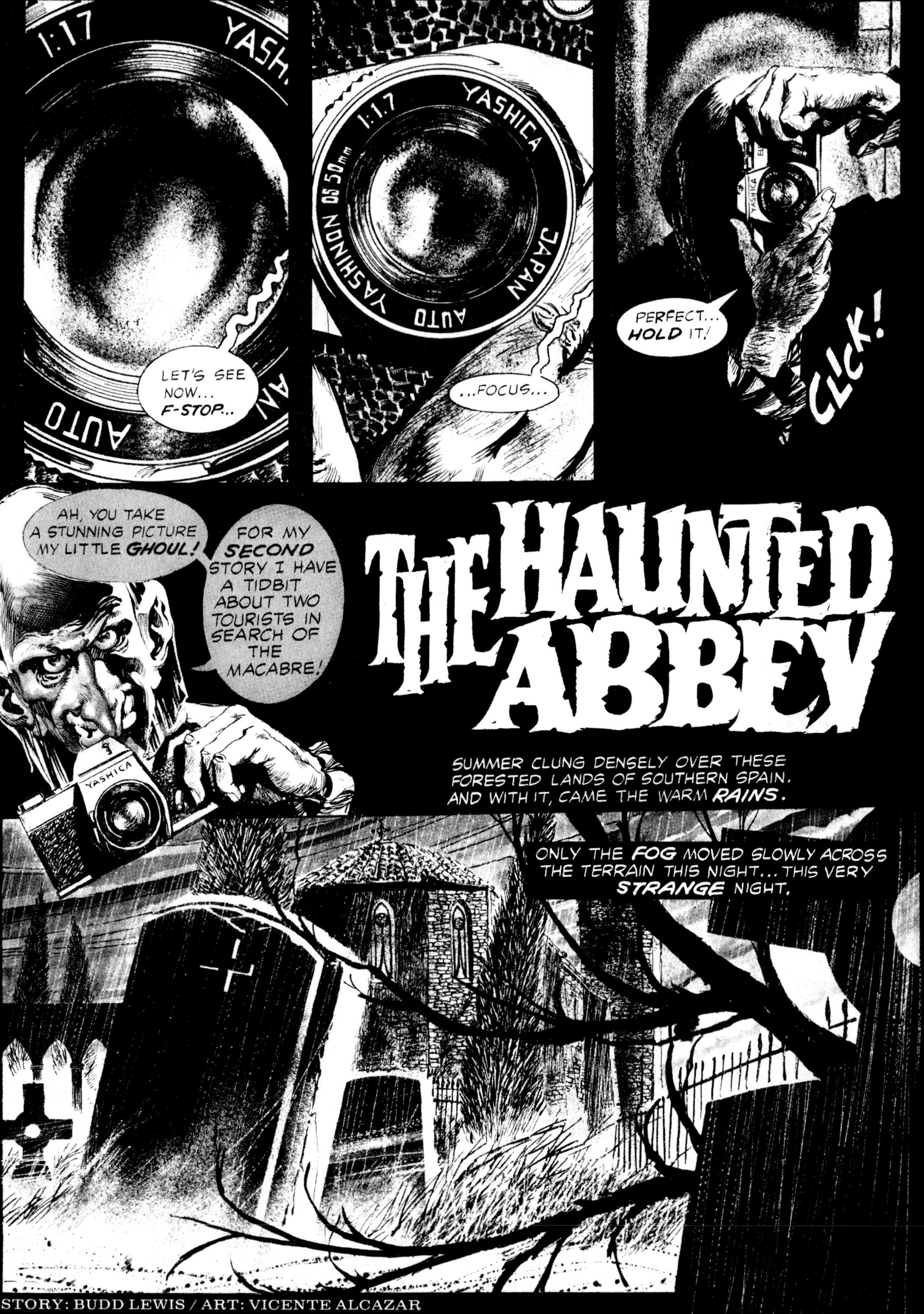
1:17 YASHICA
AUTO
LET'S SEE NOW... F-STOP...
1:1.7 YASHICA
YASHINON DS 50mm JAPAN AUTO
...FOCUS...
PERFECT... HOLD IT!
CLICK!
AH, YOU TAKE A STUNNING PICTURE MY LITTLE GHOUL!
FOR MY SECOND STORY I HAVE A TIDBIT ABOUT TWO TOURISTS IN SEARCH OF THE MACABRE!
YASHICA
THE HAUNTED ABBEY
SUMMER CLUNG DENSELY OVER THESE FORESTED LANDS OF SOUTHERN SPAIN. AND WITH IT, CAME THE WARM RAINS.
ONLY THE FOG MOVED SLOWLY ACROSS THE TERRAIN THIS NIGHT... THIS VERY STRANGE NIGHT.

STORY: BUDD LEWIS / ART: VICENTE ALCAZAR

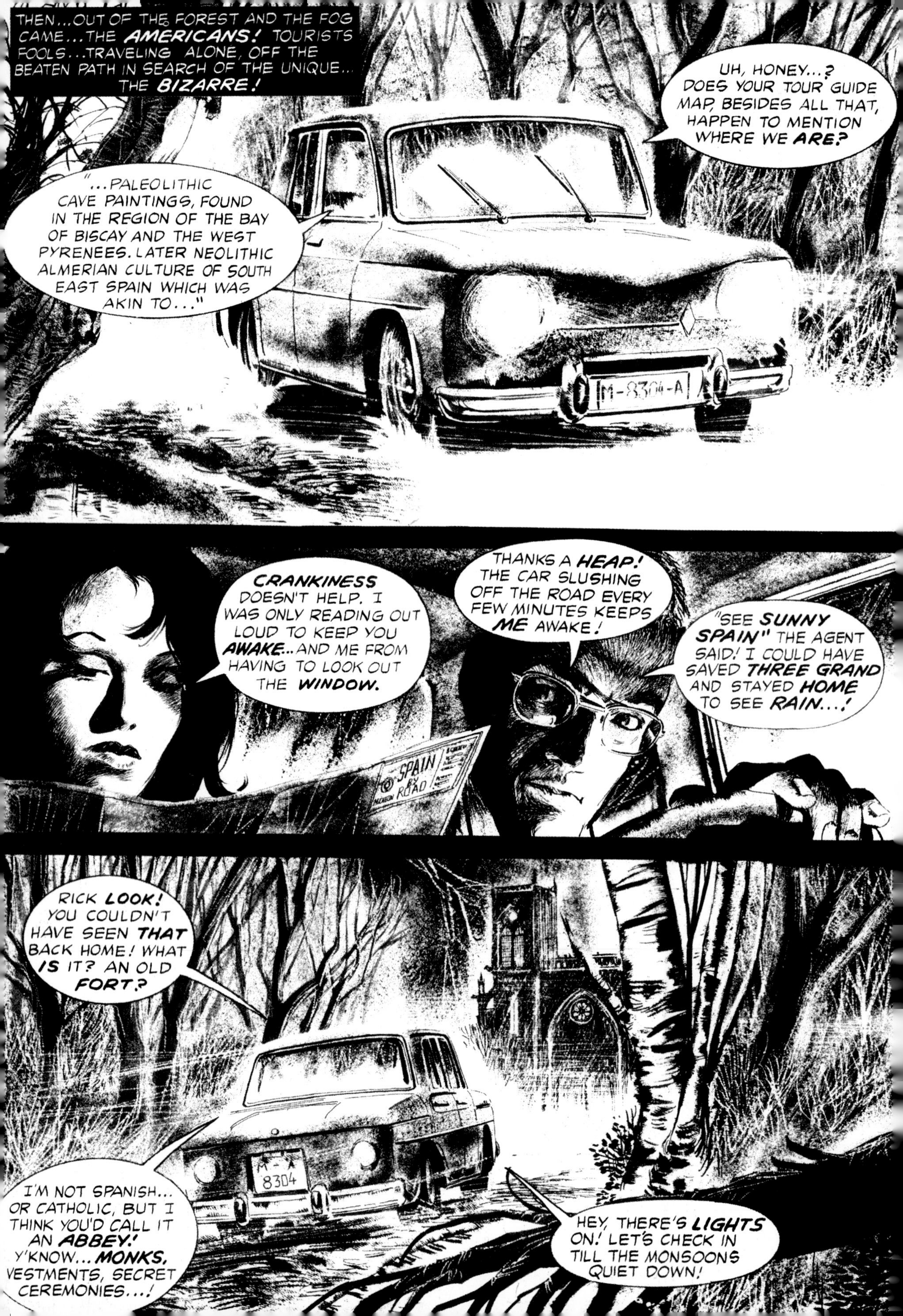
THEN...OUT OF THE FOREST AND THE FOG CAME...THE AMERICANS! TOURISTS FOOLS...TRAVELING ALONE, OFF THE BEATEN PATH IN SEARCH OF THE UNIQUE... THE BIZARRE!
"...PALEOLITHIC CAVE PAINTINGS, FOUND IN THE REGION OF THE BAY OF BISCAY AND THE WEST PYRENEES. LATER NEOLITHIC ALMERIAN CULTURE OF SOUTH EAST SPAIN WHICH WAS AKIN TO..."
UH, HONEY...? DOES YOUR TOUR GUIDE MAP, BESIDES ALL THAT, HAPPEN TO MENTION WHERE WE ARE?
M-8304-A
CRANKINESS DOESN'T HELP. I WAS ONLY READING OUT LOUD TO KEEP YOU AWAKE...AND ME FROM HAVING TO LOOK OUT THE WINDOW.
THANKS A HEAP! THE CAR SLUSHING OFF THE ROAD EVERY FEW MINUTES KEEPS ME AWAKE!
"SEE SUNNY SPAIN" THE AGENT SAID! I COULD HAVE SAVED THREE GRAND AND STAYED HOME TO SEE RAIN...!
SPAIN BY ROAD
RICK LOOK! YOU COULDN'T HAVE SEEN THAT BACK HOME! WHAT IS IT? AN OLD FORT?
I'M NOT SPANISH... OR CATHOLIC, BUT I THINK YOU'D CALL IT AN ABBEY! Y'KNOW...MONKS, VESTMENTS, SECRET CEREMONIES...!
M - A 8304
HEY, THERE'S LIGHTS ON! LET'S CHECK IN TILL THE MONSOONS QUIET DOWN!

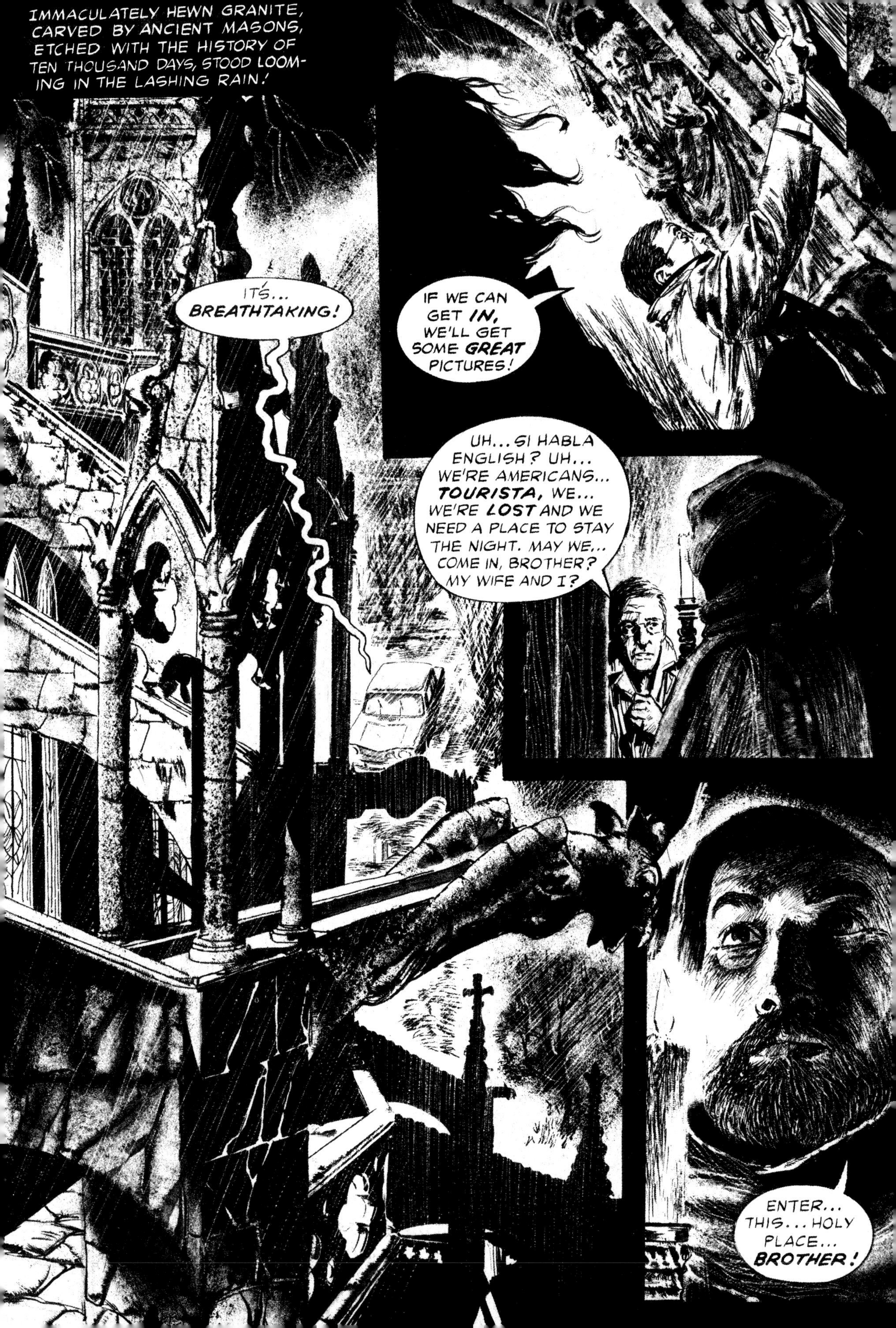
IMMACULATELY HEWN GRANITE, CARVED BY ANCIENT MASONS, ETCHED WITH THE HISTORY OF TEN THOUSAND DAYS, STOOD LOOMING IN THE LASHING RAIN!
IT'S... BREATHTAKING!
IF WE CAN GET IN, WE'LL GET SOME GREAT PICTURES!
UH... SI HABLA ENGLISH? UH... WE'RE AMERICANS... TOURISTA, WE... WE'RE LOST AND WE NEED A PLACE TO STAY THE NIGHT. MAY WE... COME IN, BROTHER? MY WIFE AND I?
ENTER... THIS... HOLY PLACE... BROTHER!

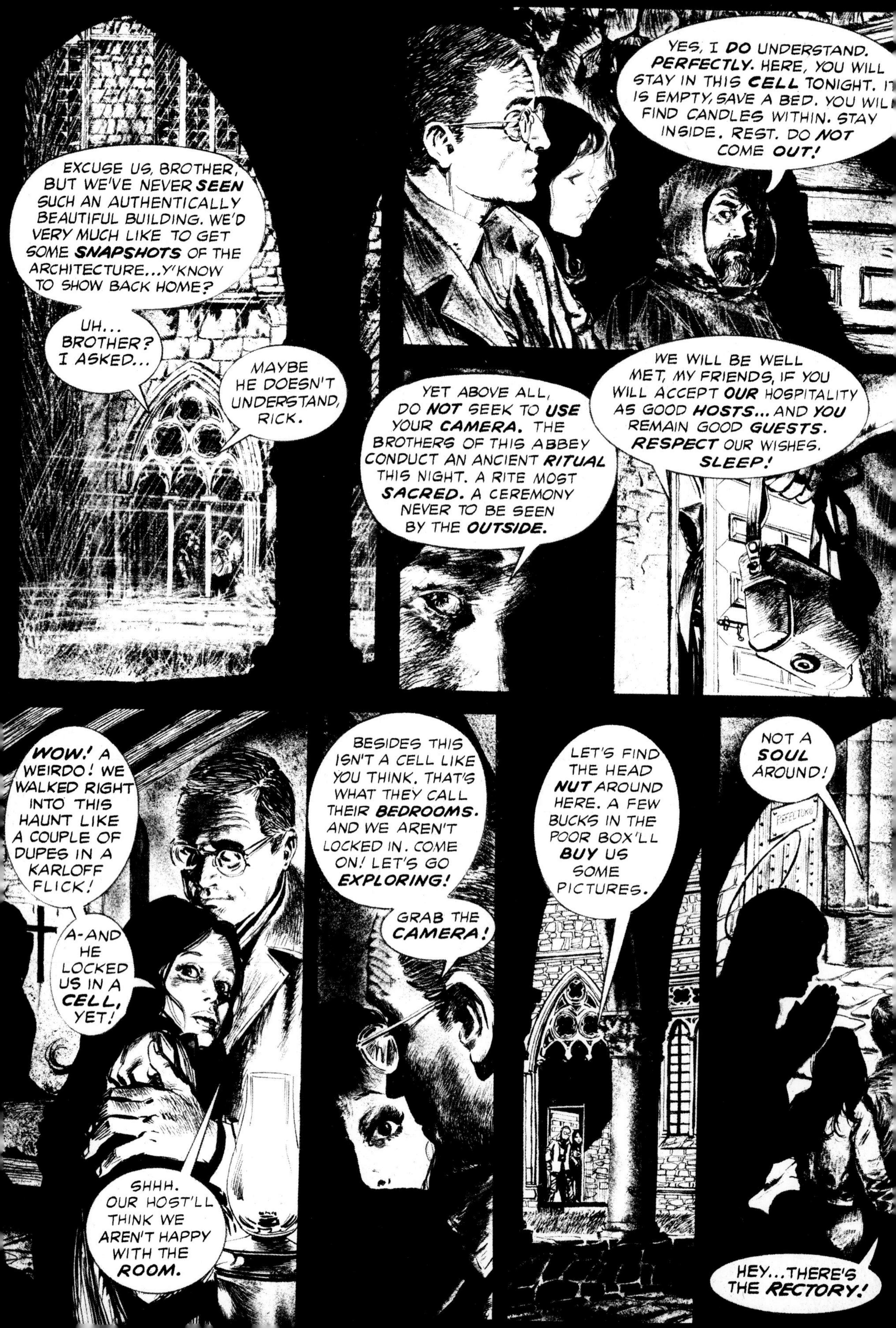
EXCUSE US, BROTHER, BUT WE'VE NEVER SEEN SUCH AN AUTHENTICALLY BEAUTIFUL BUILDING. WE'D VERY MUCH LIKE TO GET SOME SNAPSHOTS OF THE ARCHITECTURE...Y'KNOW TO SHOW BACK HOME?
UH... BROTHER? I ASKED...
MAYBE HE DOESN'T UNDERSTAND, RICK.
YES, I DO UNDERSTAND. PERFECTLY. HERE, YOU WILL STAY IN THIS CELL TONIGHT. IT IS EMPTY, SAVE A BED. YOU WILL FIND CANDLES WITHIN. STAY INSIDE. REST. DO NOT COME OUT!
YET ABOVE ALL, DO NOT SEEK TO USE YOUR CAMERA. THE BROTHERS OF THIS ABBEY CONDUCT AN ANCIENT RITUAL THIS NIGHT. A RITE MOST SACRED. A CEREMONY NEVER TO BE SEEN BY THE OUTSIDE.
WE WILL BE WELL MET, MY FRIENDS, IF YOU WILL ACCEPT OUR HOSPITALITY AS GOOD HOSTS... AND YOU REMAIN GOOD GUESTS. RESPECT OUR WISHES. SLEEP!
WOW! A WEIRDO! WE WALKED RIGHT INTO THIS HAUNT LIKE A COUPLE OF DUPES IN A KARLOFF FLICK!
A-AND HE LOCKED US IN A CELL, YET!
SHHH. OUR HOST'LL THINK WE AREN'T HAPPY WITH THE ROOM.
BESIDES THIS ISN'T A CELL LIKE YOU THINK. THAT'S WHAT THEY CALL THEIR BEDROOMS. AND WE AREN'T LOCKED IN. COME ON! LET'S GO EXPLORING!
GRAB THE CAMERA!
LET'S FIND THE HEAD NUT AROUND HERE. A FEW BUCKS IN THE POOR BOX'LL BUY US SOME PICTURES.
NOT A SOUL AROUND!
HEY...THERE'S THE RECTORY!

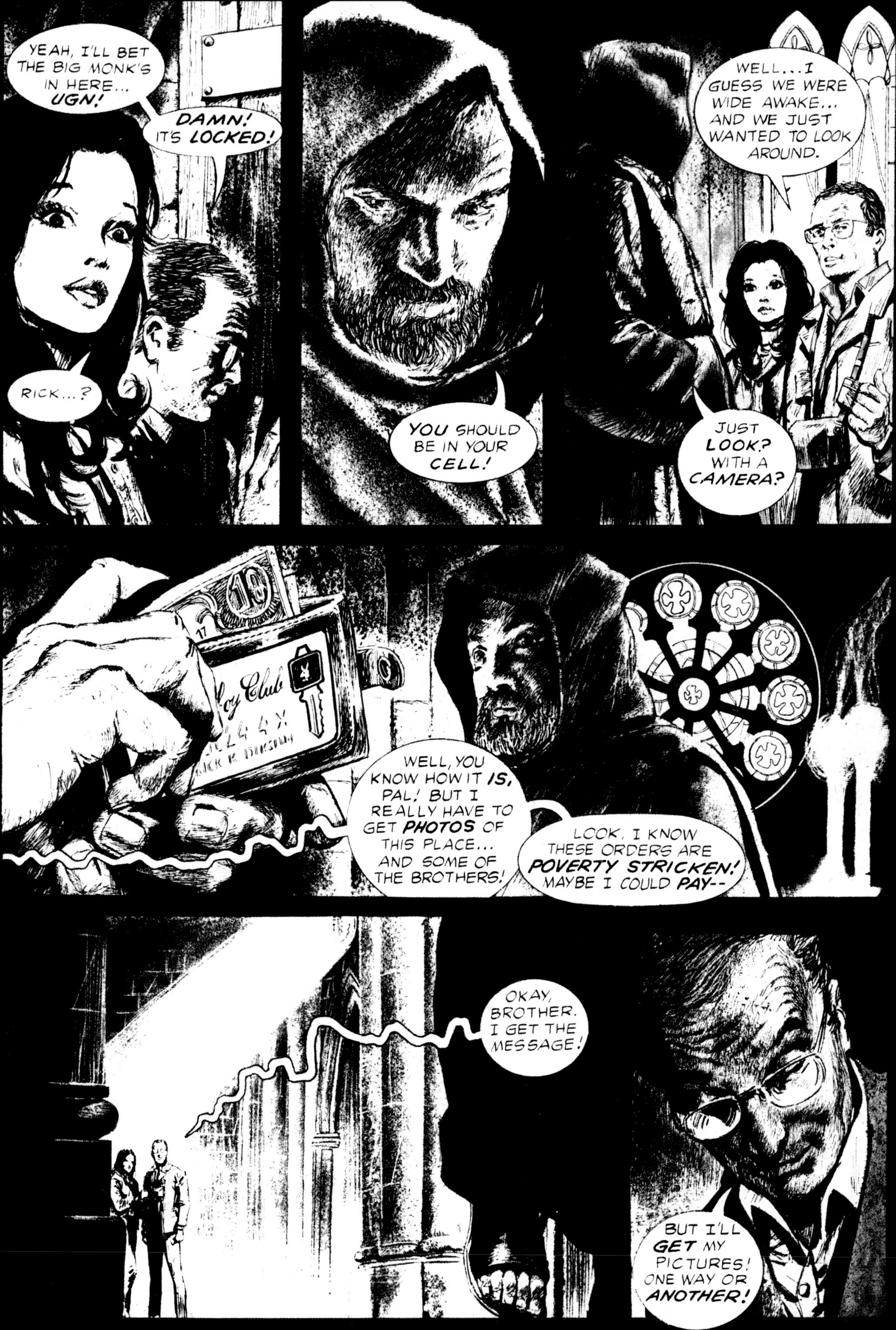
YEAH, I'LL BET THE BIG MONK'S IN HERE... UGN!
DAMN! IT'S LOCKED!
RICK...?
YOU SHOULD BE IN YOUR CELL!
WELL...I GUESS WE WERE WIDE AWAKE... AND WE JUST WANTED TO LOOK AROUND.
JUST LOOK? WITH A CAMERA?
WELL, YOU KNOW HOW IT IS, PAL! BUT I REALLY HAVE TO GET PHOTOS OF THIS PLACE... AND SOME OF THE BROTHERS!
LOOK, I KNOW THESE ORDERS ARE POVERTY STRICKEN! MAYBE I COULD PAY--
OKAY, BROTHER. I GET THE MESSAGE!
BUT I'LL GET MY PICTURES! ONE WAY OR ANOTHER!

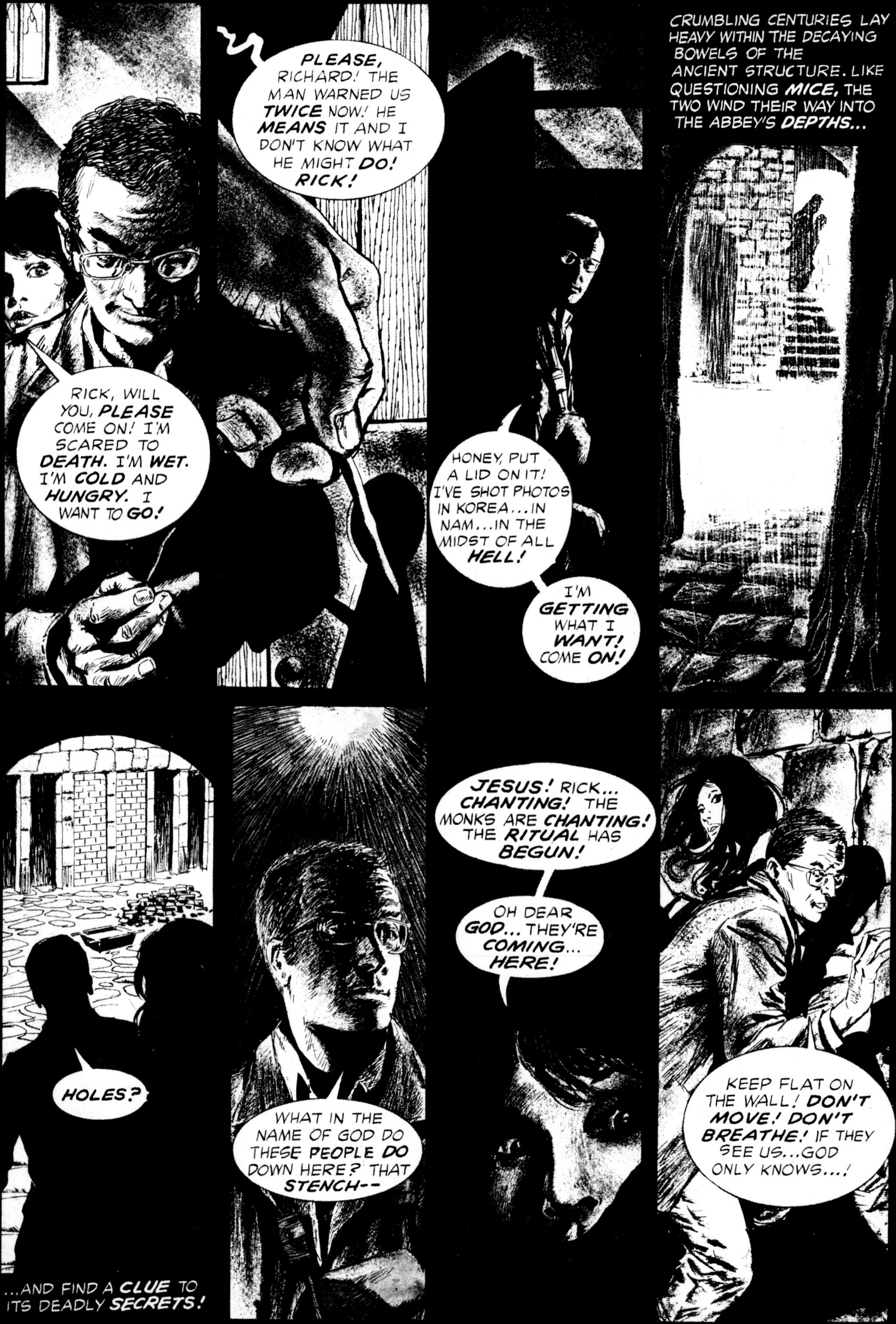
RICK, WILL YOU, PLEASE COME ON! I'M SCARED TO DEATH. I'M WET. I'M COLD AND HUNGRY. I WANT TO GO!
PLEASE, RICHARD! THE MAN WARNED US TWICE NOW! HE MEANS IT AND I DON'T KNOW WHAT HE MIGHT DO! RICK!
HONEY, PUT A LID ON IT! I'VE SHOT PHOTOS IN KOREA... IN NAM... IN THE MIDST OF ALL HELL!
I'M GETTING WHAT I WANT! COME ON!
CRUMBLING CENTURIES LAY HEAVY WITHIN THE DECAYING BOWELS OF THE ANCIENT STRUCTURE. LIKE QUESTIONING MICE, THE TWO WIND THEIR WAY INTO THE ABBEY'S DEPTHS...
HOLES?
...AND FIND A CLUE TO ITS DEADLY SECRETS!
WHAT IN THE NAME OF GOD DO THESE PEOPLE DO DOWN HERE? THAT STENCH--
JESUS! RICK... CHANTING! THE MONKS ARE CHANTING! THE RITUAL HAS BEGUN!
OH DEAR GOD... THEY'RE COMING... HERE!
KEEP FLAT ON THE WALL! DON'T MOVE! DON'T BREATHE! IF THEY SEE US...GOD ONLY KNOWS...!

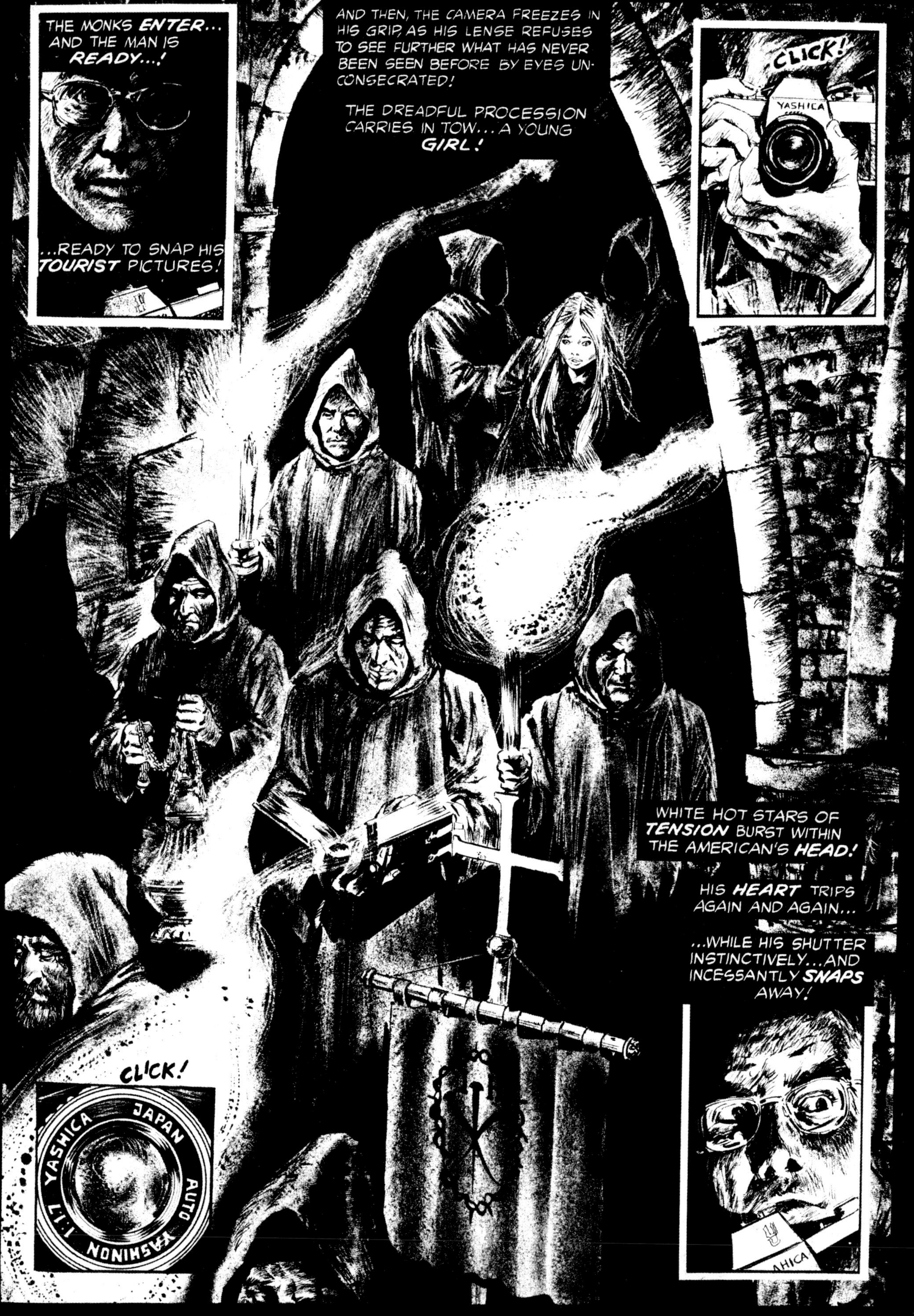
THE MONKS ENTER... AND THE MAN IS READY...!
...READY TO SNAP HIS TOURIST PICTURES!
AND THEN, THE CAMERA FREEZES IN HIS GRIP, AS HIS LENSE REFUSES TO SEE FURTHER WHAT HAS NEVER BEEN SEEN BEFORE BY EYES UN-CONSECRATED!
THE DREADFUL PROCESSION CARRIES IN TOW... A YOUNG GIRL!
CLICK!
YASHICA
WHITE HOT STARS OF TENSION BURST WITHIN THE AMERICAN'S HEAD!
HIS HEART TRIPS AGAIN AND AGAIN...
...WHILE HIS SHUTTER INSTINCTIVELY...AND INCESSANTLY SNAPS AWAY!
CLICK!
YASHICA JAPAN AUTO YASHINON 1:1.7

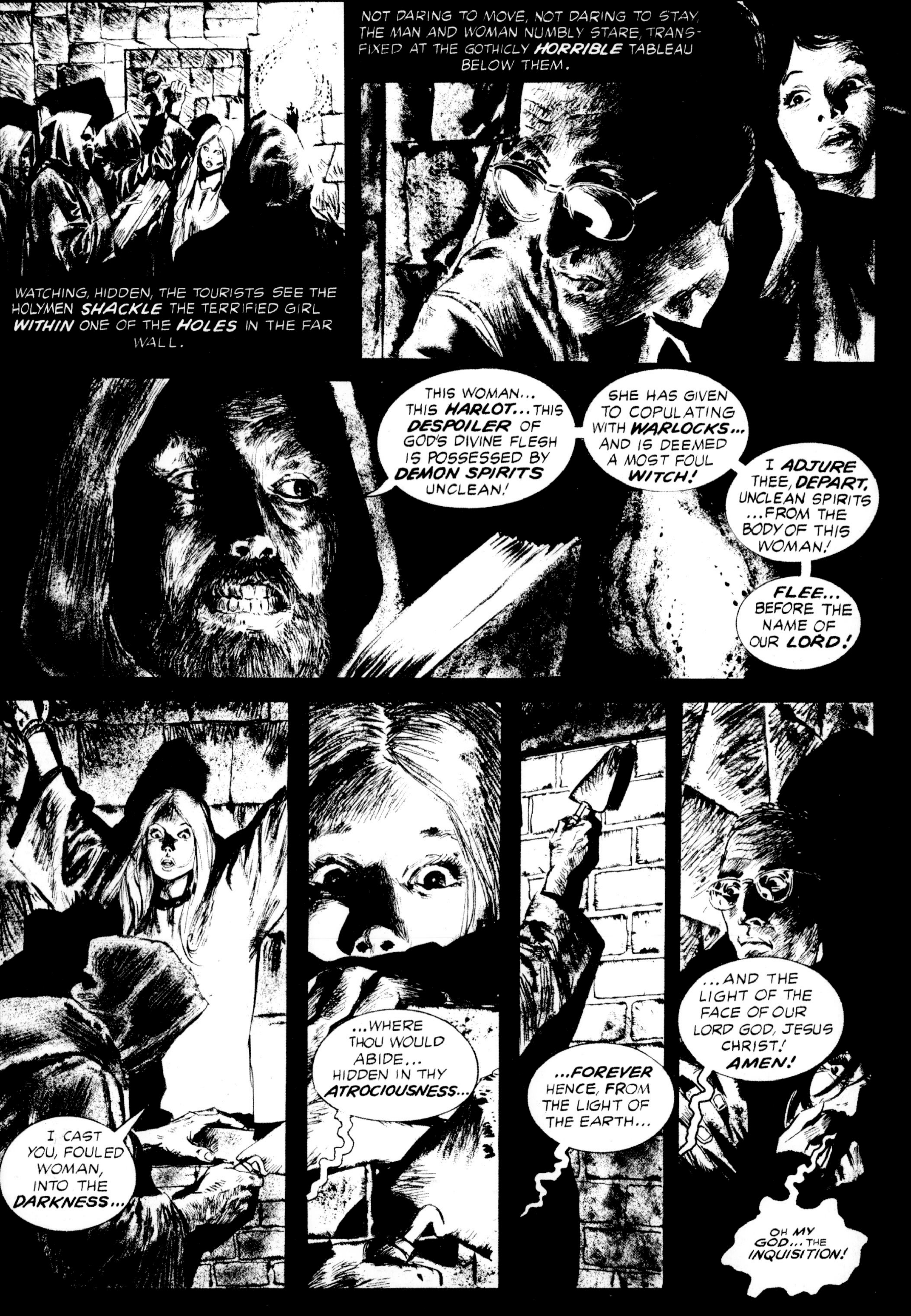

WATCHING, HIDDEN, THE TOURISTS SEE THE HOLYMEN SHACKLE THE TERRIFIED GIRL WITHIN ONE OF THE HOLES IN THE FAR WALL.
NOT DARING TO MOVE, NOT DARING TO STAY, THE MAN AND WOMAN NUMBLY STARE, TRANSFIXED AT THE GOTHICLY HORRIBLE TABLEAU BELOW THEM.
THIS WOMAN... THIS HARLOT... THIS DESPOILER OF GOD'S DIVINE FLESH IS POSSESSED BY DEMON SPIRITS UNCLEAN!
SHE HAS GIVEN TO COPULATING WITH WARLOCKS... AND IS DEEMED A MOST FOUL WITCH!
I ADJURE THEE, DEPART, UNCLEAN SPIRITS ...FROM THE BODY OF THIS WOMAN!
FLEE... BEFORE THE NAME OF OUR LORD!
I CAST YOU, FOULED WOMAN, INTO THE DARKNESS...
...WHERE THOU WOULD ABIDE... HIDDEN IN THY ATROCIOUSNESS...
...FOREVER HENCE, FROM THE LIGHT OF THE EARTH...
...AND THE LIGHT OF THE FACE OF OUR LORD GOD, JESUS CHRIST! AMEN!
OH MY GOD... THE INQUISITION!

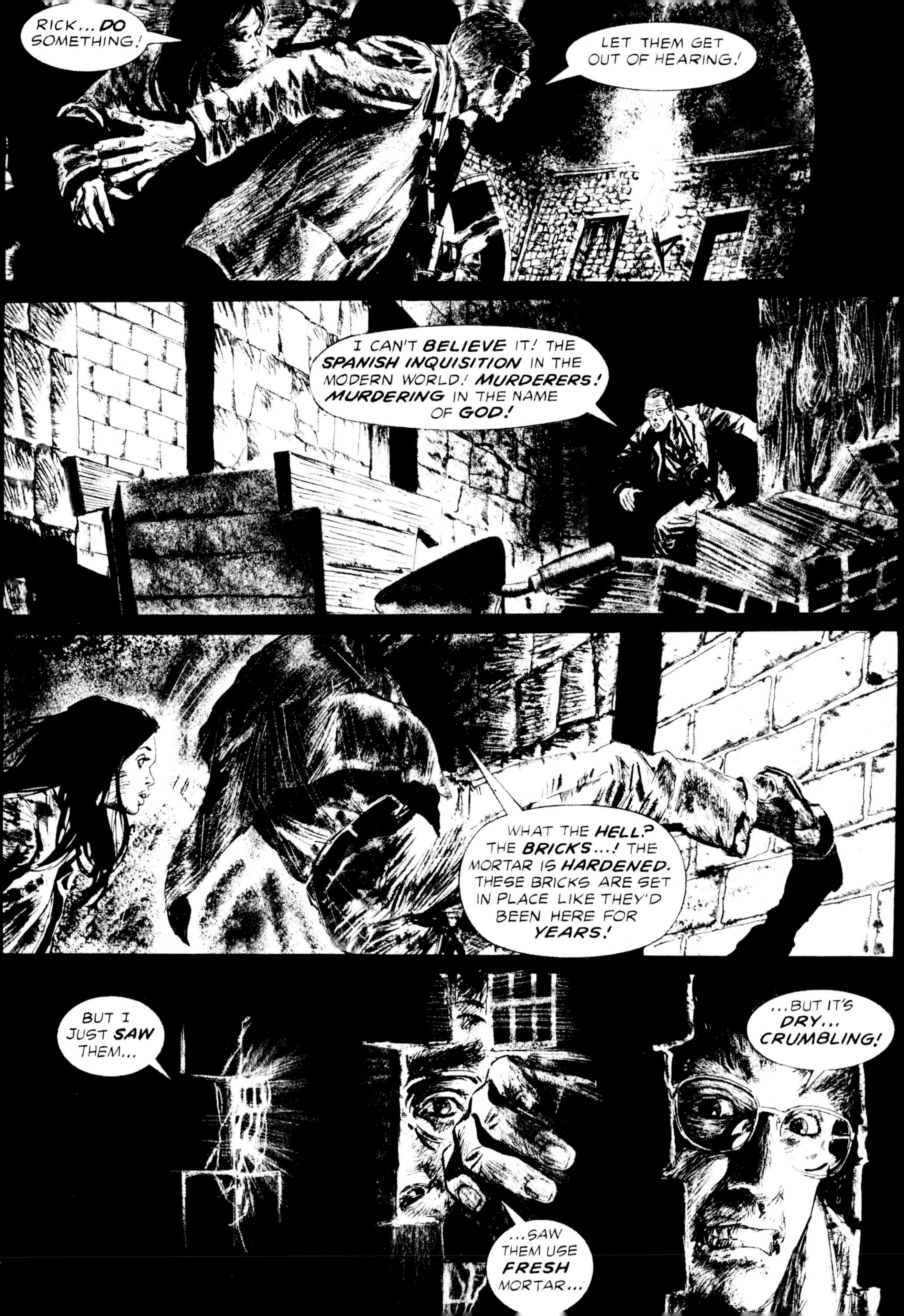
RICK... DO SOMETHING!
LET THEM GET OUT OF HEARING!
I CAN'T BELIEVE IT! THE SPANISH INQUISITION IN THE MODERN WORLD! MURDERERS! MURDERING IN THE NAME OF GOD!
WHAT THE HELL? THE BRICKS...! THE MORTAR IS HARDENED. THESE BRICKS ARE SET IN PLACE LIKE THEY'D BEEN HERE FOR YEARS!
BUT I JUST SAW THEM...
...SAW THEM USE FRESH MORTAR...
...BUT IT'S DRY... CRUMBLING!

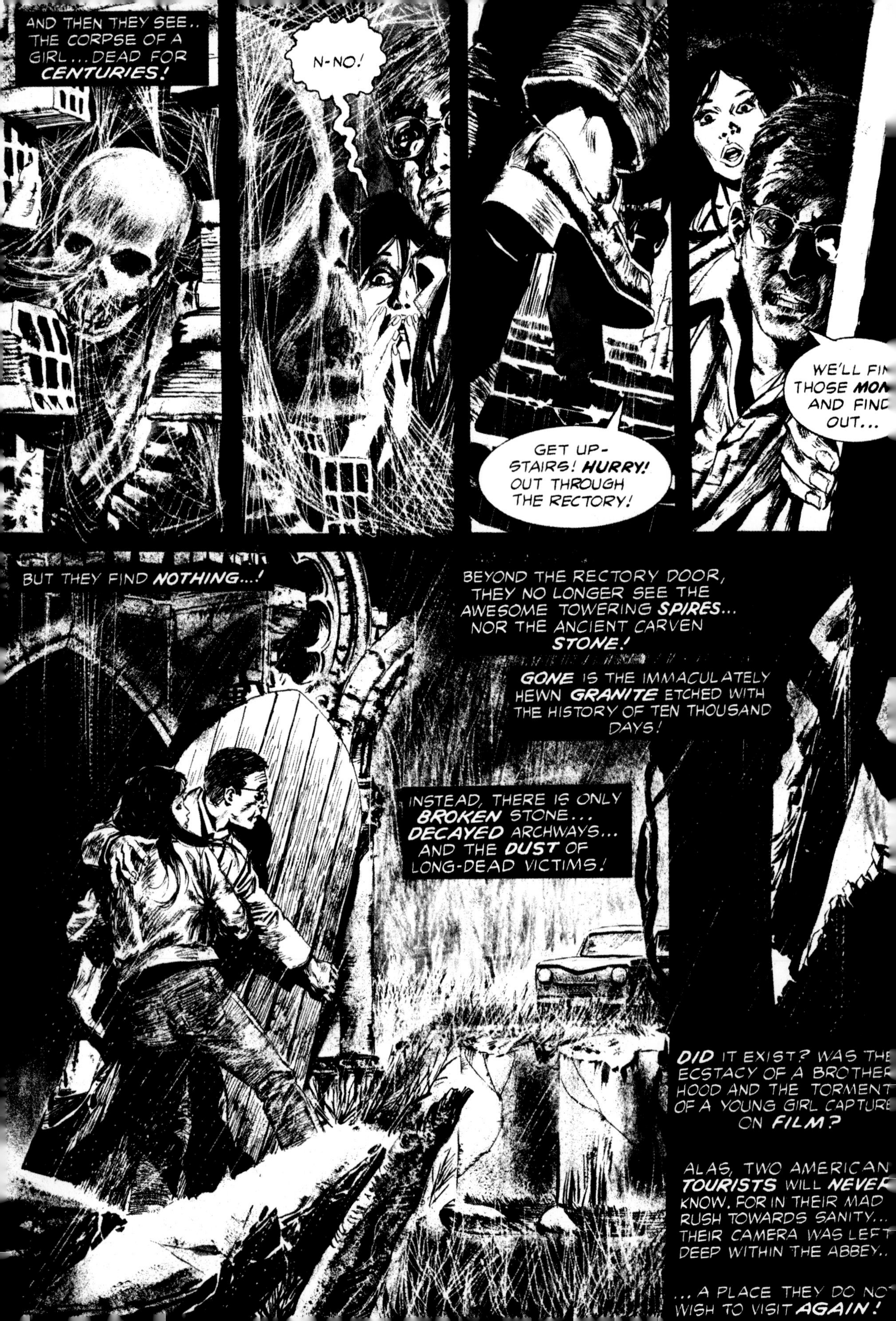
AND THEN THEY SEE.. THE CORPSE OF A GIRL...DEAD FOR CENTURIES!
N-NO!
GET UP-STAIRS! HURRY! OUT THROUGH THE RECTORY!
WE'LL FIN THOSE MON AND FINC OUT...
BUT THEY FIND NOTHING...!
BEYOND THE RECTORY DOOR, THEY NO LONGER SEE THE AWESOME TOWERING SPIRES... NOR THE ANCIENT CARVEN STONE!
GONE IS THE IMMACULATELY HEWN GRANITE ETCHED WITH THE HISTORY OF TEN THOUSAND DAYS!
INSTEAD, THERE IS ONLY BROKEN STONE... DECAYED ARCHWAYS... AND THE DUST OF LONG-DEAD VICTIMS!
DID IT EXIST? WAS THE ECSTACY OF A BROTHER HOOD AND THE TORMENT OF A YOUNG GIRL CAPTURE ON FILM?
ALAS, TWO AMERICAN TOURISTS WILL NEVER KNOW. FOR IN THEIR MAD RUSH TOWARDS SANITY... THEIR CAMERA WAS LEFT DEEP WITHIN THE ABBEY..
... A PLACE THEY DO NOT WISH TO VISIT AGAIN!

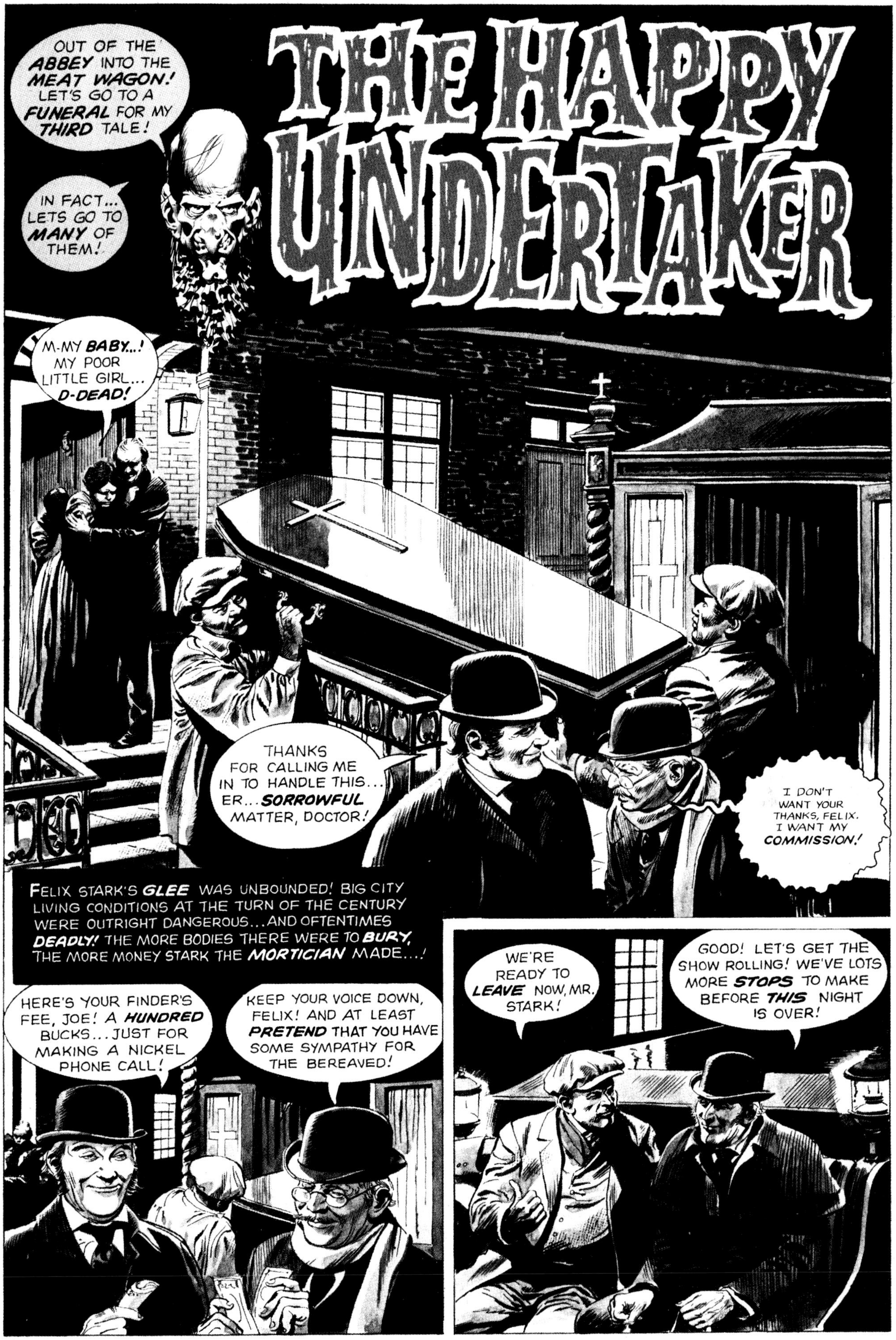
OUT OF THE ABBEY INTO THE MEAT WAGON! LET'S GO TO A FUNERAL FOR MY THIRD TALE!
IN FACT... LETS GO TO MANY OF THEM!
THE HAPPY UNDERTAKER
M-MY BABY...! MY POOR LITTLE GIRL... D-DEAD!
THANKS FOR CALLING ME IN TO HANDLE THIS... ER...SORROWFUL MATTER, DOCTOR!
I DON'T WANT YOUR THANKS, FELIX. I WANT MY COMMISSION!
FELIX STARK'S GLEE WAS UNBOUNDED! BIG CITY LIVING CONDITIONS AT THE TURN OF THE CENTURY WERE OUTRIGHT DANGEROUS...AND OFTENTIMES DEADLY! THE MORE BODIES THERE WERE TO BURY, THE MORE MONEY STARK THE MORTICIAN MADE...!
HERE'S YOUR FINDER'S FEE, JOE! A HUNDRED BUCKS...JUST FOR MAKING A NICKEL PHONE CALL!
KEEP YOUR VOICE DOWN, FELIX! AND AT LEAST PRETEND THAT YOU HAVE SOME SYMPATHY FOR THE BEREAVED!
WE'RE READY TO LEAVE NOW, MR. STARK!
GOOD! LET'S GET THE SHOW ROLLING! WE'VE LOTS MORE STOPS TO MAKE BEFORE THIS NIGHT IS OVER!

STORY: CARL WESSLER / ART: MARTIN SALVADOR

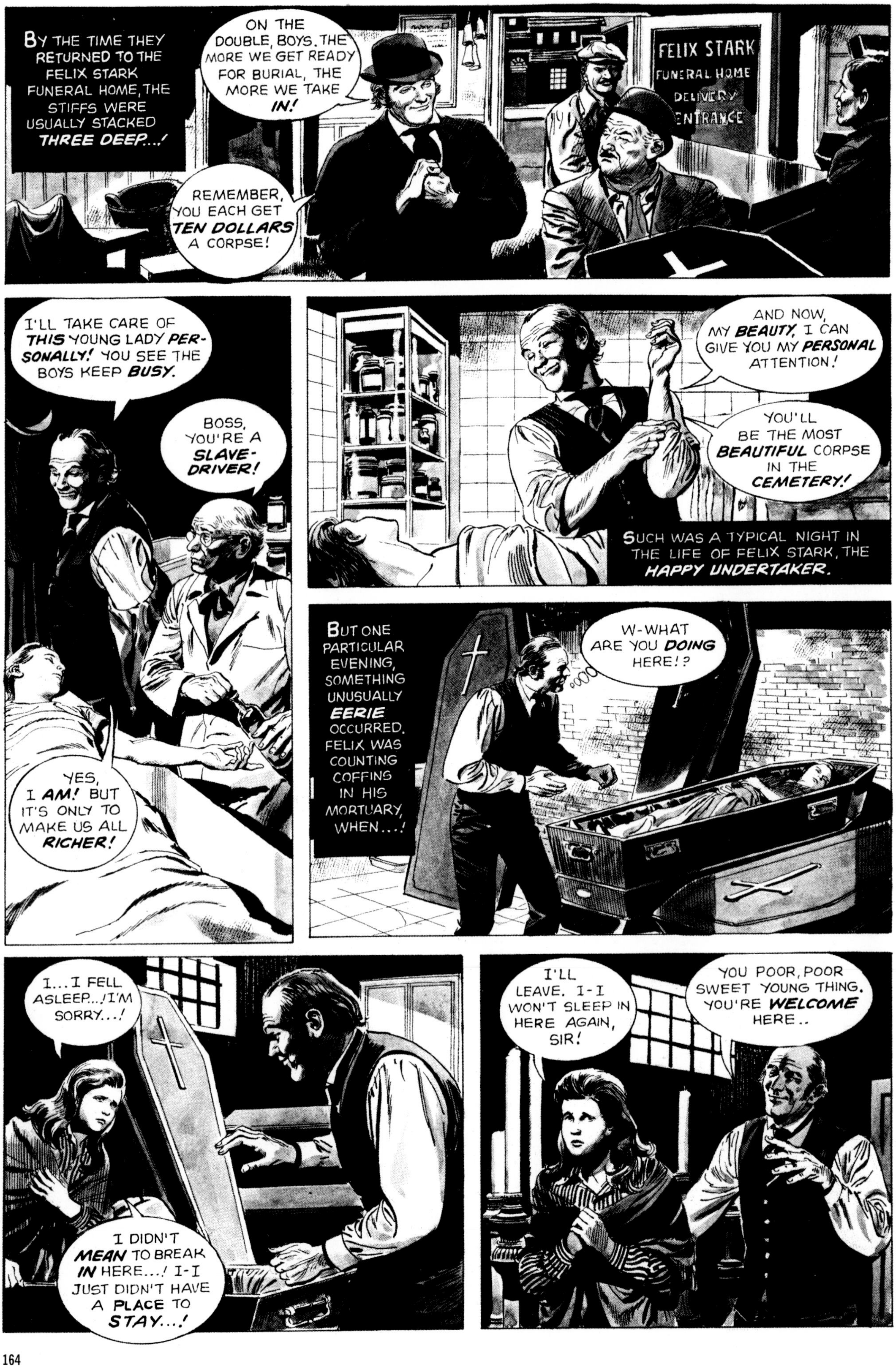
BY THE TIME THEY RETURNED TO THE FELIX STARK FUNERAL HOME, THE STIFFS WERE USUALLY STACKED THREE DEEP...!
ON THE DOUBLE, BOYS. THE MORE WE GET READY FOR BURIAL, THE MORE WE TAKE IN!
REMEMBER, YOU EACH GET TEN DOLLARS A CORPSE!
FELIX STARK FUNERAL HOME DELIVERY ENTRANCE
I'LL TAKE CARE OF THIS YOUNG LADY PERSONALLY! YOU SEE THE BOYS KEEP BUSY.
BOSS, YOU'RE A SLAVE-DRIVER!
YES, I AM! BUT IT'S ONLY TO MAKE US ALL RICHER!
AND NOW, MY BEAUTY, I CAN GIVE YOU MY PERSONAL ATTENTION!
YOU'LL BE THE MOST BEAUTIFUL CORPSE IN THE CEMETERY!
SUCH WAS A TYPICAL NIGHT IN THE LIFE OF FELIX STARK, THE HAPPY UNDERTAKER.
BUT ONE PARTICULAR EVENING, SOMETHING UNUSUALLY EERIE OCCURRED. FELIX WAS COUNTING COFFINS IN HIS MORTUARY, WHEN...!
W-WHAT ARE YOU DOING HERE!?
I...I FELL ASLEEP...!I'M SORRY...!
I DIDN'T MEAN TO BREAK IN HERE...! I-I JUST DIDN'T HAVE A PLACE TO STAY...!
I'LL LEAVE. I-I WON'T SLEEP IN HERE AGAIN, SIR!
YOU POOR, POOR SWEET YOUNG THING. YOU'RE WELCOME HERE..

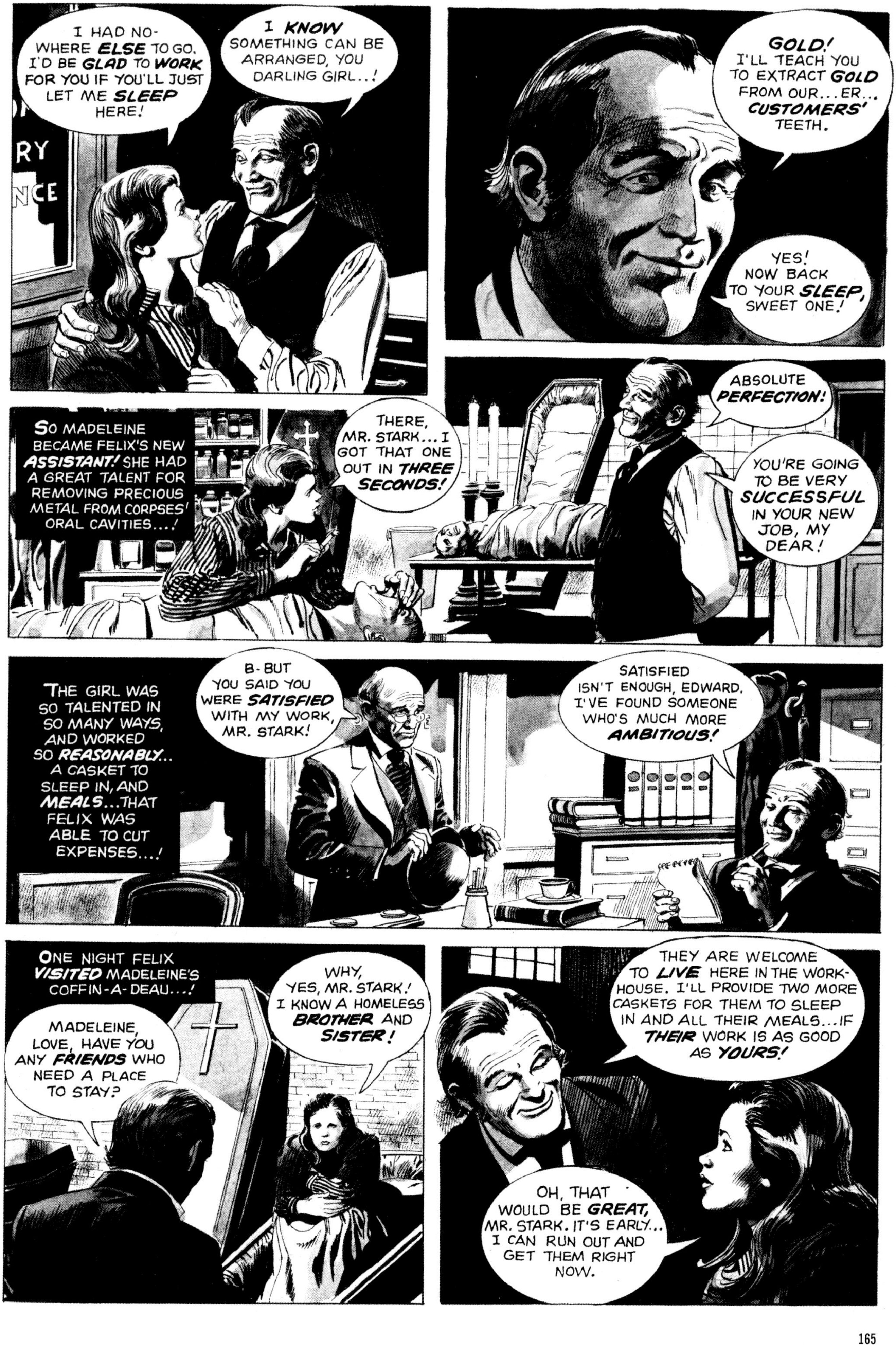
I HAD NO-WHERE ELSE TO GO. I'D BE GLAD TO WORK FOR YOU IF YOU'LL JUST LET ME SLEEP HERE!
I KNOW SOMETHING CAN BE ARRANGED, YOU DARLING GIRL...!
GOLD! I'LL TEACH YOU TO EXTRACT GOLD FROM OUR... ER... CUSTOMERS' TEETH.
YES! NOW BACK TO YOUR SLEEP, SWEET ONE!
SO MADELEINE BECAME FELIX'S NEW ASSISTANT! SHE HAD A GREAT TALENT FOR REMOVING PRECIOUS METAL FROM CORPSES' ORAL CAVITIES...!
THERE, MR. STARK... I GOT THAT ONE OUT IN THREE SECONDS!
ABSOLUTE PERFECTION!
YOU'RE GOING TO BE VERY SUCCESSFUL IN YOUR NEW JOB, MY DEAR!
THE GIRL WAS SO TALENTED IN SO MANY WAYS, AND WORKED SO REASONABLY... A CASKET TO SLEEP IN, AND MEALS... THAT FELIX WAS ABLE TO CUT EXPENSES...!
B-BUT YOU SAID YOU WERE SATISFIED WITH MY WORK, MR. STARK!
SATISFIED ISN'T ENOUGH, EDWARD. I'VE FOUND SOMEONE WHO'S MUCH MORE AMBITIOUS!
ONE NIGHT FELIX VISITED MADELEINE'S COFFIN-A-DEAU...!
MADELEINE, LOVE, HAVE YOU ANY FRIENDS WHO NEED A PLACE TO STAY?
WHY, YES, MR. STARK! I KNOW A HOMELESS BROTHER AND SISTER!
THEY ARE WELCOME TO LIVE HERE IN THE WORK-HOUSE. I'LL PROVIDE TWO MORE CASKETS FOR THEM TO SLEEP IN AND ALL THEIR MEALS... IF THEIR WORK IS AS GOOD AS YOURS!
OH, THAT WOULD BE GREAT, MR. STARK. IT'S EARLY... I CAN RUN OUT AND GET THEM RIGHT NOW.

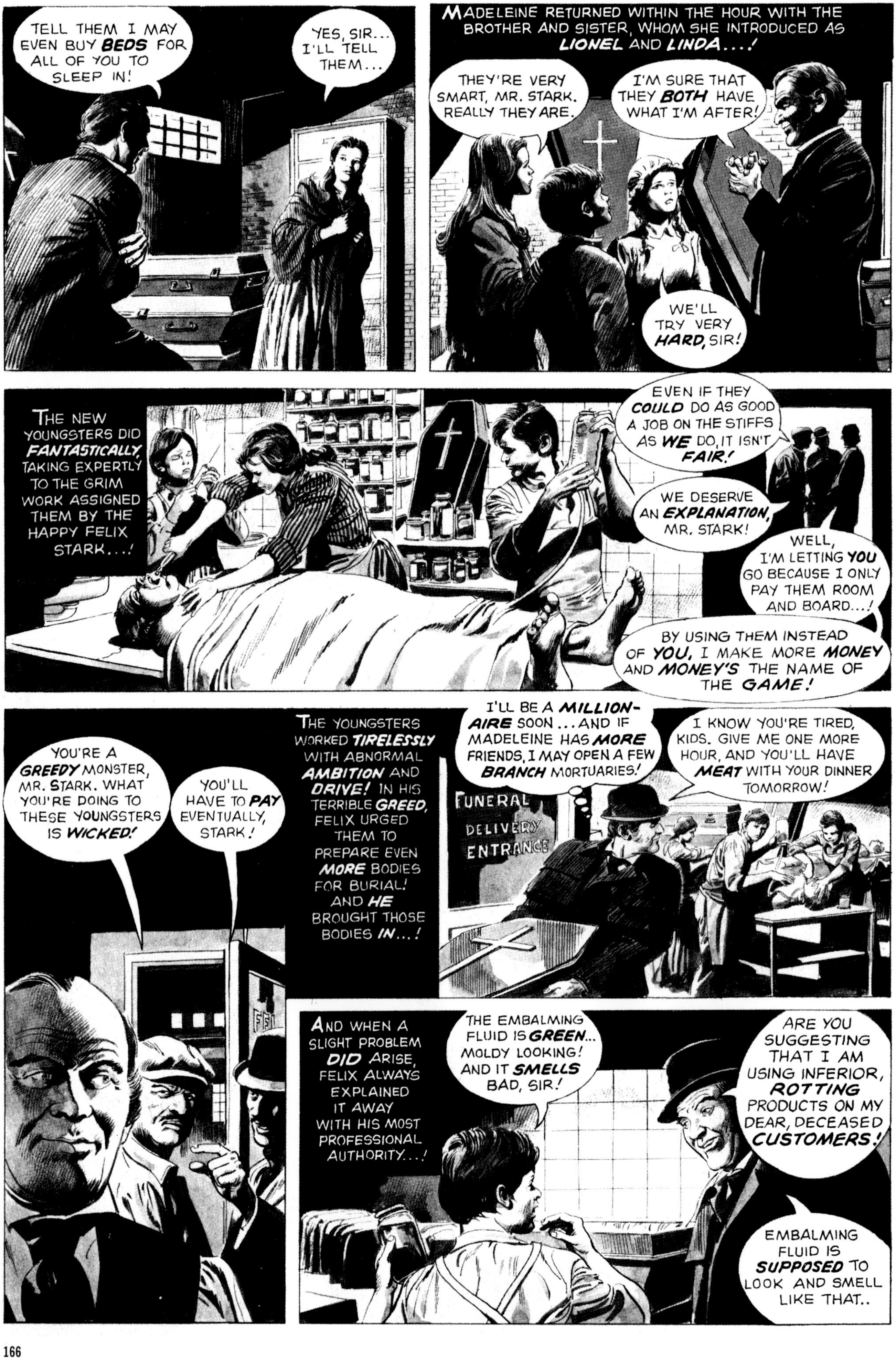
TELL THEM I MAY EVEN BUY BEDS FOR ALL OF YOU TO SLEEP IN!
YES, SIR... I'LL TELL THEM...
MADELEINE RETURNED WITHIN THE HOUR WITH THE BROTHER AND SISTER, WHOM SHE INTRODUCED AS LIONEL AND LINDA...!
THEY'RE VERY SMART, MR. STARK. REALLY THEY ARE.
I'M SURE THAT THEY BOTH HAVE WHAT I'M AFTER!
WE'LL TRY VERY HARD, SIR!
THE NEW YOUNGSTERS DID FANTASTICALLY, TAKING EXPERTLY TO THE GRIM WORK ASSIGNED THEM BY THE HAPPY FELIX STARK...!
EVEN IF THEY COULD DO AS GOOD A JOB ON THE STIFFS AS WE DO, IT ISN'T FAIR!
WE DESERVE AN EXPLANATION, MR. STARK!
WELL, I'M LETTING YOU GO BECAUSE I ONLY PAY THEM ROOM AND BOARD...!
BY USING THEM INSTEAD OF YOU, I MAKE MORE MONEY AND MONEY'S THE NAME OF THE GAME!
YOU'RE A GREEDY MONSTER, MR. STARK. WHAT YOU'RE DOING TO THESE YOUNGSTERS IS WICKED!
YOU'LL HAVE TO PAY EVENTUALLY, STARK!
THE YOUNGSTERS WORKED TIRELESSLY WITH ABNORMAL AMBITION AND DRIVE! IN HIS TERRIBLE GREED, FELIX URGED THEM TO PREPARE EVEN MORE BODIES FOR BURIAL! AND HE BROUGHT THOSE BODIES IN...!
I'LL BE A MILLION-AIRE SOON... AND IF MADELEINE HAS MORE FRIENDS, I MAY OPEN A FEW BRANCH MORTUARIES!
I KNOW YOU'RE TIRED, KIDS. GIVE ME ONE MORE HOUR, AND YOU'LL HAVE MEAT WITH YOUR DINNER TOMORROW!
FUNERAL DELIVERY ENTRANCE
AND WHEN A SLIGHT PROBLEM DID ARISE, FELIX ALWAYS EXPLAINED IT AWAY WITH HIS MOST PROFESSIONAL AUTHORITY...!
THE EMBALMING FLUID IS GREEN... MOLDY LOOKING! AND IT SMELLS BAD, SIR!
ARE YOU SUGGESTING THAT I AM USING INFERIOR, ROTTING PRODUCTS ON MY DEAR, DECEASED CUSTOMERS!
EMBALMING FLUID IS SUPPOSED TO LOOK AND SMELL LIKE THAT..

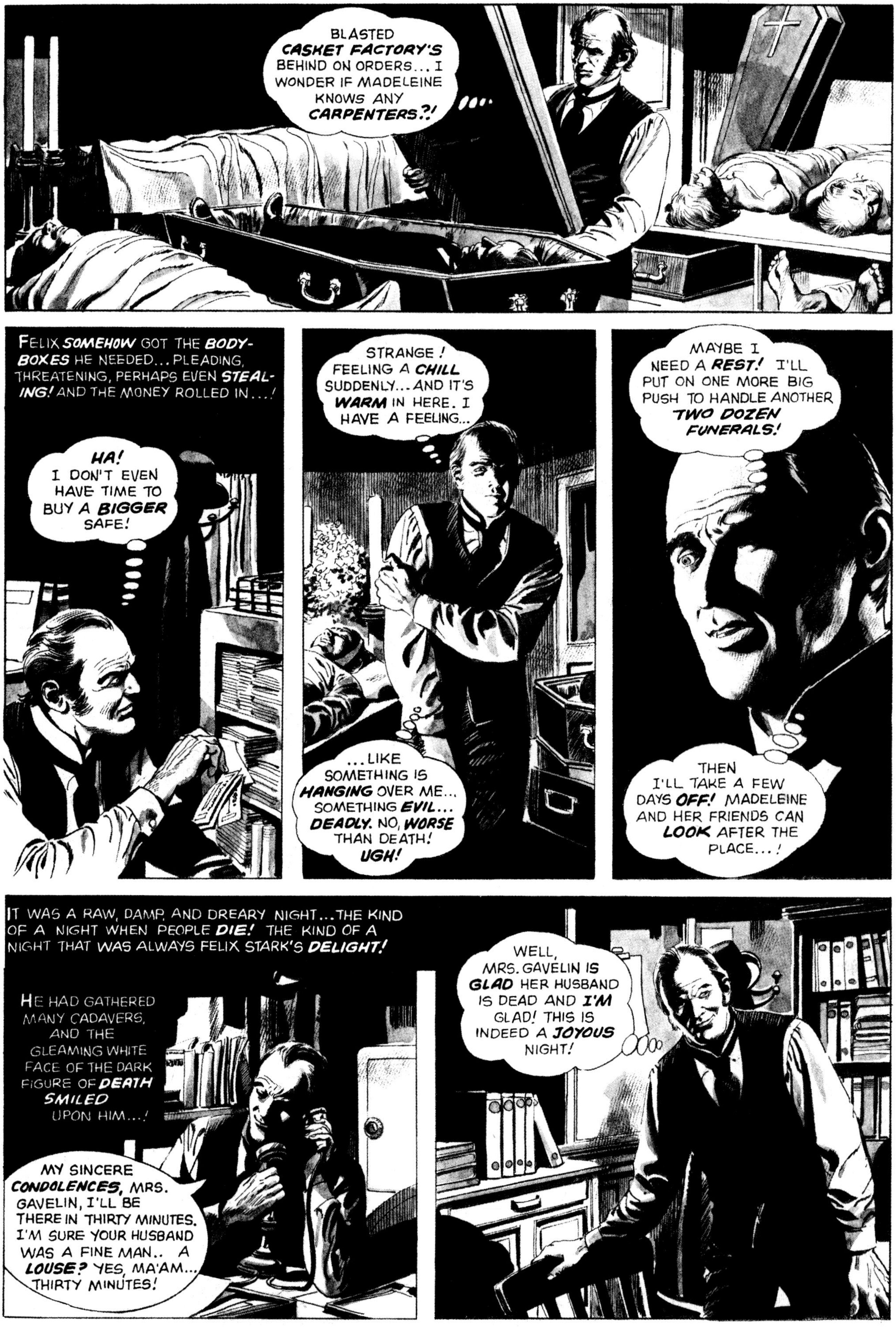
BLASTED CASKET FACTORY'S BEHIND ON ORDERS... I WONDER IF MADELEINE KNOWS ANY CARPENTERS?!
FELIX SOMEHOW GOT THE BODY-BOXES HE NEEDED... PLEADING, THREATENING, PERHAPS EVEN STEALING! AND THE MONEY ROLLED IN...!
HA! I DON'T EVEN HAVE TIME TO BUY A BIGGER SAFE!
STRANGE! FEELING A CHILL SUDDENLY... AND IT'S WARM IN HERE. I HAVE A FEELING...
...LIKE SOMETHING IS HANGING OVER ME... SOMETHING EVIL... DEADLY. NO, WORSE THAN DEATH! UGH!
MAYBE I NEED A REST! I'LL PUT ON ONE MORE BIG PUSH TO HANDLE ANOTHER TWO DOZEN FUNERALS!
THEN I'LL TAKE A FEW DAYS OFF! MADELEINE AND HER FRIENDS CAN LOOK AFTER THE PLACE...!
IT WAS A RAW, DAMP, AND DREARY NIGHT... THE KIND OF A NIGHT WHEN PEOPLE DIE! THE KIND OF A NIGHT THAT WAS ALWAYS FELIX STARK'S DELIGHT!
HE HAD GATHERED MANY CADAVERS, AND THE GLEAMING WHITE FACE OF THE DARK FIGURE OF DEATH SMILED UPON HIM...!
MY SINCERE CONDOLENCES, MRS. GAVELIN, I'LL BE THERE IN THIRTY MINUTES. I'M SURE YOUR HUSBAND WAS A FINE MAN.. A LOUSE? YES, MA'AM... THIRTY MINUTES!
WELL, MRS. GAVELIN IS GLAD HER HUSBAND IS DEAD AND I'M GLAD! THIS IS INDEED A JOYOUS NIGHT!

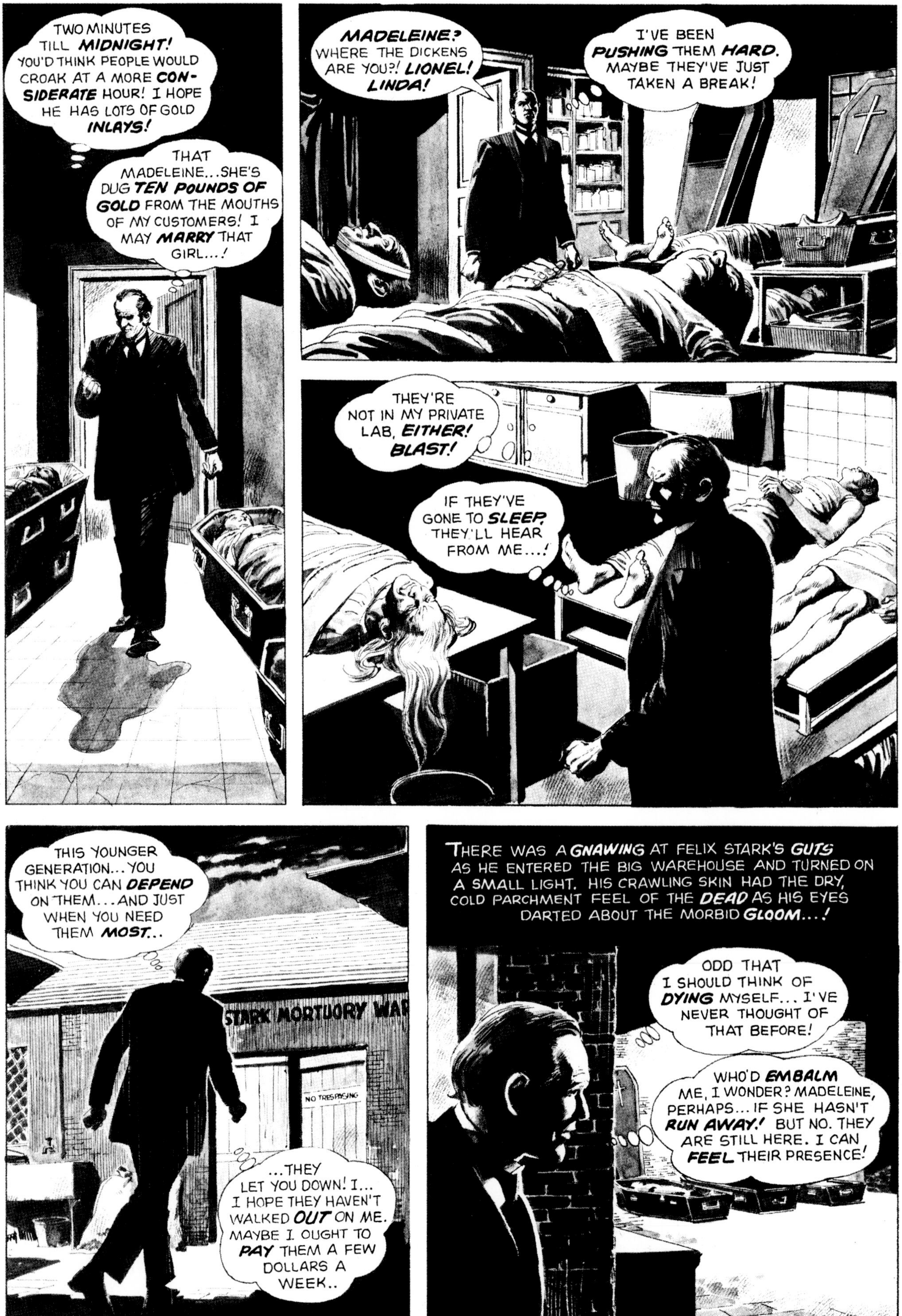
TWO MINUTES TILL MIDNIGHT! YOU'D THINK PEOPLE WOULD CROAK AT A MORE CONSIDERATE HOUR! I HOPE HE HAS LOTS OF GOLD INLAYS!
THAT MADELEINE...SHE'S DUG TEN POUNDS OF GOLD FROM THE MOUTHS OF MY CUSTOMERS! I MAY MARRY THAT GIRL...!
MADELEINE? WHERE THE DICKENS ARE YOU?! LIONEL! LINDA!
I'VE BEEN PUSHING THEM HARD. MAYBE THEY'VE JUST TAKEN A BREAK!
THEY'RE NOT IN MY PRIVATE LAB, EITHER! BLAST!
IF THEY'VE GONE TO SLEEP, THEY'LL HEAR FROM ME...!
THIS YOUNGER GENERATION... YOU THINK YOU CAN DEPEND ON THEM... AND JUST WHEN YOU NEED THEM MOST..
STARK MORTUARY WA
NO TRESPASSING
...THEY LET YOU DOWN! I... I HOPE THEY HAVEN'T WALKED OUT ON ME. MAYBE I OUGHT TO PAY THEM A FEW DOLLARS A WEEK..
THERE WAS A GNAWING AT FELIX STARK'S GUTS AS HE ENTERED THE BIG WAREHOUSE AND TURNED ON A SMALL LIGHT. HIS CRAWLING SKIN HAD THE DRY, COLD PARCHMENT FEEL OF THE DEAD AS HIS EYES DARTED ABOUT THE MORBID GLOOM...!
ODD THAT I SHOULD THINK OF DYING MYSELF... I'VE NEVER THOUGHT OF THAT BEFORE!
WHO'D EMBALM ME, I WONDER? MADELEINE, PERHAPS... IF SHE HASN'T RUN AWAY! BUT NO. THEY ARE STILL HERE. I CAN FEEL THEIR PRESENCE!

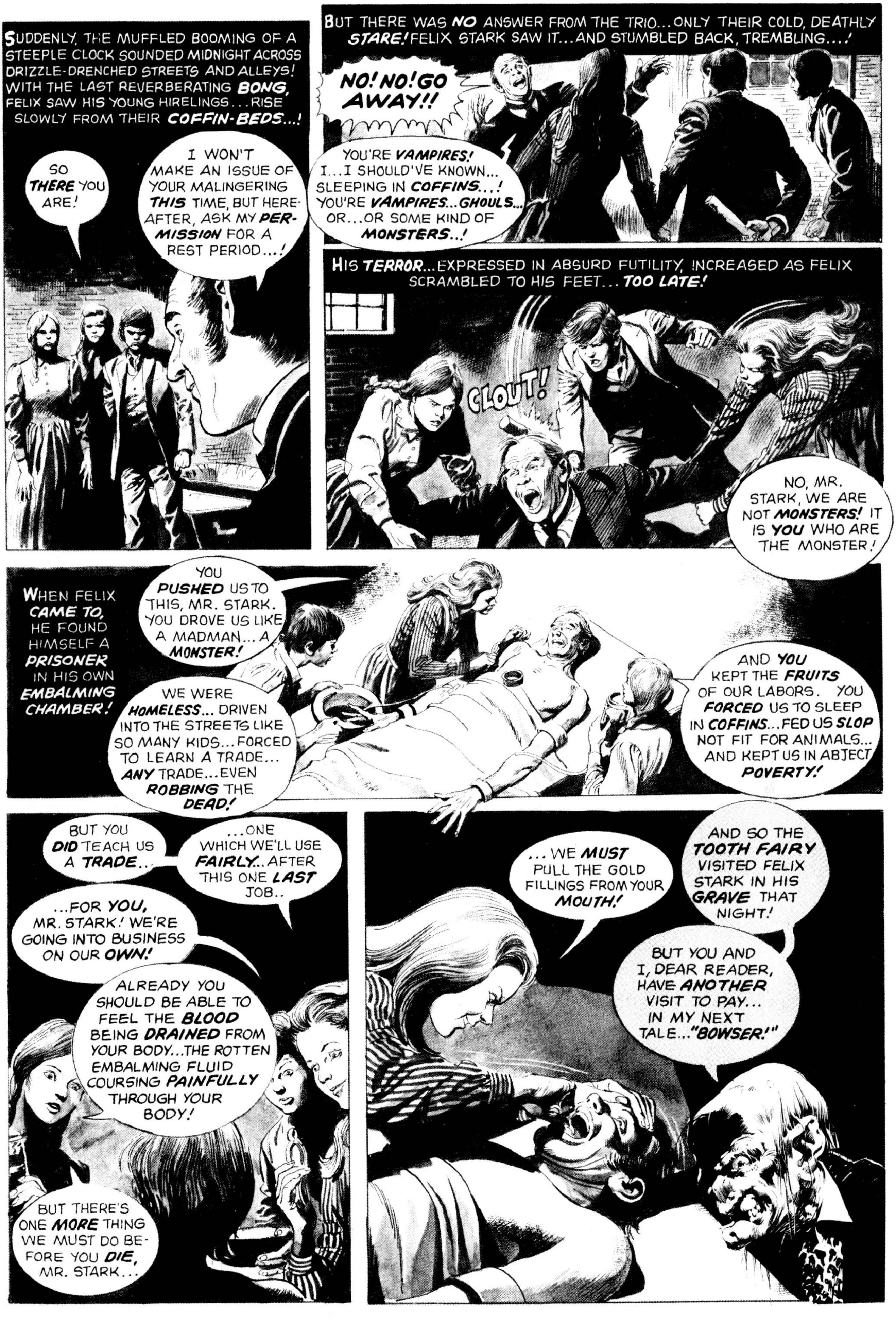
SUDDENLY, THE MUFFLED BOOMING OF A STEEPLE CLOCK SOUNDED MIDNIGHT ACROSS DRIZZLE-DRENCHED STREETS AND ALLEYS! WITH THE LAST REVERBERATING BONG, FELIX SAW HIS YOUNG HIRELINGS... RISE SLOWLY FROM THEIR COFFIN-BEDS...!
SO THERE YOU ARE!
I WON'T MAKE AN ISSUE OF YOUR MALINGERING THIS TIME, BUT HERE-AFTER, ASK MY PER-MISSION FOR A REST PERIOD...!
BUT THERE WAS NO ANSWER FROM THE TRIO... ONLY THEIR COLD, DEATHLY STARE! FELIX STARK SAW IT... AND STUMBLED BACK, TREMBLING...!
NO! NO! GO AWAY!!
YOU'RE VAMPIRES! I... I SHOULD'VE KNOWN... SLEEPING IN COFFINS...! YOU'RE VAMPIRES... GHOULS... OR... OR SOME KIND OF MONSTERS..!
HIS TERROR... EXPRESSED IN ABSURD FUTILITY, INCREASED AS FELIX SCRAMBLED TO HIS FEET... TOO LATE!
CLOUT!
NO, MR. STARK, WE ARE NOT MONSTERS! IT IS YOU WHO ARE THE MONSTER!
WHEN FELIX CAME TO, HE FOUND HIMSELF A PRISONER IN HIS OWN EMBALMING CHAMBER!
YOU PUSHED US TO THIS, MR. STARK. YOU DROVE US LIKE A MADMAN... A MONSTER!
WE WERE HOMELESS... DRIVEN INTO THE STREETS LIKE SO MANY KIDS... FORCED TO LEARN A TRADE... ANY TRADE... EVEN ROBBING THE DEAD!
AND YOU KEPT THE FRUITS OF OUR LABORS. YOU FORCED US TO SLEEP IN COFFINS... FED US SLOP NOT FIT FOR ANIMALS... AND KEPT US IN ABJECT POVERTY!
BUT YOU DID TEACH US A TRADE...
...ONE WHICH WE'LL USE FAIRLY... AFTER THIS ONE LAST JOB..
...FOR YOU, MR. STARK! WE'RE GOING INTO BUSINESS ON OUR OWN!
ALREADY YOU SHOULD BE ABLE TO FEEL THE BLOOD BEING DRAINED FROM YOUR BODY... THE ROTTEN EMBALMING FLUID COURSING PAINFULLY THROUGH YOUR BODY!
BUT THERE'S ONE MORE THING WE MUST DO BE-FORE YOU DIE, MR. STARK...
...WE MUST PULL THE GOLD FILLINGS FROM YOUR MOUTH!
AND SO THE TOOTH FAIRY VISITED FELIX STARK IN HIS GRAVE THAT NIGHT!
BUT YOU AND I, DEAR READER, HAVE ANOTHER VISIT TO PAY... IN MY NEXT TALE..."BOWSER!"

MOVIE MONSTER KITS!

Create your own Classic Horror Film Characters! Authentic life-like Model Kits made of Styrene plastic. You paint them yourself with quick dry enamel and watch them Glow in the Dark. Fantastic!

"GLOW" FRANKENSTEIN

The most famous Movie Monster that Karloffornia's movie studios ever produced! Now you can have him walk right across your bookshelf! Turn to last page of this magazine & order this 10-1/2" high monstrosity! #2402 FRANKENSTEIN $2.50

"GLOW" DRACULA

Nine inches of nerve numbling terror! That's what this model of the nefarious Count is! His hands are outstretched, as he beckons his next victim! It might be YOU! Help a vampire get together, kitwise! Certainly a MUST for terror freaks! Order #2404 DRACULA $2.50

"GLOW" PHANTOM OF THE OPERA

Erik, the vile and tortured Mad Phantom of the great Paris Opera House! Horrid Glow in the Dark face of sheer Terror! Scarred and torn damaged face! Eyes popping in hatred for all the world! 9" high! Order #2405 PHANTOM OF THE OPERA $2.50

"GLOW" FORGOTTEN PRISONER OF CASTLEMARE

He resides, now and forever, he chained to his prison wall in the dungeon of the Cursed Castle! The man cursed wrongfully will send his curse back upon the unlucky! #2406 FORGOTTEN PRISONER OF CASTLEMARE $2.50

"GLOW" MUMMY

Stalking stealthily forth from the tomb of the evil Pharoahs, he plods! His shroudlike bandages that now hang in foul tatters woven when Dark magic ruled the World! Now he crawls and creeps onward . . . plodding . . . TO KILL YOU! #2403 MUMMY $2.50

"GLOW" WEREWOLF

It's a bad moon on the rise! The sore wind now rustles a tree branch—the ghostly gray evening air is all filled with the sound of the rugged pantings of a ferocious wild beast . . . THEN HE STRIKES! His fangs glowing at you! Talons sink into your throat . . . #2407 WOLFMAN $2.50

"GLOW" CREATURE FROM THE BLACK LAGOON

Now you can build the gurgling gill-man who's merely 300,000 years old! One of the finniest folk-heroes of the Frightful Fifties is recreated to perfection! #2409 CREATURE FROM THE BLACK LAGOON $2.50

"GLOW" DR. JEKYLL AS MR. HYDE

He clutches his neck in agony! The serum is taking effect! His skin feels strange, now "crawling," as bestial hair is sprouting quickly from all the pores of his transforming hide! His soul, too, is warping, growing malignant! #2401 DR. JEKYLL AS MR. HYDE $2.50

"GLOW" HUNCHBACK OF NOTRE DAME

QUASIMODO! Ringing church bells and kidnapping Gypsy damsels, suffering for tortures his deformity! Scene is of Quasimodo in torment. #2408 HUNCHBACK OF NOTRE DAME $2.50

"GLOW" GODZILLA

Atomic Energy has brought him back to life, after a long million years of extinction! Now he prowls, rampages through cities, nations, continents and maybe your own bookshelf! The most popular Japanese film monster ever! 8-1/2" tall of the Big "G" town-terrorizing! #2413 GLOW GODZILLA $2.50

"GLOW" OLD WITCH

You've seen her everywhere, from Macbeth to OZ to the House on Haunted Hill! No curse is complete without her! What complete hobbyist can look into his broken mirror each sunset and admit he doesn't own this spell-bopper? Over 8" high! #2427 THE OLD WITCH $2.50

"GLOW" KING KONG

The Kong of Kongs! The 1st & best beast of them all! He's the giant, and he lumbers over 9" tall, with a tiny female victim writhing in his paw! You can bring Kong back to life to prowl forever on your hobby shelf! Don't hesitate another moment to get this one! Order #2414 KING KONG $2.50

To order any of these items, please see last page of this magazine for convenient RUSH ORDER FORM.

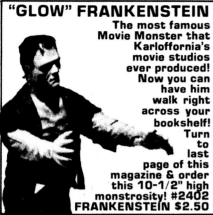

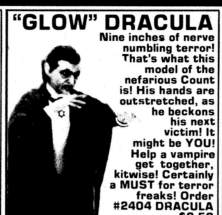

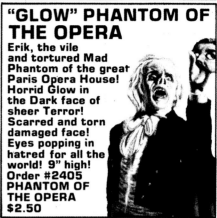

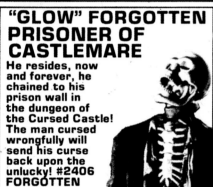

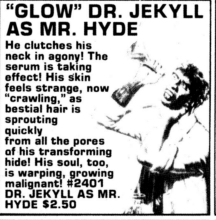

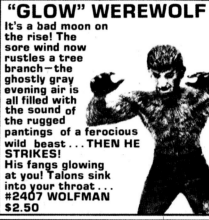

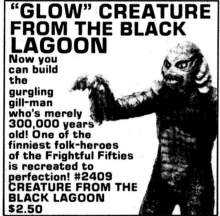

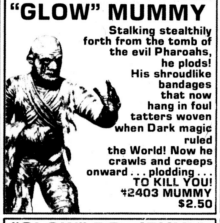

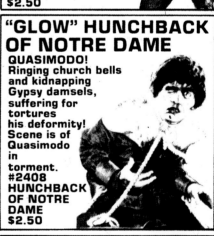

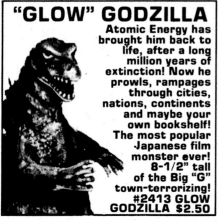

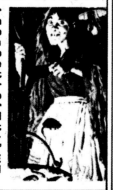

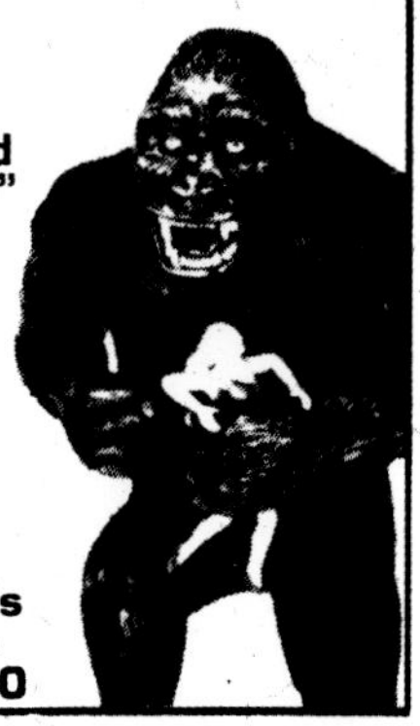

ONCE UPON A MIDNIGHT DREARY, WHILE I PONDERED WEAK AND WEARY, OVER MANY A QUAINT AND CURIOUS VOLUME OF FORGOTTEN LORE...
WHILE I NODDED, NEARLY NAPPING, SUDDENLY THERE CAME A TAPPING AS OF SOME ONE GENTLY RAPPING, RAPPING AT MY CHAMBER DOOR.
"'TIS SOME VISITOR," I MUTTERED, "TAPPING AT MY CHAMBER DOOR. ONLY THIS AND NOTHING MORE."
TAP! TAP! TAP!
EDGAR ALLAN POE'S
THE RAVEN
ART: RICH CORBEN

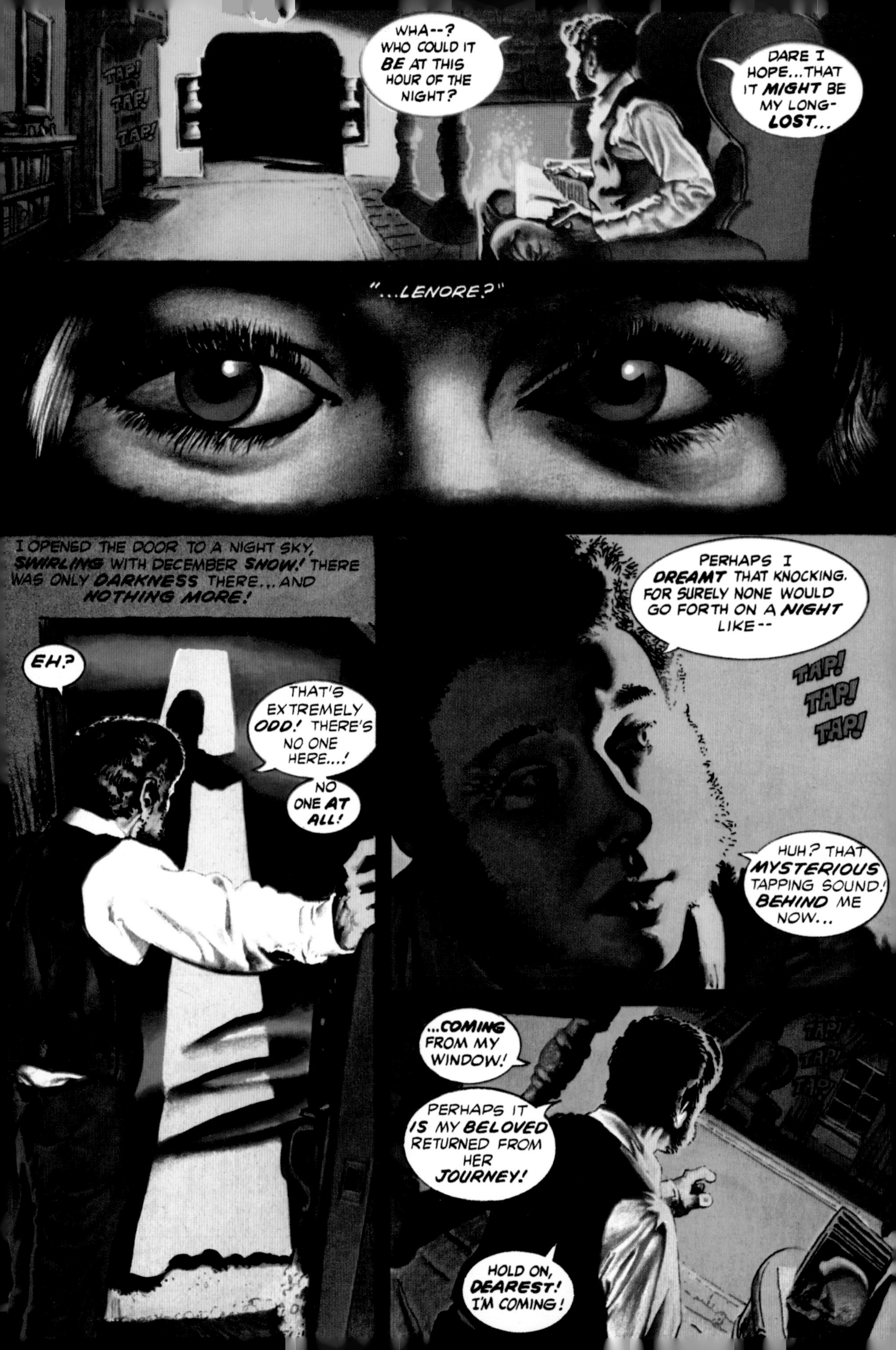

TAP! TAP! TAP!
WHA--? WHO COULD IT BE AT THIS HOUR OF THE NIGHT?
DARE I HOPE...THAT IT MIGHT BE MY LONG-LOST...
"...LENORE?"
I OPENED THE DOOR TO A NIGHT SKY, SWIRLING WITH DECEMBER SNOW! THERE WAS ONLY DARKNESS THERE... AND NOTHING MORE!
EH?
THAT'S EXTREMELY ODD! THERE'S NO ONE HERE...!
NO ONE AT ALL!
PERHAPS I DREAMT THAT KNOCKING. FOR SURELY NONE WOULD GO FORTH ON A NIGHT LIKE--
TAP! TAP! TAP!
HUH? THAT MYSTERIOUS TAPPING SOUND! BEHIND ME NOW...
...COMING FROM MY WINDOW!
TAP! TAP! TAP!
PERHAPS IT IS MY BELOVED RETURNED FROM HER JOURNEY!
HOLD ON, DEAREST! I'M COMING!

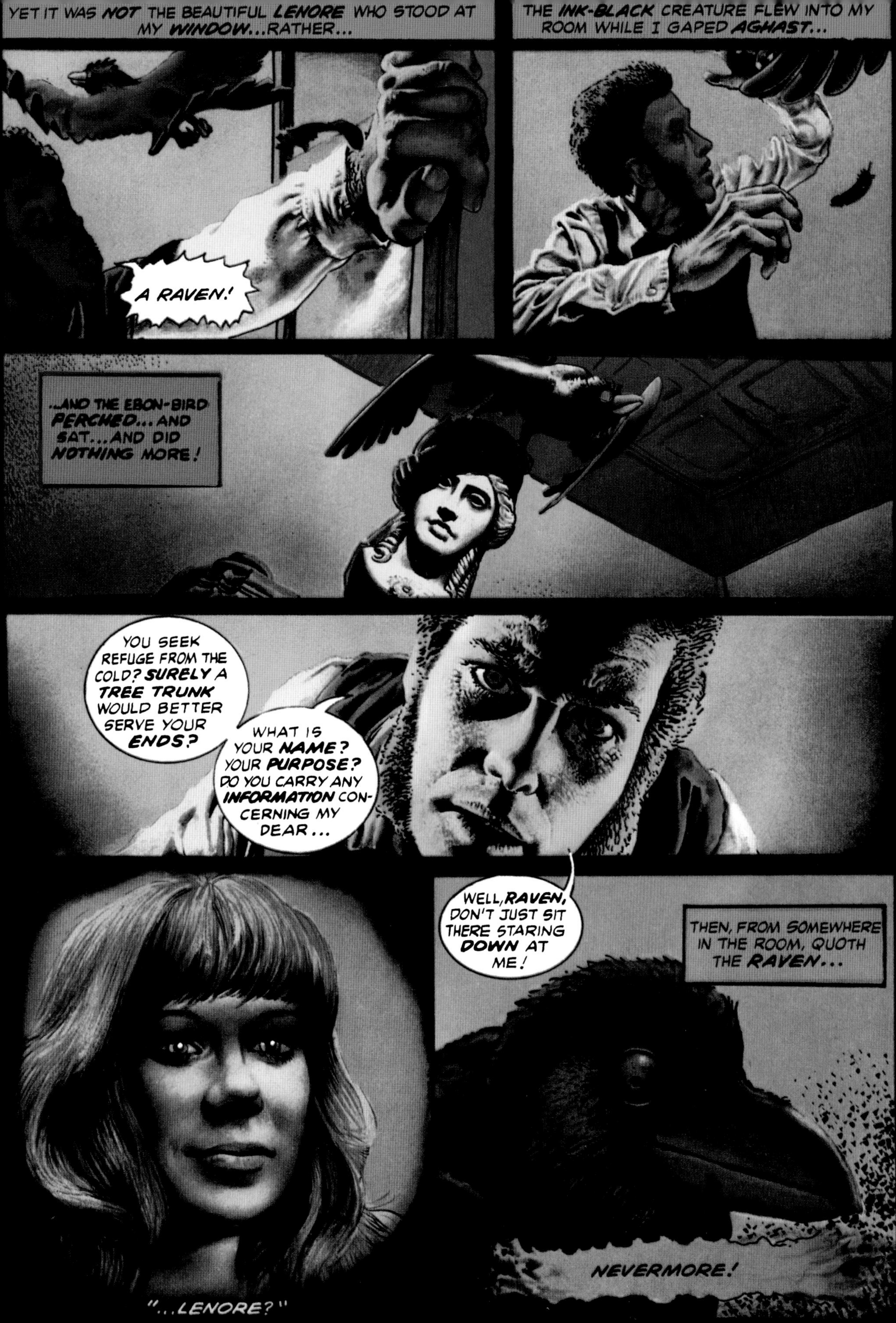
YET IT WAS NOT THE BEAUTIFUL LENORE WHO STOOD AT MY WINDOW...RATHER...
A RAVEN!
THE INK-BLACK CREATURE FLEW INTO MY ROOM WHILE I GAPED AGHAST...
...AND THE EBON-BIRD PERCHED... AND SAT... AND DID NOTHING MORE!
YOU SEEK REFUGE FROM THE COLD? SURELY A TREE TRUNK WOULD BETTER SERVE YOUR ENDS?
WHAT IS YOUR NAME? YOUR PURPOSE? DO YOU CARRY ANY INFORMATION CONCERNING MY DEAR...
"...LENORE?"
WELL, RAVEN, DON'T JUST SIT THERE STARING DOWN AT ME!
THEN, FROM SOMEWHERE IN THE ROOM, QUOTH THE RAVEN...
NEVERMORE!

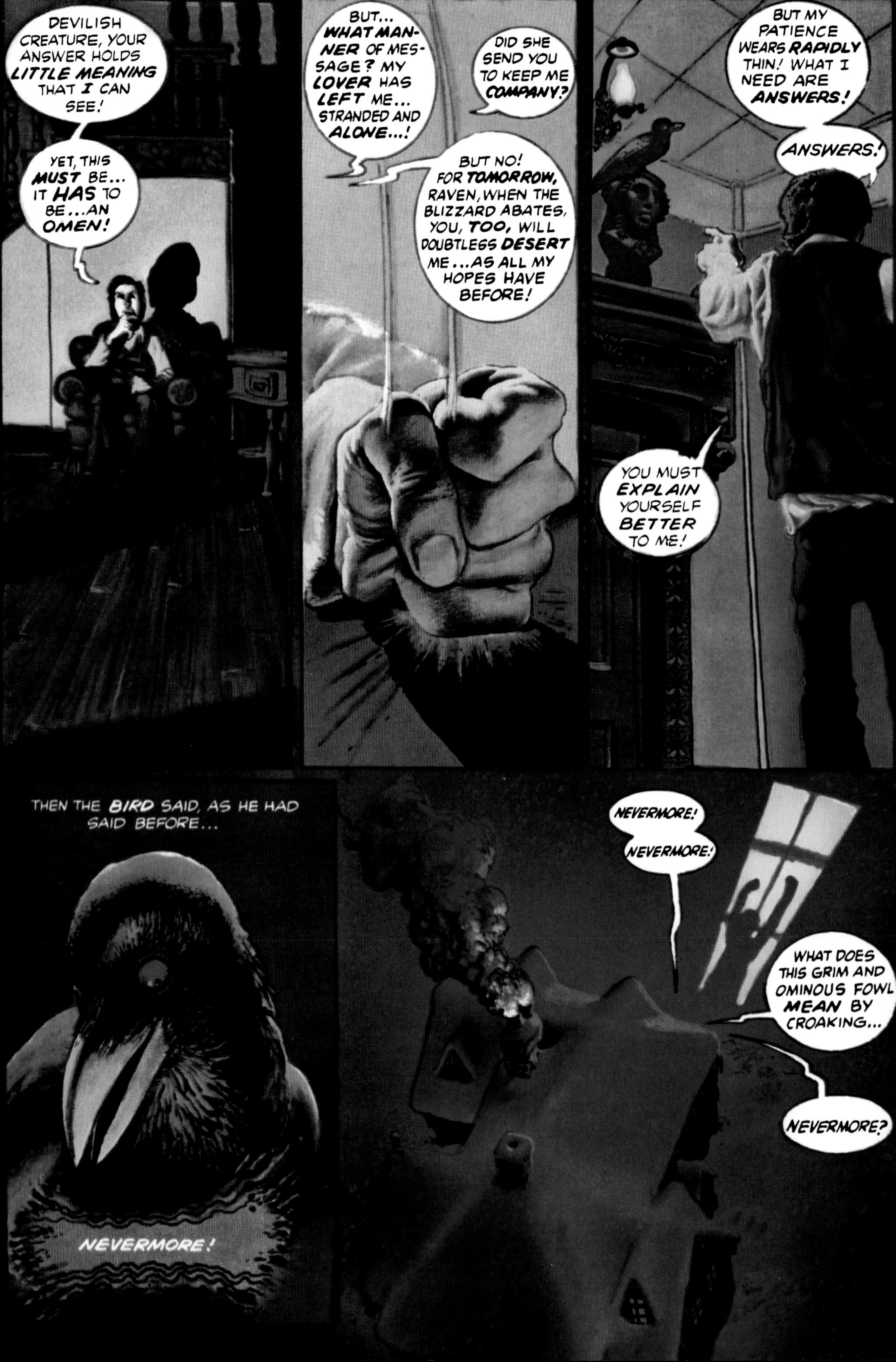
DEVILISH CREATURE, YOUR ANSWER HOLDS LITTLE MEANING THAT I CAN SEE!
YET, THIS MUST BE... IT HAS TO BE...AN OMEN!
BUT... WHAT MANNER OF MESSAGE? MY LOVER HAS LEFT ME... STRANDED AND ALONE...!
DID SHE SEND YOU TO KEEP ME COMPANY?
BUT NO! FOR TOMORROW, RAVEN, WHEN THE BLIZZARD ABATES, YOU, TOO, WILL DOUBTLESS DESERT ME...AS ALL MY HOPES HAVE BEFORE!
BUT MY PATIENCE WEARS RAPIDLY THIN! WHAT I NEED ARE ANSWERS!
ANSWERS!
YOU MUST EXPLAIN YOURSELF BETTER TO ME!
THEN THE BIRD SAID, AS HE HAD SAID BEFORE...
NEVERMORE!
NEVERMORE!
NEVERMORE!
WHAT DOES THIS GRIM AND OMINOUS FOWL MEAN BY CROAKING...
NEVERMORE?

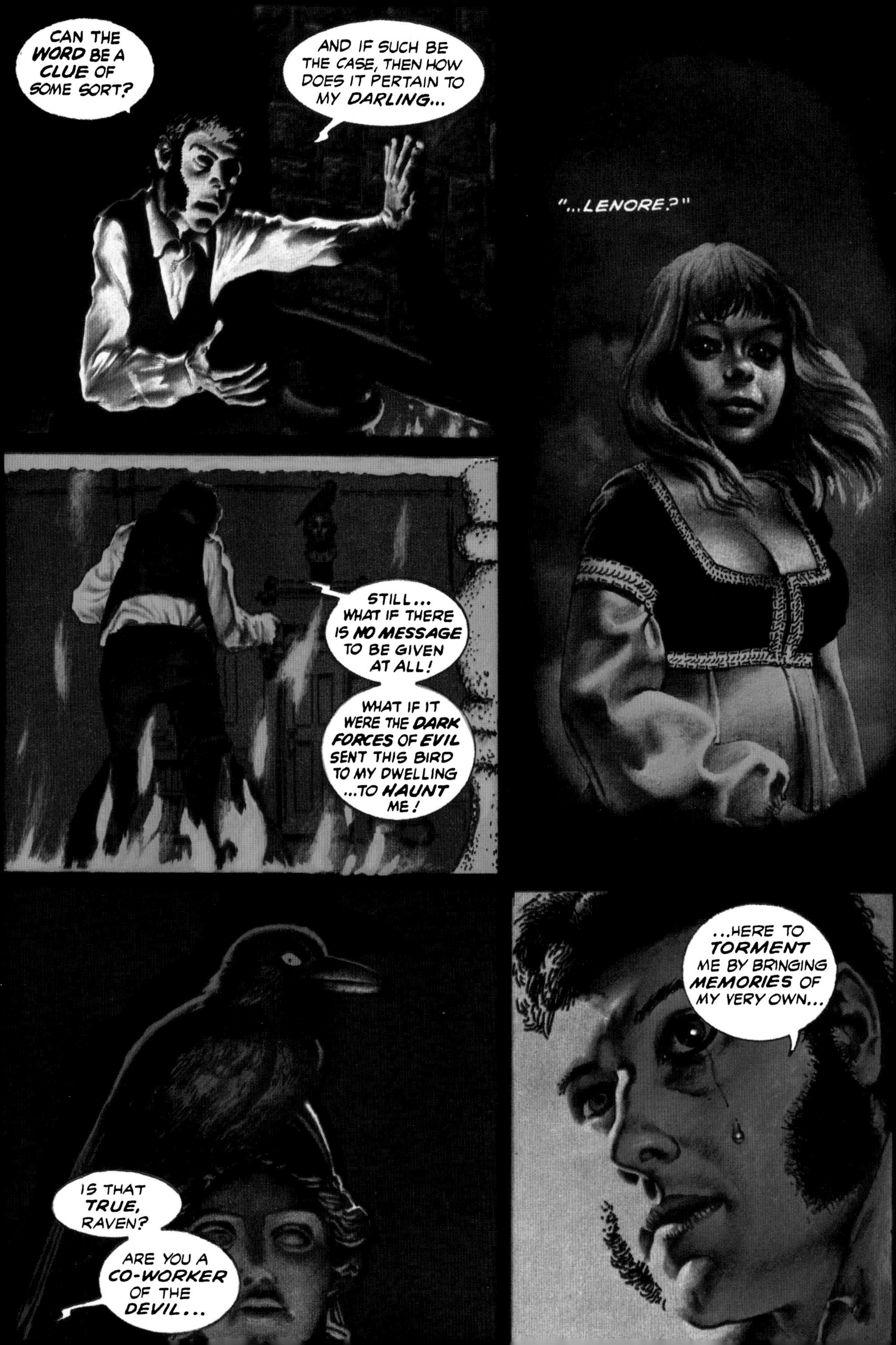
CAN THE WORD BE A CLUE OF SOME SORT?
AND IF SUCH BE THE CASE, THEN HOW DOES IT PERTAIN TO MY DARLING...
"...LENORE?"
STILL... WHAT IF THERE IS NO MESSAGE TO BE GIVEN AT ALL!
WHAT IF IT WERE THE DARK FORCES OF EVIL SENT THIS BIRD TO MY DWELLING ...TO HAUNT ME!
IS THAT TRUE, RAVEN?
ARE YOU A CO-WORKER OF THE DEVIL...
...HERE TO TORMENT ME BY BRINGING MEMORIES OF MY VERY OWN...

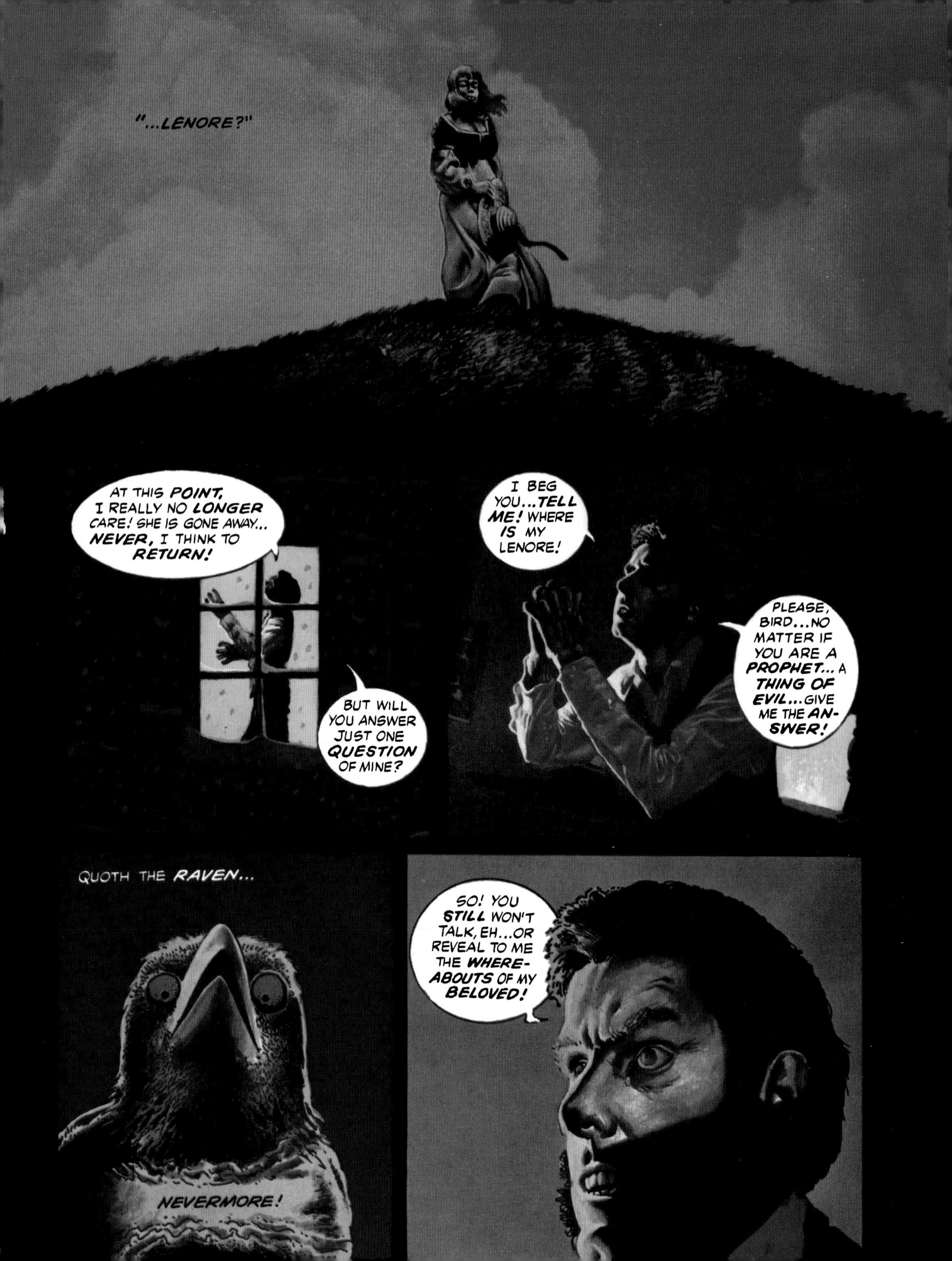
"...LENORE?"
AT THIS POINT, I REALLY NO LONGER CARE! SHE IS GONE AWAY... NEVER, I THINK TO RETURN!
BUT WILL YOU ANSWER JUST ONE QUESTION OF MINE?
I BEG YOU...TELL ME! WHERE IS MY LENORE!
PLEASE, BIRD...NO MATTER IF YOU ARE A PROPHET... A THING OF EVIL...GIVE ME THE AN-SWER!
QUOTH THE RAVEN...
NEVERMORE!
SO! YOU STILL WON'T TALK, EH...OR REVEAL TO ME THE WHERE-ABOUTS OF MY BELOVED!

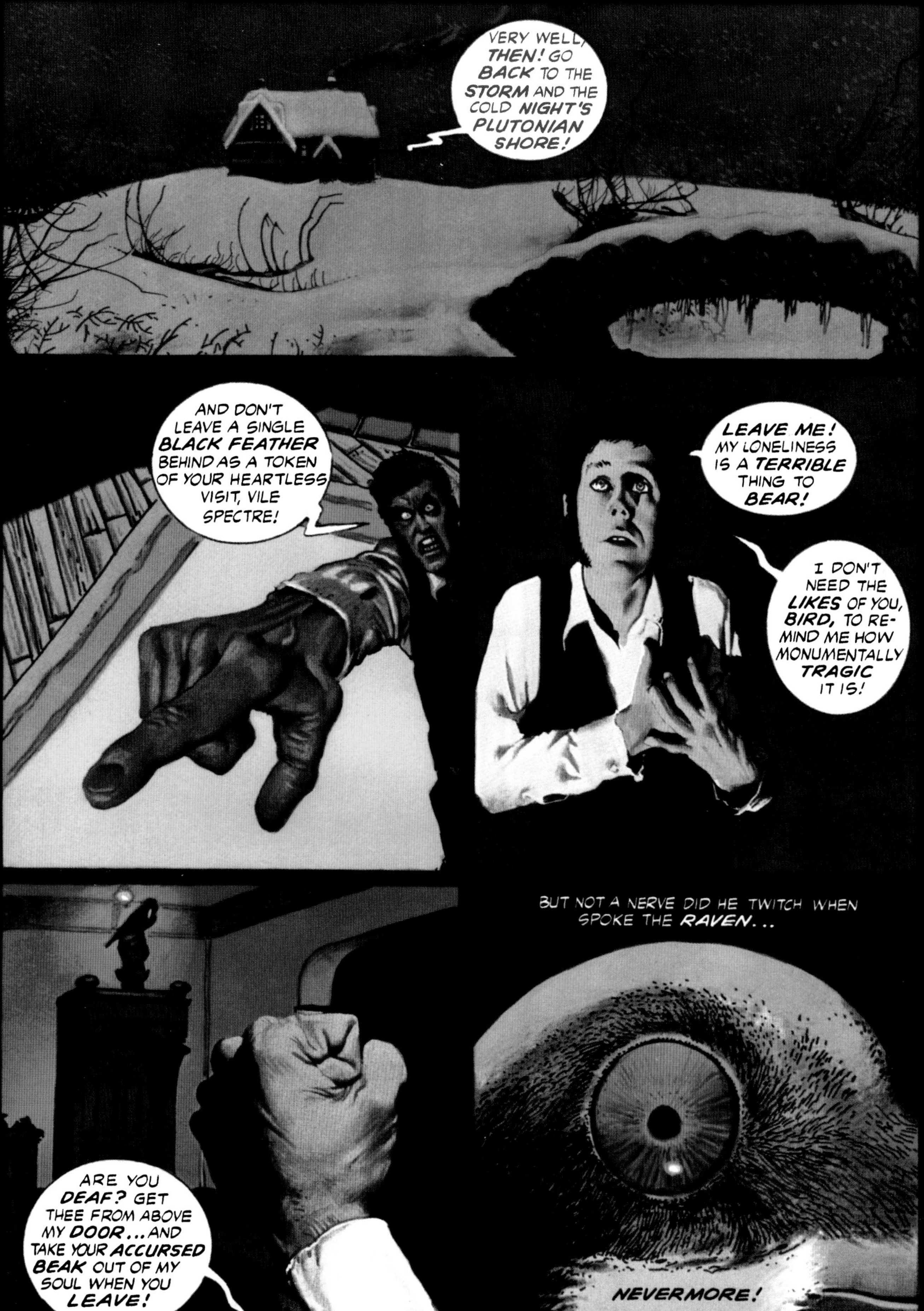
VERY WELL, THEN! GO BACK TO THE STORM AND THE COLD NIGHT'S PLUTONIAN SHORE!
AND DON'T LEAVE A SINGLE BLACK FEATHER BEHIND AS A TOKEN OF YOUR HEARTLESS VISIT, VILE SPECTRE!
LEAVE ME! MY LONELINESS IS A TERRIBLE THING TO BEAR!
I DON'T NEED THE LIKES OF YOU, BIRD, TO RE-MIND ME HOW MONUMENTALLY TRAGIC IT IS!
ARE YOU DEAF? GET THEE FROM ABOVE MY DOOR... AND TAKE YOUR ACCURSED BEAK OUT OF MY SOUL WHEN YOU LEAVE!
BUT NOT A NERVE DID HE TWITCH WHEN SPOKE THE RAVEN...
NEVERMORE!

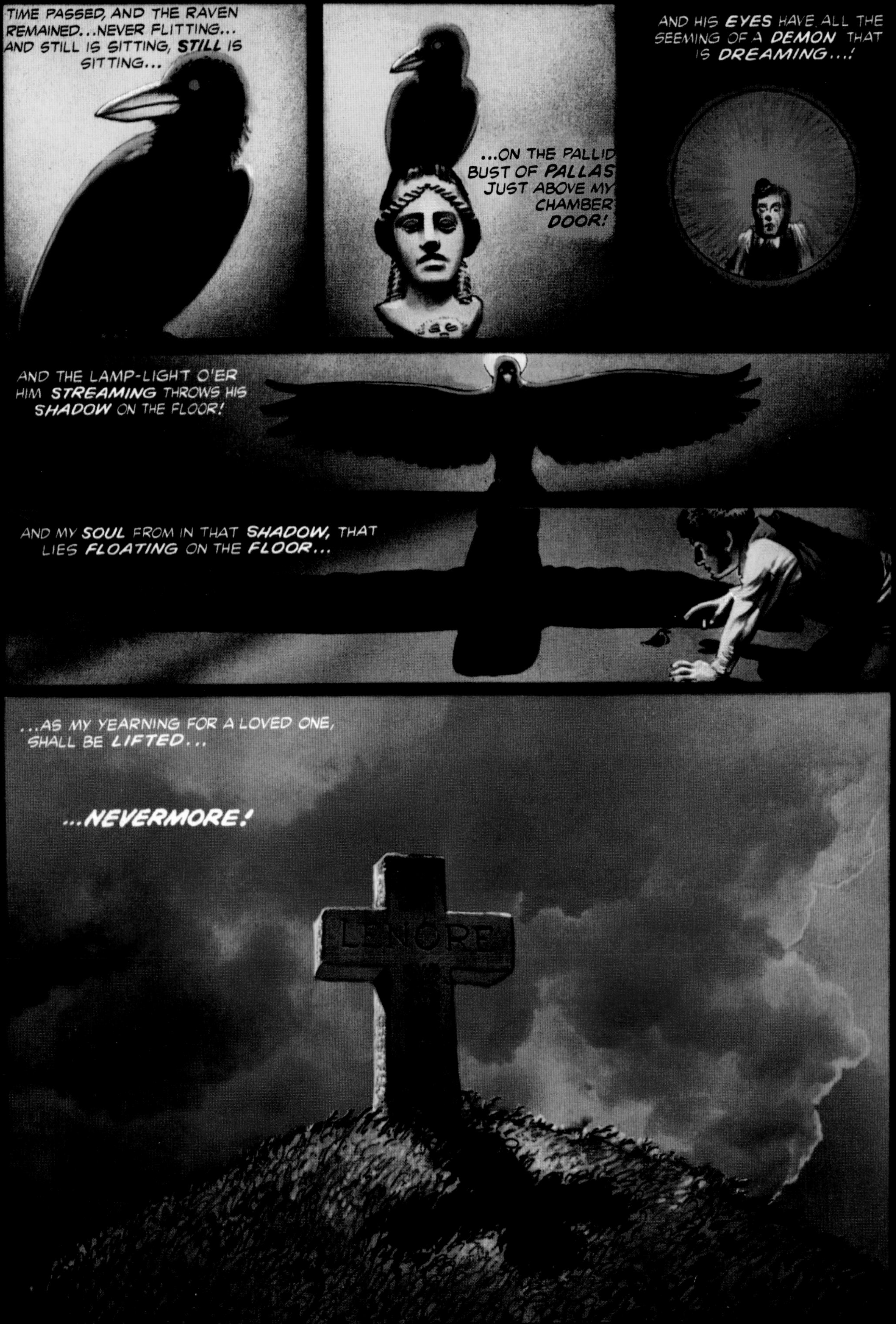
TIME PASSED, AND THE RAVEN REMAINED...NEVER FLITTING... AND STILL IS SITTING, STILL IS SITTING...
...ON THE PALLID BUST OF PALLAS JUST ABOVE MY CHAMBER DOOR!
AND HIS EYES HAVE ALL THE SEEMING OF A DEMON THAT IS DREAMING...!
AND THE LAMP-LIGHT O'ER HIM STREAMING THROWS HIS SHADOW ON THE FLOOR!
AND MY SOUL FROM IN THAT SHADOW, THAT LIES FLOATING ON THE FLOOR...
...AS MY YEARNING FOR A LOVED ONE, SHALL BE LIFTED...
...NEVERMORE!
LENORE

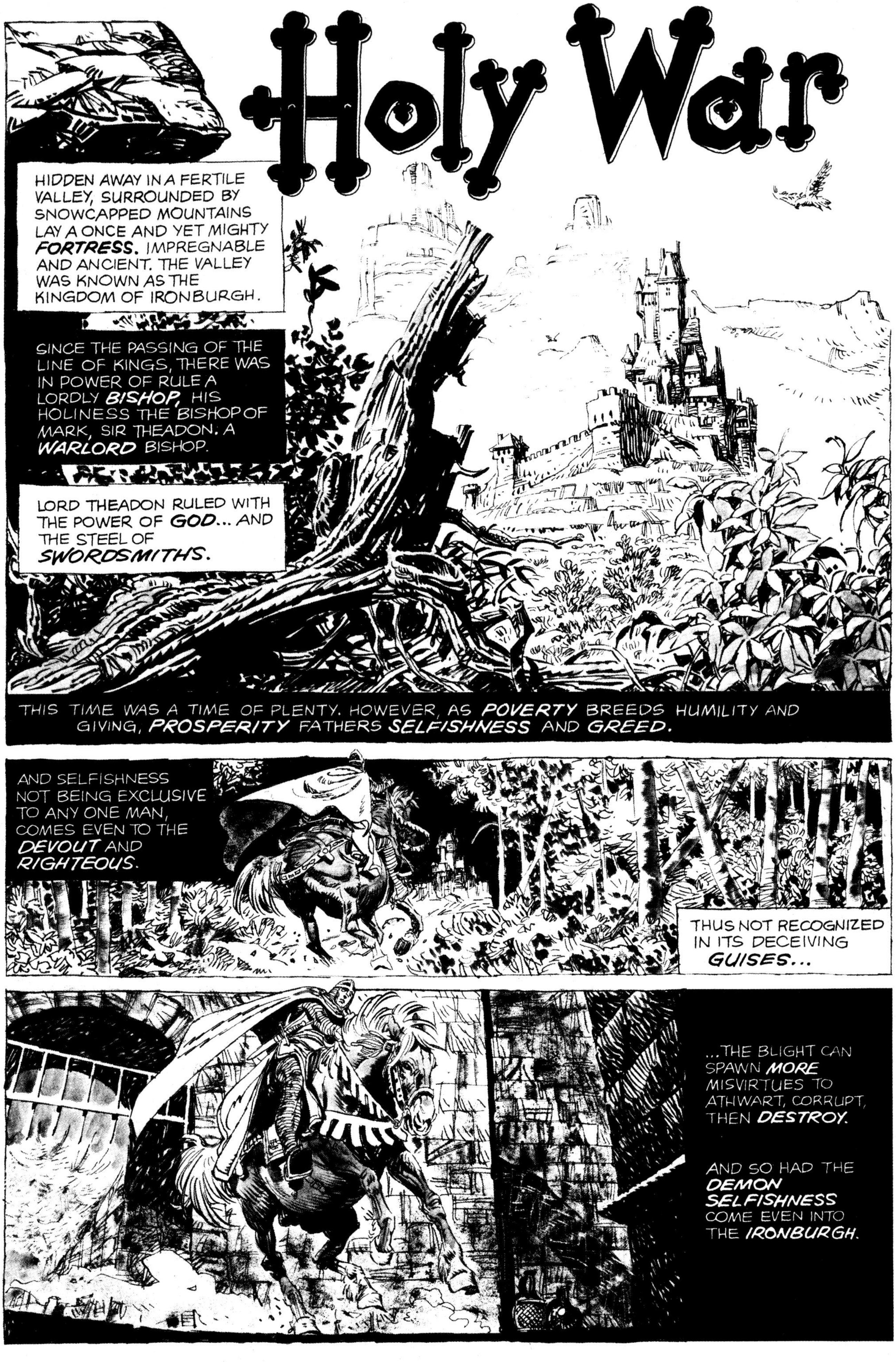
Holy War
HIDDEN AWAY IN A FERTILE VALLEY, SURROUNDED BY SNOWCAPPED MOUNTAINS LAY A ONCE AND YET MIGHTY FORTRESS. IMPREGNABLE AND ANCIENT. THE VALLEY WAS KNOWN AS THE KINGDOM OF IRONBURGH.
SINCE THE PASSING OF THE LINE OF KINGS, THERE WAS IN POWER OF RULE A LORDLY BISHOP, HIS HOLINESS THE BISHOP OF MARK, SIR THEADON. A WARLORD BISHOP.
LORD THEADON RULED WITH THE POWER OF GOD... AND THE STEEL OF SWORDSMITHS.
THIS TIME WAS A TIME OF PLENTY. HOWEVER, AS POVERTY BREEDS HUMILITY AND GIVING, PROSPERITY FATHERS SELFISHNESS AND GREED.
AND SELFISHNESS NOT BEING EXCLUSIVE TO ANY ONE MAN, COMES EVEN TO THE DEVOUT AND RIGHTEOUS.
THUS NOT RECOGNIZED IN ITS DECEIVING GUISES...
...THE BLIGHT CAN SPAWN MORE MISVIRTUES TO ATHWART, CORRUPT, THEN DESTROY.
AND SO HAD THE DEMON SELFISHNESS COME EVEN INTO THE IRONBURGH.

STORY: BUDD LEWIS / ART: ADOLFO ABELLAN

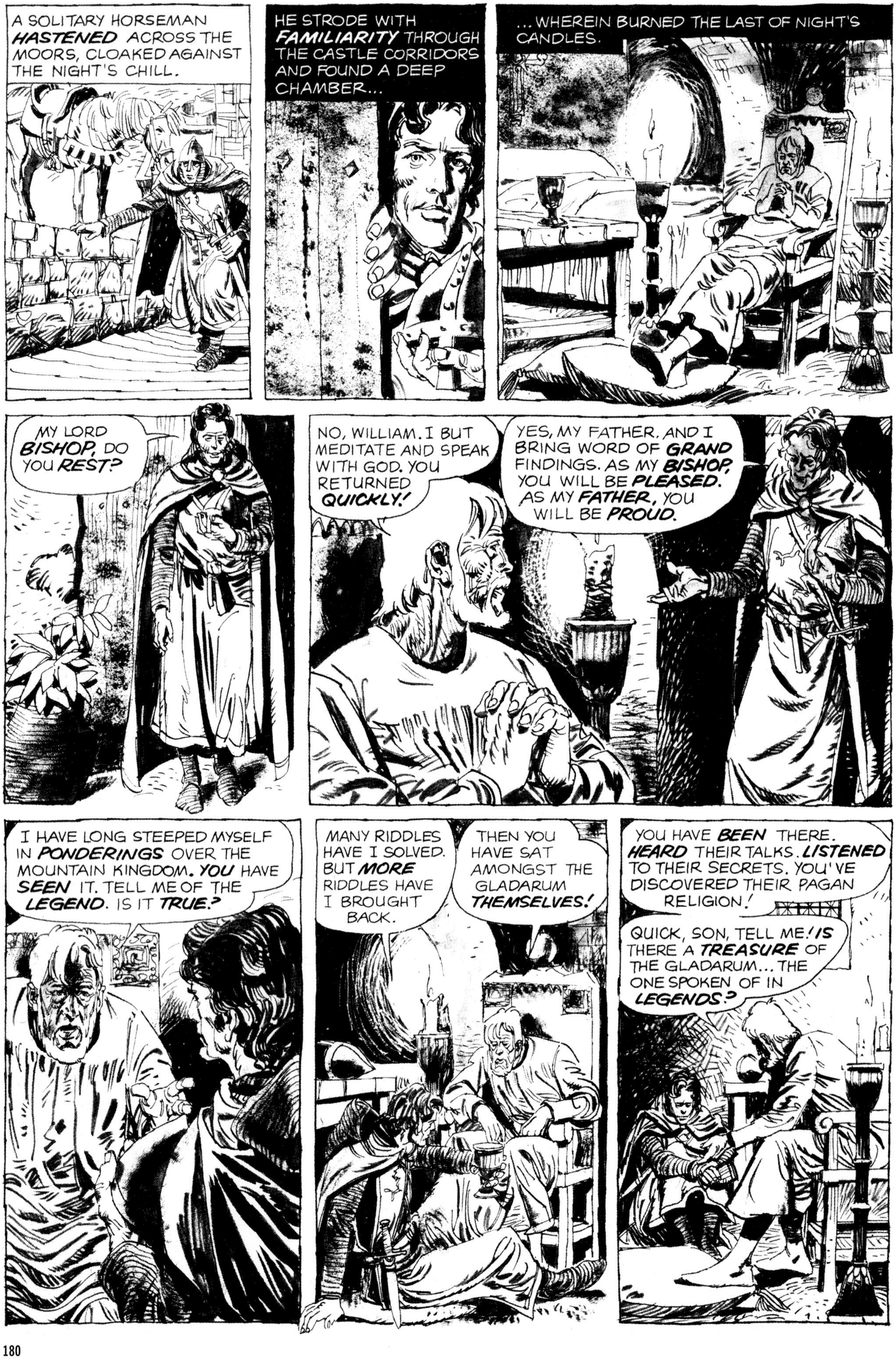
A SOLITARY HORSEMAN HASTENED ACROSS THE MOORS, CLOAKED AGAINST THE NIGHT'S CHILL.
HE STRODE WITH FAMILIARITY THROUGH THE CASTLE CORRIDORS AND FOUND A DEEP CHAMBER...
...WHEREIN BURNED THE LAST OF NIGHT'S CANDLES.
MY LORD BISHOP, DO YOU REST?
NO, WILLIAM. I BUT MEDITATE AND SPEAK WITH GOD. YOU RETURNED QUICKLY!
YES, MY FATHER. AND I BRING WORD OF GRAND FINDINGS. AS MY BISHOP, YOU WILL BE PLEASED. AS MY FATHER, YOU WILL BE PROUD.
I HAVE LONG STEEPED MYSELF IN PONDERINGS OVER THE MOUNTAIN KINGDOM. YOU HAVE SEEN IT. TELL ME OF THE LEGEND. IS IT TRUE?
MANY RIDDLES HAVE I SOLVED. BUT MORE RIDDLES HAVE I BROUGHT BACK.
THEN YOU HAVE SAT AMONGST THE GLADARUM THEMSELVES!
YOU HAVE BEEN THERE. HEARD THEIR TALKS. LISTENED TO THEIR SECRETS. YOU'VE DISCOVERED THEIR PAGAN RELIGION!
QUICK, SON, TELL ME! IS THERE A TREASURE OF THE GLADARUM... THE ONE SPOKEN OF IN LEGENDS?

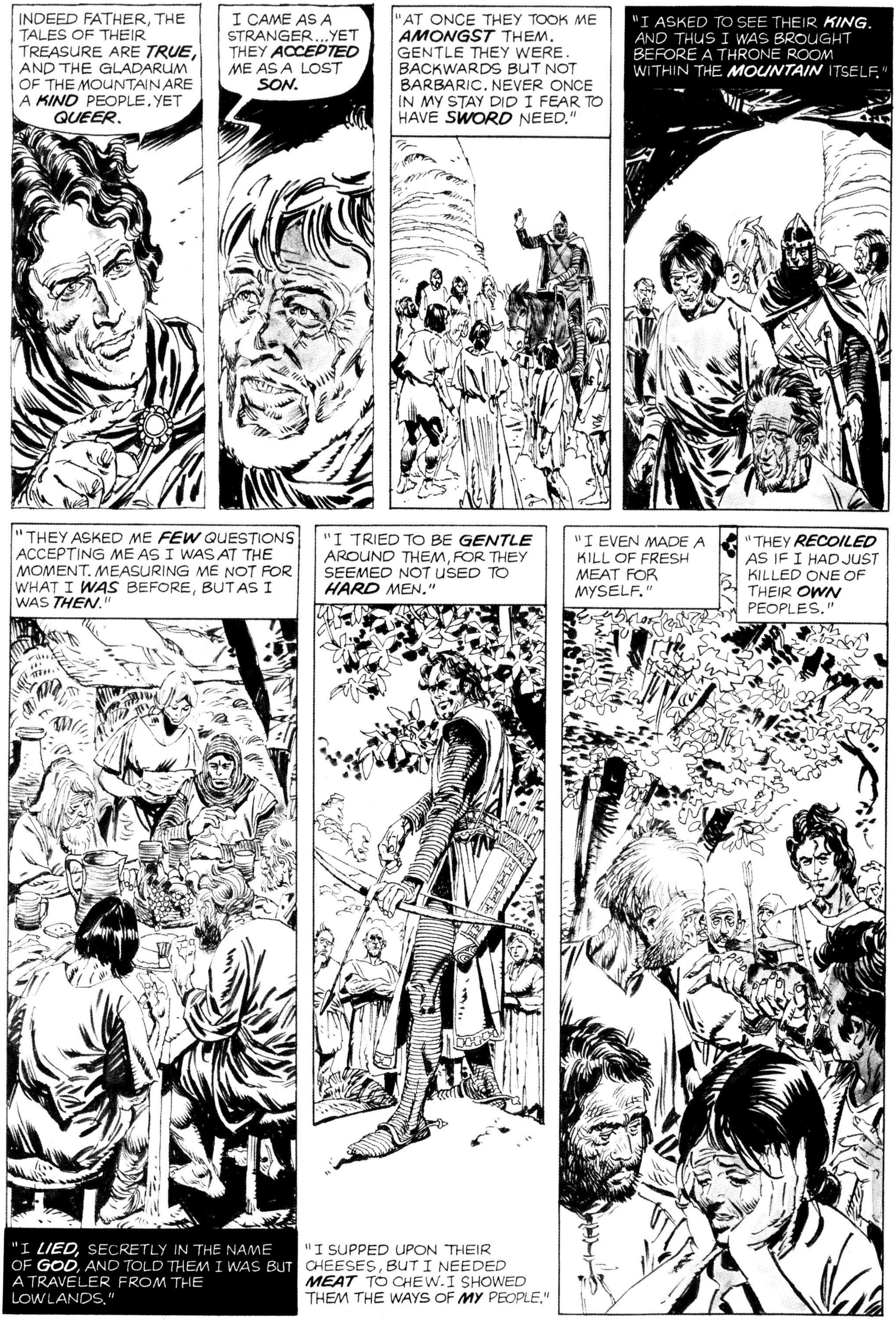
INDEED FATHER, THE TALES OF THEIR TREASURE ARE TRUE, AND THE GLADARUM OF THE MOUNTAIN ARE A KIND PEOPLE. YET QUEER.
I CAME AS A STRANGER...YET THEY ACCEPTED ME AS A LOST SON.
"AT ONCE THEY TOOK ME AMONGST THEM. GENTLE THEY WERE. BACKWARDS BUT NOT BARBARIC. NEVER ONCE IN MY STAY DID I FEAR TO HAVE SWORD NEED."
"I ASKED TO SEE THEIR KING. AND THUS I WAS BROUGHT BEFORE A THRONE ROOM WITHIN THE MOUNTAIN ITSELF."
"THEY ASKED ME FEW QUESTIONS ACCEPTING ME AS I WAS AT THE MOMENT. MEASURING ME NOT FOR WHAT I WAS BEFORE, BUT AS I WAS THEN."
"I LIED, SECRETLY IN THE NAME OF GOD, AND TOLD THEM I WAS BUT A TRAVELER FROM THE LOWLANDS."
"I TRIED TO BE GENTLE AROUND THEM, FOR THEY SEEMED NOT USED TO HARD MEN."
"I SUPPED UPON THEIR CHEESES, BUT I NEEDED MEAT TO CHEW. I SHOWED THEM THE WAYS OF MY PEOPLE."
"I EVEN MADE A KILL OF FRESH MEAT FOR MYSELF."
"THEY RECOILED AS IF I HAD JUST KILLED ONE OF THEIR OWN PEOPLES."

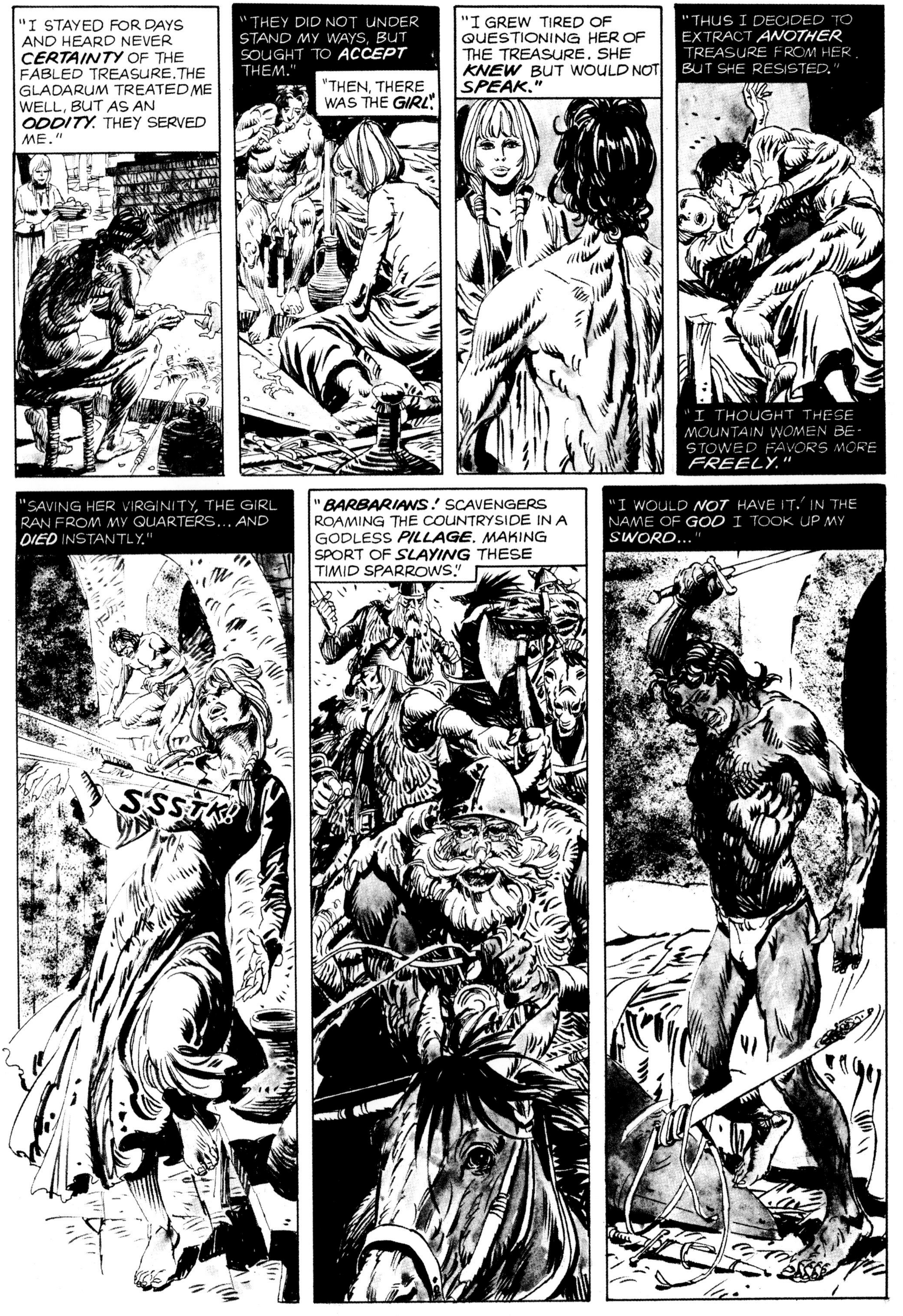
"I STAYED FOR DAYS AND HEARD NEVER CERTAINTY OF THE FABLED TREASURE. THE GLADARUM TREATED ME WELL, BUT AS AN ODDITY. THEY SERVED ME."
"THEY DID NOT UNDER STAND MY WAYS, BUT SOUGHT TO ACCEPT THEM."
"THEN, THERE WAS THE GIRL."
"I GREW TIRED OF QUESTIONING HER OF THE TREASURE. SHE KNEW BUT WOULD NOT SPEAK."
"THUS I DECIDED TO EXTRACT ANOTHER TREASURE FROM HER. BUT SHE RESISTED."
"I THOUGHT THESE MOUNTAIN WOMEN BE- STOWED FAVORS MORE FREELY."
"SAVING HER VIRGINITY, THE GIRL RAN FROM MY QUARTERS... AND DIED INSTANTLY."
SSSTK!
"BARBARIANS! SCAVENGERS ROAMING THE COUNTRYSIDE IN A GODLESS PILLAGE, MAKING SPORT OF SLAYING THESE TIMID SPARROWS."
"I WOULD NOT HAVE IT! IN THE NAME OF GOD I TOOK UP MY SWORD..."

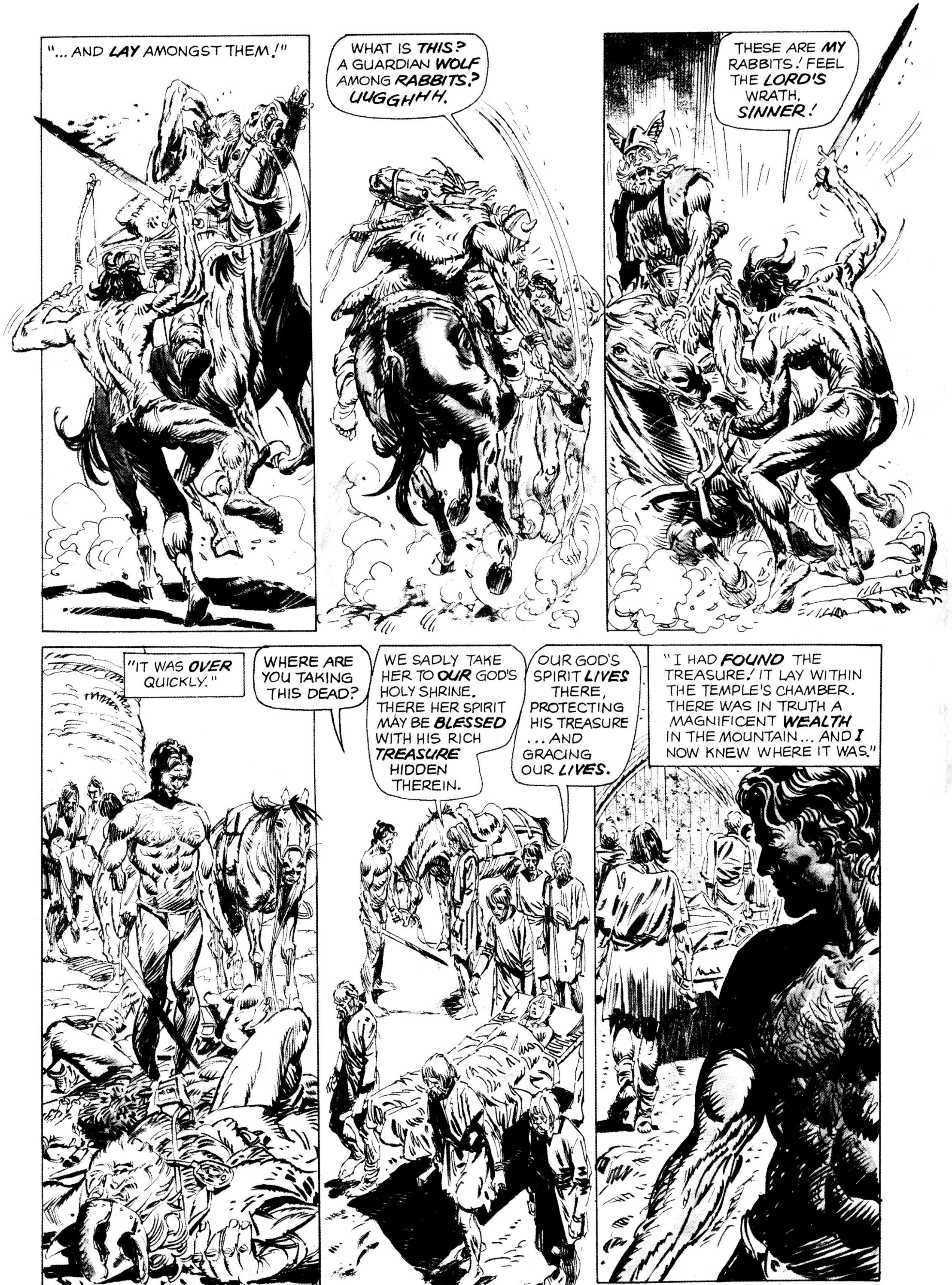
"... AND LAY AMONGST THEM!"
WHAT IS THIS? A GUARDIAN WOLF AMONG RABBITS? UUGGHHH.
THESE ARE MY RABBITS! FEEL THE LORD'S WRATH, SINNER!
"IT WAS OVER QUICKLY."
WHERE ARE YOU TAKING THIS DEAD?
WE SADLY TAKE HER TO OUR GOD'S HOLY SHRINE. THERE HER SPIRIT MAY BE BLESSED WITH HIS RICH TREASURE HIDDEN THEREIN.
OUR GOD'S SPIRIT LIVES THERE, PROTECTING HIS TREASURE ... AND GRACING OUR LIVES.
"I HAD FOUND THE TREASURE! IT LAY WITHIN THE TEMPLE'S CHAMBER. THERE WAS IN TRUTH A MAGNIFICENT WEALTH IN THE MOUNTAIN ... AND I NOW KNEW WHERE IT WAS."

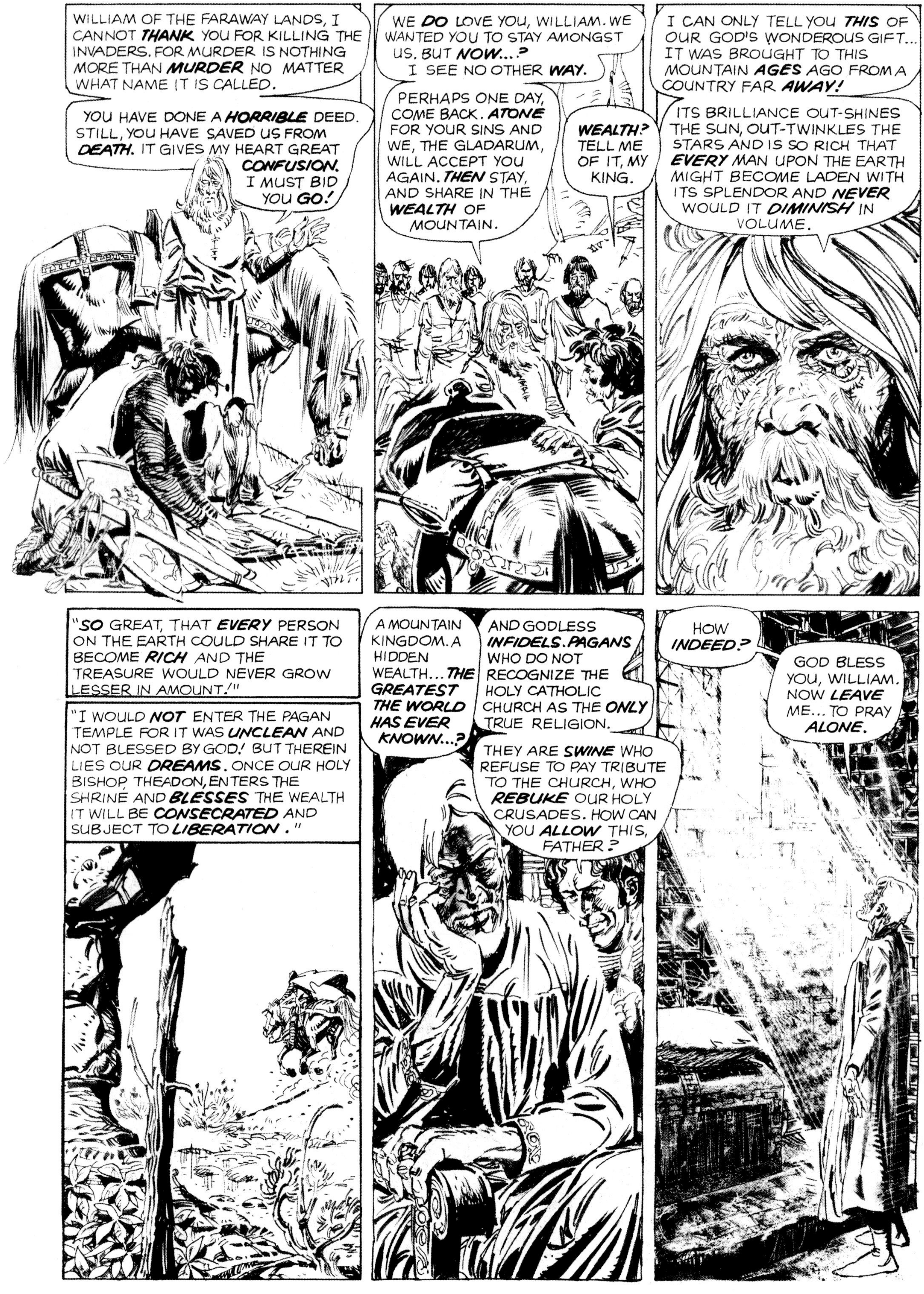
WILLIAM OF THE FARAWAY LANDS, I CANNOT THANK YOU FOR KILLING THE INVADERS. FOR MURDER IS NOTHING MORE THAN MURDER NO MATTER WHAT NAME IT IS CALLED.
YOU HAVE DONE A HORRIBLE DEED. STILL, YOU HAVE SAVED US FROM DEATH. IT GIVES MY HEART GREAT CONFUSION. I MUST BID YOU GO!
WE DO LOVE YOU, WILLIAM. WE WANTED YOU TO STAY AMONGST US. BUT NOW...? I SEE NO OTHER WAY.
PERHAPS ONE DAY, COME BACK. ATONE FOR YOUR SINS AND WE, THE GLADARUM, WILL ACCEPT YOU AGAIN. THEN STAY, AND SHARE IN THE WEALTH OF MOUNTAIN.
WEALTH? TELL ME OF IT, MY KING.
I CAN ONLY TELL YOU THIS OF OUR GOD'S WONDEROUS GIFT... IT WAS BROUGHT TO THIS MOUNTAIN AGES AGO FROM A COUNTRY FAR AWAY!
ITS BRILLIANCE OUT-SHINES THE SUN, OUT-TWINKLES THE STARS AND IS SO RICH THAT EVERY MAN UPON THE EARTH MIGHT BECOME LADEN WITH ITS SPLENDOR AND NEVER WOULD IT DIMINISH IN VOLUME.
"SO GREAT, THAT EVERY PERSON ON THE EARTH COULD SHARE IT TO BECOME RICH AND THE TREASURE WOULD NEVER GROW LESSER IN AMOUNT!"
"I WOULD NOT ENTER THE PAGAN TEMPLE FOR IT WAS UNCLEAN AND NOT BLESSED BY GOD! BUT THEREIN LIES OUR DREAMS. ONCE OUR HOLY BISHOP, THEADON, ENTERS THE SHRINE AND BLESSES THE WEALTH IT WILL BE CONSECRATED AND SUBJECT TO LIBERATION."
A MOUNTAIN KINGDOM. A HIDDEN WEALTH... THE GREATEST THE WORLD HAS EVER KNOWN...?
AND GODLESS INFIDELS. PAGANS WHO DO NOT RECOGNIZE THE HOLY CATHOLIC CHURCH AS THE ONLY TRUE RELIGION.
THEY ARE SWINE WHO REFUSE TO PAY TRIBUTE TO THE CHURCH, WHO REBUKE OUR HOLY CRUSADES. HOW CAN YOU ALLOW THIS, FATHER?
HOW INDEED?
GOD BLESS YOU, WILLIAM. NOW LEAVE ME... TO PRAY ALONE.

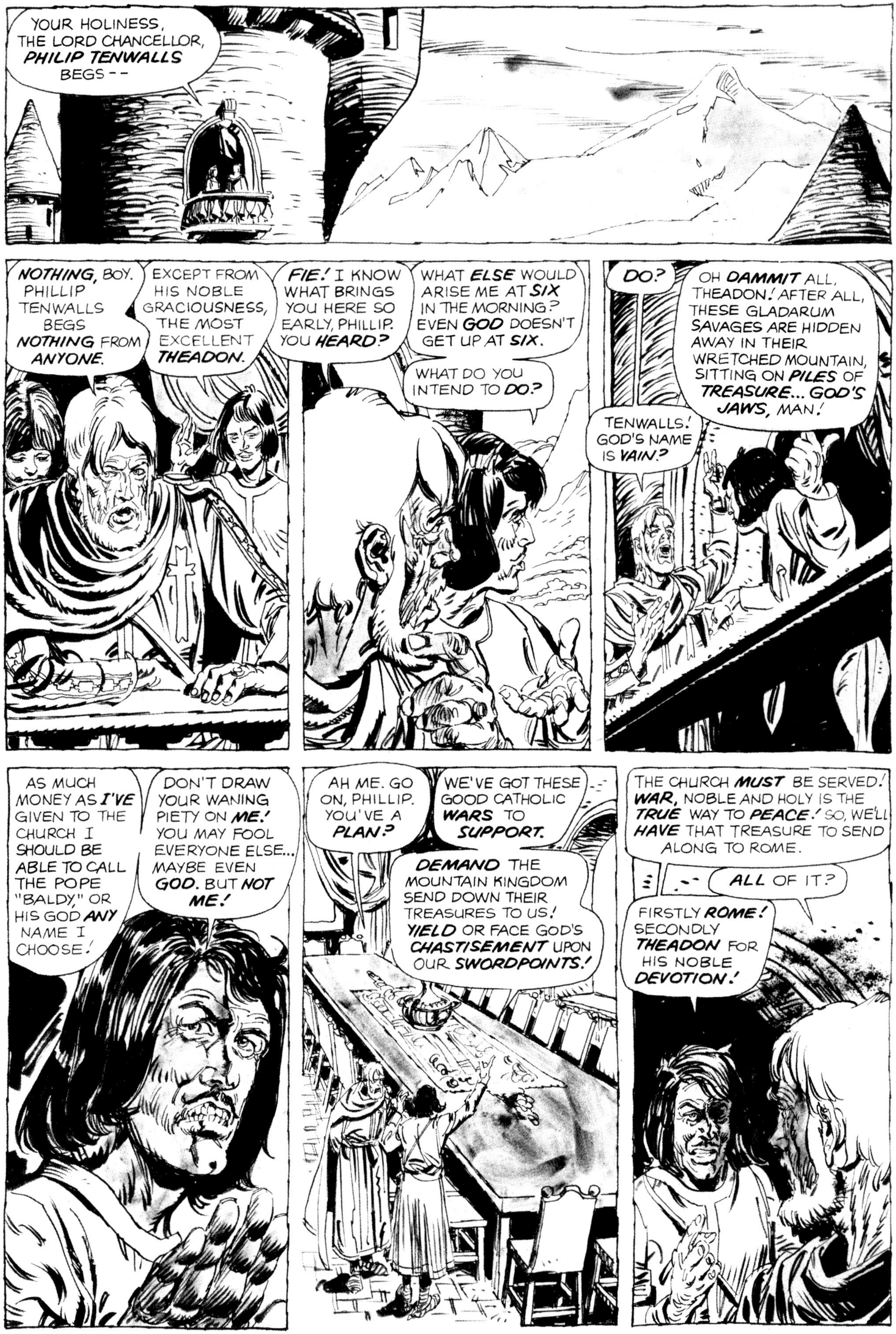

YOUR HOLINESS, THE LORD CHANCELLOR, PHILIP TENWALLS BEGS --
NOTHING, BOY. PHILLIP TENWALLS BEGS NOTHING FROM ANYONE.
EXCEPT FROM HIS NOBLE GRACIOUSNESS, THE MOST EXCELLENT THEADON.
FIE! I KNOW WHAT BRINGS YOU HERE SO EARLY, PHILLIP. YOU HEARD?
WHAT ELSE WOULD ARISE ME AT SIX IN THE MORNING? EVEN GOD DOESN'T GET UP AT SIX.
WHAT DO YOU INTEND TO DO?
DO?
OH DAMMIT ALL, THEADON! AFTER ALL, THESE GLADARUM SAVAGES ARE HIDDEN AWAY IN THEIR WRETCHED MOUNTAIN, SITTING ON PILES OF TREASURE... GOD'S JAWS, MAN!
TENWALLS! GOD'S NAME IS VAIN?
AS MUCH MONEY AS I'VE GIVEN TO THE CHURCH I SHOULD BE ABLE TO CALL THE POPE "BALDY," OR HIS GOD ANY NAME I CHOOSE!
DON'T DRAW YOUR WANING PIETY ON ME! YOU MAY FOOL EVERYONE ELSE... MAYBE EVEN GOD. BUT NOT ME!
AH ME. GO ON, PHILLIP. YOU'VE A PLAN?
WE'VE GOT THESE GOOD CATHOLIC WARS TO SUPPORT.
DEMAND THE MOUNTAIN KINGDOM SEND DOWN THEIR TREASURES TO US! YIELD OR FACE GOD'S CHASTISEMENT UPON OUR SWORDPOINTS!
THE CHURCH MUST BE SERVED! WAR, NOBLE AND HOLY IS THE TRUE WAY TO PEACE! SO, WE'LL HAVE THAT TREASURE TO SEND ALONG TO ROME.
ALL OF IT?
FIRSTLY ROME! SECONDLY THEADON FOR HIS NOBLE DEVOTION!

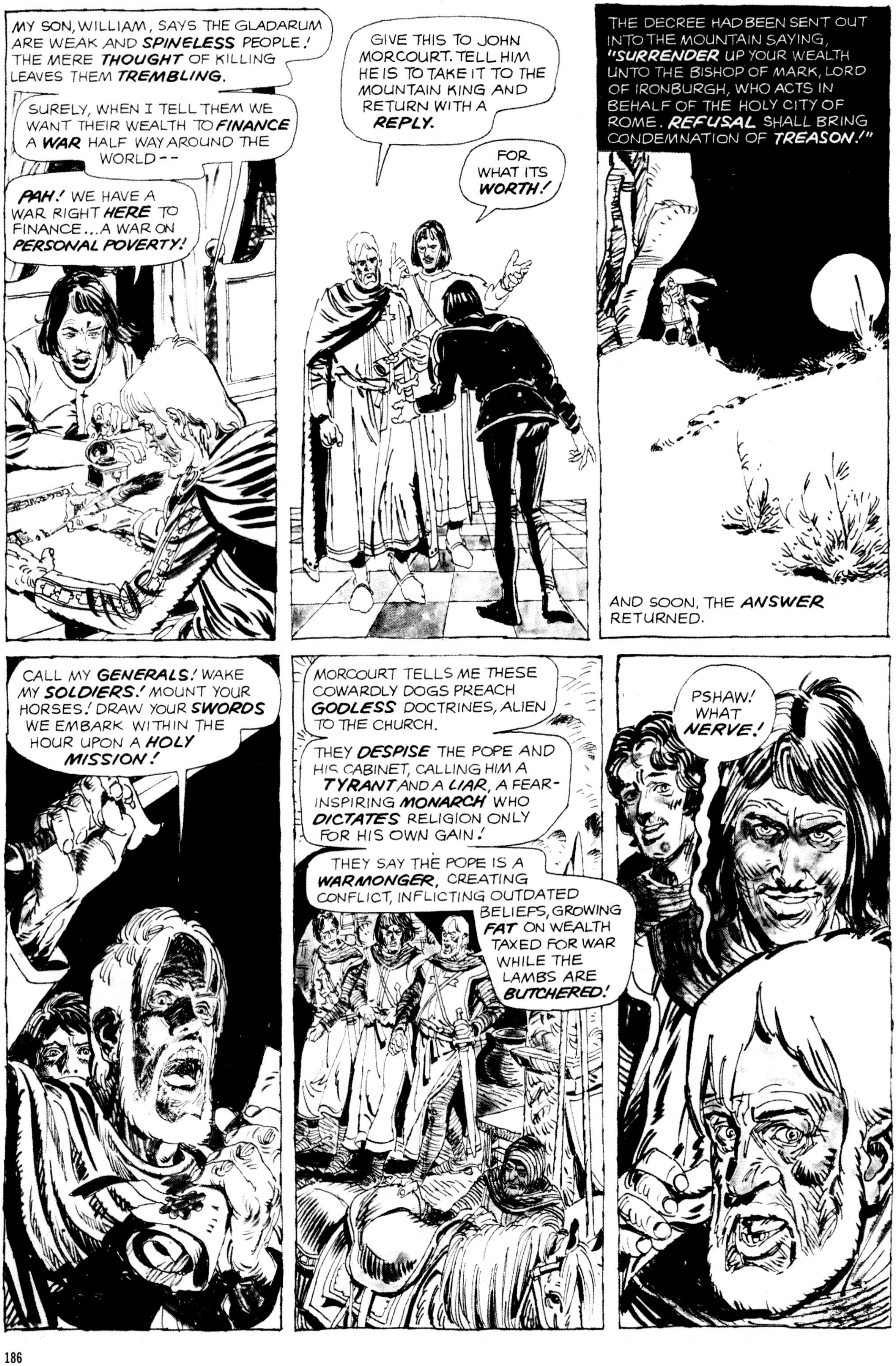
MY SON, WILLIAM, SAYS THE GLADARUM ARE WEAK AND SPINELESS PEOPLE! THE MERE THOUGHT OF KILLING LEAVES THEM TREMBLING.
SURELY, WHEN I TELL THEM WE WANT THEIR WEALTH TO FINANCE A WAR HALF WAY AROUND THE WORLD--
PAH! WE HAVE A WAR RIGHT HERE TO FINANCE...A WAR ON PERSONAL POVERTY!
GIVE THIS TO JOHN MORCOURT. TELL HIM HE IS TO TAKE IT TO THE MOUNTAIN KING AND RETURN WITH A REPLY.
FOR WHAT ITS WORTH!
THE DECREE HAD BEEN SENT OUT INTO THE MOUNTAIN SAYING, "SURRENDER UP YOUR WEALTH UNTO THE BISHOP OF MARK, LORD OF IRONBURGH, WHO ACTS IN BEHALF OF THE HOLY CITY OF ROME. REFUSAL SHALL BRING CONDEMNATION OF TREASON!"
AND SOON, THE ANSWER RETURNED.
CALL MY GENERALS! WAKE MY SOLDIERS! MOUNT YOUR HORSES! DRAW YOUR SWORDS WE EMBARK WITHIN THE HOUR UPON A HOLY MISSION!
MORCOURT TELLS ME THESE COWARDLY DOGS PREACH GODLESS DOCTRINES, ALIEN TO THE CHURCH.
THEY DESPISE THE POPE AND HIS CABINET, CALLING HIM A TYRANT AND A LIAR, A FEAR-INSPIRING MONARCH WHO DICTATES RELIGION ONLY FOR HIS OWN GAIN!
THEY SAY THE POPE IS A WARMONGER, CREATING CONFLICT, INFLICTING OUTDATED BELIEFS, GROWING FAT ON WEALTH TAXED FOR WAR WHILE THE LAMBS ARE BUTCHERED!
PSHAW! WHAT NERVE!

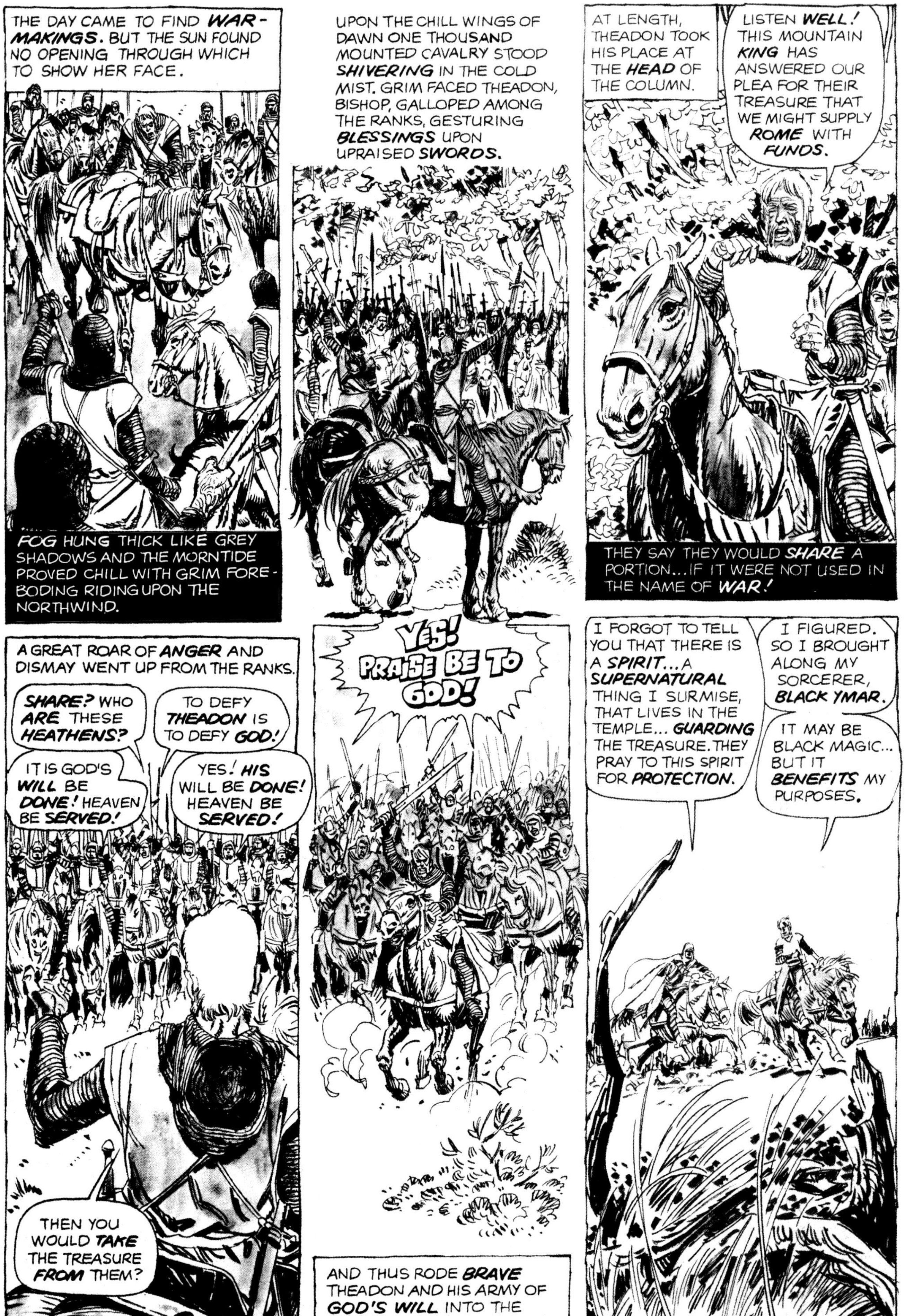

THE DAY CAME TO FIND WAR-MAKINGS. BUT THE SUN FOUND NO OPENING THROUGH WHICH TO SHOW HER FACE.
FOG HUNG THICK LIKE GREY SHADOWS AND THE MORNTIDE PROVED CHILL WITH GRIM FORE-BODING RIDING UPON THE NORTHWIND.
UPON THE CHILL WINGS OF DAWN ONE THOUSAND MOUNTED CAVALRY STOOD SHIVERING IN THE COLD MIST. GRIM FACED THEADON, BISHOP, GALLOPED AMONG THE RANKS, GESTURING BLESSINGS UPON UPRAISED SWORDS.
AT LENGTH, THEADON TOOK HIS PLACE AT THE HEAD OF THE COLUMN.
LISTEN WELL! THIS MOUNTAIN KING HAS ANSWERED OUR PLEA FOR THEIR TREASURE THAT WE MIGHT SUPPLY ROME WITH FUNDS.
THEY SAY THEY WOULD SHARE A PORTION... IF IT WERE NOT USED IN THE NAME OF WAR!
A GREAT ROAR OF ANGER AND DISMAY WENT UP FROM THE RANKS.
SHARE? WHO ARE THESE HEATHENS?
TO DEFY THEADON IS TO DEFY GOD!
IT IS GOD'S WILL BE DONE! HEAVEN BE SERVED!
YES! HIS WILL BE DONE! HEAVEN BE SERVED!
THEN YOU WOULD TAKE THE TREASURE FROM THEM?
YES! PRAISE BE TO GOD!
AND THUS RODE BRAVE THEADON AND HIS ARMY OF GOD'S WILL INTO THE MOUNTAIN.
I FORGOT TO TELL YOU THAT THERE IS A SPIRIT... A SUPERNATURAL THING I SURMISE, THAT LIVES IN THE TEMPLE... GUARDING THE TREASURE. THEY PRAY TO THIS SPIRIT FOR PROTECTION.
I FIGURED. SO I BROUGHT ALONG MY SORCERER, BLACK YMAR.
IT MAY BE BLACK MAGIC... BUT IT BENEFITS MY PURPOSES.

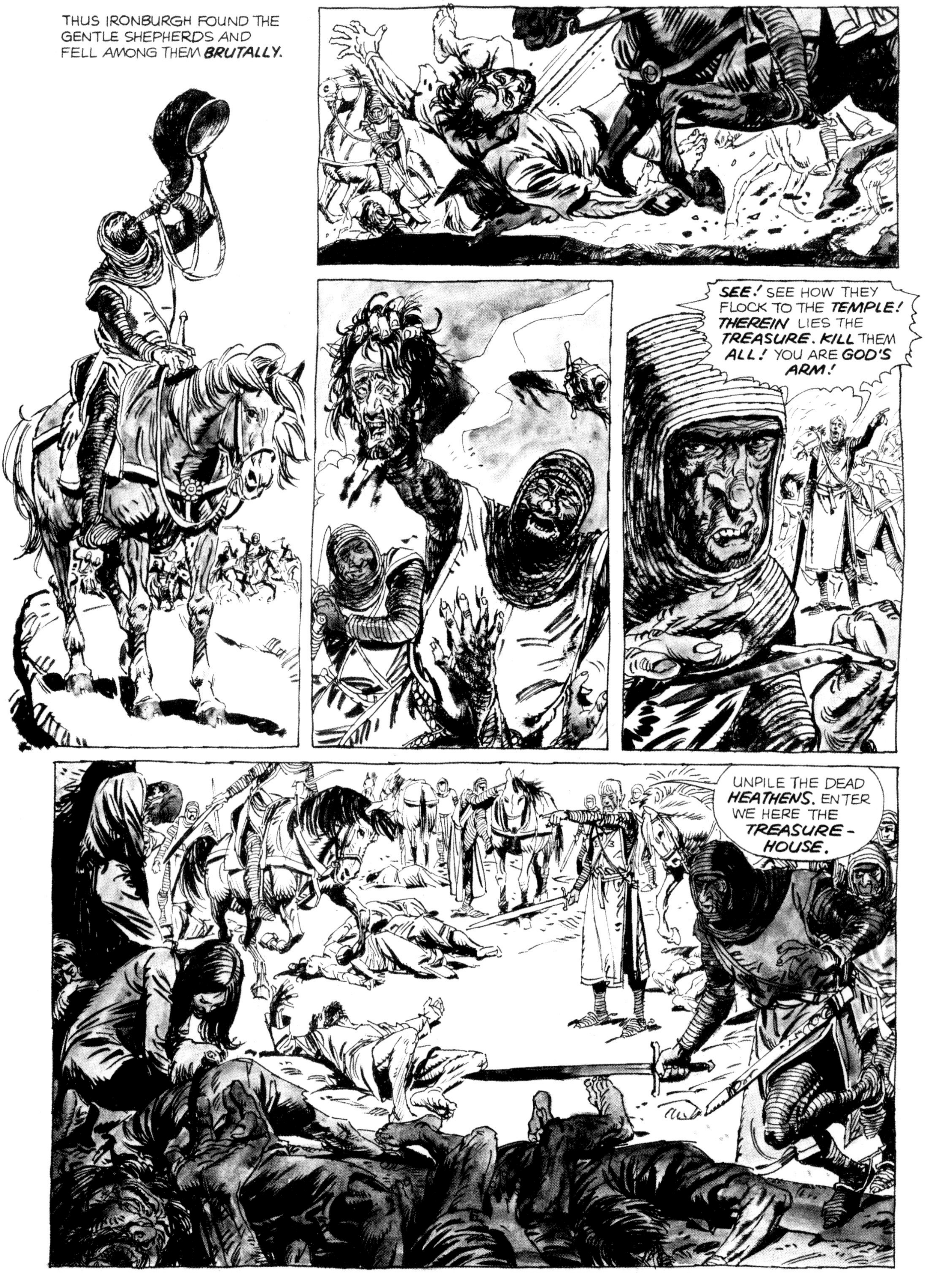
THUS IRONBURGH FOUND THE GENTLE SHEPHERDS AND FELL AMONG THEM BRUTALLY.
SEE! SEE HOW THEY FLOCK TO THE TEMPLE! THEREIN LIES THE TREASURE. KILL THEM ALL! YOU ARE GOD'S ARM!
UNPILE THE DEAD HEATHENS. ENTER WE HERE THE TREASURE-HOUSE.

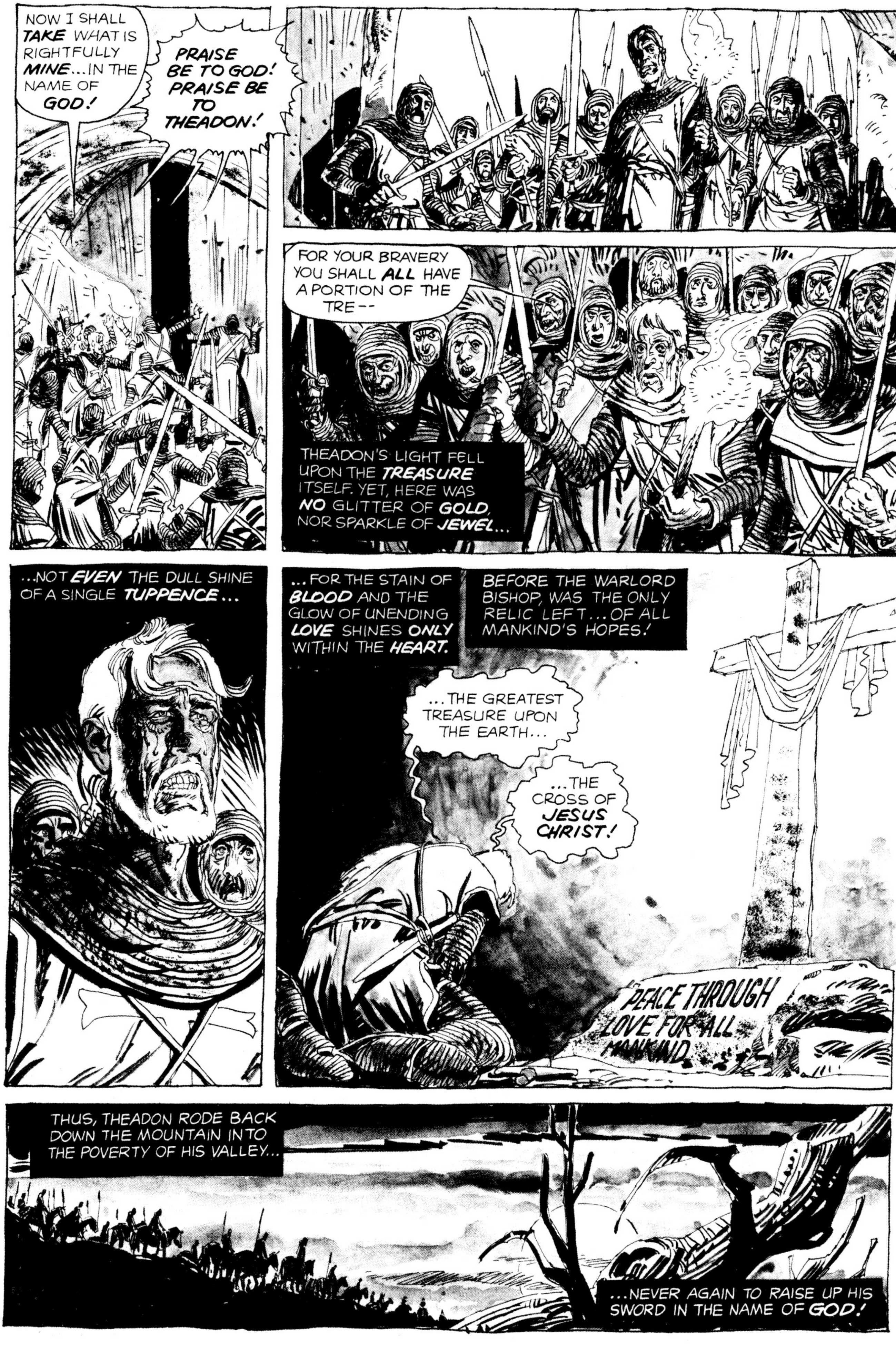
NOW I SHALL TAKE WHAT IS RIGHTFULLY MINE... IN THE NAME OF GOD!
PRAISE BE TO GOD! PRAISE BE TO THEADON!
FOR YOUR BRAVERY YOU SHALL ALL HAVE A PORTION OF THE TRE--
THEADON'S LIGHT FELL UPON THE TREASURE ITSELF. YET, HERE WAS NO GLITTER OF GOLD, NOR SPARKLE OF JEWEL...
...NOT EVEN THE DULL SHINE OF A SINGLE TUPPENCE...
...FOR THE STAIN OF BLOOD AND THE GLOW OF UNENDING LOVE SHINES ONLY WITHIN THE HEART.
BEFORE THE WARLORD BISHOP, WAS THE ONLY RELIC LEFT... OF ALL MANKIND'S HOPES!
INRI
...THE GREATEST TREASURE UPON THE EARTH...
...THE CROSS OF JESUS CHRIST!
PEACE THROUGH LOVE FOR ALL MANKIND
THUS, THEADON RODE BACK DOWN THE MOUNTAIN INTO THE POVERTY OF HIS VALLEY...
...NEVER AGAIN TO RAISE UP HIS SWORD IN THE NAME OF GOD!

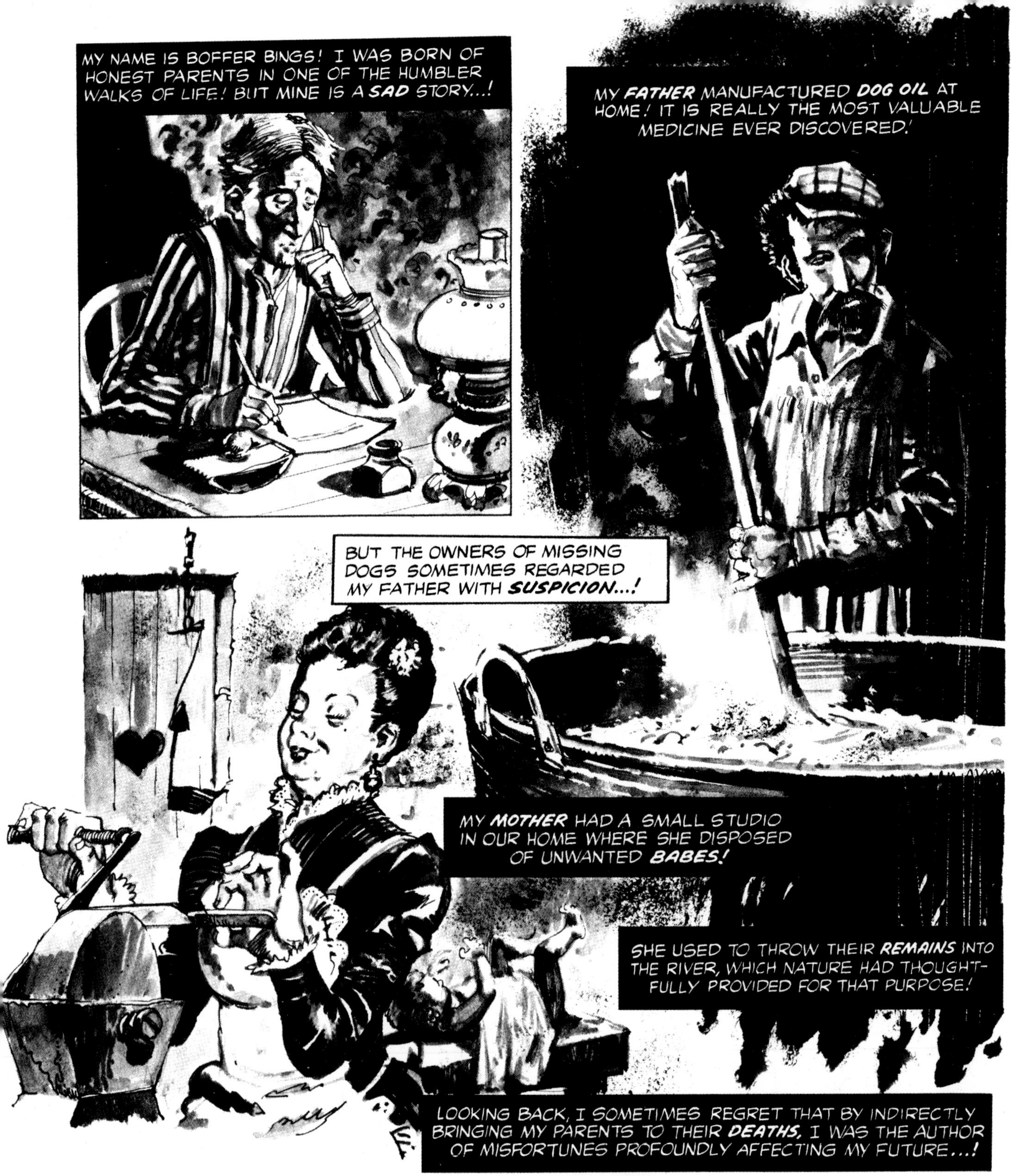
MY NAME IS BOFFER BINGS! I WAS BORN OF HONEST PARENTS IN ONE OF THE HUMBLER WALKS OF LIFE! BUT MINE IS A SAD STORY...!
MY FATHER MANUFACTURED DOG OIL AT HOME! IT IS REALLY THE MOST VALUABLE MEDICINE EVER DISCOVERED!
BUT THE OWNERS OF MISSING DOGS SOMETIMES REGARDED MY FATHER WITH SUSPICION...!
MY MOTHER HAD A SMALL STUDIO IN OUR HOME WHERE SHE DISPOSED OF UNWANTED BABES!
SHE USED TO THROW THEIR REMAINS INTO THE RIVER, WHICH NATURE HAD THOUGHTFULLY PROVIDED FOR THAT PURPOSE!
LOOKING BACK, I SOMETIMES REGRET THAT BY INDIRECTLY BRINGING MY PARENTS TO THEIR DEATHS, I WAS THE AUTHOR OF MISFORTUNES PROFOUNDLY AFFECTING MY FUTURE...!

AMBROSE BIERCE'S

OIL OF DOG!

STORY ADAPTATION: JACK BUTTERWORTH / ART: ISIDRO MONES

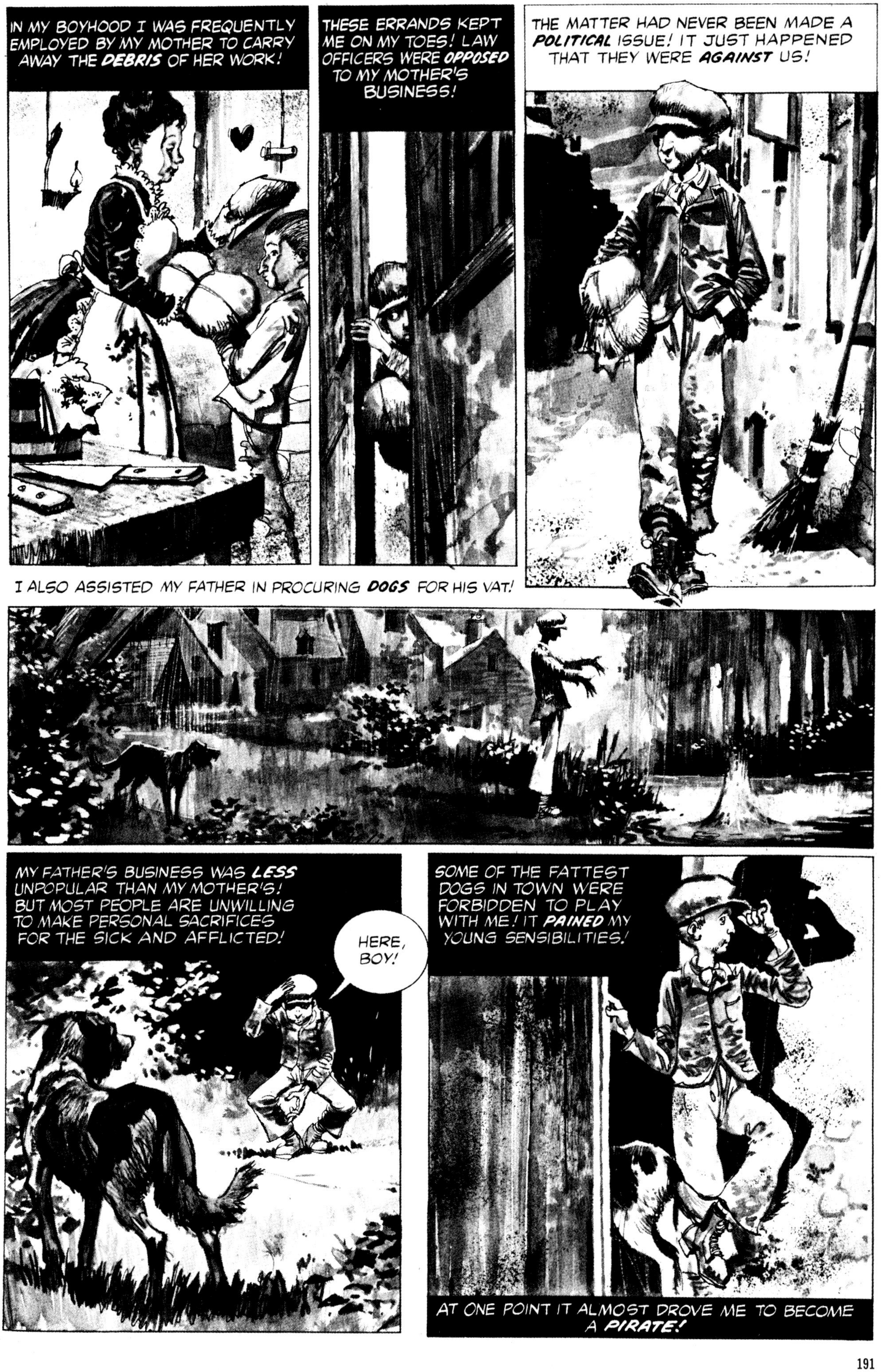
IN MY BOYHOOD I WAS FREQUENTLY EMPLOYED BY MY MOTHER TO CARRY AWAY THE **DEBRIS** OF HER WORK!
THESE ERRANDS KEPT ME ON MY TOES! LAW OFFICERS WERE **OPPOSED** TO MY MOTHER'S BUSINESS!
THE MATTER HAD NEVER BEEN MADE A **POLITICAL** ISSUE! IT JUST HAPPENED THAT THEY WERE **AGAINST** US!
I ALSO ASSISTED MY FATHER IN PROCURING **DOGS** FOR HIS VAT!
MY FATHER'S BUSINESS WAS **LESS** UNPOPULAR THAN MY MOTHER'S! BUT MOST PEOPLE ARE UNWILLING TO MAKE PERSONAL SACRIFICES FOR THE SICK AND AFFLICTED!
HERE, BOY!
SOME OF THE FATTEST DOGS IN TOWN WERE FORBIDDEN TO PLAY WITH ME! IT **PAINED** MY YOUNG SENSIBILITIES!
AT ONE POINT IT ALMOST DROVE ME TO BECOME A **PIRATE!**

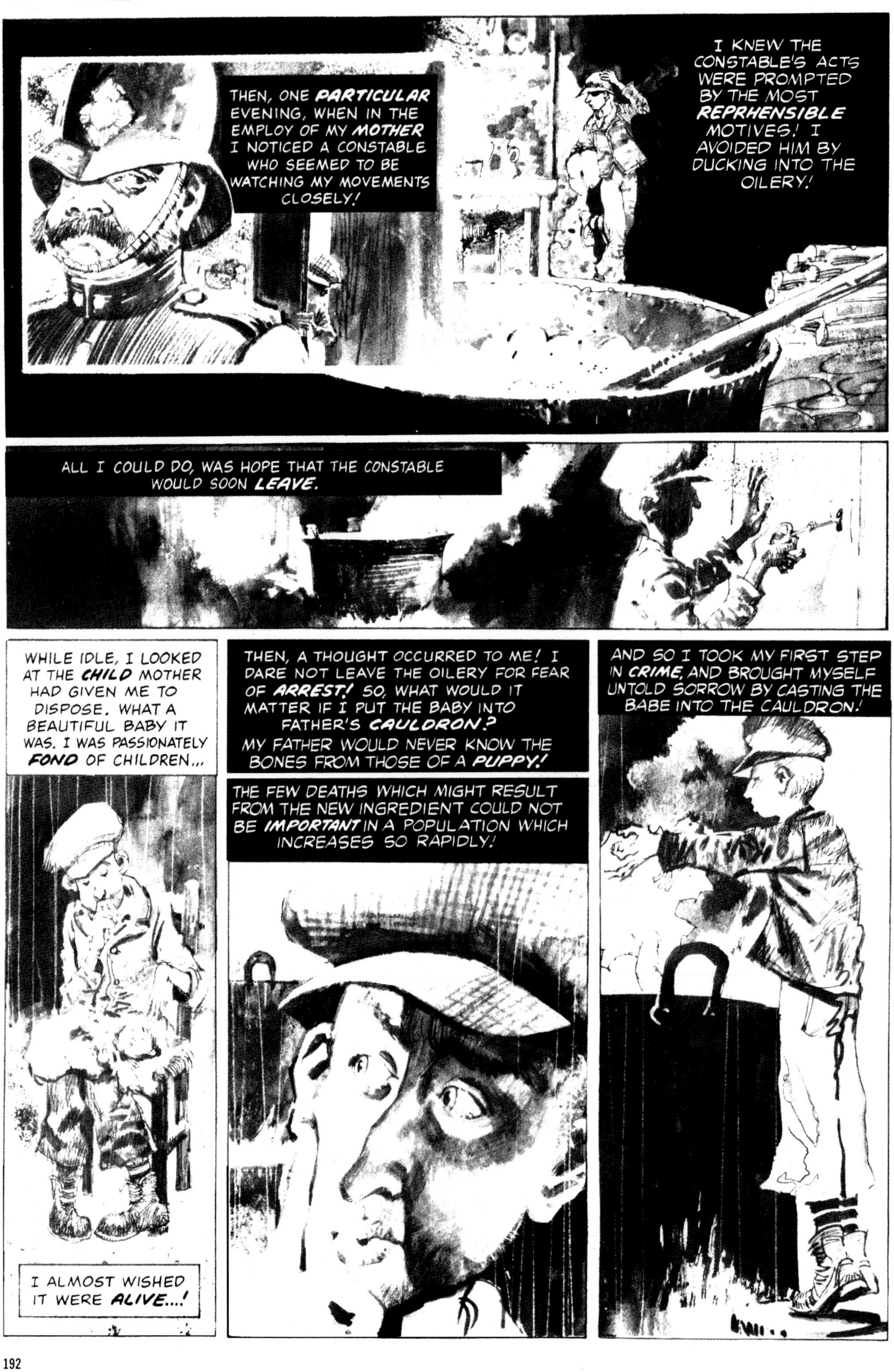
THEN, ONE PARTICULAR EVENING, WHEN IN THE EMPLOY OF MY MOTHER I NOTICED A CONSTABLE WHO SEEMED TO BE WATCHING MY MOVEMENTS CLOSELY!
I KNEW THE CONSTABLE'S ACTS WERE PROMPTED BY THE MOST REPRHENSIBLE MOTIVES! I AVOIDED HIM BY DUCKING INTO THE OILERY!
ALL I COULD DO, WAS HOPE THAT THE CONSTABLE WOULD SOON LEAVE.
WHILE IDLE, I LOOKED AT THE CHILD MOTHER HAD GIVEN ME TO DISPOSE. WHAT A BEAUTIFUL BABY IT WAS. I WAS PASSIONATELY FOND OF CHILDREN...
I ALMOST WISHED IT WERE ALIVE...!
THEN, A THOUGHT OCCURRED TO ME! I DARE NOT LEAVE THE OILERY FOR FEAR OF ARREST! SO, WHAT WOULD IT MATTER IF I PUT THE BABY INTO FATHER'S CAULDRON?
MY FATHER WOULD NEVER KNOW THE BONES FROM THOSE OF A PUPPY!
THE FEW DEATHS WHICH MIGHT RESULT FROM THE NEW INGREDIENT COULD NOT BE IMPORTANT IN A POPULATION WHICH INCREASES SO RAPIDLY!
AND SO I TOOK MY FIRST STEP IN CRIME, AND BROUGHT MYSELF UNTOLD SORROW BY CASTING THE BABE INTO THE CAULDRON!

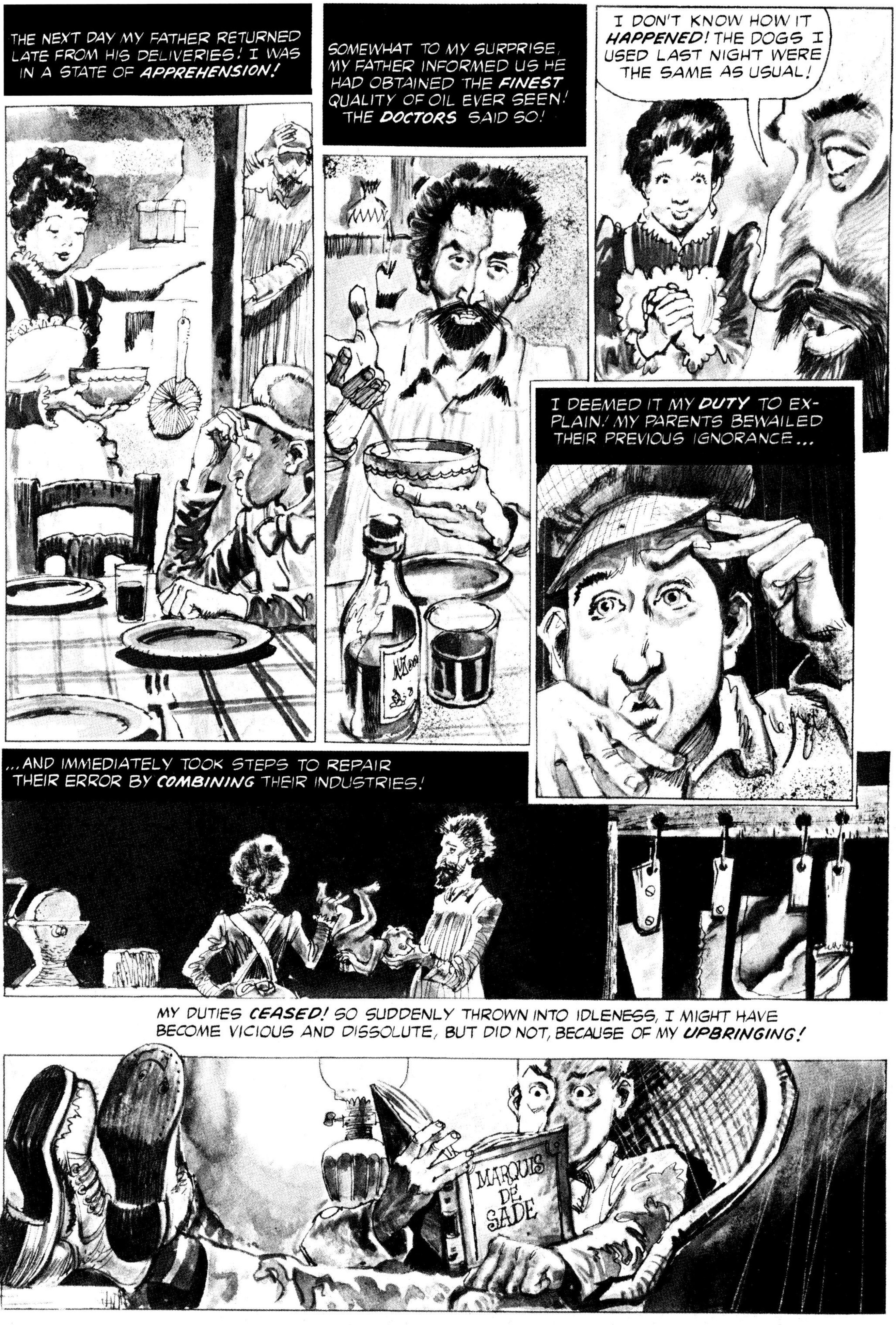
THE NEXT DAY MY FATHER RETURNED LATE FROM HIS DELIVERIES! I WAS IN A STATE OF APPREHENSION!
SOMEWHAT TO MY SURPRISE, MY FATHER INFORMED US HE HAD OBTAINED THE FINEST QUALITY OF OIL EVER SEEN! THE DOCTORS SAID SO!
I DON'T KNOW HOW IT HAPPENED! THE DOGS I USED LAST NIGHT WERE THE SAME AS USUAL!
I DEEMED IT MY DUTY TO EXPLAIN! MY PARENTS BEWAILED THEIR PREVIOUS IGNORANCE...
...AND IMMEDIATELY TOOK STEPS TO REPAIR THEIR ERROR BY COMBINING THEIR INDUSTRIES!
MY DUTIES CEASED! SO SUDDENLY THROWN INTO IDLENESS, I MIGHT HAVE BECOME VICIOUS AND DISSOLUTE, BUT DID NOT, BECAUSE OF MY UPBRINGING!
MARQUIS DE SADE

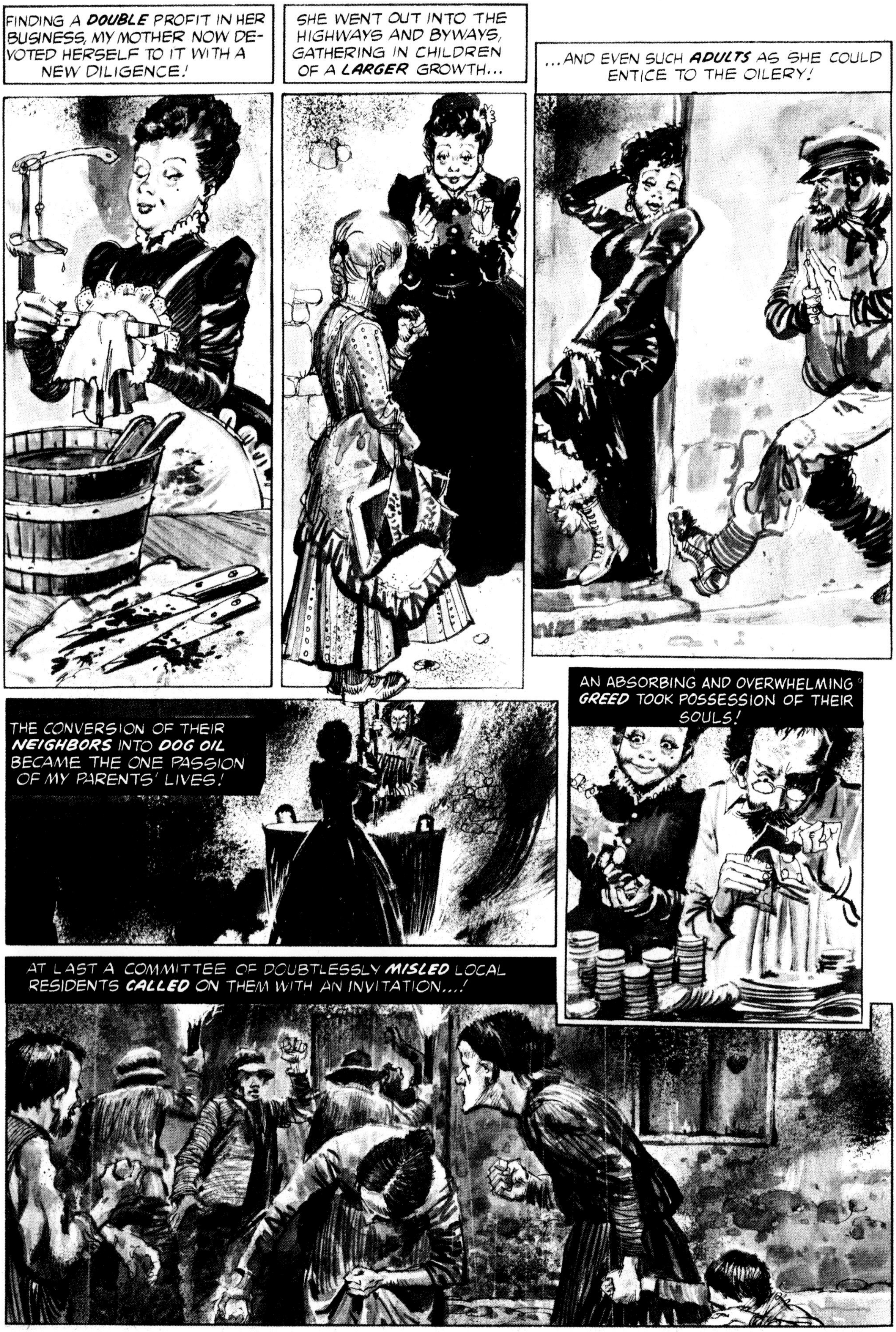
FINDING A DOUBLE PROFIT IN HER BUSINESS, MY MOTHER NOW DEVOTED HERSELF TO IT WITH A NEW DILIGENCE!
SHE WENT OUT INTO THE HIGHWAYS AND BYWAYS, GATHERING IN CHILDREN OF A LARGER GROWTH...
...AND EVEN SUCH ADULTS AS SHE COULD ENTICE TO THE OILERY!
THE CONVERSION OF THEIR NEIGHBORS INTO DOG OIL BECAME THE ONE PASSION OF MY PARENTS' LIVES!
AN ABSORBING AND OVERWHELMING GREED TOOK POSSESSION OF THEIR SOULS!
AT LAST A COMMITTEE OF DOUBTLESSLY MISLED LOCAL RESIDENTS CALLED ON THEM WITH AN INVITATION...!

THAT NIGHT THEY ATTENDED A PUBLIC *MEETING!* THEIR ATTEMPTS AT RATIONAL DIALOGUE WERE UNSUCCESSFUL!

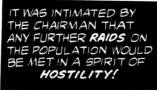

RESOLUTIONS WERE PASSED SEVERELY *CENSURING* THEM!

IT WAS INTIMATED BY THE CHAIRMAN THAT ANY FURTHER *RAIDS* ON THE POPULATION WOULD BE MET IN A SPIRIT OF *HOSTILITY!*

MY POOR PARENTS LEFT THE MEETING BROKEN-HEARTED, DESPERATE AND, I BELIEVE, NOT ALTOGETHER *SANE!*

ANYHOW, I DEEMED IT PRUDENT NOT TO STAY IN THE HOUSE THAT NIGHT, BUT SLEPT *OUTSIDE* INSTEAD!

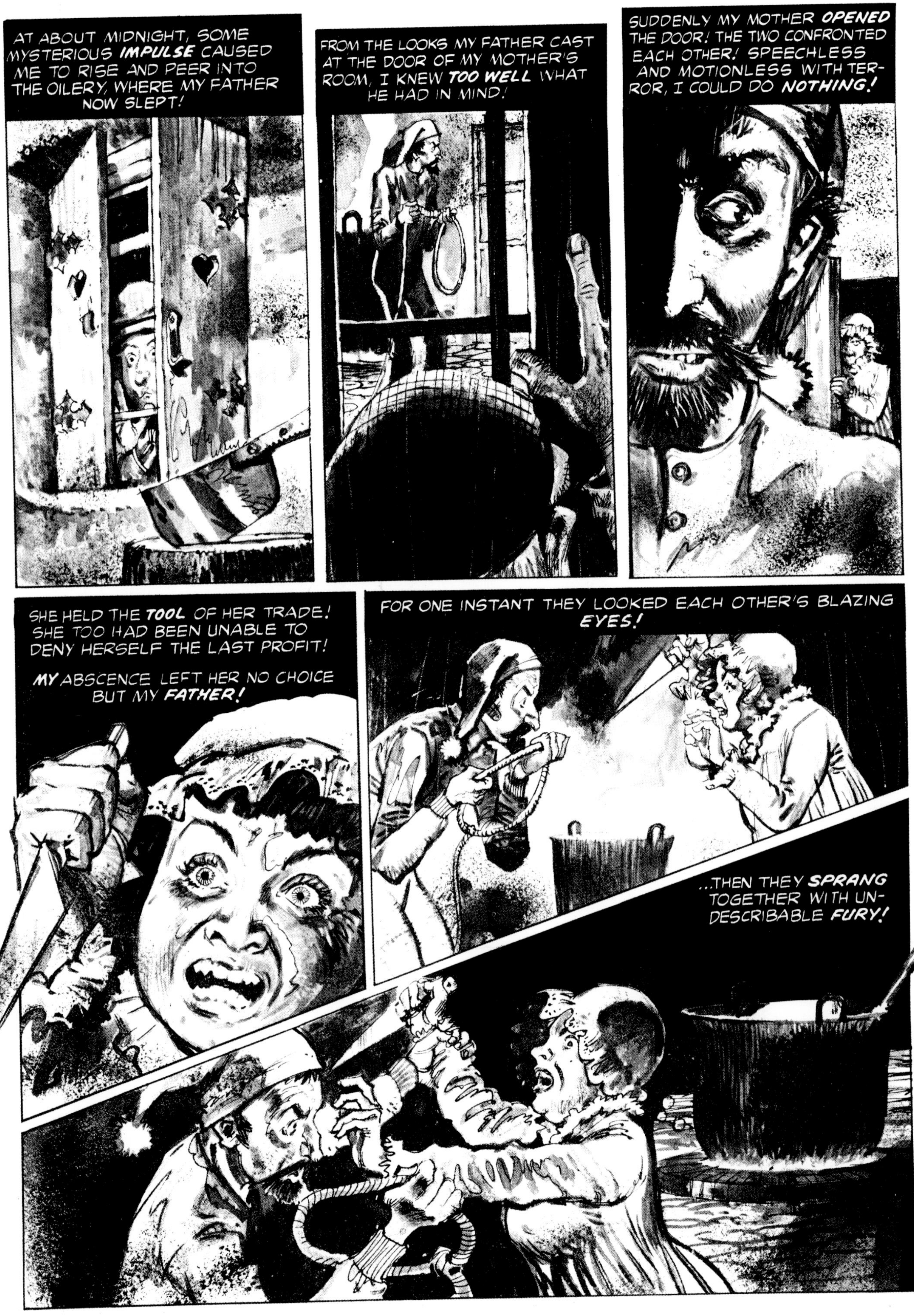

AT ABOUT MIDNIGHT, SOME MYSTERIOUS IMPULSE CAUSED ME TO RISE AND PEER INTO THE OILERY, WHERE MY FATHER NOW SLEPT!
FROM THE LOOKS MY FATHER CAST AT THE DOOR OF MY MOTHER'S ROOM, I KNEW TOO WELL WHAT HE HAD IN MIND!
SUDDENLY MY MOTHER OPENED THE DOOR! THE TWO CONFRONTED EACH OTHER! SPEECHLESS AND MOTIONLESS WITH TERROR, I COULD DO NOTHING!
SHE HELD THE TOOL OF HER TRADE! SHE TOO HAD BEEN UNABLE TO DENY HERSELF THE LAST PROFIT!
MY ABSCENCE LEFT HER NO CHOICE BUT MY FATHER!
FOR ONE INSTANT THEY LOOKED EACH OTHER'S BLAZING EYES!
...THEN THEY SPRANG TOGETHER WITH UNDESCRIBABLE FURY!

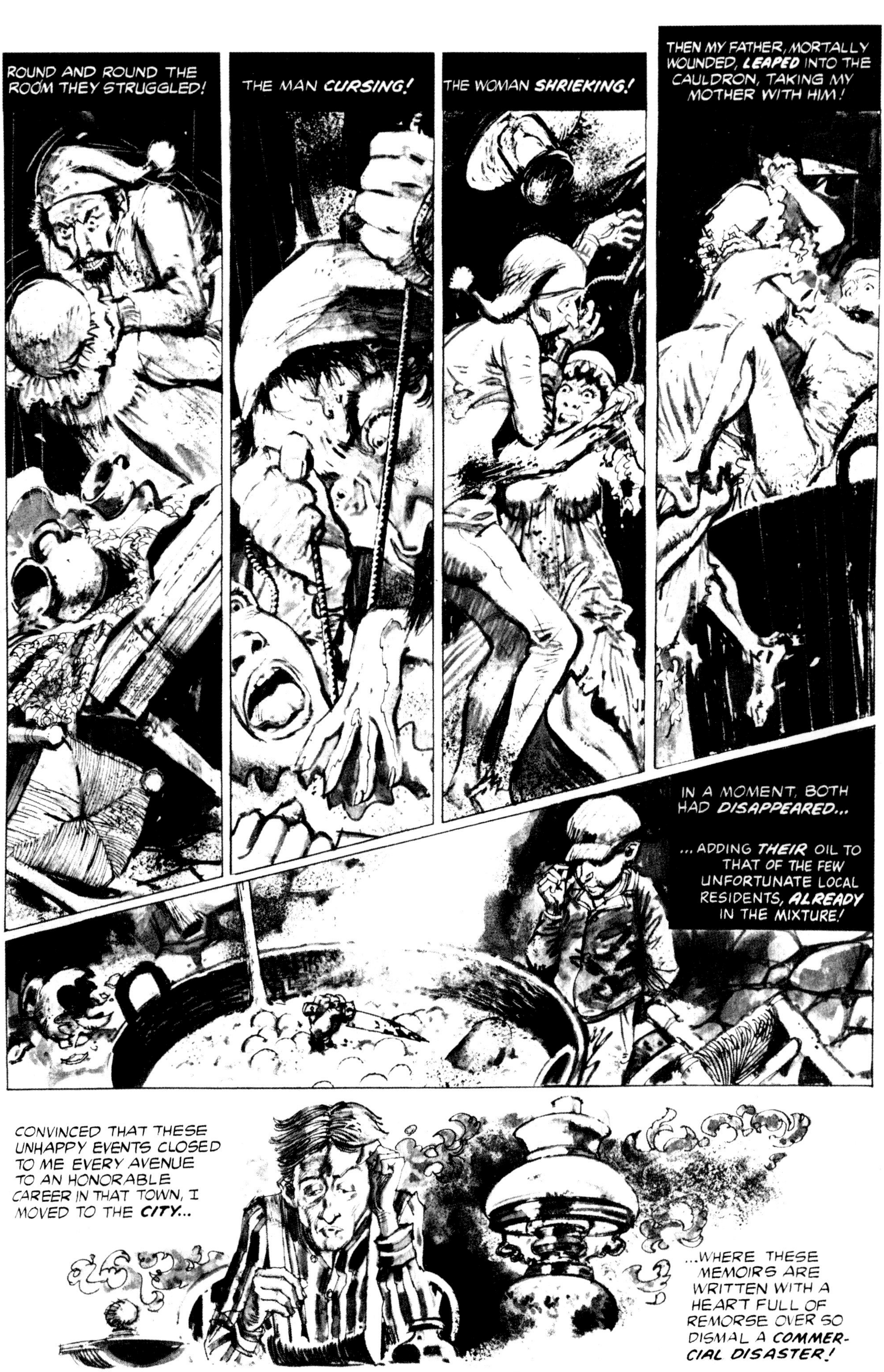
ROUND AND ROUND THE ROOM THEY STRUGGLED!
THE MAN CURSING!
THE WOMAN SHRIEKING!
THEN MY FATHER, MORTALLY WOUNDED, LEAPED INTO THE CAULDRON, TAKING MY MOTHER WITH HIM!
IN A MOMENT, BOTH HAD DISAPPEARED...
...ADDING THEIR OIL TO THAT OF THE FEW UNFORTUNATE LOCAL RESIDENTS, ALREADY IN THE MIXTURE!
CONVINCED THAT THESE UNHAPPY EVENTS CLOSED TO ME EVERY AVENUE TO AN HONORABLE CAREER IN THAT TOWN, I MOVED TO THE CITY...
...WHERE THESE MEMOIRS ARE WRITTEN WITH A HEART FULL OF REMORSE OVER SO DISMAL A COMMERCIAL DISASTER!

FIVE COLOSSAL MONSTER GAMES!

MONSTER'S CASTLE

A $2.50 FIASCO!

Now you can own all five of the exciting Warren Monster Madness games! Find the monstrous lycanthrope in WEREWOLF! Amass an army of fiendish beasties in the MONSTER MATCH! Run from hideous horrors in the MONSTER'S CASTLE! Become a misshapen horror in the CREEPY CRAWLEY CASTLE! And duel mysterious menaces in Vampirella's enthralling game of CAPTURE! All five games come complete with tokens, instructions, spinners and playing surfaces. Big games. Thrill-packed fun for the entire family designed by Warren's own Bill DuBay. Order set of five games now. Only $2.50/#2661

CREEPY CASTLE

MONSTER MATCH

MONSTER MATCH GAME

WEREWOLF GAME

CAPTURE GAME

CAPTURE

SUPER-DELUXE SPOOKTACULAR CREEPY & EERIE MASKS!

UNCLE CREEPY DELUXE MASK

Specially made by Don Post! Finely executed with Creepish Craftsmanship to look just like our old Ugly Unc! High quality latex rubber and a ghastly, ghostly and realistic thatch of pale hair to top him off! A Morbid Masterwork! Order #2544 UNCLE CREEPY DELUXE MASK $14.95

COUSIN EERIE DELUXE MASK

Heavy, durable, whole-headed mask of our half-wit fiend! COUSIN EERIE is Scarily Sculpted in high quality latex rubber, with some hellishly red and realistic hair atop his hand-painted face! A Clammy Classic! Order #2545 COUSIN EERIE DELUXE MASK $14.95

PLUS TWO TYPES CREEPY & EERIE BUDGET MASKS VINYL & RUBBER

BOTH BUDGET MASKS CAST FROM SAME MOLD! ONLY ONE IS VINYL, ONE IS RUBBER!

Both the vinyl & the rubber Budget masks, represented above, look alike, but the vinyl is sturdier, more heavy-duty. Both these makes of mask cover the entire head, too. Each is a bargain! You'll probably want all six: Deluxe, Vinyl & Rubber, to hold super CREEPY & EERIE parties!

#2566 CREEPY VINYL MASK $8.95
#2567 EERIE VINYL MASK $8.95

#2509 CREEPY RUBBER MASK $4.95
#2510 EERIE RUBBER MASK $4.95

HERE ARE 3 FABULOUS SETS OF CREEPY-EERIE MASKS!

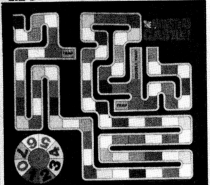

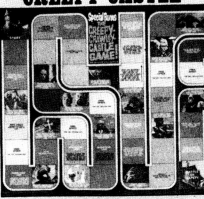

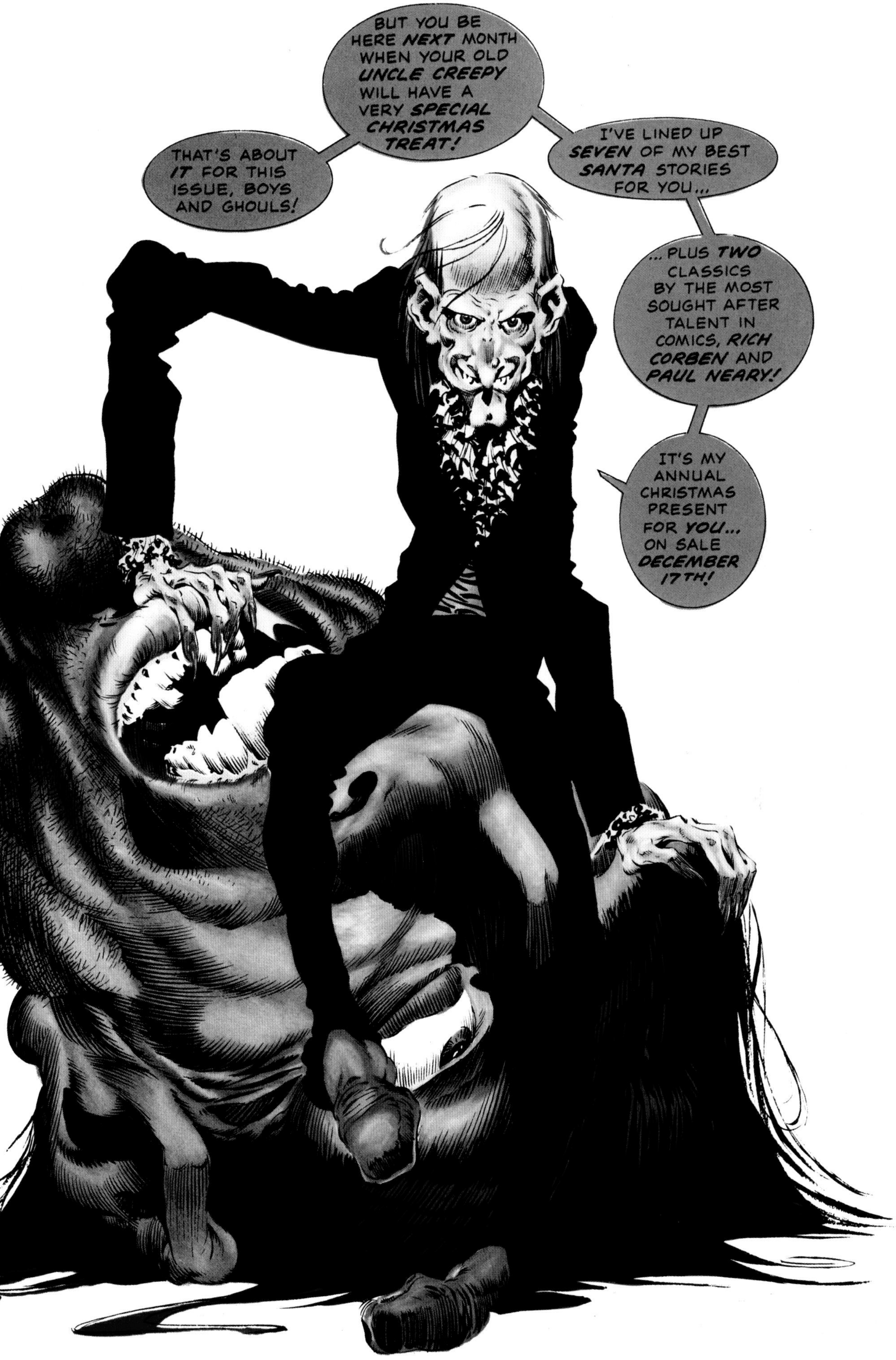
THAT'S ABOUT IT FOR THIS ISSUE, BOYS AND GHOULS!
BUT YOU BE HERE NEXT MONTH WHEN YOUR OLD UNCLE CREEPY WILL HAVE A VERY SPECIAL CHRISTMAS TREAT!
I'VE LINED UP SEVEN OF MY BEST SANTA STORIES FOR YOU...
... PLUS TWO CLASSICS BY THE MOST SOUGHT AFTER TALENT IN COMICS, RICH CORBEN AND PAUL NEARY!
IT'S MY ANNUAL CHRISTMAS PRESENT FOR YOU... ON SALE DECEMBER 17TH!

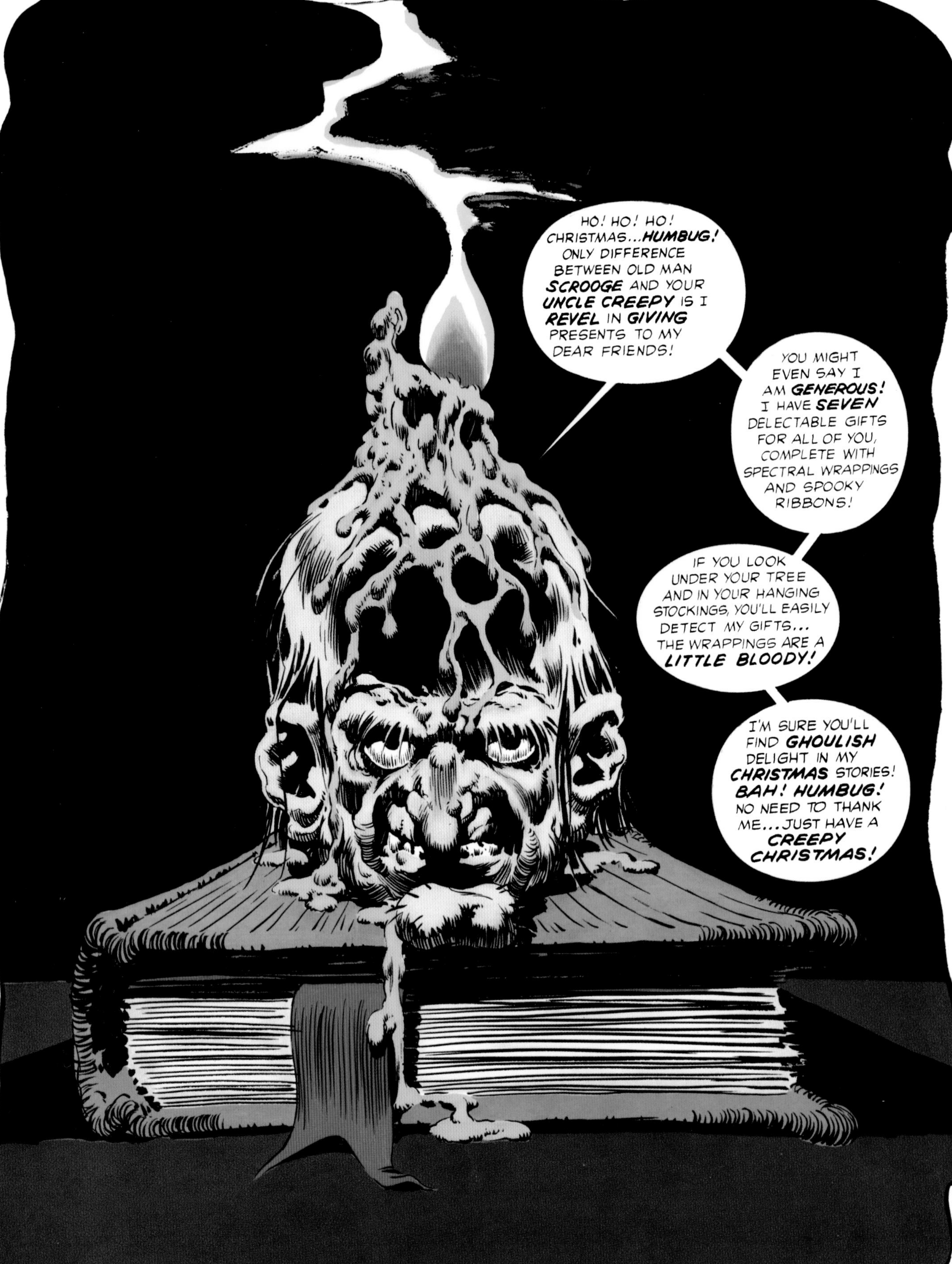
HO! HO! HO! CHRISTMAS...HUMBUG! ONLY DIFFERENCE BETWEEN OLD MAN SCROOGE AND YOUR UNCLE CREEPY IS I REVEL IN GIVING PRESENTS TO MY DEAR FRIENDS!
YOU MIGHT EVEN SAY I AM GENEROUS! I HAVE SEVEN DELECTABLE GIFTS FOR ALL OF YOU, COMPLETE WITH SPECTRAL WRAPPINGS AND SPOOKY RIBBONS!
IF YOU LOOK UNDER YOUR TREE AND IN YOUR HANGING STOCKINGS, YOU'LL EASILY DETECT MY GIFTS... THE WRAPPINGS ARE A LITTLE BLOODY!
I'M SURE YOU'LL FIND GHOULISH DELIGHT IN MY CHRISTMAS STORIES! BAH! HUMBUG! NO NEED TO THANK ME...JUST HAVE A CREEPY CHRISTMAS!

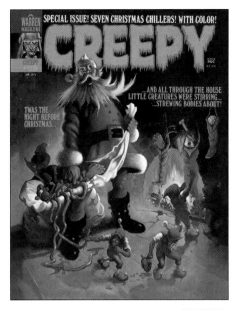

SPECIAL ISSUE! SEVEN CHRISTMAS CHILLERS! WITH COLOR!
WARREN MAGAZINE
CREEPY
...AND ALL THROUGH THE HOUSE LITTLE CREATURES WERE STIRRING... ...STREWING BODIES ABOUT!
TWAS THE NIGHT BEFORE CHRISTMAS...

OUR COVER:
A very special holiday gift is left by "The Christmas Gnome of Timothy Brayle." A macabre classic by Budd Lewis. A shocking painting by Ken Kelly.

Editor-In-Chief
& Publisher
JAMES WARREN

Editor
W.B. DuBAY

Production Manager
W.R. MOHALLEY

Circulation Director
AB SIDEMAN

Interior Color
RICH CORBEN

Cover
KEN KELLY

Back Cover
SANJULIAN

Artists This Issue
ADOLFO ABELLAN
VICENTE ALCAZAR
RICH CORBEN
ISIDRO MONES
MARTIN SALVADOR
LEOPOLD SANCHEZ
JOHN SEVERIN
BERNI WRIGHTSON

Writers This Issue
GERRY BOUDREAU
BUDD LEWIS
DOUG MOENCH

SANTA CLAUS SUIT

CREEPY®

CONTENTS

ISSUE NO. 68
JANUARY 1975

DEAR UNCLE CREEPY

"What matters is that an artist is the best!"

With current competition so keen, **Warren Publishing** can't afford to make a bad business move. So what's the matter with you guys? Why are you **sitting still? Expansion** seems to be in order. And I don't mean by publishing **reprint** books like **Comic International.**

The science fiction magazine that fans have been clamoring for for years now would be a nice addition to the **Warren** line. And the market for such a magazine is already being tested . . . by your leading competitor.

Sword and sorcery seems too, to have proven itself a healthy seller. So why not a magazine in that vein?

Adventure, war, westerns . . . are all successful nowadays . . . all moneymakers. Why not give us a magazine in that genre?

Big name artists and writers are also an incentive to magazine readers. I'm not saying to ignore the unknown or upcoming talent, but you should cling tenaciously to your "name" creators, who have proven to be good, competent **salesmen,** as well. **Berni Wrightson, Wally Wood, Archie Goodwin** and **Esteban Maroto** are such people. They look good in the present **Warren** magazines. They'd look **better** in a new **Warren** title.

TONY DALEY
Chicago, Ill.

The cover to CREEPY #66 was very good. Another beautiful painting by **Ken Kelly.** The inside cover by **Berni Wrightson** was good too.

"Desecration" was fantastic! It was exciting, and held my interest thoroughly. And the ending was clever. Strike up another point for **Doug Moench. Jose Ortiz** did a good job on the artwork, too. The Egyptian drawings were exquisite.

The idea behind "Portrait of Death" was just average. But the execution of the story . . . the **Poe**-like narrative was beautiful. Only a **Warren** writer could pull it off. And **Budd Lewis** is the **best** there is! A genius.

"Solitude" was great. The story was exciting and the ending was a total surprise. Even **Martin Salvador's** art was nice . . . for a change.

"Pinball Wizard" was unique. I'm glad the boy got his revenge, and the ending a happy one. I prefer your stories with upbeat conclusions. **Rich Corben's** art was classical. His work in black and white is as good as his art in color.

"Relatively Axe-Cidental" was another good story by the great **Greg Potter. Adolfo Abellan's** art was okay. But I'm not crazy about the way he draws. He's a little too sloppy for me.

"Nightmare" was good, too. **Isidro Mones** never fails in the art department. Now we know he can also **write!**

A fine issue. What more can one **do** but praise!?

RUSSELL KALTSCHMIDT
Long Island, N.Y.

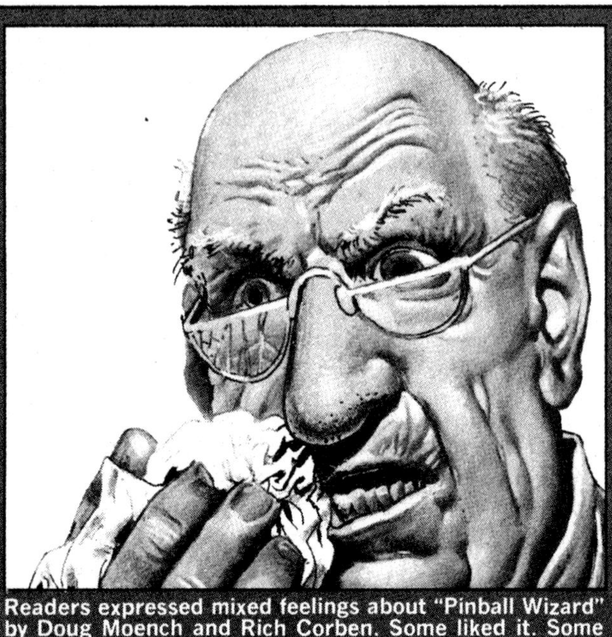

Readers expressed mixed feelings about "Pinball Wizard" by Doug Moench and Rich Corben. Some liked it. Some didn't. Many asked for more Corben art in exciting color!

A few comments on CREEPY #66. First, the cover: Isn't there something missing? The body of the man being executed should be visible. It isn't. This single blooper aside, it's still one of **Ken Kelly's** most effective covers. He's one of the few artists in the horror field who isn't afraid to use bright colors. **Basil Gogos** is another.

Two stories in this issue deserve special comment. "Desecration" was a good idea, poorly developed. If the thesis of **Chariot of the Gods** is correct, and the mythological deities were really astronauts from another world, how would they have handled matters when someone like **Akhenaton** denied their very existence? Unfortunately, this is not explored in great depth, and the story is ruined by a trite ending. Also, the god pictures is actually **Anubis** . . . which is puzzling, since **Jose Ortiz** drew **Amon-Ra** correctly in VAMPIRELLA #36.

"Solitude" offered the finest art yet from **Martin Salvador.** There were a few panels which even reminded me of **Reed Crandall's** old work! There seemed to be the same sense of composition, the same attention to authentic detail. **Archie Goodwin's** writing made a work of art out of what, in lesser hands, would have been a formula plot.

In regards to this month's editorial: have we run out of **genuine** controversies after only ten years of publishing? I'm speaking, of course, of the letters that sparked **Bill DuBay's** fiery attitude in his defense of **Warren's** Spanish illustrators. Graphic literature is one of the last fields in which I would have expected to find the kind of "jingoism" displayed by readers who do not like your art . . . because the artists are Spanish. Good illustrators are rare in any country. **Warren** deserves credit for making the readership aware of the great work being done abroad.

Nowadays, almost every publisher has a multi-national staff, and the field as a whole has profited. If there is a good artist in Lower Slobbovia, I, for one, hope that you spare no expense to hire him.

I missed the color section this time, but I presume that it will reappear next month. Heaven help you if it **doesn't!** At least there was no cut in the number of pages. However, as long as you continue to present the best in black and white illustration, **I'll** be satisfied.

BRIAN CADEN
Cincinnati, Ohio

Truth to tell, CREEPY #66 wasn't very impressive. Most of the stories were minor variations on hackneyed themes, and as such, were quite unimaginative and predictable.

But **Doug Moench's** tale, "Pinball Wizard" stands out as a fine example of poetic justice with some fine lyrical discriptions of classic horror. **Rich Corben's** art was good, but it **virtually dried out for color.** It's impact would have been immeasurably greater with **Corben's** dynamic colors. **Bill DuBay** deserves a huge demerit for not recognizing this.

ED O'REILLY
Ada, Ohio

Doug Moench did a good job on "Pinball Wizard." But it could have had a better ending. "Pinball Wizard of Hell?" That wasn't up to **Warren's** standards. But **Rich Corben's** artwork made up for it. I would rank that story first in CREEPY #66, despite the fact that the plot was swiped from an old **Jimmy Cagney** movie.

Then comes "Relatively Axe-Cidental!" **Greg Potter** really had it on the ball with this one. It's one of the best stories he ever stole. Credit to "The Third Night of Mourning" by **Jim Stenstrum. Adolfo Abellan's** art wasn't up to snuff, either.

I thought "Solitude" was an awfully cliche story. What happened to the once-great **Archie Goodwin?** As usual, **Martin Salvador's** art was superb. It saved the story for me.

"Portrait of Death" was a real loser. **Vicente Alcazar** is the poorest excuse for an artist I've ever seen. It's too bad **Budd Lewis'** superb narration was ruined by weak "art."

"Desecration" featured the issue's best art. Please give us much more of **Jose Ortiz.** Unfortunately, the story was the issue's worst. I don't think I've yet to see an **original** script come from the pen of **Doug Moench.** If he isn't stealing from old **movies** he's stealing from **novels.** But you can be thankful for one thing: **Moench's** most recent work for your competitors is even worse than his earlier work for you. For **Warren,** he stole from the best films and the best novels. For his present employer, he's swiping the storylines of grade B movies and 1950 smut-back books. It's downright sinful to see how the mighty have fallen.

But then I guess that goes for CREEPY, too. This issue was a **bomb!**

KEMPER WHITE
North Branford, Conn.

"Ken Kelly is first-rate!"

To be quite honest, all of your magazines have seen better days. But perhaps CREEPY has fallen the hardest.

Your defense of the Spanish artists is well taken. It doesn't matter what race, nationality, creed, sex or planet one belongs to. If one is the best qualified, he should be utilized. Unfortunately, to a large degree, you are now employing **second** class talent, as differentiated from your competitors who employ **third** class talent.

The only area in which you have shown improvement recently is with covers. **Ken Kelly** is a true talent. He has a total command over the human figure and the most imaginative color this side of **Rich Corben**.

But the **interior** artwork for the most part, has suffered greatly. The additions of **Berni Wrightson** and **Corben** to your art staff have partially filled a need . . . but the need **remains**. The loss of the color section has hurt **Corben's** work. He isn't as **shocking** in black and white. Also, it is hard to justify the dollar cost of the book without color.

People like **Jose Ortiz, Martin Salvador, Ramon Torrents** and **Gonzalo Mayo** are mediocre artists who are excellent for a change of pace. But they are not top notch artists or even average story-tellers. **Adolfo Abellan** and **Vicente Alcazar** are a step below the above mentioned gentlemen. Their stories are unreadable. These artists simply do not meet the standard of quality CREEPY has been known for.

The writing quality has also dropped considerably as of late. Gone are the sensitive, thought-provoking and truly horrible tales of **T. Casey Brennan, Don McGregor** and **Archie Goodwin**. They have been replaced by a collection of hacked, formula-written, boring stories scripted by a crew of inexperienced newcomers. I like **Gerry Boudreau, Steve Skeates** and some of **Doug Moench's** stories. But their bylines have been appearing less and less lately.

Ten years ago, you entered the comics field, wanting to publish something worthwhile. Perhaps you wanted to publish something to show the public that comic books were indeed **art**.

Perhaps you're no longer willing to strive for uncomquered heights. If so, I think the comic book reading public needs a new **Warren Publishing**.

MARK GASPER
Flushing, N.Y.

I would like to challenge the editorial in CREEPY #66 "In Defense of a Name."

I can't say any of your foreign artists produce substandard art. But I suspect that you use them because they can be paid **less** than most artists closer to home.

TOM NESTOR
Alberta, Canada

Your challenge is accepted, Tom. Warren artists, whether they come from Spain, England or America, are all paid one rate: the highest in the history of American comic art publishing!

As we stated in our editorial, no expense is spared in bringing to our readers the finest artists available in the WORLD!

Those readers who claim you've been over-using Spanish artists in your magazines, make a valid point. There are some very fine Spanish artists working for **Warren Publishing. Esteban Maroto, Felix Mas, Ramon Torrents** and **Sanjulian** continually amaze me with their ever-increasing quality work. However, an overwhelming number of your other Spanish artists are **awful**.

In the flood that has opened up from the Philippines and Spain in recent years, a lot of second and third rate artists have slipped through. The thing is, many of these fellows have similar art styles. It leaves one with the feeling of being **bombarded** with often times **inferior** foreign work.

Of course, **Warren** isn't the only company using foreign artists. They **all** do. This must be discouraging to young American artists who'd like to break into comic illustrating. There must be dozens of young **Joe Kuberts, Alex Toths,** and **Mike Kalutas** out there. But is there any American comic publisher willing to **use** these youngsters instead of importing foreign talent?

On the other side of the coin though, there are some overseas artists **Warren** should be using, but isn't. Where are **Alfredo Alcala, Alex Nino** and **Nestor Redondo** in the **Warren** titles? Make room for them. Dump **Adolfo Abellan, Jose Gual** and this new guy, **Luis Bermejo**. And above all else . . . give the **new** guys a break.

GARY KIMBER
Ontario, Canada

We only wish there WERE dozens of young Kuberts, Toths and Kalutas out there, Gary. This industry would then have the QUALITY talent it so needs.

Letters tell us that readers don't care where an artist comes from. "If his work is the best around, use him!"

About CREEPY #66. Pretty sneaky, I say! I mean even **Alfred Hitchcock** appears at least once in every one of his movies. I can understand your wanting to have your name in your own magazine, Uncle CREEPY, but signing it to a document putting a man to death? Shame, shame! But surely, it's all "Relatively Axecidental?"

This issue had a great cover . . . with one small problem: where's the body the head came from? Other than that, give **Ken Kelly** my praises. He's doing fine.

"Desecration" with **Jose Ortiz'** art was okay. The story though, just wasn't up to the CREEPY tradition. "Portrait of Death" had so-so-art, and a "no-comment" story. Same for "Solitude."

I've seldom read as good a story as "Pinball Wizard." The combination of **Doug Moench** and **Rich Corben** could never fail.

As for the final tale . . . I couldn't sleep, thinking about "Nightmare."

Aside from the great art, great stories, great ads, great letters (such as this), great inside covers by the great **Berni Wrightson**, this issue was just normal for CREEPY. Great!

DON CLARK
Wolfeboro, N.H.

I used to really like your magazine. Now the first thing I look at are the advertisements. Are they getting better, or are the stories getting worse?

More ads!

JAMES P. EZUFOM
Cicero, Ill.

Thanks to Captain Company Art Director, Sherry Berne, the ads are actually getting better!

I would like to bring up the subject of **Rich Corben's** artwork. **Corben** is a genius, there's no denying it. No one even comes close to his storytelling, drama or excitement.

But it seems to me that he colors only the poorly written stories he is forced to illustrate. His better scripted stories are always published in black and white.

For example, in CREEPY #54, #58 and #66, each **Corben** story was good, but uncolored. In issue #63, however, the story "Demon in the Cockpit" was lousy. It was also **colored**.

Corben is the greatest acquired talent of the century. It seems to me that when you use him, you ought to use him **correctly**.

MIKE J. KAROL
Taunton, Mass.

Let me make this perfectly clear!

Why not take a chance on a 300 year-old creep? Write! Send letters to:

205

CREEPY'S CATACOMBS

BERNI WRIGHTSON

There is an unfounded rumor (possibly started by **Wrightson** himself) that **Berni Wrightson** was actually killed in an automobile accident in 1968. His friends, unable to bear the loss, re-create a **Berni** each month, to collaborate on a strip drawn under his name. In essence, they have assured **Berni's** immortality.

Is there any basis for this ridiculous rumor?

Is the slender young man who signs autographs to that effect, the same **Berni Wrightson** who spent his early childhood in a haunted roadhouse in Maryland and played among the tombstones in a nearby cemetery? The kid **born** knowing how to draw?

Berni says the fact that ninety per-cent of his work concerns disfigured liches and animated corpses is only **natural**. For **more** information, he suggests, with a pale bony smile, that we querie some of his **friends**.

No one denies the rumor. In fact, many suggested that it might be **true**.

Berni has always had lots of friends . . . and a lots of people claim to have helped make him the man he is today.

His first published work was on an early CREEPY fan page. From there, **Berni** moved to Manhattan and immediately found work at National Comics.

Several years later, **Berni** and **Vaughn Bode** collaborated on the color comic strip "Purple Pictography" for **Swank Magazine.**

While working on the first issues of **Swamp Thing** for **DC** color comics, **Berni** moved to upstate New York.

Swamp Thing was an immediate success . . . **Berni** says, because he has an affinity for "dead things."

Soon after his move, **Berni** produced some surprisingly professional paintings for several paperback book companies . . . though he had never painted before that time. Again the work of his friends?

In early 1974, **Berni** moved again . . . this time to **Warren Publishing.** Since then he has given us many fine stories about monsters, the living dead and other macabre creatures. Among them is the terrifying classic "Jennifer" written by **Berni's** good friend, artist **Bruce Jones.**

Berni has now returned to New York City. When not lurking around his own apartment, he can often be found visiting some of the people who help make him the **Berni** you know today.

Did **Warren**, realizing his profit potential, really have him rebuilt from spare parts? Did his buddies at **Neal Adams'** Continuity Studios, recreate him, the way they created, in the great tradition of **Dr. Frankenstein,** the inking identity, **Crusty Bunkers?**

When asked these questions, **Berni** only laughs (as who wouldn't?) and asks if we would like to see the seams where they stitched him together?

ACCEPT NO SUBSTITUTES!

Why buy CREEPY? EERIE? VAMPIRELLA? Why not one of the other black and white horror comic magazines that have proliferated in the past few months? Why buy an original when you can get a "clever" copy at sometimes slightly less cost?

Well, for one thing, a real **connoisseur** knows about **quality.** He doesn't shop at the Five & Dime for a Ming vase or at a used car dealer for a Rolls Royce. The seeker of quality is adventurous . . . he looks around before he buys. And then he buys the **best.**

That might be one reason why the **Warren** magazines sell better than any other black and white comic in America.

Warren Publishing has been around for a long time. We've tried a lot of different things. Some of them worked and have been kept; some of them didn't and were thrown out. We've been able to publish magazines that have had the approval of thousands of readers for a whole lot of years. We know they've approved because they have continued to buy **Warren** magazines, in ever increasing numbers, through rising prices caused by inflation and temptations posed by "clever" competitors.

We'd like to think that **Warren** publications simply have **more** to offer. We have more stories (usually **six** per issue to any competitors' average **four**); more pages (devoted to graphic horror, not filler text). We even have more and better letters on our letters pages (possible, because **Warren's** readers are more vocal . . . or possibly because of their higher level of intelligence). And with all that space devoted to readers' opinion, our readers know they have had a hand in shaping the kind of magazines **Warren** publishes.

We take ourselves seriously. In an editorial last month, we promised you more realistic, more contemporary, more controversial horror. We want to do more than **just** entertain you (though entertaining you is certainly our **major** goal). We want to interest and involve you as well. And from the letters we've been receiving recently, readers seem to think we're doing a pretty good job of it.

Of course, part of entertaining you and keeping your interest is employing the finest writers and artists available.

Warren brings you the best from around the world . . . internationally famous artists like **Esteban Maroto, Jose Ortiz** and **Paul Neary** plus the finest American talents available. **Berni Wrightson** and **Rich Corben** are both gifted artists **and** writers. Possibly this is what makes them two of the best storytellers around . . . even when they're telling someone **else's** story.

We have the best writers in the country as well: **Bill DuBay, Budd Lewis, Bruce Bezaire, Gerry Boudreau** are a few. From time to time we even feature adaptations of the best loved horror classics from the pen of **H.P. Lovecraft, Edgar Allen Poe** and **Ambrose Bierce.** You could find no finer collections of writers in **any** publishers' magazines.

One huge advantage CREEPY, EERIE and VAMPIRELLA have over rival publications are their fantastic color sections with hand separated color by **Rich Corben** and **Michele Brand.** Competitors imitate our artists and writers . . . they don't even **try** to duplicate our color sections.

Warren's magazines come to you with **more** stories per issue, plus a **color section,** for the **same** price you pay for **fewer** stories and **no** color in the magazines of some competitors.

And, we have an unbeatable inside front and back cover in two colors . . . instead of the eternal black and white muscle **advertisements** on the inside covers of competitive magazines.

If the **facts** haven't convinced you to remain a lifelong **Warren** reader, maybe our statement of policy **will:** At Warren, we pledge to give you our **best** . . . 100% of the time. We hope it's good enough.

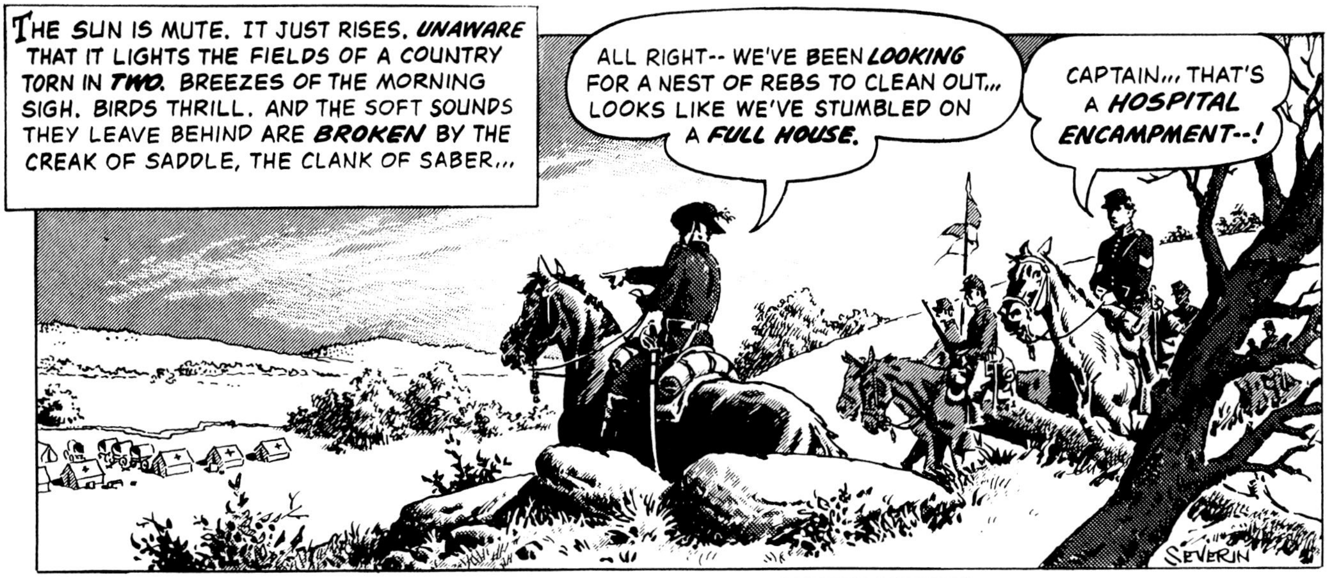
THE SUN IS MUTE. IT JUST RISES. UNAWARE THAT IT LIGHTS THE FIELDS OF A COUNTRY TORN IN TWO. BREEZES OF THE MORNING SIGH. BIRDS THRILL. AND THE SOFT SOUNDS THEY LEAVE BEHIND ARE BROKEN BY THE CREAK OF SADDLE, THE CLANK OF SABER...
ALL RIGHT-- WE'VE BEEN LOOKING FOR A NEST OF REBS TO CLEAN OUT... LOOKS LIKE WE'VE STUMBLED ON A FULL HOUSE.
CAPTAIN... THAT'S A HOSPITAL ENCAMPMENT--!
SEVERIN

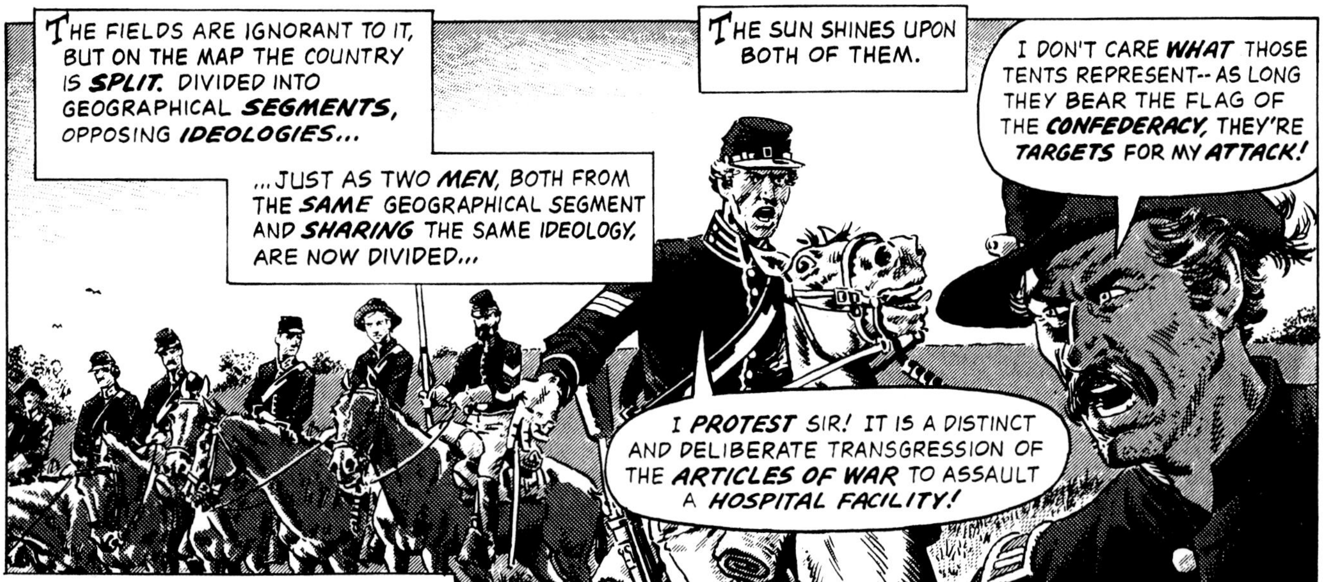
THE FIELDS ARE IGNORANT TO IT, BUT ON THE MAP THE COUNTRY IS SPLIT. DIVIDED INTO GEOGRAPHICAL SEGMENTS, OPPOSING IDEOLOGIES...
...JUST AS TWO MEN, BOTH FROM THE SAME GEOGRAPHICAL SEGMENT AND SHARING THE SAME IDEOLOGY, ARE NOW DIVIDED...
THE SUN SHINES UPON BOTH OF THEM.
I DON'T CARE WHAT THOSE TENTS REPRESENT-- AS LONG THEY BEAR THE FLAG OF THE CONFEDERACY, THEY'RE TARGETS FOR MY ATTACK!
I PROTEST SIR! IT IS A DISTINCT AND DELIBERATE TRANSGRESSION OF THE ARTICLES OF WAR TO ASSAULT A HOSPITAL FACILITY!

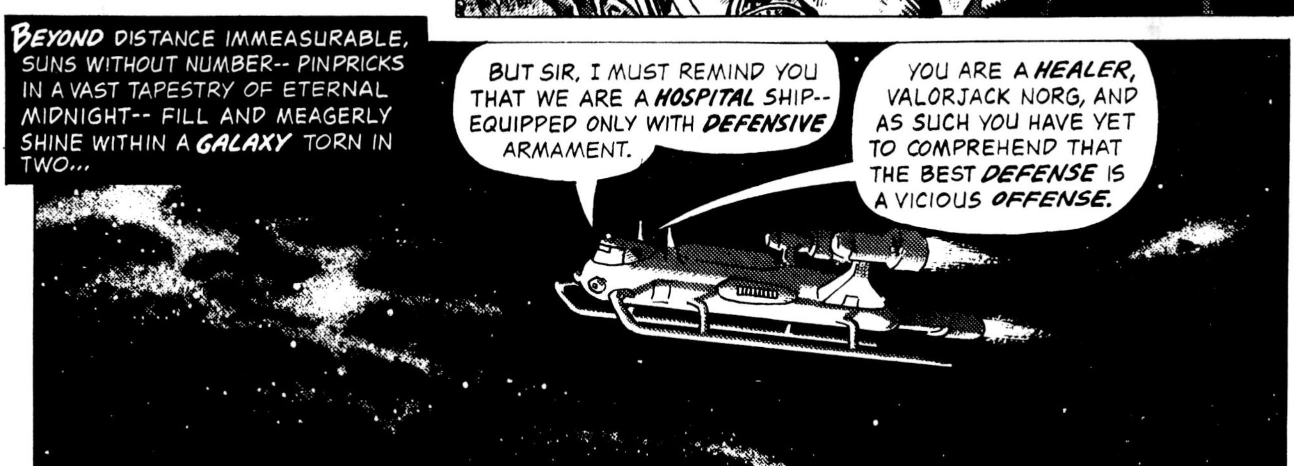
BEYOND DISTANCE IMMEASURABLE, SUNS WITHOUT NUMBER-- PINPRICKS IN A VAST TAPESTRY OF ETERNAL MIDNIGHT-- FILL AND MEAGERLY SHINE WITHIN A GALAXY TORN IN TWO...
BUT SIR, I MUST REMIND YOU THAT WE ARE A HOSPITAL SHIP-- EQUIPPED ONLY WITH DEFENSIVE ARMAMENT.
YOU ARE A HEALER, VALORJACK NORG, AND AS SUCH YOU HAVE YET TO COMPREHEND THAT THE BEST DEFENSE IS A VICIOUS OFFENSE.

READY FOR *BLASTOFF,* GALAXY-GALLOPERS? THIS TALE'S A *LOADED* ONE... AND JUST TO GET *THROUGH* THIS STARDUSTED STRIFE I MAY HAVE TO FALL BACK ON...

The STARS MY SALVATION

STORY: DOUG MOENCH / ART: JOHN SEVERIN

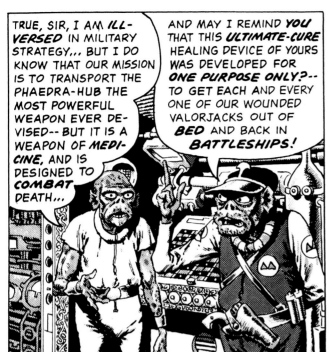

TRUE, SIR, I AM *ILL-VERSED* IN MILITARY STRATEGY... BUT I DO KNOW THAT OUR MISSION IS TO TRANSPORT THE PHAEDRA-HUB THE MOST POWERFUL WEAPON EVER DEVISED-- BUT IT IS A WEAPON OF *MEDICINE*, AND IS DESIGNED TO *COMBAT* DEATH...

AND MAY I REMIND *YOU* THAT THIS *ULTIMATE-CURE* HEALING DEVICE OF YOURS WAS DEVELOPED FOR *ONE PURPOSE ONLY?*-- TO GET EACH AND EVERY ONE OF OUR WOUNDED VALORJACKS OUT OF *BED* AND BACK IN *BATTLESHIPS!*

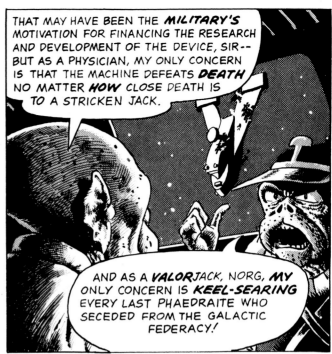

THAT MAY HAVE BEEN THE *MILITARY'S* MOTIVATION FOR FINANCING THE RESEARCH AND DEVELOPMENT OF THE DEVICE, SIR-- BUT AS A PHYSICIAN, MY ONLY CONCERN IS THAT THE MACHINE DEFEATS *DEATH* NO MATTER *HOW* CLOSE DEATH IS TO A STRICKEN JACK.

AND AS A *VALOR*JACK, NORG, *MY* ONLY CONCERN IS *KEEL-SEARING* EVERY LAST PHAEDRAITE WHO SECEDED FROM THE GALACTIC FEDERACY!

THAT SHIP'S *PHAEDRAN*-- WHY WASN'T IT DETECTED BY THE *SENSORS?!* NO MATTER-- WE'LL *BLAST* IT INTO FREE-FLOATING *MESONS!*

BUT SIR-- IT'S *CRIPPLED*... JUST A GUTTED *HULK!* WE ARE MANNING A SHIP DEDICATED TO *SAVING PRESERVING* LIVES, NOT *TAKING* LIVES-- EVEN IF THEY'RE THE LIVES OF THE *ENEMY!*

I *DEMAND* THAT WE *ASSIST* THE WOUNDED ON THAT SHIP.

YOU *WHAT*, PLANKTON?!? YOU *PROTEST*--?!

LISTEN TO ME, PLANKTON, AND LISTEN WITH *MORE* THAN BOTH EARS IF YOU WANT TO *KEEP* THEM ON THE SIDES OF YOUR *HEAD* -- THE UNION WILL *NOT* TOLERATE GROSS INSUBORDINATION FROM ITS SOLDIERS!

NOR WILL IT TOLERATE A DELIBERATE VIOLATION OF THE RULES OF WAR! THE REBS IN THOSE MEDICAL TENTS ARE WOUNDED-- *DYING*...THEY'RE *HELPLESS!*

ONE MORE *WORD* FROM YOU, PLANKON, AND THOSE STINKING REBS DOWN THERE WILL DIE UNDER A SABER FIRST STAINED WITH *UNION* BLOOD! NOW GET YOURSELF INTO *ATTACK FORMATION*--

SORRY, CAPTAIN, BUT...

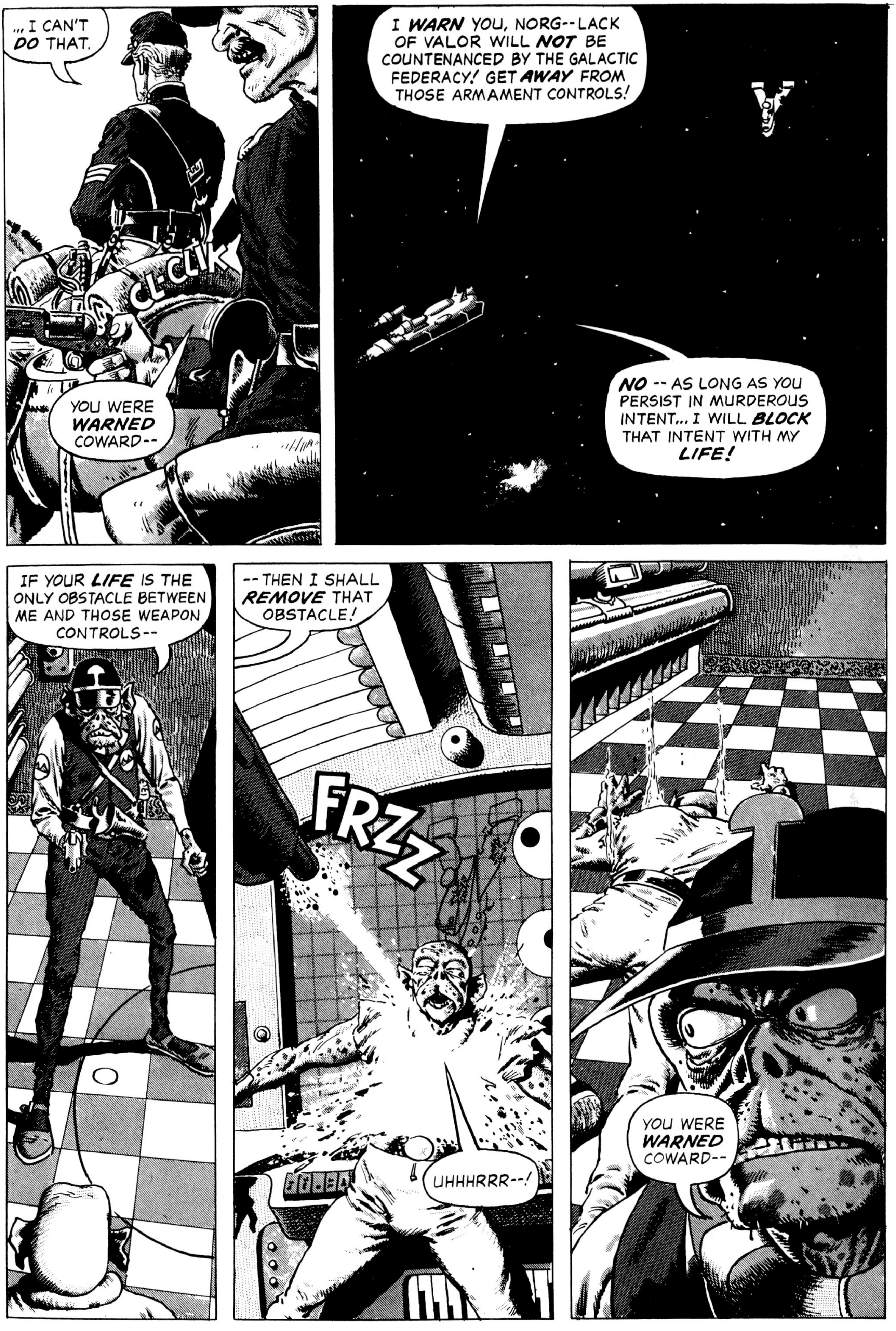

...I CAN'T DO THAT.
CL-CLIK
YOU WERE WARNED COWARD--
I WARN YOU, NORG--LACK OF VALOR WILL NOT BE COUNTENANCED BY THE GALACTIC FEDERACY! GET AWAY FROM THOSE ARMAMENT CONTROLS!
NO -- AS LONG AS YOU PERSIST IN MURDEROUS INTENT... I WILL BLOCK THAT INTENT WITH MY LIFE!
IF YOUR LIFE IS THE ONLY OBSTACLE BETWEEN ME AND THOSE WEAPON CONTROLS--
--THEN I SHALL REMOVE THAT OBSTACLE!
FRZZ
UHHHRRR--!
YOU WERE WARNED COWARD--

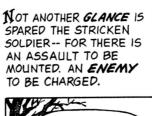

IF A DESERTER WON'T *FACE* FIGHT--

--HE *DESERVES* TO GET IT IN THE *BACK*--!

*N*OT ANOTHER *GLANCE* IS SPARED THE STRICKEN SOLDIER-- FOR THERE IS AN ASSAULT TO BE MOUNTED. AN *ENEMY* TO BE CHARGED.

*B*UT THE ORB OF THE *SUN* LOOKS DOWN. CAUGHT IN ITS PASSIVE GAZE ARE *MOUNTED* FORMS,...AND A *SPRAWLED* ONE.

DRAW SABERS--

--CHARRRGE!!!

*F*LASHING HOOVE'S RAVAGE THE TURF ON THE HILL. CLOTS OF DIRT SPEW BEHIND THE THUNDERING ASSAULT. HELPLESS HOSPITAL TENTS LOOM *NEARER*, SILENT, *IMPASSIVE*, AWAITING THE FRENETIC DISPLAY OF MARAUDING FORCE,...

...AND THEN THE TENTS *BREAK* THEIR SILENCE-- WITH THE HISS AND CRACK OF CANVAS ABRUPTLY WHIPPED *BACK*...

...TO REVEAL WAITING ROWS OF HIGHLY-DISCIPLINED, *GRIM-FACED* MEN--

BAM BAM BA-BAM-BAM BAM

...THE KIND OF MEN WHO WOULD *NOT NORMALLY* BE FOUND IN A *HOSPITAL* ENVIRONMENT.

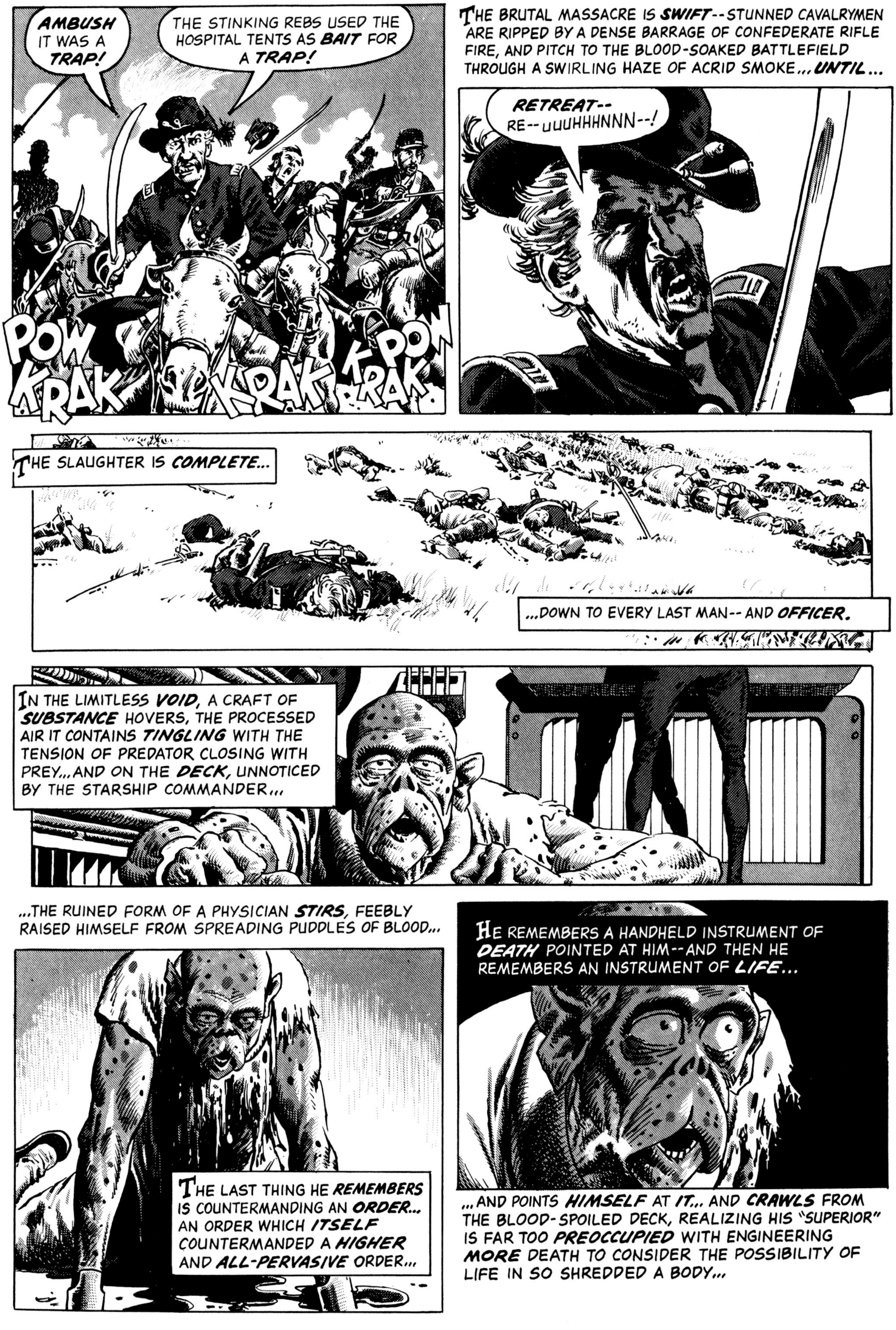
AMBUSH IT WAS A TRAP!
THE STINKING REBS USED THE HOSPITAL TENTS AS BAIT FOR A TRAP!
POW
KRAK
KRAK
POW
KRAK
THE BRUTAL MASSACRE IS SWIFT--STUNNED CAVALRYMEN ARE RIPPED BY A DENSE BARRAGE OF CONFEDERATE RIFLE FIRE, AND PITCH TO THE BLOOD-SOAKED BATTLEFIELD THROUGH A SWIRLING HAZE OF ACRID SMOKE... UNTIL...
RETREAT-- RE--UUUHHHHNNN--!
THE SLAUGHTER IS COMPLETE...
...DOWN TO EVERY LAST MAN-- AND OFFICER.
IN THE LIMITLESS VOID, A CRAFT OF SUBSTANCE HOVERS, THE PROCESSED AIR IT CONTAINS TINGLING WITH THE TENSION OF PREDATOR CLOSING WITH PREY... AND ON THE DECK, UNNOTICED BY THE STARSHIP COMMANDER...
...THE RUINED FORM OF A PHYSICIAN STIRS, FEEBLY RAISED HIMSELF FROM SPREADING PUDDLES OF BLOOD...
THE LAST THING HE REMEMBERS IS COUNTERMANDING AN ORDER... AN ORDER WHICH ITSELF COUNTERMANDED A HIGHER AND ALL-PERVASIVE ORDER...
HE REMEMBERS A HANDHELD INSTRUMENT OF DEATH POINTED AT HIM--AND THEN HE REMEMBERS AN INSTRUMENT OF LIFE...
...AND POINTS HIMSELF AT IT... AND CRAWLS FROM THE BLOOD-SPOILED DECK, REALIZING HIS "SUPERIOR" IS FAR TOO PREOCCUPIED WITH ENGINEERING MORE DEATH TO CONSIDER THE POSSIBILITY OF LIFE IN SO SHREDDED A BODY...

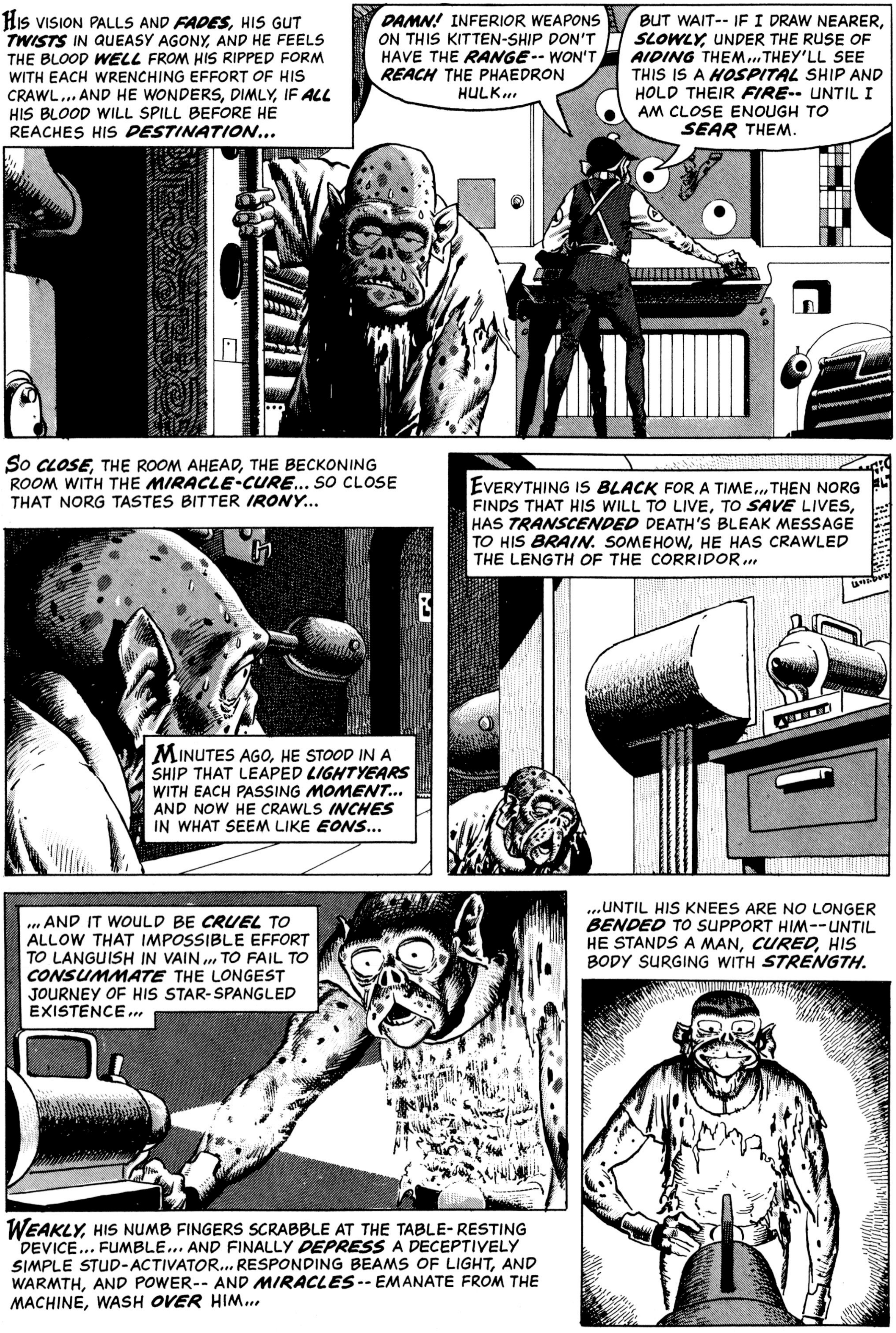
HIS VISION PALLS AND FADES, HIS GUT TWISTS IN QUEASY AGONY, AND HE FEELS THE BLOOD WELL FROM HIS RIPPED FORM WITH EACH WRENCHING EFFORT OF HIS CRAWL... AND HE WONDERS, DIMLY, IF ALL HIS BLOOD WILL SPILL BEFORE HE REACHES HIS DESTINATION...
DAMN! INFERIOR WEAPONS ON THIS KITTEN-SHIP DON'T HAVE THE RANGE-- WON'T REACH THE PHAEDRON HULK...
BUT WAIT-- IF I DRAW NEARER, SLOWLY, UNDER THE RUSE OF AIDING THEM... THEY'LL SEE THIS IS A HOSPITAL SHIP AND HOLD THEIR FIRE-- UNTIL I AM CLOSE ENOUGH TO SEAR THEM.
SO CLOSE, THE ROOM AHEAD, THE BECKONING ROOM WITH THE MIRACLE-CURE... SO CLOSE THAT NORG TASTES BITTER IRONY...
MINUTES AGO, HE STOOD IN A SHIP THAT LEAPED LIGHTYEARS WITH EACH PASSING MOMENT... AND NOW HE CRAWLS INCHES IN WHAT SEEM LIKE EONS...
EVERYTHING IS BLACK FOR A TIME... THEN NORG FINDS THAT HIS WILL TO LIVE, TO SAVE LIVES, HAS TRANSCENDED DEATH'S BLEAK MESSAGE TO HIS BRAIN. SOMEHOW, HE HAS CRAWLED THE LENGTH OF THE CORRIDOR...
...AND IT WOULD BE CRUEL TO ALLOW THAT IMPOSSIBLE EFFORT TO LANGUISH IN VAIN... TO FAIL TO CONSUMMATE THE LONGEST JOURNEY OF HIS STAR-SPANGLED EXISTENCE...
WEAKLY, HIS NUMB FINGERS SCRABBLE AT THE TABLE-RESTING DEVICE... FUMBLE... AND FINALLY DEPRESS A DECEPTIVELY SIMPLE STUD-ACTIVATOR... RESPONDING BEAMS OF LIGHT, AND WARMTH, AND POWER-- AND MIRACLES-- EMANATE FROM THE MACHINE, WASH OVER HIM...
...UNTIL HIS KNEES ARE NO LONGER BENDED TO SUPPORT HIM--UNTIL HE STANDS A MAN, CURED, HIS BODY SURGING WITH STRENGTH.

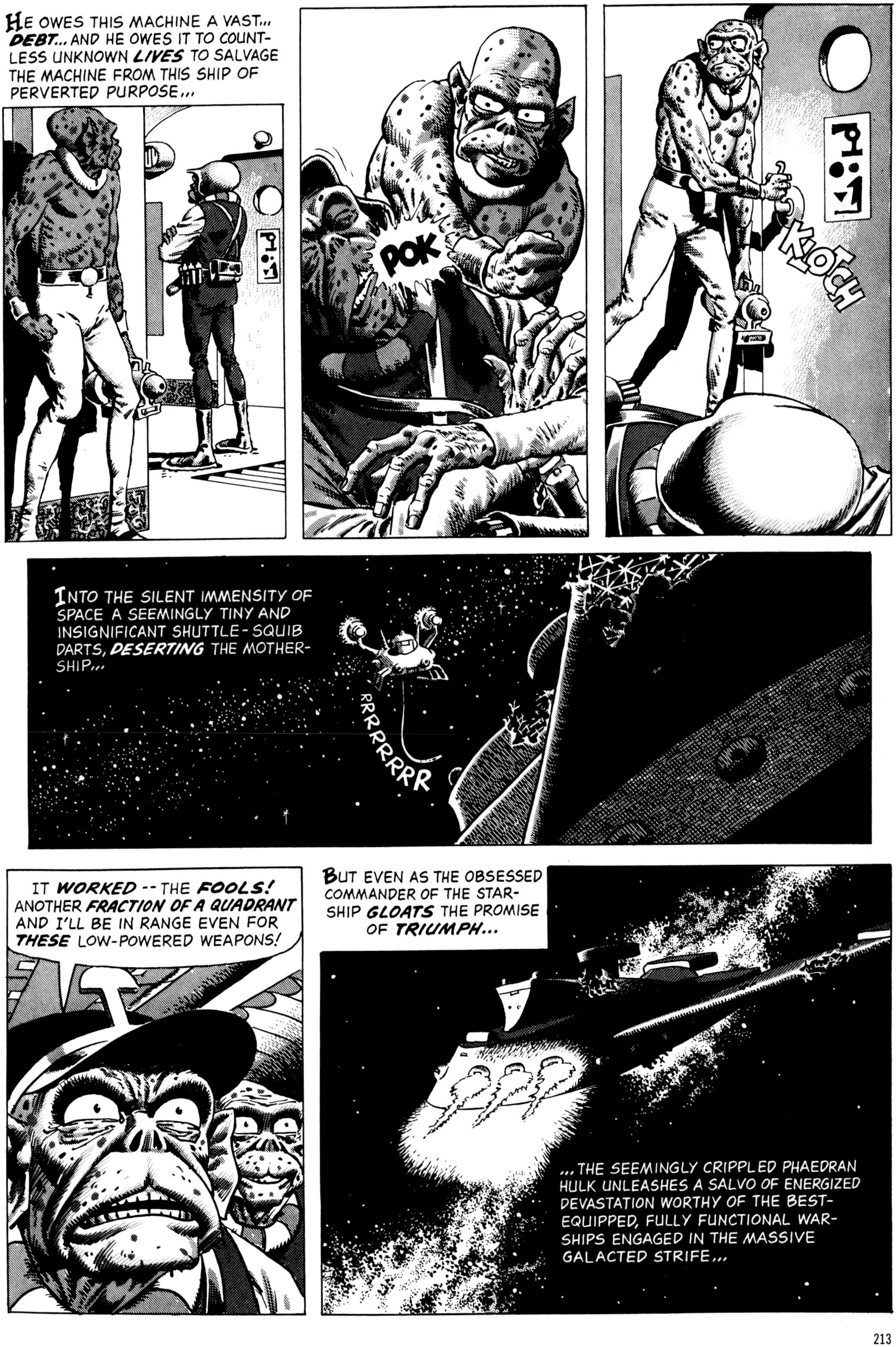
HE OWES THIS MACHINE A VAST... DEBT... AND HE OWES IT TO COUNTLESS UNKNOWN LIVES TO SALVAGE THE MACHINE FROM THIS SHIP OF PERVERTED PURPOSE...
POK
KLOTCH
INTO THE SILENT IMMENSITY OF SPACE A SEEMINGLY TINY AND INSIGNIFICANT SHUTTLE-SQUIB DARTS, DESERTING THE MOTHER-SHIP...
RRRRRRRRR
IT WORKED -- THE FOOLS! ANOTHER FRACTION OF A QUADRANT AND I'LL BE IN RANGE EVEN FOR THESE LOW-POWERED WEAPONS!
BUT EVEN AS THE OBSESSED COMMANDER OF THE STAR-SHIP GLOATS THE PROMISE OF TRIUMPH...
...THE SEEMINGLY CRIPPLED PHAEDRAN HULK UNLEASHES A SALVO OF ENERGIZED DEVASTATION WORTHY OF THE BEST-EQUIPPED, FULLY FUNCTIONAL WAR-SHIPS ENGAGED IN THE MASSIVE GALACTED STRIFE...

NO!!!

IT WAS A **BAIT**--THE SHIP'S **NOT** CRIPPLED-- IT WAS DISGUISED FOR AN **AMBUSH!** **NOOOOOOOO!**

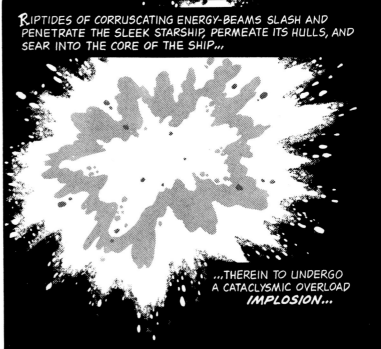

RIPTIDES OF CORRUSCATING ENERGY-BEAMS SLASH AND PENETRATE THE SLEEK STARSHIP, PERMEATE ITS HULLS, AND SEAR INTO THE CORE OF THE SHIP...

...THEREIN TO UNDERGO A CATACLYSMIC OVERLOAD **IMPLOSION**...

SPACE IS INSTANTLY LITTERED WITH CAREENING DEBRIS,,,FLOTSAM DESTINED TO SHOOT THROUGH AN **INFINITY** OF SPACE-- UNLESS STOPPED BY AN **EQUAL FORCE**... OR AN **IMMOVABLE OBJECT**...

...**NEITHER** OF WHICH THE SMALL SHUTTLECRAFT **IS**. THE COLLISION IS NEGLIGIBLE, A **GLANCING** BLOW... BUT THE IMPLOSION-PROPELLED STARSHIP-FRAGMENT **DOES** STRIKE WITH ENOUGH FORCE TO,,,

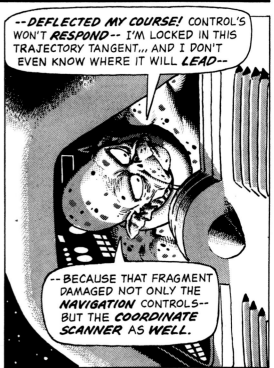

--**DEFLECTED MY COURSE!** CONTROL'S WON'T **RESPOND** -- I'M LOCKED IN THIS TRAJECTORY TANGENT,,, AND I DON'T EVEN KNOW WHERE IT WILL **LEAD**--

-- BECAUSE THAT FRAGMENT DAMAGED NOT ONLY THE **NAVIGATION** CONTROLS-- BUT THE **COORDINATE SCANNER** AS **WELL**.

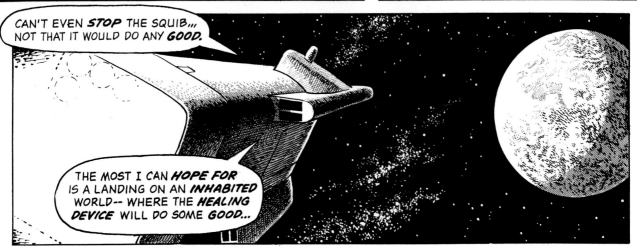

CAN'T EVEN **STOP** THE SQUIB,,, NOT THAT IT WOULD DO ANY **GOOD**.

THE MOST I CAN **HOPE FOR** IS A LANDING ON AN **INHABITED** WORLD-- WHERE THE **HEALING DEVICE** WILL DO SOME **GOOD**...

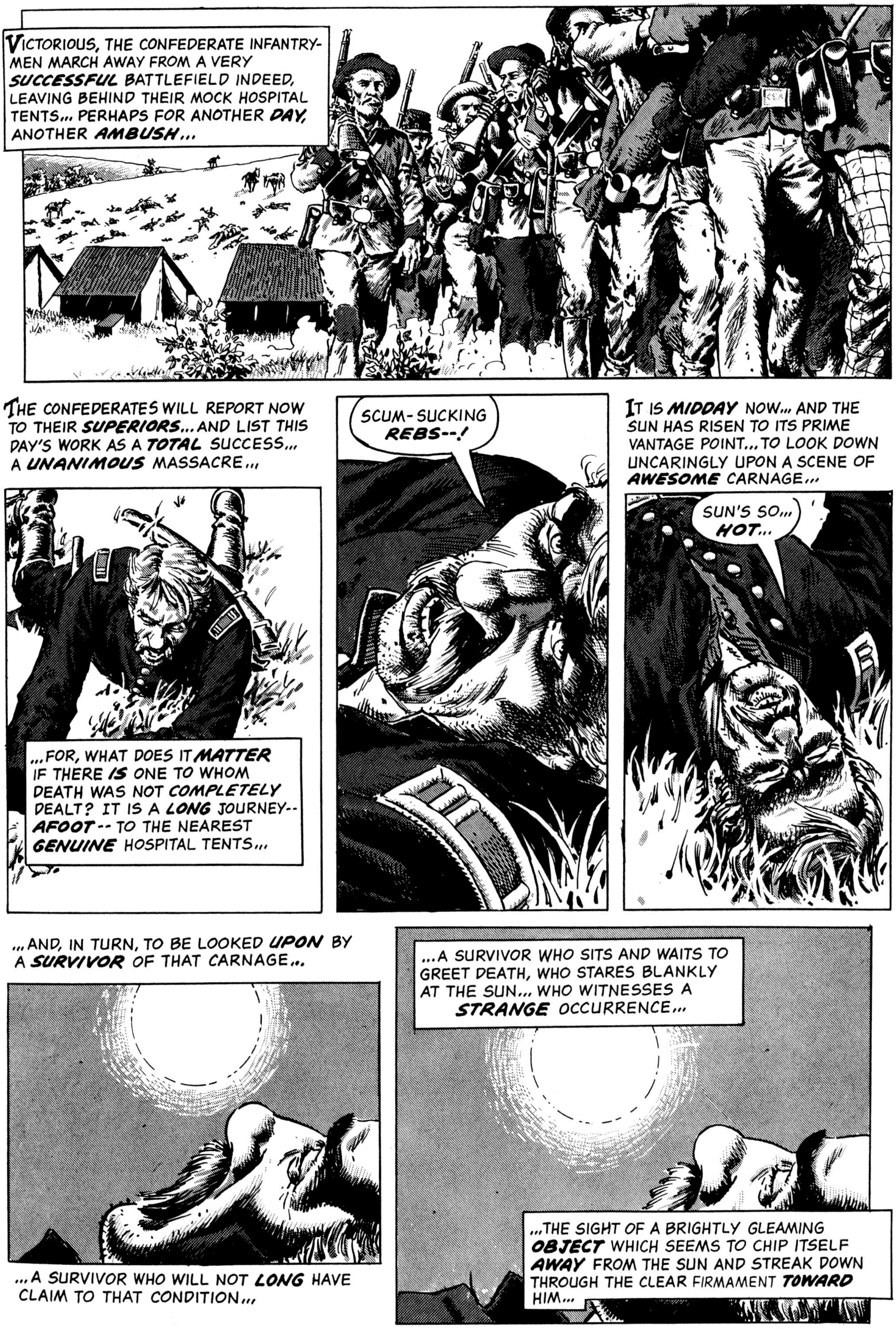

VICTORIOUS, THE CONFEDERATE INFANTRYMEN MARCH AWAY FROM A VERY SUCCESSFUL BATTLEFIELD INDEED, LEAVING BEHIND THEIR MOCK HOSPITAL TENTS... PERHAPS FOR ANOTHER DAY, ANOTHER AMBUSH...
THE CONFEDERATES WILL REPORT NOW TO THEIR SUPERIORS... AND LIST THIS DAY'S WORK AS A TOTAL SUCCESS... A UNANIMOUS MASSACRE...
...FOR, WHAT DOES IT MATTER IF THERE IS ONE TO WHOM DEATH WAS NOT COMPLETELY DEALT? IT IS A LONG JOURNEY-- AFOOT-- TO THE NEAREST GENUINE HOSPITAL TENTS...
SCUM-SUCKING REBS--!
IT IS MIDDAY NOW... AND THE SUN HAS RISEN TO ITS PRIME VANTAGE POINT... TO LOOK DOWN UNCARINGLY UPON A SCENE OF AWESOME CARNAGE...
SUN'S SO... HOT...
...AND, IN TURN, TO BE LOOKED UPON BY A SURVIVOR OF THAT CARNAGE...
...A SURVIVOR WHO WILL NOT LONG HAVE CLAIM TO THAT CONDITION...
...A SURVIVOR WHO SITS AND WAITS TO GREET DEATH, WHO STARES BLANKLY AT THE SUN... WHO WITNESSES A STRANGE OCCURRENCE...
...THE SIGHT OF A BRIGHTLY GLEAMING OBJECT WHICH SEEMS TO CHIP ITSELF AWAY FROM THE SUN AND STREAK DOWN THROUGH THE CLEAR FIRMAMENT TOWARD HIM...

...ULTIMATELY SLAMMING TO THE GROUND *NEARBY*...

DYING... *SEEING* THINGS... SEEMED LIKE SOMETHING FELL FROM THE *SKY*... CRASHED OVER THERE...*CLOSE*...

THEN, FOR THE CAPTAIN, THE WORLD *REELS* AND TUMBLES DOWN A WHIRLPOOL TO SWIRLING, LIQUID *BLACK*...

...AND WHEN HIS EYES AGAIN *OPEN* -- FOR ONE *FINAL* TIME -- HE SEES HIS DESTINY ETCHED IN A FORM WHICH IS *UNIMAGINABLY* HIDEOUS...TO *HIM*.

ᏌᎫᏋᏋᎷᏇ ᎷᎯᏝᎫᏝᏇᎯ ᎮᏋᎶᎲᎾᎾ:·.

A... A *MONSTER*... AM ...AM I IN... *HELL*--?

THE LOATHSOME MONSTROSITY PLAINLY INTENDS TO DO THE CAPTAIN *HARM*...

ᎯᎫ ᎫᏌᎲᎮᎾᎲ :·.·:·.

...AS ATTESTED BY THE STRANGE *WEAPON* IT LIFTS AND POINTS *TOWARD* HIM...

CL-CLIK

NO-- IT'S *NOT* HELL! IT...IT'S *REAL*--!

...AND THE CAPTAIN IS NOT A MAN TO ALLOW WEAPONS TO BE POINTED AT HIM IF HE CAN *PREVENT* IT...

BLAM

NORG DIES *INSTANTLY*...DIES WITHIN *INCHES* OF THE HEALING DEVICE HE WAS ON THE VERGE OF *ACTIVATING*... THE HEALING DEVICE HE WISHED TO USE ON THE STRANGE CAPTAIN-CREATURE OBVIOUSLY NEARING DEATH...

KNIK

...THE HEALING DEVICE WHICH IS ACTIVATED *NEVERTHELESS*... BY *FATE* -- FATE, AND THE FACT THAT IT FALLS TO THE GROUND *STUD-SIDE DOWN*...

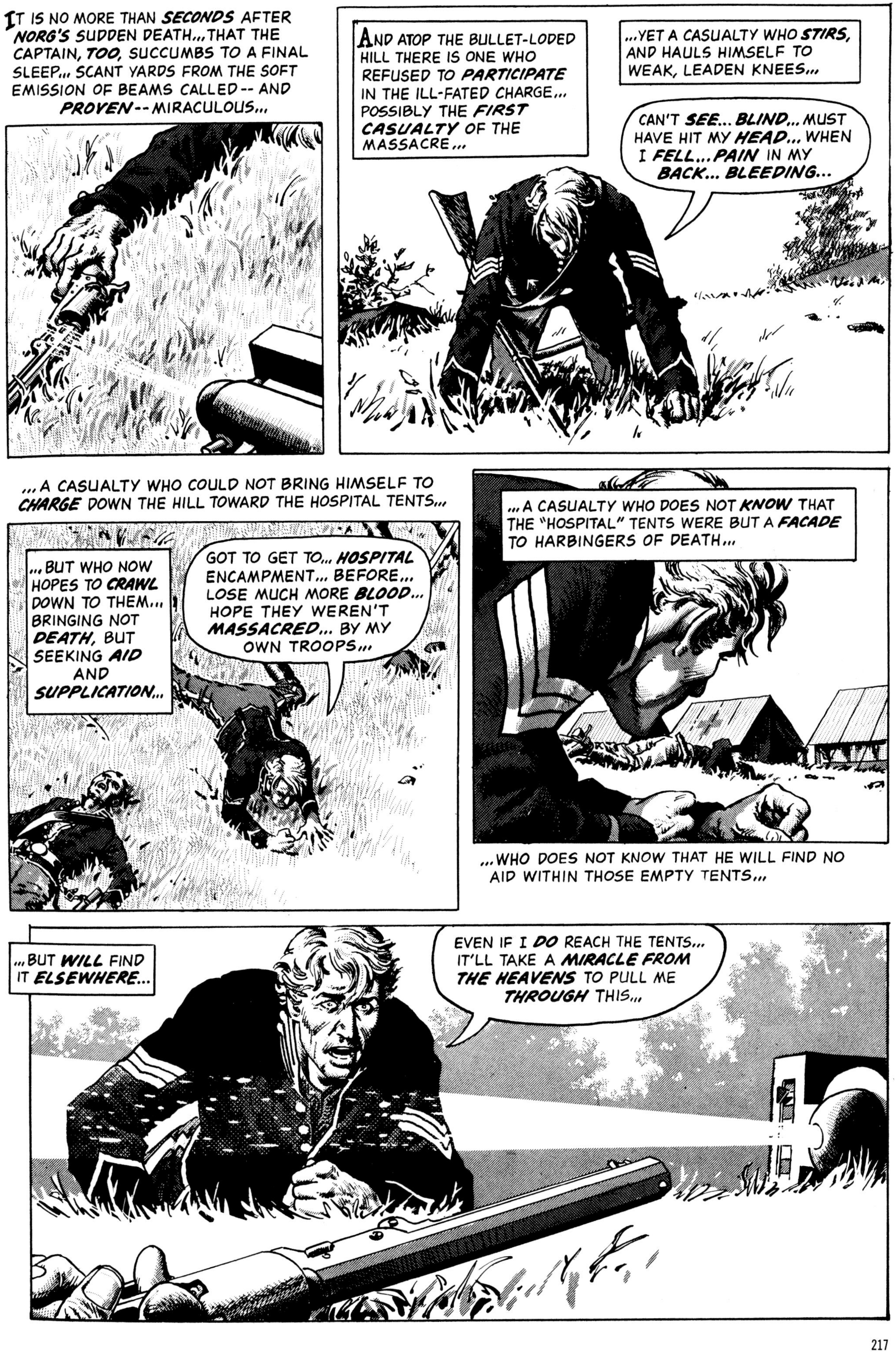
IT IS NO MORE THAN SECONDS AFTER NORG'S SUDDEN DEATH... THAT THE CAPTAIN, TOO, SUCCUMBS TO A FINAL SLEEP... SCANT YARDS FROM THE SOFT EMISSION OF BEAMS CALLED -- AND PROVEN -- MIRACULOUS...
AND ATOP THE BULLET-LODED HILL THERE IS ONE WHO REFUSED TO PARTICIPATE IN THE ILL-FATED CHARGE... POSSIBLY THE FIRST CASUALTY OF THE MASSACRE...
...YET A CASUALTY WHO STIRS, AND HAULS HIMSELF TO WEAK, LEADEN KNEES...
CAN'T SEE... BLIND... MUST HAVE HIT MY HEAD... WHEN I FELL... PAIN IN MY BACK... BLEEDING...
...A CASUALTY WHO COULD NOT BRING HIMSELF TO CHARGE DOWN THE HILL TOWARD THE HOSPITAL TENTS...
...BUT WHO NOW HOPES TO CRAWL DOWN TO THEM... BRINGING NOT DEATH, BUT SEEKING AID AND SUPPLICATION...
GOT TO GET TO... HOSPITAL ENCAMPMENT... BEFORE... LOSE MUCH MORE BLOOD... HOPE THEY WEREN'T MASSACRED... BY MY OWN TROOPS...
...A CASUALTY WHO DOES NOT KNOW THAT THE "HOSPITAL" TENTS WERE BUT A FACADE TO HARBINGERS OF DEATH...
...WHO DOES NOT KNOW THAT HE WILL FIND NO AID WITHIN THOSE EMPTY TENTS...
...BUT WILL FIND IT ELSEWHERE...
EVEN IF I DO REACH THE TENTS... IT'LL TAKE A MIRACLE FROM THE HEAVENS TO PULL ME THROUGH THIS...

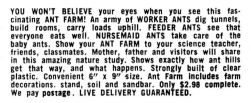

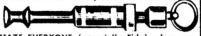

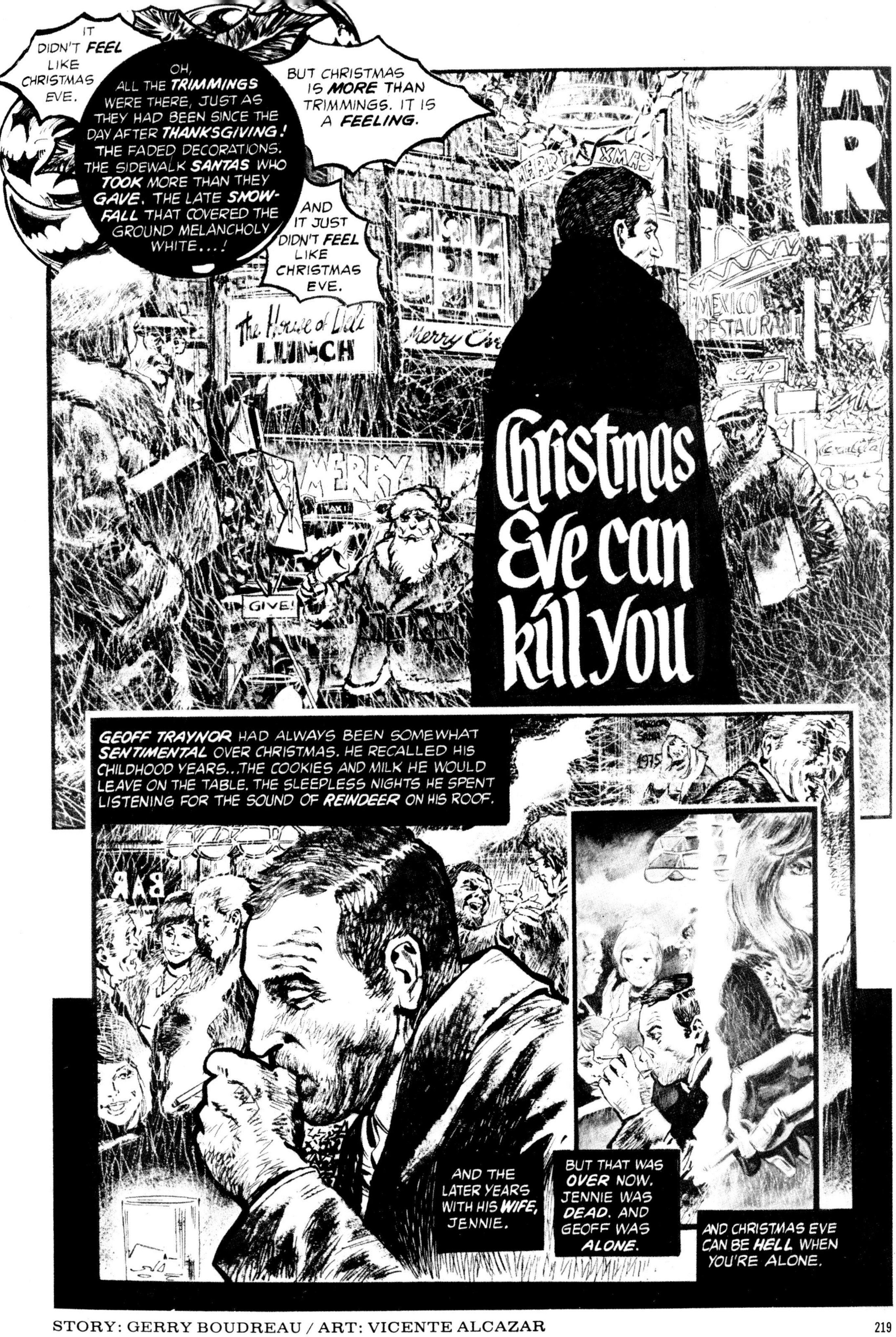

IT DIDN'T FEEL LIKE CHRISTMAS EVE.
OH, ALL THE TRIMMINGS WERE THERE, JUST AS THEY HAD BEEN SINCE THE DAY AFTER THANKSGIVING! THE FADED DECORATIONS. THE SIDEWALK SANTAS WHO TOOK MORE THAN THEY GAVE. THE LATE SNOW-FALL THAT COVERED THE GROUND MELANCHOLY WHITE...!
BUT CHRISTMAS IS MORE THAN TRIMMINGS. IT IS A FEELING.
AND IT JUST DIDN'T FEEL LIKE CHRISTMAS EVE.
The House of Lili LUNCH
Merry Chr
MERRY XMAS
MEXICO RESTAURANT
MERRY
GIVE!
Christmas Eve can kill you
GEOFF TRAYNOR HAD ALWAYS BEEN SOMEWHAT SENTIMENTAL OVER CHRISTMAS. HE RECALLED HIS CHILDHOOD YEARS...THE COOKIES AND MILK HE WOULD LEAVE ON THE TABLE. THE SLEEPLESS NIGHTS HE SPENT LISTENING FOR THE SOUND OF REINDEER ON HIS ROOF.
1975
BAR
AND THE LATER YEARS WITH HIS WIFE, JENNIE.
BUT THAT WAS OVER NOW. JENNIE WAS DEAD. AND GEOFF WAS ALONE.
AND CHRISTMAS EVE CAN BE HELL WHEN YOU'RE ALONE.

STORY: GERRY BOUDREAU / ART: VICENTE ALCAZAR

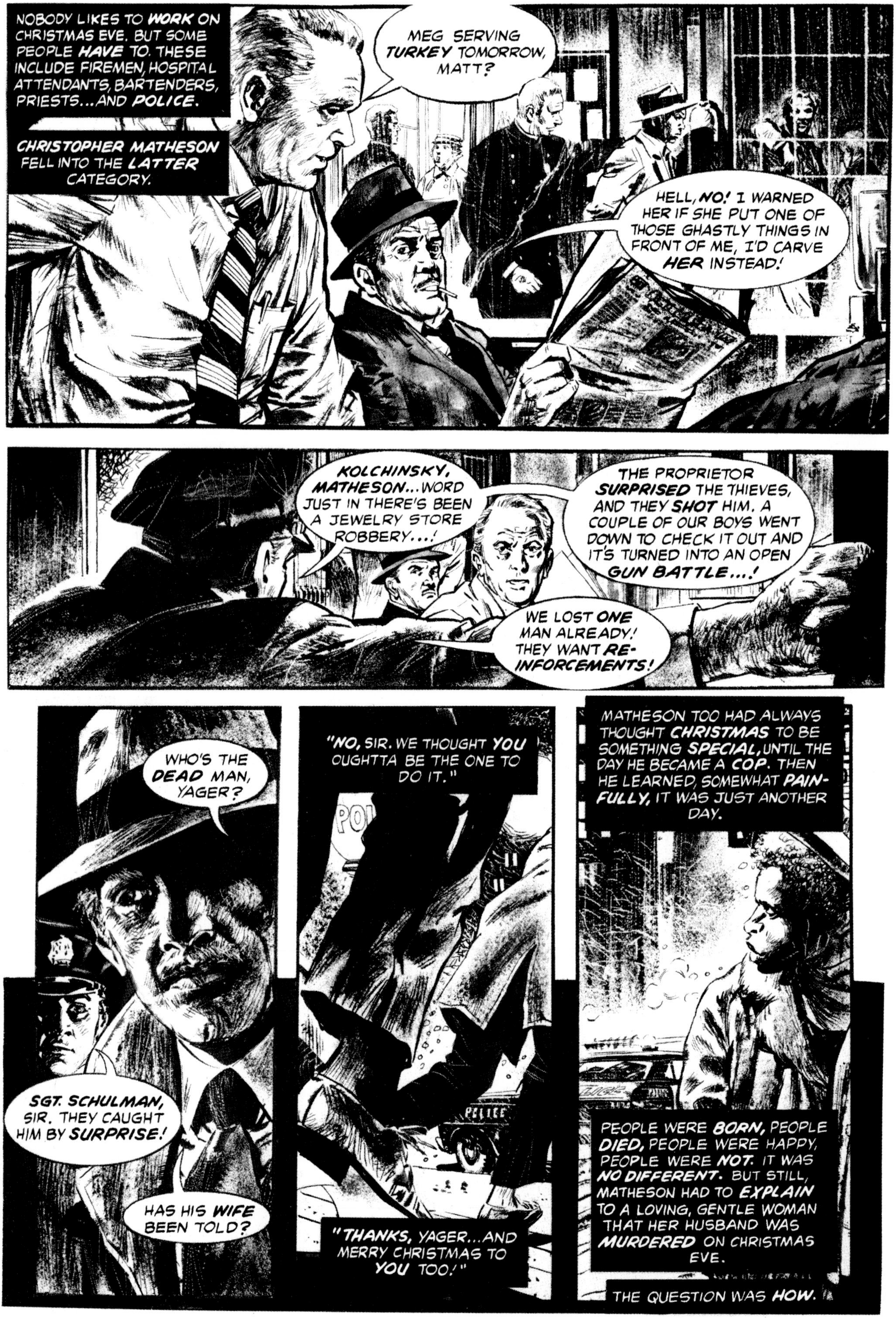
NOBODY LIKES TO WORK ON CHRISTMAS EVE. BUT SOME PEOPLE HAVE TO. THESE INCLUDE FIREMEN, HOSPITAL ATTENDANTS, BARTENDERS, PRIESTS...AND POLICE.
CHRISTOPHER MATHESON FELL INTO THE LATTER CATEGORY.
MEG SERVING TURKEY TOMORROW, MATT?
HELL, NO! I WARNED HER IF SHE PUT ONE OF THOSE GHASTLY THINGS IN FRONT OF ME, I'D CARVE HER INSTEAD!
KOLCHINSKY, MATHESON...WORD JUST IN THERE'S BEEN A JEWELRY STORE ROBBERY...!
THE PROPRIETOR SURPRISED THE THIEVES, AND THEY SHOT HIM. A COUPLE OF OUR BOYS WENT DOWN TO CHECK IT OUT AND IT'S TURNED INTO AN OPEN GUN BATTLE...!
WE LOST ONE MAN ALREADY! THEY WANT RE-INFORCEMENTS!
WHO'S THE DEAD MAN, YAGER?
SGT. SCHULMAN, SIR. THEY CAUGHT HIM BY SURPRISE!
HAS HIS WIFE BEEN TOLD?
"NO, SIR. WE THOUGHT YOU OUGHTTA BE THE ONE TO DO IT."
"THANKS, YAGER...AND MERRY CHRISTMAS TO YOU TOO!"
MATHESON TOO HAD ALWAYS THOUGHT CHRISTMAS TO BE SOMETHING SPECIAL, UNTIL THE DAY HE BECAME A COP. THEN HE LEARNED, SOMEWHAT PAIN-FULLY, IT WAS JUST ANOTHER DAY.
PEOPLE WERE BORN, PEOPLE DIED, PEOPLE WERE HAPPY, PEOPLE WERE NOT. IT WAS NO DIFFERENT. BUT STILL, MATHESON HAD TO EXPLAIN TO A LOVING, GENTLE WOMAN THAT HER HUSBAND WAS MURDERED ON CHRISTMAS EVE.
THE QUESTION WAS HOW.

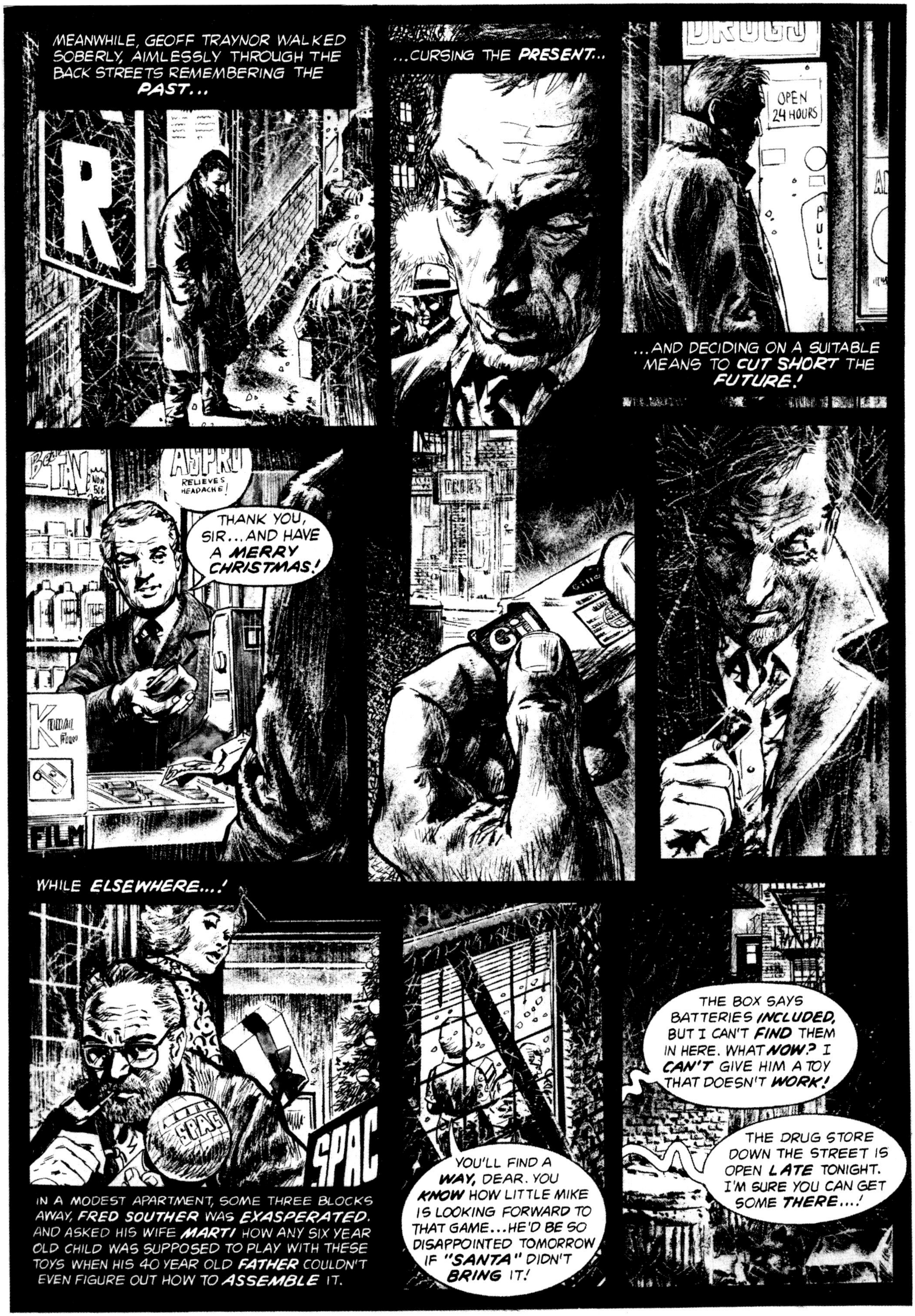
MEANWHILE, GEOFF TRAYNOR WALKED SOBERLY, AIMLESSLY THROUGH THE BACK STREETS REMEMBERING THE PAST...
...CURSING THE PRESENT...
DRUGS
OPEN 24 HOURS
PULL
...AND DECIDING ON A SUITABLE MEANS TO CUT SHORT THE FUTURE!
ASPRO RELIEVES HEADACHE!
THANK YOU, SIR... AND HAVE A MERRY CHRISTMAS!
FILM
WHILE ELSEWHERE...!
SPAC
IN A MODEST APARTMENT, SOME THREE BLOCKS AWAY, FRED SOUTHER WAS EXASPERATED. AND ASKED HIS WIFE MARTI HOW ANY SIX YEAR OLD CHILD WAS SUPPOSED TO PLAY WITH THESE TOYS WHEN HIS 40 YEAR OLD FATHER COULDN'T EVEN FIGURE OUT HOW TO ASSEMBLE IT.
YOU'LL FIND A WAY, DEAR. YOU KNOW HOW LITTLE MIKE IS LOOKING FORWARD TO THAT GAME... HE'D BE SO DISAPPOINTED TOMORROW IF "SANTA" DIDN'T BRING IT!
THE BOX SAYS BATTERIES INCLUDED, BUT I CAN'T FIND THEM IN HERE. WHAT NOW? I CAN'T GIVE HIM A TOY THAT DOESN'T WORK!
THE DRUG STORE DOWN THE STREET IS OPEN LATE TONIGHT. I'M SURE YOU CAN GET SOME THERE...!

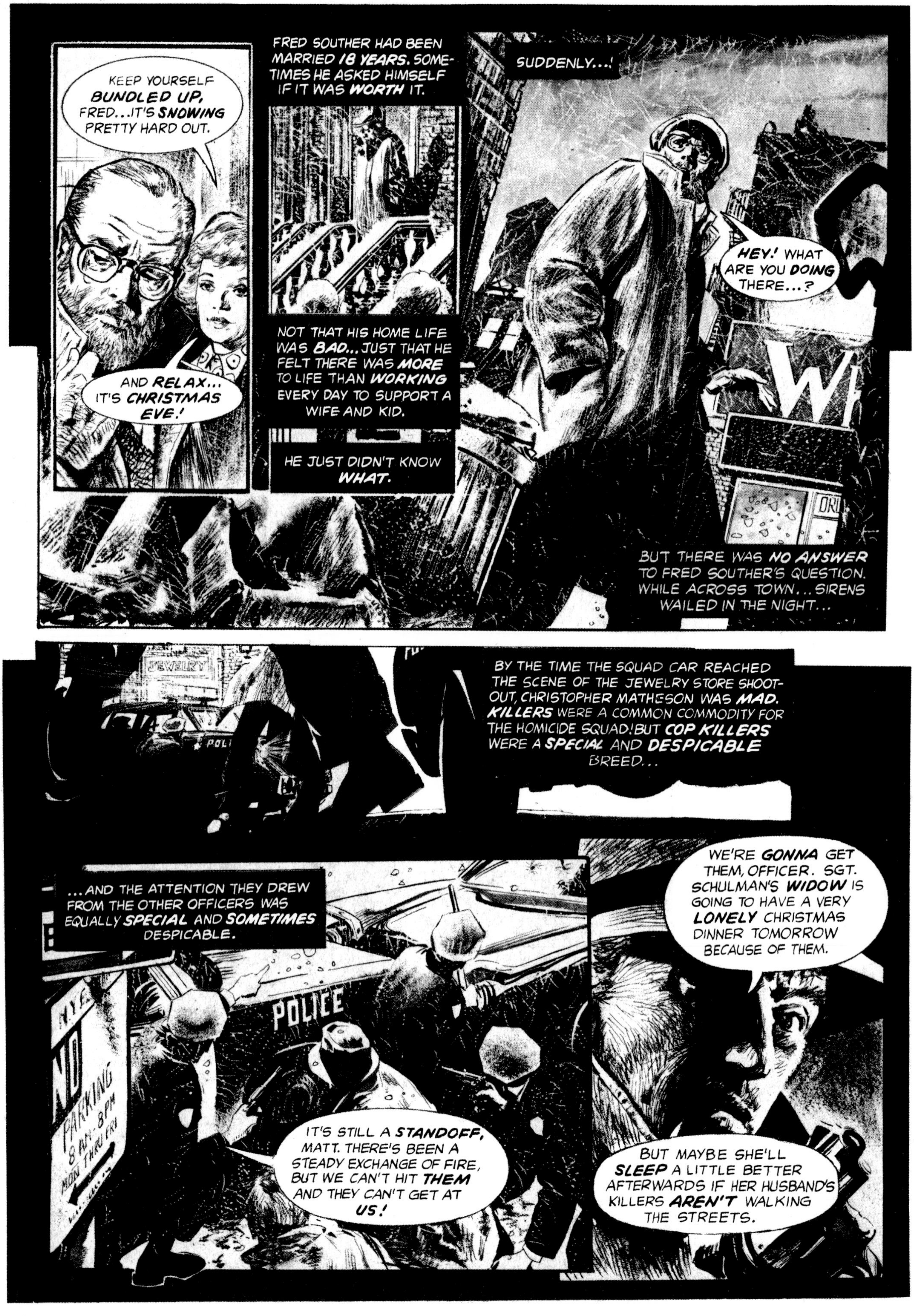
KEEP YOURSELF BUNDLED UP, FRED...IT'S SNOWING PRETTY HARD OUT.
AND RELAX... IT'S CHRISTMAS EVE!
FRED SOUTHER HAD BEEN MARRIED 18 YEARS. SOMETIMES HE ASKED HIMSELF IF IT WAS WORTH IT.
NOT THAT HIS HOME LIFE WAS BAD... JUST THAT HE FELT THERE WAS MORE TO LIFE THAN WORKING EVERY DAY TO SUPPORT A WIFE AND KID.
HE JUST DIDN'T KNOW WHAT.
SUDDENLY...!
HEY! WHAT ARE YOU DOING THERE...?
BUT THERE WAS NO ANSWER TO FRED SOUTHER'S QUESTION. WHILE ACROSS TOWN... SIRENS WAILED IN THE NIGHT...
JEWELRY
BY THE TIME THE SQUAD CAR REACHED THE SCENE OF THE JEWELRY STORE SHOOT-OUT, CHRISTOPHER MATHESON WAS MAD. KILLERS WERE A COMMON COMMODITY FOR THE HOMICIDE SQUAD! BUT COP KILLERS WERE A SPECIAL AND DESPICABLE BREED...
...AND THE ATTENTION THEY DREW FROM THE OTHER OFFICERS WAS EQUALLY SPECIAL AND SOMETIMES DESPICABLE.
POLICE
NO PARKING 8 AM - 8 PM MON THRU FRI
IT'S STILL A STANDOFF, MATT. THERE'S BEEN A STEADY EXCHANGE OF FIRE, BUT WE CAN'T HIT THEM AND THEY CAN'T GET AT US!
WE'RE GONNA GET THEM, OFFICER. SGT. SCHULMAN'S WIDOW IS GOING TO HAVE A VERY LONELY CHRISTMAS DINNER TOMORROW BECAUSE OF THEM.
BUT MAYBE SHE'LL SLEEP A LITTLE BETTER AFTERWARDS IF HER HUSBAND'S KILLERS AREN'T WALKING THE STREETS.

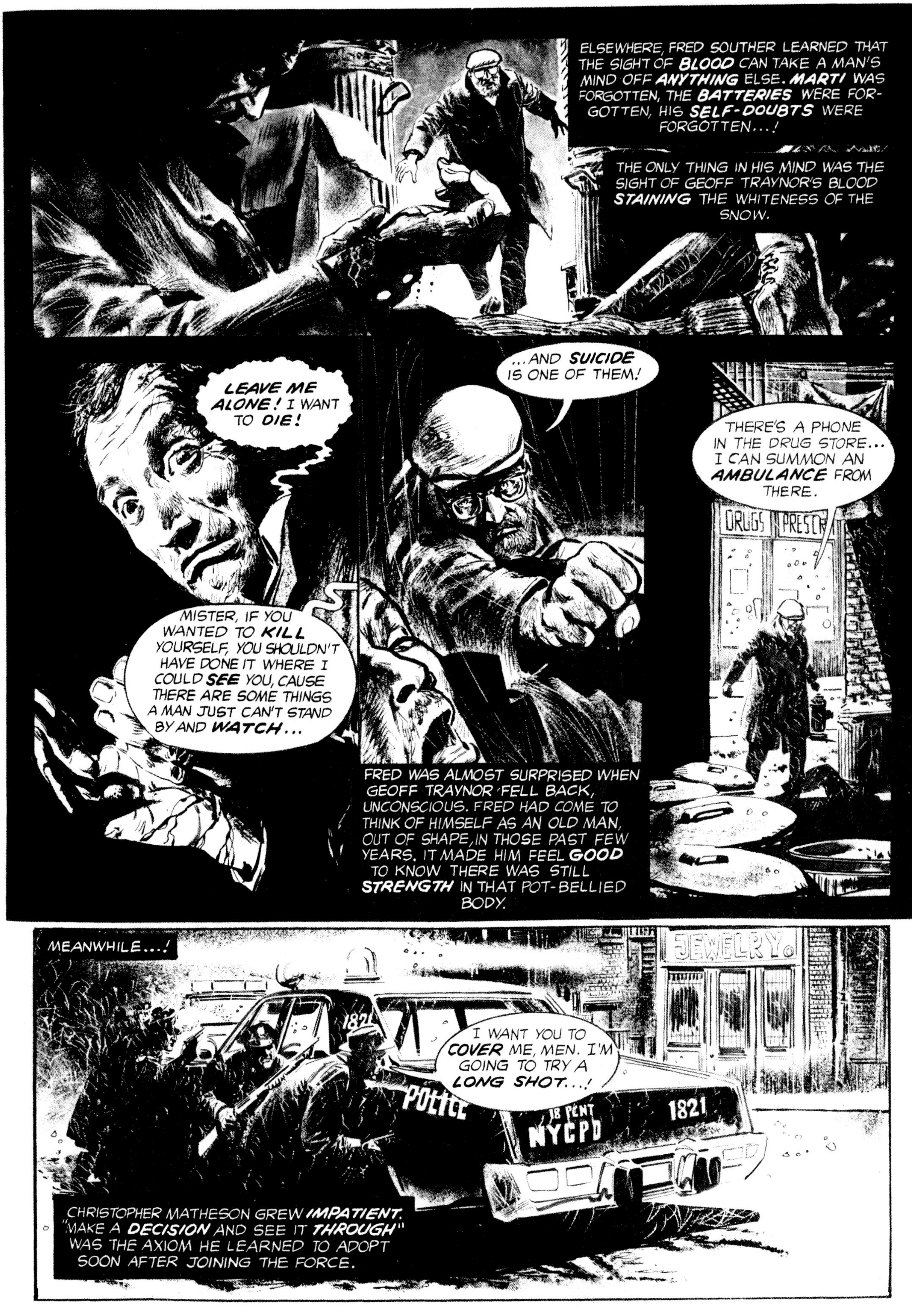

ELSEWHERE, FRED SOUTHER LEARNED THAT THE SIGHT OF BLOOD CAN TAKE A MAN'S MIND OFF ANYTHING ELSE. MARTI WAS FORGOTTEN, THE BATTERIES WERE FORGOTTEN, HIS SELF-DOUBTS WERE FORGOTTEN...!
THE ONLY THING IN HIS MIND WAS THE SIGHT OF GEOFF TRAYNOR'S BLOOD STAINING THE WHITENESS OF THE SNOW.
LEAVE ME ALONE! I WANT TO DIE!
MISTER, IF YOU WANTED TO KILL YOURSELF, YOU SHOULDN'T HAVE DONE IT WHERE I COULD SEE YOU, CAUSE THERE ARE SOME THINGS A MAN JUST CAN'T STAND BY AND WATCH...
...AND SUICIDE IS ONE OF THEM!
FRED WAS ALMOST SURPRISED WHEN GEOFF TRAYNOR FELL BACK, UNCONSCIOUS. FRED HAD COME TO THINK OF HIMSELF AS AN OLD MAN, OUT OF SHAPE, IN THOSE PAST FEW YEARS. IT MADE HIM FEEL GOOD TO KNOW THERE WAS STILL STRENGTH IN THAT POT-BELLIED BODY.
THERE'S A PHONE IN THE DRUG STORE... I CAN SUMMON AN AMBULANCE FROM THERE.
DRUGS
PRESC
MEANWHILE...!
JEWELRY
I WANT YOU TO COVER ME, MEN. I'M GOING TO TRY A LONG SHOT...!
POLICE
18 PCNT
NYCPD
1821
CHRISTOPHER MATHESON GREW IMPATIENT. "MAKE A DECISION AND SEE IT THROUGH" WAS THE AXIOM HE LEARNED TO ADOPT SOON AFTER JOINING THE FORCE.

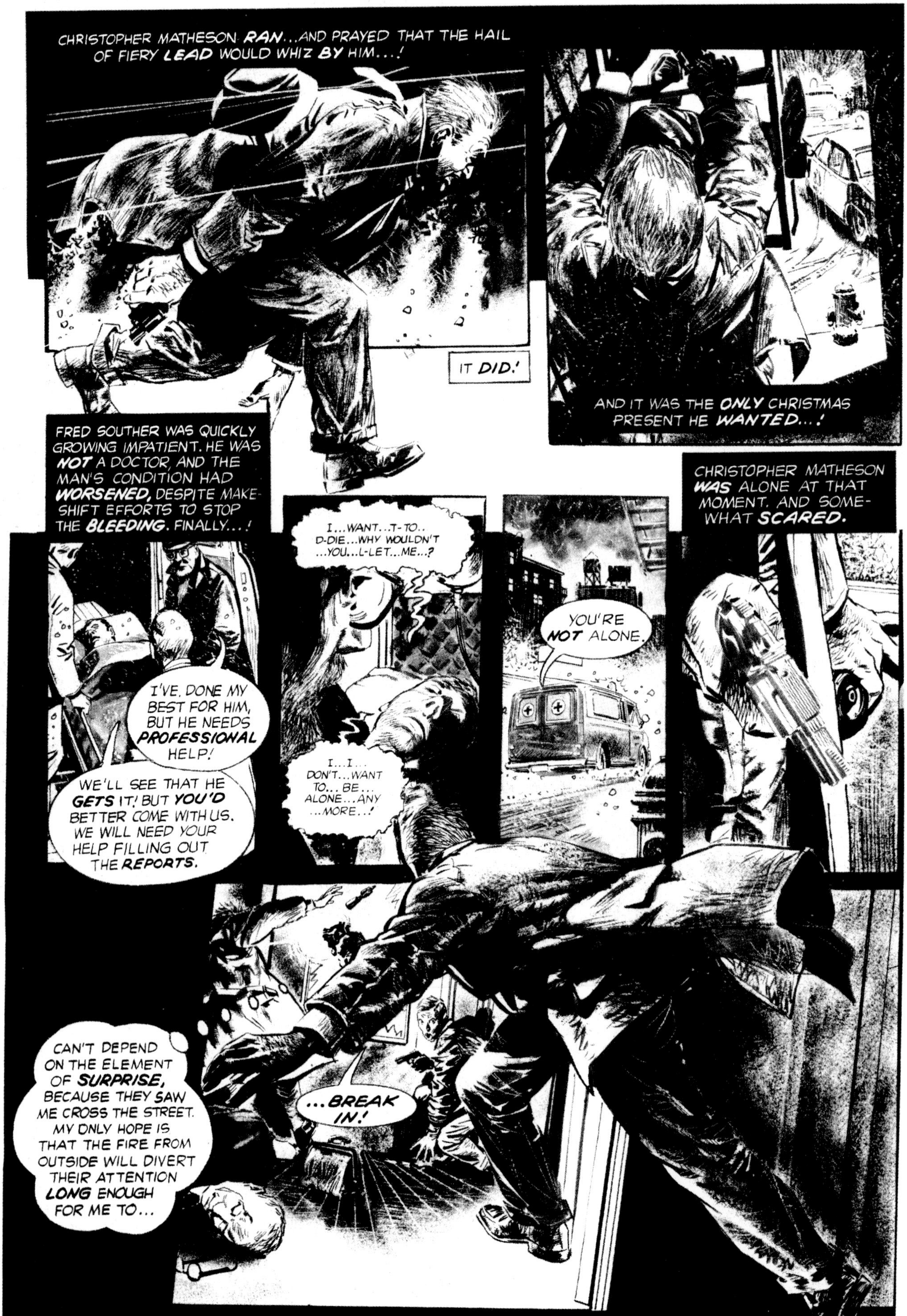

CHRISTOPHER MATHESON RAN...AND PRAYED THAT THE HAIL OF FIERY LEAD WOULD WHIZ BY HIM...!
IT DID!
AND IT WAS THE ONLY CHRISTMAS PRESENT HE WANTED...!
FRED SOUTHER WAS QUICKLY GROWING IMPATIENT. HE WAS NOT A DOCTOR, AND THE MAN'S CONDITION HAD WORSENED, DESPITE MAKE-SHIFT EFFORTS TO STOP THE BLEEDING. FINALLY...!
I'VE DONE MY BEST FOR HIM, BUT HE NEEDS PROFESSIONAL HELP!
WE'LL SEE THAT HE GETS IT! BUT YOU'D BETTER COME WITH US. WE WILL NEED YOUR HELP FILLING OUT THE REPORTS.
I...WANT...T-TO.. D-DIE...WHY WOULDN'T ...YOU...L-LET...ME...?
I...I... DON'T...WANT TO... BE... ALONE...ANY ...MORE...!
YOU'RE NOT ALONE.
CHRISTOPHER MATHESON WAS ALONE AT THAT MOMENT, AND SOME-WHAT SCARED.
CAN'T DEPEND ON THE ELEMENT OF SURPRISE, BECAUSE THEY SAW ME CROSS THE STREET. MY ONLY HOPE IS THAT THE FIRE FROM OUTSIDE WILL DIVERT THEIR ATTENTION LONG ENOUGH FOR ME TO...
...BREAK IN!

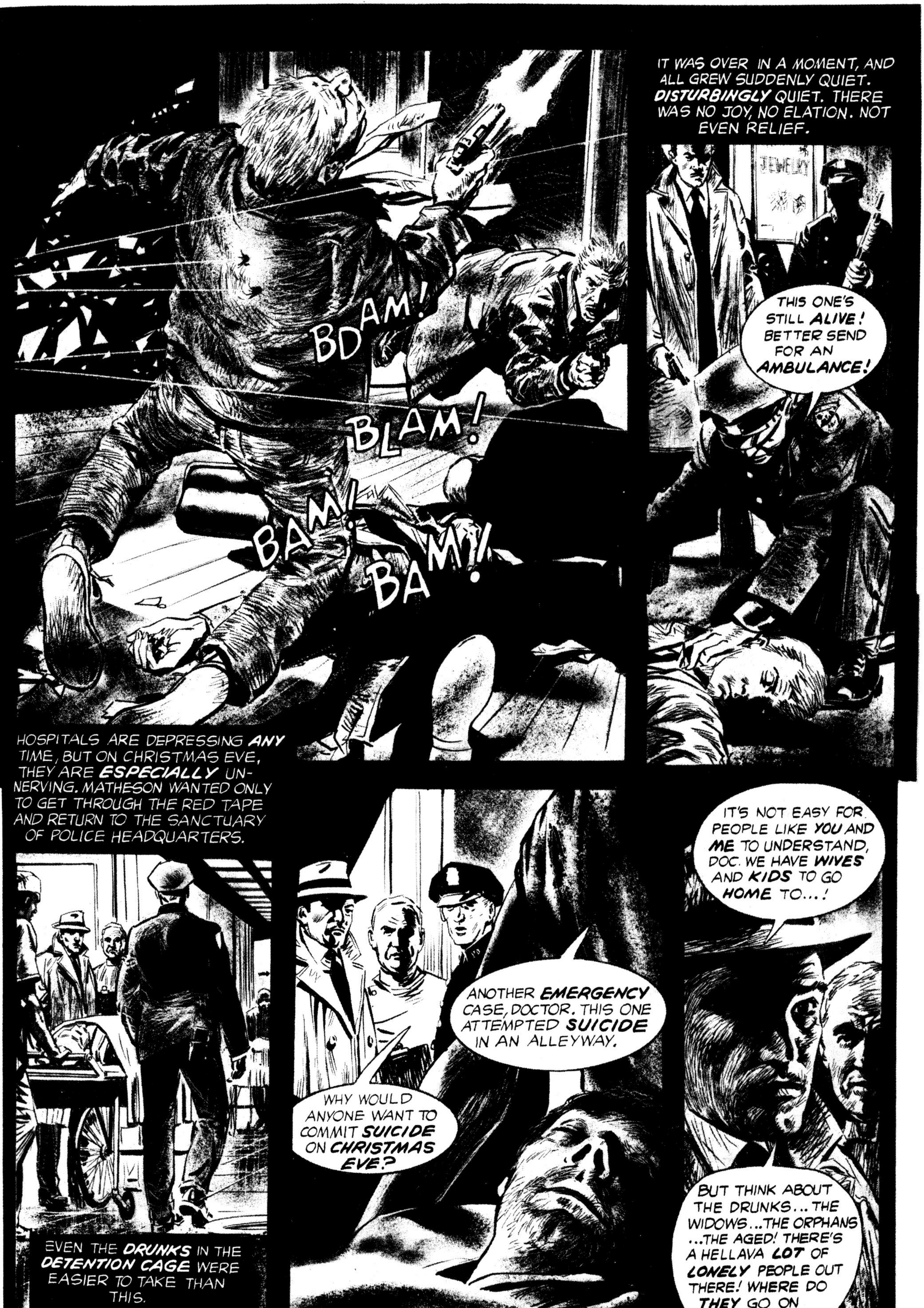
BDAM!
BLAM!
BAM!
BAM!
IT WAS OVER IN A MOMENT, AND ALL GREW SUDDENLY QUIET. DISTURBINGLY QUIET. THERE WAS NO JOY, NO ELATION. NOT EVEN RELIEF.
JEWELRY
THIS ONE'S STILL ALIVE! BETTER SEND FOR AN AMBULANCE!
HOSPITALS ARE DEPRESSING ANY TIME, BUT ON CHRISTMAS EVE, THEY ARE ESPECIALLY UNNERVING. MATHESON WANTED ONLY TO GET THROUGH THE RED TAPE AND RETURN TO THE SANCTUARY OF POLICE HEADQUARTERS.
EVEN THE DRUNKS IN THE DETENTION CAGE WERE EASIER TO TAKE THAN THIS.
ANOTHER EMERGENCY CASE, DOCTOR. THIS ONE ATTEMPTED SUICIDE IN AN ALLEYWAY.
WHY WOULD ANYONE WANT TO COMMIT SUICIDE ON CHRISTMAS EVE?
IT'S NOT EASY FOR PEOPLE LIKE YOU AND ME TO UNDERSTAND, DOC. WE HAVE WIVES AND KIDS TO GO HOME TO...!
BUT THINK ABOUT THE DRUNKS... THE WIDOWS...THE ORPHANS ...THE AGED! THERE'S A HELLAVA LOT OF LONELY PEOPLE OUT THERE! WHERE DO THEY GO ON CHRISTMAS?

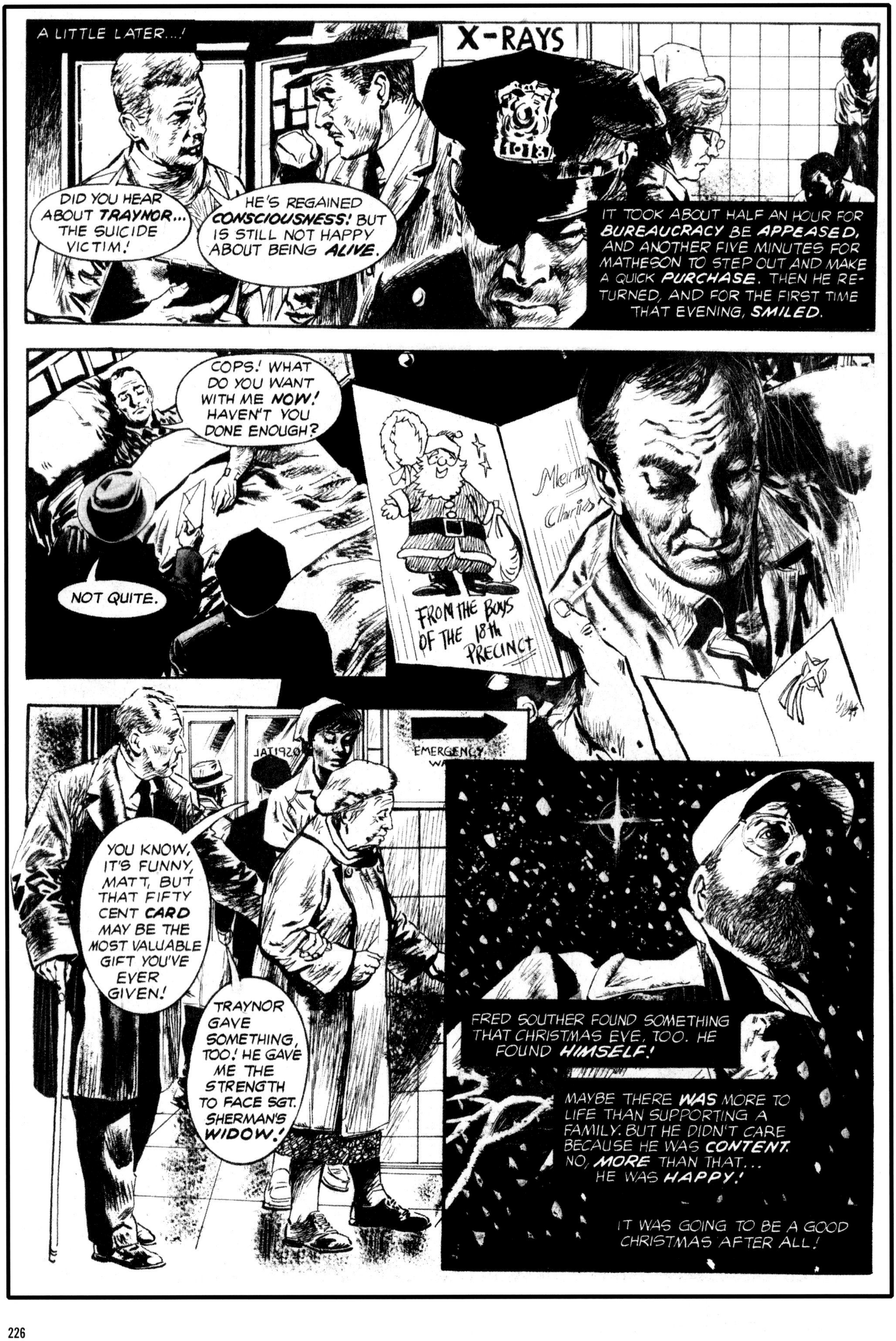
A LITTLE LATER...!
X-RAYS
DID YOU HEAR ABOUT TRAYNOR... THE SUICIDE VICTIM!
HE'S REGAINED CONSCIOUSNESS! BUT IS STILL NOT HAPPY ABOUT BEING ALIVE.
IT TOOK ABOUT HALF AN HOUR FOR BUREAUCRACY BE APPEASED, AND ANOTHER FIVE MINUTES FOR MATHESON TO STEP OUT AND MAKE A QUICK PURCHASE. THEN HE RETURNED, AND FOR THE FIRST TIME THAT EVENING, SMILED.
COPS! WHAT DO YOU WANT WITH ME NOW! HAVEN'T YOU DONE ENOUGH?
NOT QUITE.
FROM THE BOYS OF THE 18th PRECINCT
EMERGENCY
YOU KNOW, IT'S FUNNY, MATT, BUT THAT FIFTY CENT CARD MAY BE THE MOST VALUABLE GIFT YOU'VE EVER GIVEN!
TRAYNOR GAVE SOMETHING, TOO! HE GAVE ME THE STRENGTH TO FACE SGT. SHERMAN'S WIDOW!
FRED SOUTHER FOUND SOMETHING THAT CHRISTMAS EVE, TOO. HE FOUND HIMSELF!
MAYBE THERE WAS MORE TO LIFE THAN SUPPORTING A FAMILY. BUT HE DIDN'T CARE BECAUSE HE WAS CONTENT. NO, MORE THAN THAT... HE WAS HAPPY!
IT WAS GOING TO BE A GOOD CHRISTMAS AFTER ALL!

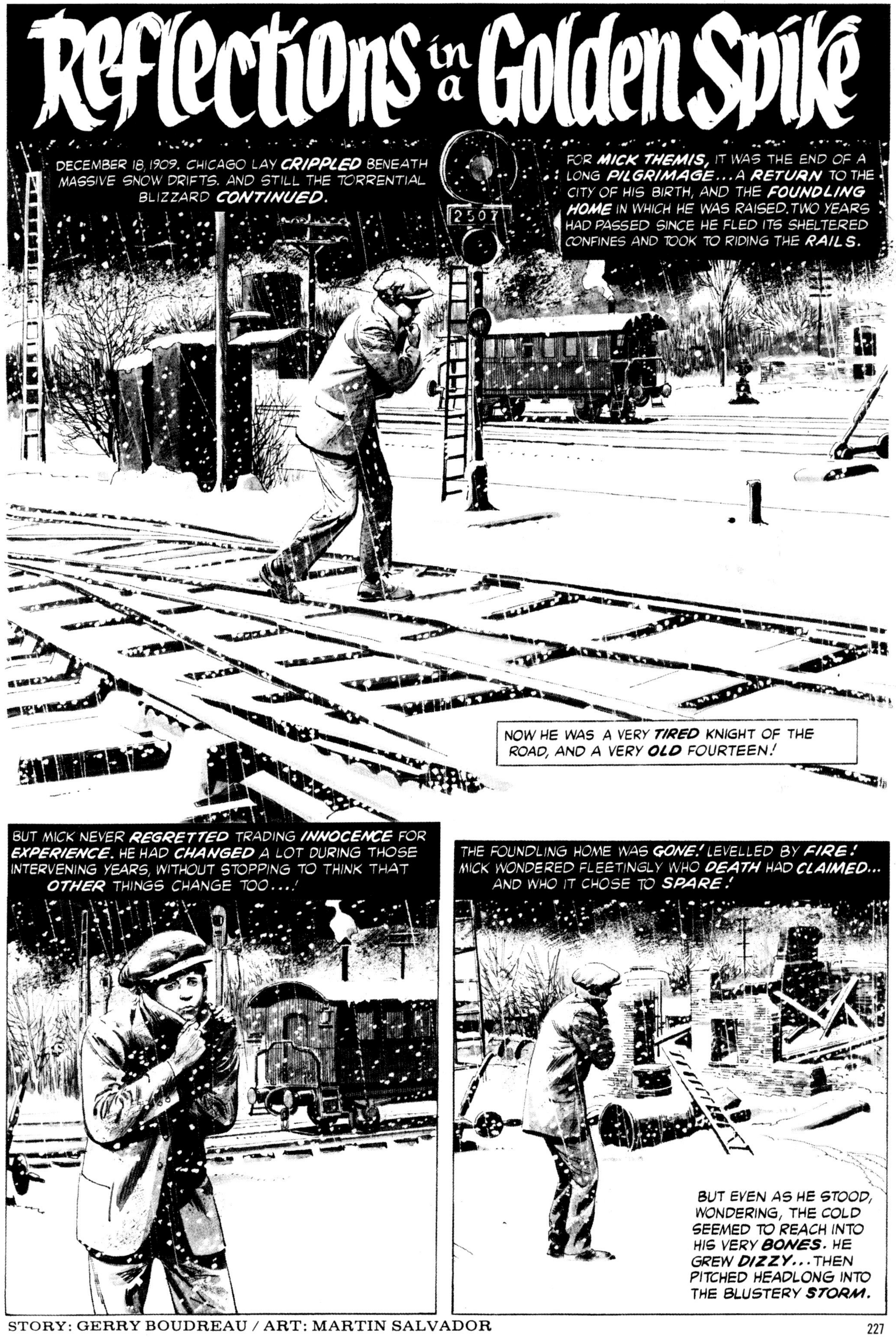
Reflections in a Golden Spike
DECEMBER 18, 1909. CHICAGO LAY CRIPPLED BENEATH MASSIVE SNOW DRIFTS. AND STILL THE TORRENTIAL BLIZZARD CONTINUED.
FOR MICK THEMIS, IT WAS THE END OF A LONG PILGRIMAGE... A RETURN TO THE CITY OF HIS BIRTH, AND THE FOUNDLING HOME IN WHICH HE WAS RAISED. TWO YEARS HAD PASSED SINCE HE FLED ITS SHELTERED CONFINES AND TOOK TO RIDING THE RAILS.
2507
NOW HE WAS A VERY TIRED KNIGHT OF THE ROAD, AND A VERY OLD FOURTEEN!
BUT MICK NEVER REGRETTED TRADING INNOCENCE FOR EXPERIENCE. HE HAD CHANGED A LOT DURING THOSE INTERVENING YEARS, WITHOUT STOPPING TO THINK THAT OTHER THINGS CHANGE TOO...!
THE FOUNDLING HOME WAS GONE! LEVELLED BY FIRE! MICK WONDERED FLEETINGLY WHO DEATH HAD CLAIMED... AND WHO IT CHOSE TO SPARE!
BUT EVEN AS HE STOOD, WONDERING, THE COLD SEEMED TO REACH INTO HIS VERY BONES. HE GREW DIZZY... THEN PITCHED HEADLONG INTO THE BLUSTERY STORM.

STORY: GERRY BOUDREAU / ART: MARTIN SALVADOR

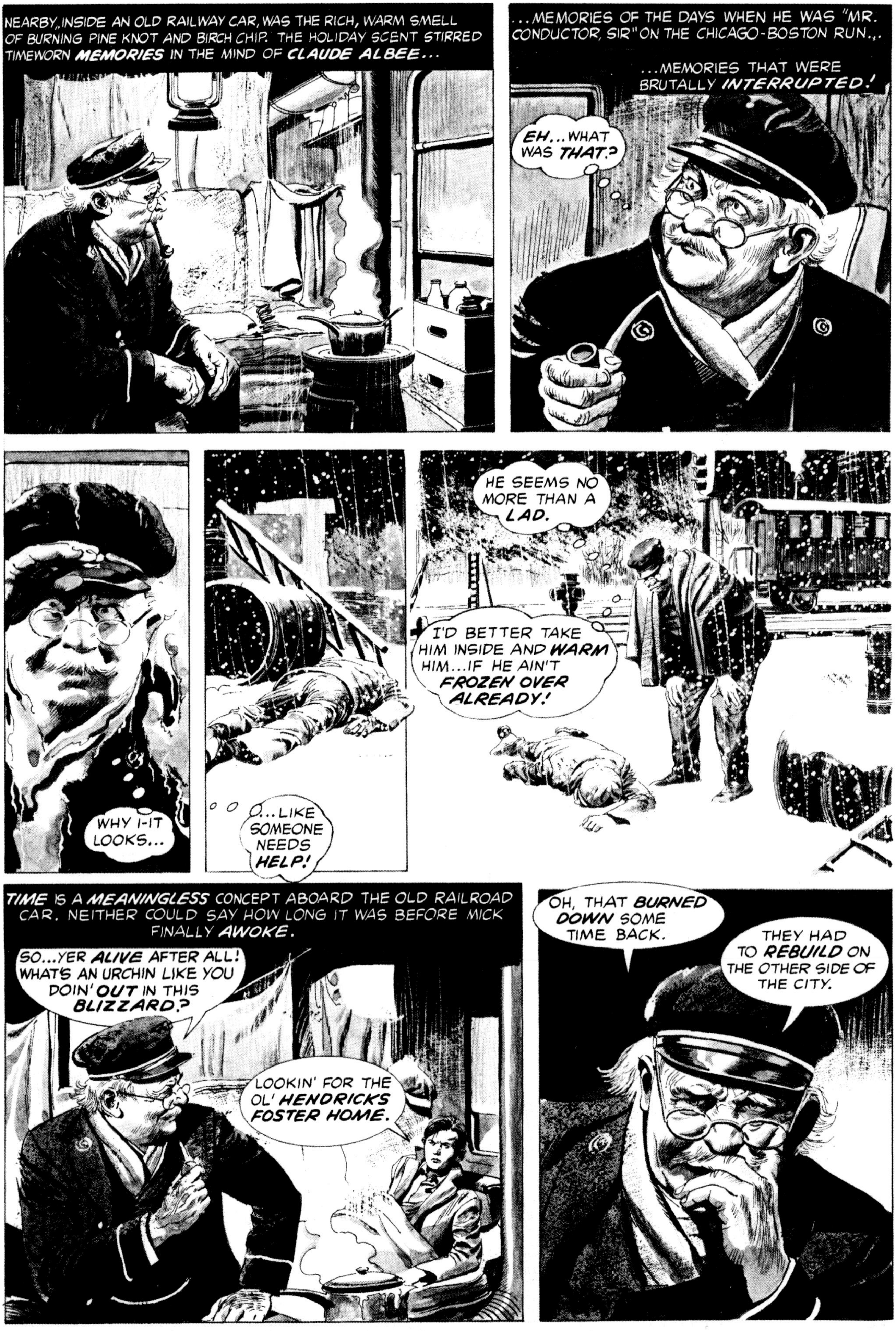
NEARBY, INSIDE AN OLD RAILWAY CAR, WAS THE RICH, WARM SMELL OF BURNING PINE KNOT AND BIRCH CHIP. THE HOLIDAY SCENT STIRRED TIMEWORN MEMORIES IN THE MIND OF CLAUDE ALBEE...
...MEMORIES OF THE DAYS WHEN HE WAS "MR. CONDUCTOR, SIR" ON THE CHICAGO-BOSTON RUN...
...MEMORIES THAT WERE BRUTALLY INTERRUPTED!
EH...WHAT WAS THAT?
WHY I-IT LOOKS...
...LIKE SOMEONE NEEDS HELP!
HE SEEMS NO MORE THAN A LAD.
I'D BETTER TAKE HIM INSIDE AND WARM HIM...IF HE AIN'T FROZEN OVER ALREADY!
TIME IS A MEANINGLESS CONCEPT ABOARD THE OLD RAILROAD CAR. NEITHER COULD SAY HOW LONG IT WAS BEFORE MICK FINALLY AWOKE.
SO...YER ALIVE AFTER ALL! WHAT'S AN URCHIN LIKE YOU DOIN' OUT IN THIS BLIZZARD?
LOOKIN' FOR THE OL' HENDRICKS FOSTER HOME.
OH, THAT BURNED DOWN SOME TIME BACK.
THEY HAD TO REBUILD ON THE OTHER SIDE OF THE CITY.

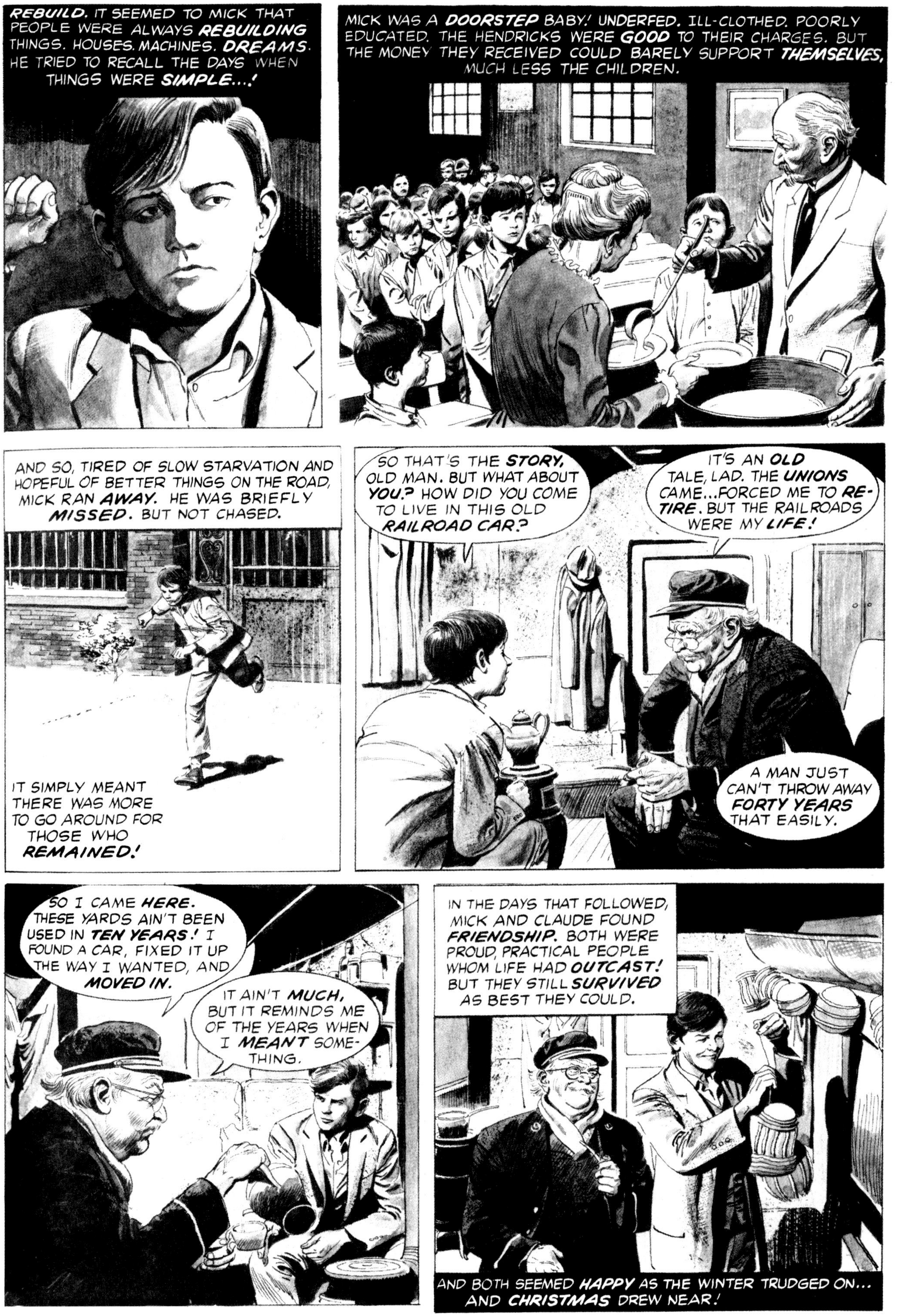
REBUILD. IT SEEMED TO MICK THAT PEOPLE WERE ALWAYS REBUILDING THINGS. HOUSES. MACHINES. DREAMS. HE TRIED TO RECALL THE DAYS WHEN THINGS WERE SIMPLE...!
MICK WAS A DOORSTEP BABY! UNDERFED. ILL-CLOTHED. POORLY EDUCATED. THE HENDRICKS WERE GOOD TO THEIR CHARGES. BUT THE MONEY THEY RECEIVED COULD BARELY SUPPORT THEMSELVES, MUCH LESS THE CHILDREN.
AND SO, TIRED OF SLOW STARVATION AND HOPEFUL OF BETTER THINGS ON THE ROAD, MICK RAN AWAY. HE WAS BRIEFLY MISSED. BUT NOT CHASED.
IT SIMPLY MEANT THERE WAS MORE TO GO AROUND FOR THOSE WHO REMAINED!
SO THAT'S THE STORY, OLD MAN. BUT WHAT ABOUT YOU? HOW DID YOU COME TO LIVE IN THIS OLD RAILROAD CAR?
IT'S AN OLD TALE, LAD. THE UNIONS CAME...FORCED ME TO RETIRE. BUT THE RAILROADS WERE MY LIFE!
A MAN JUST CAN'T THROW AWAY FORTY YEARS THAT EASILY.
SO I CAME HERE. THESE YARDS AIN'T BEEN USED IN TEN YEARS! I FOUND A CAR, FIXED IT UP THE WAY I WANTED, AND MOVED IN.
IT AIN'T MUCH, BUT IT REMINDS ME OF THE YEARS WHEN I MEANT SOMETHING.
IN THE DAYS THAT FOLLOWED, MICK AND CLAUDE FOUND FRIENDSHIP. BOTH WERE PROUD, PRACTICAL PEOPLE WHOM LIFE HAD OUTCAST! BUT THEY STILL SURVIVED AS BEST THEY COULD.
AND BOTH SEEMED HAPPY AS THE WINTER TRUDGED ON... AND CHRISTMAS DREW NEAR!

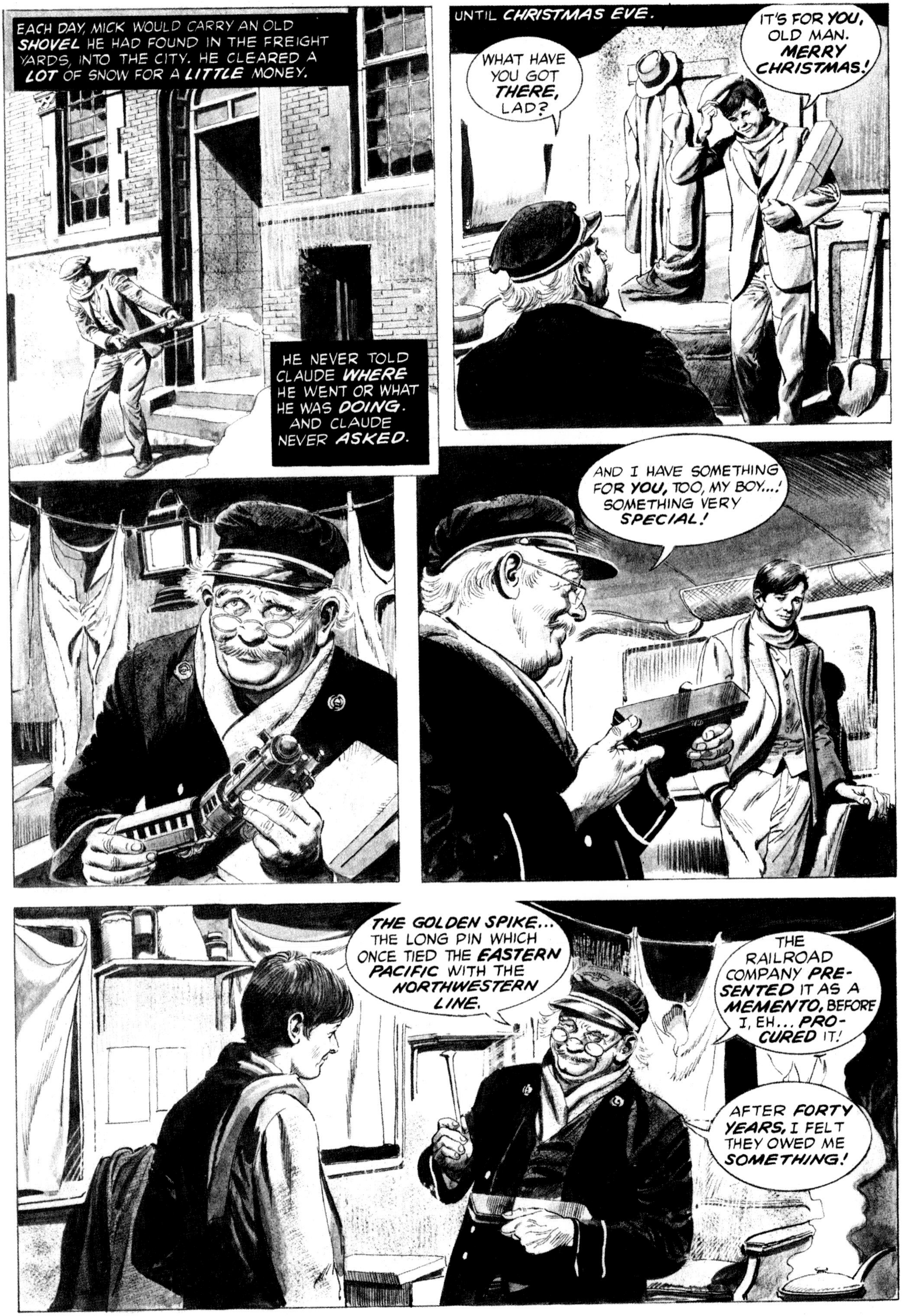
EACH DAY, MICK WOULD CARRY AN OLD SHOVEL HE HAD FOUND IN THE FREIGHT YARDS, INTO THE CITY. HE CLEARED A LOT OF SNOW FOR A LITTLE MONEY.
HE NEVER TOLD CLAUDE WHERE HE WENT OR WHAT HE WAS DOING. AND CLAUDE NEVER ASKED.
UNTIL CHRISTMAS EVE.
WHAT HAVE YOU GOT THERE, LAD?
IT'S FOR YOU, OLD MAN. MERRY CHRISTMAS!
AND I HAVE SOMETHING FOR YOU, TOO, MY BOY...! SOMETHING VERY SPECIAL!
THE GOLDEN SPIKE... THE LONG PIN WHICH ONCE TIED THE EASTERN PACIFIC WITH THE NORTHWESTERN LINE.
THE RAILROAD COMPANY PRESENTED IT AS A MEMENTO, BEFORE I, EH... PROCURED IT!
AFTER FORTY YEARS, I FELT THEY OWED ME SOMETHING!

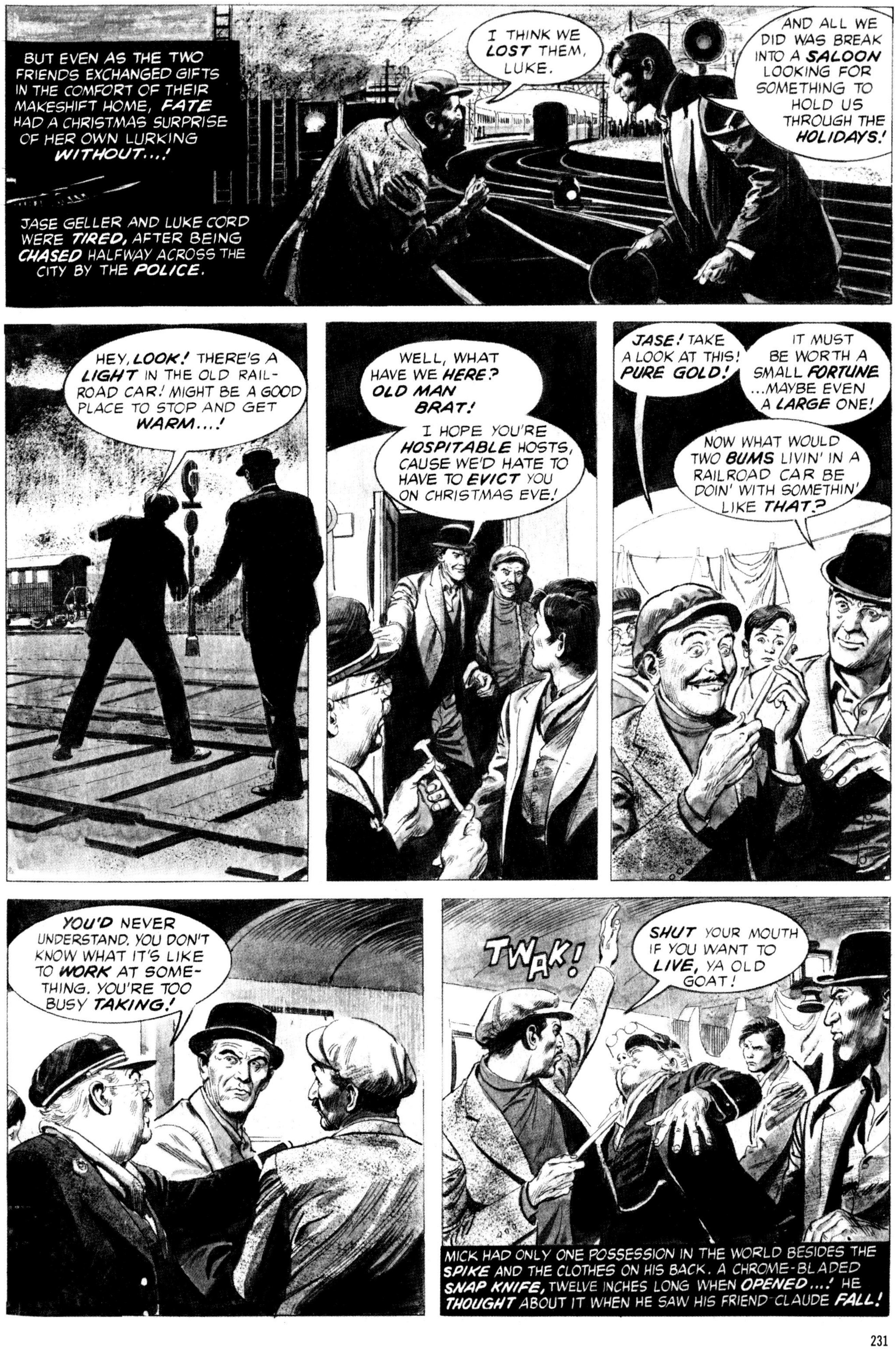

BUT EVEN AS THE TWO FRIENDS EXCHANGED GIFTS IN THE COMFORT OF THEIR MAKESHIFT HOME, FATE HAD A CHRISTMAS SURPRISE OF HER OWN LURKING WITHOUT...!
JASE GELLER AND LUKE CORD WERE TIRED, AFTER BEING CHASED HALFWAY ACROSS THE CITY BY THE POLICE.
I THINK WE LOST THEM, LUKE.
AND ALL WE DID WAS BREAK INTO A SALOON LOOKING FOR SOMETHING TO HOLD US THROUGH THE HOLIDAYS!
HEY, LOOK! THERE'S A LIGHT IN THE OLD RAIL-ROAD CAR! MIGHT BE A GOOD PLACE TO STOP AND GET WARM...!
WELL, WHAT HAVE WE HERE? OLD MAN BRAT!
I HOPE YOU'RE HOSPITABLE HOSTS, CAUSE WE'D HATE TO HAVE TO EVICT YOU ON CHRISTMAS EVE!
JASE! TAKE A LOOK AT THIS! PURE GOLD!
IT MUST BE WORTH A SMALL FORTUNE ...MAYBE EVEN A LARGE ONE!
NOW WHAT WOULD TWO BUMS LIVIN' IN A RAILROAD CAR BE DOIN' WITH SOMETHIN' LIKE THAT?
YOU'D NEVER UNDERSTAND. YOU DON'T KNOW WHAT IT'S LIKE TO WORK AT SOME-THING. YOU'RE TOO BUSY TAKING!
TWAK!
SHUT YOUR MOUTH IF YOU WANT TO LIVE, YA OLD GOAT!
MICK HAD ONLY ONE POSSESSION IN THE WORLD BESIDES THE SPIKE AND THE CLOTHES ON HIS BACK. A CHROME-BLADED SNAP KNIFE, TWELVE INCHES LONG WHEN OPENED...! HE THOUGHT ABOUT IT WHEN HE SAW HIS FRIEND CLAUDE FALL!

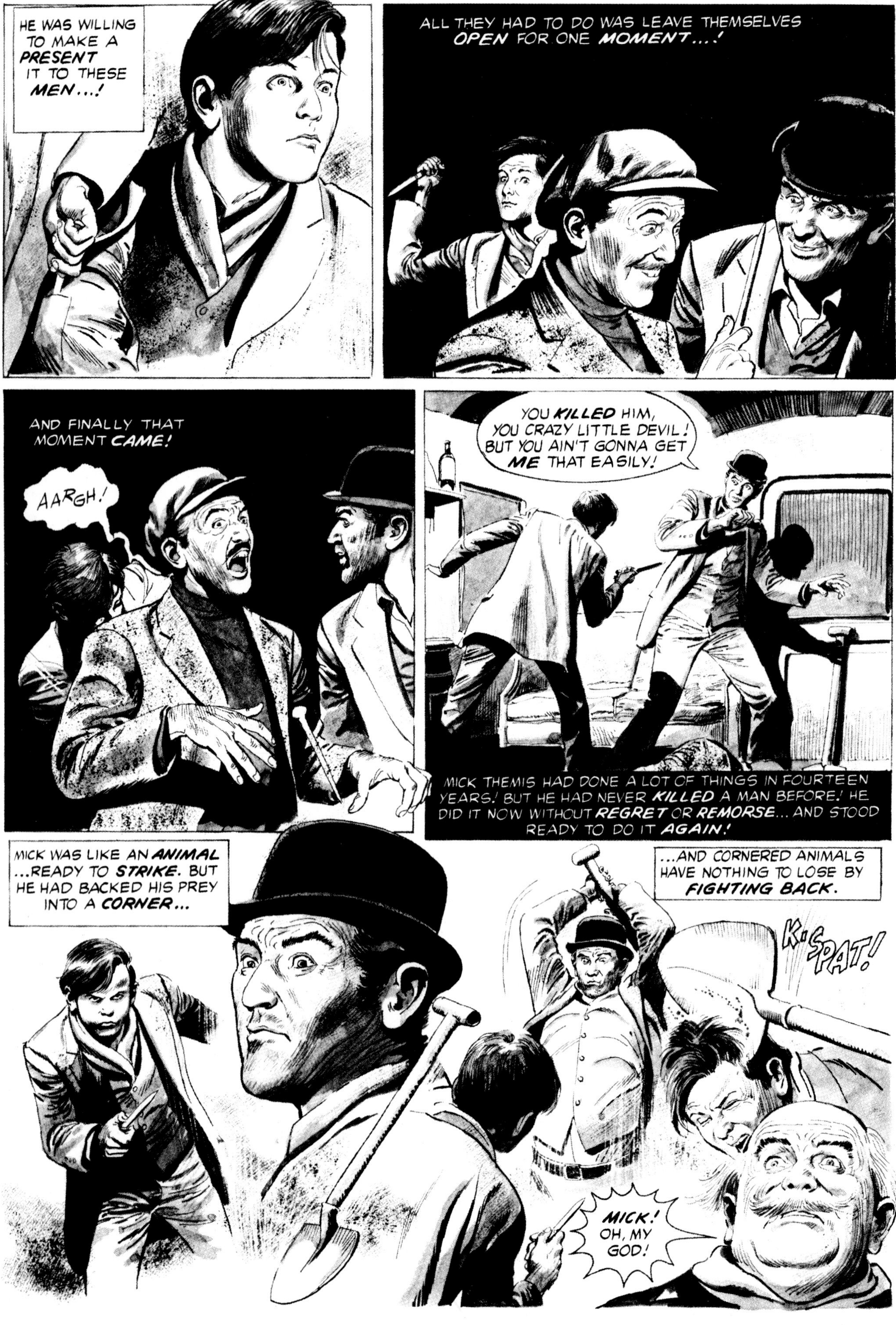
HE WAS WILLING TO MAKE A PRESENT IT TO THESE MEN...!
ALL THEY HAD TO DO WAS LEAVE THEMSELVES OPEN FOR ONE MOMENT...!
AND FINALLY THAT MOMENT CAME!
AARGH!
YOU KILLED HIM, YOU CRAZY LITTLE DEVIL! BUT YOU AIN'T GONNA GET ME THAT EASILY!
MICK THEMIS HAD DONE A LOT OF THINGS IN FOURTEEN YEARS! BUT HE HAD NEVER KILLED A MAN BEFORE! HE DID IT NOW WITHOUT REGRET OR REMORSE... AND STOOD READY TO DO IT AGAIN!
MICK WAS LIKE AN ANIMAL ...READY TO STRIKE. BUT HE HAD BACKED HIS PREY INTO A CORNER...
...AND CORNERED ANIMALS HAVE NOTHING TO LOSE BY FIGHTING BACK.
K-SPAT!
MICK! OH, MY GOD!

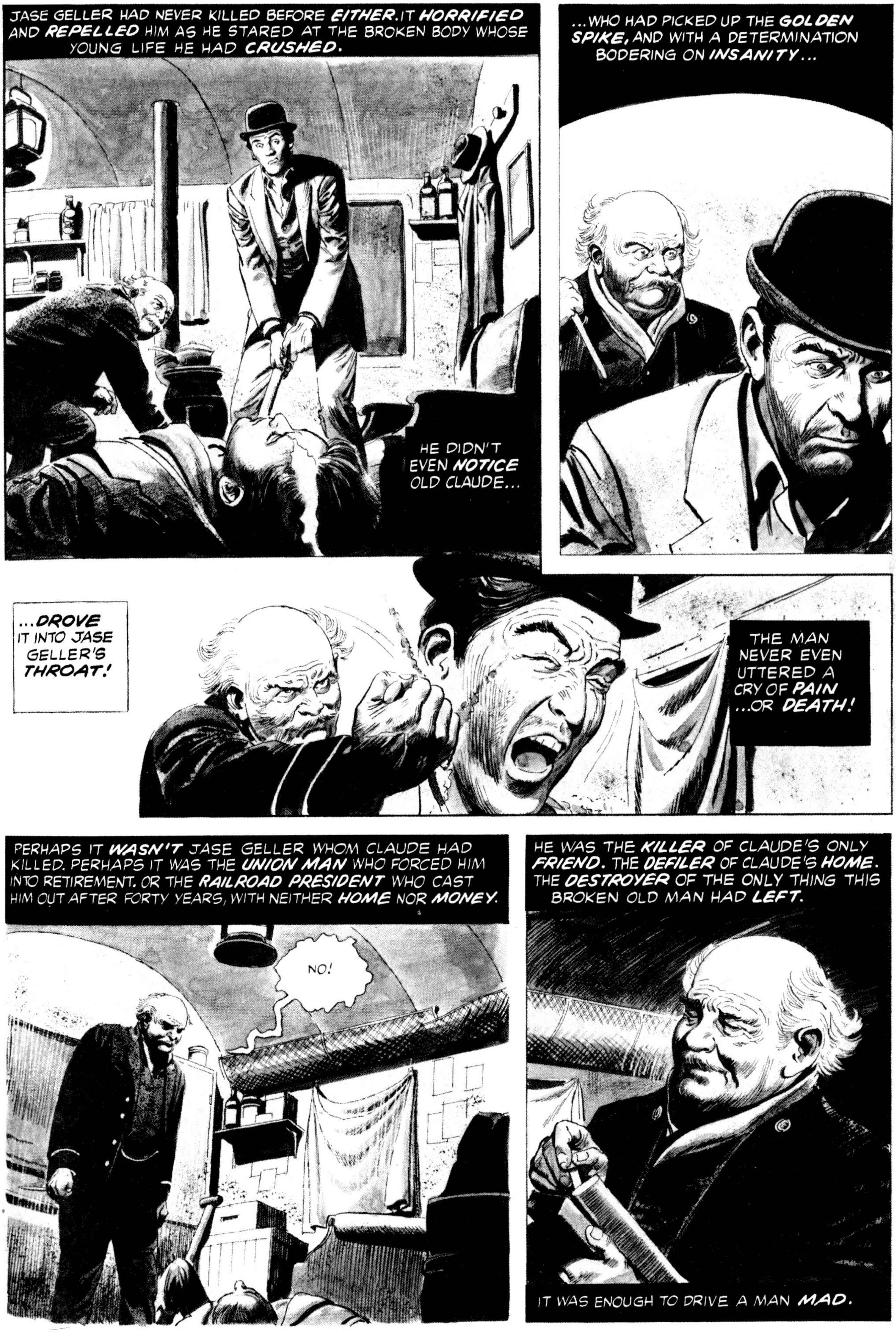

JASE GELLER HAD NEVER KILLED BEFORE EITHER. IT HORRIFIED AND REPELLED HIM AS HE STARED AT THE BROKEN BODY WHOSE YOUNG LIFE HE HAD CRUSHED.
HE DIDN'T EVEN NOTICE OLD CLAUDE...
...WHO HAD PICKED UP THE GOLDEN SPIKE, AND WITH A DETERMINATION BODERING ON INSANITY...
...DROVE IT INTO JASE GELLER'S THROAT!
THE MAN NEVER EVEN UTTERED A CRY OF PAIN ...OR DEATH!
PERHAPS IT WASN'T JASE GELLER WHOM CLAUDE HAD KILLED. PERHAPS IT WAS THE UNION MAN WHO FORCED HIM INTO RETIREMENT. OR THE RAILROAD PRESIDENT WHO CAST HIM OUT AFTER FORTY YEARS, WITH NEITHER HOME NOR MONEY.
NO!
HE WAS THE KILLER OF CLAUDE'S ONLY FRIEND. THE DEFILER OF CLAUDE'S HOME. THE DESTROYER OF THE ONLY THING THIS BROKEN OLD MAN HAD LEFT.
IT WAS ENOUGH TO DRIVE A MAN MAD.

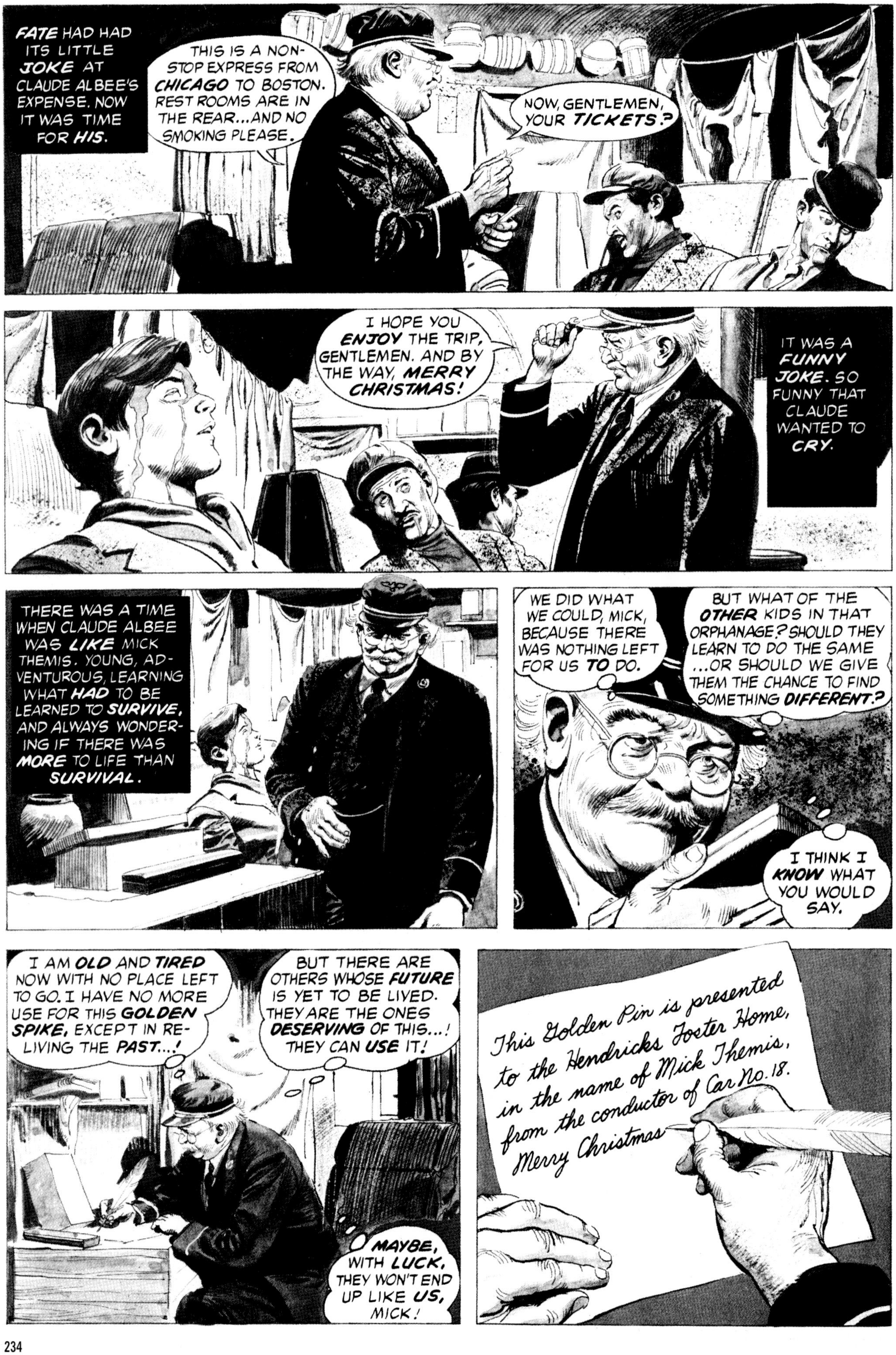
FATE HAD HAD ITS LITTLE JOKE AT CLAUDE ALBEE'S EXPENSE. NOW IT WAS TIME FOR HIS.
THIS IS A NON-STOP EXPRESS FROM CHICAGO TO BOSTON. REST ROOMS ARE IN THE REAR...AND NO SMOKING PLEASE.
NOW, GENTLEMEN, YOUR TICKETS?
I HOPE YOU ENJOY THE TRIP, GENTLEMEN. AND BY THE WAY, MERRY CHRISTMAS!
IT WAS A FUNNY JOKE. SO FUNNY THAT CLAUDE WANTED TO CRY.
THERE WAS A TIME WHEN CLAUDE ALBEE WAS LIKE MICK THEMIS. YOUNG, ADVENTUROUS, LEARNING WHAT HAD TO BE LEARNED TO SURVIVE, AND ALWAYS WONDERING IF THERE WAS MORE TO LIFE THAN SURVIVAL.
WE DID WHAT WE COULD, MICK, BECAUSE THERE WAS NOTHING LEFT FOR US TO DO.
BUT WHAT OF THE OTHER KIDS IN THAT ORPHANAGE? SHOULD THEY LEARN TO DO THE SAME ...OR SHOULD WE GIVE THEM THE CHANCE TO FIND SOMETHING DIFFERENT?
I THINK I KNOW WHAT YOU WOULD SAY.
I AM OLD AND TIRED NOW WITH NO PLACE LEFT TO GO. I HAVE NO MORE USE FOR THIS GOLDEN SPIKE, EXCEPT IN RELIVING THE PAST...!
BUT THERE ARE OTHERS WHOSE FUTURE IS YET TO BE LIVED. THEY ARE THE ONES DESERVING OF THIS...! THEY CAN USE IT!
MAYBE, WITH LUCK, THEY WON'T END UP LIKE US, MICK!
This Golden Pin is presented
to the Hendricks Foster Home,
in the name of Mick Themis,
from the conductor of Car No. 18.
Merry Christmas

Anti-Christmas

"YOU HAVE HEARD THAT THE *ANTICHRIST* IS COMING... THEREFORE WE KNOW THAT IT IS THE *LAST HOUR...!* (JOHN 2:18)

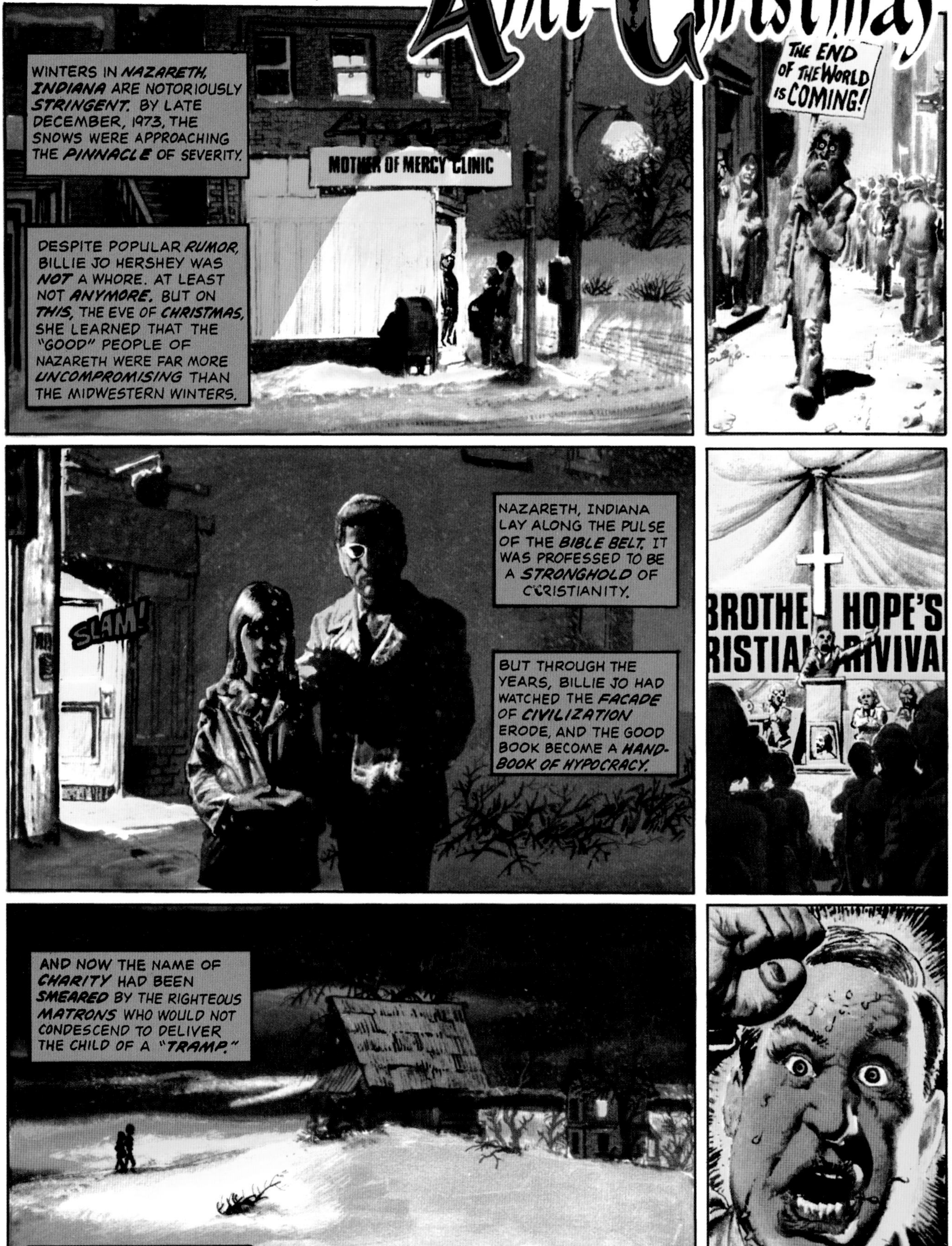

WINTERS IN *NAZARETH, INDIANA* ARE NOTORIOUSLY *STRINGENT.* BY LATE DECEMBER, 1973, THE SNOWS WERE APPROACHING THE *PINNACLE* OF SEVERITY.
MOTHER OF MERCY CLINIC
DESPITE POPULAR *RUMOR,* BILLIE JO HERSHEY WAS *NOT* A WHORE. AT LEAST NOT *ANYMORE.* BUT ON *THIS,* THE EVE OF *CHRISTMAS,* SHE LEARNED THAT THE "*GOOD*" PEOPLE OF NAZARETH WERE FAR MORE *UNCOMPROMISING* THAN THE MIDWESTERN WINTERS.
THE END OF THE WORLD IS COMING!
SLAM!
NAZARETH, INDIANA LAY ALONG THE PULSE OF THE *BIBLE BELT.* IT WAS PROFESSED TO BE A *STRONGHOLD* OF CHRISTIANITY.
BUT THROUGH THE YEARS, BILLIE JO HAD WATCHED THE *FACADE* OF *CIVILIZATION* ERODE, AND THE GOOD BOOK BECOME A *HAND-BOOK OF HYPOCRACY.*
BROTHE HOPE'S
RISTIA RIVIVA
AND NOW THE NAME OF *CHARITY* HAD BEEN *SMEARED* BY THE RIGHTEOUS *MATRONS* WHO WOULD NOT CONDESCEND TO DELIVER THE CHILD OF A "*TRAMP.*"
BILLIE JO WONDERED WHAT THIS WORLD WAS *COMING* TO.

STORY: GERRY BOUDREAU / ART: RICH CORBEN

BILLIE JO SLOWLY SUCCUMBED TO THE DEMANDS OF *UNCONSCIOUSNESS*, AND HER THOUGHTS FELL UPON *ANOTHER TIME*, SOME TWO YEARS EARLIER....!

BILLIE JO'S PAINS WERE GROWING MORE ACUTE, MORE *FREQUENT*. HER MUFFLED *CRIES* FILLED THE SILENT STABLE. JOSEPH *CLOSED* HIMSELF TO THEM, LEST THEY *CRIPPLE* HIM TO THE INEVITABLE *TASK* THAT AWAITED.

I *KNOW* THAT YOU AND THAT YOUNG HOODLUM HAVE *SINNED* AGAINST *GOD* AND AGAINST *ME!* NOW YOU *COMPOUND* THE OFFENSE BY *LYING....!*

I WILL *NOT* HAVE IT SAID THAT MY DAUGHTER IS A CHILD OF THE *DEVIL*. YOU ARE NO LONGER *WELCOME* IN MY HOUSE....!

IN THE WEEKS THAT FOLLOWED, BILLIE JO LEARNED TWO THINGS. POVERTY BEGETS *MORE* POVERTY, AND *DESTITUTION* IS A SHORT STEP FROM *PROSTITUTION*.

THEN SHE MET JOSEPH. NOT *RICH*, PERHAPS, BUT PROUD. AND PRIDE WAS SOMETHING *SHE* HAD SACRIFICED A LONG TIME AGO.

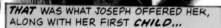

THAT WAS WHAT JOSEPH OFFERED HER, ALONG WITH HER FIRST *CHILD*...

...*THIS* CHILD, FOR WHOM JOSEPH WAS NOW THE RELUCTANT *MIDWIFE*.

ALL THOUGHT FLED FROM BILLIE JO'S MIND, AND SHE *SURRENDERED* TO THE PAIN

IT IS *DONE*, JOSEPH? THEN *GIVE* US THE CHILD...SHE WILL NEVER *KNOW* THAT THIS ONE IS NOT *HERS*.

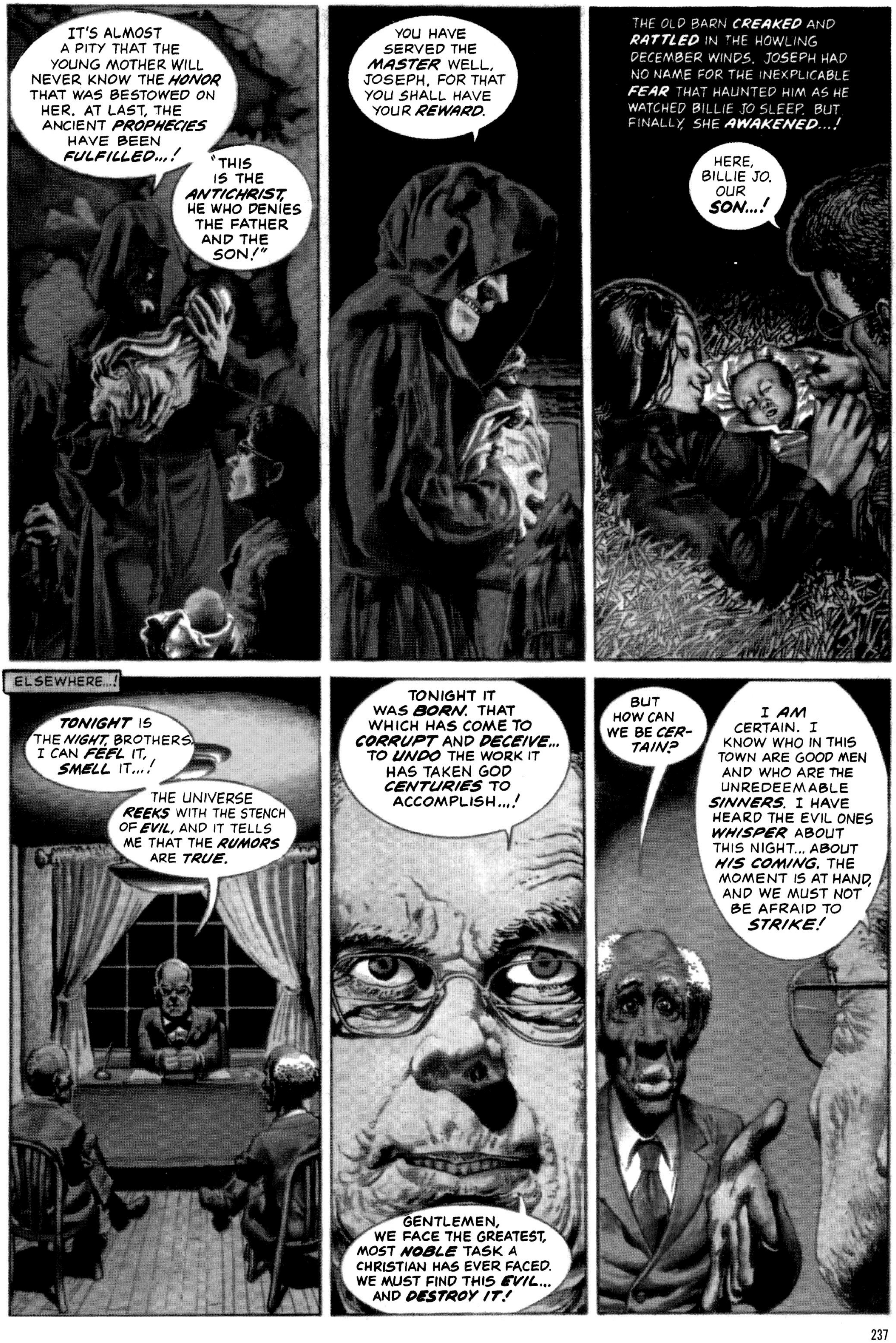
IT'S ALMOST A PITY THAT THE YOUNG MOTHER WILL NEVER KNOW THE HONOR THAT WAS BESTOWED ON HER. AT LAST, THE ANCIENT PROPHECIES HAVE BEEN FULFILLED...!
"THIS IS THE ANTICHRIST, HE WHO DENIES THE FATHER AND THE SON!"
YOU HAVE SERVED THE MASTER WELL, JOSEPH. FOR THAT YOU SHALL HAVE YOUR REWARD.
THE OLD BARN CREAKED AND RATTLED IN THE HOWLING DECEMBER WINDS. JOSEPH HAD NO NAME FOR THE INEXPLICABLE FEAR THAT HAUNTED HIM AS HE WATCHED BILLIE JO SLEEP. BUT FINALLY, SHE AWAKENED...!
HERE, BILLIE JO. OUR SON...!
ELSEWHERE...!
TONIGHT IS THE NIGHT, BROTHERS. I CAN FEEL IT, SMELL IT...!
THE UNIVERSE REEKS WITH THE STENCH OF EVIL, AND IT TELLS ME THAT THE RUMORS ARE TRUE.
TONIGHT IT WAS BORN. THAT WHICH HAS COME TO CORRUPT AND DECEIVE... TO UNDO THE WORK IT HAS TAKEN GOD CENTURIES TO ACCOMPLISH...!
GENTLEMEN, WE FACE THE GREATEST, MOST NOBLE TASK A CHRISTIAN HAS EVER FACED. WE MUST FIND THIS EVIL... AND DESTROY IT!
BUT HOW CAN WE BE CER-TAIN?
I AM CERTAIN. I KNOW WHO IN THIS TOWN ARE GOOD MEN AND WHO ARE THE UNREDEEMABLE SINNERS. I HAVE HEARD THE EVIL ONES WHISPER ABOUT THIS NIGHT... ABOUT HIS COMING. THE MOMENT IS AT HAND, AND WE MUST NOT BE AFRAID TO STRIKE!

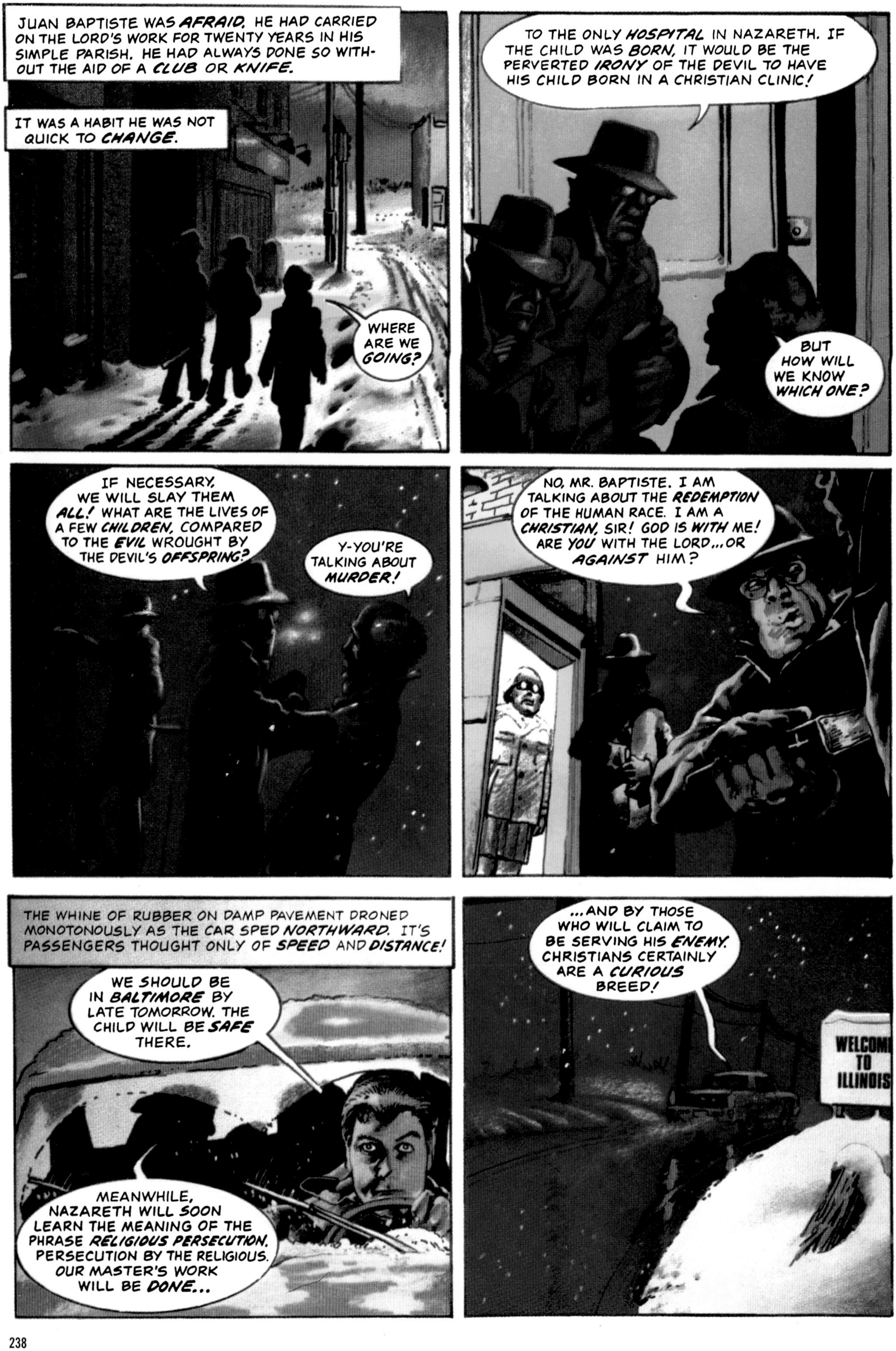
JUAN BAPTISTE WAS AFRAID. HE HAD CARRIED ON THE LORD'S WORK FOR TWENTY YEARS IN HIS SIMPLE PARISH. HE HAD ALWAYS DONE SO WITHOUT THE AID OF A CLUB OR KNIFE.
IT WAS A HABIT HE WAS NOT QUICK TO CHANGE.
WHERE ARE WE GOING?
TO THE ONLY HOSPITAL IN NAZARETH. IF THE CHILD WAS BORN, IT WOULD BE THE PERVERTED IRONY OF THE DEVIL TO HAVE HIS CHILD BORN IN A CHRISTIAN CLINIC!
BUT HOW WILL WE KNOW WHICH ONE?
IF NECESSARY, WE WILL SLAY THEM ALL! WHAT ARE THE LIVES OF A FEW CHILDREN, COMPARED TO THE EVIL WROUGHT BY THE DEVIL'S OFFSPRING?
Y-YOU'RE TALKING ABOUT MURDER!
NO, MR. BAPTISTE. I AM TALKING ABOUT THE REDEMPTION OF THE HUMAN RACE. I AM A CHRISTIAN, SIR! GOD IS WITH ME! ARE YOU WITH THE LORD...OR AGAINST HIM?
THE WHINE OF RUBBER ON DAMP PAVEMENT DRONED MONOTONOUSLY AS THE CAR SPED NORTHWARD. IT'S PASSENGERS THOUGHT ONLY OF SPEED AND DISTANCE!
WE SHOULD BE IN BALTIMORE BY LATE TOMORROW. THE CHILD WILL BE SAFE THERE.
MEANWHILE, NAZARETH WILL SOON LEARN THE MEANING OF THE PHRASE RELIGIOUS PERSECUTION. PERSECUTION BY THE RELIGIOUS. OUR MASTER'S WORK WILL BE DONE...
...AND BY THOSE WHO WILL CLAIM TO BE SERVING HIS ENEMY. CHRISTIANS CERTAINLY ARE A CURIOUS BREED!
WELCOM TO ILLINOIS

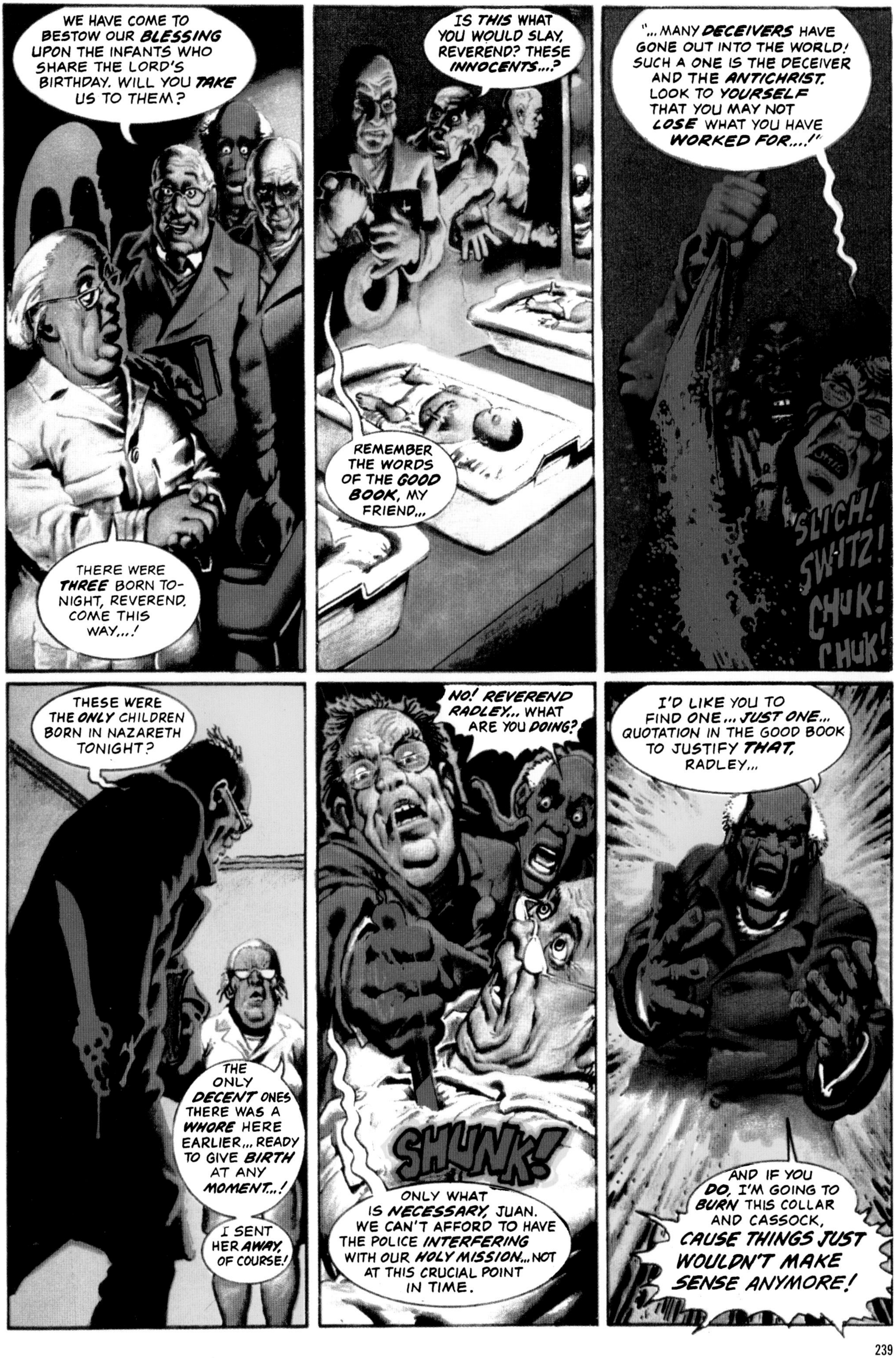
WE HAVE COME TO BESTOW OUR BLESSING UPON THE INFANTS WHO SHARE THE LORD'S BIRTHDAY. WILL YOU TAKE US TO THEM?
THERE WERE THREE BORN TO-NIGHT, REVEREND. COME THIS WAY...!
IS THIS WHAT YOU WOULD SLAY, REVEREND? THESE INNOCENTS...?
REMEMBER THE WORDS OF THE GOOD BOOK, MY FRIEND...
"...MANY DECEIVERS HAVE GONE OUT INTO THE WORLD! SUCH A ONE IS THE DECEIVER AND THE ANTICHRIST. LOOK TO YOURSELF THAT YOU MAY NOT LOSE WHAT YOU HAVE WORKED FOR...!"
SLICH! SWITZ! CHUK! CHUK!
THESE WERE THE ONLY CHILDREN BORN IN NAZARETH TONIGHT?
THE ONLY DECENT ONES. THERE WAS A WHORE HERE EARLIER... READY TO GIVE BIRTH AT ANY MOMENT...!
I SENT HER AWAY, OF COURSE!
NO! REVEREND RADLEY... WHAT ARE YOU DOING?
SHUNK!
ONLY WHAT IS NECESSARY, JUAN. WE CAN'T AFFORD TO HAVE THE POLICE INTERFERING WITH OUR HOLY MISSION... NOT AT THIS CRUCIAL POINT IN TIME.
I'D LIKE YOU TO FIND ONE... JUST ONE... QUOTATION IN THE GOOD BOOK TO JUSTIFY THAT, RADLEY...
AND IF YOU DO, I'M GOING TO BURN THIS COLLAR AND CASSOCK, CAUSE THINGS JUST WOULDN'T MAKE SENSE ANYMORE!

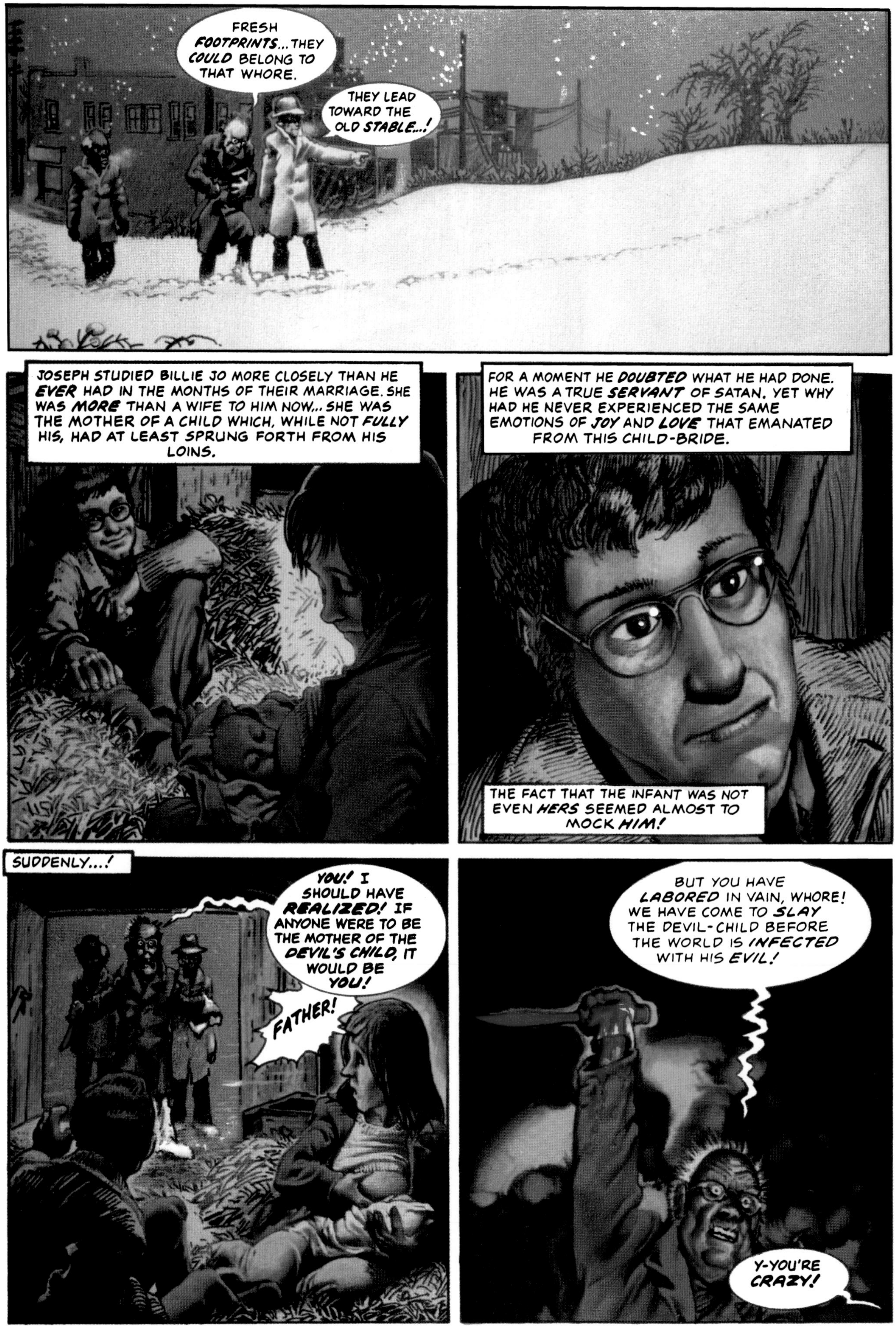

FRESH FOOTPRINTS... THEY COULD BELONG TO THAT WHORE.
THEY LEAD TOWARD THE OLD STABLE...!
JOSEPH STUDIED BILLIE JO MORE CLOSELY THAN HE EVER HAD IN THE MONTHS OF THEIR MARRIAGE. SHE WAS MORE THAN A WIFE TO HIM NOW... SHE WAS THE MOTHER OF A CHILD WHICH, WHILE NOT FULLY HIS, HAD AT LEAST SPRUNG FORTH FROM HIS LOINS.
FOR A MOMENT HE DOUBTED WHAT HE HAD DONE. HE WAS A TRUE SERVANT OF SATAN. YET WHY HAD HE NEVER EXPERIENCED THE SAME EMOTIONS OF JOY AND LOVE THAT EMANATED FROM THIS CHILD-BRIDE.
THE FACT THAT THE INFANT WAS NOT EVEN HERS SEEMED ALMOST TO MOCK HIM!
SUDDENLY...!
YOU! I SHOULD HAVE REALIZED! IF ANYONE WERE TO BE THE MOTHER OF THE DEVIL'S CHILD, IT WOULD BE YOU!
FATHER!
BUT YOU HAVE LABORED IN VAIN, WHORE! WE HAVE COME TO SLAY THE DEVIL-CHILD BEFORE THE WORLD IS INFECTED WITH HIS EVIL!
Y-YOU'RE CRAZY!

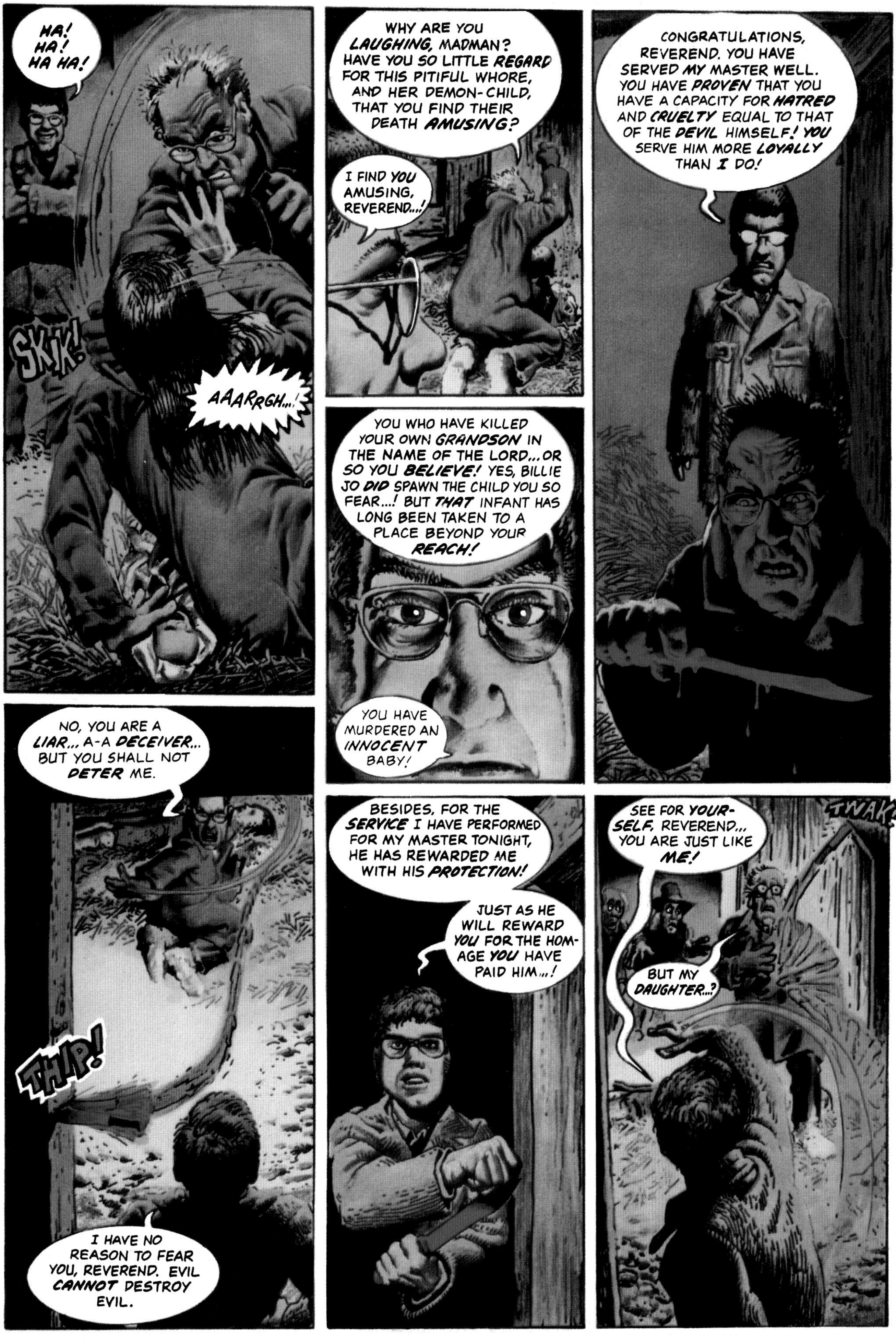
HA! HA! HA HA!
SKIK!
AAARRGH...!
WHY ARE YOU LAUGHING, MADMAN? HAVE YOU SO LITTLE REGARD FOR THIS PITIFUL WHORE, AND HER DEMON-CHILD, THAT YOU FIND THEIR DEATH AMUSING?
I FIND YOU AMUSING, REVEREND...!
YOU WHO HAVE KILLED YOUR OWN GRANDSON IN THE NAME OF THE LORD...OR SO YOU BELIEVE! YES, BILLIE JO DID SPAWN THE CHILD YOU SO FEAR...! BUT THAT INFANT HAS LONG BEEN TAKEN TO A PLACE BEYOND YOUR REACH!
YOU HAVE MURDERED AN INNOCENT BABY!
CONGRATULATIONS, REVEREND. YOU HAVE SERVED MY MASTER WELL. YOU HAVE PROVEN THAT YOU HAVE A CAPACITY FOR HATRED AND CRUELTY EQUAL TO THAT OF THE DEVIL HIMSELF! YOU SERVE HIM MORE LOYALLY THAN I DO!
NO, YOU ARE A LIAR... A-A DECEIVER... BUT YOU SHALL NOT DETER ME.
THHP!
I HAVE NO REASON TO FEAR YOU, REVEREND. EVIL CANNOT DESTROY EVIL.
BESIDES, FOR THE SERVICE I HAVE PERFORMED FOR MY MASTER TONIGHT, HE HAS REWARDED ME WITH HIS PROTECTION!
JUST AS HE WILL REWARD YOU FOR THE HOMAGE YOU HAVE PAID HIM...!
TWAK!
SEE FOR YOURSELF, REVEREND... YOU ARE JUST LIKE ME!
BUT MY DAUGHTER...?

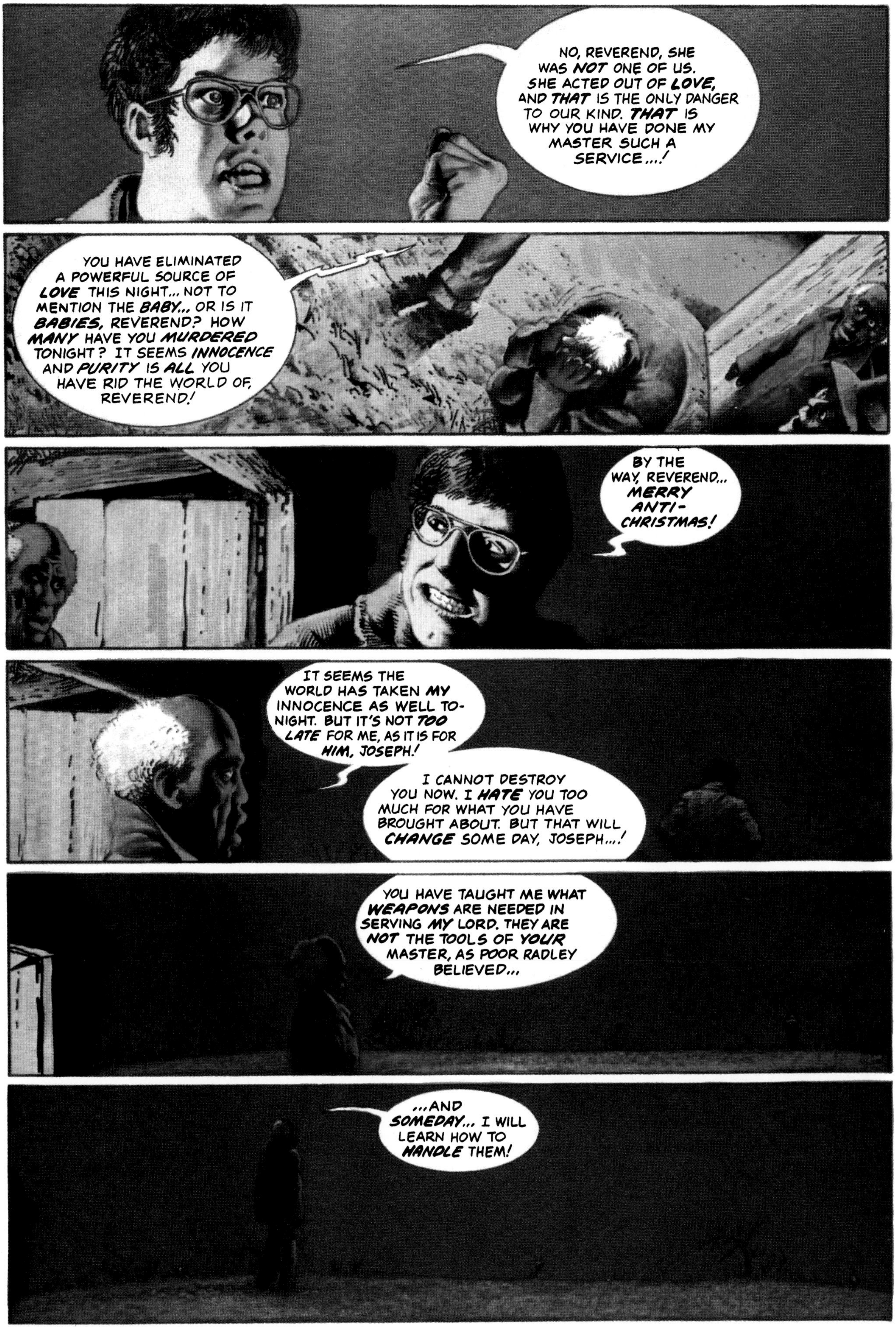
NO, REVEREND, SHE WAS NOT ONE OF US. SHE ACTED OUT OF LOVE, AND THAT IS THE ONLY DANGER TO OUR KIND. THAT IS WHY YOU HAVE DONE MY MASTER SUCH A SERVICE....!
YOU HAVE ELIMINATED A POWERFUL SOURCE OF LOVE THIS NIGHT... NOT TO MENTION THE BABY... OR IS IT BABIES, REVEREND? HOW MANY HAVE YOU MURDERED TONIGHT? IT SEEMS INNOCENCE AND PURITY IS ALL YOU HAVE RID THE WORLD OF, REVEREND!
BY THE WAY, REVEREND... MERRY ANTI-CHRISTMAS!
IT SEEMS THE WORLD HAS TAKEN MY INNOCENCE AS WELL TO-NIGHT. BUT IT'S NOT TOO LATE FOR ME, AS IT IS FOR HIM, JOSEPH!
I CANNOT DESTROY YOU NOW. I HATE YOU TOO MUCH FOR WHAT YOU HAVE BROUGHT ABOUT. BUT THAT WILL CHANGE SOME DAY, JOSEPH...!
YOU HAVE TAUGHT ME WHAT WEAPONS ARE NEEDED IN SERVING MY LORD. THEY ARE NOT THE TOOLS OF YOUR MASTER, AS POOR RADLEY BELIEVED...
...AND SOMEDAY... I WILL LEARN HOW TO HANDLE THEM!

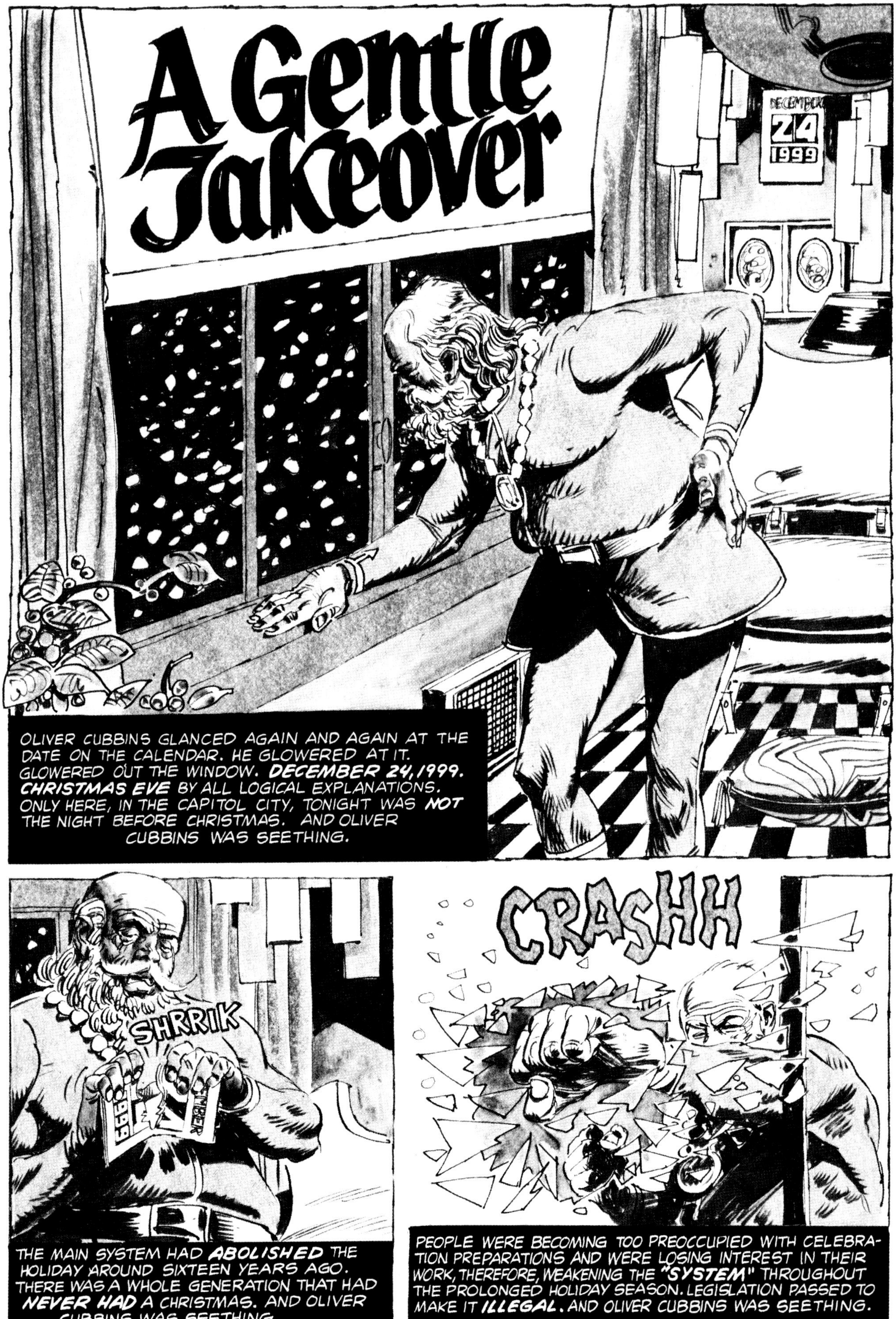
A Gentle Takeover
DECEMBER
24
1999
OLIVER CUBBINS GLANCED AGAIN AND AGAIN AT THE DATE ON THE CALENDAR. HE GLOWERED AT IT. GLOWERED OUT THE WINDOW. DECEMBER 24, 1999. CHRISTMAS EVE BY ALL LOGICAL EXPLANATIONS. ONLY HERE, IN THE CAPITOL CITY, TONIGHT WAS NOT THE NIGHT BEFORE CHRISTMAS. AND OLIVER CUBBINS WAS SEETHING.
SHRRIK
THE MAIN SYSTEM HAD ABOLISHED THE HOLIDAY AROUND SIXTEEN YEARS AGO. THERE WAS A WHOLE GENERATION THAT HAD NEVER HAD A CHRISTMAS. AND OLIVER CUBBINS WAS SEETHING.
CRASHH
PEOPLE WERE BECOMING TOO PREOCCUPIED WITH CELEBRATION PREPARATIONS AND WERE LOSING INTEREST IN THEIR WORK, THEREFORE, WEAKENING THE "SYSTEM" THROUGHOUT THE PROLONGED HOLIDAY SEASON. LEGISLATION PASSED TO MAKE IT ILLEGAL. AND OLIVER CUBBINS WAS SEETHING.

STORY: BUDD LEWIS / ART: ADOLFO ABELLAN

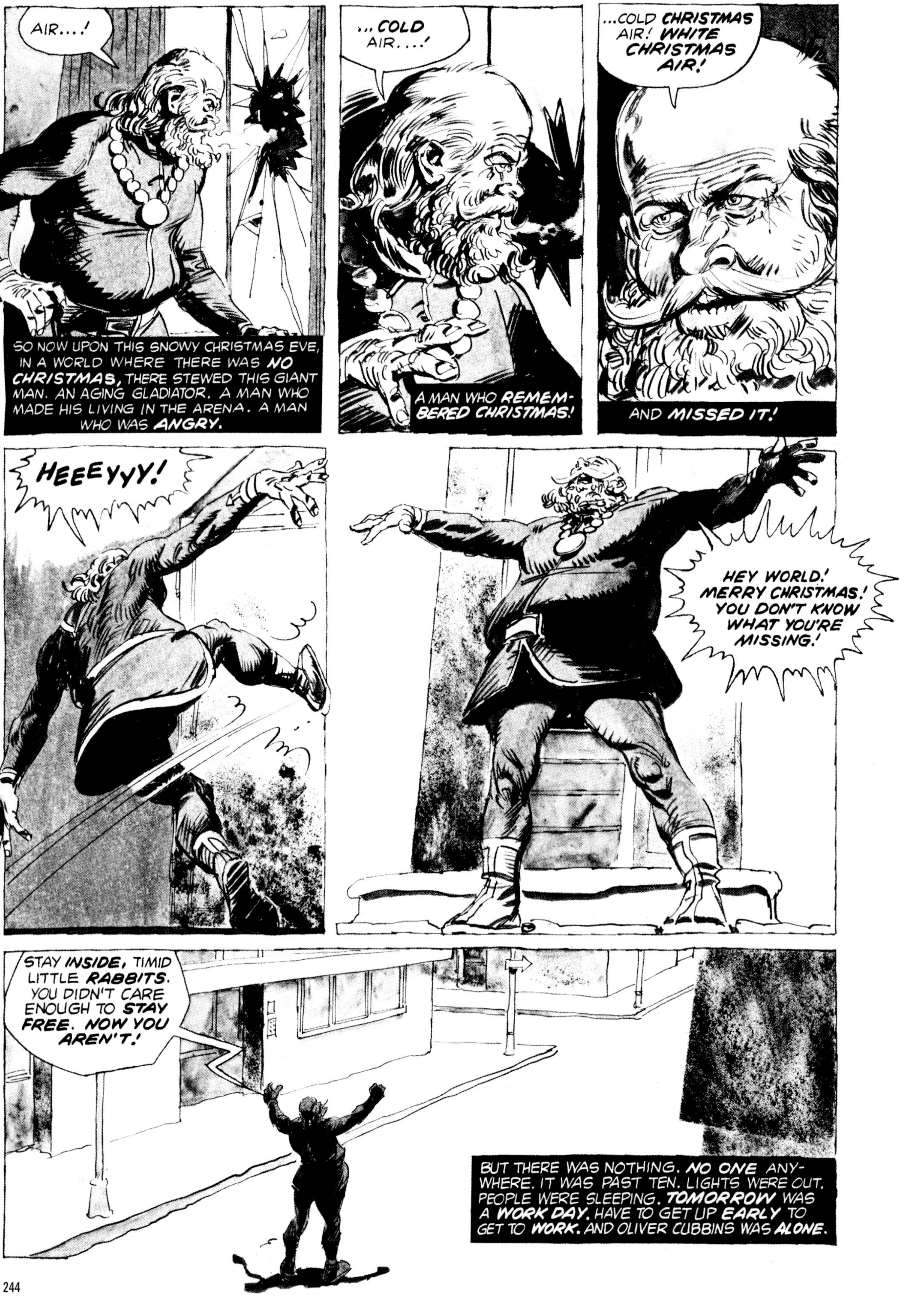

AIR....!
SO NOW UPON THIS SNOWY CHRISTMAS EVE, IN A WORLD WHERE THERE WAS NO CHRISTMAS, THERE STEWED THIS GIANT MAN. AN AGING GLADIATOR. A MAN WHO MADE HIS LIVING IN THE ARENA. A MAN WHO WAS ANGRY.
...COLD AIR....!
A MAN WHO REMEMBERED CHRISTMAS!
...COLD CHRISTMAS AIR! WHITE CHRISTMAS AIR!
AND MISSED IT!
HEEEYYY!
HEY WORLD! MERRY CHRISTMAS! YOU DON'T KNOW WHAT YOU'RE MISSING!
STAY INSIDE, TIMID LITTLE RABBITS. YOU DIDN'T CARE ENOUGH TO STAY FREE. NOW YOU AREN'T!
BUT THERE WAS NOTHING. NO ONE ANYWHERE. IT WAS PAST TEN. LIGHTS WERE OUT. PEOPLE WERE SLEEPING. TOMORROW WAS A WORK DAY. HAVE TO GET UP EARLY TO GET TO WORK. AND OLIVER CUBBINS WAS ALONE.

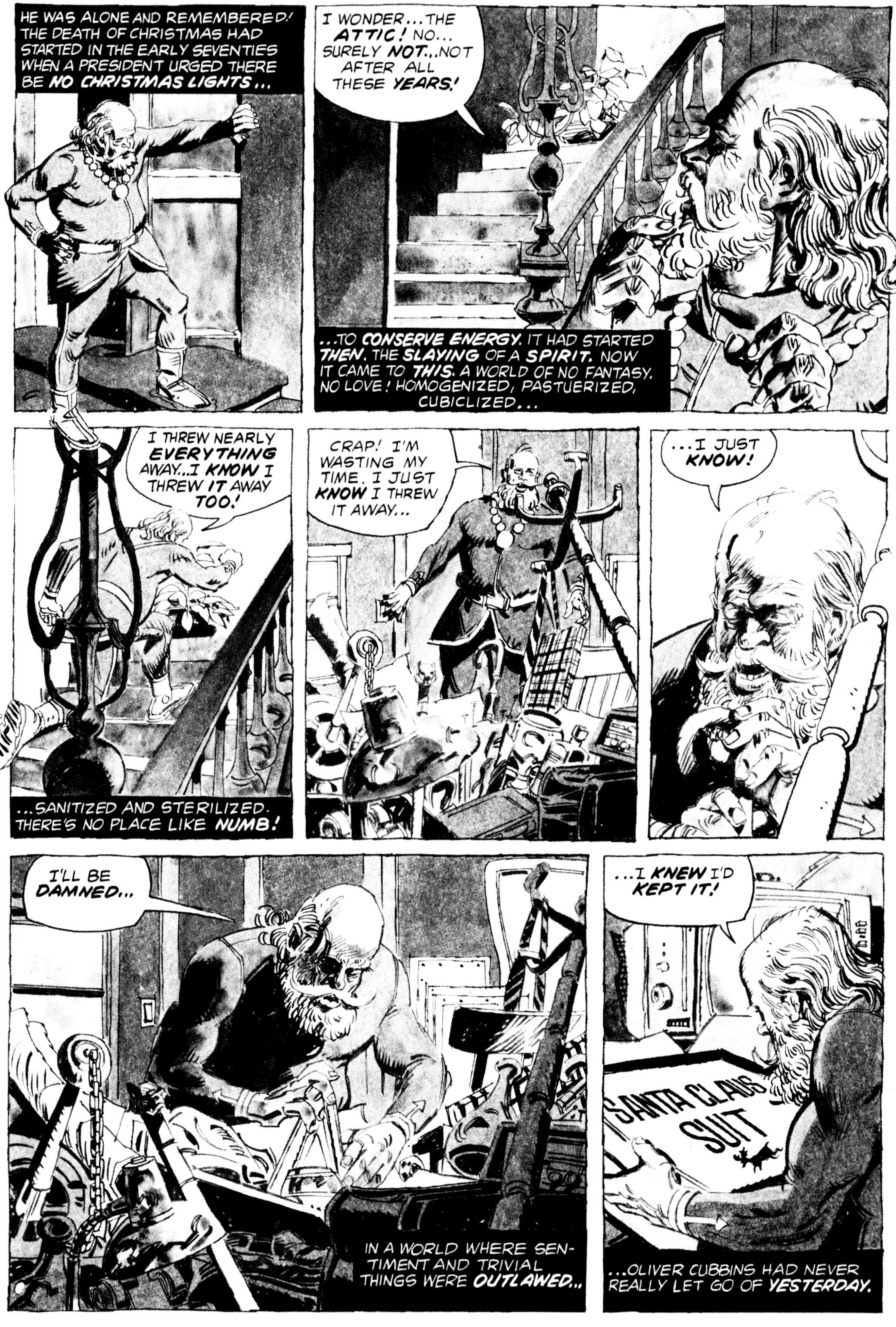
HE WAS ALONE AND REMEMBERED! THE DEATH OF CHRISTMAS HAD STARTED IN THE EARLY SEVENTIES WHEN A PRESIDENT URGED THERE BE NO CHRISTMAS LIGHTS...
I WONDER... THE ATTIC! NO... SURELY NOT... NOT AFTER ALL THESE YEARS!
...TO CONSERVE ENERGY. IT HAD STARTED THEN. THE SLAYING OF A SPIRIT. NOW IT CAME TO THIS. A WORLD OF NO FANTASY. NO LOVE! HOMOGENIZED, PASTUERIZED, CUBICLIZED...
I THREW NEARLY EVERYTHING AWAY... I KNOW I THREW IT AWAY TOO!
...SANITIZED AND STERILIZED. THERE'S NO PLACE LIKE NUMB!
CRAP! I'M WASTING MY TIME. I JUST KNOW I THREW IT AWAY...
...I JUST KNOW!
I'LL BE DAMNED...
IN A WORLD WHERE SENTIMENT AND TRIVIAL THINGS WERE OUTLAWED...
...I KNEW I'D KEPT IT!
SANTA CLAUS SUIT
...OLIVER CUBBINS HAD NEVER REALLY LET GO OF YESTERDAY.

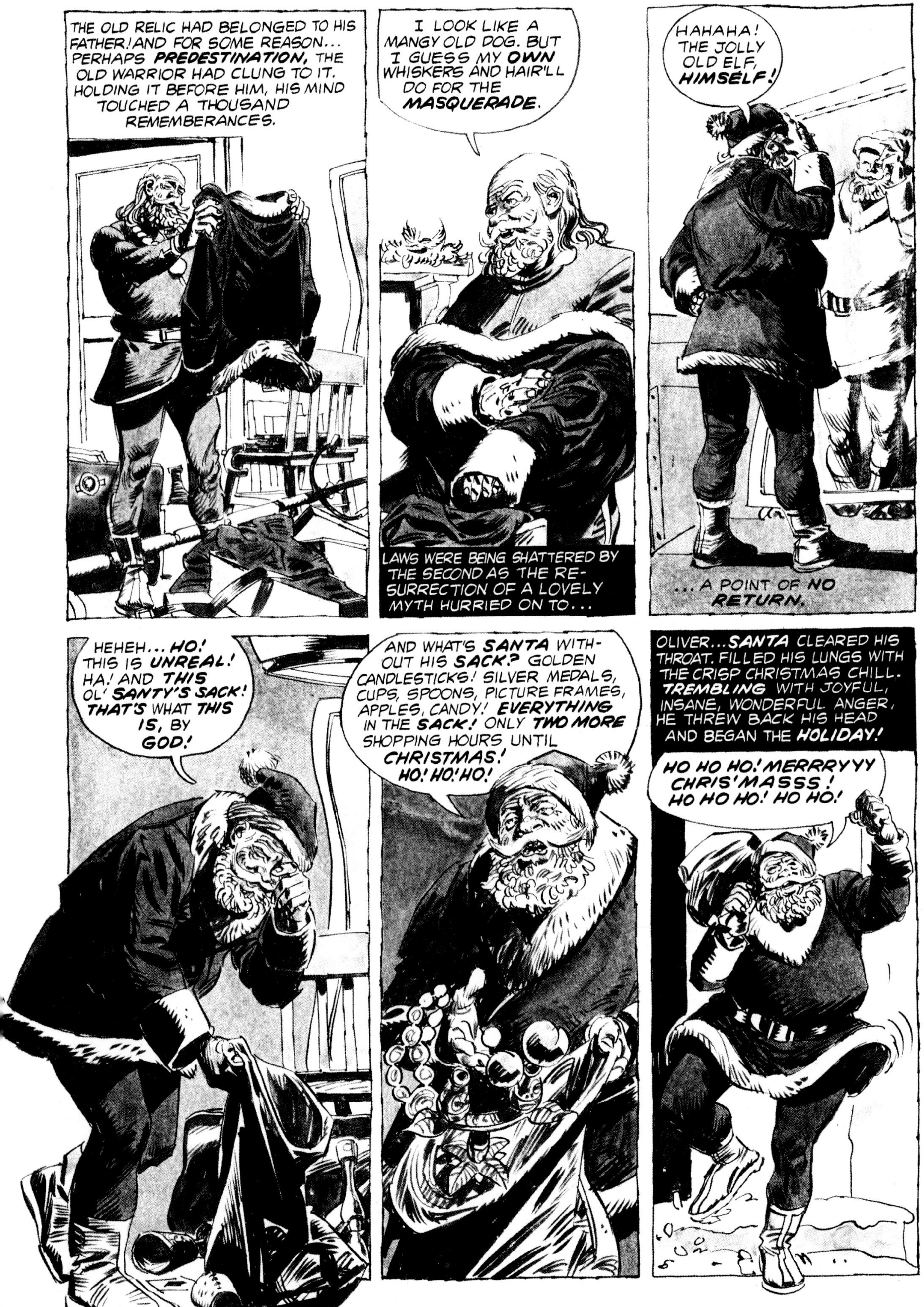
THE OLD RELIC HAD BELONGED TO HIS FATHER! AND FOR SOME REASON... PERHAPS PREDESTINATION, THE OLD WARRIOR HAD CLUNG TO IT. HOLDING IT BEFORE HIM, HIS MIND TOUCHED A THOUSAND REMEMBERANCES.
I LOOK LIKE A MANGY OLD DOG. BUT I GUESS MY OWN WHISKERS AND HAIR'LL DO FOR THE MASQUERADE.
LAWS WERE BEING SHATTERED BY THE SECOND AS THE RE-SURRECTION OF A LOVELY MYTH HURRIED ON TO...
HAHAHA! THE JOLLY OLD ELF, HIMSELF!
... A POINT OF NO RETURN.
HEHEH... HO! THIS IS UNREAL! HA! AND THIS OL' SANTY'S SACK! THAT'S WHAT THIS IS, BY GOD!
AND WHAT'S SANTA WITH-OUT HIS SACK? GOLDEN CANDLESTICKS! SILVER MEDALS, CUPS, SPOONS, PICTURE FRAMES, APPLES, CANDY! EVERYTHING IN THE SACK! ONLY TWO MORE SHOPPING HOURS UNTIL CHRISTMAS! HO! HO! HO!
OLIVER... SANTA CLEARED HIS THROAT. FILLED HIS LUNGS WITH THE CRISP CHRISTMAS CHILL. TREMBLING WITH JOYFUL, INSANE, WONDERFUL ANGER, HE THREW BACK HIS HEAD AND BEGAN THE HOLIDAY!
HO HO HO! MERRRYYY CHRIS'MASSS! HO HO HO! HO HO!

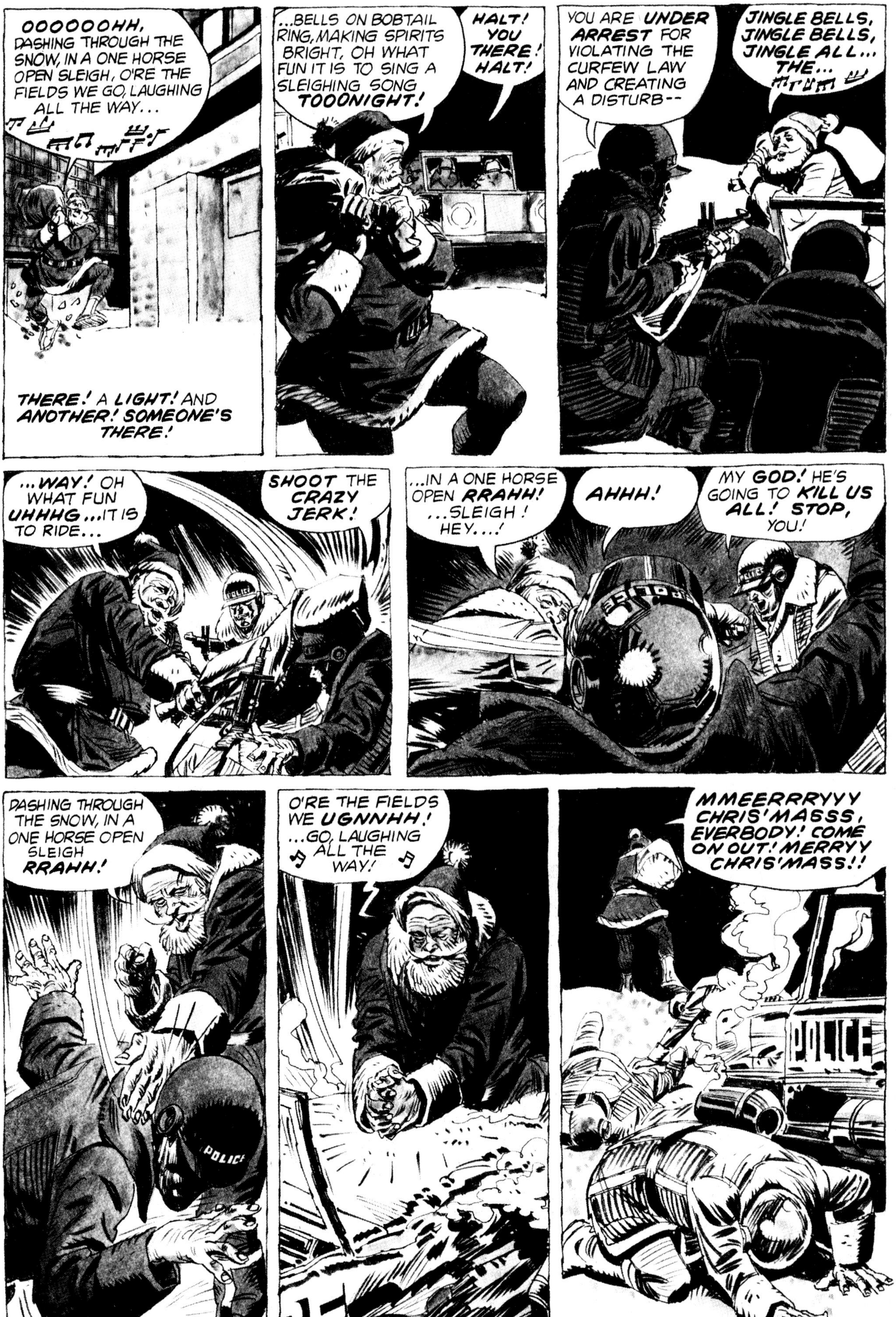
OOOOOOHH, DASHING THROUGH THE SNOW, IN A ONE HORSE OPEN SLEIGH, O'RE THE FIELDS WE GO, LAUGHING ALL THE WAY...
THERE! A LIGHT! AND ANOTHER! SOMEONE'S THERE!
...BELLS ON BOBTAIL RING, MAKING SPIRITS BRIGHT, OH WHAT FUN IT IS TO SING A SLEIGHING SONG TOOONIGHT!
HALT! YOU THERE! HALT!
YOU ARE UNDER ARREST FOR VIOLATING THE CURFEW LAW AND CREATING A DISTURB--
JINGLE BELLS, JINGLE BELLS, JINGLE ALL... THE...
...WAY! OH WHAT FUN UHHG... IT IS TO RIDE...
SHOOT THE CRAZY JERK!
...IN A ONE HORSE OPEN RRAHH! ...SLEIGH! HEY...!
AHHH!
MY GOD! HE'S GOING TO KILL US ALL! STOP, YOU!
DASHING THROUGH THE SNOW, IN A ONE HORSE OPEN SLEIGH RRAHH!
O'RE THE FIELDS WE UGNHHH! ...GO, LAUGHING ALL THE WAY!
MMEERRRYYY CHRIS'MASSS, EVERBODY! COME ON OUT! MERRYY CHRIS'MASS!!

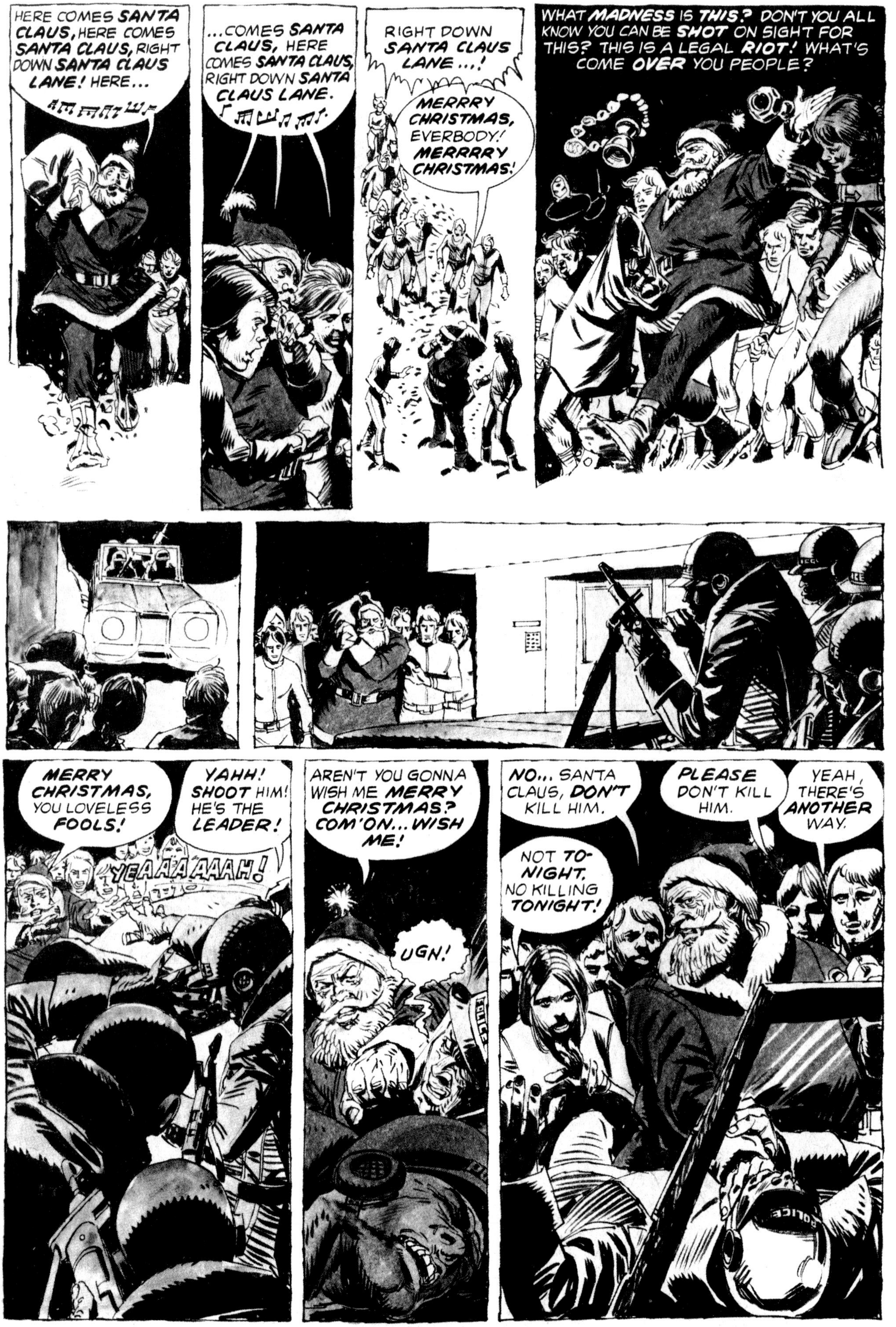
HERE COMES SANTA CLAUS, HERE COMES SANTA CLAUS, RIGHT DOWN SANTA CLAUS LANE! HERE...
...COMES SANTA CLAUS, HERE COMES SANTA CLAUS, RIGHT DOWN SANTA CLAUS LANE.
RIGHT DOWN SANTA CLAUS LANE...!
MERRY CHRISTMAS, EVERBODY! MERRRRY CHRISTMAS!
WHAT MADNESS IS THIS? DON'T YOU ALL KNOW YOU CAN BE SHOT ON SIGHT FOR THIS? THIS IS A LEGAL RIOT! WHAT'S COME OVER YOU PEOPLE?
MERRY CHRISTMAS, YOU LOVELESS FOOLS!
YAHH! SHOOT HIM! HE'S THE LEADER!
YEAAAAAAH!
AREN'T YOU GONNA WISH ME MERRY CHRISTMAS? COM'ON... WISH ME!
UGN!
NO... SANTA CLAUS, DON'T KILL HIM.
NOT TO-NIGHT, NO KILLING TONIGHT!
PLEASE DON'T KILL HIM.
YEAH, THERE'S ANOTHER WAY.

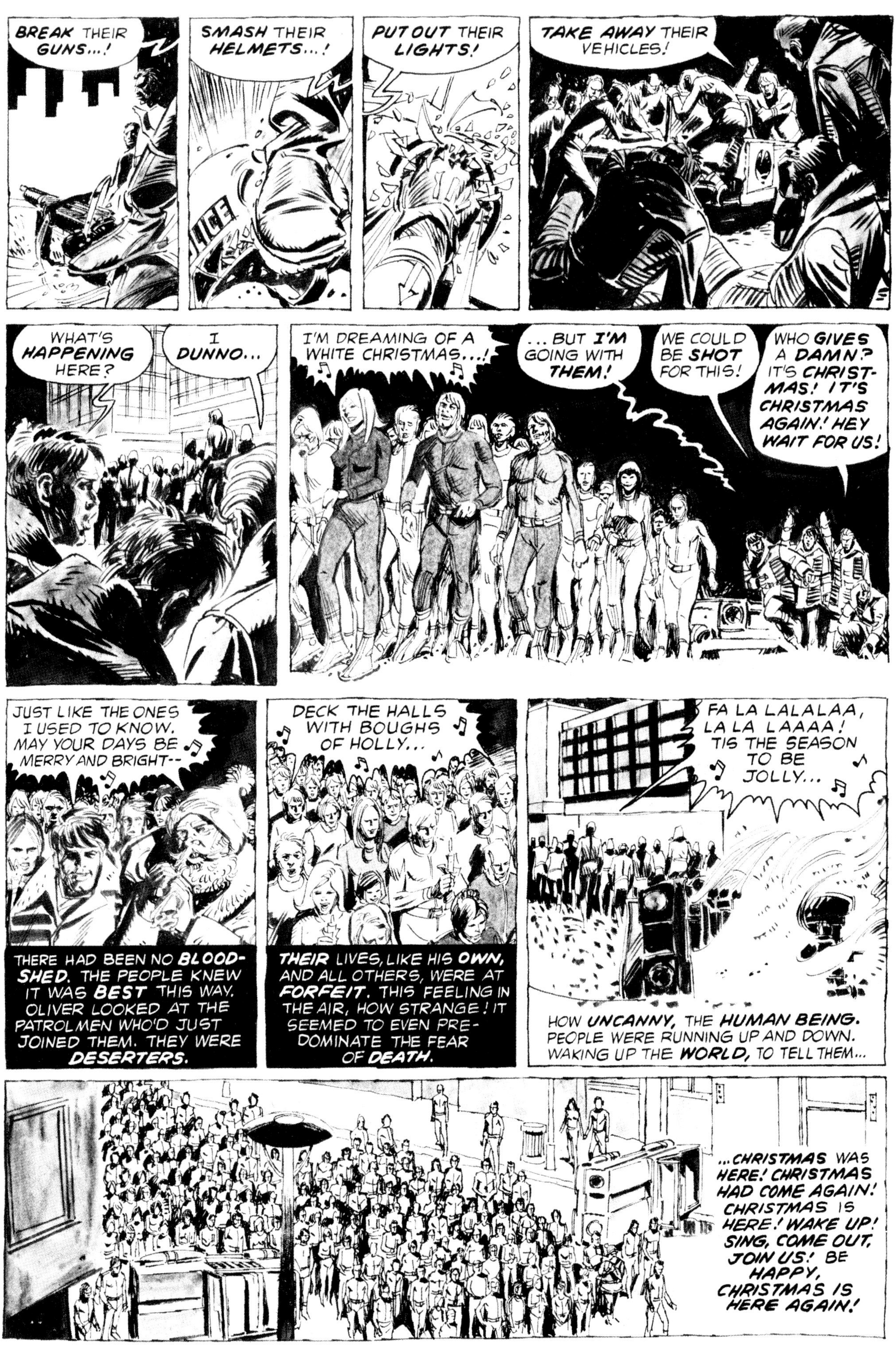
BREAK THEIR GUNS...!
SMASH THEIR HELMETS...!
PUT OUT THEIR LIGHTS!
TAKE AWAY THEIR VEHICLES!
WHAT'S HAPPENING HERE?
I DUNNO...
I'M DREAMING OF A WHITE CHRISTMAS...!
...BUT I'M GOING WITH THEM!
WE COULD BE SHOT FOR THIS!
WHO GIVES A DAMN? IT'S CHRISTMAS! IT'S CHRISTMAS AGAIN! HEY WAIT FOR US!
JUST LIKE THE ONES I USED TO KNOW. MAY YOUR DAYS BE MERRY AND BRIGHT--
THERE HAD BEEN NO BLOODSHED. THE PEOPLE KNEW IT WAS BEST THIS WAY. OLIVER LOOKED AT THE PATROLMEN WHO'D JUST JOINED THEM. THEY WERE DESERTERS.
DECK THE HALLS WITH BOUGHS OF HOLLY...
THEIR LIVES, LIKE HIS OWN, AND ALL OTHERS, WERE AT FORFEIT. THIS FEELING IN THE AIR, HOW STRANGE! IT SEEMED TO EVEN PREDOMINATE THE FEAR OF DEATH.
FA LA LALALAA, LA LA LAAAA! TIS THE SEASON TO BE JOLLY...
HOW UNCANNY, THE HUMAN BEING. PEOPLE WERE RUNNING UP AND DOWN. WAKING UP THE WORLD, TO TELL THEM...
...CHRISTMAS WAS HERE! CHRISTMAS HAD COME AGAIN! CHRISTMAS IS HERE! WAKE UP! SING, COME OUT, JOIN US! BE HAPPY, CHRISTMAS IS HERE AGAIN!

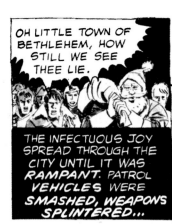

OH LITTLE TOWN OF BETHLEHEM, HOW STILL WE SEE THEE LIE.

THE INFECTUOUS JOY SPREAD THROUGH THE CITY UNTIL IT WAS *RAMPANT*. PATROL *VEHICLES* WERE *SMASHED, WEAPONS SPLINTERED...*

SILENT NIGHT, HOLY NIGHT, ALL IS CALM, ALL IS BRIGHT. ♪

...YET NO *BLOOD* WAS SHED. OLIVER CLIMBED TO THE *TOP* OF A *MONUMENT...*

HOLY INFANT SO TENDER AND MILD...

...SO THE *WHOLE CITY* COULD *SEE SANTA CLAUS* WAS *ALIVE*. AND *SO WERE THEY*.

...SLEEP IN HEAVENLY PEACE...

THE STREETS WERE FILLED WITH *THOUSANDS* OF PEOPLE. *FREE PEOPLE*. THEIR VOICES RANG OUT *TOGETHER, IN PEACE*.

...SLEEEP IN HEAVENLY PEACE, SLEEP IN HEEEAVENLY ♪ PEACE. ♪

A *NEW BORN* PEOPLE. AND *PEACE*. *PEACE*. *THAT'S* WHAT IT WAS ALL ABOUT NOW. SLEEP IN HEAVENLY PEACE.

PEACE ON EARTH AND MERCY MILD...

OLIVER THOUGHT OF ALL THE LIVES THAT HAD BEEN *RISKED*, AND IT CULMINATED IN *THIS*. THEY HAD *TAKEN OVER*. BUT GENTLY. A *GENTLE TAKE-OVER*. AND THEY'D *NEVER BE SLAVES AGAIN*.

♪ GOD AND ♪ SINNERS RECONCILED!

SUDDENLY A *SOFT LIGHT* BATHED THE THRONG OF CHRISTMAS CAROLERS. A SOFT AND GENTLE RADIANCE AS *DELICATE* AS A *SMILE*, SHONE ALL AROUND.

JOY TO THE WORLD, THE LORD HAS COME. ♪

THE JOYFUL SINGING ECHOED IN HIS HEART AND A *MILLION CANDLES* LIGHTED THE EARTH AS HE LOOKED INTO THE HEAVEN TOWARD *ANOTHER LIGHT*.

THE CLEAR COLD NIGHT SHONE FORTH A *STAR...* A STAR WHICH HAD *NOT SHONE* IN *2,000 YEARS*.

ITS WHITE BRILLANCE TOUCHED THE *FREE CITY* AND *EVERY HEART* IN IT, AND SOFTLY IN THE NIGHT, IT BEGAN TO SNOW.

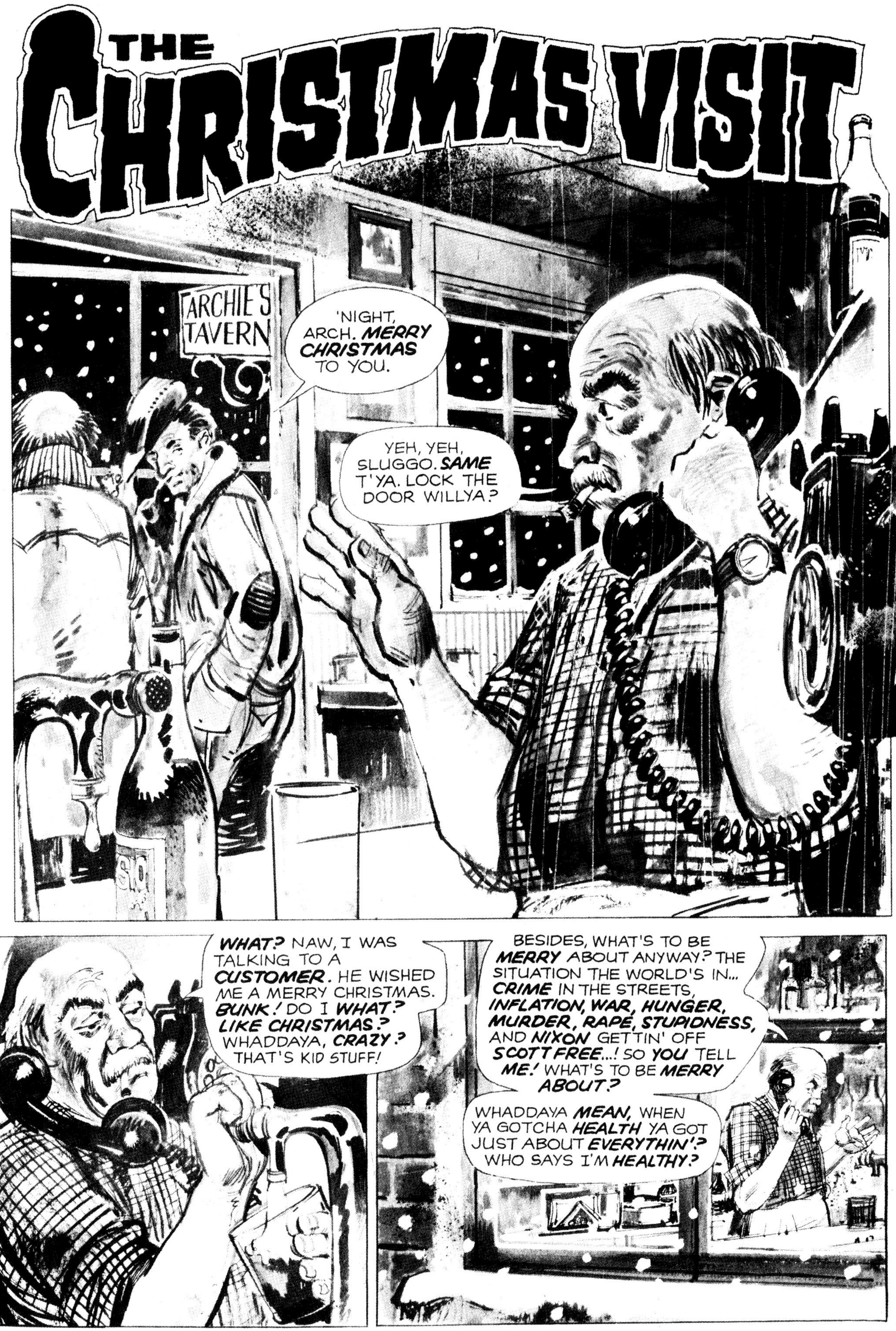
THE CHRISTMAS VISIT
ARCHIE'S TAVERN
'NIGHT, ARCH. MERRY CHRISTMAS TO YOU.
YEH, YEH, SLUGGO. SAME T'YA. LOCK THE DOOR WILLYA?
WHAT? NAW, I WAS TALKING TO A CUSTOMER. HE WISHED ME A MERRY CHRISTMAS. BUNK! DO I WHAT? LIKE CHRISTMAS? WHADDAYA, CRAZY? THAT'S KID STUFF!
BESIDES, WHAT'S TO BE MERRY ABOUT ANYWAY? THE SITUATION THE WORLD'S IN... CRIME IN THE STREETS, INFLATION, WAR, HUNGER, MURDER, RAPE, STUPIDNESS, AND NIXON GETTIN' OFF SCOTT FREE...! SO YOU TELL ME! WHAT'S TO BE MERRY ABOUT?
WHADDAYA MEAN, WHEN YA GOTCHA HEALTH YA GOT JUST ABOUT EVERYTHIN'? WHO SAYS I'M HEALTHY?

STORY: BUDD LEWIS / ART: ISIDRO MONES

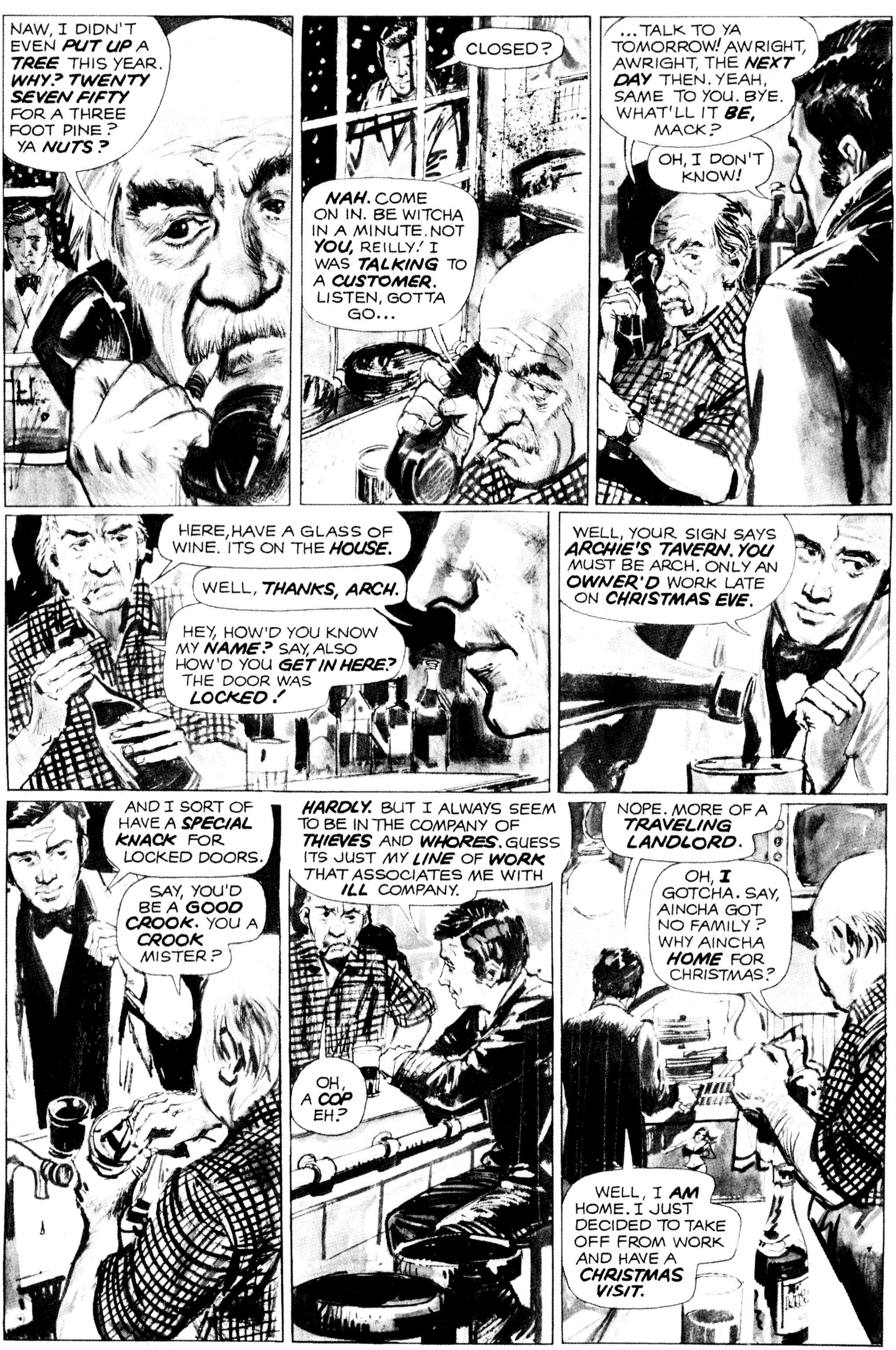
NAW, I DIDN'T EVEN PUT UP A TREE THIS YEAR. WHY? TWENTY SEVEN FIFTY FOR A THREE FOOT PINE? YA NUTS?
CLOSED?
NAH. COME ON IN. BE WITCHA IN A MINUTE. NOT YOU, REILLY! I WAS TALKING TO A CUSTOMER. LISTEN, GOTTA GO...
...TALK TO YA TOMORROW! AWRIGHT, AWRIGHT, THE NEXT DAY THEN. YEAH, SAME TO YOU. BYE. WHAT'LL IT BE, MACK?
OH, I DON'T KNOW!
HERE, HAVE A GLASS OF WINE. ITS ON THE HOUSE.
WELL, THANKS, ARCH.
HEY, HOW'D YOU KNOW MY NAME? SAY, ALSO HOW'D YOU GET IN HERE? THE DOOR WAS LOCKED!
WELL, YOUR SIGN SAYS ARCHIE'S TAVERN. YOU MUST BE ARCH. ONLY AN OWNER'D WORK LATE ON CHRISTMAS EVE.
AND I SORT OF HAVE A SPECIAL KNACK FOR LOCKED DOORS.
SAY, YOU'D BE A GOOD CROOK. YOU A CROOK MISTER?
HARDLY. BUT I ALWAYS SEEM TO BE IN THE COMPANY OF THIEVES AND WHORES. GUESS ITS JUST MY LINE OF WORK THAT ASSOCIATES ME WITH ILL COMPANY.
OH, A COP EH?
NOPE. MORE OF A TRAVELING LANDLORD.
OH, I GOTCHA. SAY, AINCHA GOT NO FAMILY? WHY AINCHA HOME FOR CHRISTMAS?
WELL, I AM HOME. I JUST DECIDED TO TAKE OFF FROM WORK AND HAVE A CHRISTMAS VISIT.

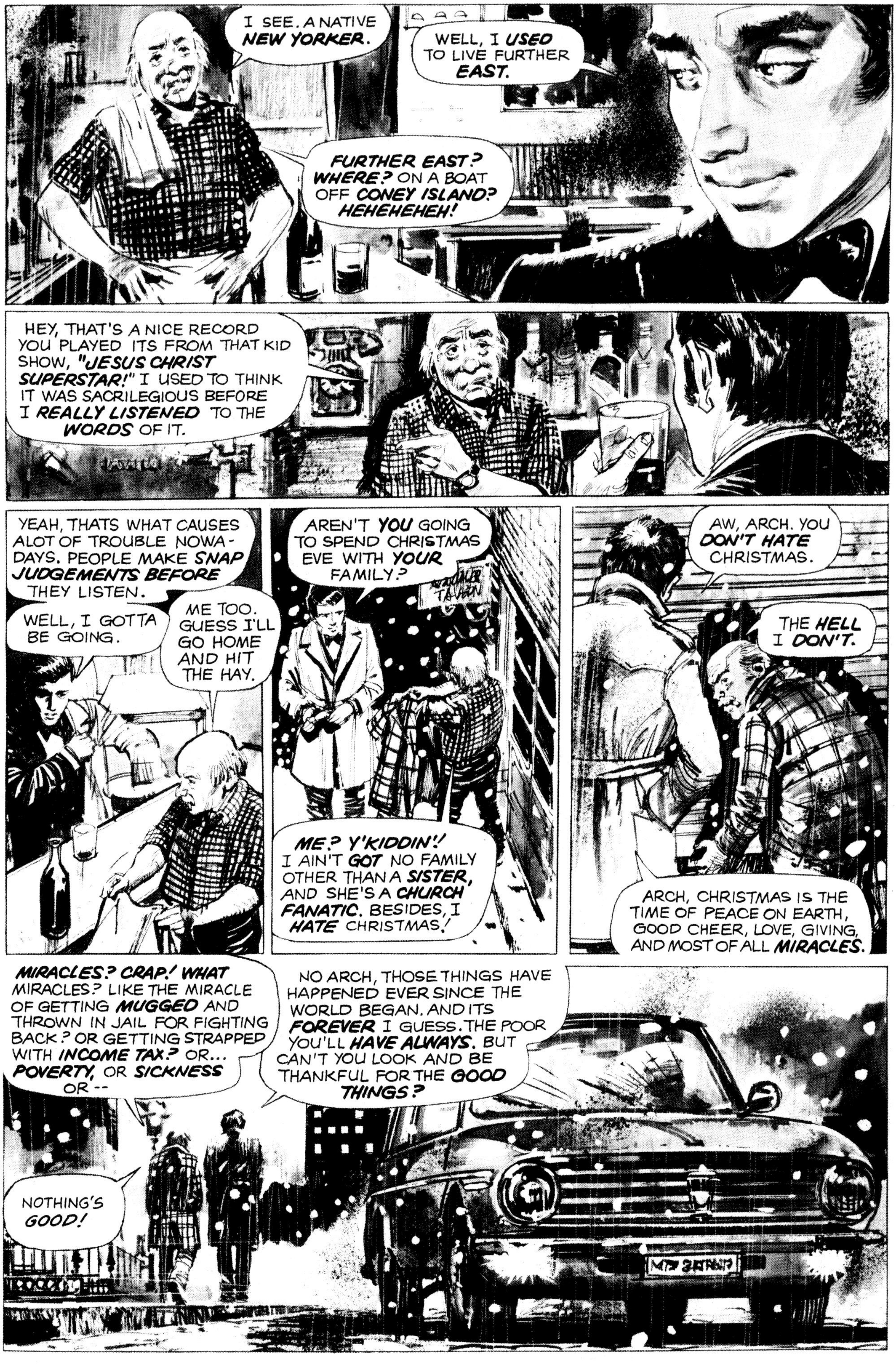
I SEE. A NATIVE NEW YORKER.
WELL, I USED TO LIVE FURTHER EAST.
FURTHER EAST? WHERE? ON A BOAT OFF CONEY ISLAND? HEHEHEHEH!
HEY, THAT'S A NICE RECORD YOU PLAYED ITS FROM THAT KID SHOW, "JESUS CHRIST SUPERSTAR!" I USED TO THINK IT WAS SACRILEGIOUS BEFORE I REALLY LISTENED TO THE WORDS OF IT.
YEAH, THATS WHAT CAUSES ALOT OF TROUBLE NOWA-DAYS. PEOPLE MAKE SNAP JUDGEMENTS BEFORE THEY LISTEN.
WELL, I GOTTA BE GOING.
ME TOO. GUESS I'LL GO HOME AND HIT THE HAY.
AREN'T YOU GOING TO SPEND CHRISTMAS EVE WITH YOUR FAMILY?
ME? Y'KIDDIN'! I AIN'T GOT NO FAMILY OTHER THAN A SISTER, AND SHE'S A CHURCH FANATIC. BESIDES, I HATE CHRISTMAS!
AW, ARCH. YOU DON'T HATE CHRISTMAS.
THE HELL I DON'T.
ARCH, CHRISTMAS IS THE TIME OF PEACE ON EARTH, GOOD CHEER, LOVE, GIVING, AND MOST OF ALL MIRACLES.
MIRACLES? CRAP! WHAT MIRACLES? LIKE THE MIRACLE OF GETTING MUGGED AND THROWN IN JAIL FOR FIGHTING BACK? OR GETTING STRAPPED WITH INCOME TAX? OR... POVERTY, OR SICKNESS OR --
NO ARCH, THOSE THINGS HAVE HAPPENED EVER SINCE THE WORLD BEGAN. AND ITS FOREVER I GUESS. THE POOR YOU'LL HAVE ALWAYS. BUT CAN'T YOU LOOK AND BE THANKFUL FOR THE GOOD THINGS?
NOTHING'S GOOD!

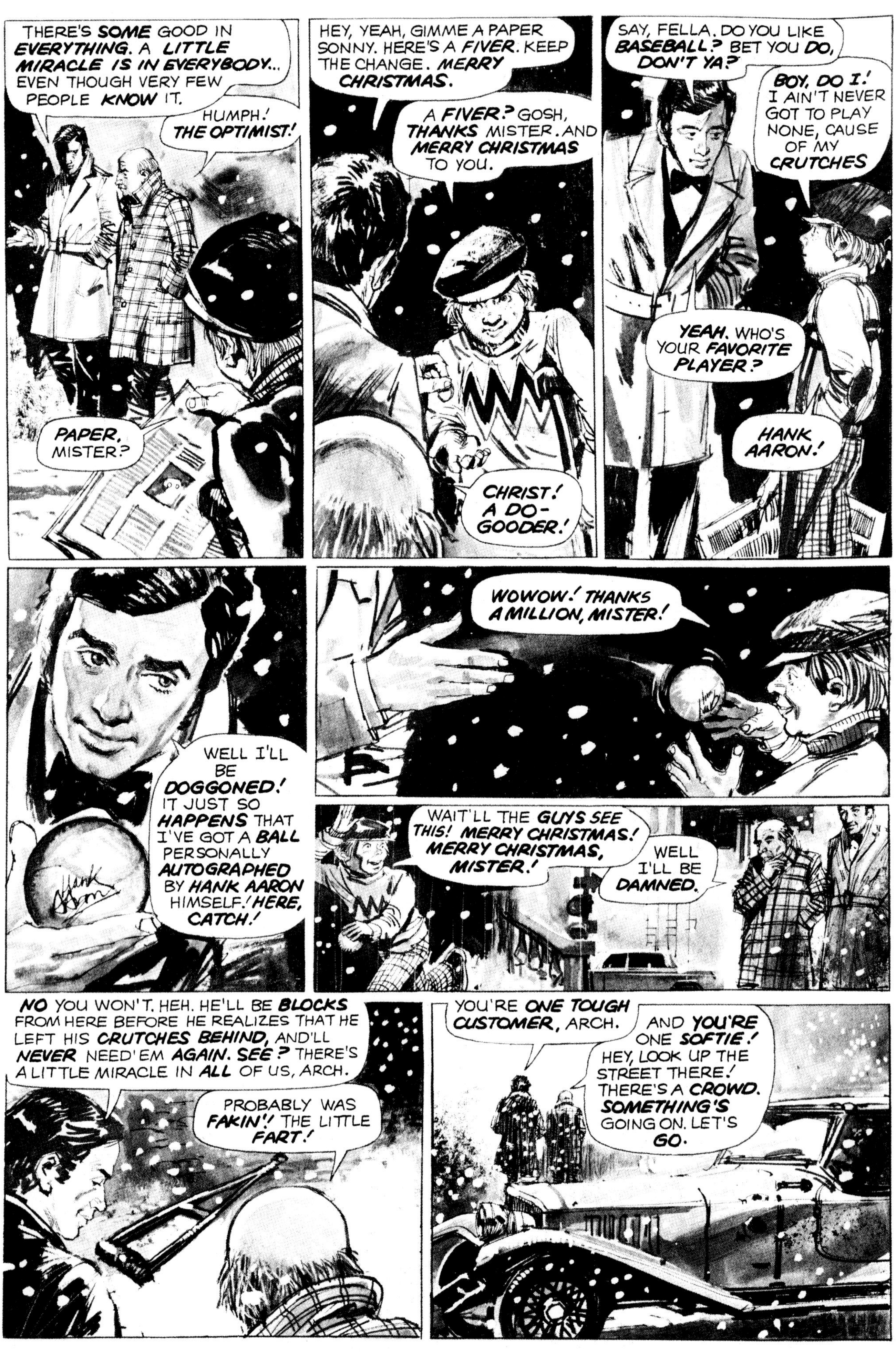

THERE'S SOME GOOD IN EVERYTHING. A LITTLE MIRACLE IS IN EVERYBODY... EVEN THOUGH VERY FEW PEOPLE KNOW IT.
HUMPH! THE OPTIMIST!
PAPER, MISTER?
HEY, YEAH, GIMME A PAPER SONNY. HERE'S A FIVER. KEEP THE CHANGE. MERRY CHRISTMAS.
A FIVER? GOSH, THANKS MISTER. AND MERRY CHRISTMAS TO YOU.
CHRIST! A DO-GOODER!
SAY, FELLA. DO YOU LIKE BASEBALL? BET YOU DO, DON'T YA?
BOY, DO I! I AIN'T NEVER GOT TO PLAY NONE, CAUSE OF MY CRUTCHES
YEAH. WHO'S YOUR FAVORITE PLAYER?
HANK AARON!
WELL I'LL BE DOGGONED! IT JUST SO HAPPENS THAT I'VE GOT A BALL PERSONALLY AUTOGRAPHED BY HANK AARON HIMSELF! HERE, CATCH!
WOWOW! THANKS A MILLION, MISTER!
WAIT'LL THE GUYS SEE THIS! MERRY CHRISTMAS! MERRY CHRISTMAS, MISTER!
WELL I'LL BE DAMNED.
NO YOU WON'T. HEH. HE'LL BE BLOCKS FROM HERE BEFORE HE REALIZES THAT HE LEFT HIS CRUTCHES BEHIND, AND'LL NEVER NEED'EM AGAIN. SEE? THERE'S A LITTLE MIRACLE IN ALL OF US, ARCH.
PROBABLY WAS FAKIN'! THE LITTLE FART!
YOU'RE ONE TOUGH CUSTOMER, ARCH.
AND YOU'RE ONE SOFTIE! HEY, LOOK UP THE STREET THERE! THERE'S A CROWD. SOMETHING'S GOING ON. LET'S GO.

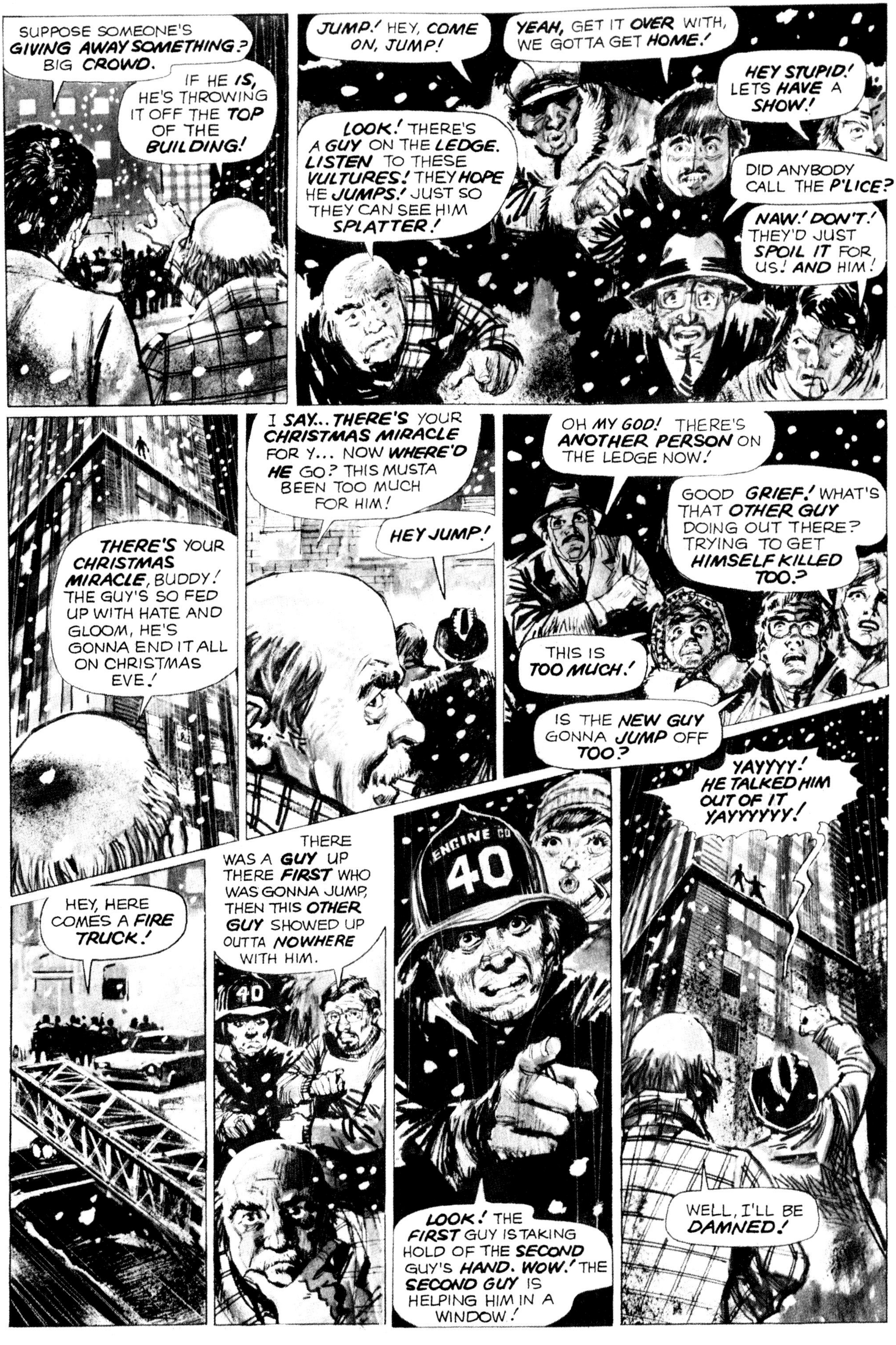
SUPPOSE SOMEONE'S GIVING AWAY SOMETHING? BIG CROWD.
IF HE IS, HE'S THROWING IT OFF THE TOP OF THE BUILDING!
JUMP! HEY, COME ON, JUMP!
YEAH, GET IT OVER WITH, WE GOTTA GET HOME!
HEY STUPID! LETS HAVE A SHOW!
LOOK! THERE'S A GUY ON THE LEDGE. LISTEN TO THESE VULTURES! THEY HOPE HE JUMPS! JUST SO THEY CAN SEE HIM SPLATTER!
DID ANYBODY CALL THE P'LICE?
NAW! DON'T! THEY'D JUST SPOIL IT FOR US! AND HIM!
THERE'S YOUR CHRISTMAS MIRACLE, BUDDY! THE GUY'S SO FED UP WITH HATE AND GLOOM, HE'S GONNA END IT ALL ON CHRISTMAS EVE!
I SAY... THERE'S YOUR CHRISTMAS MIRACLE FOR Y... NOW WHERE'D HE GO? THIS MUSTA BEEN TOO MUCH FOR HIM!
HEY JUMP!
OH MY GOD! THERE'S ANOTHER PERSON ON THE LEDGE NOW!
GOOD GRIEF! WHAT'S THAT OTHER GUY DOING OUT THERE? TRYING TO GET HIMSELF KILLED TOO?
THIS IS TOO MUCH!
IS THE NEW GUY GONNA JUMP OFF TOO?
HEY, HERE COMES A FIRE TRUCK!
THERE WAS A GUY UP THERE FIRST WHO WAS GONNA JUMP, THEN THIS OTHER GUY SHOWED UP OUTTA NOWHERE WITH HIM.
ENGINE CO 40
40
LOOK! THE FIRST GUY IS TAKING HOLD OF THE SECOND GUY'S HAND. WOW! THE SECOND GUY IS HELPING HIM IN A WINDOW!
YAYYYY! HE TALKED HIM OUT OF IT YAYYYYYY!
WELL, I'LL BE DAMNED!

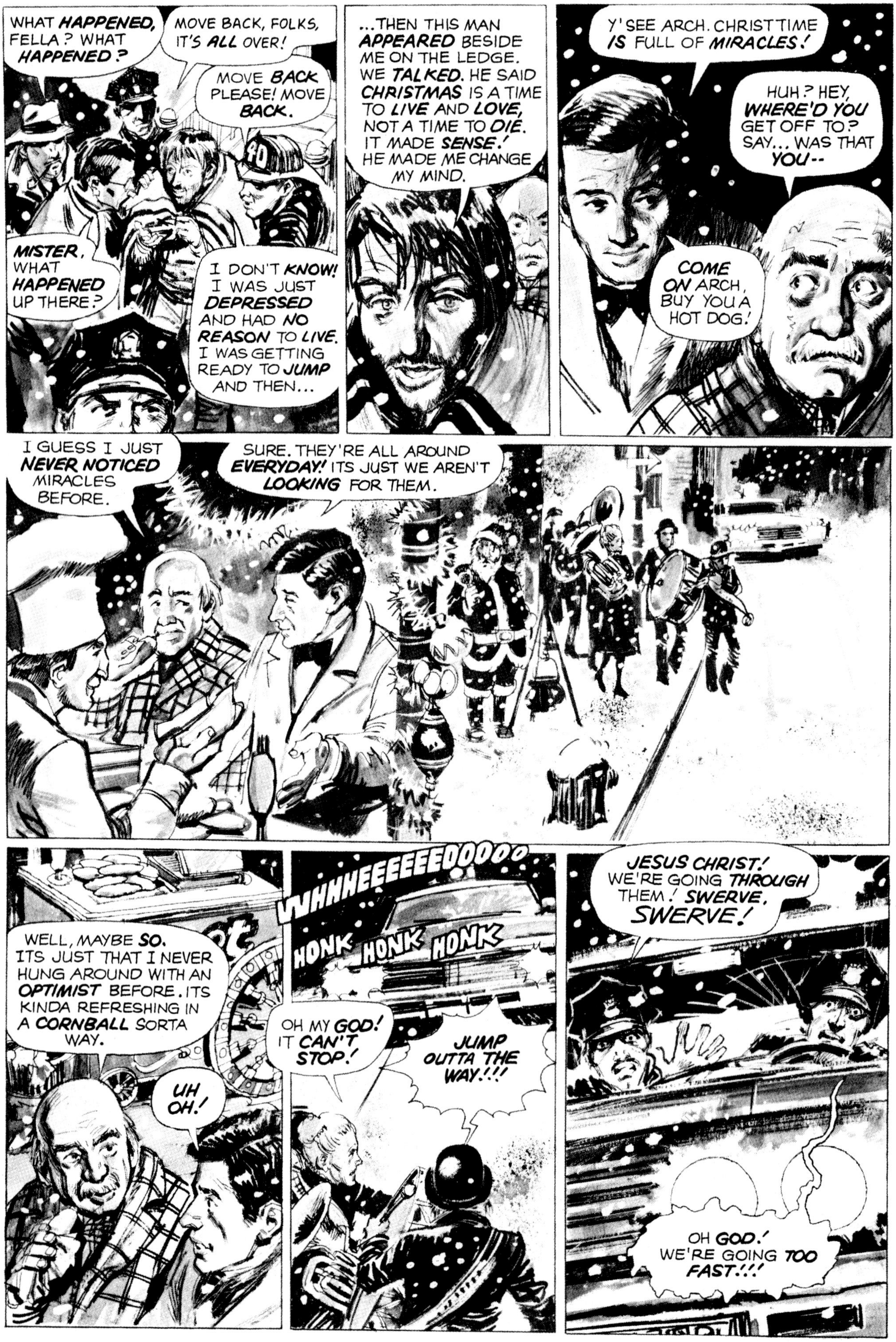
WHAT HAPPENED, FELLA? WHAT HAPPENED?
MOVE BACK, FOLKS, IT'S ALL OVER!
MOVE BACK PLEASE! MOVE BACK.
MISTER, WHAT HAPPENED UP THERE?
I DON'T KNOW! I WAS JUST DEPRESSED AND HAD NO REASON TO LIVE. I WAS GETTING READY TO JUMP AND THEN...
...THEN THIS MAN APPEARED BESIDE ME ON THE LEDGE. WE TALKED. HE SAID CHRISTMAS IS A TIME TO LIVE AND LOVE, NOT A TIME TO DIE. IT MADE SENSE! HE MADE ME CHANGE MY MIND.
Y'SEE ARCH. CHRISTTIME IS FULL OF MIRACLES!
HUH? HEY, WHERE'D YOU GET OFF TO? SAY... WAS THAT YOU--
COME ON ARCH, BUY YOU A HOT DOG!
I GUESS I JUST NEVER NOTICED MIRACLES BEFORE.
SURE. THEY'RE ALL AROUND EVERYDAY! ITS JUST WE AREN'T LOOKING FOR THEM.
WELL, MAYBE SO. ITS JUST THAT I NEVER HUNG AROUND WITH AN OPTIMIST BEFORE. ITS KINDA REFRESHING IN A CORNBALL SORTA WAY.
UH OH!
WHHHEEEEEEEOOOOO
HONK HONK HONK
OH MY GOD! IT CAN'T STOP!
JUMP OUTTA THE WAY!!!
JESUS CHRIST! WE'RE GOING THROUGH THEM! SWERVE, SWERVE!
OH GOD! WE'RE GOING TOO FAST!!!

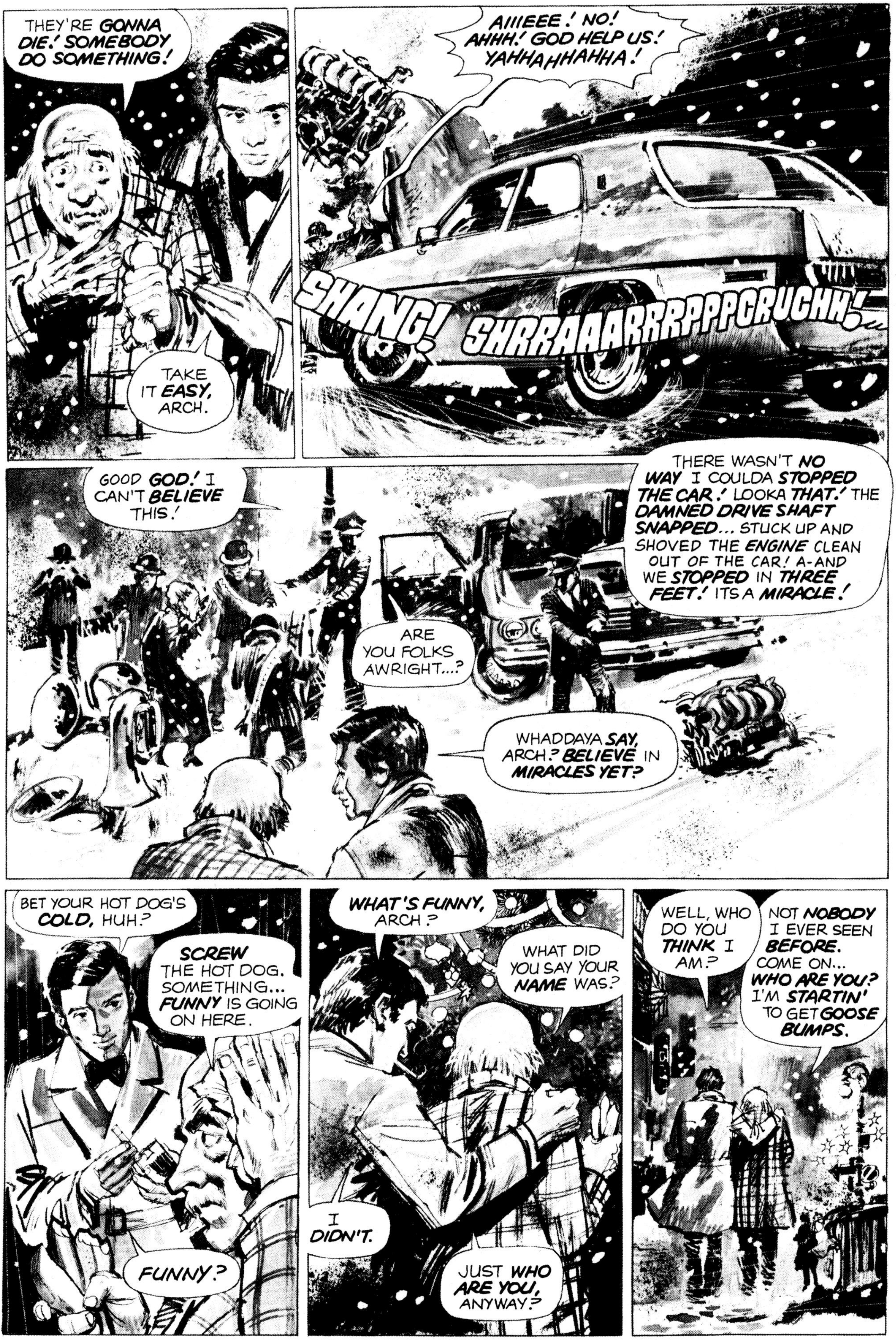
THEY'RE GONNA DIE! SOMEBODY DO SOMETHING!
TAKE IT EASY, ARCH.
AIIIEEE! NO! AHHH! GOD HELP US! YAHHAHHAHHA!
SHANG! SHRRAAARRRPPPCRUCHH!
GOOD GOD! I CAN'T BELIEVE THIS!
THERE WASN'T NO WAY I COULDA STOPPED THE CAR! LOOKA THAT! THE DAMNED DRIVE SHAFT SNAPPED... STUCK UP AND SHOVED THE ENGINE CLEAN OUT OF THE CAR! A-AND WE STOPPED IN THREE FEET! ITS A MIRACLE!
ARE YOU FOLKS AWRIGHT...?
WHADDAYA SAY, ARCH? BELIEVE IN MIRACLES YET?
BET YOUR HOT DOG'S COLD, HUH?
SCREW THE HOT DOG. SOMETHING... FUNNY IS GOING ON HERE.
FUNNY?
WHAT'S FUNNY, ARCH?
WHAT DID YOU SAY YOUR NAME WAS?
I DIDN'T.
JUST WHO ARE YOU, ANYWAY?
WELL, WHO DO YOU THINK I AM?
NOT NOBODY I EVER SEEN BEFORE. COME ON... WHO ARE YOU? I'M STARTIN' TO GET GOOSE BUMPS.

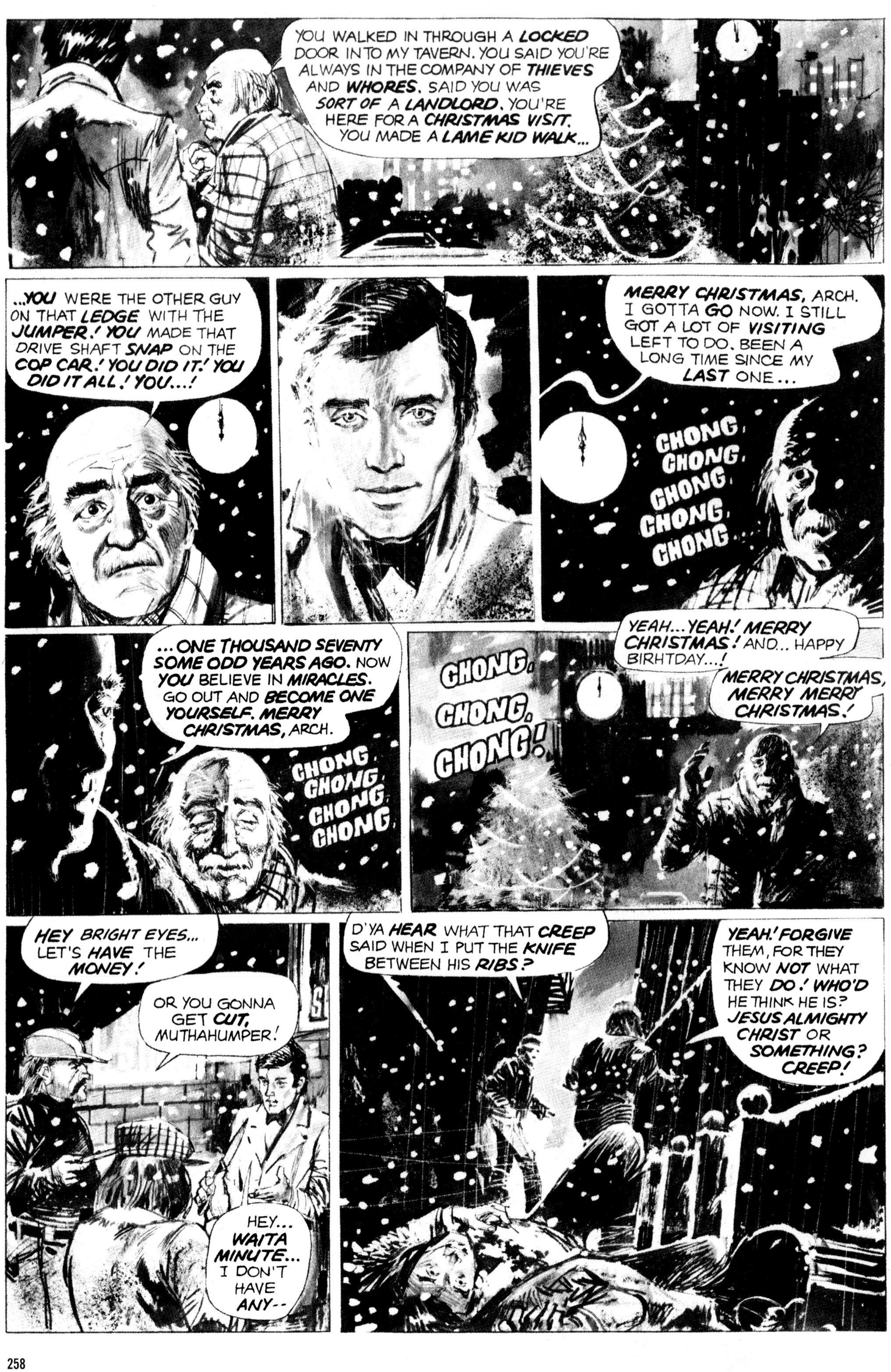
YOU WALKED IN THROUGH A LOCKED DOOR INTO MY TAVERN. YOU SAID YOU'RE ALWAYS IN THE COMPANY OF THIEVES AND WHORES. SAID YOU WAS SORT OF A LANDLORD. YOU'RE HERE FOR A CHRISTMAS VISIT. YOU MADE A LAME KID WALK...
...YOU WERE THE OTHER GUY ON THAT LEDGE WITH THE JUMPER! YOU MADE THAT DRIVE SHAFT SNAP ON THE COP CAR! YOU DID IT! YOU DID IT ALL! YOU...!
MERRY CHRISTMAS, ARCH. I GOTTA GO NOW. I STILL GOT A LOT OF VISITING LEFT TO DO. BEEN A LONG TIME SINCE MY LAST ONE...
CHONG CHONG CHONG CHONG CHONG
...ONE THOUSAND SEVENTY SOME ODD YEARS AGO. NOW YOU BELIEVE IN MIRACLES. GO OUT AND BECOME ONE YOURSELF. MERRY CHRISTMAS, ARCH.
CHONG CHONG CHONG CHONG
YEAH...YEAH! MERRY CHRISTMAS! AND... HAPPY BIRHTDAY...!
MERRY CHRISTMAS, MERRY MERRY CHRISTMAS!
CHONG, CHONG, CHONG!
HEY BRIGHT EYES... LET'S HAVE THE MONEY!
OR YOU GONNA GET CUT, MUTHAHUMPER!
HEY... WAITA MINUTE... I DON'T HAVE ANY--
D'YA HEAR WHAT THAT CREEP SAID WHEN I PUT THE KNIFE BETWEEN HIS RIBS?
YEAH! FORGIVE THEM, FOR THEY KNOW NOT WHAT THEY DO! WHO'D HE THINK HE IS? JESUS ALMIGHTY CHRIST OR SOMETHING? CREEP!

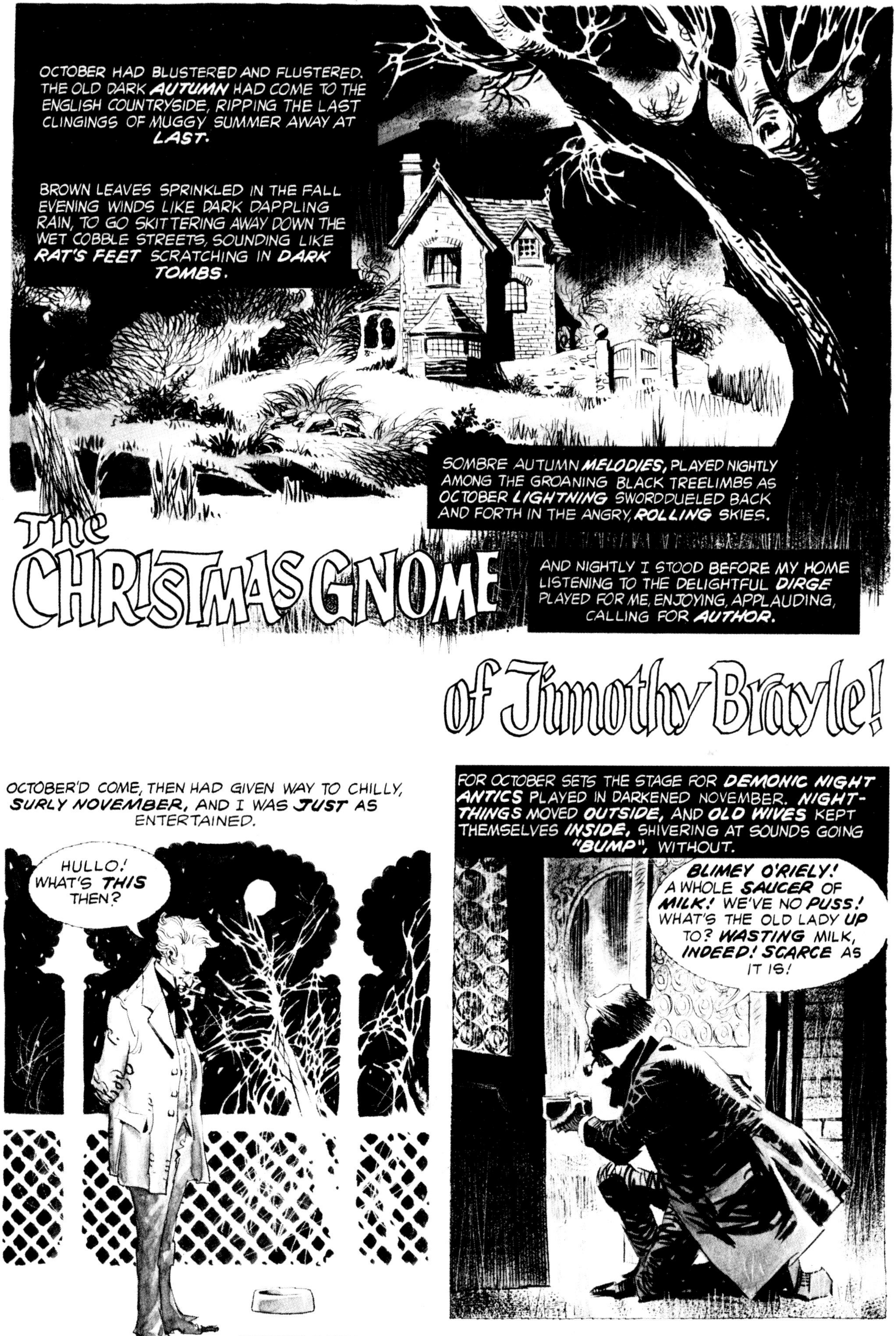

OCTOBER HAD BLUSTERED AND FLUSTERED. THE OLD DARK AUTUMN HAD COME TO THE ENGLISH COUNTRYSIDE, RIPPING THE LAST CLINGINGS OF MUGGY SUMMER AWAY AT LAST.
BROWN LEAVES SPRINKLED IN THE FALL EVENING WINDS LIKE DARK DAPPLING RAIN, TO GO SKITTERING AWAY DOWN THE WET COBBLE STREETS, SOUNDING LIKE RAT'S FEET SCRATCHING IN DARK TOMBS.
SOMBRE AUTUMN MELODIES, PLAYED NIGHTLY AMONG THE GROANING BLACK TREELIMBS AS OCTOBER LIGHTNING SWORDDUELED BACK AND FORTH IN THE ANGRY, ROLLING SKIES.
The CHRISTMAS GNOME
AND NIGHTLY I STOOD BEFORE MY HOME LISTENING TO THE DELIGHTFUL DIRGE PLAYED FOR ME, ENJOYING, APPLAUDING, CALLING FOR AUTHOR.
of Timothy Brayle!
OCTOBER'D COME, THEN HAD GIVEN WAY TO CHILLY, SURLY NOVEMBER, AND I WAS JUST AS ENTERTAINED.
HULLO! WHAT'S THIS THEN?
FOR OCTOBER SETS THE STAGE FOR DEMONIC NIGHT ANTICS PLAYED IN DARKENED NOVEMBER. NIGHT-THINGS MOVED OUTSIDE, AND OLD WIVES KEPT THEMSELVES INSIDE, SHIVERING AT SOUNDS GOING "BUMP", WITHOUT.
BLIMEY O'RIELY! A WHOLE SAUCER OF MILK! WE'VE NO PUSS! WHAT'S THE OLD LADY UP TO? WASTING MILK, INDEED! SCARCE AS IT IS!

STORY: BUDD LEWIS / ART: LEOPOLD SANCHEZ

MMM. SWEET AS **MOTHER'S KISS.** HATE TO **WASTE** IT! TIM, MY BOY, **INDULGE** YOURSELF!

IT'D NEVER BEEN **CLEAR** TO ME BEFORE THAT **OLD WIVES TALES** ARE SUPPORTED BY **OLD WIVES,** LIKE **MINE.** BUT, HERE IT **WAS...**

...MAGGIE BRAYLE'S **OFFERING** TO THE **DARK SPIRITS** OF THE **NIGHT.** A FRESH BOWL OF MILK FOR THE IMPS, SPRITES AND GNOMES.

THAT'S WHAT SHE'S DOING... LEAVING MILK FOR THE TROUBLEMAKING **ELVES!** AH, MY DEAR, SWEET **DUMB** WIFE, MAGGIE!

AHHH, WELL! THE OLD WOMAN'D BE DISAPPOINTED IF HER OFFERING WASN'T **TOUCHED** IN THE MORNING. THE EARLY **GNOME** GETS THE **CREAM!**

IT MUST HAVE BEEN ONE OF THOSE **EVES** WHEN THE WEE **SPIRITS** WERE ON THE **PROWL.** AND, THE **ONLY** WAY TO KEEP THEM **HAPPY** WAS **BRIBERY.**

HERE, LET THE LITTLE DEVILS DRINK **THIS!** FAR LESS **SCARCE** THAN MILK AND FAR MORE **FUN!**

NOTHING LIKE A GOOD SLUG OF MILK BEFORE TURNING IN!

I'D NEVER LOST WHAT MUM CALLED ME **MILK TOOTH.** THUS, I MADE AN AGREEABLE **EXCHANGE.** BESIDES, I WAS A BIT VEXED AT MAGS FOR LEAVING **BRIBES** TO FAIRIES AND **ELVES.** THOUGHT SHE'D GROWN OUT OF **THAT** THINKING.

RECALLING BITS AND FLASHES OF LOCAL **LORE,** ON **CERTAIN EVENINGS** WHEN THE PIXIES PROWLED, IF A HOUSE DID NOT LEAVE SOMETHING TO EAT FOR THEM, THEY'D CAUSE **CHAOS.**

OH NOTHING **MONUMENTAL,** BUT **PRANKS,** SUCH AS CURDLING THE MILK, STOPPING UP THE FIREPLACE, MAKING THE BABIES CRY AND SUCH.

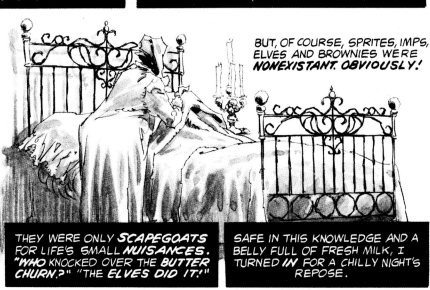

BUT, OF COURSE, SPRITES, IMPS, ELVES AND BROWNIES WERE **NONEXISTANT. OBVIOUSLY!**

THEY WERE ONLY **SCAPEGOATS** FOR LIFE'S SMALL **NUISANCES.** "**WHO** KNOCKED OVER THE **BUTTER CHURN?**" "THE **ELVES** DID IT!"

SAFE IN THIS KNOWLEDGE AND A BELLY FULL OF FRESH MILK, I TURNED **IN** FOR A CHILLY NIGHT'S REPOSE.

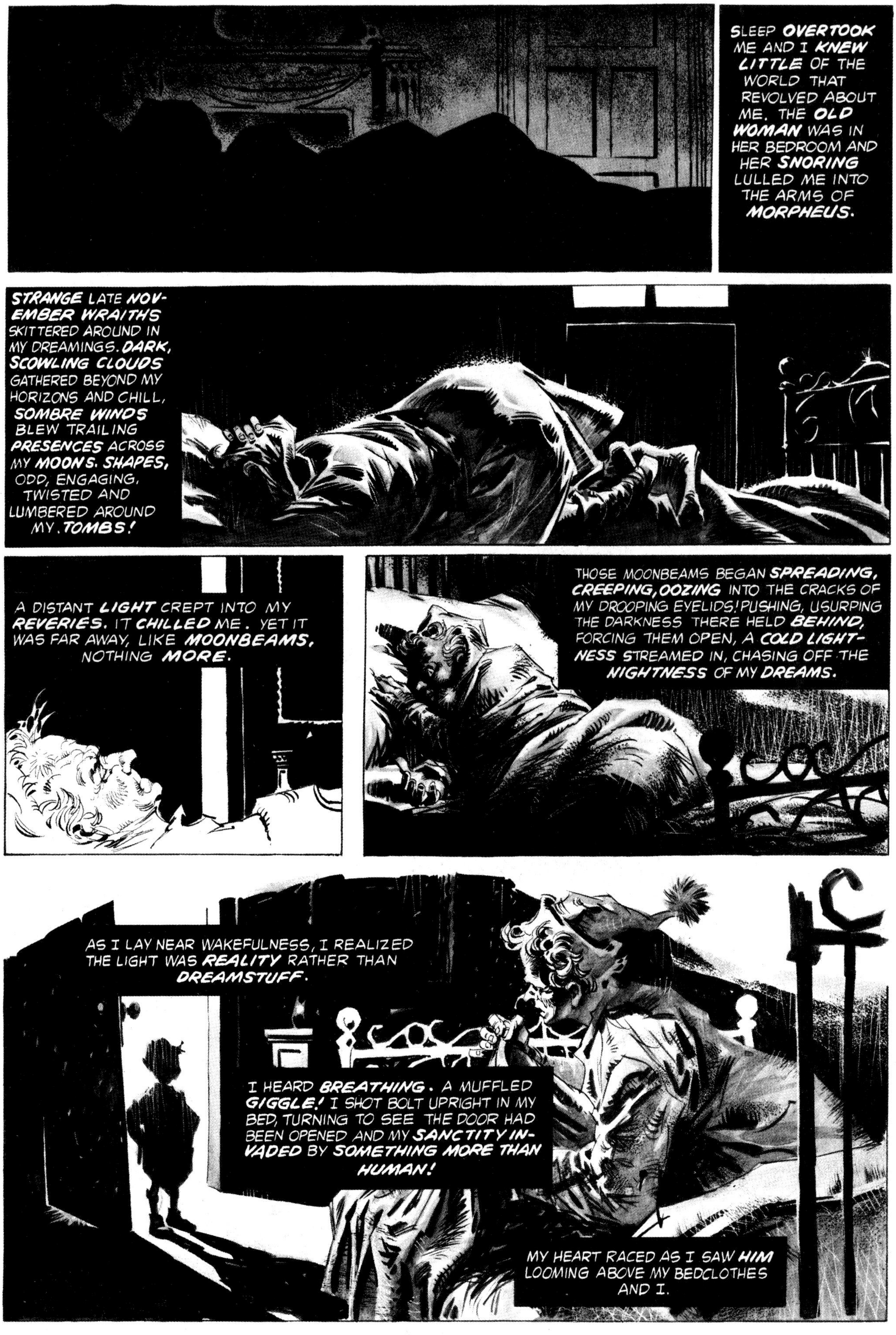
SLEEP OVERTOOK ME AND I KNEW LITTLE OF THE WORLD THAT REVOLVED ABOUT ME. THE OLD WOMAN WAS IN HER BEDROOM AND HER SNORING LULLED ME INTO THE ARMS OF MORPHEUS.
STRANGE LATE NOVEMBER WRAITHS SKITTERED AROUND IN MY DREAMINGS. DARK, SCOWLING CLOUDS GATHERED BEYOND MY HORIZONS AND CHILL, SOMBRE WINDS BLEW TRAILING PRESENCES ACROSS MY MOONS. SHAPES, ODD, ENGAGING, TWISTED AND LUMBERED AROUND MY .TOMBS!
A DISTANT LIGHT CREPT INTO MY REVERIES. IT CHILLED ME. YET IT WAS FAR AWAY, LIKE MOONBEAMS, NOTHING MORE.
THOSE MOONBEAMS BEGAN SPREADING, CREEPING, OOZING INTO THE CRACKS OF MY DROOPING EYELIDS! PUSHING, USURPING THE DARKNESS THERE HELD BEHIND, FORCING THEM OPEN, A COLD LIGHTNESS STREAMED IN, CHASING OFF THE NIGHTNESS OF MY DREAMS.
AS I LAY NEAR WAKEFULNESS, I REALIZED THE LIGHT WAS REALITY RATHER THAN DREAMSTUFF.
I HEARD BREATHING. A MUFFLED GIGGLE! I SHOT BOLT UPRIGHT IN MY BED, TURNING TO SEE THE DOOR HAD BEEN OPENED AND MY SANCTITY INVADED BY SOMETHING MORE THAN HUMAN!
MY HEART RACED AS I SAW HIM LOOMING ABOVE MY BEDCLOTHES AND I.

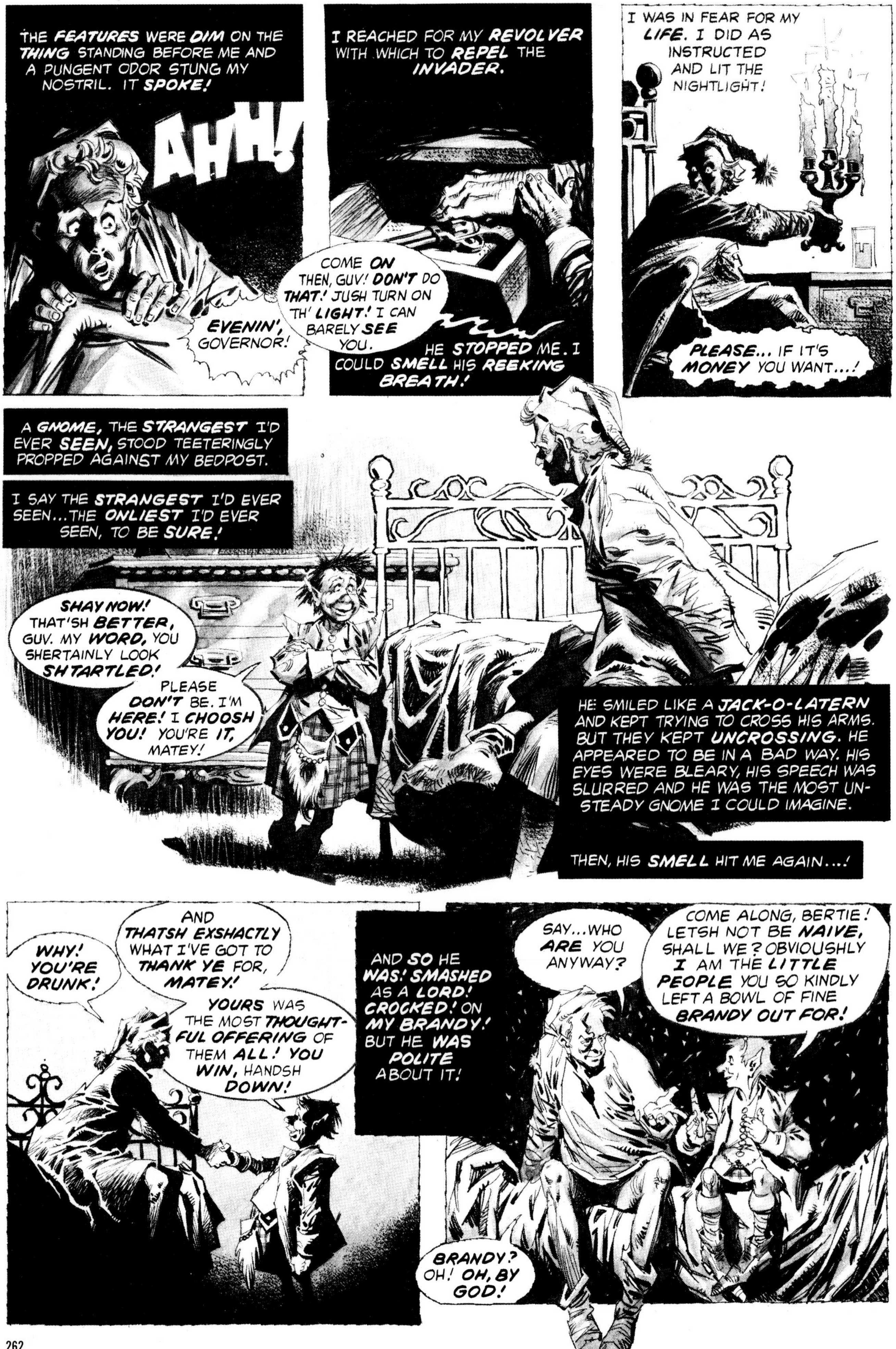
THE FEATURES WERE DIM ON THE THING STANDING BEFORE ME AND A PUNGENT ODOR STUNG MY NOSTRIL. IT SPOKE!
AHH!
EVENIN', GOVERNOR!
I REACHED FOR MY REVOLVER WITH WHICH TO REPEL THE INVADER.
COME ON THEN, GUV! DON'T DO THAT! JUSH TURN ON TH' LIGHT! I CAN BARELY SEE YOU.
HE STOPPED ME. I COULD SMELL HIS REEKING BREATH!
I WAS IN FEAR FOR MY LIFE. I DID AS INSTRUCTED AND LIT THE NIGHTLIGHT!
PLEASE... IF IT'S MONEY YOU WANT...!
A GNOME, THE STRANGEST I'D EVER SEEN, STOOD TEETERINGLY PROPPED AGAINST MY BEDPOST.
I SAY THE STRANGEST I'D EVER SEEN...THE ONLIEST I'D EVER SEEN, TO BE SURE!
SHAY NOW! THAT'SH BETTER, GUV. MY WORD, YOU SHERTAINLY LOOK SHTARTLED!
PLEASE DON'T BE. I'M HERE! I CHOOSH YOU! YOU'RE IT, MATEY!
HE SMILED LIKE A JACK-O-LATERN AND KEPT TRYING TO CROSS HIS ARMS. BUT THEY KEPT UNCROSSING. HE APPEARED TO BE IN A BAD WAY. HIS EYES WERE BLEARY, HIS SPEECH WAS SLURRED AND HE WAS THE MOST UNSTEADY GNOME I COULD IMAGINE.
THEN, HIS SMELL HIT ME AGAIN...!
WHY! YOU'RE DRUNK!
AND THATSH EXSHACTLY WHAT I'VE GOT TO THANK YE FOR, MATEY!
YOURS WAS THE MOST THOUGHTFUL OFFERING OF THEM ALL! YOU WIN, HANDSH DOWN!
AND SO HE WAS! SMASHED AS A LORD! CROCKED! ON MY BRANDY! BUT HE WAS POLITE ABOUT IT!
SAY...WHO ARE YOU ANYWAY?
COME ALONG, BERTIE! LETSH NOT BE NAIVE, SHALL WE? OBVIOUSHLY I AM THE LITTLE PEOPLE YOU SO KINDLY LEFT A BOWL OF FINE BRANDY OUT FOR!
BRANDY? OH! OH, BY GOD!

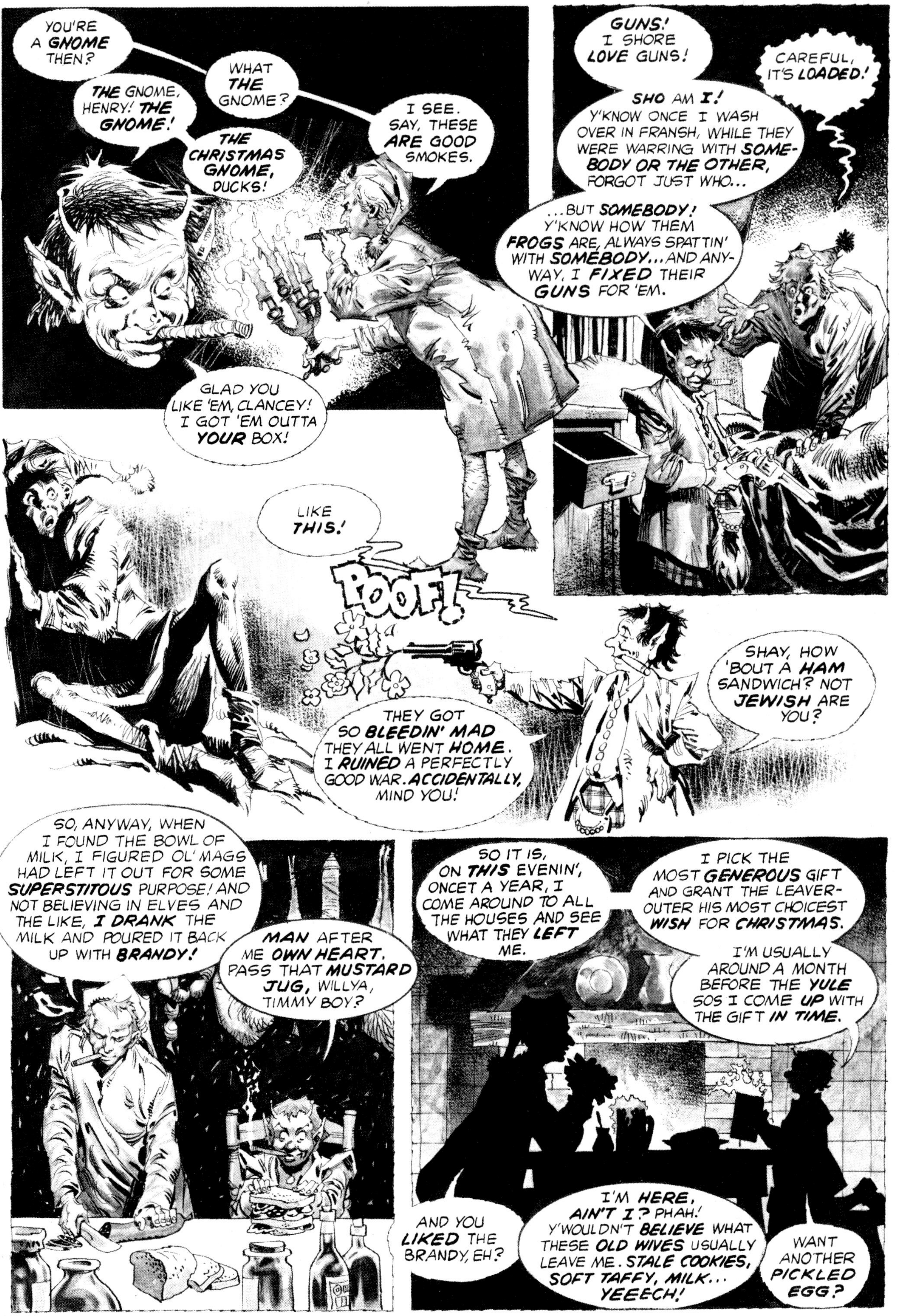
YOU'RE A GNOME THEN?
WHAT THE GNOME?
THE GNOME, HENRY! THE GNOME!
THE CHRISTMAS GNOME, DUCKS!
I SEE. SAY, THESE ARE GOOD SMOKES.
GLAD YOU LIKE 'EM, CLANCEY! I GOT 'EM OUTTA YOUR BOX!
GUNS! I SHORE LOVE GUNS!
CAREFUL, IT'S LOADED!
SHO AM I! Y'KNOW ONCE I WASH OVER IN FRANSH, WHILE THEY WERE WARRING WITH SOMEBODY OR THE OTHER, FORGOT JUST WHO...
...BUT SOMEBODY! Y'KNOW HOW THEM FROGS ARE, ALWAYS SPATTIN' WITH SOMEBODY... AND ANYWAY, I FIXED THEIR GUNS FOR 'EM.
LIKE THIS!
POOF!
THEY GOT SO BLEEDIN' MAD THEY ALL WENT HOME. I RUINED A PERFECTLY GOOD WAR. ACCIDENTALLY, MIND YOU!
'SHAY, HOW 'BOUT A HAM SANDWICH? NOT JEWISH ARE YOU?
SO, ANYWAY, WHEN I FOUND THE BOWL OF MILK, I FIGURED OL' MAGS HAD LEFT IT OUT FOR SOME SUPERSTITOUS PURPOSE! AND NOT BELIEVING IN ELVES AND THE LIKE, I DRANK THE MILK AND POURED IT BACK UP WITH BRANDY!
MAN AFTER ME OWN HEART. PASS THAT MUSTARD JUG, WILLYA, TIMMY BOY?
SO IT IS, ON THIS EVENIN', ONCET A YEAR, I COME AROUND TO ALL THE HOUSES AND SEE WHAT THEY LEFT ME.
I PICK THE MOST GENEROUS GIFT AND GRANT THE LEAVER-OUTER HIS MOST CHOICEST WISH FOR CHRISTMAS.
I'M USUALLY AROUND A MONTH BEFORE THE YULE SOS I COME UP WITH THE GIFT IN TIME.
AND YOU LIKED THE BRANDY, EH?
I'M HERE, AIN'T I? PHAH! Y'WOULDN'T BELIEVE WHAT THESE OLD WIVES USUALLY LEAVE ME. STALE COOKIES, SOFT TAFFY, MILK... YEEECH!
WANT ANOTHER PICKLED EGG?

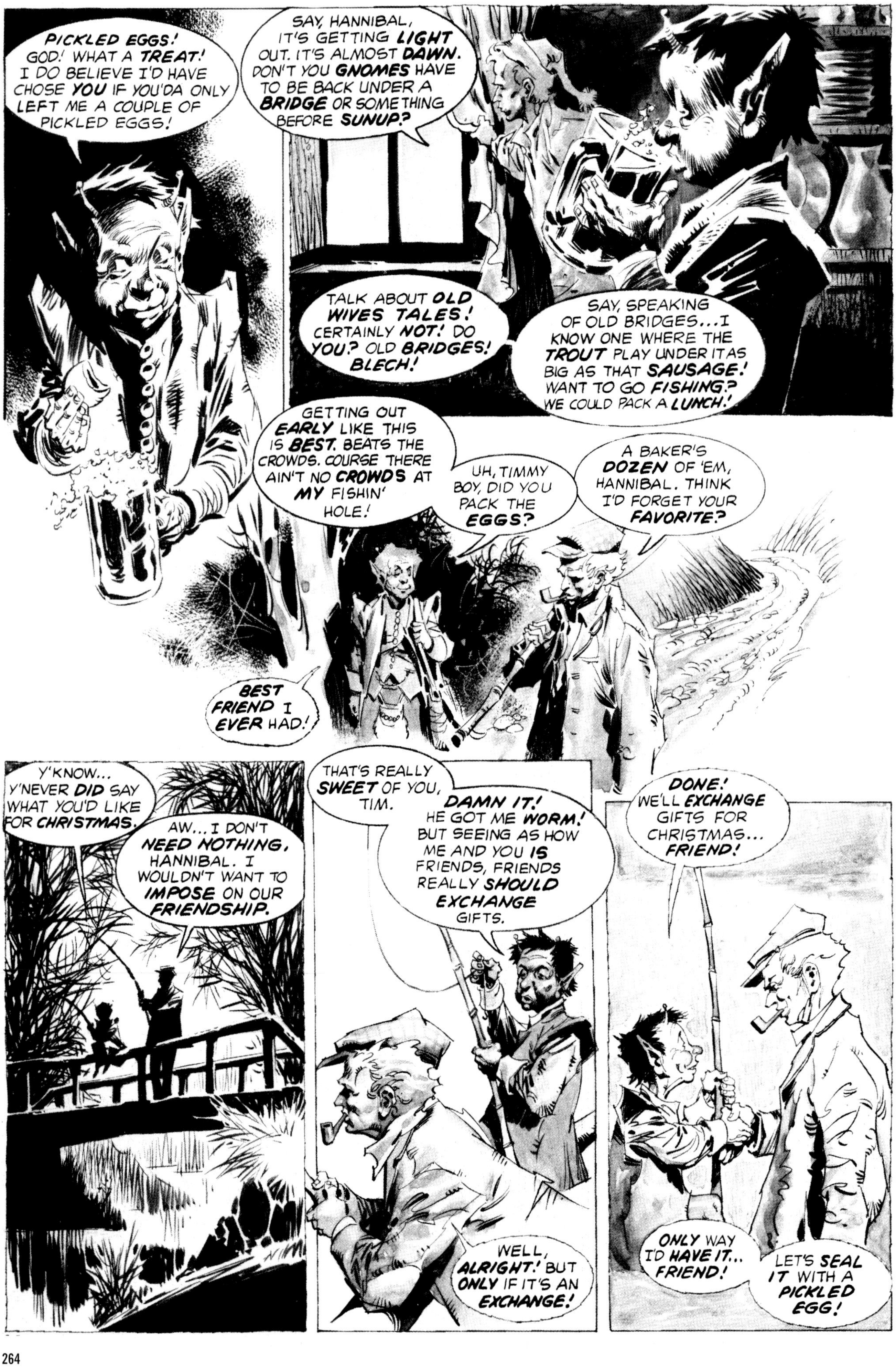
PICKLED EGGS! GOD! WHAT A TREAT! I DO BELIEVE I'D HAVE CHOSE YOU IF YOU'DA ONLY LEFT ME A COUPLE OF PICKLED EGGS!
SAY, HANNIBAL, IT'S GETTING LIGHT OUT. IT'S ALMOST DAWN. DON'T YOU GNOMES HAVE TO BE BACK UNDER A BRIDGE OR SOMETHING BEFORE SUNUP?
TALK ABOUT OLD WIVES TALES! CERTAINLY NOT! DO YOU? OLD BRIDGES! BLECH!
SAY, SPEAKING OF OLD BRIDGES... I KNOW ONE WHERE THE TROUT PLAY UNDER IT AS BIG AS THAT SAUSAGE! WANT TO GO FISHING? WE COULD PACK A LUNCH!
GETTING OUT EARLY LIKE THIS IS BEST. BEATS THE CROWDS. COURSE THERE AIN'T NO CROWDS AT MY FISHIN' HOLE!
UH, TIMMY BOY, DID YOU PACK THE EGGS?
A BAKER'S DOZEN OF 'EM, HANNIBAL. THINK I'D FORGET YOUR FAVORITE?
BEST FRIEND I EVER HAD!
Y'KNOW... Y'NEVER DID SAY WHAT YOU'D LIKE FOR CHRISTMAS.
AW... I DON'T NEED NOTHING, HANNIBAL. I WOULDN'T WANT TO IMPOSE ON OUR FRIENDSHIP.
THAT'S REALLY SWEET OF YOU, TIM.
DAMN IT! HE GOT ME WORM! BUT SEEING AS HOW ME AND YOU IS FRIENDS, FRIENDS REALLY SHOULD EXCHANGE GIFTS.
WELL, ALRIGHT! BUT ONLY IF IT'S AN EXCHANGE!
DONE! WE'LL EXCHANGE GIFTS FOR CHRISTMAS... FRIEND!
ONLY WAY I'D HAVE IT... FRIEND!
LET'S SEAL IT WITH A PICKLED EGG!

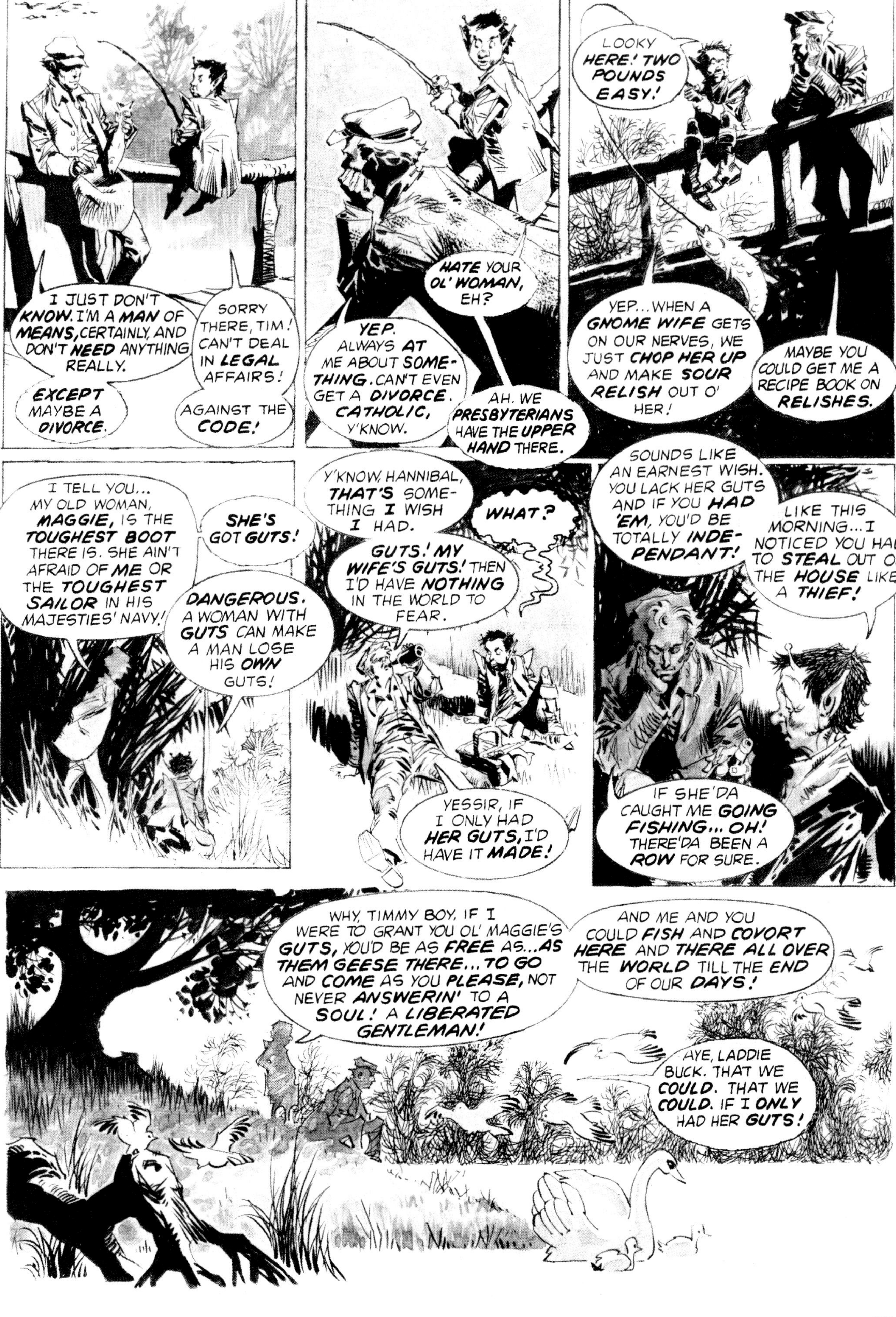
I JUST DON'T KNOW. I'M A MAN OF MEANS, CERTAINLY, AND DON'T NEED ANYTHING REALLY.
EXCEPT MAYBE A DIVORCE.
SORRY THERE, TIM! CAN'T DEAL IN LEGAL AFFAIRS!
AGAINST THE CODE!
HATE YOUR OL' WOMAN, EH?
YEP. ALWAYS AT ME ABOUT SOMETHING. CAN'T EVEN GET A DIVORCE. CATHOLIC, Y'KNOW.
AH. WE PRESBYTERIANS HAVE THE UPPER HAND THERE.
LOOKY HERE! TWO POUNDS EASY!
YEP... WHEN A GNOME WIFE GETS ON OUR NERVES, WE JUST CHOP HER UP AND MAKE SOUR RELISH OUT O' HER!
MAYBE YOU COULD GET ME A RECIPE BOOK ON RELISHES.
I TELL YOU... MY OLD WOMAN, MAGGIE, IS THE TOUGHEST BOOT THERE IS. SHE AIN'T AFRAID OF ME OR THE TOUGHEST SAILOR IN HIS MAJESTIES' NAVY!
SHE'S GOT GUTS!
DANGEROUS. A WOMAN WITH GUTS CAN MAKE A MAN LOSE HIS OWN GUTS!
Y'KNOW, HANNIBAL, THAT'S SOMETHING I WISH I HAD.
WHAT?
GUTS! MY WIFE'S GUTS! THEN I'D HAVE NOTHING IN THE WORLD TO FEAR.
YESSIR, IF I ONLY HAD HER GUTS, I'D HAVE IT MADE!
SOUNDS LIKE AN EARNEST WISH. YOU LACK HER GUTS AND IF YOU HAD 'EM, YOU'D BE TOTALLY INDEPENDANT!
LIKE THIS MORNING... I NOTICED YOU HAD TO STEAL OUT OF THE HOUSE LIKE A THIEF!
IF SHE'DA CAUGHT ME GOING FISHING... OH! THERE'DA BEEN A ROW FOR SURE.
WHY, TIMMY BOY, IF I WERE TO GRANT YOU OL' MAGGIE'S GUTS, YOU'D BE AS FREE AS...AS THEM GEESE THERE... TO GO AND COME AS YOU PLEASE, NOT NEVER ANSWERIN' TO A SOUL! A LIBERATED GENTLEMAN!
AND ME AND YOU COULD FISH AND COVORT HERE AND THERE ALL OVER THE WORLD TILL THE END OF OUR DAYS!
AYE, LADDIE BUCK. THAT WE COULD. THAT WE COULD. IF I ONLY HAD HER GUTS!

WELL, A *BARGAIN* WAS HIT UPON...MY *WISH* WAS *MADE* FOR MY CHRISTMAS *PRESENT* AND HANNIBAL HAD TO BE ON HIS WAY FOR AWHILE. *BUSY* PEOPLE *CHRISTMAS GNOMES.*

DECK THE HALLS WITH BOUGHS OF *HOLLY,* FALALALA *LA LALA ♪ LAAAA! ♪*

I'D *RECEIVED* SEVERAL CARDS FROM HANNIBAL FROM THE CONTINENT. HIS CARDS WERE ALWAYS FULL OF *GOOD CHEER* AND *FRIENDSHIP.*

HERE'S *YOURS,* HANNIBAL. THE *BEST* TO BE *BOUGHT.*

Merry Christmas to Hannibal Your [illegible]

BRANDY IMPORTED FRAGILE 24 BOT COUNT

SAID HE'D BE *BACK* FOR *CHRISTMAS!* AND IF HE COULD ARRANGE TO GIVE ME THE *GUTS* I NEEDED, WE'D BE *OFF TOGETHER* FOR A *YEAR LONG HOLIDAY AROUND THE WORLD. WINE, WOMEN AND SONG!* AND *MAGGIE'D NEVER* COMPLAIN!

I *MISSED* MY FRIEND *SORELY.* THOUGHT ABOUT HIM EVERYDAY. BUT I KNEW HE WAS A GENTLEMANLY GNOME OF HIS *WORD,* AND I KNEW HE'D GET HIS BUSINESS IN ORDER IN TIME TO COME *BACK* FOR *CHRISTMAS.*

I DID SO *LONG* FOR *SOMEONE* TO *SHARE* THE HAPPY SEASON *WITH,* AS MAGGIE'D SHUT HERSELF *AWAY.* SHE *HATED CHRISTMAS.*

CHRISTMAS *DAWN* EDGED INTO MY ROOM AND I SLIPPED DOWNSTAIRS TO SEE WHAT *MIGHT* BE UNDER THE *TREE.*

WELL, I'LL BE *DAMNED!*

AND THERE, SURE ENOUGH, WAS A *SIGHT* TO *DELIGHT* MY *EYES* AND *HEART.*

MERRY CHRISTMAS, TO TIM. HERE'S YOUR WIFE'S GUTS. YOURS, HANNIBAL

MERRY CHRISTMAS, TIMMY BOY!

AND A *MERRY CHRISTMAS* TO YOU, HANNIBAL! LET'S HAVE SOME *EGGS!*

IT WAS THE *MERRIEST CHRISTMAS* OF *ALL.* WE *LAUGHED* AND *SANG* AND *TOASTED* EACH OTHER ALL *DAY* AND *NIGHT.* IT WAS THE *MERRIEST OF GIFT EXCHANGES!*

I HAVE TO *CLOSE* THIS NOW, TO FINISH *PACKING.* HANNIBAL WENT TO BUY *STEAMSHIP PASSAGE* FOR *TWO.* WE PLAN TO BE IN *PARIS* BY *NEW YEARS. MY...HOW THEY DO CELEBRATE NEW YEARS IN PARIS!*

MERRY CHRISTMAS TO YOU ALL!

CREEPY FAN CLUB

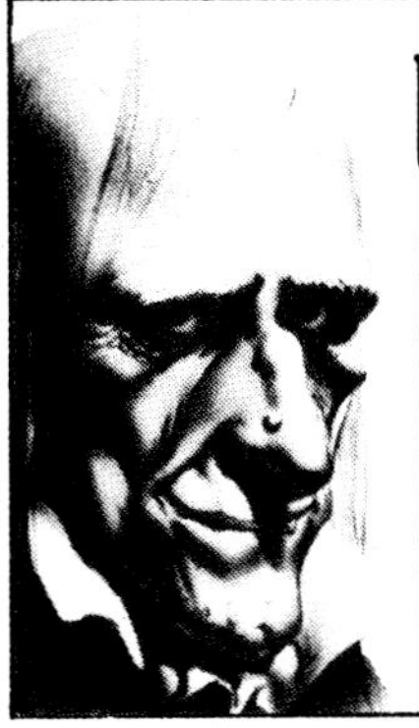

UNCLE CREEPY'S VERY OWN FANG CLUB!—AND IT'S A MUST-JOIN THING FOR ALL OUR RABID READERS!! Take a good look at the Funtastic couple of goodies you get when you join! A foul, full-color UNCLE CREEPY membership badge, with eye-catching art by JACK DAVIS! And an UNCLE CREEPY FAN CLUB MEMBERSHIP CARD, WITH KNEAT GLOSSY FINISH AND YOUR OWN SPECIALLY PRINTED IDENTIFICATION NUMBER ON IT! Order Today! #2642, UNCLE CREEPY FAN CLUB, $2.00

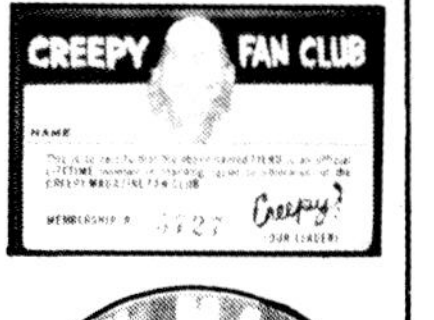
CREEPY
FAN CLUB

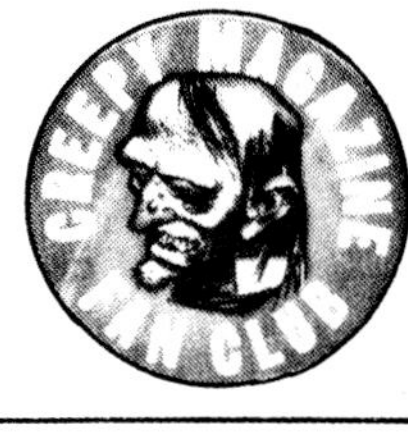
CREEPY MAGAZINE
FAN CLUB

PATCHES

3-INCH CREEPY AND EERIE EMBLEMS IN COLOR!

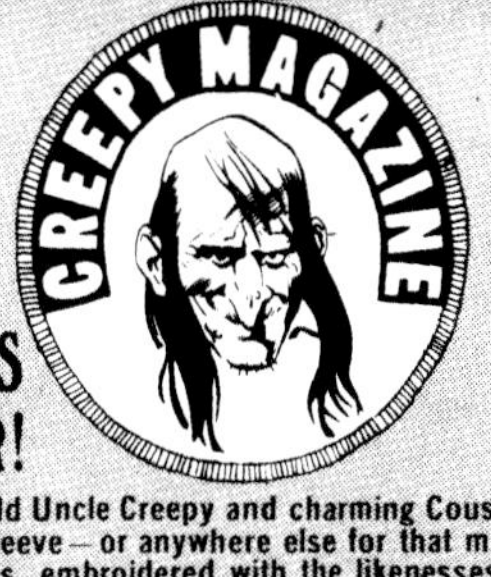
CREEPY MAGAZINE

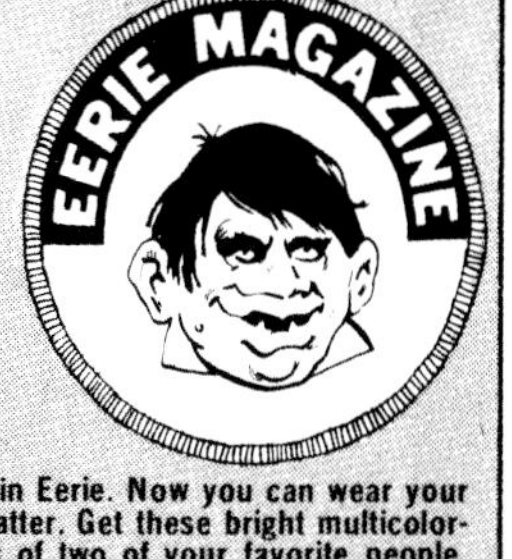
EERIE MAGAZINE

You love dear old Uncle Creepy and charming Cousin Eerie. Now you can wear your heart on your sleeve—or anywhere else for that matter. Get these bright multicolored cloth patches, embroidered with the likenesses of two of your favorite people. Sew them on your jacket, jeans, T-shirt, cap or anyplace. Patches are three inches tall. Eerie patch is aqua with green face. Creepy patch, orange with yellow face. Heavy duty, machine washable, satin bound. Buy a batch! #2621 CREEPY PATCH $1.00/ #2623 EERIE PATCH $1.00.

CREEPY & EERIE RINGS

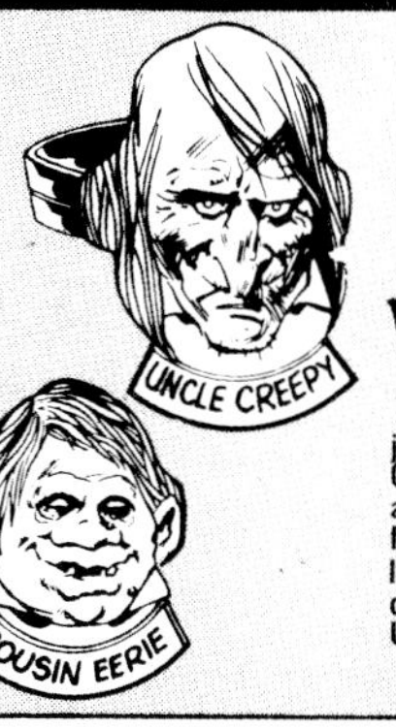
UNCLE CREEPY
COUSIN EERIE

QUALITY JEWELRY COLLECTOR'S ITEM! FITS ANY FINGER

You asked for it, and here they are! These magnificently burnished Gold Finish Rings cover HALF your finger! They are specially made for us by a quality jewelry manufacturer & are adjustable to fit any finger. Guaranteed to become Collector's Items! The faces of CREEPY & EERIE are over 1-1/2" long, majestically sculptured in fine detail. You'll be proud to wear these costly-looking fine rings for any occasion. Refer to the coupon last page of this magazine to order. #2610 UNCLE CREEPY RING $1.25; and #2611 COUSIN RING $1.25!

SAVE YOUR CREEPY

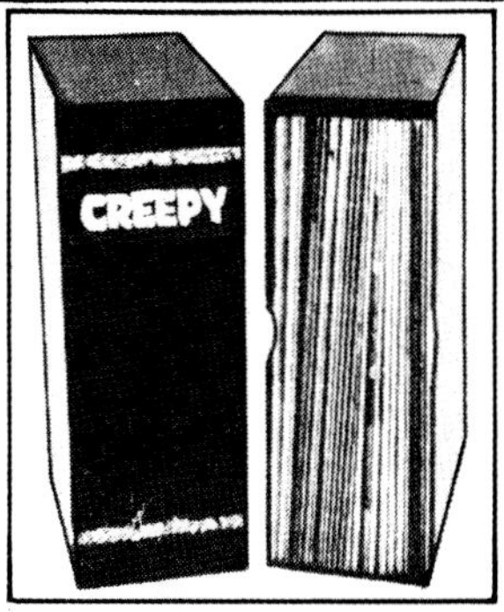
CREEPY

BACK ISSUES IN CUSTOM-DESIGNED LIBRARY CASES!

You must know how valuable Warren magazines are. You know how back issues increase in desirability and price as the supply of mint copies dwindles. So, you serious collectors of our books must be pleased to know that we're bringing out a whole fantastic line of CUSTOM-DESIGNED LEATHERETTE FINISH LIBRARY CASES. Each one holds a one-year run of this, your favorite imaginative horror mag, and keeps that run in superb condition. And has our title in gold type right on the spine! Fantastic! Order today!

This CREEPY LIBRARY CASE features a Navy-Blue spine and black leatherette body. #2635 CREEPY LIBRARY CASE $4.95

SUPER-DELUXE SPOOKTACULAR CREEPY & EERIE MASKS!

PLUS TWO TYPES CREEPY & EERIE BUDGET MASKS VINYL & RUBBER

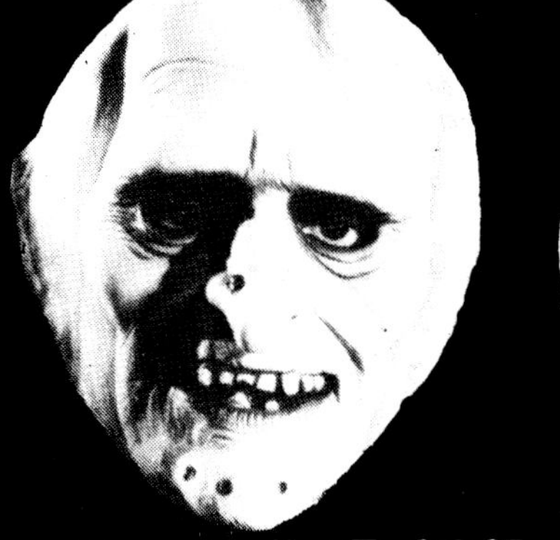

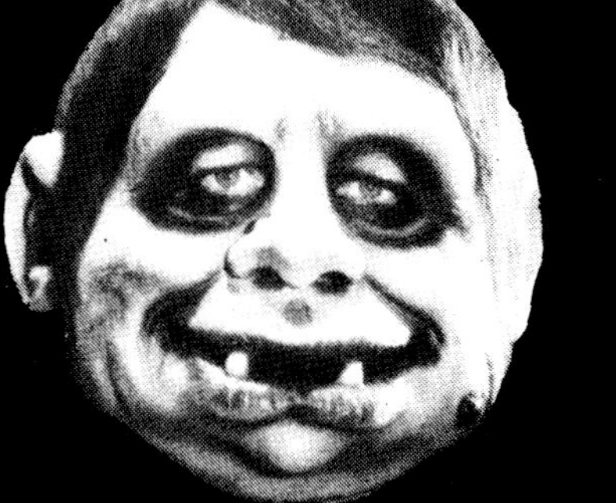

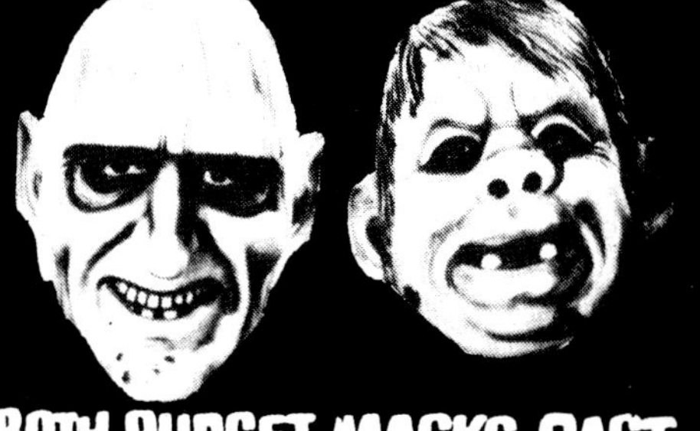

BOTH BUDGET MASKS CAST FROM SAME MOLD! ONLY ONE IS VINYL, ONE IS RUBBER!

UNCLE CREEPY DELUXE MASK

Specially made by Don Post! Finely executed with Creepish Craftsmanship to look just like our old Ugly Unc! High quality latex rubber and a ghastly, ghostly and realistic thatch of pale hair to top him off! A Morbid Masterwork! Order #2544 UNCLE CREEPY DELUXE MASK $14.95

COUSIN EERIE DELUXE MASK

Heavy, durable, whole-headed mask of our half-wit fiend! COUSIN EERIE is Scarily Sculpted in high quality latex rubber, with some hellishly red and realistic hair atop his hand-painted face! A Clammy Classic! Order #2545 COUSIN EERIE DELUXE MASK $14.95

Both the vinyl & the rubber Budget masks, represented above, look alike, but the vinyl is sturdier, more heavy-duty. Both these makes of mask cover the entire head, too. Each is a bargain! You'll probably want all six: Deluxe, Vinyl & Rubber, to hold super CREEPY & EERIE parties!

#2566 CREEPY VINYL MASK $8.95
#2567 EERIE VINYL MASK $8.95

#2509 CREEPY RUBBER MASK $4.95
#2510 EERIE RUBBER MASK $4.95

HERE ARE 3 FABULOUS SETS OF CREEPY-EERIE MASKS!

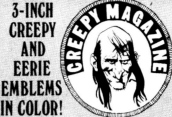

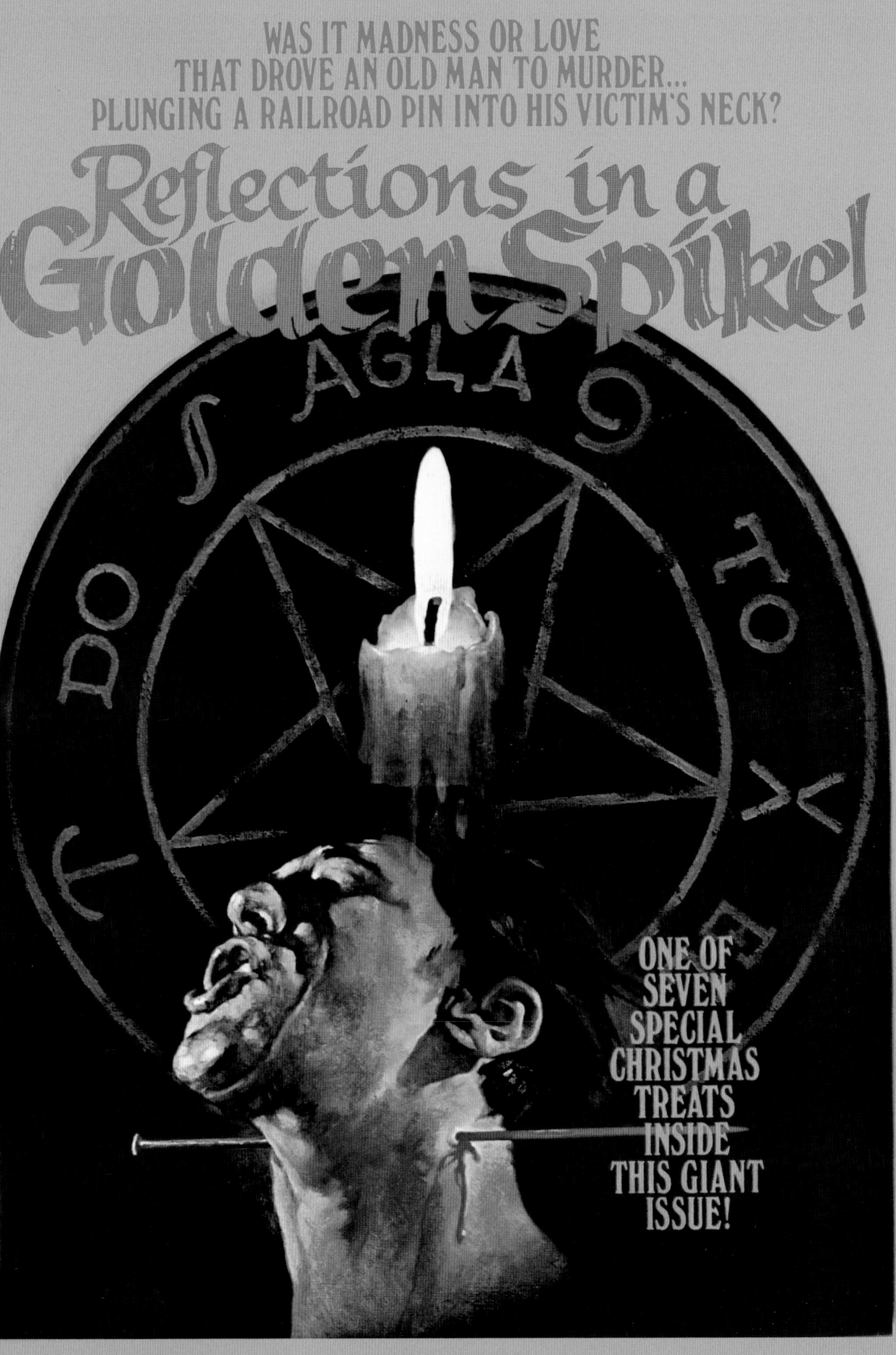
WAS IT MADNESS OR LOVE
THAT DROVE AN OLD MAN TO MURDER...
PLUNGING A RAILROAD PIN INTO HIS VICTIM'S NECK?
Reflections in a Golden Spike!
AGLA
DO
TO
ONE OF SEVEN SPECIAL CHRISTMAS TREATS INSIDE THIS GIANT ISSUE!

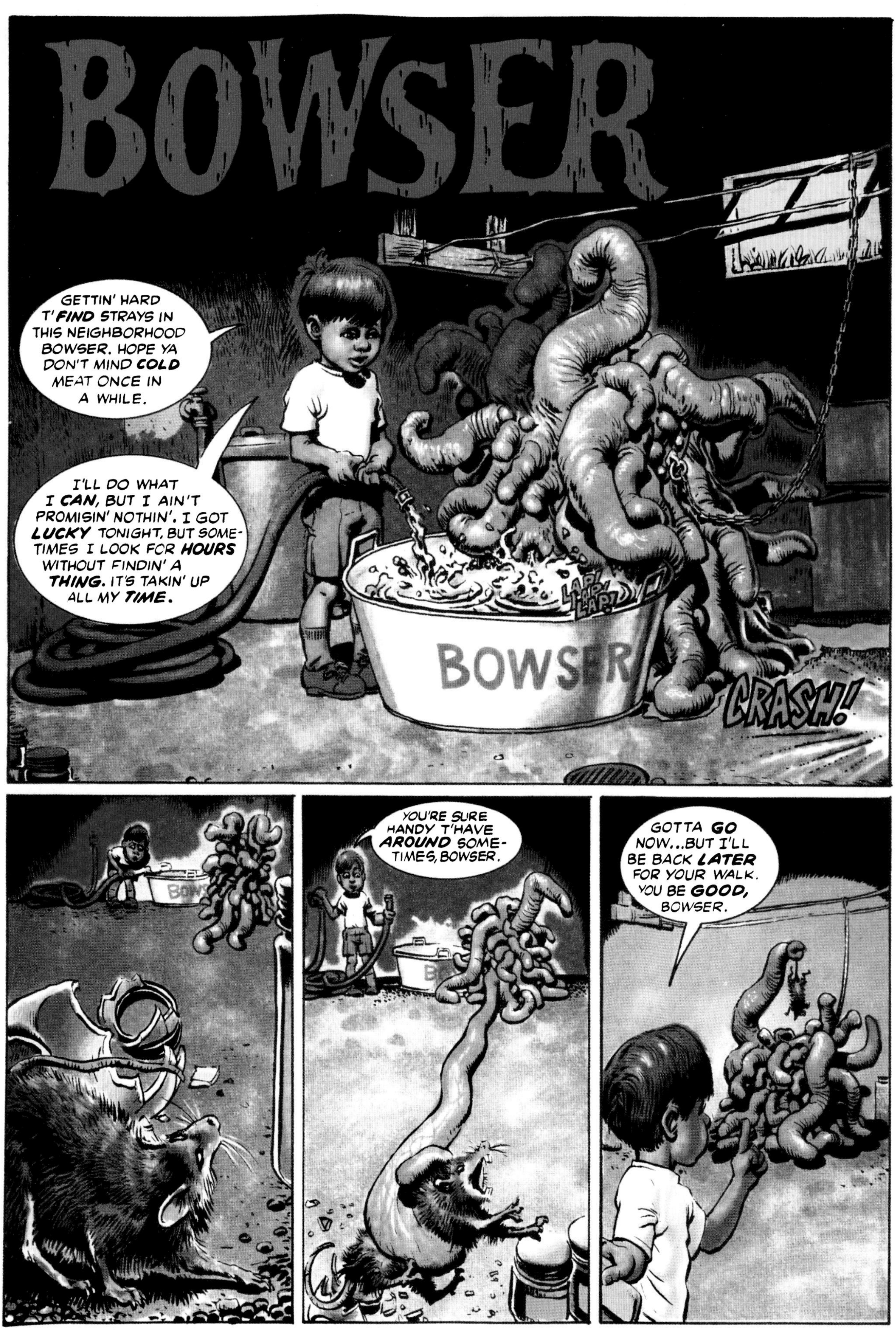
BOWSER
GETTIN' HARD T'FIND STRAYS IN THIS NEIGHBORHOOD BOWSER. HOPE YA DON'T MIND COLD MEAT ONCE IN A WHILE.
I'LL DO WHAT I CAN, BUT I AIN'T PROMISIN' NOTHIN'. I GOT LUCKY TONIGHT, BUT SOMETIMES I LOOK FOR HOURS WITHOUT FINDIN' A THING. IT'S TAKIN' UP ALL MY TIME.
LAP! LAP! LAP!
BOWSER
CRASH!
YOU'RE SURE HANDY T'HAVE AROUND SOMETIMES, BOWSER.
GOTTA GO NOW...BUT I'LL BE BACK LATER FOR YOUR WALK. YOU BE GOOD, BOWSER.

STORY: JAN STRNAD/ART: RICH CORBEN

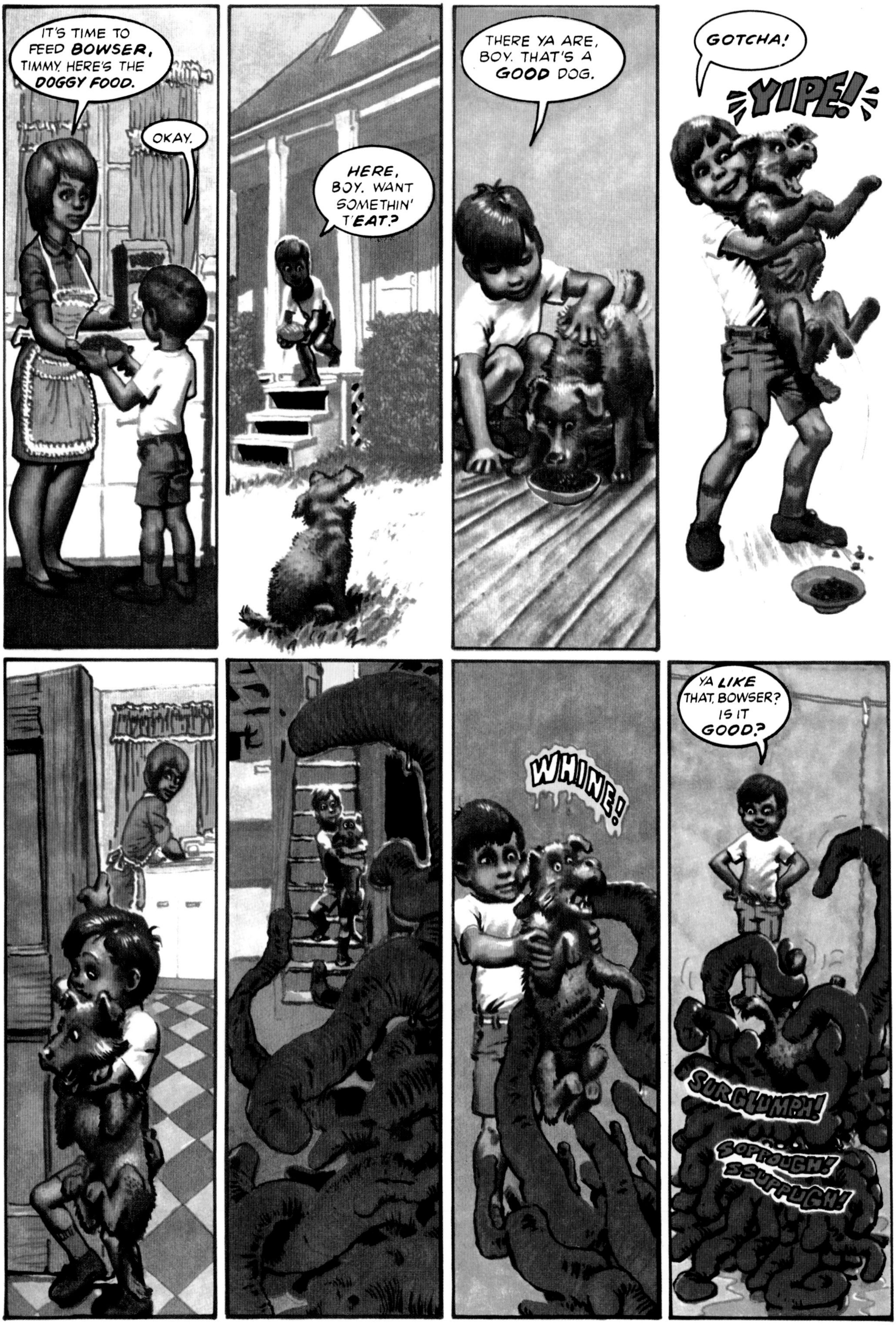

IT'S TIME TO FEED BOWSER, TIMMY. HERE'S THE DOGGY FOOD.
OKAY.
HERE, BOY. WANT SOMETHIN' T'EAT?
THERE YA ARE, BOY. THAT'S A GOOD DOG.
GOTCHA!
YIPE!
WHINE!
YA LIKE THAT, BOWSER? IS IT GOOD?
SURGLUMPH!
SOPROUGH!
SSUPPLUGH!

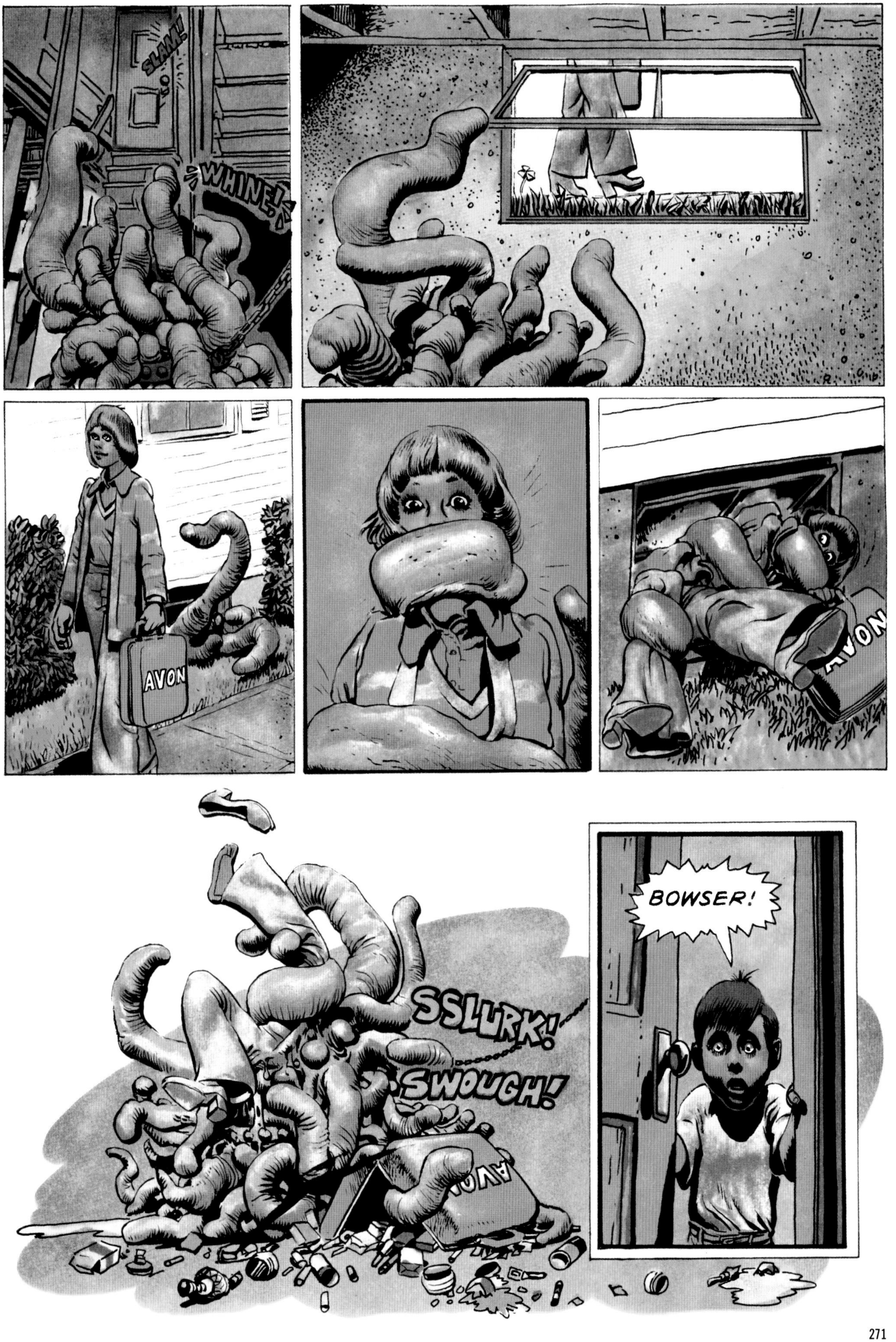
SLAM!
WHINE!
AVON
AVON
SSLURK!
SWOUGH!
AVON
BOWSER!

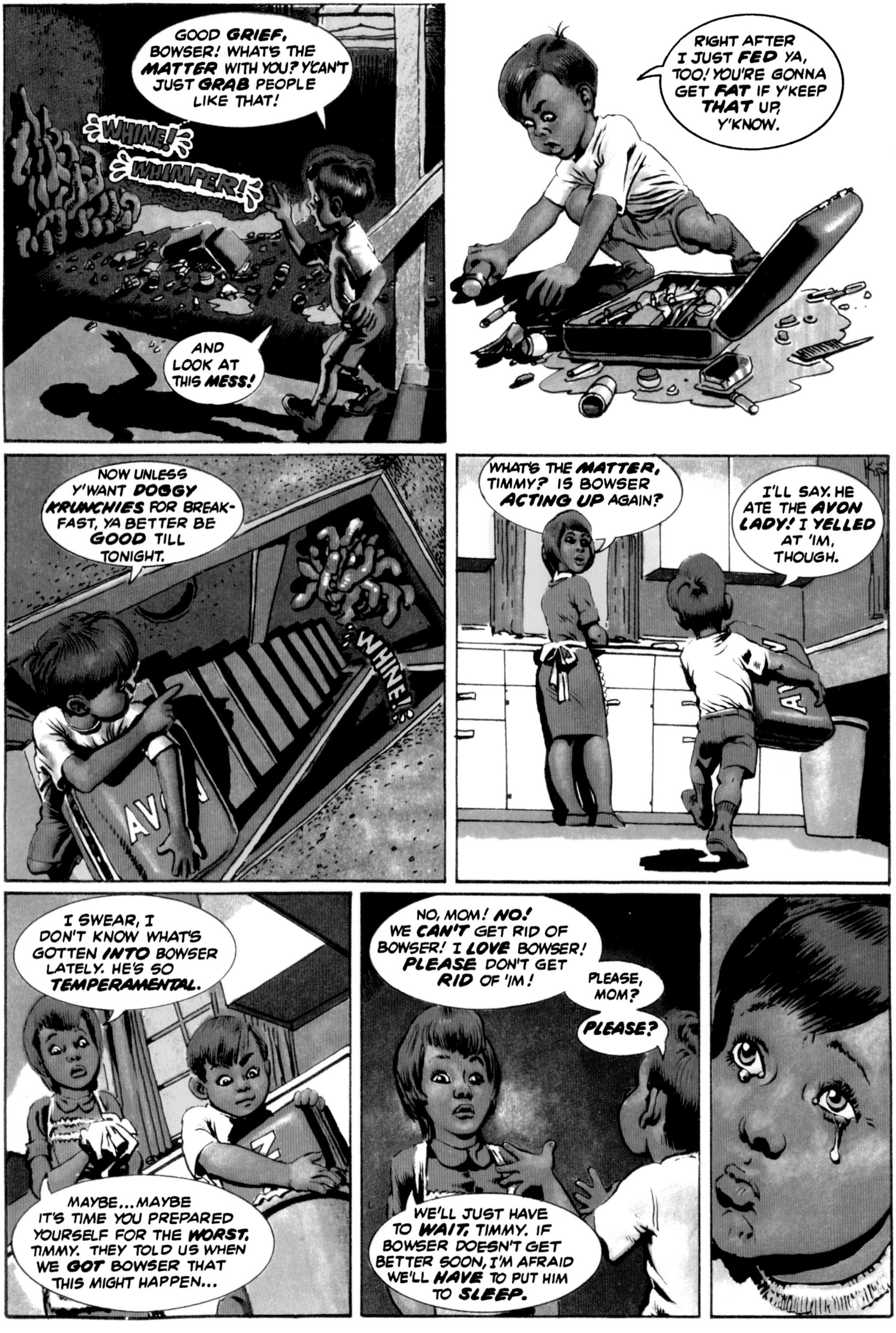
GOOD GRIEF, BOWSER! WHAT'S THE MATTER WITH YOU? Y'CAN'T JUST GRAB PEOPLE LIKE THAT!
WHINE!
WHIMPER!
AND LOOK AT THIS MESS!
RIGHT AFTER I JUST FED YA, TOO! YOU'RE GONNA GET FAT IF Y'KEEP THAT UP, Y'KNOW.
NOW UNLESS Y'WANT DOGGY KRUNCHIES FOR BREAK-FAST, YA BETTER BE GOOD TILL TONIGHT.
WHINE!
AVON
WHAT'S THE MATTER, TIMMY? IS BOWSER ACTING UP AGAIN?
I'LL SAY. HE ATE THE AVON LADY! I YELLED AT 'IM, THOUGH.
I SWEAR, I DON'T KNOW WHAT'S GOTTEN INTO BOWSER LATELY. HE'S SO TEMPERAMENTAL.
MAYBE...MAYBE IT'S TIME YOU PREPARED YOURSELF FOR THE WORST, TIMMY. THEY TOLD US WHEN WE GOT BOWSER THAT THIS MIGHT HAPPEN...
NO, MOM! NO! WE CAN'T GET RID OF BOWSER! I LOVE BOWSER! PLEASE DON'T GET RID OF 'IM!
PLEASE, MOM?
PLEASE?
WE'LL JUST HAVE TO WAIT, TIMMY. IF BOWSER DOESN'T GET BETTER SOON, I'M AFRAID WE'LL HAVE TO PUT HIM TO SLEEP.

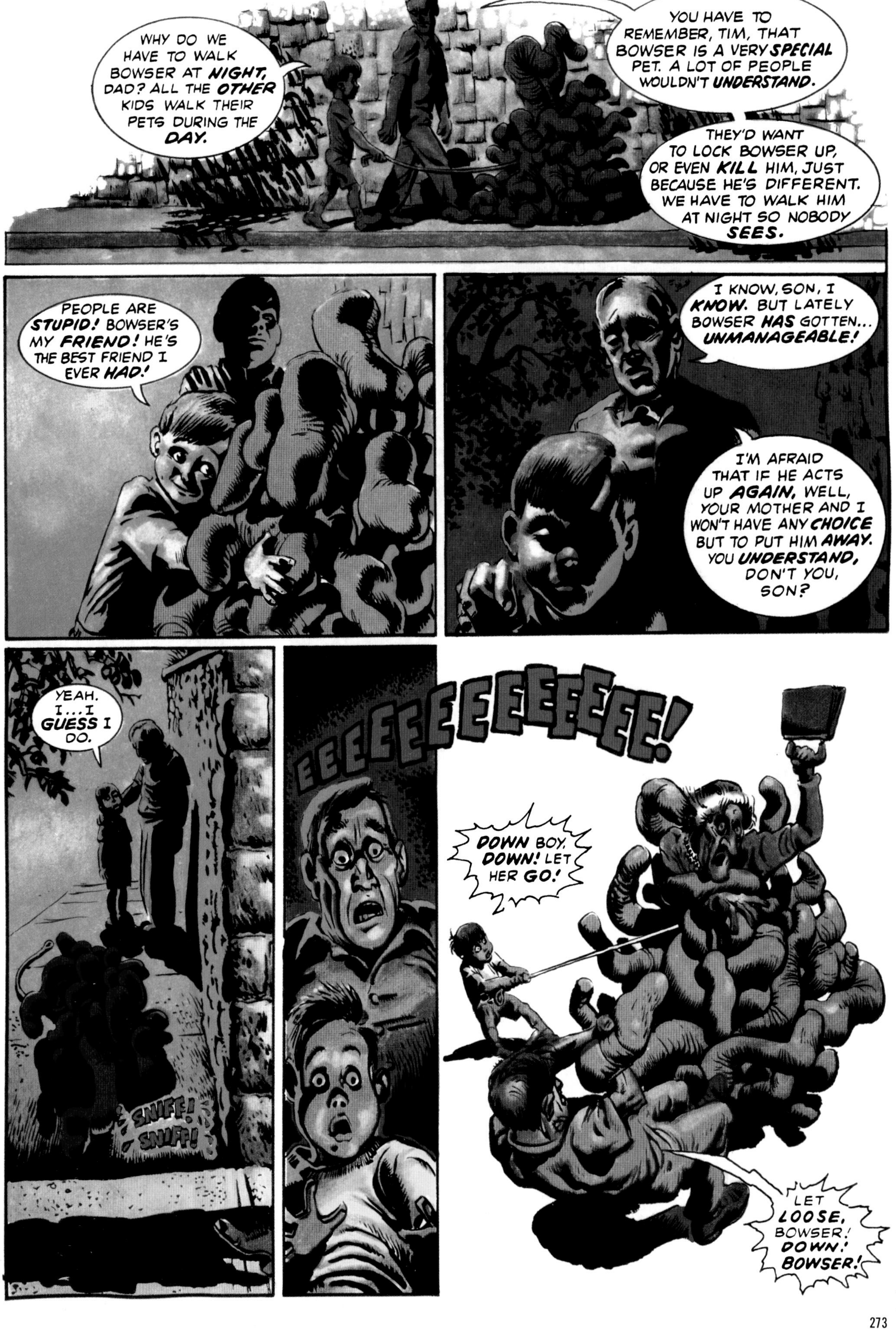
WHY DO WE HAVE TO WALK BOWSER AT NIGHT, DAD? ALL THE OTHER KIDS WALK THEIR PETS DURING THE DAY.
YOU HAVE TO REMEMBER, TIM, THAT BOWSER IS A VERY SPECIAL PET. A LOT OF PEOPLE WOULDN'T UNDERSTAND.
THEY'D WANT TO LOCK BOWSER UP, OR EVEN KILL HIM, JUST BECAUSE HE'S DIFFERENT. WE HAVE TO WALK HIM AT NIGHT SO NOBODY SEES.
PEOPLE ARE STUPID! BOWSER'S MY FRIEND! HE'S THE BEST FRIEND I EVER HAD!
I KNOW, SON, I KNOW. BUT LATELY BOWSER HAS GOTTEN... UNMANAGEABLE!
I'M AFRAID THAT IF HE ACTS UP AGAIN, WELL, YOUR MOTHER AND I WON'T HAVE ANY CHOICE BUT TO PUT HIM AWAY. YOU UNDERSTAND, DON'T YOU, SON?
YEAH. I...I GUESS I DO.
SNIFF! SNIFF!
EEEEEEEEEEEEEE!
DOWN BOY, DOWN! LET HER GO!
LET LOOSE, BOWSER! DOWN! BOWSER!

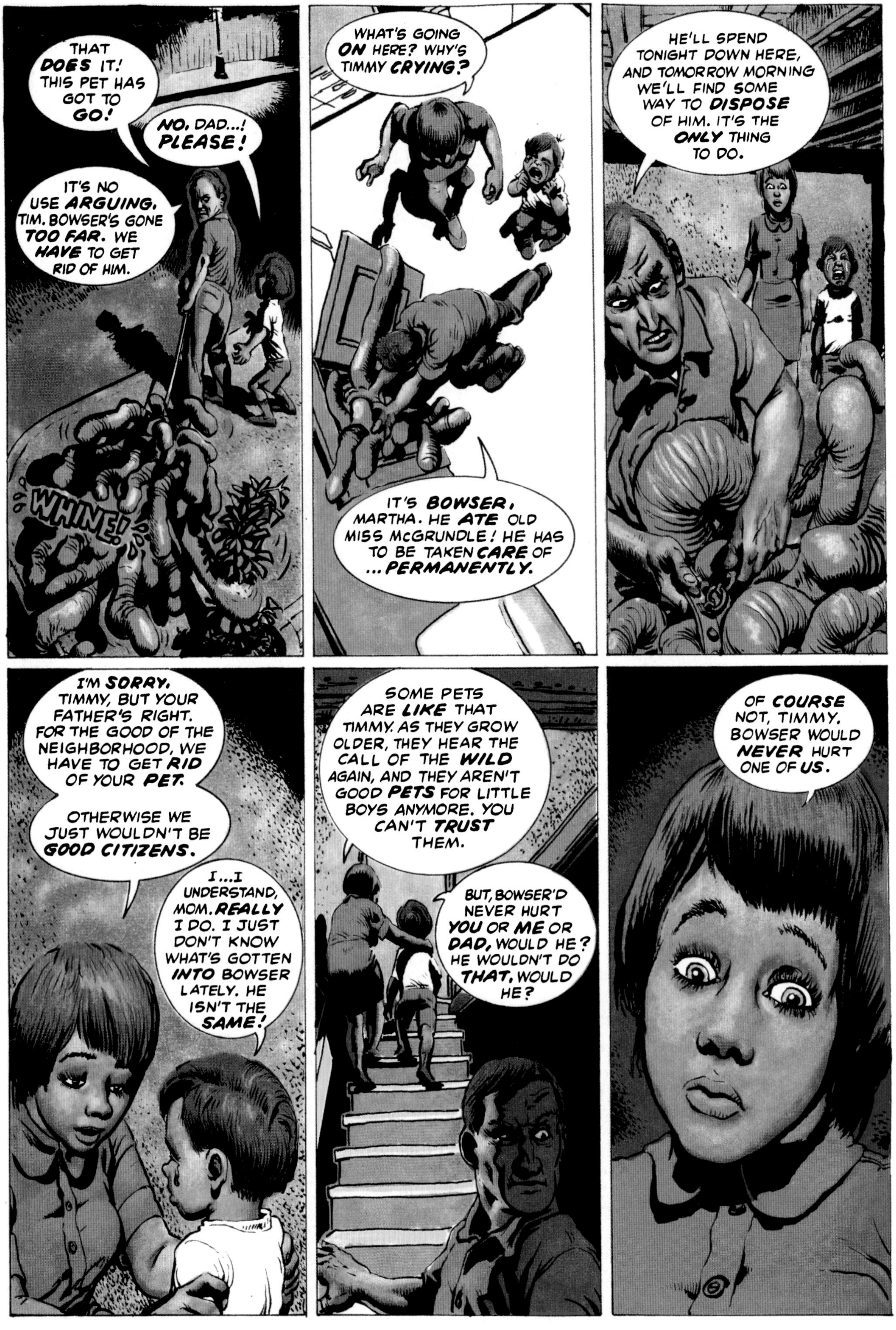
THAT DOES IT! THIS PET HAS GOT TO GO!
NO, DAD...! PLEASE!
IT'S NO USE ARGUING, TIM. BOWSER'S GONE TOO FAR. WE HAVE TO GET RID OF HIM.
WHINE!
WHAT'S GOING ON HERE? WHY'S TIMMY CRYING?
IT'S BOWSER, MARTHA. HE ATE OLD MISS McGRUNDLE! HE HAS TO BE TAKEN CARE OF ...PERMANENTLY.
HE'LL SPEND TONIGHT DOWN HERE, AND TOMORROW MORNING WE'LL FIND SOME WAY TO DISPOSE OF HIM. IT'S THE ONLY THING TO DO.
I'M SORRY, TIMMY, BUT YOUR FATHER'S RIGHT. FOR THE GOOD OF THE NEIGHBORHOOD, WE HAVE TO GET RID OF YOUR PET.
OTHERWISE WE JUST WOULDN'T BE GOOD CITIZENS.
I...I UNDERSTAND, MOM. REALLY I DO. I JUST DON'T KNOW WHAT'S GOTTEN INTO BOWSER LATELY. HE ISN'T THE SAME!
SOME PETS ARE LIKE THAT TIMMY. AS THEY GROW OLDER, THEY HEAR THE CALL OF THE WILD AGAIN, AND THEY AREN'T GOOD PETS FOR LITTLE BOYS ANYMORE. YOU CAN'T TRUST THEM.
BUT, BOWSER'D NEVER HURT YOU OR ME OR DAD, WOULD HE? HE WOULDN'T DO THAT, WOULD HE?
OF COURSE NOT, TIMMY. BOWSER WOULD NEVER HURT ONE OF US.

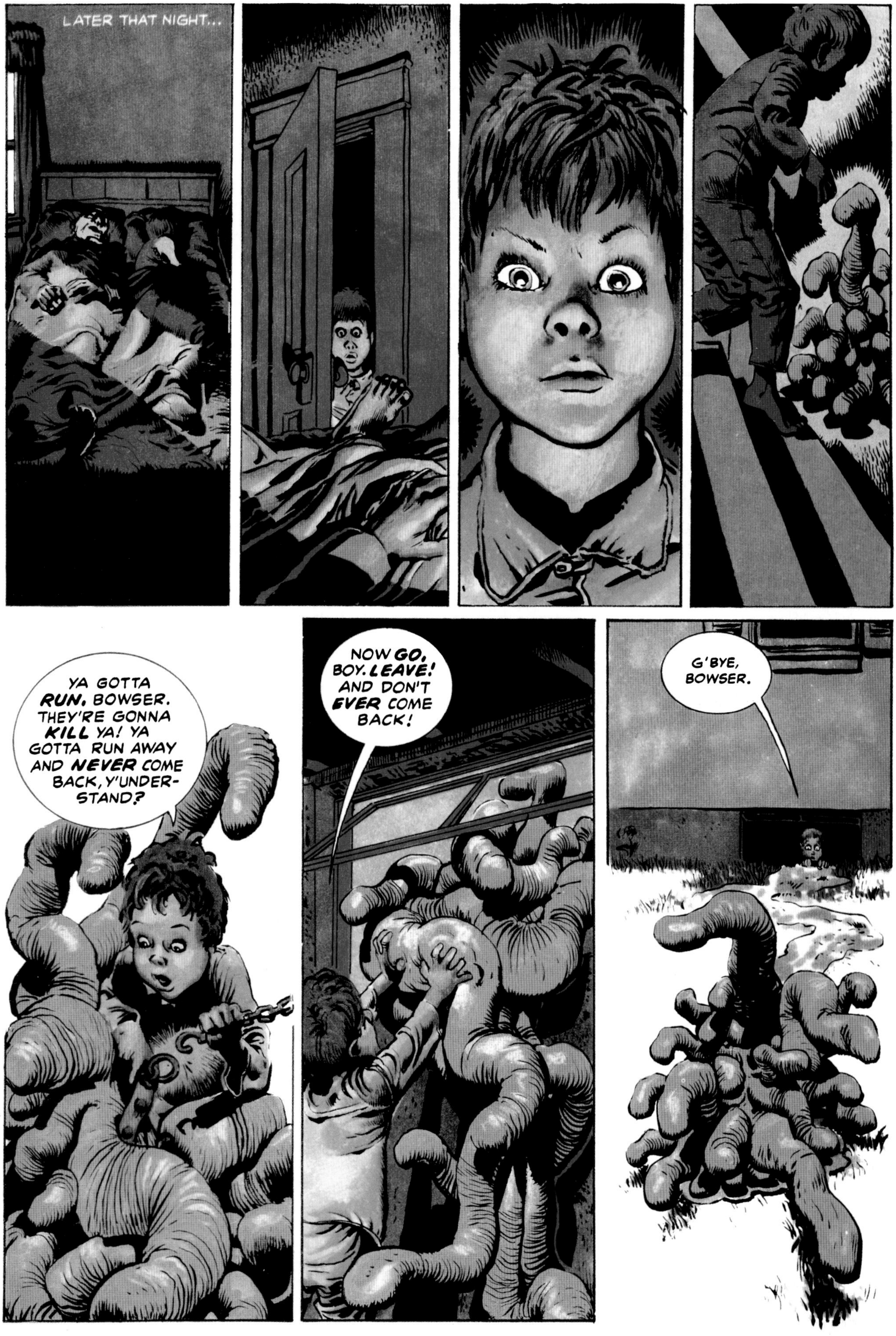
LATER THAT NIGHT...
YA GOTTA RUN, BOWSER. THEY'RE GONNA KILL YA! YA GOTTA RUN AWAY AND NEVER COME BACK, Y'UNDER-STAND?
NOW GO, BOY. LEAVE! AND DON'T EVER COME BACK!
G'BYE, BOWSER.

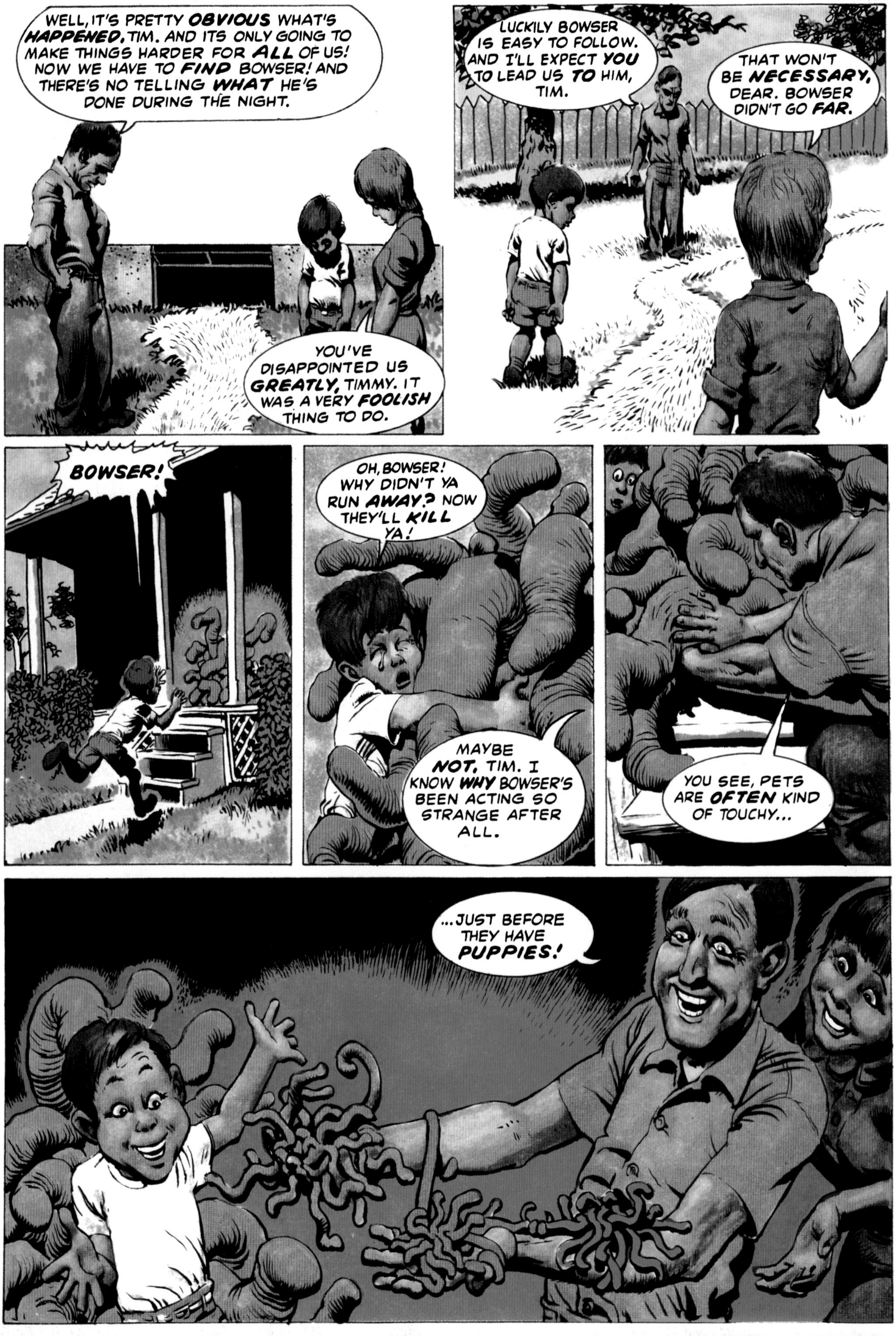
WELL, IT'S PRETTY OBVIOUS WHAT'S HAPPENED, TIM. AND ITS ONLY GOING TO MAKE THINGS HARDER FOR ALL OF US! NOW WE HAVE TO FIND BOWSER! AND THERE'S NO TELLING WHAT HE'S DONE DURING THE NIGHT.
YOU'VE DISAPPOINTED US GREATLY, TIMMY. IT WAS A VERY FOOLISH THING TO DO.
LUCKILY BOWSER IS EASY TO FOLLOW. AND I'LL EXPECT YOU TO LEAD US TO HIM, TIM.
THAT WON'T BE NECESSARY, DEAR. BOWSER DIDN'T GO FAR.
BOWSER!
OH, BOWSER! WHY DIDN'T YA RUN AWAY? NOW THEY'LL KILL YA!
MAYBE NOT, TIM. I KNOW WHY BOWSER'S BEEN ACTING SO STRANGE AFTER ALL.
YOU SEE, PETS ARE OFTEN KIND OF TOUCHY...
...JUST BEFORE THEY HAVE PUPPIES!

CREEPY™ AND EERIE™

PRESENTS

Bringing you the finest compilations of the
best-known names in horror comics!

BERNIE WRIGHTSON

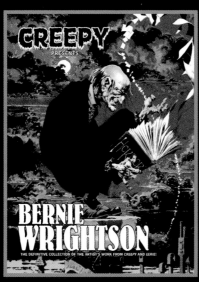

ISBN 978-1-59582-809-5 $19.99

RICHARD CORBEN

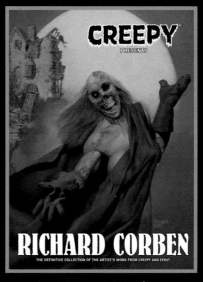

ISBN 978-1-59582-919-1 $29.99

HUNTER

ISBN 978-1-59582-810-1 $19.99

EL CID

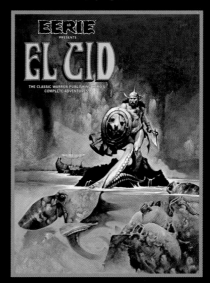

ISBN 978-1-61655-015-8 $15.99

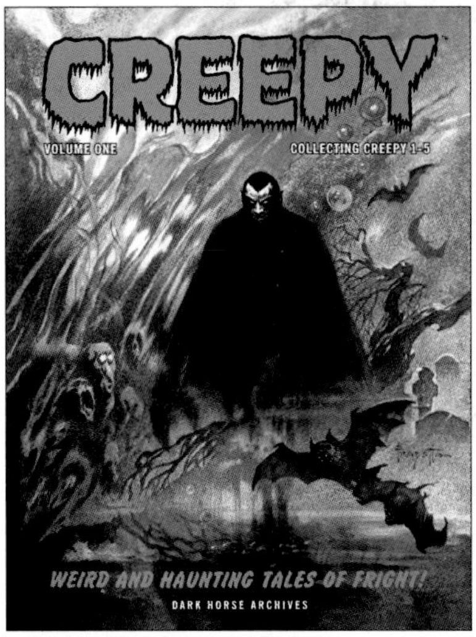
CREEPY
VOLUME ONE
COLLECTING CREEPY 1-5
WEIRD AND HAUNTING TALES OF FRIGHT!
DARK HORSE ARCHIVES

Volume 1 ISBN 978-1-59307-973-4

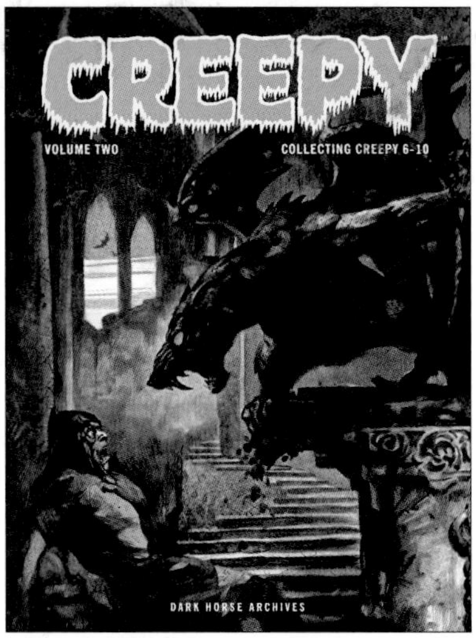
CREEPY
VOLUME TWO
COLLECTING CREEPY 6-10
DARK HORSE ARCHIVES

Volume 2 ISBN 978-1-59582-168-3

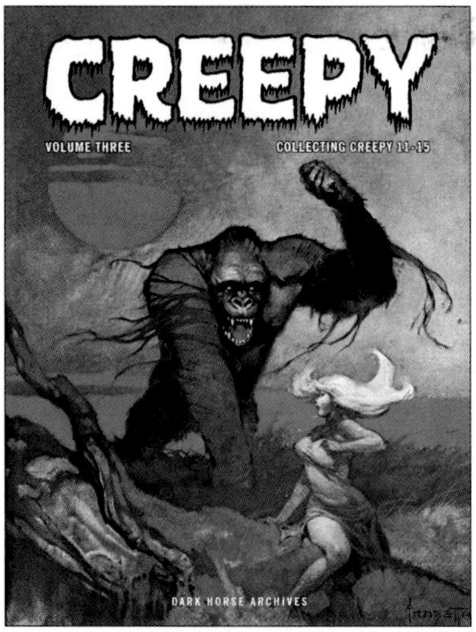
CREEPY
VOLUME THREE
COLLECTING CREEPY 11-15
DARK HORSE ARCHIVES

Volume 3 ISBN 978-1-59582-259-8

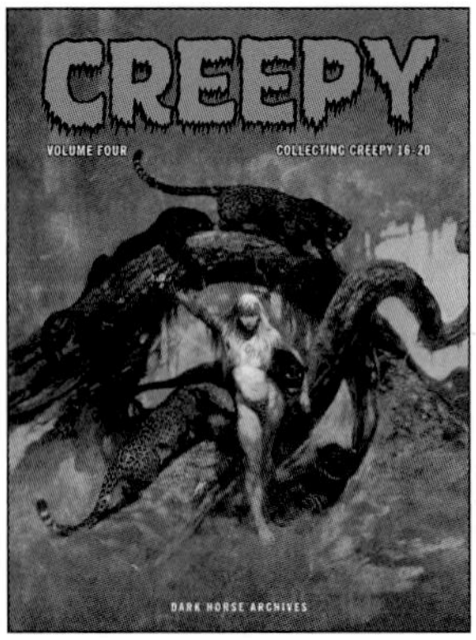
CREEPY
VOLUME FOUR
COLLECTING CREEPY 16-20
DARK HORSE ARCHIVES

Volume 4 ISBN 978-1-59582-308-3

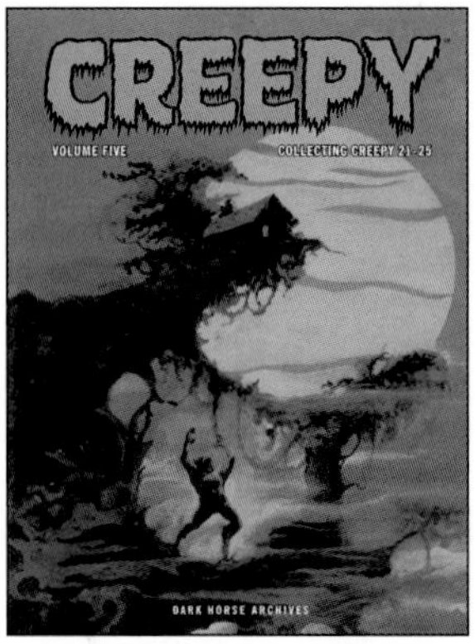
CREEPY
VOLUME FIVE
COLLECTING CREEPY 21-25
DARK HORSE ARCHIVES

Volume 5 ISBN 978-1-59582-353-3

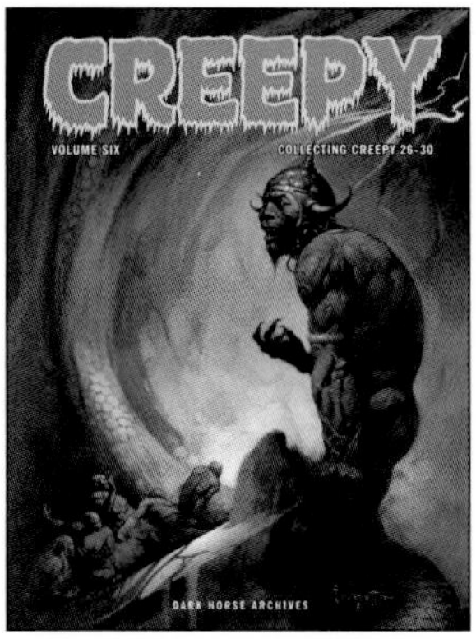
CREEPY
VOLUME SIX
COLLECTING CREEPY 26-30
DARK HORSE ARCHIVES

Volume 6 ISBN 978-1-59582-354-0

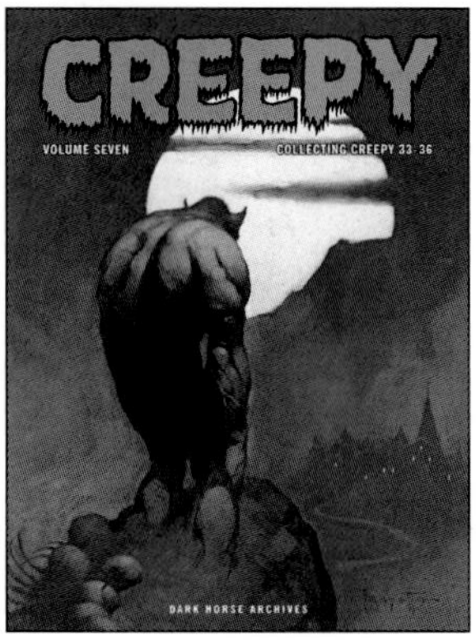
CREEPY
VOLUME SEVEN
DARK HORSE ARCHIVES

Volume 7 ISBN 978-1-59582-516-2

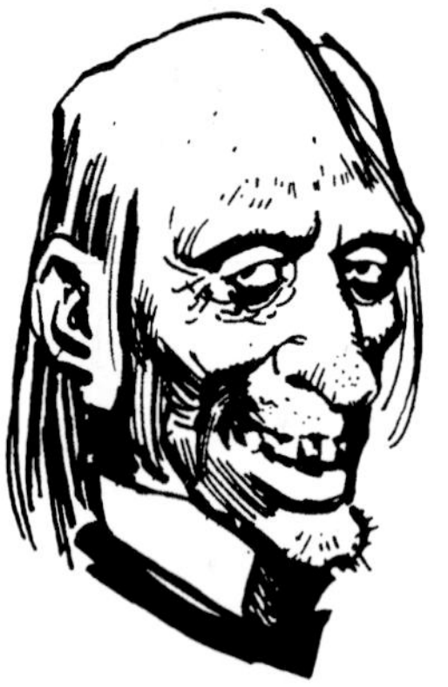

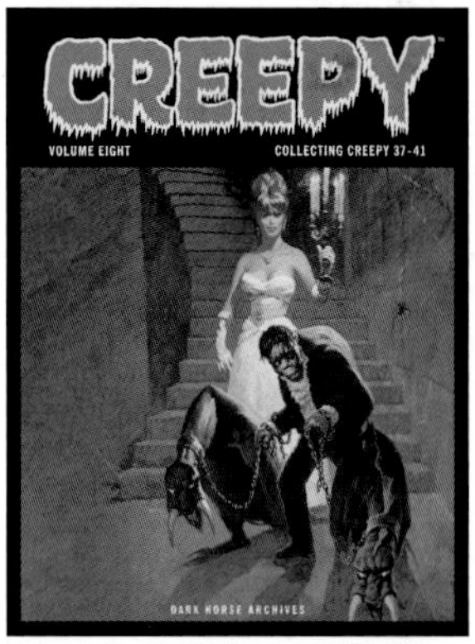
CREEPY
VOLUME EIGHT
COLLECTING CREEPY 37-41
DARK HORSE ARCHIVES

Volume 8 ISBN 978-1-59582-568-1

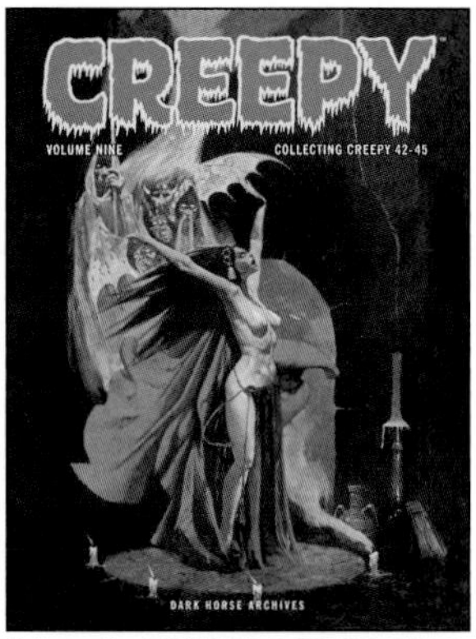
CREEPY
VOLUME NINE
COLLECTING CREEPY 42-45
DARK HORSE ARCHIVES

Volume 9 ISBN 978-1-59582-693-0

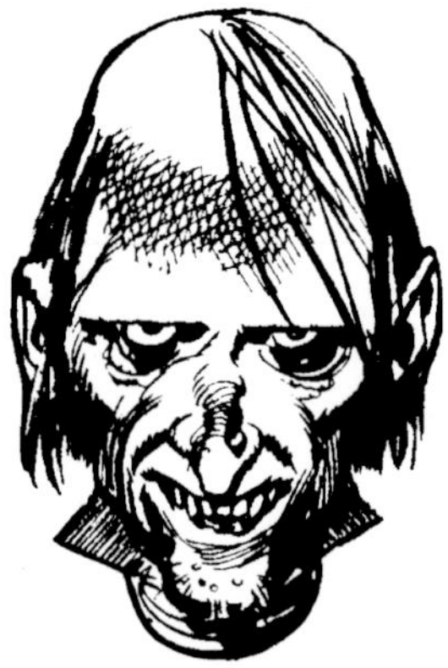

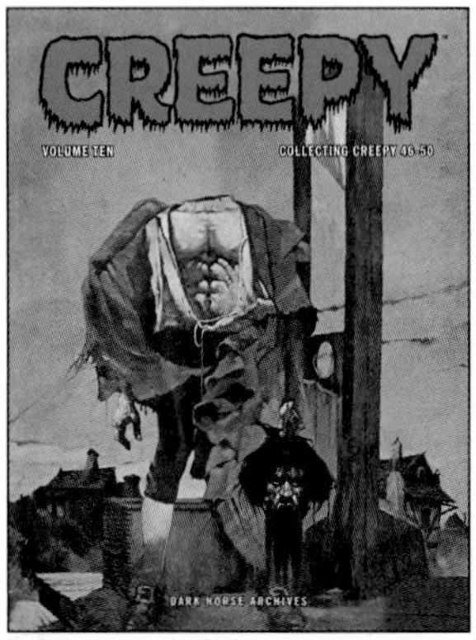
CREEPY
VOLUME TEN
COLLECTING CREEPY 46-50
DARK HORSE ARCHIVES

Volume 10 ISBN 978-1-59582-719-7

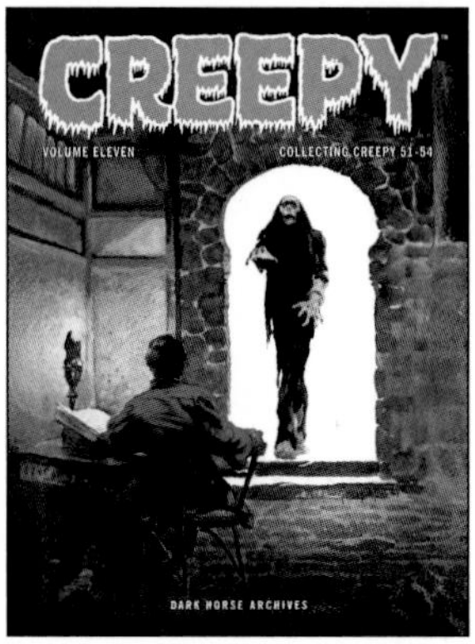
CREEPY
VOLUME ELEVEN
COLLECTING CREEPY 51-54
DARK HORSE ARCHIVES

Volume 11 ISBN 978-1-59582-761-6

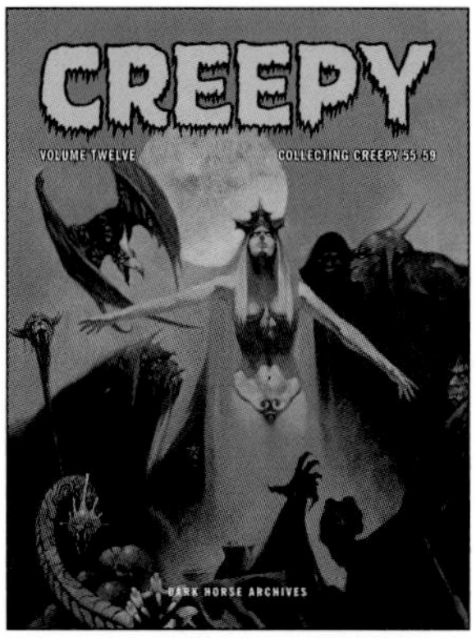
CREEPY
VOLUME TWELVE
COLLECTING CREEPY 55-59
DARK HORSE ARCHIVES

Volume 12 ISBN 978-1-59582-770-8

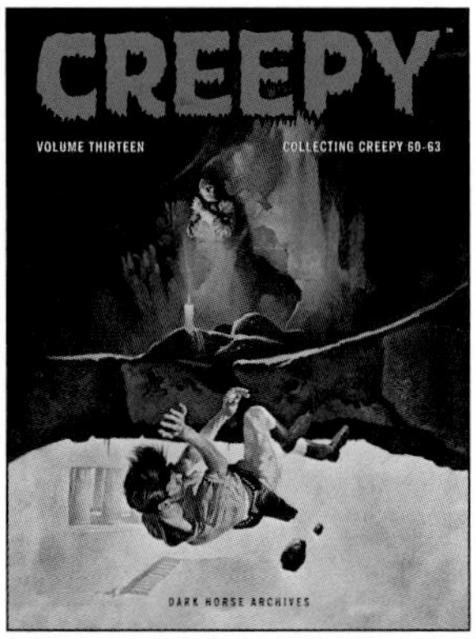
CREEPY
VOLUME THIRTEEN
COLLECTING CREEPY 60-63
DARK HORSE ARCHIVES

Volume 13 ISBN 978-1-59582-771-5

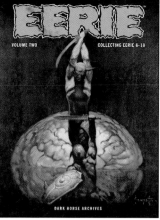